BLACK THUNDER

GENERAL HAG'S SKEEZAG
by Amiri Baraka

Baraka stands as a giant in Black Theater over the past three decades. With a craft as exciting as that in his early *Dutchman* and *The Toilet,* this new play again stuns the audience with its anger, biting satire and dialogue.

MA RAINEY'S BLACK BOTTOM
by August Wilson

A highlight of the 1984 Broadway season, this wonderful presentation of the legendary blues singer, her entourage, and Ma's music is a searing exploration of the Black American search for identity.

LONG TIME SINCE YESTERDAY
by P.J. Gibson

Gibson brings the special resonance of the Black woman's voice to this award-winning play, as a group of Black career women speak of love, men, taking risks, looking back . . . and moving forward fighting for a place in this world.

AND SIX MORE OUTSTANDING CONTEMPORARY PLAYS

WILLIAM B. BRANCH, Professor of Theater and Communications at the Africana Studies & Research Center, Cornell University, is a playwright, journalist, and media writer-producer. His plays include *A Medal for Willie, Baccalaureate* (included in this collection), *A Wreath for Udomo,* and *In Splendid Error*. Among his awards are a Guggenheim fellowship in playwriting and a Robert E.Sherwood television award for his NBC drama "Light in the Southern Sky."

BLACK THUNDER

An Anthology of Contemporary African American Drama

EDITED AND WITH AN INTRODUCTION
BY
WILLIAM B. BRANCH

A MENTOR BOOK

MENTOR
Published by the Penguin Group
Penguin Books USA Inc., 375 Hudson Street,
New York, New York 10014, U.S.A.
Penguin Books Ltd, 27 Wrights Lane, London W8 5TZ, England
Penguin Books Australia Ltd, Ringwood, Victoria, Australia
Penguin Books Canada Ltd, 10 Alcorn Avenue, Toronto, Ontario,
Canada M4V 3B2
Penguin Books (N.Z.) Ltd, 182–190 Wairau Road, Auckland 10,
New Zealand

Penguin Books Ltd, Registered Offices:
Harmondsworth, Middlesex, England

First published by Mentor, an imprint of New American Library,
a division of Penguin Books USA Inc.

First Printing, February, 1992

10 9 8 7 6 5 4 3 2

To my daughter, Rochelle

Contents

Foreword

The plays collected in *Black Thunder*[1] were all originally produced in the fifteen-year time span between 1975 and 1990. In effect, they may be referred to as a *post*-civil-rights-era collection, since, by 1975, most of the *de jure* goals of the great 1960s movement by African Americans and their allies—encompassing marches, sit-ins, freedom rides and other demonstrations—had been achieved: school desegregation, voting rights, equal access to public accommodations, equal-employment-opportunity statutes, etc. (It goes without saying, of course, that *de facto* racial discrimination did not wholly end by then—nor has it to this day.)

Does this, then, mark a turning point in outlooks and concerns by African American dramatists? Does it spell an end to what has long been called Black "protest" drama, and usher in a new era of less confrontational, more "universal" works than many of those written and produced heretofore? Have the playwrights in this collection reached a stage in which race plays less of a part in their grappling with issues of the human heart and spirit? In short, does this constitute the vanguard of a *new* African American drama, which strives to transcend race as a thematic necessity and to point unmistakably toward a "humanistic" aesthetic?

Well . . . Pleasant as that report might seem to some, the fact is that it would not be candid. Race has always been, and continues to be, a dominant factor in American life, and any serious Black American writer—in charge of his senses—who tries to ignore or avoid it does so at a fundamental compromise to his/her integrity. Moreover, the universal and humanistic in art have always been rooted in the particular, and this is no less so for African American theater than for any other artistic entity. It is no less theater because it is African American, and should be expected to reflect no less an African American perspective because it is theater.

Though differing widely in themes, styles and aims, the playwrights in this volume have chosen not to compromise, but to meet head-on the challenge of expressing truth and honesty

about the society in which they live. In their individual ways,
they illuminate aspects of life in an historically and fundamen-
tally racist U. S. of A. Even when that fact of life is not
overtly mentioned at all, there are nonetheless—for those
with eyes to see—the omnipresent racial realities of American history, politics, economics and sociology hovering in the
not too distant background, acknowledgment of which is
essential for a true understanding of the work at hand.

This is not to say that African American playwrights are
unconcerned with elements of characterization, plot, dialogue,
dramatic action, style and all the other facets of good storytell-
ing required for a successful theatrical realization. Mastering,
and individualizing, the crafts and arts of dramatic expression
have been amply demonstrated by Black dramatists long before
the Tony Awards and Pulitzer Prize committees began taking
notice of the rich contributions to American theater and literature they had been overlooking. African American drama can
be—and oft-times is—as touching and as exhilarating as the
spirit of the people from which it springs. As Ossie Davis
observed in his classic play, *Purlie Victorious*: "Bein' colored
can be a whole lotta fun—when ain't nobody lookin'."

Herewith, then, is a varied collection of plays by contemporary African American dramatists. Included are plays that easily rank among the best work being done in the American
theater. Some are published here for the first time. Most exciting of all, however, is the realization that they do not stand
alone; there are many more where these came from.

> —William B. Branch
> New Rochelle, New York
> August 24, 1990

[1]In the long-established multi-cultural traditions of West Africa—from
which the ancestors of most African Americans were abducted during
the three-centuries-long holocaust of the European slave trade—the
symbol of power, authority and rule is often the god of thunder: sometimes called "Shango," especially by the Yoruba peoples of Nigeria
and other nations. Increasingly recognized and respected in other areas
of the world as well—in the U.S., the Caribbean and particularly Brazil,
which has the largest population of African descent (acknowledged and otherwise)—this deity is prominently invoked on occasions calling for affirmations of truth, vision and service to one's communal grouping.

In the spirit of this active connection with the African diaspora, then,
this anthology has been titled *Black Thunder*.

Introduction

THE LEGACY OF THE AFRICAN GROVE: FROM *KING SHOTAWAY* TO *THE PIANO LESSON*

When the ubiquitous Mr. Brown opened a tea garden behind his home on Thomas Street in lower Manhattan, New York City, in the early nineteenth century, and began presenting "acts" and "exhibitionists" for his customers' entertainment, little could he have realized that he was about to launch an artistic and cultural tradition that was to last far beyond his own lifetime, and that today has become known as Black Theater—or, as the term is increasingly re-employed, African American Theater.

Mr. Brown (his given names are apparently still in some question among theater historians, although at least one has identified him as William Henry Brown)[1] was at first seeking merely to broaden the cordiality of his modest establishment, which catered to a small but growing community of free African Americans in the City, and possibly to enhance his economic situation somewhat as well. But by 1821, when these occasional entertainments of song, recitals and skits had expanded and grown into a formal organization called the African Company—which, under its leading actor, James Hewlett, had established its own facility at Mercer and Bleecker Streets named the African Grove Theater[2]—Mr. Brown found himself presiding over not only a proud and popular entertainment attraction, but also an activity perceived as a potential threat to a long-established white theatrical enterprise in the area: the Park Theater, run by one Stephen Price.

It appears that Price and a powerful friend—a local newspaper editor, politician and sometime playwright named Mordecai Noah—took umbrage at the audacity of former slaves and their descendants presuming to undertake the high Caucasian challenge of the introspections of Shakespeare's *Macbeth* and *Richard III*, let alone the dire threat to Western civilization—particularly the sanctity of white womanhood—posed by the "miscegeny" implicit in *Othello*. In addition, Mr. Brown's thriving enterprise had become so popular, despite denunciations by the white press (including *The National Advocate*, edited by Mordecai Noah), that white people were clamoring to pay good money to be let in—albeit in a segregated area set aside by Brown because, as he saw it, some whites did not know "how to behave themselves at entertainments designed for ladies and gentlemen of color."[3] Further, these black pretenders to the art of dramaturgy had had the nerve to fashion a play of their own, entitled *The Drama of King Shotaway*, in which they called upon their enslaved brethren in the U.S. to emulate the Caravs of the Caribbean and revolt against their masters.

But worst of all, as a politician, Noah was alarmed about a pending proposal before the New York State constitutional convention that would open the franchise to African Americans, fearing that local Black folk, if enfranchised, would vote for his political opponents. "These people do not want to vote," he editorialized in his paper. "They are perfectly happy to visit the African Grove [theater] and talk scandal."[4]

Something had to be done—and, of course, it was. Whether at the direct instigation of Mr. Brown's competitors or not, white hoodlums began to heckle and disrupt the troupe's performances, and when the police were summoned—you guessed it!—they arrested and carted off not the white hooligans, but the black actors on the stage. (It seems Mr. Noah had been appointed sheriff!)[5] The African Grove Theater ceased to exist in 1823, closed by the authorities as a public nuisance.

Importantly, it must be added that Ira Aldridge, a young actor with the African Company, migrated to London, where in short order he became a stellar attraction as a Shakespearean actor—for example, playing Othello to Ellen Tree's Desdemona. Later, as head of his own troupe, Aldridge toured the leading theaters of Britain and Europe, garnering high praise from critics and decorations from royalty until his death on tour in Lodz, Poland, in 1867. To this day, his portrait hangs in a place of honor in the Bakhrushin Theatrical Museum in Moscow, and a chair adorned with a plaque in his name is to be found in the fourth row of stalls at the Shakespeare Memorial Theater in Stratford-upon-Avon. Ironically, though records and references to Aldridge's extraordinary career are readily found in numerous European theater histories and reviews, Ira Aldridge remains little known in this, the country of his birth, having been left out of many works on European theater by white American writers.[6]

Nonetheless, by establishing the short-lived African Grove Theater, Mr. Brown had succeeded in providing an invaluable legacy. In initiating an African American theatrical tradition that refused to accomodate to pressure, he ennobled himself and his peers, and left to his many unborn heirs an inspiration, and a challenge, that is no less vital today than it was in 1823—a tradition which, though oft-times sputtering, gasping and wheezing, has managed, against both the usual artistic odds and those additional roadblocks created by prejudice, to survive and occasionally even to flourish in the nearly two centuries succeeding.

The long and detailed history of African American Theater since the demise of the African Grove has been ably chronicled by Loften Mitchell in *Black Drama: The Story of the American Negro in the Theatre*, and by others, and no comprehensive duplication will be attempted here. It may be desirable, however, to review briefly some background accenting the African American *playwright* in particular, and to survey that entity's contributions in the decades since, in order to approach in perspective the dramatists and their plays appearing in this collection.[7]

After *King Shotaway*, no script of which is extant (though authorship is credited to Mr. Brown), the record of African American playwrights is exceedingly sparse for the rest of the nineteenth century, during which minstrelsy reigned supreme. This theater form, based upon evenings of entertainment by slaves for the white ruling class on Southern plantations, was first commercialized by white performers in blackface, and only later by Blacks, who often were obliged to black their faces, too, in order to be accepted as "authentic" minstrels—prompting critic James Weldon Johnson to label this "a caricature of a caricature."[8] There was little opportunity or motivation for "serious" efforts in drama by Blacks, either in the white-oriented theatrical institutions of the time (from which they were barred) or in African American cultural circles. Higher on Blacks' priority lists were abolition of slavery, basic economic survival, obtaining educational opportunities, gaining citizenship rights and, not infrequently, avoiding lynch mobs.

Before the Civil War, however, an escaped slave named William Wells Brown developed an interest in using the form of legitimate theater to propagandize openly for abolition. His resulting 1858 play, *The Escape: or a Leap to Freedom*, was read from Anti-Slavery Society platforms rather than performed in stage productions, and its author joined the great Black orator Frederick Douglass as a frequent attraction at abolitionist gatherings, reading *The Escape* to the audiences himself. In England, Ira Aldridge became a playwright of sorts by adapting and performing a French play entitled *The Black Doctor*, while in France itself, an African American from New Orleans, Victor Sejour, carved out a remarkable career in the Parisian theater, with some twenty-one "white" plays staged during his lifetime (1817–74). In addition to these, on record are two verse plays about leading figures in the successful revolution against Napoleon by Blacks in Haiti, *Dessalines* and *Christophe* by William Easton, who wrote in 1893 that, in contrast to the "buffoonery" of minstrelsy, he hoped to see launched "a happier era inaugurated by the constant production of legitimate drama written exclusively for Negro players."[9]

Easton may have been reacting to the rise, and popularity among whites, of Negro musicals in New York City during the 1890s, when such Black entrepreneurs as Bob Cole, Will Marion Cook, J. Rosamund Johnson and poet Paul Lawrence Dunbar successfully wrote and produced a series of musicals for downtown white audiences. With titles such as *A Trip to Coontown*, *The Octoroons*, *The Shoefly Regiment* and *Jes Lak White Folks*, they often appeared to some Black observers as little advanced beyond actual minstrelsy itself. Still, these and other shows by African Americans are credited with an attempt, at least, to break the stranglehold of minstrel expectations whenever Black performers appeared onstage.

In 1901, a Louisville, Kentucky, school principal named Joseph S. Cotter Sr., a great admirer of Booker T. Washington, published a full-length play called *Caleb the Degenerate*. Although there appears to be no record of its actually having been performed, in it he contrasted what he considered to be a backwardness among Black Americans with his advocacy of a simplistic faith in a Horatio Alger–Booker T. Washington work ethic. However, the man who did much to oppose Washington's essentially accommodationist philosophy, Dr. William Edward Burghardt DuBois, next appeared on the theatrical scene with an expansive pageant, *The Star of Ethiopia*, in 1913, which with varying casts of hundreds was staged in New York, Washington, D.C., Los Angeles and other cities before huge audiences. It was a studied attempt by the preeminent African American scholar and activist to counter some of the many negative images of Blacks then constantly encountered in America's press, literature, theater and emerging film industry (even before the notorious *The Birth of a Nation* was released in 1915) by offering a sweeping overview of Black accomplishments from ancient Egypt to the present era.

Dr. DuBois, who apparently never thought of himself as a playwright as such, nonetheless proved to be a seminal figure in the field of Black Theater. In the pages of *The Crisis* magazine, which he founded and edited as research director of the National Association for the Advancement of Colored People (NAACP), he called for others to join in combatting harmful portrayals by writing their own fiction, essays and plays. DuBois established prizes in *The Crisis* for these efforts and even founded his own little theater group in Harlem, the Krigwa Players ("Krigwa" being an anagram for *Crisis* Guild of Writers and Artists).

The first produced play to result from Dr. DuBois's call was *Rachel* by Angelina Grimke (not to be confused with her celebrated abolitionist great-aunt of the same name). Produced by the Washington, D.C., branch of the NAACP—which declared the event its first attempt to "use the stage for race propaganda in order to enlighten the American people relative to the lamentable condition of ten millions of Colored citizens in this free republic"[10]—*Rachel* projected a decidedly negative assessment of prospects for a middle-class African American family to advance in a racist and openly hostile U.S. In it, the young woman protagonist decides to remain forever loveless and childless rather than bring into the world a child destined to be "blighted . . . blasted by the white man's prejudice." (Interestingly, a number of Washington NAACP members objected to this "propaganda" approach and were instrumental in founding a drama group at Howard University devoted to promoting "purely artistic" goals.)[11] *Rachel* is believed to be the first straight play (i.e., non-musical) by an African American playwright to be produced in the U.S. with an all-Black cast (save, perhaps, for Mr. Brown's *King Shotaway*, the details of whose cast remain unknown).

From this somewhat controversial beginning, a body of work by African American playwrights gradually took shape during the first two decades of the twentieth century. Often they were short one-act plays written for high schools, colleges and little theater groups. Often, too, they were by Black women schoolteachers, reacting to the lack of educational materials specifically reflecting the realities of the Black experience in

America. Some were in the category of what became known as "Negro folk plays," attempts to bring to the stage aspects of a Southern rural background which most Black Americans then shared. Some were comedies, imbued with rich folk humor or scathing satire, while others sought to document the historical record of Black heroes and heroines. Some grappled with the intense racism of the period, protesting against lynchings—of both the body and the spirit—by the dominant society, thus earning the title "protest drama."

By the end of the 1920s, according to African American Theater historian Samuel Hay, hundreds of such plays had been entered in the playwriting contests of *The Crisis* and the Urban League's *Opportunity* magazine.[12] Few were actually produced or published, but scripts by Alice Dunbar Nelson (*Mine Eyes Have Seen*), Georgia Douglas Johnson (*A Sunday Morning in the South*), Willis Richardson (*The Chip Woman's Fortune*), Randolph Edmonds (*Nat Turner*) and others demonstrate the growing confidence and purposefulness of Black dramatists, often operating without any hope or expectation of actual realization in stage productions. In 1923, however, Richardson's one-act play became the first drama by an African American to be produced on Broadway. It was followed two years later by *Appearances*, a full-length drama about a Black man falsely accused of the rape of a white woman, written by a San Francisco bellhop named Garland Anderson. Far from accenting a racial theme in his play, however, Anderson seemed intent upon advancing his personal philosophy of accommodation with a smile. (Actually, Anderson's hustling to get the play produced is a far more interesting story than that contained in the play itself.)

An African American actor, Frank Wilson, tried his hand at writing for his fellow thespians, and the result, *Meek Mose* (later retitled *Brother Mose*), an attempt at a serious study of Black American life, was seen on Broadway briefly in 1928. A fourth play, *Harlem*, by Harlem Renaissance writer Wallace Thurman (with white writer Jourdan Rapp) also enjoyed a modest Broadway run in 1929, purporting to give white theatergoers a voyeuristic view of life in what was then regarded as the "Black capitol of the world." (One saying during the period was that if a white man could get to spend one Saturday night as a Black man in Harlem, he'd never want to be white again!)

The Depression years of the 1930s saw an apparent slackening of activity by Black playwrights. While the record shows no evidence of any African Americans jumping out of Wall

Street windows after the stock market crash on so-called "Black Monday," the economic crisis which gripped the nation impacted even more severely upon Black communities than upon whites. Nonetheless, the creation of a Federal Theater Project in 1935 provided opportunities for a number of African American playwrights—albeit in segregated "Negro units" of the U.S. government-funded program. *Walk Together Children* by Frank Wilson, *Conjure Man Dies* by Rudolph Fisher and *Natural Man* by Theodore Browne were staged under these auspices, as was *The Trial of Dr. Beck* by Hughes Allison, a murder mystery involving skin-color differences among African Americans, which moved to Broadway after its premiere at Newark's Federal Theater. *Run Little Chillun*, a musical folk play by choral director Hall Johnson, and *Turpentine*, a social drama by J. Augustus Smith (with Peter Morrell) were also taken to Broadway.

Another important Federal Theater Negro Unit drama was *Big White Fog*, a controversial political play by Chicago playwright Theodore Ward. Ward's play appeared to suggest to some that Black Americans, fed up with segregation and discrimination, just might turn toward communism if conditions were not improved. It took the personal intervention of Hattie Flanigan, the national director of the Federal Theater Project, to afford *Big White Fog* a staging. (It was later revived by the short-lived Negro Playwrights Theatre in Harlem in 1940.)

It was Langston Hughes, however, operating outside the Federal Theater, whose star as playwright shone most brightly during the thirties. After an ill-fated attempt at a play collaboration with folklorist Zora Neale Hurston, entitled *Mule Bone*, Hughes wrote his own first play, initially titled *Cross: A Play of the Deep South*, based upon his poem *Cross*, on the theme of the tragic mulatto. Retitled *Mulatto*, Hughes' drama was taken to Broadway in 1935. A hoary tale of lust, revenge and miscegenation in the early twentieth-century South, *Mulatto* was bastardized to some extent by its white producer-director, but nonetheless became the longest-running Broadway play by an African American until eclipsed by Lorraine Hansberry's *A Raisin in the Sun* nearly twenty-five years later.

Other theater works by Hughes in the thirties include *Little Ham* and *Joy to My Soul*, two grass roots urban comedies; *Troubled Island* (also later billed as *Emperor of Haiti* and *Drums of Haiti*), an historical tragedy; *When the Jack Hollers*, a folk comedy written with Arna Bontemps; and *Front Porch*, a depiction of the erstwhile Black bourgeoisie—all written while playwright-in-residence for his hometown (Cleveland, Ohio) Karamu Theater. In Harlem, where he founded his own group, the Suitcase Theater, his poetry play with blues and spirituals, *Don't You Want to Be Free?* opened in 1935 and played both uptown and downtown (on what is now called Off-Broadway) for over a year, with several later revivals.

Another poet-playwright emerging during the 1930s was Owen Dodson, with a timely consideration of African American religious cults, centered on evangelist Father Divine and his fervent flock. Entitled *Divine Comedy*, it was written at the Yale University School of Drama in 1938, where Dodson was the only Black student, and was first staged there with an all-white cast in brownface!

World War II dominated the first half of the 1940s, which saw little advance upon the activity of Black playwrights of the thirties. Richard Wright's best-selling novel about an interracial murder in Chicago, *Native Son*, was adapted for the Broadway stage by Wright and white playwright Paul Green. Theodore Ward's Federal Theater drama of thwarted Black hopes during Reconstruction, *Our Lan'*, was brought to Broadway briefly. And Abram Hill—who co-founded the American Negro Theater (ANT) with actors Frederick O'Neal and Austin Briggs-Hall—wrote two original dramas for the group: *On Strivers Row*, a farce about Harlem's Black bourgeoisie; and *Walk Hard*, a consideration of the plight of an African American prizefighter, which moved briefly to Broadway. In addition, Hill is known to have largely re-written white writer Philip Yordan's play about a Polish American prostitute, *Anna Lucasta*, into the long-running Broadway and London hit it became after being brought to ANT and refashioned for an all-Black cast.

In addition, three graduates of the famed Harlem Renaissance of the 1920s—when Negroes were supposedly "in vogue"—were involved in prominent musicals of the forties. Arna Bontemps and Countee Cullen supplied the book for the Broadway musical *St. Louis Woman*, based upon Bontemps' novel, *God Sends Sunday*; and Langston Hughes wrote the lyrics for the Kurt Weill opera *Street Scene*. However, the dislocation of the war effort, followed by an often bitter scramble for jobs and basic human dignity, especially by returning African American veterans (in one incident, former soldier Isaac Woodard had his eyes gouged out by a white policeman), apparently left little incentive for Black writers to set sights on the theater, as the record of the 1940s suggests.

Samuel Hay has referred to the 1950s (and early sixties) as "the Golden Era of [Black] protest drama"[13]—a characterization which, for obvious reasons, this writer will leave to others to assess. Other African American critics, however, have branded the same period one of "integrationist" drama—whatever that is supposed to mean. Insofar as the dramatists of the fifties sometimes achieved a measure of recognition and success in mainstream theater circles previously little experienced by their forebears, perhaps both terms have some validity. What is *not* valid, however, is any supposition that these playwrights were obliged to "tone down" their racial or political points of view in order to make their work "acceptable" to the white drama establishment—an assumption raised from time to time by some latter-day, misguided academics, who apparently have difficulty comprehending that intellectual honesty and unswerving devotion to racial justice could possibly have existed before they were born. One playwright of the period, Alice Childress, has tellingly referred to the fact that she broke off negotiations for a Broadway production when the white producers insisted upon changes she felt would compromise the racial realities of her play. And on several occasions, white film and television producers have urged yours truly to "forget about writing about Negroes and write about just *people*." My reply has been to the effect that, while admittedly I may not be an expert on anthropology, it has always been my impression that African Americans *are* people. That often spelled the end of both the conversation and any interest either of us might have had in working together. (Since then, of course, it has been fairly firmly established that the people of Africa, Black Americans' direct ancestors, are the oldest *people* on the face of the globe—humankind itself, Homo sapiens, having originated in East Africa.)

Nonetheless, a marked increase in activity for this period was led off in 1950 by Alice Childress, who penned an intellectual race confrontation in one act, entitled *Florence*, and adapted several Langston Hughes' newspaper columns into a musical named *Just a Little Simple* (not to be confused with Hughes' own subsequent 1957 musical entitled *Simply Heavenly*). Childress was later to have *Trouble in Mind* (1955), a full-length play about black actors in a white playwright's production, win an Obie (Off-Broadway) Award. The play was believed to be based upon Childress's experiences with the white director of *Anna Lucasta*, in whose cast she acted for several years.

A Medal for Willie, a play by yours truly (William Branch), appeared in Harlem in 1951, raising questions about wartime service by African Americans in the U.S. armed forces while Black soldiers and their families were still openly denied equal rights here at home—a theme which predated the widespread anti-Vietnam War protests of the late 1960s by well over a decade. (Ironically, the morning after the play opened, its author was promptly inducted into the U.S. Army!) In 1954, Branch (now out of the army) was again represented in New York with *In Splendid Error*, an historical drama with contemporary overtones, about Frederick Douglass's indecision over joining John Brown in his ill-fated Harper's Ferry insurrection. Louis Peterson's *Take a Giant Step*, an evocation of a troubled Black adolescent's coming of age, was produced on Broadway in 1953. *A Land Beyond the River* by Loften Mitchell, dealing with a Southern civil-rights struggle which contributed to the U.S. Supreme Court school-desegregation decision of 1954, saw production Off-Broadway in 1957. The same year, *Simply Heavenly*, Langston Hughes' own musical about a Harlem bar-fly philosopher from his syndicated newspaper column, moved from Off-Broadway to Broadway, played the West Coast, and then was staged in London.

Other dramatists who first surfaced during the fifties included Julian Mayfield, with two one-acts: *The Other Foot*, a sexual comedy, and *World Full of Men*; and actor Ossie Davis, with the one-act *Alice in Wonder*, later expanded into the full-length *The Big Deal*. A play involving African American actors blacklisted during the McCarthyism Red-scare witch hunts of the time, Davis's play—along with works by a number of those already mentioned which were also racially and politically outspoken—have led still other observers to characterize this period as one of a distinctly *political* Black drama.

It was, however, the great, popular success of Lorraine Hansberry's Chicago family drama, *A Raisin in the Sun*, which opened on Broadway in 1958 with a cast headed by film star Sidney Poitier, which brought widespread consideration of the proposition that the Black playwright might, indeed, have a role to play in so-called mainstream theater. Hansberry's drama won the New York Drama Critics Circle Award—a first for an African American dramatist—was filmed by Hollywood, and has since become probably the best-known work by a Black playwright. (A later, musical version entitled *Raisin*, largely fashioned by whites, appeared on Broadway in 1973 to repeated success.) Combining intra-family conflicts with a white–black confrontation, Hansberry both entertained and educated with her drama of under-privileged, but aspiring, African Americans who inherit a modest legacy, while nonetheless prodding the consciences of her largely white Broadway audience by spotlighting that same audience's NIMBY fears ("Not in my back yard!") when the Black family seeks to move out of the ghetto.

The 1960s was, of course, a period of great racial and social upheaval in the U.S., and this was to be reflected in African American theater as well as at lunch counters, bus stations, county jails and polling places. One of the earliest plays by Black playwrights during this decade was Ossie Davis's 1961 Broadway farce, *Purlie Victorious*, in which Davis himself starred (with his wife, Ruby Dee) as a flamboyant Southern preacher intent upon restructuring the Southern social order. A year before, the college sit-in movement was utilized by William Branch as a framework (prologue and epilogue) for *To Follow the Phoenix*, a drama about civil-rights pioneer Mary Church Terrell. The same author's *A Wreath for Udomo*, based upon a novel by Black South African writer Peter Abrahams, which dealt with the rise and fall of an African prime minister, was staged in London in 1961 after a showing in Cleveland the year before.

Lorraine Hansberry's second Broadway play, *The Sign in Sidney Brustein's Window*, appeared in 1965. A socio-political drama, set in New York's Greenwich Village with a nearly all-white cast, it marked the tragic end of its author's promising career, closing the day after she died at age thirty-four. Posthumously, Hansberry was again heard from in *To Be Young, Gifted and Black*, a potpourri of scenes, letters, and other writings put together by her husband, Robert Nemiroff, in 1969 (later filmed for the Public Broadcasting Corporation); and *Les Blancs*, a play on colonial Africa, which was seen briefly on Broadway the following year.

Langston Hughes was active in theater until shortly before his death in 1967, with *Black Nativity*, the first of several "gospel" musicals he authored, which toured the U.S. and Europe off and on for several years; *Jericho Jim Crow*, which combined gospel music with civil-rights songs of the day; and *Tambourines to Glory*, a play with music involving both religious fervor and fakery, aided and abetted by a contemporary Black Beelzebub, which moved to Broadway briefly in 1965. Among other musicals which enlivened the decade were *Ballad for Bimshire*, a Caribbean satire by Loften Mitchell and Irving Burgie; *Kicks and Company*, a Chicago offering by Oscar Brown, Jr., which also featured a modern Mephistopheles; and *Fly Blackbird*, a West Coast-originated look at the "Freedom Now!" youth movement, by the interracial team of C. Bernard Jackson and James Hatch.

Novelist and essayist James Baldwin turned to the theater and wrote two works which saw production on Broadway during the sixties: *Blues for Mister Charlie*, an angry reflection upon the shocking lynching of fourteen-year-old Emmett Till in Mississippi, and *The Amen Corner*, a re-examination of the world of poor Blacks in storefront churches he had previously explored in his autobiographical novel, *Go Tell It on the Mountain*. *The Amen Corner*, which was first staged at Howard University by Owen Dodson in 1954, has since become a staple of the African American Theater repertoire, perhaps second only to *A Raisin in the Sun* in revivals by Black Theater groups.

Other works coming to attention during this period were *Happy Ending* and *Day of Absence*, a double bill by Douglas Turner Ward, humorously but sharply aimed at whites' complacency toward their Negro domestics (which led to the founding, with Ford Foundation money, of the Negro Ensemble Company); *Moon on a Rainbow Shawl*, a Caribbean drama by Errol John; *The Tumult and the Shouting* by Thomas Pawley, a glimpse into the lives of professors on a Black college campus; and *Ceremonies in Dark Old Men*, Lonne Elder III's consideration of morality as applied to struggling ghetto dwellers—which in 1968 became the first play by an African American to be nominated for a Pulitzer Prize.

It was, however, the emergence and rapid growth of a new genre of Black plays, from what came to be called the "Black Arts Movement"—itself an outgrowth and ally of the Black Power and Black Consciousness phenomenon sweeping younger Black Americans—that marked a different milestone in African American Theater during the sixties. Central to that development were the New York Off-Broadway premieres of three short plays by poet LeRoi Jones (later known as Amiri Baraka): *Dutchman*, *The Slave* and *The Toilet*. Each examined aspects of Black-white relationships in America with scathing, often profane attacks upon white liberals and Black integrationists alike—especially with prognostications in *The Slave* of an eventual racial Armageddon. Later founding his own group, the Black Arts Theatre in Harlem, with grants from the antipoverty program, Jones churned out a stream of short, agitprop "street" plays which eventually brought down the wrath of government inspectors, who cut off the funding.

Nonetheless, Jones's work is often credited with sparking the new Black Arts Movement, which mirrored, if not actually advanced, the widespread rise in Black grass roots militancy in wake of increasing television news footage of the bombings, murders, fire hoses, police dogs and other outrages against participants in the ongoing civil-rights struggle. Trumpeting their genre as "the Black Revolutionary Theater," new Black playwrights mushroomed seemingly overnight, with a proliferation of works proclaimed to be tuned to a new Black aesthetic. Though sometimes uneven in execution and craftsmanship, these mainly one-act pieces were uncompromising in their attacks upon both white racism and Black Uncle-Tomism in what they often perceived to be an outright war between the races—echoing Jones's *The Slave*. Though criticized by some in the African American community as mainly "Get Whitey" and "Blacker Than Thou" plays, often with more profanity than profundity, this genre nonetheless proved highly popular with the growing grass roots Black Theater audiences, which delighted in seeing reflections of themselves, their viewpoints and their life-styles portrayed onstage—often in makeshift theaters in their own communities—as opposed to the usual television and film diet of near lily-white offerings and perspectives.

Who's Got His Own by Ron Milner depicted an African American family struggling for self-definition after a funeral. *Requiem for Brother X* was one of the first in a number of plays memorializing the assassinated Malcolm X, this one by William Wellington Mackey. *Sister Sonji* was poet Sonia Sanchez's espousal of the new militancy. Charles (Oyamo) Gordon dealt with the volatile prison scene in *The Breakout*. *Black Quartet*, a bill of one acts, consisted of *Prayer Meeting Or, the First Militant Minister* by Ben Caldwell, a satirical comedy reflecting the times; *The Warning—A Theme for Linda* by Milner, which explored a young Black woman's emerging sexuality; *The Gentleman Caller* by Ed Bullins, with a different slant on the Black Mammy; and *Great Goodness of Life (A Coon Show)* by LeRoi Jones, which zeroed in on the Black bourgeoisie.

Bullins—at one time Minister of Culture of the Black Panther Party in California—found inspiration in the writings of LeRoi Jones and turned his considerable energies to Black Theater, quickly establishing himself as a force to be reckoned with. From absurdist plays such as *How Do You Do?* and *The Electronic Nigger*, to his naturalistic "Theatre of Reality" dramas, *In the Wine Time, In New England Winter, Goin' A Buffalo* and others, Bullins mined a rich lode of characters and themes from grass roots African American street corners and dives and projected them into what Black critic Clayton Riley characterized as "street nigger royalty."[14] *Goin A Buffalo*, for example, dealt with a hapless group of so-called "underclass" urban Blacks, striving desperately to "make it" on the periphery of American society, whether to them that called for hold-ups, pimping, prostitution, drugs, or even betrayal of their fellow unfortunates. (Bullins may have been influenced by Maxim Gorky's classic, *The Lower Depths*, an adaptation of which he worked on while briefly employed by the New York Shakespeare Festival.)

Other plays which added spice to the sixties scene—to name only a few—were *Funnyhouse of a Negro* and *A Rat's Mass*, two works which introduced the avant-garde fantasy of Adrienne Kennedy to theater audiences; *Gabriel*, an historical drama about a Virginia slave revolt, and *Sister Sadie*, a contemporary "in-group" satire, both by Clifford Mason; *Tell Pharaoh* and *Star of the Morning*, two history plays by Loften Mitchell—the latter a biography of minstrel Bert Williams; and *Dr. B.S. Black*, a contemporary "soul" reworking of Moliere's *The Doctor in Spite of Himself*, by Carlton Molette (later also staged as a musical). Needless to say, there were many more.

At decade's end (1969), a play by actor Chuck Gordon—corrected to "Charles Gordone" for his playwriting credit—appeared Off-Broadway and went on to make theatrical history in 1970 by becoming the first work by an African American playwright to win the Pulitzer Prize for Drama (then only recently extended to consider Off-Broadway offerings). The play, entitled *No Place to Be Somebody*, was an interracial barroom melodrama, set in New York's bohemian Greenwich Village district, which blended aspects of Black aspirations with intrigues involving the local Mafia. Gordone's play toured, then played Broadway briefly. (Gordone has continued to write, but his only play to be staged professionally in New York since—at this writing—was *The Last Chord*, set in Harlem in the 1940s, which was seen briefly in Brooklyn in 1975.)

The vitality and dynamism which marked the great burst in the growth of African American Theater during the sixties swept on into the 1970s, at first seemingly without abatement. Funds tapped from anti-poverty programs and foundations had resulted in the establishment and flowering of Black Theater groups and organizations from coast to coast. Black playwrights were being nurtured to some extent with grants and college residencies. Scholarly assessments of this heretofore neglected body of work began appearing in critical dissertations, leading journals, and anthologies issued by important publishers. As opportunities for college enrollment by African Americans increased markedly, "Black Theater" courses made their debuts on college and university campuses, often accompanied by Black Theater workshops which produced plays from the growing Black Theater repertoire.

Despite these hopeful signs, however, the millenium had not yet arrived, and as America's political climate swung sharply rightward, funding began to shrivel and dry up, programs were curtailed or erased entirely, and Black Theater—along with every other African American institution—soon felt the freeze.

Still, the accomplishments of Black playwrights during the decade are impressive. Early on, prominently produced Off-Broadway (and later on network television) was Alice Childress's *Wedding Band*, an early twentieth-century interracial love story, said to be based upon her Charleston, S.C., forebears. *Wine in the Wilderness*, a second Childress work (originally written for public television), dealt with an inadvertent Black victim of the "Burn, Baby, burn" urban riots which had swept the country. The Negro Ensemble Company (NEC), founded by actor-playwright Douglas Turner Ward (with actor Robert Hooks and accountant Gerald Krone) mounted season after season of works by African American dramatists, among them: *The Sty of the Blind Pig*, Philip Hayes Dean's study of unrequited Black love; Leslie Lee's *The First Breeze of Summer*, a Southern generation-gap conflict with interracial skeletons in the closet; *Man Better Man*, a Caribbean folk musical by Errol Hill; and *The Great Macdaddy*, a far-ranging fantasy with music by Paul Carter Harrison. Other works staged by NEC during the period included *Eden*, Steve Carter's drama of a clash of cultures between U.S.-born African Americans and West Indians in the 1920s; *Home*, Samm-Art Williams's imaginative evocation of his North Carolina roots, which moved to Broadway; and *The River Niger* by Joseph Walker, a Black family drama with poetic overtones, which was awarded the 1975 Antoinette Perry ("Tony") Award for Best Play, the first such for an African American playwright. Walker's play was eventually filmed.

Black producer Woodie King, Jr., managed to tap into the

grant-proposal system and, with a bow to the 1930s institution, established the *New* Federal Theater (NFT) in downtown Manhattan, where he also presented play after play by African American writers. Included were: *Black Girl*, an urban ghetto drama by J. E. Franklin, which was later filmed by Ossie Davis; poet Larry Neal's *The Glorious Monster in the Bell of a Horn*, an imaginative and promising effort not long before Neal's untimely death; *Cotillion*, a musical satirizing Brooklyn's rising West Indian middle class, based by novelist John O. Killens on his book of the same name; and Ron Milner's *What the Wine-sellers Buy*, a revealing study of the influence of a pimp on neighborhood youngsters, which was moved to Lincoln Center and later taken on national tour by King. Another NFT production, *The Taking of Miss Janie*, by Ed Bullins—a consideration of cross-racial sexual attractions as a metaphor for U.S. race relations—after also moving to Lincoln Center, won the New York Drama Critics Circle Award for 1974–75. King's best-known presentation, however, was Ntozake Shange's *For Colored Girls Who Have Considered Suicide/When the Rainbow Is Enuf*, a Black feminist "choreopoem" which was moved first to the New York Shakespeare Festival, then to Broadway, where it ran for more than a year, and then went on national tour. Ms. Shange's offering, which appeared to evince a harsh perspective on African American *men*, predictably caused considerable controversy.

Other plays which also reflected the events, moods and changing life-styles of the volatile sixties and seventies appeared in rapid succession. William Wellington Mackey's *Behold! Cometh the Vanderkellans* visited a Black college campus in revolt not only against the white establishment, but also against the college's Black president. *Five on the Black Hand Side*, a family comedy by Charles Russell involving the new Black consciousness, was filmed by actor Brock Peters. Don Evans' *Showdown* played a similarly humorous theme, while Martie Evans-Childs' *Jamimma* took a more pointed view of Black family life. Ted Shine's one-act dramas, *Contribution* and *Herbert III*, were comedies evoking nostalgia for the days of the civil-rights movement, but *Rosalee Pritchett* by Carlton and Barbara Molette dealt harshly with upper-middle-class African Americans who looked down on ghetto rioters. Actor J. E. (Sonny Jim) Gaines depicted small-town "sporting" life in the sixties in *Don't Let it Go to Your Head*. And recalling Baldwin's *Blues for Mister Charlie* of a decade before, Edgar White's *The Burghers of Calais* questioned America's handling of interracial rape charges, reaching all the way back to the case of the Scottsboro boys in the 1930s.

The Black Revolutionary Theater thrived as well. *El Hajj Malik* by N. R. Davidson, a dramatization of the life of the then still highly controversial Malcolm X, appeared in 1971. The same year, Richard Wesley, a protégé of Ed Bullins, startled many, both Black and white, with his Armageddon drama *The Black Terror*. Bullins himself (apparently) sang a similar theme of Black-white warfare—under the nom de plume of "Kingsley Bass, Jr."—in a work entitled *We Righteous Bombers*, said by some to be an unabashed reworking of Albert Camus' *The Just Assassins*. Another "urban guerilla" offering popular with Black Theater groups in the seventies was Jimmy Garret's *We Own the Night*, which, like a number of others of this genre, seemed more intent upon eliminating uncooperative Black people—in Garret's play, the revolutionist's own mother—than in "getting Whitey."

But it was LeRoi Jones—by now renamed Amiri Baraka—whose work in this area continued to set the pace, especially with *Slaveship*, a searing ceremonial drama which conjured up the horrific sights, sounds, and smells of a journey on the Middle Passage. Other Baraka plays during this period bore titles such as *Experimental Death Unit #1, Junkies Are Full of (Shhh . . .), The Motion of History* and *Sidnee Poet Heroical*—the latter a withering comment upon the film career of Sidney Poitier. Baraka also revived what apparently were bitter memories of his U.S. Air Force days in *A Recent Killing*.

Noteworthy also during the seventies was the rise and brief flourishing of a distinctive Black Theater form called "the rituals." Largely improvised, often varying from performance to performance, these presentations combined elements of the African background, the Black church, revolutionary ideology, and music and dance, in an effort to involve Black audiences both spiritually and physically in their presentations. The New Lafayette Theater in Harlem, founded by director Robert McBeth and with Ed Bullins as resident playwright, developed several such rituals which were eventually scripted and made available to other production groups. With arresting titles such as *A Ritual to Bind Together and Strengthen Black People So That They Can Survive the Long Struggle That Is to Come* and *To Raise the Dead and Foretell the Future*, these cooperatively developed offerings sparked others by Black companies the country over. The word was out, in the vernacular, that "you ain' hittin' on nuthin' 'less you be doin' the rituals, Baby!"

More orthodox dramas to surface during the seventies were
The Duplex and *The Fabulous Miss Marie*, two further entries
in Ed Bullins's "Twentieth Century Cycle" of plays involving
characters first encountered in *In the Wine Time*; *The Rise and
The Brownsville Raid*, two plays of African American history
by Charles Fuller, the former devoted to Marcus Garvey and
the latter to an incident involving mistreatment of Black soldiers
by the U.S. government; *Freeman*, a psychological study
of an unorthodox African American, by Philip Hayes Dean;
and *Black Picture Show* by Bill Gunn, in which an African
American who briefly tasted success in Hollywood winds up in
a psychiatric ward in the Bronx. Still others were *Fount of the
Nation*, a drama of government intrigue in Africa by Julian
Mayfield; *Baccalaureate*, a glimpse into the aspiring Black
bourgeoisie by William Branch, which premiered in Bermuda;
and *The Mighty Gents* (formerly titled *The Last Street Play*) by
Richard Wesley, a drama of the perils of young black manhood,
which was briefly on Broadway. Also produced on
Broadway, and later in London, was Philip Hayes Dean's
monodrama *Paul Robeson*, with James Earl Jones in the title
role.

An important development in African American Theater in
the 1970s was a renaissance of sorts of the Black-written, Black-
produced and Black-performed musical on Broadway. Film
director Melvin Van Peebles led off the decade with two of his
own: *Ain't Supposed to Die a Natural Death*, a Black
"underclass" statement of accusation and confrontation, based
upon two of his record albums; and *Don't Play Us Cheap*, a
Harlem fantasy adapted from a Van Peebles novel. Rejected by
white critics and regular (white) audiences alike, Van Peebles
nevertheless kept both shows running on Broadway for
weeks—at one time simultaneously—reportedly by subsidizing
them with earnings from his hit film, *Sweet Sweetback's Baad-
asssss Song*.

Bubbling Brown Sugar, with a book by Loften Mitchell based
upon a concept by Rosetta LeNoire, successfully navigated the
dangerous Broadway waters, offering a nostalgic review of Harlem
nightlife during the Harlem Renaissance. Director Vinnette
Carroll and writer-singer Micki Grant, collaborators in an
Urban Arts Corps youth program, fashioned two musicals
which fared well when moved to Broadway: *Don't Bother Me,
I Can't Cope*, an inner-city medley of skits and songs; and *Your
Arm's Too Short to Box With God*, a gospel musical whose
title was taken from one of James Weldon Johnson's poetic

Negro sermons in his book, *God's Trombones*. Most successful of all, however, was *The Wiz*, an African American version of the popular film *The Wizard of Oz*. Produced by neophyte Black producer Ken Harper, who managed to talk Twentieth Century-Fox into investing $650,000 in the show, *The Wiz* won seven Tony Awards in 1975, ran on Broadway for nearly four years, and was prominently filmed (by Twentieth Century-Fox, of course), despite its initial lukewarm reception by white critics, some of whom voiced offense at the "blackening" of what they regarded as a white classic. William F. Brown is credited with the book, based upon the original story by white writer Frank Baum.

Two other hit musicals on Broadway in the seventies were based upon successful plays by African Americans: *Purlie*, fashioned from Ossie Davis's *Purlie Victorious*, and *Raisin*, developed from Lorraine Hansberry's *A Raisin in the Sun*. In both cases, however, the book and lyrics were credited to whites. In addition, *Ain't Misbehavin'*, an all-Black musical revue produced by whites, utilizing Fats Waller's music—but with no book—thrived on Broadway and toured for years, while a similar offering, *One Mo' Time*, was an Off-Broadway hit before also touring the U.S. and abroad. In addition, famed ragtime composer Scott Joplin's folk opera, *Treemonisha*, written and composed nearly sixty years before, was finally staged in New York in 1975, though its creator had long since gone to his creator.

By the time the 1980s rolled around, African American Theater was in another of its periodic slumps, occasioned not by any fall-off of interest or desire on the part of Black playwrights or other theater professionals, but largely by the sharply escalating costs of production, paired with a decline in support from government, foundations and other funding sources. Since this was true of American theater in general, it goes without saying that white producers and theatrical institutions were not overly inclined toward utilizing their shrinking resources in support of offerings arising from the African American experience. Black production circles, traditionally gasping for breath, were forced to scale back even further—that is, if they were able to survive at all. Many didn't. That the eighties nonetheless eventually proved to be a watershed of achievement by Black playwrights in the American theater is an anomaly.

Charles Fuller, produced by the Negro Ensemble Company, led things off with his *Zooman and the Sign*, a discomforting clash of values between contemporary "street dudes" and middle-class strivers within an urban Black community. Two years later, in 1982, came Fuller's *A Soldier's Play*, an involved "whodunnit," set in a U.S. Army camp during World War II, which probed issues of race, class and group responsibility within the American context. Following Charles Gordone's *No Place to Be Somebody* of twelve years earlier, *A Soldier's Play* became the second work by an African American playwright to be awarded the Pulitzer Prize for Drama. (Oddly enough, it never played on Broadway.) When later filmed by Hollywood under the title *A Soldier's Story*, it was nominated for an Academy Award for best picture of the year.

In 1983, veteran Broadway production stage manager Charles Blackwell played a chief role in bringing to Broadway *The Tap Dance Kid*, a musical based upon a novel by African American writer Louise Fitzhugh. In it, the young son of Black urban professionals living in a predominantly white New York City condominium complex rebels against his expected path in life, and aided by a sympathetic if ne'er-do-well showbiz uncle, sets his sights on a career as a tap dancer. Though mildly received by critics, *The Tap Dance Kid* ran for two years on Broadway and toured the country, in the process earning Blackwell a Tony nomination as author of the book. A second musical with an African American theme, *Amen Corner*, based by its white adapters upon James Baldwin's earlier play, found neither favor nor audiences on the Great White Way.

Checkmates, a drama by Ron Milner, also made it to Broadway in the eighties and enjoyed a substantial run—no mean feat given the sharp escalation in production costs and resulting ticket prices, which had drastically limited production on Broadway of plays other than musicals. It, too—though in a markedly different way from *The Tap Dance Kid*—explored a contrast between affluent "buppies" and more ordinary members of the Black community. Actress Ruby Dee and film stars Paul Winfield and Denzel Washington were in the cast.

Unquestionably, however, the decade's strongest impression by any playwright, Black or white, was made by a relative newcomer to the scene, a midwesterner named August Wilson. Shepherded by veteran Black director Lloyd Richards from the Eugene O'Neill Playwrights Center to the Yale School of Drama (of which Richards was dean), and then, often with interim productions in regional theaters across the country, to Broadway stages, this writer's works became the most critically acclaimed and honored of any American dramatist since Eugene O'Neill, Arthur Miller or Tennessee Williams. Indeed, in one instance, a play by Wilson won more awards and had the highest grosses of any straight drama ever produced on Broadway.

The procession began in 1984 with *Ma Rainey's Black Bottom*, a work set in the early days of blues and jazz recordings ("Black Bottom" is a song sung by Rainey), which ultimately comments on the pent-up frustrations of African Americans living constricted lives in a prejudiced U.S. Two years later, *Fences* conquered the Broadway scene. With Pittsburgh in the 1950s as its setting, Wilson explored the "fences"—both external and internal—of an African American garbage collector and his family. James Earl Jones starred as the former Negro Leagues baseball player reduced to working for the sanitation department. (Jones was succeeded for the second year on Broadway by film star Billy Dee Williams.) While *Fences* was still running, *Joe Turner's Come and Gone* was brought to Broadway. An ensemble work of mystery and suspense amid interactions within a Black boardinghouse in 1911, *Joe Turner* evoked symbolic links with the African past.

Then, in 1990, after incubating in productions at Yale and in regional theaters over a two-year period, Wilson's *The Piano Lesson* arrived in New York. Also set in Pittsburgh, this time in the 1930s, it unfolded a saga of a Southern Black family—as personified by Boy Willie and his sister, Berniece—whose legacy from the days of slavery is represented by a piano, originally bought by their ancestors' slaveowner by selling two slaves. Posing conflicts between the consequences of holding on to often painful memories of the slave heritage and cashing them in for more tangible assets, *The Piano Lesson* revealed still more complexities of Wilson's ponderings on the promises versus the realities of the Black experience in America.

Each of the four plays received the New York Drama Critics Circle Award as best play of the season. Both *Fences* and *The Piano Lesson* were also awarded the Pulitzer Prize for Drama. *Fences* additionally received a long list of other awards, prompting the producers to claim in an advertisement in *The New York Times* that it was the most honored play in the history of Broadway.[15] Further, other press reports revealed that box-office receipts for *Fences* made it the highest-grossing straight play in Broadway history[16]—a staggering feat given the usual racial dynamics at work in the U.S., including the theater. (The *Times* suggested—but seemed reluctant to assert—that a large, perhaps predominant, portion of that gross was realized by the attendance of many thousands of Black patrons—few among them regular Broadway theatergoers, but people who were not hesitant to pay Broadway prices for a tasteful presentation to which they, as African Americans, could relate in a positive sense.[17] The same appears to be the case with *The Piano Lesson*.) As this was being written, Wilson had two more plays completed and waiting in the wings: *Two Trains Running*, set in the 1960s, and *Moon Going Down*, the working title of his forties play.

These high-profile commercial successes were not the only achievements by African American playwrights during the eighties, however. Woodie King (who also directed Ron Milner's *Checkmates* on Broadway in 1987) continued to present work by Black writers Off-Broadway, through his nonprofit New Federal Theater, that was often just as deserving of attention as that seen commercially. Included were: *Long Time Since Yesterday*, P. J. Gibson's drama of the varying life-styles of a group of African American female college graduates; *Boogie Woogie and Booker T.*, by Wesley Brown, which placed several icons of the past—including W.E.B. DuBois, Ida B. Wells, and Booker T. Washington—on stage together at a strategy conference in 1904; Clifford Mason's *Time Out of Time*, exploring the class and racial ambivalance of a Jamaican aristocrat; and *Welcome to Black River* by Samm-Art Williams, retracing Williams's roots in rural North Carolina that he previously evoked in *Home*. Lawrence Holder's double-bill of *Zora* and *When the Chickens Come Home to Roost* were also NFT entries, the former profiling Black writer Zora Neale Hurston and the second addressing Malcolm X. Still another King production was *The Meeting* by Jeff Stetson, which imagined a secret private conference in Harlem between Malcolm X and Martin Luther King, Jr., and was eventually seen on public television.

Douglas Turner Ward's Negro Ensemble Company was no slouch, either, staging among others: *Two Can Play*, a West Indian comedy by Trevor Rhone; *House of Shadows* by Steve Carter, which offered a unique twist to the interracial liaison theme; *Colored People's Time*, Leslie Lee's pot pourri of scenes from African American history; and play after play by Charles Fuller, including his four-play history cycle, collectively titled *We*. Spanning a period from before emancipation through the tragic end of Reconstruction, Fuller's four dramas—*Sally*, *Prince*, *Jonquil* and *Burner's Frolic*—follow a diverse group of African Americans as they grapple with the opportunities and frustrations of a people newly freed, but unsupported and unprotected by any other than themselves.

A decidedly unique accomplishment of the 1980s was *Mama*,

I Want to Sing, a musical written and produced by the interracial team of Vy Higgenson and Kenneth Wydro. Begun as a showcase production, it established itself at an Off-Broadway theater in 1983, caught on, and ran and ran—at this writing, still on the boards and alternating with a second installment, *Mama, I Want to Sing II*. A gospel and pop-soul account of the rise of a recording star, *Mama* has toured the nation, sent companies to Europe and Japan, and grossed millions of dollars, despite its modest production and unpretentious demeanor. Much of its audience in New York came from out of town on bus charters by Black church, fraternal, school and social groups.

Other eighties presentations of interest (again, due to space limitations, to name only a few) were: *The Colored Museum* by George C. Wolfe, a satirical review which came to Off-Broadway from the rising Black production house, the Crossroads Theater of New Brunswick, New Jersey; *Spell #7*, Ntozake Shange's fantasy spinoff from minstrelsy; *Williams and Walker* by Vincent Smith, about the early twentieth-century Black minstrel team Bert Williams and George Walker; and *The Forbidden City*, a withering portrait of a Philadelphia Black middle-class mother by Bill Gunn. Still others were *Tutankh-amon, the Boy King*, a depiction of the ancient Egyptian pharaoh by Garland Thompson; *Do Lord Remember Me* by James de Jongh, based upon actual narratives from former slaves; *Splendid Mummer* by Lonne Elder III, a one-man tour de force on the nineteenth-century Black Shakespearean actor, Ira Aldridge; and *Sherlock Holmes and the Hands of Othello* by Alexander Simmons, another play evoking the spirit of Aldridge, set in London, with the legendary fictional British sleuth involved as well.

As the last decade of the twentieth century begins, two new offerings by African American playwrights are attracting attention: *The Talented Tenth*, by Richard Wesley, and *Spunk*, by George C. Wolfe. Wesley's drama is a look at the Black civil-rights college generation twenty years later, and Wolfe's play is a dramatization of three folk short stories by Zora Neale Hurston.

Were a reincarnated Mr. Brown able to appear upon the scene today and look back upon what has transpired in African American Theater since *King Shotaway* was presented by the African Company in 1823, what would be his reaction? Amazement, certainly. And pride, great pride. Concern, perhaps, at continuing difficulties—inevitably inseparable from the status of Black people in the U.S. as a whole. But also, I think, great curiosity as to where African American theater goes from here. Having achieved important milestones in several directions— (1) as a means of racial enlightenment and protest to the dominant European American community; (2) as an in-house communication among African Americans; (3) as an "equal opportunity" partner with mainstream American theater; (4) as a means of reinforcing ancestral ties with other Africans in the diaspora—what will be its directions as the twenty-first century fast approaches? A new century in which, the demographers tell us, European Americans will soon lose their numerical dominance of the U.S. population; a century in which Blacks, Latinos, native Americans, Asians and other "peoples of color" will collectively come to dominate the U.S. work force; a century in which Womanpower will undoubtedly come into its own; a new century with new challenges, new problems and new opportunities—for progress, for disaster, for something in between, perhaps.

There is much to ponder. For instance, how can African American playwrights contribute importantly to the great task of revising, for a changing population, the educational, economic, political and cultural perspectives of the society in which we live—which have largely been promulgated and propagandized in the past by, and for the primary advantage of, European Americans? What themes should Black dramatists consider, what forces of history must they re-examine, and how will they reconcile the great need to *counter*-propagandize with the essential focus of theater as a means of entertainment rather than sermonizing? Even beyond that, as we contemplate a world of rapidly realigning forces and values, what of the need for African Americans—and others—to develop a greater global consciousness—a *Weltanschauung*, if you please—given that over four-fifths of the world's citizens are people of color, and considering what is sometimes referred to as the never ending reality of the struggle for power?

These and other questions await examination by African American playwrights of the present and the future. As for the *first* African American playwright, I'm sure it will be at least as interesting to Mr. Brown to see what occurs in the next one-hundred and seventy years as in the last.

—William B. Branch
New Rochelle, New York
July 30, 1990

NOTES

1. Errol Hill, *Shakespeare and the Black Actor* (Amherst, Mass.: University of Massachusetts Press, 1984), p. 11.
2. Herbert Marshall and Mildred Stock, *Ira Aldridge, the Negro Tragedian* (New York: Macmillan, 1958), pp. 28–47.
3. Loften Mitchell, *Black Drama: The Story of the American Negro in the Theatre* (New York: Hawthorne, 1967), p. 25.
4. Samuel A. Hay, "The African American Theatre Company: An Overview," Monograph in the program for the Fourth Annual National Conference on African American Theatre, April 9–10, 1987, Morgan State University, Baltimore, Md. Hay quotes from an article by Mordecai Noah in *The National Advocate*.
5. *Ibid*.
6. Marshall and Stock, pp. 7–10. Also, *Sherlock Holmes and the Hands of Othello*, by Alexander Simmons—included in this collection—reflects Ira Aldridge's career in fictional terms.
7. Of necessity, many of the plays referred to in this introduction were produced in New York City, which—despite Black Theater activity all across the country nowadays—remains more-or-less the definitive "proving ground" for U.S. dramatists of all backgrounds.
   Also, this survey focuses principally upon "straight" plays—i.e., non-musicals. For a detailed account of musicals, see *Black Musical Theatré* by Allen Wohl (Baton Rouge: Louisiana State University Press, 1989).
8. Mitchell, p. 40.
9. James V. Hatch, ed., *Black Drama U.S.A.: 45 Plays by Black Americans, 1847–1974* (New York: Free Press, 1974), p. 137.
10. *Ibid*.
11. *Ibid*.
12. Samuel A. Hay, "African American Theater: A Critical History, 1821–1972," 1987. At this writing, an unpublished manuscript.
13. *Ibid*.
14. Caldwell, Milner, Bullins and Jones, *A Black Quartet* (New York: New American Library, 1970), from the introduction by Clayton Riley, p. xx.
15. *The New York Times*, Sun. Jun. 14, 1987, p. H-7.
16. Liz Smith, *The New York Daily News*, Mar. 28, 1988, p. 8.
17. "Broadway Is Offering Black Theatergoers More Reason to Go," *The New York Times*, March 29, 1988, p. C-13.

THE COLORED MUSEUM

A PLAY

by George C. Wolfe

The Colored Museum was first produced at the Crossroads Theater in New Brunswick, New Jersey, by the Crossroads Theater Company on March 26, 1986, and opened at the New York Shakespeare Festival on November 2 of the same year.

GEORGE C. WOLFE

Born in Frankfort, Kentucky, George C. Wolfe received a
B.A. in directing from Pomona College, where he was twice
winner of the regional festival of the American College Theatre
Festival (ACTF); and an M.F.A. in dramatic writing/musical
theater from New York University. Associated with the Inner
City Cultural Center in Los Angeles during the 1970s, he currently resides in New York City. He is a recipient of a CBS/
Foundation of the Dramatists Guild Playwriting Award for *The
Colored Museum*, and grants from the Rockefeller Foundation,
the National Endowment for the Arts, and the National Institute for Musical Theatre.

   Among Wolfe's other works are *Up for Grabs*, a comedy-
satire; *Block Party*, a play with music; the musicals *Back Alley
Tales, Paradise,* and *Queenie Pie*—the latter to music by Duke
Ellington, which was produced at the Kennedy Center in Washington, D.C., in 1986; and *Spunk*, a dramatization with music
of three short stories by Zora Neale Hurston, which was moved
to the New York Shakespeare Festival in New York City after
premiering at the Crossroads Theatre Company in New Brunswick, New Jersey, in 1990.

CHARACTERS

Git on Board
  MISS PAT
Cookin' with Aunt Ethel
  AUNT ETHEL
The Photo Session
  GIRL
  GUY
Soldier with a Secret
  JUNIE ROBINSON
The Gospel According to Miss Roj
  MISS ROJ
  WAITER
The Hairpiece
  THE WOMAN
  JANINE
  LAWANDA
The Last Mama-on-the-Couch Play
  NARRATOR
  MAMA

WALTER-LEE-BEAU-WILLIE-JONES
LADY IN PLAID
MEDEA JONES
Symbiosis
THE MAN
THE KID
Lala's Opening
LALA LAMAZING GRACE
ADMONIA
FLO'RANCE
THE LITTLE GIRL
Permutations
NORMAL JEAN REYNOLDS
The Party
TOPSY WASHINGTON
MISS PAT
MISS ROJ
LALA LAMAZING GRACE
THE MAN (*From* "Symbiosis")

THE EXHIBITS

Git on Board
Cookin' with Aunt Ethel
The Photo Session
Soldier with a Secret
The Gospel According to Miss Roj
The Hairpiece
The Last Mama-on-the-Couch Play
Symbiosis
Lala's Opening
Permutations
The Party

THE CAST: An ensemble of five, two men and three women, all black, who perform all the characters that inhabit the exhibits.*

THE STAGE: White walls and recessed lighting. A starkness befitting a museum where the myths and madness of black/Negro/colored Americans are stored.

*A LITTLE GIRL, seven to twelve years old, is needed for a walk-on part in "Lala's Opening."

Built into the walls are a series of small panels, doors, revolving walls, and compartments from which actors can retrieve key props and make quick entrances.

A revolve is used, which allows for quick transitions from one exhibit to the next.

MUSIC: All of the music for the show should be prerecorded. Only the drummer, who is used in "Git on Board," and then later in "Permutations" and "The Party," is live.

There is no intermission.

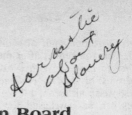

Git on Board

(Blackness. Cut by drums pounding. Then slides, rapidly flashing before us. Images we've all seen before, of African slaves being captured, loaded onto ships, tortured. The images flash, flash, flash. The drums crescendo. Blackout. And then lights reveal MISS PAT, frozen. She is black, pert, and cute. She has a flip to her hair and wears a hot pink mini-skirt stewardess uniform.)

(She stands in front of a curtain which separates her from an offstage cockpit.)

(An electronic bell goes "ding" and MISS PAT comes to life, presenting herself in a friendly but rehearsed manner, smiling and speaking as she has done so many times before.)

MISS PAT: Welcome aboard Celebrity Slaveship, departing the Gold Coast and making short stops at Bahia, Port au Prince, and Havana, before our final destination of Savannah.

Hi. I'm Miss Pat and I'll be serving you here in Cabin A. We will be crossing the Atlantic at an altitude that's pretty high, so you must wear your shackles at all times. *(She removes a shackle from the overhead compartment and demonstrates.)*

To put on your shackle, take the right hand and close the metal ring around your left hand like so. Repeat the action using your left hand to secure the right. If you have any trouble bonding yourself, I'd be more than glad to assist.

Once we reach the desired altitude, the captain will turn off the "Fasten Your Shackle" sign . . . *(She efficiently points out the "FASTEN YOUR SHACKLE" signs on either side of her, which light up.)* . . . allowing you a chance to stretch and dance in the aisles a bit. But otherwise, shackles must be worn at all times.

(The "FASTEN YOUR SHACKLE" signs go off.)

MISS PAT: Also, we ask that you please refrain from call-and-response singing between cabins, as that sort of thing can

5

lead to rebellion. And, of course, no drums are allowed on board. Can you repeat after me, "No drums." (*She gets the audience to repeat.*) With a little more enthusiasm, please. "No drums." (*After the audience repeats it.*) That was great!

Once we're airborne, I'll be by with magazines, and ear-phones can be purchased for the price of your first-born male.

If there's anything I can do to make this middle passage more pleasant, press the little button overhead and I'll be with you faster than you can say, "Go down, Moses." (*She laughs at her "little joke."*) Thanks for flying Celebrity and here's hoping you have a pleasant takeoff.

(*The engines surge, the "FASTEN YOUR SHACKLE" signs go on, and over-articulate Muzak voices are heard singing as* MISS PAT *pulls down a bucket seat and "shackles-up" for takeoff.*)

VOICES:
Get on board Celebrity slaveship
Get on board Celebrity slaveship
Get on board Celebrity slaveship
There's room for many a more

(*The engines reach an even, steady hum. Just as* MISS PAT *rises and replaces the shackles in the overhead compartment, the faint sound of African drumming is heard.*)

MISS PAT: Hi. Miss Pat again. I'm sorry to disturb you, but someone is playing drums. And what did we just say . . . "No drums." It must be someone in Coach. But we here in Cabin A are not going to respond to those drums. As a matter of fact, we don't even hear them. Repeat after me. "I don't hear any drums." (*The audience repeats.*) And "I will not rebel."

(*The audience repeats. The drumming grows.*)

MISS PAT: (*Placating.*) OK, now I realize some of us are a bit edgy after hearing about the tragedy on board The Laughing Mary, but let me assure you Celebrity has no intention of throwing you overboard and collecting the insurance. We value you!

(She proceeds to single out individual passengers/audience members.)

Why, the songs *you* are going to sing in the cotton fields, under the burning heat and stinging lash, will metamorphose and give birth to the likes of James Brown and the Fabulous Flames. And you, yes, *you*, are going to come up with some of the best dances! The best dances! The Watusi! The Funky Chicken! And just think of what *you* are going to mean to William Faulkner.

All right, so you're gonna have to suffer for a few hundred years, but from your pain will come a culture so complex. *And*, with this little item here . . . *(She removes a basketball from the overhead compartment.)* . . . you'll become millionaires!

(There is a roar of thunder. The lights quiver and the "FASTEN YOUR SHACKLE" signs begin to flash. MISS PAT quickly replaces the basketball in the overhead compartment and speaks very reassuringly.)

MISS PAT: No, don't panic. We're just caught in a little thunderstorm. Now, the only way you're going to make it through is if you abandon your God and worship a new one. So, on the count of three, let's all sing. One, two, three . . .

Nobody knows de trouble I seen . . .

Oh, I forgot to mention, when singing, omit the T-H sound. "The" becomes "de." "They" becomes "dey." Got it? Good!

Nobody knows . . .
Nobody knows . . .

Oh, so you don't like that one? Well then let's try another—

Summer time and de livin' is easy—

Gershwin. He comes from another oppressed people so he understands.

Fish are jumpin' . . .

Come on.

And de cotton is high.
And de cotton is . . .

Sing, damnit!

(Lights begin to flash, the engines surge, and there is wild drumming. MISS PAT sticks her head through the curtain and speaks with an offstage CAPTAIN.)

MISS PAT: What?
VOICE OF CAPTAIN: *(Offstage.)* Time warp!
MISS PAT: Time warp! *(She turns to the audience and puts on a pleasant face.)* The captain has assured me everything is fine. We're just caught in a little time warp. *(Trying to fight her growing hysteria.)* On your right you will see the American Revolution, which will give the U.S. of A. exclusive rights to your life. And on your left, the Civil War, which means you will vote Republican until F.D.R. comes along. And now we're passing over the Great Depression, which means everybody gets to live the way you've been living. *(There is a blinding flash of light, and an explosion. She screams.)* Ahhhhhhhhh! That was World War I, which is not to be confused with World War II . . . *(There is a larger flash of light, and another explosion.)* . . . Ahhhhh! Which is not to be confused with the Korean War or the Vietnam War, all of which you will play a major role in.

Oh, look, now we're passing over the sixties. Martha and the Vandellas . . . "Julia" with Miss Diahann Carroll . . . Malcom X . . . those five little girls in Alabama . . . Martin Luther King . . . Oh no! The Supremes broke up! *(The drumming intensifies.)* Stop playing those drums! Those drums will be confiscated once we reach Savannah. You can't change history! You can't turn back the clock! *(To the audience.)* Repeat after me, I don't hear any drums! I will not rebel! I will not rebel! I will not re—

(The lights go out, she screams, and the sound of a plane landing and screeching to a halt is heard. After a beat, lights reveal a wasted, disheveled MISS PAT, but perky nonetheless.)

MISS PAT: Hi. Miss Pat here. Things got a bit jumpy back there, but the captain has just informed me we have safely landed in Savannah. Please check the overhead before exiting, as any baggage you don't claim, we trash.

It's been fun, and we hope the next time you consider travel, it's with Celebrity.

(*Luggage begins to revolve onstage from offstage left, going past* MISS PAT *and revolving offstage right. Mixed in with the luggage are two male slaves and a woman slave, complete with luggage and ID tags around their necks.*)

MISS PAT: (*With routine, rehearsed pleasantness.*) Have a nice day. Bye bye.
Button up that coat, it's kind of chilly.
Have a nice day. Bye bye.
You take care now.
See you.
Have a nice day.
Have a nice day.
Have a nice day.

Cookin' with Aunt Ethel

(*As the slaves begin to revolve off, a low-down, gut-bucket blues is heard.* AUNT ETHEL, *a down-home black woman with a bandana on her head, revolves to center stage. She stands behind a big black pot and wears a reassuring grin.*)

AUNT ETHEL: Welcome to "Aunt Ethel's Down-Home Cookin' Show," where we explores the magic and mysteries of colored cuisine.
Today, we gonna be servin' ourselves up some . . . (*She laughs.*) I'm not gonna tell you. That's right! I'm not gonna tell you what it is till after you done cooked it. Child, on "The Aunt Ethel Show" we loves to have ourselves some fun. Well, are you ready? Here goes.

(*She belts out a hard-drivin' blues and throws invisible ingredients into the big, black pot.*)

First ya add a pinch of style
And then a dash of flair
Now ya stir in some preoccupation
With the texture of your hair

Next ya add all kinds of rhythms
Lots of feelings and pizzazz

Then hunny throw in some rage
Till it congeals and turns to jazz

Now you cookin'
Cookin' with Aunt Ethel
You really cookin'
Cookin' with Aunt Ethel, oh yeah

Now ya add a heap of survival
And humility, just a touch
Add some attitude
Oops! I put too much
And now a whole lot of humor
Salty language, mixed with sadness
Then throw in a box of blues
And simmer to madness

Now you cookin'
Cookin' with Aunt Ethel, oh yeah!

Now you beat it—really work it
Discard and disown
And in a few hundred years
Once it's aged and fully grown
Ya put it in the oven
Till it's black
And has a sheen
Or till it's nice and yella
Or any shade in between

Next ya take 'em out and cool 'em
'Cause they no fun when they hot
And won't you be surprised
At the concoction you got

You have baked
Baked yourself a batch of Negroes
Yes, you have baked yourself
Baked yourself a batch of Negroes

(*She pulls from the pot a handful of Negroes, black dolls.*)

But don't ask me what to do with 'em now that you got
'em, 'cause, child, that's your problem. (*She throws the dolls*

back into the pot.) But in any case, yaw be sure to join Aunt Ethel next week, when we gonna be servin' ourselves up some chitlin quiche . . . some grits-under-glass,

And a sweet potato pie
And you'll be cookin'
Cookin' with Aunt Ethel
Oh yeah!

(*On* AUNT ETHEL'S *final rift, lights reveal . . .*)

The Photo Session

(*. . . a very glamorous, gorgeous, black couple, wearing the best of everything and perfect smiles. The stage is bathed in color and bright white light. Disco music with the chant "We're fabulous" plays in the background. As they pose, larger-than-life images of their perfection are projected on the museum walls. The music quiets and the images fade away as they begin to speak and pose.*)

GIRL: The world was becoming too much for us.
GUY: We couldn't resolve the contradictions of our existence.
GIRL: And we couldn't resolve yesterday's pain.
GUY: So we gave away our life and we now live inside *Ebony Magazine*.
GIRL: Yes, we live inside a world where everyone is beautiful and wears fabulous clothes.
GUY: And no one says anything profound.
GIRL: Or meaningful.
GUY: Or contradictory.
GIRL: Because no one talks. Everyone just smiles and shows off their cheekbones.

(*They adopt a profile pose.*)

GUY: Last month I was black and fabulous while holding up a bottle of vodka.
GIRL: This month we get to be black and fabulous together.

(*They dance/pose. The "We're fabulous" chant builds and then fades as they start to speak again.*)

GIRL: There are of course setbacks.

GUY: We have to smile like this for a whole month.

GIRL: And we have no social life.

GUY: And no sex.

GIRL: And at times it feels like we're suffocating, like we're not human anymore.

GUY: And everything is rehearsed, including this other kind of pain we're starting to feel.

GIRL: The kind of pain that comes from feeling no pain at all.

(They then speak and pose with a sudden burst of energy.)

GUY: But one can't have everything.

GIRL: Can one?

GUY: So if the world is becoming too much for you, do like we did.

GIRL: Give away your life and come be beautiful with us.

GUY: We guarantee, no contradictions.

GIRL/GUY: Smile/click, smile/click, smile/click.

GIRL: And no pain.

(They adopt a final pose and revolve off as the "We're fabulous" chant plays and fades into the background.)

A Soldier with a Secret

(Projected onto the museum walls are the faces of black soldiers—from the Spanish-American through the Vietnam War. Lights slowly reveal JUNIE ROBINSON, a black combat soldier, posed on an onyx plinth. He comes to life and smiles at the audience. Somewhat dim-witted, he has an easygoing charm about him.)

JUNIE: Pst. Pst. Guess what? I know the secret. The secret to your pain. 'Course, I didn't always know. First I had to die, then come back to life, 'fore I had the gift.

   Ya see, the Cappin sent me off up ahead to scout for screamin' yella bastards. 'Course, for the life of me I couldn't understand why they'd be screamin', seein' as how we was tryin' to kill them and they us.

   But anyway, I'm off lookin', when all of a sudden I find myself caught smack dead in the middle of this explosion. This blindin', burnin', scaldin' explosion. Musta been a booby trap or something, 'cause all around me is fire. Hell, I'm on fire. Like a piece of chicken dropped in a skillet of cracklin' grease. Why, my flesh was justa peelin' off of my bones.

But then I says to myself, "Junie, if yo' flesh is on fire, how come you don't feel no pain!" And I didn't. I swear as I'm standin' here, I felt nuthin'. That's when I sort of put two and two together and realized I didn't feel no whole lot of hurtin' 'cause I done died.

Well, I just picked myself up and walked right on out of that explosion. Hell, once you know you dead, why keep on dyin', ya know?

So, like I say, I walk right outta that explosion, fully expectin' to see white clouds, Jesus, and my mama, only all I saw was more war. Shootin' goin' on way off in this direction and that direction. And there, standin' around, was all the guys. Hubert, J. F., the Cappin. I guess the sound of the explosion must of attracted 'em, and they all starin' at me like I'm some kind of ghost.

So I yells to 'em, "Hey there, Hubert! Hey there, Cappin!" But they just stare. So I tells 'em how I'd died and how I guess it wasn't my time 'cause here I am, "fully in the flesh and not a scratch to my bones." And they still just stare. So I took to starin' back.

(The expression on JUNIE'S *face slowly turns to horror and disbelief.)*

Only what I saw . . . well, I can't exactly to this day describe it. But I swear, as sure as they was wearin' green and holdin' guns, they was each wearin' a piece of the future on their faces.

Yeah. All the hurt that was gonna get done to them and they was gonna do to folks was right there clear as day.

I saw how J. F., once he got back to Chicago, was gonna get shot dead by this po-lice, and I saw how Hubert was gonna start beatin' up on his old lady, which I didn't understand 'cause all he could do was talk on and on about how much he loved her. Each and every one of 'em had pain in his future and blood on his path. And God or the Devil one spoke to me and said, "Junie, these colored boys ain't gonna be the same after this war. They ain't gonna have no kind of happiness."

Well, right then and there it comes to me. The secret to their pain.

Late that night, after the medics done checked me over and found me fit for fightin', after everybody done settle down for the night, I sneaked over to where Hubert was sleepin', and with a needle I stole from the medics . . . pst, pst . . . I shot a little air into his veins. The second he died, all the hurtin'-to-come just left his face.

Two weeks later I got J. F. and after that Woodrow . . . Jimmy Joe . . . I even spent all night waitin' by the latrine 'cause I knew the Cappin always made a late-night visit and . . . pst, pst . . . I got him.

(*Smiling, quite proud of himself.*) That's how come I died and come back to life. 'Cause just like Jesus went around healin' the sick, I'm supposed to go around healin' the hurtin' all these colored boys wearin' from the war.

Pst, pst. I know the secret. The secret to your pain. The secret to yours, and yours. Pst. Pst. Pst. Pst.

(*The lights slowly fade.*)

The Gospel According to Miss Roj

(*The darkness is cut by electronic music. Cold, pounding, unrelenting. A neon sign which spells out "THE BOTTOMLESS PIT" clicks on. There is a lone bar stool. Lights flash on and off, pulsating to the beat. There is a blast of smoke, and from the haze MISS ROJ appears. He is dressed in striped patio pants, white go-go boots, a halter, and cat-shaped sunglasses. What would seem ridiculous on anyone else, MISS ROJ wears as if it were high fashion. He carries himself with total elegance and absolute arrogance.*)

MISS ROJ: God created black people and black people created style. The name's Miss Roj . . . that's R.O.J., thank you, and you can find me every Wednesday, Friday, and Saturday nights at The Bottomless Pit, the watering hole for the wild and weary which asks the question, "Is there life after Jheri-curl?"

(*A waiter enters, hands MISS ROJ a drink, and then exits.*)

Thanks, doll. *Yes*, if they be black and swish, the B.P. has seen them, which is not to suggest the Pit is lacking in cultural diversity. Oh no. There are your dinge queens, white men who like their chicken legs dark. (*He winks/flirts with a man in the audience.*) And let's not forget "Los Muchachos de la Neighborhood." But the speciality of the house is the Snap Queens. (*He snaps his fingers.*) We are a rare breed.

For, you see, when something strikes our fancy, when the truth comes piercing through the dark, well, you just can't let it pass unnoticed. No, darling. You must pronounce it with a snap. (*He snaps.*)

Snapping comes from another galaxy, as do all Snap Queens. That's right. I ain't just your regular oppressed American Negro. No-no-no! I am an extraterrestial. And I ain't talkin' none of that shit you seen in the movies! I have real power.

(*The waiter enters.* MISS ROJ *stops him.*)

Speaking of no power, will you please tell Miss Stingy-with-the-rum that if Miss Roj had wanted to remain sober, she could have stayed home and drank Kool-Aid. (*He snaps.*) Thank you.

(*The waiter exits.* MISS ROJ *crosses and sits on bar stool.*)

Yes, I was placed here on Earth to study the life habits of a deteriorating society, and child, when we talkin' New York City, we are discussing the Queen of Deterioration. Miss New York is doing a slow dance with death, and I am here to warn you all, but before I do, I must know: don't you just love my patio pants? Annette Funicello immortalized them in *Beach Blanket Bingo*, and I have continued the legacy. And my go-gos? I realize white after Labor Day is very gauche, but as the saying goes, if you've got it, flaunt it. If you don't, front it and snap to death any bastard who dares to defy you. (*Laughing.*) Oh ho! My demons are showing. Yes, my demons live at the bottom of my Bacardi and Coke.

Let's just hope for all concerned I dance my demons out before I drink them out 'cause child, dancing demons take you on a ride, but those drinkin' demons just take you, and you find yourself doing the strangest things. Like the time I locked my father in the broom closet. Seems the liquor made his tongue real liberal and he decided he was gonna baptize me with the word *faggot* over and over. Well, he's just going on and on and with "faggot this" and "faggot that," all the while walking toward the broom closet to piss. So the demons just took hold of my wedges and forced me to kick the drunk son of a bitch into the closet and lock the door. (*Laughter.*) Three days later I remembered he was there. (*He snaps.*)

(The waiter enters. MISS ROJ *takes a drink and downs it.)*

Another!

(The waiter exits.)

(*Dancing about.*) Oh yes yes yes! Miss Roj is quintessential style. I corn row the hairs on my legs so that they spell out M.I.S.S. R.O.J. And I dare any bastard to fuck with me because I will snap your ass into oblivion.

I have the power, you know. Everytime I snap, I steal one beat of your heart. So if you find yourself gasping for air in the middle of the night, chances are you fucked with Miss Roj and she didn't like it.

Like the time this asshole at Jones Beach decided to take issue with my coulotte-sailor ensemble. This child, this muscle-bound Brooklyn thug in a skin-tight bikini, very skin-tight so the whole world can see that instead of a brain, God gave him an extra thick piece of sausage. You know, the kind who beat up on their wives for breakfast. Snap your fingers if you know what I'm talking about . . . Come on and snap, child. (*He gets the audience to snap.*) Well, he decided to blurt out when I walked by, "Hey, look at da monkey coon in da faggit suit." Well, I walked up to the poor dear, very calmly lifted my hand, and. . . . (*He snaps in rapid succession.*) A heart attack, right there on the beach. (*He singles out someone in the audience.*) You don't believe it? Cross me! Come on! Come on!

(The waiter enters, hands MISS ROJ *a drink.* MISS ROJ *downs it. The waiter exits.)*

(*Looking around.*) If this place is the answer, we're asking all the wrong questions. The only reason I come here is to communicate with my origins. The flashing lights are signals from my planet way out there. Yes, girl, even farther than Flatbush. We're talking another galaxy. The flashing lights tell me how much time is left before the end.

(*Very drunk and loud by now.*) I hate the people here. I hate the drinks. But most of all I hate this goddamn music. That ain't music. Give me Aretha Franklin any day. (*Singing.*) "Just a little respect. R.E.S.P.E.C.T." Yeah! Yeah!

Come on and dance your last dance with Miss Roj. Last call is but a drink away, and each snap puts you one step closer to the end.

A high-rise goes up. You can't get no job. Come on, everybody, and dance. A whole race of people gets trashed and debased. Snap those fingers and dance. Some sick bitch throws her baby out the window 'cause she thinks it's the Devil. Everybody snap! *The New York Post.* Snap!

Snap for every time you walk past someone lying in the street, smelling like frozen piss and shit and you don't see it. Snap for every crazed bastard who kills himself so as to get the jump on being killed. And snap for every sick mutha-fucker who, bored with carrying around his fear, takes to shooting up other people.

Yeah, snap your fingers and dance with Miss Roj. But don't be fooled by the banners and balloons 'cause, child, this ain't no party going on. Hell no! It's a wake. And the casket's made out of stone, steel, and glass, and the people are racing all over the pavement like maggots on a dead piece of meat.

Yeah, dance! But don't be surprised if there ain't no beat holding you together 'cause we traded in our drums for respectability. So now it's just words. Words rappin'. Words screechin'. Words flowin' instead of blood 'cause you know that don't work. Words cracklin' instead of fire 'cause by the time a match is struck on 125th Street and you run to Mid-town, the flame has been blown away.

So come on and dance with Miss Roj and her demons. We don't ask for acceptance. We don't ask for approval. We know who we are and we move on it!

I guarantee you will never hear two fingers put together in a snap and not think of Miss Roj. That's power, baby. Patio pants and all.

(The lights begin to flash in rapid succession.)

So let's dance! And snap! And dance! And snap!

(MISS ROJ *begins to dance as if driven by his demons. There is a blast of smoke and when the haze settles,* MISS ROJ *has revolved off and in place of him is a recording of Aretha Frank-lin singing "Respect.")*

The Hairpiece

(As "Respect" fades into the background, a vanity revolves to center stage. On this vanity are two wigs, an Afro wig circa 1968 and a long, flowing wig, both resting on wig stands. A black WOMAN *enters, her head and body wrapped in towels. She picks up a framed picture and after a few moments of hesitation, throws it into a small trashcan. She then removes one of her towels to reveal a totally bald head. Looking into a mirror on the "fourth wall," she begins applying makeup.)*

(The wig stand holding the Afro wig opens her eyes. Her name is JANINE. *She stares in disbelief at the bald woman.)*

JANINE: *(Calling to the other wig stand.)* LaWanda. LaWanda, girl, wake up.

(The other wig stand, the one with the long, flowing wig, opens her eyes. Her name is LAWANDA.*)*

LAWANDA: What? What is it?

JANINE: Check out girlfriend.

LAWANDA: Oh, girl, I don't believe it.

JANINE: *(Laughing.)* Just look at the poor thing, trying to paint some life onto that face of hers. You'd think by now she'd realize it's the hair. It's all about the hair.

LAWANDA: What hair! She ain't got no hair! She done fried, dyed, de-chemicalized her shit to death.

JANINE: And all that's left is that buck-naked scalp of hers, sittin' up there apologizin' for being odd-shaped and ugly.

LAWANDA: *(Laughing with* JANINE.*)* Girl, stop!

JANINE: I ain't sayin' nuthin' but the truth.

LAWANDA/JANINE: The bitch is bald! *(They laugh.)*

JANINE: And all over some man.

LAWANDA: I tell ya, girl, I just don't understand it. I mean, look at her. She's got a right nice face, a good head on her shoulders. A good job even. And she's got to go fall in love with that fool.

JANINE: That political quick-change artist. Every time the nigga went and changed his ideology, she went and changed her hair to fit the occasion.

LAWANDA: Well, at least she's breaking up with him.

JANINE: Hunny, no!

LaWANDA: Yes, child.

JANINE: Oh, girl, dish me the dirt!

LaWANDA: Well, you see, I heard her on the phone, talking to one of her girlfriends, and she's meeting him for lunch today to give him the ax.

JANINE: Well, it's about time.

LaWANDA: I hear ya. But don't you worry 'bout a thing, girlfriend. I'm gonna tell you all about it.

JANINE: Hunny, you won't have to tell me a damn thing 'cause I'm gonna be there, front row, center.

LaWANDA: You?

JANINE: Yes, child, she's wearing me to lunch.

LaWANDA: (*Outraged.*) I don't think so!

JANINE: (*With an attitude.*) What do you mean, you don't think so?

LaWANDA: Exactly what I said, "I don't think so." Damn, Janine, get real. How the hell she gonna wear both of us?

JANINE: She ain't wearing both of us. She's wearing me.

LaWANDA: Says who?

JANINE: Says me! Says her! Ain't that right, girlfriend?

(*The* WOMAN *stops putting on makeup, looks around, sees no one, and goes back to her makeup.*)

JANINE: I said, ain't that right!

(*The* WOMAN *picks up the phone.*)

WOMAN: Hello . . . hello . . .

JANINE: Did you hear the damn phone ring?

WOMAN: No.

JANINE: Then put the damn phone down and talk to me.

WOMAN: I, ah . . . don't understand.

JANINE: It ain't deep, so don't panic. Now, you're having lunch with your boyfriend, right?

WOMAN: (*Breaking into tears.*) I think I'm having a nervous breakdown.

JANINE: (*Impatient.*) I said, you're having lunch with your boyfriend, right!

WOMAN: (*Scared, pulling herself together.*) Yes, right . . . right.

JANINE: To break up with him.

WOMAN: How did you know that?

LaWANDA: I told her.

WOMAN: (*Stands and screams.*) Help! Help!

JANINE: Sit down. I said, sit your ass down!

(*The* WOMAN *does.*)

JANINE: Now set her straight and tell her you're wearing me.
LaWANDA: She's the one that needs to be set straight, so go on and tell her you're wearing me.
JANINE: No, tell her you're wearing me.

(*There is a pause.*)

LaWANDA: Well?
JANINE: Well?
WOMAN: I, ah . . . actually hadn't made up my mind.
JANINE: (*Going off.*) What do you mean, you ain't made up your mind! After all that fool has put you through, you gonna need all the attitude you can get, and there is nothing like attitude and a healthy head of kinks to make his shit shrivel like it should!

That's right! When you wearin' me, you lettin' him know he ain't gonna get no sweet-talkin' comb through your love without some serious resistance. No-no! The kink of my head is like the kink of your heart, and neither is about to be hot-pressed into surrender.
LaWANDA: That shit is so tired. The last time attitude worked on anybody was 1968. Janine girl, you need to get over it and get on with it. (*To the* WOMAN.) And you need to give the nigga a good-bye he will never forget.

I say give him hysteria! Give him emotion! Give him rage! And there is nothing like a toss of the tresses to make your emotional outburst shine with emotional flair.

You can toss me back, shake me from side to side, all the while screaming, "I want you out of my life forever!!!" And not only will I come bouncing back for more, but you just might win an Academy Award for best performance by a head of hair in a dramatic role.
JANINE: Miss Hunny, please! She don't need no Barbie doll dipped in chocolate telling her what to do. She needs a head of hair that's coming from a fo' real place.
LaWANDA: Don't you dare talk about nobody coming from a "fo' real place," Miss Made-in-Taiwan!
JANINE: Hey! I ain't ashamed of where I come from. Besides, it don't matter where you come from as long as you end up in the right place.

LaWanda: And it don't matter the grade as long as the point gets made. So go on and tell her you're wearing me.
Janine: No, tell her you're wearing me.

(The Woman, unable to take it, begins to bite off her fake nails as LaWanda and Janine go at each other.)

LaWanda: Set the bitch straight. Let her know there is no way she could even begin to compete with me. I am quality. She is kink. I am exotic. She is common. I am class and she is trash. That's right. T.R.A.S.H. We're talking three strikes and you're out. So go on and tell her you're wearing me. Go on, tell her! Tell her! Tell her!

Janine: Who you callin' a bitch? Why, if I had hands I'd knock you clear into next week. You think you cute. She thinks she's cute just 'cause that synthetic mop of hers blows in the wind. She looks like a fool and you look like an even bigger fool when you wear her, so go on and tell her you're wearing me. Go on, tell her! Tell her! Tell her!

(The Woman screams and pulls the two wigs off the wig stands as the lights go to black on three bald heads.)

The Last Mama-on-the-Couch Play

(A Narrator, dressed in a black tuxedo, enters through the audience and stands center stage. He is totally solemn.)

Narrator: We are pleased to bring you yet another Mama-on-the-Couch play. A searing domestic drama that tears at the very fabric of racist America. *(He crosses upstage center and sits on a stool and reads from a playscript.)* Act One. Scene One.

(Mama revolves on stage left, sitting on a couch reading a large, oversized Bible. A window is placed stage right. Mama's dress, the couch, and drapes are made from the same material. A doormat lays down center.)

Narrator: Lights up on a dreary, depressing, but with middle-class aspirations tenement slum. There is a couch, with a Mama on it. Both are well worn. There is a picture of Jesus on the wall . . . *(A picture of Jesus is instantly revealed.)* . . .

and a window which looks onto an abandoned tenement. It is late spring.

Enter Walter-Lee-Beau-Willie-Jones. (SON *enters through the audience.*) He is Mama's thirty-year-old son. His brow is heavy from three hundred years of oppression.

MAMA: (*Looking up from her Bible, speaking in a slow manner.*) Son, did you wipe your feet?

SON: (*An ever erupting volcano.*) No, Mama, I didn't wipe my feet! Out there, every day, Mama, is the Man. The Man, Mama. Mr. Charlie! Mr. Boss Man! And he's wipin' his feet on me. On me, Mama, every damn day of my life. Ain't that enough for me to deal with? Ain't that enough?

MAMA: Son, wipe your feet.

SON: I wanna dream. I wanna be somebody. I wanna take charge of my life.

MAMA: You can do all of that, but first you got to wipe your feet.

SON: (*As he crosses to the mat, mumbling and wiping his feet.*) Wipe my feet . . . wipe my feet . . . wipe my feet . . .

MAMA: That's a good boy.

SON: (*Exploding.*) Boy! Boy! I don't wanna be nobody's good boy, Mama. I wanna be my own man!

MAMA: I know, son, I know. God will show the way.

SON: God, Mama! Since when did your God ever do a damn thing for the Black man? Huh, Mama, huh? You tell me. When did your God ever help me?

MAMA: (*Removing her wire-rim glasses.*) Son, come here. (SON *crosses to* MAMA, *who slowly stands and in an exaggerated stage slap, backhands* SON *clear across the stage. The* NARRATOR *claps his hands to create the sound for the slap.* MAMA *then lifts her clenched fists to the heavens.*) Not in my house, my house, will you ever talk that way again!

(*The* NARRATOR, *so moved by her performance, erupts in applause and encourages the audience to do so.*)

NARRATOR: Beautiful. Just stunning.

(*He reaches into one of the secret compartments of the set and gets an award which he ceremoniously gives to* MAMA *for her performance. She bows and then returns to the couch.*)

NARRATOR: Enter Walter-Lee-Beau-Willie's wife, the Lady in Plaid.

(Music from nowhere is heard, a jazzy pseudo-abstract intro as the LADY IN PLAID *dances in through the audience, wipes her feet, and then twirls about.)*

LADY:
She was a creature of regal beauty
who in ancient time graced the temples of the Nile
with her womanliness
But here she was, stuck being colored
and a woman in a world that valued neither.

SON: You cooked my dinner?

LADY: *(Oblivious to* SON.)
Feet flat, back broke,
she looked at the man who, though he be thirty,
still ain't got his own apartment.
Yeah, he's still livin' with his mama!
And she asked herself, was this the life
for a Princess Colored, who by the
translucence of her skin, knew the
universe was her sister?

(The LADY IN PLAID *twirls and dances.)*

SON: *(Becoming irate.)* I've had a hard day of dealin' with the Man. Where's my damn dinner? Woman, stand still when I'm talkin' to you!

LADY: And she cried for her sisters in Detroit
Who knew, as she, that their souls belonged
in ancient temples on the Nile.
And she cried for her sisters in Chicago
who, like her, their life has become
one colored hell.

SON: There's only one thing gonna get through to you.

LADY: And she cried for her sisters in New Orleans
And her sisters in Trenton and Birmingham,
and
Poughkeepsie and Orlando and Miami Beach
and
Las Vegas, Palm Springs.

(As she continues to call out cities, he crosses offstage and returns with two black dolls and then crosses to the window.)

SON: Now are you gonna cook me dinner?

LADY: Walter-Lee-Beau-Willie-Jones, no! Not my babies.

(SON throws them out the window. The LADY IN PLAID then lets out a primal scream.)

LADY: He dropped them!!!!

(The NARRATOR breaks into applause.)

NARRATOR: Just splendid. Shattering.

(He then crosses and after an intense struggle with MAMA, he takes the award from her and gives it to the LADY IN PLAID, who is still suffering primal pain.)

LADY: Not my babies . . . not my . . . *(Upon receiving the award, she instantly recovers.)* Help me up, sugar. *(She then bows and crosses and stands behind the couch.)*

NARRATOR: Enter Medea Jones, Walter-Lee-Beau-Willie's sister.

(MEDEA moves very ceremoniously, wiping her feet and then speaking and gesturing as if she just escaped from a Greek tragedy.)

MEDEA:
Ah, see how the sun kneels to speak
her evening vespers, exaulting all
in her vision, even lowly tenement
long abandoned.

Mother, wife of brother, I trust
the approaching darkness finds you
safe in Hestia's bosom.

Brother, why wear the face of a man
in anguish. Can the garment of thine
feelings cause the shape of your
countenance to disfigure so?
SON: *(At the end of his rope.)* Leave me alone, Medea.
MEDEA: *(To MAMA.)*
Is good brother still going on and on and on about He and
the Man.
MAMA/LADY: What else?

MEDEA: Ah brother, if with our thoughts and
    words we could cast thine oppressors
    into the lowest bowels of wretched
    hell, would that make us more like the
    gods or more like our oppressors.

    No, brother, no, do not let thy rage
    choke the blood which anoints thy
    heart with love. Forgo thine darkened
    humor and let love shine on your
    soul, like a jewel on a young maiden's hand.

    (Dropping to her knees.)

    I beseech thee, forgo thine
    anger and leave wrath to the gods!
SON: Girl, what has gotten into you?
MEDEA: Juliard, good brother. For I am no
    longer bound by rhythms of race or
    region. Oh, no. My speech, like my
    pain and suffering, have become
    classical and therefore universal.
LADY: I didn't understand a damn thing she said, but girl, you
    usin' them words.

*(LADY IN PLAID crosses and gives MEDEA the award and
everyone applauds.)*

SON: *(Trying to stop the applause.)* Wait one damn minute!
    This my play. It's about me and the Man. It ain't got nuthin'
    to do with no ancient temples on the Nile and it ain't got
    nuthin' to do with Hestia's bosom. And it ain't got nuthin'
    to do with you slappin' me across no room. *(His gut-
    wrenching best.)* It's about me. Me and my pain! My pain!
THE VOICE OF THE MAN: Walter-Lee-Beau-Willie, this is the
    Man. You have been convicted of overacting. Come out with
    your hands up.

(SON starts to cross to the window.)

SON: Well now, that does it.
MAMA: Son, no, don't go near that window. Son, no!

(Gunshots ring out and SON falls dead.)

MAMA: (*Crossing to the body, too emotional for words.*) My son, he was a good boy. Confused. Angry. Just like his father. And his father's father. And his father's father's father. And now he's dead.

(*Seeing she's about to drop to her knees, the* NARRATOR *rushes and places a pillow underneath her just in time.*)

If only he had been born into a world better than this. A world where there are no well-worn couches and no well-worn mamas and nobody over-emotes.
If only he had been born into an all-black musical.

(*A song intro begins.*)

Nobody ever dies in an all-black musical.

(MEDEA *and* LADY IN PLAID *pull out church fans and begin to fan themselves.*)

MAMA: (*Singing a soul-stirring gospel.*)
Oh why couldn't he
Be born
Into a show with lots of singing
And dancing

I say why
Couldn't he
Be born . . .
LADY: Go ahead, hunny. Take your time.
MAMA:
. . . into a show where everybody
Is happy
NARRATOR/MEDEA: Preach! Preach!
MAMA:
Oh why couldn't he be born with the chance
To smile a lot and sing and dance
Oh why
Oh why

Oh why
Couldn't he
Be born

Into an all-black show
Woah-woah

(*The* CAST *joins in, singing do-wop gospel background to* MAMA'S *lament.*)

Oh why
Couldn't he
Be born
(He be born)
Into a show where everybody
Is happy

Why couldn't he be born with the chance
To smile a lot and sing and dance
Wanna know why
Wanna know why

Oh why
Couldn't he
Be born
Into an all-black show
A-men

(*A singing/dancing, spirit-raising revival begins.*)

Oh, son, get up
Get up and dance
We say, get up
This is your second chance

Don't shake a fist
Just shake a leg
And do the twist
Don't scream and beg
Son son son
Get up and dance

Get
Get up
Get up and
Get up and dance—all right!
Get up and dance—all right!
Get up and dance!!

*(*WALTER-LEE-BEAU-WILLIE *springs to life and joins in the dancing. A foot-stomping, hand-clapping production number takes off, which encompasses myriad black-Broadwayesque dancing styles—shifting speeds and styles with exuberant abandonment.)*

MAMA: *(Bluesy.)*
  Why couldn't he be born into an all-black show
CAST:
  With singing and dancing
MAMA:
  Black show

*(*MAMA *scats and the dancing becomes manic and just a little too desperate to please.)*

CAST:
  We gotta dance
  We gotta dance
  Get up get up get up and dance
  We gotta dance
  We gotta dance
  Gotta dance!

(Just at the point the dancing is about to become violent, the CAST *freezes and pointedly, simply sings:)*

  If we want to live
  We have got to
  We have got to
  Dance . . . and dance . . . and dance . . .

(As they continue to dance with zombie-like frozen smiles and faces, around them images of coon performers flash as the lights slowly fade.)

Symbiosis

(The Temptations singing "My Girl" are heard as lights reveal a BLACK MAN *in corporate dress standing before a large trash can, throwing objects from a Saks Fifth Avenue bag into it. Circling around him with his every emotion on his face is* THE KID, *who is dressed in a late-sixties street style. His moves are slightly heightened. As the scene begins the music fades.)*

MAN: *(With contained emotions.)*
My first pair of Converse All-stars. Gone.
My first Afro comb. Gone.
My first dashiki. Gone.
My autographed pictures of Stokley Carmichael, Jomo Kenyatta, and Donna Summer. Gone.

KID: *(Near tears, totally upset.)* This shit's not fair, man. Damn! Hell! Shit! Shit! It's not fair!

MAN:
My first jar of Murray's Pomade.
My first can of Afro sheen.
My first box of curl relaxer. Gone! Gone! Gone!
Eldridge Cleaver's *Soul on Ice.*

KID: Not *Soul on Ice!*

MAN: It's been replaced on my bookshelf by *The Color Purple.*

KID: *(Horrified.)* No!

MAN: Gone!

KID: But—

MAN:
Jimi Hendrix's "Purple Haze." Gone.
Sly Stone's "There's a Riot Goin' on." Gone.
The Jackson Five's "I Want You Back."

KID: Man, you can't throw that away. It's living proof Michael had a black nose.

MAN: It's all going. Anything and everything that connects me to you, to who I was, to what we were, is out of my life.

KID: You've got to give me another chance.

MAN: "Fingertips Part 2."

KID: Man, how can you do that? That's vintage Stevie Wonder.

MAN: You want to know how, Kid? You want to know how? Because my survival depends on it. Whether you know it or not, the Ice Age is upon us.

KID: *(Jokingly.)* Man, what the hell you talkin' about? It's ninety-five damn degrees.

MAN: The climate is changing, Kid, and either you adjust or you end up extinct. A sociological dinosaur. Do you understand what I'm trying to tell you? King Kong would have made it to the top if only he had taken the elevator. Instead he brought attention to his struggle and ended up dead.

KID: *(Pleading.)* I'll change. I swear I'll change. I'll maintain a low profile. You won't even know I'm around.

MAN: If I'm to become what I'm to become, then you've got to go. . . . I have no history. I have no past.

KID: Just like that?

MAN: (*Throwing away a series of buttons.*) Free Angela! Free Bobby! Free Huey, Dewey, and Louie! U.S. out of Vietnam. U.S. out of Cambodia. U.S. out of Harlem, Detroit, and Newark. Gone! . . . *The Temptations Greatest Hits!*

KID: (*Grabbing the album.*) No!!!

MAN: Give it back, Kid.

KID: No.

MAN: I said, give it back!

KID: No. I can't let you trash this. Johnny man, it contains fourteen classic cuts by the tempting Temptations. We're talking, "Ain't Too Proud to Beg," "Papa Was a Rolling Stone," "My Girl."

MAN: (*Warning.*) I don't have all day.

KID: For God's sake, Johnny man, "My Girl" is the jam to end all jams. It's what we are. Who we are. It's a way of life. Come on, man, for old times sake. (*Singing.*)

> I got sunshine on a cloudy day
> Bum-da-dum-da-dum-da-bum
> And when it's cold outside

Come on, Johnny man, you ain't, "bummin'," man.

> I got the month of May

Here comes your favorite part. Come on, Johnny man, sing.

> I guess you say
> What can make me feel this way?
> My girl, my girl, my girl
> Talkin' 'bout

MAN: (*Exploding.*) I said, give it back!

KID: (*Angry.*) I ain't givin' you a muthafuckin' thing!

MAN: Now you listen to me!

KID: No, you listen to me. This is the kid you're dealin' with, so don't fuck with me!

(*He hits his fist into his hand, and* THE MAN *grabs for his heart.* THE KID *repeats with two more hits, which causes* THE MAN *to drop to the ground, grabbing his heart.*)

KID: Jai! Jai! Jai!

MAN: Kid, please.

KID: Yeah. Yeah. Now who's begging who. . . . Well, well, well, look at Mr. Cream-of-the-Crop, Mr. Colored-Man-on-Top. Now that he's making it, he no longer wants anything to do with the Kid. Well, you may put all kinds of silk ties 'round your neck and white lines up your nose, but the Kid

is here to stay. You may change your women as often as you
change your underwear, but the Kid is here to stay. And
regardless of how much of your past that you trash, I ain't
goin' no-damn-where. Is that clear? Is that clear?

MAN: (*Regaining his strength, beginning to stand.*) Yeah.

KID: Good. (*After a beat.*) You all right, man? You all right?
I don't want to hurt you, but when you start all that talk
about getting rid of me, well, it gets me kind of crazy. We
need each other. We are one . . .

(*Before* THE KID *can complete his sentence,* THE MAN *grabs
him around his neck and starts to choke him violently.*)

MAN: (*As he strangles him.*) The . . . Ice . . . Age . . . is . . .
upon us . . . and either we adjust . . . or we end up . . .
extinct.

(THE KID *hangs limp in* THE MAN'S *arms.*)

MAN: (*Laughing*) Man kills his own rage. Film at eleven. (*He
then dumps* THE KID *into the trash can, and closes the lid.
He speaks in a contained voice.*) I have no history. I have no
past. I can't. It's too much. It's much too much. I must be
able to smile on cue. And watch the news with an impersonal
eye. I have no stake in the madness.
Being black is too emotionally taxing; therefore I will be
black only on weekends and holidays.

(*He then turns to go, but sees the Temptations album lying
on the ground. He picks it up and sings quietly to himself.*)

I guess you say
What can make me feel this way?

(*He pauses, but then crosses to the trash can, lifts the lid, and
just as he is about to toss the album in, a hand reaches from
inside the can and grabs hold of* THE MAN'S *arm.* THE KID *then
emerges from the can with a death grip on* THE MAN'S *arm.*)

KID: (*Smiling.*) What's happenin'?

(*Blackout.*)

Lala's Opening

(Roving follow spots. A timpani drum roll. As we hear the voice of the ANNOUNCER, *outrageously glamorous images of* LALA *are projected onto the museum walls.)*

VOICE OF ANNOUNCER: From Rome to Rangoon! Paris to Prague! We are pleased to present the American debut of the one! the only! the breathtaking! the astounding! the stupendous! the incredible! the magnificent! Lala Lamazing Grace!

(Thunderous applause as LALA *struts on, the definitive black diva. She has long, flowing hair, an outrageous lamé dress, and an affected French accent which she loses when she's upset.)*

LALA:
Everybody loves Lala
Everybody loves me
Paris! Berlin! London! Rome!
No matter where I go
I always feel at home

Ohhhh
Everybody loves Lala
Everybody loves me
I'm *très magnifique*
And oh so unique
And when it comes to glamour
I'm chic-er than chic

   (She giggles.)

That's why everybody
Everybody
Everybody-everybody-everybody
Loves me

(She begins to vocally reach for higher and higher notes, until she has to point to her final note. She ends the number with a grand flourish and bows to thunderous applause.)

LALA: Yes, it's me! Lala Lamazing Grace and I have come home. Home to the home I never knew as home. Home to you, my people, my blood, my guts.

My story is a simple one, full of fire, passion, *magique*. You may ask how did I, a humble girl from the backwoods of Mississippi, come to be the ninth wonder of the modern world. Well, I can't take all of the credit. Part of it goes to him. (*She points toward the heavens.*)

No, not the light man, darling, but God. For, you see, Lala is a star. A very big star. Let us not mince words, I'm a fucking meteorite. (*She laughs.*) But He is the universe and just like my sister, Aretha la Franklin, Lala's roots are in the black church. (*She sings in a showy gospel style.*)

That's why everybody loves
Swing low sweet chariot
That's why everybody loves
Go down Moses way down in Egypt land
That's why everybody everybody loves me!!!

(*Once again she points to her final note and then basks in applause.*)

I love that note. I just can't hit it.

Now, before I dazzle you with more of my limitless talent, tell me something, America. (*Musical underscoring.*) Why has it taken you so long to recognize my artistry? Mother France opened her loving arms and Lala came running. All over the world Lala was embraced. But here, ha! You spat at Lala. Was I too exotic? Too much woman, or what?

Diana Ross you embrace. A two-bit nobody from Detroit, of all places. Now, I'm not knocking la Ross. She does the best she can with the little she has. (*She laughs.*) But the Paul la Robesons, the James la Baldwins, the Josephine la Bakers, who was my godmother, you know. The Lala Lamazing Graces you kick out. You drive . . .

Away
I am going away
Hoping to find a better day
What do you say
Hey hey
I am going away
Away

(LALA, *caught up in the drama of the song, doesn't see* ADMONIA, *her maid, stick her head out from offstage. Once she is sure* LALA *isn't looking, she wheels onto stage right* FLO'-RANCE, LALA's *lover, who wears a white mask/blond hair. He is gagged and tied to a chair.* ADMONIA *places him on stage and then quickly exits.*)

LALA:
Au revoir—je vais partir maintenant
Je veux dire maintenant
Au revoir
Au revoir
Au revoir
Au revoir
A-Ma-vie

(On her last note, she see FLO'RANCE *and, in total shock, crosses to him.)*

LALA: Flo'rance, what the hell are you doing out here, looking like that. I haven't seen you for three days and you decide to show up now?

(He mumbles.)

I don't want to hear it!

(He mumbles.)

I said, shut up!

(ADMONIA *enters from stage right and has a letter opener on a silver tray.*)

ADMONIA: Pst!
LALA: (*Embarrassed by the presence of* ADMONIA *on stage, smiles apologetically at the audience.*) Un momento. (*She then pulls* ADMONIA *to the side.*) Darling, have you lost your mind coming on stage while I'm performing? And what have you done to Flo'rance? When I asked you to keep him tied up, I didn't mean to tie him up.

(ADMONIA *gives her the letter opener.*)

LALA: Why are you giving me this? I have no letters to open. I'm in the middle of my American debut. Admonia, take Flo'rance off this stage with you! Admonia!

(ADMONIA *is gone.* LALA *turns to the audience and tries to make the best of it.*)

LALA: That was Admonia, my slightly overweight black maid, and this is Flo'rance, my amour. I remember how we met, don't you, Flo'rance? I was sitting in a café on the Left Bank, when I looked up and saw the most beautiful man staring down at me.

"Who are you," he asked. I told him my name . . . whatever my name was back then. And he said, "No, that cannot be your name. Your name should fly, like Lala." And the rest is la history.

Flo'rance molded me into the woman I am today. He is my Svengali, my reality, my all. And I thought I was all to him, until we came here to America, and he fucked that bitch. Yeah, you fucked 'em all. Anything black and breathing. And all this time I thought you loved me for being me. (*She holds the letter opener to his neck.*)

You may think you made me, but I'll have you know I was who I was, whoever that was, long before you made me what I am. So there! (*She stabs him and breaks into song.*)

Oh, love can drive a woman to madness
To pain and sadness
I know
Believe me, I know
I know
I know

(LALA *sees what she's done and is about to scream but catches herself and tries to play it off.*)

LALA: Moving right along.
ADMONIA: (*Enters with a telegram on a tray.*) Pst.
LALA: (*Anxious/hostile.*) What is it now?

(ADMONIA *hands* LALA *a telegram.*)

LALA: (*Excited.*) Oh, la telegram from one of my fans and the concert isn't even over yet. Get me the letter opener. It's in Flo'rance.

(ADMONIA *hands* LALA *the letter opener*.)

LALA: Next I am going to do for you my immortal hit song, "The Girl Inside." But first we open the telegram. (*She quickly reads it and is outraged*.) What! Which pig in la audience wrote this trash? (*Reading*.) "Dear Sadie, I'm so proud. The show's wonderful, but talk less and sing more. Love, Mama."

First off, no one calls me Sadie. Sadie died the day Lala was born. And secondly, my mama's dead. Anyone who knows anything about Lala Lamazing Grace knows that my mother and Josephine Baker were French patriots together. They infiltrated a carnival rumored to be the center of Nazi intelligence, disguised as Hottentot Siamese twins. You may laugh but it's true. Mama died a heroine. It's all in my autobiography, *Voilá Lala*! So whoever sent this telegram is a liar!

(ADMONIA *promptly presents her with another telegram*.)

LALA: This had better be an apology. (*To* ADMONIA.) Back up, darling. (*Reading*.) "Dear Sadie, I'm not dead. P.S. Your child misses you." What? (*She squares off at the audience*.) Well, now, that does it! If you are my mother, which you are not. And this alleged child is my child, then that would mean I am a mother and I have never given birth. I don't know nothin' 'bout birthin' no babies! (*She laughs*.) Lala made a funny.

So whoever sent this, show me the child! Show me!

(ADMONIA *offers another telegram*.)

LALA: (*To* ADMONIA.) You know, you're gonna get fired! (*She reluctantly opens it*.) "The child is in the closet." What closet?

ADMONIA: Pst. (*Pushes a button and the center wall unit revolves around to reveal a large black door*. ADMONIA *exits, taking* FLO'RANCE *with her, leaving* LALA *alone*.)

LALA: (*Laughing*.) I get it. It's a plot, isn't it? A nasty little CIA, FBI kind of plot. Well, let me tell you muthafuckers one thing, there is nothing in that closet, real or manufactured, that will be a dimmer to the glimmer of Lamé the star. You may have gotten Billie and Bessie and a little piece of everyone else who's come along since, but you won't get Lala. My clothes are too fabulous! My hair is too long! My accent too French. That's why I came home to America. To prove you ain't got nothing on me!

(The music for her next song starts, but LALA *is caught up in her tirade, and talks/screams over the music.)*

My mother and Josephine Baker were French patriots together! I've had brunch with the Pope! I've dined with the Queen! Everywhere I go I cause riots! Hunny, I am a star! I have transcended pain! So there! *(Yelling.)* Stop the music! Stop that goddamn music.

(The music stops. LALA *slowly walks downstage and singles out someone in the audience.)*

Darling, you're not looking at me. You're staring at that damn door. Did you pay to stare at some fucking door or be mesmerized by my talent?
(To the whole audience.) Very well! I guess I am going to have to go to the closet door, fling it open, in order to dispel all the nasty little thoughts these nasty little telegrams have planted in your nasty little minds. *(Speaking directly to someone in the audience.)* Do you want me to open the closet door? Speak up, darling, this is live. *(Once she gets the person to say yes.)* I will open the door, but before I do, let me tell you bastards one last thing. To hell with coming home and to hell with lies and insinuations!

*(*LALA *goes into the closet and after a short pause comes running out, ready to scream, and slams the door. Traumatized to the point of no return, she tells the following story as if it were a jazz solo of rushing, shifting emotions.)*

LALA: I must tell you this dream I had last night. Simply *magnifique*. In this dream, I'm running naked in Sammy Davis Junior's hair. *(Crazed laughter.)*
Yes! I'm caught in this larger-than-life, deep, dark forest of savage, nappy-nappy hair. The kinky-kinks are choking me, wrapped around my naked arms, thighs, breast, face. I can't breathe. And there was nothing in that closet!
And I'm thinking if only I had a machete, I could cut away the kinks. Remove once and for all the roughness. But then I look up and it's coming toward me. Flowing like lava. It's pomade! Ohhh, Sammy!

Yes, cakes and cakes of pomade. Making everything nice and white and smooth and shiny, like my black/white/black/white/black behiney.

Mama, no!

And then spikes start cutting through the pomade. Combing the coated kink. Cutting through the kink, into me. There are bloodlines on my back. On my thighs.

It's all over. All over . . . all over me. All over for me.

(LALA *accidentally pulls off her wig to reveal her real hair. Stripped of her "disguise," she recoils like a scared little girl and sings.*)

Mommy and Daddy
Meet and mate
The child that's born
Is torn with love and with hate
She runs away to find her own
And tries to deny
What she's always known
The girl inside

(*The closet door opens.* LALA *runs away, and a* LITTLE BLACK GIRL *emerges from the closet. Standing behind her is* ADMONIA.)

(*The* LITTLE GIRL *and* LALA *are in two isolated pools of light, and mirror each other's moves until* LALA *reaches past her reflection and the* LITTLE GIRL *comes to* LALA *and they hug.* ADMONIA *then joins them as* LALA *sings. Music underscored.*)

LALA:
What's left is the girl inside
The girl who died
So a new girl could be born

(*Slow fade to black.*)

Permutations

(*Lights up on* NORMAL JEAN REYNOLDS. *She is very Southern/country and very young. She wears a simple faded print dress and her hair, slightly mussed, is in plaits. She sits, her dress covering a large oval object.*)

NORMAL: My mama used to say, God made the exceptional, then God made the special, and when God got bored, he made me. 'Course, she don't say too much of nuthin' no more, not since I lay me this egg.

(She lifts her dress to uncover a large white egg lying between her legs.)

Ya see, it all got started when I had me sexual relations with the garbage man. Ooowee, did he smell.

No, not bad. No! He smelled of all the good things folks never shoulda thrown away. His sweat was like cantaloupe juice. His neck was like a ripe-red strawberry. And the water that fell from his eyes was like a deep, dark, juicy-juicy grape. I tell ya, it was like fuckin' a fruit salad, only I didn't spit out the seeds. I kept them here, deep inside. And three days later, my belly commence to swell, real big like.

Well, my mama locked me off in some dark room, refusin' to let me see light of day 'cause "What would the neighbors think." At first I cried a lot, but then I grew used to livin' my days in the dark, and my nights in the dark. . . . *(She hums.)* And then it wasn't but a week or so later, my mama off at church, that I got this hurtin' feelin' down here. Worse than anything I'd ever known. And then I started bleedin', real bad. I mean, there was blood everywhere. And the pain had me howlin' like a near dead dog. I tell ya, I was yellin' so loud, I couldn't even hear myself. Nooooooooo! Noooooo! Carrying on something like that.

And I guess it was just too much for the body to take, 'cause the next thing I remember . . . is me coming to and there's this big white egg layin' 'tween my legs. First I thought somebody musta put it there as some kind of joke. But then I noticed that all 'round this egg were thin lines of blood that I could trace to back between my legs.

(Laughing.) Well, when my mama come home from church she just about died. "Normal Jean, what's that thing 'tween your legs? Normal Jean, you answer me, girl!" It's not a thing, Mama. It's an egg. And I laid it.

She tried separatin' me from it, but I wasn't havin' it. I stayed in that dark room, huggin', holdin' onto it.

And then I heard it. It wasn't anything that coulda been heard 'round the world, or even in the next room. It was kinda like layin' back in the bathtub, ya know, the water just coverin' your ears . . . and if you lay real still and listen real close, you can hear the sound of your heart movin' the water. You ever done that? Well, that's what it sounded like. A heart movin' water. And it was happenin' inside here.

Why, I'm the only person I know who ever lay themselves an egg before, so that makes me special. You hear that, Mama? I'm special and so's my egg! And special things supposed to be treated like they matter. That's why every night I count to it, so it knows nuthin' never really ends. And I sing it every song I know so that when it comes out, it's full of all kinds of feelings. and I tell it secrets and laugh with it and . . .

(She suddenly stops and puts her ear to the egg and listens intently.)

Oh! I don't believe it! I thought I heard . . . yes! (*Excited.*) Can you hear it? Instead of one heart, there's two. Two little hearts just pattering away. Boom-boom-boom. Boom-boom-boom. Talkin' to each other like old friends. Racin' toward the beginnin' of their lives.

(Listening.) Oh, no, now there's three . . . four . . . five, six. More hearts than I can count. And they're all alive, beatin' out life inside my egg.

(We begin to hear the heartbeats, drums, alive inside NORMAL'S *egg.)*

Any day now, this egg is gonna crack open and what's gonna come out a be the likes of which nobody has ever seen. My babies! And their skin is gonna turn all kinds of shades in the sun and their hair a be growin' every which-a-way. And it won't matter and they won't care 'cause they know they are so rare and so special 'cause it's not everyday a bunch of babies break outa a white egg and start to live.

And nobody better not try and hurt my babies 'cause if they do, they gonna have to deal with me.

Yes, any day now, this shell's gonna crack and my babies are gonna fly. Fly! Fly!

(She laughs at the thought, but then stops and says the word as if it's the most natural thing in the world.) Fly.

(Blackout.)

The Party

(Before we know what's hit us, a hurricane of energy comes bounding into the space. It is TOPSY WASHINGTON. *Her hair and dress are a series of stylistic contradictions which are hip, black, and unencumbered. Music, spiritual and funky, underscores.)*

TOPSY: *(Dancing about.)* Yoho! Party! Party! Turn up the music! Turn up the music!

Have yaw ever been to a party where there was one fool in the middle of the room, dancing harder and yelling louder than everybody in the entire place? Well, hunny, that fool was me!

Yes, child! The name is Topsy Washington and I love to party. As a matter of fact, when God created the world, on the seventh day he didn't rest. No, child, he P-A-R-T-I-E-D. Partied!

But now let me tell you 'bout this function I went to the other night, way uptown. And baby, when I say way uptown, I mean way-way-way-way-way-way-way-way uptown. Somewhere's between 125th Street and infinity.

Inside was the largest gathering of black/Negro/colored Americans you'd ever want to see. Over in one corner you got Nat Turner sippin' champagne out of Eartha Kitt's slipper. And over in another corner, Bert Williams and Malcom X was discussing existentialism as it relates to the shuffle-ball-change. Girl, Aunt Jemima and Angela Davis was in the kitchen sharing a plate of greens and just goin' off about South Africa.

And then Fats sat down and started to work them eighty-eights. And then Stevie joined in. And then Miles and Duke and Ella and Jimi and Charlie and Sly and Lightin' and Count and Louie!

And then everybody joined in. I tell you all the children was just all up in there, dancing to the rhythm of one beat. Dancing to the rhythm of their own definition. Celebrating in their cultural madness.

And then the floor started to shake. And the walls started to move. And before anybody knew what was happening, the entire room lifted up off the ground. The whole place just took off and went flying through space—defying logic and limitations. Just a spinning and a spinning and a spinning until it disappeared inside of my head.

(TOPSY *stops dancing and regains her balance and begins to listen to the music in her head. Slowly we begin to hear it, too.*)

That's right, girl, there's a party goin' on inside of here. That's why when I walk down the street my hips just sashay all over the place. 'Cause I'm dancing to the music of the madness in me.

And whereas I used to jump into a rage anytime anybody tried to deny who I was, now all I got to do is give attitude, quicker than light, and then go on about the business of being me. 'Cause I'm dancing to the music of the madness in me.

(*As* TOPSY *continues to speak,* MISS ROJ, LALA, MISS PAT, *and* THE MAN *from "Symbiosis" revolve on, frozen like soft sculptures.*)

TOPSY: And here, all this time I been thinking we gave up our drums. But, naw, we still got 'em. I know I got mine. They're here, in my speech, my walk, my hair, my God, my style, my smile, and my eyes. And everything I need to get over in this world, is inside here, connecting me to everybody and everything that's ever been.

So, hunny, don't waste your time trying to label or define me.

(*The sculptures slowly begin to come to "life" and they mirror/echo* TOPSY'S *words.*)

TOPSY/EVERYBODY: . . . 'cause I'm not what I was ten years ago or ten minutes ago. I'm all of that and then some. And whereas I can't live inside yesterday's pain, I can't live without it.

(*All of a sudden, madness erupts on the stage. The sculptures begin to speak all at once. Images of black/Negro/colored Americans begin to flash—images of them dancing past the madness, caught up in the madness, being lynched, rioting, partying, surviving. Mixed in with these images are all the characters from the exhibits. Through all of this* TOPSY *sings. It is a vocal and visual cacophony which builds and builds.*)

LALA:
I must tell you about this dream I had last night. Simply *magnifique*. In this dream I'm running naked in Sammy Davis Junior's hair. Yes. I'm caught in this larger-than-life, deep, dark tangled forest of savage, nappy-nappy hair. Yes, the kinky-kinks are choking me, are wrapped around my naked arms, my naked thighs, breast, and face, and I can't breathe and there was nothing in that closet.

THE MAN:
I have no history. I have no past. I can't. It's too much. It's much too much. I must be able to smile on cue and watch the news with an impersonal eye. I have no stake in the madness. Being black is too emotionally taxing, therefore I will be black only on weekends and holidays.

MISS ROJ:
Snap for every time you walk past someone lying in the street smelling like frozen piss and shit and you don't see it. Snap for every crazed bastard who kills himself so as to get the jump on being killed. And snap for every sick muthafucker who, bored with carrying about his fear, takes to shooting up other people.

MISS PAT:
Stop playing those drums. I said, stop playing those damn drums. You can't stop history. You can't stop time. Those drums will be confiscated once we reach Savannah, so give them up now. Repeat after me: I don't hear any drums and I will not rebel. I will not rebel!

TOPSY: (*Singing*)
There's madness in me
And that madness sets me free
There's madness in me
And that madness sets me free
There's madness in me
And that madness sets me free
There's madness in me
And that madness sets me free
There's madness in me
And that madness sets me free
TOPSY: My power is in my . . .

EVERYBODY: *Madness!*
TOPSY: And my colored contradictions.

(The sculptures freeze with a smile on their faces as we hear the voice of MISS PAT.)

VOICE OF MISS PAT: Before exiting, check the overhead as any baggage you don't claim, we trash.

(Blackout.)

THE FIRST BREEZE OF SUMMER

A DRAMA IN TWO ACTS

by Leslie Lee

The First Breeze of Summer was first produced at the St. Marks Playhouse in New York City on March 2, 1975, by the Negro Ensemble Company in association with Woodie King, Jr., and won an Obie Award as Best Play of 1974–75. It also received a Tony nomination and won for its author a John Gassner Medallion for Playwriting, awarded by the Outer Circle Critics. Transferred to Broadway, it opened at the Palace Theater on June 10 of the same year. It was later seen in a public television adaptation on the PBS *Theater in America* series in 1976, for which it won a Mississippi ETV Award.

LESLIE LEE

A native of Bryn Mawr, Pennsylvania, Leslie Lee earned his B.A. at the University of Pennsylvania and an M.A. in the-ater at Villanova. Originally planning for a medical career, he worked for several years as a research technician, but began writing plays while attending Villanova. His first plays were produced at Ellen Stewart's La Mama E.T.C. in down-town New York City, for which he worked briefly, gaining theatrical experience. Lee has taught playwriting at the Col-lege of Old Westbury, New York, and the Frederick Doug-lass Creative Arts Center in New York City; served as playwright-in-residence at the University of Pennsylvania; was playwriting coordinator at the Negro Ensemble Com-pany's Playwriting Workshop; and has been a theater panelist with the New York State Council on the Arts. He has received playwriting grant awards from the Shubert Founda-tion (twice), the Rockefeller Foundation and the National Endowment for the Arts, as well as a playwriting fellowship from the Eugene O'Neill Playwriting Conference in Water-ford, Connecticut.

Author of two novellas: *The Day After Tomorrow* and *Never the Time and Place*, Lee also writes for television and films. *Almos' a Man*, his adaptation for public television of the short story by Richard Wright, was selected by the U.S. State Department and shown at the Ionesco Film Festival in Paris. *The Killing Floor*, a film drama, was shown at the New York, Locarno, Sundance, and Cannes film festivals, and won first prize at the National Black Film Consortium. He also adapted James Baldwin's novel *Go Tell It on the Mountain* for PBS (in collaboration with Gus Edwards); wrote a semi-documentary, *Langston Hughes*, about the poetry of Hughes, also for PBS; and contributed scripts to the NBC television daytime series "Another World."

Besides *The First Breeze of Summer*, Lee's work for the theater includes: *Elegy to a Down Queen*, a Black family tragicomedy, upon which *The First Breeze of Summer* was later based; *Cops and Robbers*, an absurdist tragicomedy; *Between Then and Now*, focusing upon a white man's fears of eventual mass racial assimilation; and *The War Party*, a political drama of a power struggle within a civil-rights orga-nization. Others are: *Colored People's Time*, subtitled "a his-tory play," a series of scenes depicting highlights of African American history; *Phillis*, a musical (music and lyrics by

Micki Grant) based upon the eighteenth-century African American poet Phillis Wheatley; *Hannah Davis*, a domestic drama about an upper-middle-class Black family; and *Martin Luther King, Jr.*, a musical biography for children (music and lyrics by Charles Strouse).

CHARACTERS

(In order of appearance)

GREMMAR: Milton and Edna's mother, her seventies

NATE EDWARDS: Black male, in his early to middle twenties

LOU EDWARDS: Nate's brother, seventeen or eighteen

AUNT EDNA: Black female, her mid-fifties

HATTIE: Milton's wife, her early to middle fifties

MILTON EDWARDS: Edna's brother, father of Lou and Nate, middle fifties

LUCRETIA: The young Gremmar, her late teens

SAM GREEN: Black male, his middle to late twenties

BRITON WOODWARD: White male, his late teens or very early twenties

REVEREND MOSELY: Black male, his early sixties

HOPE: Nate's girlfriend, black, her early twenties

JOE DRAKE: White male, his mid-forties

GLORIA TOWNES: Black female, in her late thirties

HARPER EDWARDS: Black male, mid-thirties

TIME: Contemporary

PLACE: A small city in the Northeast

ACT ONE: Thursday afternoon through Friday night in June

ACT TWO: The following Saturday afternoon through Sunday night

ACT ONE

(*It is mid-June, Thursday afternoon, the Edwards' home. A porch, stage left, takes up only a small area of the stage. It has a cement floor. A bench in the center of the porch constitutes the porch furniture. A door at the right of the porch leads into the living room, a modest area larger than the porch, with a writing desk, upstage right; a dining table with chairs, stage center; an armchair, downstage right; and an armchair, upstage left. Upstage right is an upright piano; up center, a low bench; and up left, a small side table. A flight of stairs, up right, leads to* GREMMAR'S *room, which is also the room where the flashbacks take place. The room contains a bed, stage right; a chair, stage center; and a dresser, down left.*)

(*At rise,* GREMMAR *is standing at the bed, removing a pair of house slippers from a suitcase, which is on the bed. She is singing a hymn as she moves around the room. She puts on the slippers and closes the suitcase and puts it under the bed. As she does, she has an attack of dizziness and falls on the bed. She rises finally and crosses to the dresser to get a fan, discovering a photograph and a string of pearls. She fondles the picture affectionately.*)

GREMMAR: Sam Green, Sam Green. (*Stands the photograph on the dresser and looks at the string of pearls longingly.*) Sam, Sam, I've never had something like this in my whole life—pearls, real pearls.

(*She puts the pearls on, picks up the fan, which she had placed on the dresser top, and starts out of the room. As she does, lights rise in the living room and porch areas. Simultaneously we hear the sounds of* LOU *and* NATE *playing a game of sidewalk tennis, offstage right. As* GREMMAR *reaches the bottom of the stairs* LOU *and* NATE *enter from downstage right.*)

LOU: (*Following* NATE.) Where are you going?

49

NATE: (*At stage center.*) Man, later for that—it's too hot!

LOU: Come on, Nate, we're not finished the game yet!

NATE: It's too hot, Lou!

LOU: Nate, its only 18–15. The game goes up to twenty-one!—

NATE: I know what the game goes up to!

LOU: Come on, Nate, it's not that hot!—

NATE: (*Lying on the couch, pulling at his clothing and fanning.*) The hell it isn't!

LOU: Three more points!—

NATE: You beat me, man—you won—all right?

LOU: One more serve then—one more.

NATE: Later, nigger. Shoot!—no way. That's why the old man and me quit early today, because of this heat, and I am playing that stupid game like some fool! I beat you twice already—what else do you want?

LOU: Just because I'm leading—

NATE: (*Crossing to the porch and sitting, stage right end of bench.*) So you beat me, all right?

LOU: (*Moving slowly toward the porch and sitting on stage left floor.*) Tomorrow don't say the game wasn't over because the score was only 18–15 either!

NATE: Man, I am smothering! . . . Shit! . . . No air— Nothing! Haven't had a decent breeze all summer, if we've had any! Stuff's enough to make you want to slap Jesus on Easter Sunday! (LOU *laughs despite being miffed.*) Can't eat . . . sleep . . . can't half breathe . . . itching all the time. Take a bath and you're still itching . . . Can't even get worked up over my woman Hope. You know I'm in trouble. (*Laughing despite his discomfort.*) You know what I oughta do? I ought to form me a march . . . get me some folks together and march on this crap! Demonstrate! Sit down in the street! "Down with heat! Heat ain't too cool! . . . Ban the good old summertime!"—a march! . . . Even in the wintertime, when somebody mentions the word *summer*, I begin to sweat. I hate the word, man!

(GREMMAR, *inside the living room, is seated on the piano stool, commencing to play a hymn.* LOU *crosses to the doorway. He pauses for a moment, listening. Finally he crosses stage left of porch.*)

LOU: Gremmar's been good to us, you know that, Nate? (NATE *nods.*) I mean, when you think of older people— right? She's so easy to talk to—I mean, you can—sit down

and talk to her about . . . anything just about, you know?
. . . Anything . . . more than Mom and Pop. (*Pause.*) You
know what I mean, Nate?

NATE: Yeah . . . yeah.

LOU: (*Sits stage left end of bench.*) Nate, do you remember
that scooter Gremmar brought you a long time ago?

NATE: (*Shifting to his back, fanning.*) Yeah, I remember . . .

LOU: (*Pause, smiling, reminiscent.*) She brought me that cow-
boy outfit, too—remember? (NATE *nods.*) Two guns and a
holster . . . and silver bullets! (LOU *rises.*) And that ten-
gallon hat!

NATE: (*Hot, shifting again.*) Yeah, Mr. Bad Nigger—the Lone
Ranger himself! Damn hat falling down all over his eyes
. . . running and bumping into shit and wondering why . . .
Couldn't half see . . . Running to Mom and crying about
hurting yourself.

LOU: (*Laughing.*) Yeah, I'd have worn them to bed at night if
Mom hadn't ripped them off me. (*Pause.*)

NATE: Man, this humidity's a regular bitch! (*They are interrupted by the appearance of* AUNT EDNA, *moving up to them
laboriously from offstage left.*)

LOU: Hi, Aunt Edna.

EDNA: Lord Jesus, I'm telling you! The Lord is punishing
somebody today, child! I just wish he wouldn't include me
in on the whipping, though. I didn't do nothing! Just minding
my own business! (*She kisses* NATE *and* LOU *on the cheek.
They assist her as she sits and begins to wipe her face with
her handkerchief.*) I'm telling you boys, it's hot out here
today! Just let me catch my breath a minute! (*Hearing*
GREMMAR *playing the piano.*) I see Mama's home from work
for the weekend a day early! . . . Lord, it feels good to get
off them feet! Things was killing me! Dogs was hurting! Yes
sir! . . . (*With feigned indignation.*) Louis looks so cool! How
come you look so cool, Louis?

NATE: You know them colored people, Aunt Edna—just love
the heat!

LOU: (*Slightly embarrassed.*) I can feel it! . . . I mean . . . it's
hot, but—

NATE: Listen at Lou, Aunt Edna—doesn't want to be accused
of being a nigger for the life of him!

LOU: I just said—

EDNA: We-ll, I guess I must not be one, because I can't stand
it—never could! No sir! Yes, Lord, this must be Egypt—
can't be the United States!

NATE: Got your flowered dress on today, huh, Aunt Edna?—
all fixed up, trying to turn some heads today? I know—I
know what you're trying to do!

EDNA: I'm glad you do, son, because I'm a wilted flower today!
My leaves done dried out today!

NATE: Oh no!

EDNA: Gets a little cooler now, then you're talking about
something else!

NATE: You don't have to tell me!—

EDNA: Might be snow on the roof, son, but there's plenty of
fire inside! (*All laugh.*)

NATE: All right, all right now!

EDNA: *Plenty* of fire inside!

NATE: Oh, I know that! I can see that! I been watching you!
"Look at old Aunt Edna fluttering and flapping her eyes at
old Mayberry."

EDNA: Lord, children, don't put that old man on me, now! I
don't deserve that now, do I? I don't want no old man. I
want a *young* man! Yes, a young man!

NATE: I don't know, Aunt Edna, maybe you'd better stick with
Mr. Mayberry. One of these young cats might be too much
for you!

EDNA: Well, too much is better than too little, and Henry
Mayberry is too little! (*They all laugh uproariously. During
the laughter, the blackout drop is flown in and the three
walls—for the flashbacks—SAM, BRITON, and HARPER are
sneaked in behind it.*) Well, I got my breath here now. (*Having difficulty rising.*) Give me a hand, son. These dogs of
mine ain't cooperating!

NATE: (*He moves to help her.*) I'm going to take another damn
shower.

(*They begin toward the door. LOU lingers outside before exiting downstage right across the apron. GREMMAR is playing and
singing "Leaning on the Everlasting Arms." NATE and EDNA
enter the living room; EDNA gives her shopping bag to NATE to
hide it from GREMMAR. NATE heads upstairs and exits stage
right. EDNA starts singing and GREMMAR looks around and sees
her. They hug and EDNA crosses to down right armchair and
sits. HATTIE enters from kitchen, which is up left. She is carrying
a tray with four glasses of iced tea. She gives one to EDNA and
one to GREMMAR and stands stage left of the piano—joining
the singing. MILTON enters from kitchen area, carrying a gar-*

*den spade and gloves. He crosses to the table and sits in stage
left chair, also joining the singing.)*

GREMMAR: *(Finishing.)* I just love that hymn!—such a beautiful song!

HATTIE: *(Crosses to the desk and puts the tray on it.)* Yes, it
was. (MILTON *and* EDNA *agree.)*

EDNA: Sounded like Mrs. Armstrong down at the church,
Momma.

GREMMAR: *(Laughing.)* Oh child, I'm just sitting here banging—just banging, that's all. I could play like that, child, I'd
be doing something.

HATTIE: *(Crossing downstage between* EDNA *and* GREMMAR.*)*
Yes, for somebody that's so disagreeable, she's certainly a
good organist—and just loves Milton!

MILTON: Oh now, Hattie!

EDNA: A little sweet on Milton, huh, Hattie?

HATTIE: Yes, Jesus! The first thing Sunday morning, here she
comes, "Hello, Hattie," and then just gab, gab, gab to
Milton!—

MILTON: Hattie—

HATTIE: The two of 'em just chin to chin! Tickles me!

EDNA: *(Winking at* HATTIE, *who laughs.)* Better keep your eye
on him, Hattie—keep your eye on him! I know Lucille—

MILTON: Hattie, you shouldn't be telling stories like that!—

HATTIE: *(Crosses to the table, gives a glass to* MILTON, *and sits
in stage right chair.)* I'm just teasing you, Milton.

GREMMAR: Yes, yes, she is, son, just teasing.

MILTON: Well, I wish she wouldn't. I'm in the Lord's house
. . . wouldn't be right to be . . . nasty to the woman . . .

GREMMAR: No, that's right . . . that's right . . .

HATTIE: Milton can tease but can't stand nobody to tease him.

EDNA: *(Laughing.)* Just chin to chin, huh, Hattie? Lucille is
something else! Yes, Lord! *(They are silent a moment as* LOU
crosses apron from stage right to sit on porch bench.)

HATTIE: Well, did Tom show up today?

MILTON: Half drunk as usual . . . I'd just as soon do without
the man . . . Been advertising for somebody for two weeks
now, and we haven't had one call—not one! (MILTON *rises,
and crosses to* GREMMAR *stage right between the armchair
and piano.)* Can't get young people interested in plastering
today . . . Don't want to do a day's work—want something
for nothing—fast cars and loud radios! . . . Haven't had one
call! (LOU *rises, enters, and stands at the door.)* Louis comes

this summer, that'll be somebody at least. Lord knows we
need the help. (LOU *frowns, sighing heavily.* HATTIE *looks
at him.*)

HATTIE: (*Starts toward the kitchen with two empty glasses from
the table, sees* LOUIS, *and stops.*) Louis, what are you frowning about? You aren't coming down with something, are
you?

EDNA: This kinda weather—

LOU: (*Sighing heavily again.*) I was . . . thinking about . . .
about working someplace else this summer.

(*There is a moment of strained silence, and glances are
exchanged by the others.* HATTIE *puts the glasses on the small
side table up left.*)

MILTON: Somewhere else? Where else?

LOU: (*Shrugging, peeved.*) I don't know . . . just . . . somewhere . . . else, that's all . . .

MILTON: Lord knows, Louis, I certainly was depending on you.
Nathan and I could use all the help we can get, for all Tom
is worth.

LOU: For goodness sakes, do I have to plaster every summer?

HATTIE: (*Steps to* LOUIS.) You don't have to do anything but
die, Louis.

MILTON: Is there something wrong with the way I make my
living?

LOU: I didn't say that!—

HATTIE: (*As* EDNA *concurs.*) He certainly didn't, Milton, now
don't start exaggerating—

GREMMAR: No, he didn't now . . . he didn't . . .

LOU: It's . . . it's—all I said was—

MILTON: All the work we have—people calling me up and me
promising, and here I am trying to plan ahead—can't get
nobody to work for me and—

EDNA: Milton, if the child don't want to—

MILTON: It's not a question of wanting to—

LOU: Pop—

MILTON: His brother didn't want to drop outa school to help
me, but he did. Louis is only in high school. It's not like I
was asking him to sacrifice his education—

LOU: Well, I'm not Nate—

GREMMAR: Louis, son—

MILTON: What's the matter, don't I treat you right?

LOU: Pop, I'd rather do something else—

MILTON: (*Steps toward* LOUIS.) I can't help what you want to do. You're working with Nate and me this summer! (*Cutting him off as he starts to speak.*) I'm still the father of this house!

LOU: How can anybody forget it!

MILTON: Now, that's enough back talk from you, young man!—that's enough! Here—here I am sweating to put food on the table—providing—we need the help—you wanting me to help you with your college tuition next year and—

LOU: (*Crosses downstage center to the dining table.*) All right, I'll pay for it, then!—

GREMMAR: (*Trying to lighten the atmosphere.*) Come on, you all. Let's not fight. Let's be happy—let's be happy now. (*She begins playing softly.*)

LOU: Gremmar, I will pay for it!

MILTON: (*Crossing downstage center to* LOUIS.) I don't care what you do next summer—that's your business! This summer you're working for me, and I don't want to hear another word about it! (*MILTON starts toward kitchen.*) Louis just wants to be the black sheep of the family—

LOU: (*Starting for the porch.*) Oh, for goodness sakes! Just because— (LOU *storms out.* MILTON, EDNA, *and* HATTIE *exit kitchen arguing about* LOU.)

GREMMAR: Louis! Son?—Sam! Sam!

(GREMMAR *crosses to stage center. She stops suddenly, faint, and sits in the stage center chair at table—holding the pearls. The lights dim in living room to special on* GREMMAR, *and blackout drop is flown out to reveal Wall No. 1* [SAM]. *As lights rise in the bedroom,* LUCRETIA *enters from stage left—stands at the dresser holding a hand mirror.* SAM *enters from upstage right and crosses to stand at foot of bed.*)

LUCRETIA: Oh, Sam, these are lovely!—they really are! They're so pretty!

SAM: You like 'em, huh, babe?

LUCRETIA: Oh, Sam, you know I do—I really do! (*Looking almost in awe at herself.*) They're so pretty!— What are these—pearls, Sam? Is that—

SAM: (*Proudly, cockily.*) They're pearls . . .

LUCRETIA: Oh . . . (*Continuing to look at herself and then giggling nervously.*) I—I've never had something like these before, Sam—real pearls . . . Makes me feel like a . . . a . . . rich lady or something . . . (*She laughs, glancing at him*

*for his approval, and then looks again in the mirror, gently
fingering the pearls.*) They're so beautiful . . . tiny . . . spar-
kling-like . . . Pearls! (*She stops, a look of horror on her
face.*) Sam, how much did these things cost you?

SAM: (*Laughing.*) Come on, babe, you're not supposed to be
asking me no questions like that! What's the matter, don't
you have no manners? Your momma didn't bring you up no
better than that? Don't worry about it!

LUCRETIA: (*Laughing.*) Lord, Momma's eyes'll pop wide open
when she sees this. She think's everything's supposed to be
so simple. Nothing flashy. These certainly would be flashy
to her. Probably just jealous, I guess, Poppa not being able
to give her nothing like this . . . (*Pause, stepping to* SAM.)
They didn't cost a lot, did they, Sam? Just tell me that. You
don't have to tell me nothing more—all right? They weren't,
were they?

SAM: (*Shrugging, nonchalant.*) Oh . . . not too . . .

LUCRETIA: (*Watching him.*) That's the truth?

SAM: Baby, you asked me, and I just told you—

LUCRETIA: All right, all right— (*Looking down at the pearls
again.*) Sam . . . I—I'm going to have to hide these things—

SAM: Hide 'em? . . . Huh? . . . Baby, what are you talking—

LUCRETIA: Sam, I know—I know they'll make me give 'em
back to you. I know they will!—

SAM: Give 'em back? How come you're going to have to give
'em back? It's my money. I do with it what I want. Nobody—

LUCRETIA: Sam, it's not that! . . . That's not it . . . not it at
all . . . Sam, I'm only seventeen . . . They—they might think
I shouldn't be . . . be having things like this—so expensive-
looking. I mean, you know the way things are around here—
work so slow—you know what I mean? I mean, they're kinda
funny that way . . . So afraid somebody's going to be showing off with something new—

SAM: For Pete's sake, babe! I—I didn't buy them things for
you to have to hide—

LUCRETIA: I—I'll wear 'em only around you, Sam. (*She hugs
him.*) When we're together—all right? Momma and them
don't ever have to know. Sam, it's either that or I'm going
to—to have to give 'em back to you. (*She crosses to the
dresser and looks in the hand mirror.*) I mean . . . pearls,
Sam! Who around here has some pearls?

SAM: (*Sighing heavily, helplessly.*) Lu, baby . . . Look,
sugar . . .

LUCRETIA: What's the matter?

SAM: Well . . . (*Pausing, shrugging, and then blurting out.*) Look, sugar, they—they ain't—ain't no real pearls! (*He sighs, looking at her and then dropping his eyes, expecting the worst.*) They . . . ain't . . .

LUCRETIA: (*Surprised.*) Oh . . . they're not?

SAM: (*Sighing heavily.*) They're not real . . . They're . . . imitation—that's what the woman said—imitation . . .

LUCRETIA: You mean they're . . . fakes or something?

SAM: (*Quickly.*) No, they're not fakes . . . I mean, you know, they're supposed to be pearls, but they're not, you know? . . . I mean, they look like 'em, but they're not. You know what I mean, babe? I mean, they're supposed to look like pearls, but they're something else— (*Stopping, exasperated.*) Oh, I don't know, baby, they're just—just . . . imitation, whatever the hell that is! How should I know! (*Pause.*) I— I just . . . I just don't want you to think you got something you don't, that's all . . . And there's no sense anybody else thinking it too . . . I certainly don't want you hiding them . . . (*Sighing heavily.*)

LUCRETIA: (*Turning to the mirror again.*) They sure do look real if they aren't . . . They cost a couple of dollars, then?

SAM: (*Turns and steps stage right.*) Yeah . . . yeah . . . a couple, you know . . .

LUCRETIA: Well, Sam, that's better then, isn't it? I mean, if Momma and Poppa think they're fakes—I mean, imitation— then they won't mind then, will they?

SAM: I don't know. You know your people better than I do.

LUCRETIA: Oh, Sam, thank you!— Thank you, Sam! (*Rushing to, embracing, and kissing him.*) I'll wear 'em—okay?

SAM: (*Somewhat bewildered.*) Damn, lady, you sure did put me through the mill over them things—

LUCRETIA: (*Pulling away.*) Sam, where's your uniform? I thought there was something funny about you! Sam, how come you're not at work? It's not time yet for—

SAM: (*Turning downstage.*) They—they give me the afternoon off—

LUCRETIA: The afternoon? How come?

SAM: (*Hesitant, shrugging.*) I—I don't know, baby . . . Man come up and told me . . . Some . . . some kinda slow-up on the tracks somewhere—accident—trains wasn't coming in . . . tied up . . . Didn't need all the porters in the station . . . Said to take the afternoon off. So I took it. (*Laughing nervously.*) Didn't have to tell me twice . . .

LUCRETIA: (*Not really comprehending.*) You get paid for it, don't you?

SAM: (*Boldly.*) Oh yeah . . . oh yeah . . . Something like this . . . wasn't our fault . . . they pay us . . .

LUCRETIA: (*Watching him.*) Oh . . . (LUCRETIA *starts to the dresser as* SAM *sits dejectedly on the foot of the bed. She crosses to him.*) Sam . . . are you all right? What—what are you telling me? I know—I know you're trying to tell me something—

SAM: (*Rising.*) Yeah . . . yeah, I'm trying to tell you something! . . . Yeah! . . . I'm trying to tell you I ain't been to work in two days, babe—two days! . . . Yeah, I got the afternoon off. Yeah, I get the rest of my life off as far as those people are concerned down there— (*He crosses left center.*)

LUCRETIA: (*Sighing heavily and then looking away.*) Oh, Sam! . . . Sam, what happened? Sam, you haven't been to work in—in . . . *two* days, and you're just telling me?—

SAM: There wasn't no need, baby—

LUCRETIA: What do you mean no need? Don't you think—

SAM: I thought I could get another one! . . . I thought I could . . .

LUCRETIA: Sam, what happened? (*With great consternation.*)

SAM: (*Slowly.*) Babe, do you remember me telling you about Pop?

LUCRETIA: You mean that old man at the station—the porter?

SAM: The man's a doctor, Lu! (*She looks at him, amazed.*) He's a doctor, baby! So help me! You should hear him rattle off that stuff! I mean the man knows it backward and forward—he is! He doesn't have no reason to lie to me, babe! Look, I see his—whatever they call the damn thing—his degree—all in Latin and junk! He carries it with him—no lie!—in his back pocket! He showed me!

LUCRETIA: A doctor? Lord Jesus!

SAM: You never heard nothing like that in your whole life, have you? A porter!

LUCRETIA: What—what in the world is he doing down there at the station, Sam?

SAM: (*Crossing stage right to the foot of the bed.*) He told me one day—quiet-like . . . We was sitting there eating lunch. He likes me, you see. I don't know why. We just kinda took a shine to one another—right away. I don't know . . . Maybe because I didn't ask him to explain hisself, you know? I mean, I didn't try to take nothing away from him, that's what he told me . . . (*Pause.*) He couldn't get no work, babe—

LUCRETIA: Sam, there's plenty of need for doctors around here—

SAM: He couldn't make it, baby. You have to eat. What are you going to eat—promises? Damn right we get sick. But who the hell can pay for it? He couldn't make it. The man had to eat! A hell of a lot of sick people, but no cash, babe! (LUCRETIA *sits on the bed as* SAM *crosses stage center.*) Colored people weren't ready for colored doctors, or maybe colored doctors weren't ready for colored people. I forget the way he put it, but something like that . . . He said he didn't mind helping folks, but he didn't realize how much it was necessary for him not to be hungry—to not be worrying about next month all the time . . . (*Pauses.*) Wanted it simple, he said . . . just plain simple, you know, babe . . . Didn't want to have to think . . . or feel . . . or even care . . . the hell with it . . . Gave it up . . . He's a porter, so help me God, a porter, down at the station. (*Pause.*) He was . . . you know . . . doing his job . . . He's pushing this cracker's bags . . . Cracker's got enough bags for everybody in this whole town piled up on top of Pop's cart. He's pushing the damn thing, and it's heavy, but he's pushing, smiling and whistling, happy-like . . . And I don't know, for some reason one of the bags comes tumbling down and falls on the floor. The thing is, it splits— A couple of things break. The cracker claims they're from— I don't know whether he's lying or not—from Paris or Europe, one of them damn places. And all of a sudden he's getting red in the face. He's yelling and making a big stew, calling Doc names! Calling him boy this and nigger that, and Pop—Pop is just . . . just standing there—like he's supposed to take it, smiling and apologizing. (*Pause.*) He's got his mind—Pop—on what he is now, not what he was. He ain't no goddamn porter, but he don't want nobody to change it. He's got it all figured out! So that stupid, dumb, doctor-porter is taking all the cracker's crap! Taking it, talking to himself, reciting that stuff from his medical books! . . . Well, I couldn't take it! So I hightail it over to where they standing, and—and before I could catch myself, I'm telling this cracker off! I got my hand, my fist, my nose into his, and I'm screaming at him—yelling at him—calling him the names he's calling Pop. And that stupid Pop—Doc—is pulling at me—yanking at me, because he knows, because he's made it all so simple! And he's struggling with me! And I'm yelling at the cracker: "This man's a doctor, goddammit! You oughta be carrying his bags, you sonofabitch! Don't you talk to Dr. Savage that way! And Pop is crying almost, because I promised I wouldn't say nothing to nobody! That's what's getting him! He's begging me and half crying for me to shut up! And then all of a sudden he pulls out that damn piece of paper and tears it into shreds—just rips it up! (*Pauses.*) Well . . . to make a long story short . . . that's it. I mean, that's it . . . I wasn't worth a good minute after that . . . Right on the spot . . . on the damn spot! (*Pauses*) I turn around . . . on my way out . . . and there's . . . *Pop* . . . doing penance for me . . . cleaning up that bastard's shit . . . smiling, apologizing . . . kissing ass! . . . If he's mad, he's mad at me and not at the cracker—for messing up his goddamn, stupid world . . . (*Laughing suddenly and sitting in the chair stage center.*) Baby, I'm so miserable, it's funny . . . miserable . . .

LUCRETIA: (*Taking the beads off and crossing to* SAM.) You—you take these things right back where you got it from! I—I'm not going to take your last penny! (*She gives the pearls to him.*) I don't care if they are fakes! (*Crosses to stage right.*)

SAM: (*Going to her with the pearls.*) They're yours, now put 'em on! I bought 'em for you! I wanted you to have 'em! I wasn't thinking about no money! I just wanted you to have 'em—because you'd look nice in 'em! . . . Now come on! (*He places them around her neck.*) That's it . . . that's it, baby . . . Yeah, now you're looking good . . . just like—like a—a plate of fried tomatoes and gravy, huh? . . . Huh? (*He forces a laugh. She crosses back to the dresser. He turns away.*) Yeah, yeah, he's got it all figured out . . . figured out . . . To him it's so simple . . . The rest of us make it so complicated . . . (*Turning to* LUCRETIA.) Lu . . . baby . . . I'm going to have to . . . to . . . pull out for a while. (*She groans softly, turning away.*) There's . . . there's nothing here, babe—nothing. Two days I been looking and hating, babe . . . But the word's out—everywhere . . . down in the fields too. They got me, babe . . . (*She is silent, choking back tears.*) Just for a while . . . won't be long . . .

LUCRETIA: (*Takes a step to him.*) Will you—will you take me with you?

SAM: Come on now, babe . . . come on! It ain't no kinda life for you, not the way—

LUCRETIA: (*Crossing to* SAM.) Sam, I want to go with you!—

SAM: No! No! . . . No! . . . You may as well stop—stop talk-

ing! It's no life, now take my word for it! . . . Running here
. . . Running there . . . riding that damn boxcar . . . (*Sighing, shaking his head.*) It'll only be a little while . . .

LUCRETIA: Oh Sam . . . Sam— (*She crosses upstage between the bed and chair.*)

SAM: (*Crosses to* LUCRETIA.) Just a while . . . What am I supposed to do, babe—stay here and . . . and . . . starve? There's nothing here! Pop's seen to that! (*Sighing.*) You think I want to go? I'll just be a . . . while, baby. You know I'm not going to stay away. (*Again trying to laugh.*)

LUCRETIA: That's probably what you told the last one where you've been.

SAM: (*Turning away and crossing downstage.*) Come on, will you, babe—

LUCRETIA: You probably got a whole string of 'em waiting for you to come home to—probably. You . . . black . . . nigger! (*He turns and slaps her face. She turns away, holding her face.*)

SAM: (*Sighing heavily.*) Oh, goddammit! (*Pause.* LUCRETIA *crosses to the dresser.*) Look, sugar, I'm sorry . . . I'm sorry . . . Don't call me stuff like that, huh? . . . Not stuff like that . . . It ain't that simple for me, babe—not like Pop . . . like Pop.

LUCRETIA: (*Crosses to* SAM.) Sam? . . . Sam, I—I want to talk to you about . . . something— (*She starts to speak, but he kisses her. They embrace, passions rising, and fall on the bed.*)

(*Blackout. In the blackout* NATE *can be heard singing offstage. The lights rise in the living room and porch, where* LOU *sits brooding.* GREMMAR *rises and crosses to the stairs—meeting* NATE *as he moves down the steps to the porch. He pinches her cheek lightly.* GREMMAR *exits upstairs and offstage right, carrying her glass and fan.*)

LOU: (*Tersely, upon* NATE'S *arriving.*) You've given it all up for Daddy, haven't you, Nate?

NATE: (*Stopping.*) Given what up?

LOU: School. I thought you wanted to teach so much. That's what you said you wanted to do before.

NATE: I know what I said—I know it. The man needs help, Lou. So what am I supposed to do, huh? Yeah, I wanted to be one. (*Crosses stage left of the porch.*) So what the hell, everybody can't be one. Besides, they have enough people doing it without me.

LOU: (*Shaking his head disconsolately.*) Gremmar told me about . . . about your dropping out of—quitting school because of me.

NATE: (*Shrugging, sitting.*) Yeah, well, I figured as long as one of us went, what the hell's the difference. You were smarter than me . . . in the long run . . . had the best chance of making it, so . . . (*Pause, wiping perspiration from his forehead.*) I suppose I was pissed off at first. You know the way the old man can make you feel guilty—like if you don't help him you're going to be cast into the fiery furnace . . . you know . . . So, who knows, maybe I didn't have any other choice. What the hell, it's a . . . trade . . . It's honest . . . making my own living . . . not cheating anybody. I don't know, I might go back someday.

LOU: You've been saying that for three years now, Nate.

NATE: And I might be saying it for five more! I *might* go back—I might! I . . . I think about it . . . Anyway, it's not that important anymore . . . not like it used to be . . . You get out of school, and you see some things different . . . Those people don't make that much bread anyway. Oh, who knows! I'm plastering—it's all right—it is . . . I'm outside a lot . . . Nobody but the old man standing over me, and . . . I can handle him . . . I'm better than he is anyway. He knows it. He may not admit it, but damned if he doesn't know it! . . . He knows it . . . So I'm no teacher . . . I'm a plasterer.

LOU: (*Softly, intensely.*) I . . . I could've gotten a job in the hospital this summer—in the lab maybe . . . an orderly or something . . . Instead I—I have to do what?—plaster! I could be picking up some experience maybe—something that has to do with what I want to do in . . . college. But no . . . I have to fool around working for him—

NATE: That's between you and him, Lou. I—

LOU: (*Rises, crosses to downstage edge of porch.*) Don't remind me! (*Softly, agitated.*) Riding in the back of that . . . truck . . . like some . . . dope!

NATE: (*Crossing downstage to level with* LOU.) So ride in the front—all right? I'll ride in the damn back! I don't give a shit if people think I'm a dope! Let 'em think what they please!

LOU: Oh, it's—it's not just . . . that! (*Sighing heavily.*) Plaster

. . . you get sores all over your hands . . . stuff all in your eyes! . . . Damp . . . dirty! . . . It's—

NATE: Man, you can wear some gloves—and we have a pair of goggles, if that's what's bothering you. I used to wear 'em when I first started. (LOU *sits on the edge of porch downstage.*) It's not too bad, Lou . . . Shit, I have a business . . . I'm saving a little bread . . . Don't have the damn bill collectors on my tail . . . I have enough threads and all that . . . It's no big deal . . . not worth all that. Shit, you are what you are, you know? (*There is a sudden, loud, crashing noise—the sound of breaking glass.* NATE *and* LOU *both jerk around, startled, toward the noise.*) What the hell— (*The noise also startles* MILTON, *who is just entering from the kitchen.*)

MILTON: (*Crossing stage center of living room.*) What in the world?—

(NATE *moves quickly off the porch, around the side of the house, exiting downstage right from apron.*)

NATE: Come on, man! (LOU *follows, as* HATTIE *rushes into the living room from upstage right, followed by* GREMMAR.)

HATTIE: Milton, a rock! A rock! Just come flying through the window, breaking glass all over the place!

MILTON: A rock?

GREMMAR: Lord have mercy!

HATTIE: A big piece of rock!

MILTON: Those two boys! Louis! Nate! (NATE, *again followed by* LOU, *moves back onto the porch and into the living room, meeting* MILTON.)

NATE: Pop, it was Tom!

LOU: We just saw him running down the street!

MILTON: Tom? What in the world is Tom throwing stuff through my window for?—

GREMMAR: Trash, nothing but trash, that's all. It's a shame!

NATE: I don't know. He's mad, that's all, I guess. I stopped down at the Picket Post for a couple of seconds after work. Tom was there—drunk, as usual. Already drunk up his pay. And he started bugging me to lend him some money. I told him I wasn't going to give him one red cent. I told him you weren't either, so there was no sense asking. He got teed off, and I guess he still is.

MILTON: That man! I'm going to break his neck!

NATE: He's probably back at the Post.

MILTON: (*Moving toward the kitchen area exit with* NATE *and* LOU *leading.*) Break his neck! Fool man!

HATTIE: Milton!

GREMMAR: Come on back, son.

MILTON: I—I'm just going to talk to the man, Momma. (*He continues out with the boys.*)

HATTIE: Milton, Tom ain't worth you getting in trouble about.

GREMMAR: (*Rising, moving after him, preceded by* HATTIE.) Milton, there's no sense going down there and getting yourself in a lot of trouble over that man. It's not worth it, son. Just because he wants to show his ignorance is no reason why you have to. Use your head now, Milton. Use your head.— Don't leave with anger in your heart, son— Don't go—don't go— (*She stands in the kitchen area looking helplessly after them. Her thoughts turn inward as she continues to mutter softly,* "Don't leave." *The lights fade to special on* GREMMAR. *Lights rise in* LUCRETIA'S *room. She enters from stage left and stands at the dresser in same position as* GREMMAR, *then crosses to the bed, as special on* GREMMAR *fades out. She sits on the bed, staring emptily.* SAM *appears at the door, upstage right, a traveling bag in his hand. He stands with uncertainty before stepping into the room and setting down the bag.*)

LUCRETIA: (*Without looking up.*) Are you leaving now, Sam?

SAM: In—in a minute.

LUCRETIA: (*Rises and crosses to the dresser.*) I . . . I know . . . I know you'll be gone forever.

SAM: (*Attempting lightness, steps to* LUCRETIA.) I'll be back . . . just as soon as I get me a job . . . Won't take me long. (*Laughing.*) Soon as I get me a job . . . be right back here! . . . Maybe—maybe in one of them brand-new buggies! (*Forcing more laughter.*)

LUCRETIA: (*Despondently, crossing to the bed.*) You must be getting touched in the head, Sam. (*She is silent for a moment, and then quickly without looking.*) Sam? (*He stops. She places her hand on her belly and sits on the foot of the bed.*) Sam, feel here please!

SAM: Do what?

LUCRETIA: Feel here—right here . . . Come on, feel it, Sam!

SAM: (*Frowning, sitting beside her on the bed and putting his hand on her belly.*) What—what is it I'm supposed to be feeling?

LUCRETIA: It's your child there, Sam.

SAM: You . . . you got a . . . a . . . child in there?—a . . . baby? (*She nods.*) How you—how you—you seen a doctor?

LUCRETIA: No, but—

SAM: Then how the hell you know if you haven't—

LUCRETIA: (*Rises, crosses to the dresser.*) Sam, I know! . . . I mean . . . I know! . . . I'm a woman, ain't I? I ought to know—

SAM: (*Rises, follows her.*) Don't play with me now, Lucretia! I don't like for people to play with me like that—

LUCRETIA: Sam, I know—I know! . . . I told you! (*He turns away and crosses stage right.*)

SAM: (*Turns to* LUCRETIA.) Shit! . . . Shit! . . . Baby—baby, I have to go! . . . I—I can't stay here! I stay here . . . what . . . what's that . . . child going to live on, huh? I mean, what's he going to feed on if I don't have no work? . . . Can't have no starving child in there, now. You got one, you sure of it? (*Turning to face her.*) You ain't just . . . just doing it to me?

LUCRETIA: Sam, why do I want to lie?

SAM: (*Moving to her and sitting with her on the foot of the bed.*) Look, baby, now look . . . look . . . You—you just get in touch with me, you hear? You . . . you get on over to that doctor in town, and when you're sure—real sure— you just get in touch with me—

LUCRETIA: Sam, don't change on me—people change—

SAM: I ain't people, dammit! I'm Sam Green . . . Ain't nobody but Sam Green! Now . . . now you do what I tell you, Lu, you hear? I'll—I'll let you know where I am, and you get word to me the first thing—

LUCRETIA: (*Standing, moving away from him stage left.*) Oh, man, just . . . just . . . just . . . get out of here before I start bawling, please! Please? . . .

SAM: (*Watching her for a moment, and then rises and crosses downstage right.*) Yeah . . . yeah . . . Trains don't slow down much for niggers. (*He hesitates. She suddenly turns away from the dresser and rushes to him, embracing him.*) Soon— soon, sugar lump, you'll look over at that goddamn old door—

LUCRETIA: (*Whispering.*) Please don't swear, Sam—not right now . . .

SAM: (*Matching her softness.*) You'll look at that old door, and you know who'll be standing there? . . . Yeah, that's right— me! Yeah, me! And you know what? You know what, baby?

I'm going to have me a brand-new buggy outside—all shined up and ready to take you back—

LUCRETIA: Don't talk simple, Sam. Just—just come back on a mule if you have to.

SAM: I'll be back. You'll see . . . You just keep watching. (*Brings* LUCRETIA *downstage center.*) Every once in a while, you look out that old window . . . look way down the road there—way down there. You'll see me . . . see me coming back. Done struck it rich! Yeah! (*He smiles and then kisses her. She clings to him for a moment and then lets go. At first somber, he straightens and swaggers toward the door.*)

SAM: (*Turning to her.*) See you, sugar, when I'm rich! (*He moves jauntily out the door. He is gone, enveloped by the darkness.*)

LUCRETIA: (*Crosses to the doorway upstage right.*) You're touched in the head! . . . You know that, Sam? (*She stares into the darkness.*) And don't you go messing with all them other women neither, man! You're supposed to be working hard and providing for Little Sam—that's what I'm going to call him! (*She crosses back into the room, looks at the photograph on the dresser, and then sits on the bed and stares emptily.*) Sam, I'm scared . . . all of a sudden I'm scared!

(*Lights fade, and* LUCRETIA *clears upstage right. Laughter is heard. The lights rise on the porch. It is the afternoon of the next day, and Wall No. 1 is flown out to reveal Wall No. 2 [BRITON].* GREMMAR *and* LOU *sit on the porch front, playing Scrabble.* GREMMAR *is stage right, and* LOU *is stage left on bench.*)

LOU: (*Quickly.*) That's a word!

GREMMAR: It is?

LOU: Yep—cilia.

GREMMAR: Cilia? What in the world—you mean *silly*, don't you?

LOU: (*Laughing.*) No, Gremmar—*cilia*.

GREMMAR: Now, Louis, what kind of word is that? I never—

LOU: (*Straightening, reciting proudly from memory.*) Okay, let's see. It's the . . . hair-like outgrowths of certain cells, capable of vibrating—no!—vibratory movements, or the . . . small . . . hair-like . . . processes extending from certain plant cells . . . often forming a fringe or hairy surface . . . as on the underside of some leaves . . . that's a term in biology.

GREMMAR: (*Smiling, impressed.*) Yes, I figured it was something from all you were saying about it. That's what it means, huh? Yes, well, that's right, baby, learn all you can about it—learn all you can. Lord, just spouting it out like butter! (*She studies the letters on her rack and then begins to fit them into the maze.*) Is that right? . . . I don't want you to think I'm cheating now.

LOU: (*Teasing.*) Gremmar, I'm really impressed! And another thing—you didn't cheat! Yes, that's right.

GREMMAR: I know it's right . . . Beseech! . . . Bee-seech! . . . I beseech you therefore, brethren, by the mercies of God, that ye present your bodies . . . a living sacrifice, holy, acceptable unto God, which is your reasonable service . . . And be . . . and be not confirmed to this world: but . . . be ye . . . transformed by the renewing of your mind, that ye may prove—that ye may prove what is good . . . and acceptable . . . and perfect . . . will of God! . . . That's Romans, twelfth chapter—St. Paul talking . . . ! Yes, Saint Paul . . . ! Yes sir! . . . And that's what I've been trying to do all these years, abiding by the will of the Master—doing the right thing—all my life . . . Yes, abiding by the will of the Master . . . Making myself acceptable unto the Lord, which is my reasonable service! Yes sir!

LOU: (*Pause.*) Gremmar, sometimes, you know, you—you try to do the right thing— I mean, I've been trying to—just like you did—

GREMMAR: (*Reaching, patting his hand.*) I know you have, baby. I see you trying, and the Lord'll bless you—he will.

LOU: I mean, I want to be a doctor or scientist—right? And you have to study hard—right?

GREMMAR: That's right. Oh yes!

LOU: I don't know . . . The colored kids at school . . . most of 'em . . . they fool around. They don't care! And just because I don't act silly as they do—because I know what I want to do—they call me a bookworm and really— I mean, *really* get jealous because I study hard. I mean, they try to make me feel guilty. You know what I mean?

GREMMAR: I know, I know.

LOU: And next year, half of 'em, after graduation, won't be able to get near a college, and then they'll be complaining about having to work in a . . . a . . . gas station! or . . . or . . . doing construction work . . . or being a . . . garbage collector, maybe—things like that . . . Well . . . I just don't want to do things like that . . . I mean, it's . . . it's . . . you

know . . . de . . . grading . . . (*Shrugging.*) I mean, it's all
right and all, but . . . I want to be . . . better than that.
You—you know what I mean, Gremmar?

GREMMAR: I know . . . Oh yes, child, yes, I know. But that's
right . . . that's right. You strive, you hear? You just strive
on for the highest you can get. There's nothing wrong with
that. No, you've got the brains. Lord yes, you can see that
playing this here old game with me. Yes, you have the
brains. No reason why white folks have to get it all—no
reason at all! (GREMMAR *rises and crosses downstage.*)

LOU: I know . . .

GREMMAR: Yessir, keep right on striving, you hear? (*Lights
fade down to special on* GREMMAR.)

LOU: (*Nodding softly.*) Yes, ma'am.

GREMMAR: That's it, baby . . . that's it.

(*Special fades out, and* GREMMAR *and* LOU *clear stage left.
The lights rise on* LUCRETIA'S *room.* LUCRETIA, *an apron on,
runs into the room, followed by* BRITON. *He attempts to kiss
her.*)

LUCRETIA: (*Resisting.*) Mr. Briton, I—I haven't finished my
cleaning, and—and I got cooking to do—

BRITON: You've got plenty of time for that!—

LUCRETIA: Mr. Briton, please! Your father—your father finds
out—he's got a mean temper! I—I can't afford to lose my
job—my child!—

BRITON: They're gone, and you know it!—you know it! You
want to see? I'll show you, and then what kind of excuse
will you have? (*He goes to the door upstage right.*) Hey, you
old sonofabitch, are you down there? You're gone, aren't
you, you and your old bitch?—to another one of your goddamn parties! Tell this black woman here who won't kiss me
that you're gone and won't be back until after she kisses me
at least once! Tell her so she won't be scared. Tell her,
Daddy! (*He stands, feigning listening, and then laughs, moving back to her.*) You see, they're gone!

LUCRETIA: Sometimes they come back early.

BRITON: (*Crosses downstage and into the room stage center.*)
And most of the time they don't. You think they get all fixed
up like they do just to come running back to spy on us?
(*Attempting to kiss her again, but she resists.*)

LUCRETIA: Mr. Briton, I—

BRITON: You've been . . . been teasing me, that's what you've been doing—teasing this little white boy ever since you came into this house draggin' your knapsack and little kid behind you—

LUCRETIA: Mr. Briton, I haven't . . . I most certainly haven't—

BRITON: The hell you haven't! . . . You know damn well what you've been doing—the way you look at me. Those quick little glances . . . That sneaky little smile you've got—when you're serving the table—rubbing yourself against me—

LUCRETIA: Mr. Briton, you're lying, that's not true!

BRITON: Oh yes, it is!

LUCRETIA: Shhhhhh. (*Turning and stepping stage right.*) I think—

BRITON: They're gone, goddammit! (*Crossing to the chair.*) I could do something, you know? . . . I could . . . I damn sure could . . . I could tell my old man about you . . . I could walk up to him and say, "Old man, I got something to tell you, about your servant girl . . . It's about her teasing, old man. She isn't no servant girl, she's nothing but a great big tease, that's what . . ."

LUCRETIA: Mr. Briton, I'm nothing of the kind. I never did anything to make you think . . .

BRITON: (*Sensing her fear, teasing her more.*) Yep, I just might tell him—old bird . . . You can never tell about me. I'm adopted, you see, I ain't really one of theirs. They all think I'm half crazy anyway. Yeah, who knows, I might just walk on down these steps when he comes and tell him—

LUCRETIA: I'll . . . I'll . . . I'll leave . . . I'll take Little Sam, and I'll leave right now!— (*Moving toward the dresser and removing clothing from it.*)

BRITON: (*Stopping her.*) Jesus Christ!—you—you— Oh, Jesus Christ! (*Looking at her in amazement.*) Do—do you *really* think I'd do something like that— You know I wouldn't dare, don't you? (*Pause.*) Don't you? What do you take me for, huh? I'm teasing you—just teasing you, that's all! My daddy—which he really isn't—he's the one that holds threats over folks here in Roanoke. He's the one that does stuff like that! (*Pause.*) You didn't believe I was serious, did you? . . . Did you, Lucretia?

LUCRETIA: (*Softly.*) Yes . . .

BRITON: (*In animated disbelief.*) Oh, man! . . . Oh, man, I mean, what the hell do I look like—some . . . goon or something? Is that what I look like? Jeee-sus God, are you gullible! . . . I mean . . . I mean, is that why you wouldn't let me kiss you, is that why?

LUCRETIA: (*Turning away.*) Things would start . . . Things would start . . . (*Crosses stage right.*) Mr. Briton, I have to get back to work—

BRITON: (*Stopping her.*) Why do you call me that?

LUCRETIA: Your daddy said—

BRITON: My daddy, my daddy, hell! Well, he's not my daddy. He's nothing of the kind! He says he is, but he's not! My father, I don't know where the hell he is—who the hell he is! My mother either! I don't give a good damn either, for that matter! . . . My daddy thought he was impotent. That's why it's "Briton, you do this; Briton you do that!" I remind him of his impotence! . . . Every time he looks at me, that's what he sees—and he hates . . . he hates to think of it! (*Laughing ruefully.*) They never thought they were going to have anything. Ten years they did it—humping each other. They didn't give a good goddamn about each other. Ten years! And nothing, not even a dribble from his cock! . . . And so, it was me . . . me! "That one over there!"—me! . . . And then, through some miracle, Jamie comes along! No more use for me now! You—you should just see the way they go on and on about that little bastard! I'm a mistake . . . "My daddy" hates to think of himself as possibly having been so much of a weakling for so long—no, not with all his illusions of grandeur! But that's what the hell he thought, until they finally managed to scrape the bottom of the barrel of their sexual powers and dug up Jamie . . . He looks dug up too!

LUCRETIA: (*Trying to push him out of the room.*) Please go, Mr. Briton, and let me get to my work.

BRITON: (*Grabbing her arm, stopping her.*) You're . . . you're really a pretty woman, Lucretia . . . you really are. You're not . . . artificial—like those high-society dames they try to set me up with. (*Pause, looking tenderly at her.*) We have a lot in common, you and me, Lucretia! You know that? Both of us are outcasts! That's what we are around here. No wonder it's—

LUCRETIA: I—I have to go . . . I—I have to clean the upstairs and the downstairs too. And your father—Mr. Woodward likes a bite to eat when he comes in— (*He grabs her and kisses her. She starts to struggle but yields, embracing him— pulling away after a moment, turning away downstage.*)

BRITON: (*Frowning.*) What—what's the matter? . . . You—you didn't like it? . . . I—don't kiss like your . . . black friends out on the grounds?

LUCRETIA: Shhh! (*Crossing toward the door.*) It's them— I told you! I told you! And I haven't got nothing done!

BRITON: (*Following her.*) This isn't the last time, is it, Lucretia?

LUCRETIA: (*In near panic.*) I have to go! Mr. Briton, please don't let them catch you in my room!

BRITON: (*At the door, whispering.*) Tomorrow, Lucretia, do you hear? . . . Lucretia? . . . Tomorrow! We're outcasts— okay?

(*Lights fade to black offstage, we hear* REVEREND MOSELY, HATTIE, *and* MILTON *talking. As lights rise,* GREMMAR *is crossing from kitchen area into the living room, where she reaches stage center.* REV. MOSELY *enters from the kitchen carrying a cup of tea followed by* HATTIE, MILTON [*carrying a Bible*], *and* LOU, *also entering from the kitchen.* GREMMAR *sits down right armchair;* MILTON *sits stage right at table;* HATTIE *stage left of table, and* LOU *on the piano stool.*)

MOSLEY: Therefore, I said, therefore doth my soul keep them!

GREMMAR: (*Simultaneously with* MILTON *and* LOU.) Amen, Reverend. (NATE *and* HOPE *enter from porch—see* REV. MOSELY *and start to leave. They are stopped by* HATTIE, *who indicates for them to sit in up left armchair.*)

MOSLEY: (*A slight reasonance in his voice.*) The mercy of the Lord is everlasting to *everlasting* . . . Just think of it—everlasting, children, upon them that fear him—*fear* him and his righteousness unto children's children! (*Again, "amens" from the three adults.*) For no other—no *other* foundation can any man—*any* man lay than which is in the Savior! (*"Amens."*) We're here to give testimony . . . to give thanks—to say, "Thank you, Mr. Jesus, for the many blessings you bestowed upon this household this past week. Thank you, Jesus!"

MILTON: That's right, Reverend.

GREMMAR: Thank you, Jesus.

MOSLEY: (*Crossing downstage in front of the table.*) And he has—oh yes, he has! Yes sir! We must count our blessings tonight, children. Let's count 'em—count 'em—each in his own way, each in his own time. For surely, children, we are pilgrims in this strange and weary land!—

MILTON: All right, Reverend!

GREMMAR: Amen, sir—amen!

HATTIE: Have mercy, Jesus—have mercy! (*Softly.*)

MOSLEY: (*Crossing upstage center behind the table.*) And *he* is our refuge and strength, though the waters, young people, roar and be troubled, the scriptures says: "And the mountains *shake* with the swelling thereof!" (*"Amens" from* HATTIE, MILTON, *and* GREMMAR.) All right now, children, each in his own way . . . in his own time . . . let the spirit of God—let his spirit move you—let it move you, and give thanks for his bountiful goodness this past week . . . Perhaps sister Lucretia will play something on the piano now to help us feel the spirit of God moving.

GREMMAR: (*Rising, going to the piano;* LOU *rises from the piano stool and sits on the bench.*) Certainly, Reverend, be glad to.

MOSELY: Softly now . . . softly . . . Let Jesus come into your hearts tonight, now. Let him in . . . Open up your hearts now . . . Give him the key . . . Let him unlock the door of your heart and steal softly in and move you, children. (*She begins to play "Blessed Assurance," humming softly as she does. The others join in, singing softly.*) Softly . . . softly . . . each in his own way . . . his own time . . . softly . . . (NATE *coughs, shifting nervously, attempting to mask his reluctance to be present. He glances from the corner of his eyes at* HOPE, *who is less nervous.* LOU, *like* HATTIE *and* MILTON, *is pensive and stares down at the floor.*) Let him move you now . . . *move* you. Let the Father, Son, and Holy Ghost walk on into your hearts, my friends, and move you. Don't fight him . . . don't fight him . . . Let him in.

MILTON: (*Reading strongly.*) Yea, though I walk through the valley of the shadow of death, I will fear no evil, for thou art *with* me!—

MOSELY: (*Softly but intently.*) Yes, yes! (*Resuming humming.*)

MILTON: Thy rod and thy staff comfort me! . . . Thou preparest a table before me in the presence of mine enemies; thou anointest my head with oil; my cup . . . *runneth over!* (*Closing the Bible.*)

MOSELY: Yes, yes! (*In response* GREMMAR *sings louder.*)

MILTON: (*Rises and crosses behind stage right armchair.*) I want to thank the good Lord for walking with me the past week.

MOSELY: Uh-huh . . . uh-huh . . .

MILTON: As he has done each week in the past. He has been by my side—I know it!—because I know him—I know the Lord—yes, I do!

GREMMAR: All right, son! All right! (*Singing again.*)

MOSELY: Yes, yes! (*Singing.*)

MILTON: Been by my side! I know him! Many have fallen by

the wayside since last we've gathered together, through death or through the wages of sin, but the good Lord has spared this family to see another week!—

MOSELY: All right now, sir—all right!

GREMMAR: Amen, amen!

HATTIE: (*Softly.*) Have mercy, Jesus!

MILTON: And I want to let Jesus into my heart now, and I want to say, "Thank you, Jesus!"

MOSELY: Thank you, Jesus!

GREMMAR: (*Echoing him and then singing louder.*) Thank you, Jesus!

MILTON: And I want to thank you, Lord, for preparing a table . . . preparing a table and providing . . . and providing . . . (*Unable to control his emotions, stopping and crying slightly.*)

MOSELY: Take your time, brother . . . take your time . . . take all the time the spirit gives you—

GREMMAR: Bless you, son—bless you!

MILTON: (*With difficulty.*) Thank you, Lord, for . . . preparing a table and . . . and providing for me and my family (*Crosses to* GREMMAR *and hugs her.*) and looking after Momma—

GREMMAR: (*Stops playing, but everyone continues to sing.*) That's right, son . . . that's right now . . . "Looking after Momma"—that's right— (*Resuming singing.*)

MILTON: (*Standing stage left of* GREMMAR.) And . . . taking care of her needs and all . . . And we . . . we ask your continued blessings, Lord—your continued blessings . . . and ask your help—help us to grow stronger—stronger in your way, Savior—stronger, so that— (*His voice cascades into soft sobbing,* REV. MOSELY *crosses to* MILTON *and helps him to sit at table stage right chair.*)

MOSELY: That's all right, brother, that's all right . . . It's good to let the Lord fill up your heart—it's good! Let him fill up your heart as he filled up your table! Let him fill it up! For I will fill up your heart if you let me, he said! Fill it up! (*Crossing behind stage right armchair.*) Each in his own time . . . his own way . . .

HATTIE: (*After a moment, rising quickly.*) I just want to say, "Thank you, Jesus—your continued blessing!" (*Sitting.*)

MOSELY: Amen . . . amen . . . That's right, sister Hattie. Thank you, Jesus, and your continued blessings! (*Humming and then stopping.*) Softly . . . softly . . . each in his own time . . . own way . . . (*As the others sing.*) Maybe one of the young people would like to . . . would like to say something—testify.

MILTON: Amen.

MOSELY: Maybe one of the young people would like to say something . . . remember his kindness—his goodness. You don't have to be embarrassed in front of Jesus—no sir!—not in front of the Savior! No sir, children, because he understands us all . . . understands us all! (NATE *is more uneasy and sinks down in his seat.* MILTON, *attempting not to be too obvious, looks at* NATE, *who shrugs, keeping his head down.* MILTON *glares at him.*) Trust in the Lord, young people! Let him do the talking for you. Give him the key! Can't unlock your hearts unless you give him the key now! Give him the key, young people! (HATTIE *looks at* NATE *and gestures for him to rise.* HOPE *nudges him.*)

GREMMAR: All right! All right! Give him the key! All right, sir!— (NATE *stands finally, reluctant, angry, nervous, trying to conceal his feelings. He begins to mumble his words. The others continue singing.*)

NATE: I'd . . . I'd like to say . . . as a . . . young person . . . I'd like to say . . . thank God for . . . for . . . for . . .

MOSELY: Take your time, son . . . Give him the key now . . . Don't forget the key! He'll move you!

GREMMAR: That's right, Nathan—that's right.

NATE: For all his blessings . . . this week . . . (*Sighing heavily.*) And . . . last week . . . And . . . for safety . . . and . . . good health . . . and . . . for all his . . . continued blessings . . . (*He sits dropping his eyes, embarrassed.*)

MOSELY: (*Crosses stage left toward* NATE.) All right, son, all right . . . You don't have to feel no shame in front of Jesus— no shame! He promised us that! He is willing and able to do your talking if you ask him. (*Crosses stage center.*)

GREMMAR: (*Suddenly, zealously.*) Yes, he will! Yes, he will! I know—I know, 'cause I'm a child of the King!—(*She rises, crosses downstage right, in front of the armchair.* LOU *watches her, entranced and intrigued.*) A child of the *King!* And I want you to know—I want you to know that I'm walking up the *King's* highway! (*The others sing throughout her testimony, stopping to comment but always resuming singing.*)

MILTON: (*Picking up her enthusiasm.*) That's right, Momma!

MOSELY: Uh-huh, uh-huh!

GREMMAR: And ain't nothing—nothing going to stop me from making heaven my home, because he promised me a room—

MOSELY: All right, sister, let him move you!

MILTON: Go ahead, Momma!

HATTIE: (*Softly.*) Have mercy, Savior.

GREMMAR: Promised me a room in one of his many mansions!—

MOSELY: (*And* MILTON.) Yes, yes!

GREMMAR: And though the way has been long and weary, I want you to know, Lord Jesus, that I will persevere!

MOSELY: Persevere!

MILTON: Amen, Momma!

GREMMAR: Persevere, because I am sustained in *his* strength that has made me whole! Because he alone—He alone can sustain. He is the King!

MOSELY: Yes!

GREMMAR: The King! And I want to thank my King—thank you, Jesus, for your blessings—for your tenderness. Thank you, Jesus, for being a rock in a weary land full of sin and destruction! Thank you, Jesus, for letting me *lean*. You've let me lean, Jesus, on your mighty arm, and let me lay my tired body against your soft bosom!

MOSELY: Let him talk to you, sister!—let him talk!

GREMMAR: I am weak, but you are strong, Lord! And heaven is my eternal home! And I will be there—I will *be* there on Judgement Day, because I have tried to fulfill your ways! I have walked the straight and narrow path, keeping my eyes on the sparrow—on the sparrow!—ignoring the temptations along the way! I'm marching on up the King's highway with nothing but heaven on my mind—my feeble mind. I will be there!—standing in front of your judgement bar to listen—

MOSELY: To listen—

GREMMAR: To listen to your sweet and mighty voice say—

MOSELY: Tell him what it's going to say, sister!

GREMMAR: To hear your sweet and mighty voice say: "Well done, good and faithful servant—well done!" Have mercy, Jesus, and bless your precious name!

(HATTIE *starts singing "Well Done"; the others join in.* LOU *has watched* GREMMAR'S *demonstration in awe and reverence. Caught up in the fervor of the moment, he stands suddenly— crosses downstage behind* MILTON *mesmerized, trembling, almost oblivious to the others. The others, somewhat shocked, stop singing for a moment and watch him.*)

LOU: I—I want to—to thank God . . . I want to thank God! I do—I really do! (NATE *looks at him in disbelief.*) I want to thank him . . . thank him! . . . I want to thank him for sparing my family . . . for food and strength . . . for school . . . for church . . . for Gremmar . . . (*Turns to* GREMMAR *and hugs her.*) For providing a table . . . For helping me to . . . to keep Satan out of my life . . . and . . . letting me into his heart . . . and touching me!— (LOU *crosses downstage right in front of the armchair.* NATE *frowns, suddenly realizing* LOU'S *seriousness. He shifts in his seat, disturbed. The others resume singing.*) For giving me the key and . . . and . . . unlocking the door to my heart to serve him . . . And . . . and nothing's going to stop me, like Gremmar said—Satan— nothing! Because I—I want a room in one of your mansions, Jesus—I really do! And I promise—I promise to serve you, because I love you, because . . . because I . . . I love you, Lord . . . I love you and—I give myself to you, and I'll continue to do what you want me to do . . . and pray . . . and not sin . . . and obey your commandments—I really will! Because I . . . I want to go to college and study medicine and . . . science . . . and biology . . . and keep my eye on the sparrow, and pray and . . . and not get tempted . . . and trust and . . . and . . .

(GREMMAR, HATTIE, MILTON, *and* REV. MOSELY *move to him, comforting him, and take* LOU *off into the kitchen, with* GREMMAR *following.* HOPE *starts to follow, but* NATE *tugs at her and they exit stage left off porch area.* GREMMAR *stops up left and turns stage right as lights fade down to special on her. The lights rise on* LUCRETIA'S *room and special fades out.* GREMMAR *clears stage left.* BRITON *and* LUCRETIA *lie together on the bed, their clothing awry.*)

BRITON: (*Silent, and then sitting up suddenly and crossing stage center.*) I've decided, goddammit, Lucretia! Just now, laying here with you! I'm not going back to school! I don't have to! Christ, I'm over twenty-one! I don't have to go back unless I want to! The only reason I went was because he wanted me to. He wanted me to because my brother Jamie, which he's not really, didn't want to be a lawyer like him. That's why I went—to please him. Somebody—somebody in the family had to be a lawyer. Somebody—one of us—just *had* to be a lawyer because he is! Well, to hell with him! He's so proud of Jamie, let Jamie do it for him! . . . What do you think of that, lady?

LUCRETIA: If . . . if that's what you want . . .

BRITON: Well, that's what I want, lady. I want you! (*He crosses to the bed—kisses her.*) That's what I want . . . I don't want to be a crooked lawyer like him. He's a crook—I know he is! He—he carries himself too perfect—too stiff—too proud—too much like a—bigshot! (*He hops out of bed and begins strutting around the room in imitation.*) Like some—some . . . proud-assed turkey! That's how he walks. (*She laughs.*) Doesn't he?

LUCRETIA: (*Laughing.*) Yes!

BRITON: Man, you talk about somebody not knowing how to have any fun, it's that man! (*Sobering suddenly.*) Not unless he's with Jamie . . . then he laughs. (*Strutting again, laughing only slightly.*) Big, powerful, important man like him just couldn't have taken ten years to have a kid. (*He is silent and then sits on the side of the bed next to her, thinking.*) I'm not going back. (*Rising again and pacing.*) No sir . . . I'm going to . . . I'm going to . . . to just . . . I don't know—just get the hell out of here and—and . . . *bum!*—and fly high! I'm going to be like a great big bird, Lucretia, and fly all over this world! (*He spreads his arms like a bird and spins around the room, "flying."*) Fly until I get dizzy—until I see it all, and then—then I'll come flying back to wherever you are! (*He "flies" toward her, leaping on the bed beside her and tickling her.*)

LUCRETIA: (*Laughing, again resisting.*) Briton, stop!

BRITON: (*Nestling close to her.*) You like me, don't you, Lucretia?

LUCRETIA: (*Softly.*) Yes . . .

BRITON: That's good . . . yeah, that's what I need . . . yeah . . . You need it too, you know . . . outcasts like we are . . . (*He lies down with his head on her lap.*) You're soft, Lucretia . . . good and soft . . . like a pillow. (*Pretending to snore.*)

LUCRETIA: Briton . . . if . . . if you don't like them people out there in the field . . . how . . . how come—how come you like me . . . I'm no different.

BRITON: (*Sitting up.*) The hell you're not! . . . You're . . . good-looking . . . (*Rises and crosses down left center.*) And besides . . . besides . . . your face isn't always screwed up and pissed-off-looking like theirs—like they want to kill me and not my *daddy!* I'm nice to 'em. I'm polite . . . I'm always talking with them and clowning around when I'm down there—just like I do with you . . . It pisses the old man off! It really does! You should see his face, Lucretia! You've seen his face when he gets pissed off!

LUCRETIA: (*Standing suddenly at the foot of the bed.*) Shhhhhhh!

BRITON: (*Crosses to* LUCRETIA.) Oh, come on now! Every time we're together!— They went out to dinner . . . And . . . she'll get drunk and sloppy sick with her *Southern charm,* of course. And so will he. When he's ready, they'll come home bound by their drunkeness and flop into bed. We could stay here the whole night, so stop worrying. (*Sits on the bed and pulls* LUCRETIA *down beside him, and kisses her.*)

BRITON: Your mouth is really sensual, you know, Lucretia? You Negras really have sensual mouths—not like us white people—

LUCRETIA: (*With difficulty.*) Briton . . . when I was gone today—

BRITON: Hey, I was wondering where the hell you were. I was getting lonesome.

LUCRETIA: I . . . I was at . . . I was at the doctor, Briton. (*He frowns.*) He . . . he says I'm . . . going to have another baby—

BRITON: (*Turning sharply to her, stunned.*) He says you're . . . what?

LUCRETIA: That's what he told me, Briton. I—

BRITON: (*Staring hard at her and then rising.*) You—you're not saying it's . . . *mine,* are you? You're not—

LUCRETIA: Briton, it can't be nobody else's. I don't see nobody but you. I don't hardly go out of this house—

BRITON: Who—who the hell did you go to—some colored doctor across town?

LUCRETIA: Yes, but—

BRITON: Well, you—you just get yourself to a white doctor! (*Turning away, angry, trembling.*) You just get yourself to a *white* doctor!—

LUCRETIA: Briton, the man did a test or something! He—

BRITON: (*Rises and crosses stage left center.*) But I made sure!—

LUCRETIA: (*Looking toward the door.*) Briton, not so loud!

BRITON: They're gone, goddammit! I keep telling you that! I'm not going to that goddamn door again! (*Pacing.*) I made sure! I took precautions with you—every time! Unless . . . unless the—the last time—or—sometime you told me it was all right!—

LUCRETIA: I—I thought it was!

BRITON: What do you mean, you thought? Jesus Christ, Lucretia!—

LUCRETIA: I thought . . . I thought it . . . was . . .

BRITON: You're trying to trick me, aren't you? You black—

LUCRETIA: Briton, I'm not—

BRITON: (*Turning angrily away downstage center.*) Trying to trick me!— One of those—those . . . *people* out there knocked you up and now you're trying to blame it on me!—

LUCRETIA: (*Rising, straightening, and crossing to* BRITON.) I ain't one of those flighty girlfriends you bring around here, boy!—

BRITON: Wait . . . just wait . . . just let me get my mind together . . . Sometimes I have trouble getting my mind together, you know? (*Pacing.*) I have a little trouble . . . These people around here! . . . Look, Lucretia . . . that— that white doctor . . . (*Sitting on the foot of the bed and easing her downstage right of him.*) Look, we'll get you over to him—or the black one, if that's what you want, and . . . and we'll get a job done on you.

LUCRETIA: Briton, I'm not going to get rid of it, if that's what you mean—

BRITON: Oh, come on, Lucretia, you have to—

LUCRETIA: I don't believe in that kinda stuff—

BRITON: Well, you better believe in it! . . . You have to do it, Lucretia, because—Lucretia, don't tie me down to thoughts . . . Don't tie me down to something I'm not ready to think about.

LUCRETIA: (*Rises, crosses down right.*) Briton, I've thought about it— I'm going away from here—

BRITON: (*Rising.*) Where?—and saddled with two kids? Look—

LUCRETIA: I'm not going to do what you want me to! . . . I'll tell your father I have to quit—I have to go on up North, but . . . I'm not going to do it! . . . I'm not going to tell nobody if that's what you're worried about—I won't.

BRITON: (*Steps to* LUCRETIA.) No . . . no, I know you wouldn't . . . You should, but you wouldn't. (*Pacing, stage center.*) So many things I want to do . . . so many goddamn places I want to be—sometimes all at the same time. I won't have any money—just a knapsack probably, but I know I have to go, Lucretia. I know I have to get away from this goddamn place—not you—here! And . . . and even if I stayed . . . even if I did . . . you know it would be impossible, don't you?

LUCRETIA: Briton . . . don't . . . don't say no more, please?

(*He crosses to bed, sits facing downstage. She crosses to him, and he lays his head against her belly. The lights fade out.* LOU *enters the porch in darkness, and* GREMMAR *enters to the foot of the bed. The lights rise in a special on* GREMMAR *and on* LOU, *as* LOU *sits on the bench.* NATE *moves slowly up to porch from stage left.* GREMMAR *exits upstage right.*)

NATE: What's up? (LOU *shrugs.*) Everybody in bed? (LOU *nods as* NATE *moves onto the porch.*) Oh brother, I thought it would have cooled off a little by now anyway! (*He is silent a moment and then turns his head toward* LOU. *He speaks softly because of the lateness of the hour. His tones are suggestive rather than angry.*) Lou, man, I'm telling you. (*Shaking his head.*)

LOU: (*Turning, looking at him.*) Telling me what?

NATE: (*Shrugging, pause.*) Tonight . . . All that carrying on in there—

LOU: (*Tense.*) What do you mean "carrying on"?

NATE: (*Slight pause.*) All that . . . testifying, crying and falling-out nonsense. Man, come off that stuff, will you? That's . . . old folks' bullshit . . . breaking down all over the place and acting like asses!—

LOU: (*Defensively.*) I couldn't help it, Nate! I—I wasn't . . . trying to! . . . It just . . . happened, that's all! . . . I can't help it if you don't believe in it! . . . I do—all right?

NATE: I didn't say I didn't believe in it, man. You just don't have to get so carried away with it, that's all. Shit, you can do all the believing you damn well please, but it still doesn't call for all them shenanigans. No, indeed!

LOU: (*Rises and crosses downstage.*) Look, Nate, let's drop it! . . . It's my business! . . . If— if I'm supposed to be ashamed of myself, then I'm not! . . . You just do what you want, and I'll do what I want!—

NATE: (*Crosses to the bench and sits.*) So be an ass—all right? . . . Maybe you should've seen yourself.

(LOU *turns partly toward* NATE, *speaking with extreme difficulty, tension, yet softly.*)

LOU: Nate . . . you know what? . . . I . . . I . . . I really think there's . . . something wrong with me—I really do.

NATE: (*Turning slowly, frowning.*) What do you mean?

LOU: I . . . I don't know . . . There's something wrong . . .

NATE: What do you mean, you don't know? You just said there was something wrong with you, so what the hell are you talking about?

LOU: (*Crosses to the bench and sits stage left.*) It's just that . . . Last week . . . Peggy and I, well, we went out . . . parking, you know . . . in the woods . . . near Martin's Dam . . . and, well, we were there and . . . one thing led to another, and . . . we started fooling around—

NATE: Well, that's not it, is it? What the hell's wrong with that?

LOU: I'm not finished.

NATE: Because I was going to say, man—

LOU: We started . . . fooling around . . . all that stuff, and, well, you know . . . she wanted me to . . . you know? . . . I guess I wanted to . . . I guess . . . (*Pause.*) So . . . when it was time . . . even before it was time . . . before . . . she took my hand and put it . . . down there . . . and . . . I got sick . . . I got sick! . . . I vomited! I just . . . puked all over the place! . . . I just all of a sudden got this . . . sick feeling in the pit of my stomach, and . . . and it all came up—and I just couldn't do it! I couldn't! . . . I don't know what was wrong—why I got so sick—

NATE: (*Laughing.*) So you got sick—so what?

LOU: (*Angrily.*) What do you mean "so what?" I threw up!— (LOU *crosses downstage left.*)

NATE: Tell me the honest to God's truth, Lou—have you ever had any nookie before? (LOU *doesn't answer, turning away.* NATE *rises and crosses.*) I know you ain't—knowing you, you haven't. Shit, there's nothing wrong with you, nigger—not a damn thing! . . . Shit, I know your problem. Shit, man, you just have to get on that stuff and just start working out! Work out, nigger, and don't ask no questions—don't even think about it, brother. Just get on it and get the job done! That's your problem, man. You think too much about it! Just let nature take over and forget all that . . . fiery furnace stuff. Stuff'll mess you up every time, when you want some of it. Indeed, it will! I'm sorry, but that's just not the time for it. Hell, worry about it after you've busted your nuts. Get guilty later, if you want to. It'll pass, believe you me, it will pass! Just get on it and knock that shit out and chalk it up, and square it with your conscience later—much later, if that's what's bothering you. (*Sits downstage center on the edge of the porch.*) Yeah, be ready for that stuff when it comes, man because sometimes it's far and few between! Indeed!

LOU: (*Speaking softly but intensely.*) Nate . . . some—sometimes I get . . . I get so sick and tired of it all! . . . I really do! . . . Honest to God!

NATE: What's that—nookie? Shit! I don't . . . I don't never get tired of it man—never!—

LOU: Sometimes I'd . . . I'd like to . . . to . . . take a knife and . . . and just . . . rip this black stuff off!—just . . . skin myself clean! I—

NATE: You'd just bleed, man, that's all . . . just bleed . . . (NATE *rises after a moment, and then goes up to* LOU *and claps him on the shoulder, shaking him gently.*) Ease up, man . . . just ease up! . . . Fuck it, you know? I mean, just plain fuck it all! . . . Just keep moving and you don't get hurt . . . And don't let some of it hang out, let it all! You know what I mean? (NATE *puts his arm around his shoulder.*) Fuck it— just plain fuck it all! You know? (*Lights begin slow fade.*)

LOU: (*Sighing heavily, shrugging.*) Yeah . . . yeah . . .

(*Lights out and curtain falls. During Act Break No. 2 Wall is flown out to reveal No. 3 Wall for* HARPER *flashback.*)

ACT TWO

(Curtain rises. It is Saturday afternoon. The set is the same except for a tablecloth on the dining table. The Bible, cup and saucer, and tray have been struck. The bed upstairs has been made up.)

(At rise, LOU is sitting on the floor of the porch at the entrance to the house reading a biology book. MILTON and NATE are downstage of the desk in the living room, discussing a bid for a plastering job.)

NATE: Pop, the bid is way too low, for Pete's sake!

MILTON: Nathan, you don't have to get greedy about it!

NATE: Who's getting greedy? Pop, the trouble with you is you always bid too low!

MILTON: Look, Nathan, I got it figured down right here! That's why I called you in here!

NATE: Pop, you don't have a thing here for—for profit—not a thing! . . . for time and aggravation!

MILTON: Nathan, that house isn't going to take anymore than two weeks!

NATE: Pop, by the time we buy material, pay everybody, what do we have left?

MILTON: *(Giving the bid to NATE.)* Nathan, look at these figures down there again, will you?

NATE: I'm looking at them! All they're saying is that we're going to have to scramble and charge at the lumber yard for the next job, instead of charging what the job is worth. *(Crosses stage center.)* You always underbid because you're afraid of not getting the job!

MILTON: *(Steps to NATE.)* I charge what the job is worth, and that's what I've been doing all these years!—

NATE: And that's why we don't have any capital now!

MILTON: *(Crosses stage right.)* I've been able to provide for this family, haven't I? Nobody's in need of anything here, are they?

NATE: *(Steps to MILTON.)* Pop, just tell me—why do we always

83

have to submit the lowest bid, huh? No wonder we always get the job. They know they're going to get a first-class job for the least amount of money. Those white contractors, they see us coming, and they laugh all the way to the bank. (*Crosses stage center.*) As far as I'm concerned—

MILTON: (*Grabbing the bid again and studying it.*) All right, all right, let me see the paper. (*Sits at the desk and opens the ledger, which is on the desk.*)

NATE: I'd rather risk not getting the job than to— Things are going up, and here we are charging the same thing we did last year. That house has got—

(JOE DRAKE *moves up to walk onto the porch from stage left.*)

DRAKE: Hello, Nate.

LOU: (*Rising quickly, polite but attempting to mask the indignation at the mistake.*) I'm not . . . Nate . . .

DRAKE: Oh, I'm sorry . . . I—I thought you were. (DRAKE *forces a smile.*) Is . . . your father in? . . . It's Joe Drake.

LOU: (*Moving toward the porch door.*) Just a minute . . . (*Going to* MILTON.) Pop, it's Joe Drake. (NATE *crosses upstage at the desk, hovers over* MILTON.)

MILTON: Tell him I'll be there in a minute—I'm finishing up on the bid. (*Gestures for* NATE *to sit;* NATE *sits anxiously on the piano stool.*)

LOU: (*Returning to the porch.*) He'll be here in a second. (DRAKE *stands hesitantly.*) Won't you have a seat?

DRAKE: Thank you. (*He sits stage right on the bench.* LOU *crosses stage left and sits on the floor. Throughout the scene with* DRAKE, LOU *tries to be polite, though he is somewhat ill at ease.*) You must be Lou, then? (LOU *nods, grinning somewhat shyly.*) Your father and Nate are good plasterers. (*Pause.*) That Nate is the best I've ever seen—a first-class perfectionist! I have work, I try to make certain they get it.— So, how's school going?

LOU: (*Reluctantly, shrugging.*) Okay . . . so far . . .

DRAKE: (*Nodding, pause.*) Your brother tells me you want to be a doctor some day.

LOU: (*Looking directly at him.*) I hope so . . .

DRAKE: Well, that's great . . . that's great . . . Who knows, may be someday I'll be getting a checkup from you. (*He laughs, pausing as* LOU *forces a polite smile.*) My kid's in school too— Yale . . . Every once in a while he sends me stuff home to read—things he's been studying . . . Wants to make sure I don't get too complacent—wants some intelligent conversation when he comes home on vacations . . . doesn't want a dunce as a father. (*Laughing again.* LOU *is stoic.*) Your . . . father tells me you don't like plastering very much . . .

LOU: (*Softly, hesitantly.*) It's . . . all right . . .

DRAKE: Well, it's hard work . . .

LOU: I'd just . . . rather be doing . . . something else—

DRAKE: Well, I don't blame you, son—no, I don't . . . I don't blame my own kid for not wanting to go into the building business. No, let him make up his own mind what he wants to be—

MILTON: (*Turns to* NATE.) All right, seventeen hundred—(*Rises.*)

NATE: (*Rises.*) It's still not enough!

MILTON: (*Crosses stage right.*) Nathan, I can't charge that man no more than that!—

NATE: (*Following.*) Drake's got it.

MILTON: Now you're being ridiculous!

NATE: It ought to be at least two thousand!

MILTON: Nathan, I'm sorry, but I'm just not going to do it!

NATE: That old place has got closets and pipes galore—

MILTON: I know what it's got! I can see! I'm not going to charge Drake any two thousand, so you may as well stop!—

NATE: Well, I don't know why you asked my opinion in the first place.

MILTON: (*Crossing stage center.*) Nathan, I appreciate your help, but I thought you'd use better sense.

NATE: Well, maybe you'd better figure out the bids yourself from now on! (*He angrily crosses downstage right, sits in the armchair.* MILTON *stops, looks at him for a moment, and then studies the bid. Going to the table, he writes a figure on it and steps to* NATE.)

MILTON: All right, I got it up to eighteen hundred, but I certainly can't charge the man any more than that—absolutely not! (*Crosses to the porch.*)

NATE: (*Without looking up.*) Pop, it's your business . . .

MILTON: (*Appearing at the door.*) Hello, Mr. Drake, I'm sorry to keep you waiting.

DRAKE: (*Rises.*) Oh no, that's all right. Your boy and I were just out here talking.

MILTON: Come on into the living room, Mr. Drake, where it's more comfortable. It's so hot out here.

DRAKE: (*Following him.*) Okay. Nice talking to you, Lou. (*The two men go into the living room.* DRAKE *sees* NATE.) How are you doing, Nate?

NATE: (*Sullenly.*) Okay, Mr. Drake, how are you?

DRAKE: Oh, fair to middling. (*Sitting at the table stage left.*)

MILTON: (*Handing him the bid and then sitting opposite him.*) I tried to make it as fair as I could.

DRAKE: (*Putting on a pair of glasses.*) Oh, I know that—I know that. Just let me take a quick gander at it. I'm sure it'll be all right. (*He looks at the bid and then frowns.*) Milton . . . this is a little high, isn't it?

MILTON: Mr. Drake, like I said, I tried to be fair.

DRAKE: (*Reexamining the bid.*) I'm sure you did, but—

MILTON: And I'm still not making any money . . . Material's gone up. I've got my men to pay, and they have to get union scale—

DRAKE: My expenses are up too, Milton.

MILTON: I have to make some money, Mr. Drake. Both of us are after some kind of profit—

DRAKE: Agreed, Milton, but it's just that your other bids were so much lower.

MILTON: I really didn't charge what I should have then.

DRAKE: I thought you said it would take two weeks. Here you have three—

MILTON: Mr. Drake, I don't like to rush things. I want to give you a first-class job—

DRAKE: And you always do, but—

MILTON: There's a lot to be done in that house, Mr. Drake.

DRAKE: Milton, you know I have other bids?

MILTON: I'm aware of that.

DRAKE: (*Pause.*) This one is pretty steep. Milton, you know I'm not trying to beat you out of money—you know that?

MILTON: Well, I certainly hope you wouldn't.

DRAKE: Well, I wouldn't . . . And I really would like you and Nate to have this job because you do such damned good work. (*Looking slowly at the bid again.*) But . . . on the basis of this . . . I . . . I really have to consider some of the others.

MILTON: (*Shrugging.*) Well, I'm sorry, Mr. Drake . . . I gave you the figures I . . .

DRAKE: You wouldn't consider dropping it a little, would you? Sixteen hundred—how does that sound?

MILTON: Mr. Drake, I already gave you what I thought—

DRAKE: (*Rises, crosses downstage of the table to stand between* MILTON *and* NATE.) Milton, I'm trying to arrive at something equitable for both of us—so both of our purposes can be served. I really want you and Nate to have the job, and that's no joke! Sixteen hundred—no higher, no less. (MILTON *is silent, thinking.* NATE *watches anxiously.*)

MILTON: Let me see the bid.

DRAKE: I'm not trying to pressure you now— (*Handing him the bid and crossing up center behind table.*)

MILTON: (*Studying the bid.*) You're not pressuring me.

DRAKE: Sixteen hundred.

MILTON: Sixteen hundred?

DRAKE: Sixteen. . . .

MILTON: (*A lengthy pause.*) All right . . . but . . . Lord knows I can't do it any cheaper.

DRAKE: I'm not asking you to. Sixteen hundred. We have a deal then? (*Offering his hand, which* MILTON *shakes.*) Good. Have it typed up, and we'll both sign it. I'm really glad we could compromise, Milton. You guys have me spoiled when it comes to your work. (*Looking at his watch.*) Okay, then . . . I've got to get out of here. The wife and I are having some friends over tonight, and if I'm not back on time, she'll hit the roof. (MILTON *follows him to the door.* NATE *disgustedly crosses up stage to the desk.*) When do you think you can get started, Milton?

MILTON: Oh . . . Monday, I suppose . . .

DRAKE: Good . . . sounds good. (*Looking for* NATE *who is out of view.*) Okay, Milton, I'll be talking to you a little later in the week, all right?

MILTON: All right.

DRAKE: (*Shaking his hand again.*) Good night, Milton.

MILTON: Good night. (DRAKE *moves onto the porch, leaving* MILTON *in the living room studying the bid again.*)

DRAKE: Good night, Lou. Lots of luck in school, son.

LOU: (*Softly.*) Thank you.

(DRAKE *leaves stage left.* MILTON *moves into the living room and sits at the table, stage left.* NATE *turns and glares at him.*)

NATE: Pop, you had him! Why did you let that man beat you down?—

MILTON: Now, Nathan, nobody beat nobody—

NATE: Pop, he most certainly did! (*Hearing* NATE'S *loud responses,* LOU *rises and moves into the living room and sits in stage left armchair, listening.*)

MILTON: Nathan, I got a hundred dollars more than I started with! Now we can at least be thankful for that!—

NATE: Pop, you were asking for eighteen hundred, not sixteen! Maybe that's how that man can afford to send his son to Yale—by beating us down!

MILTON: Nathan—

NATE: You had him! You should've just told him to go and get somebody else if he didn't like it! Who needs— (*Turns stage right.*)

MILTON: (*Rises and crosses upstage center.*) Nathan, you don't know anything about bargaining. In business sometimes you have to compromise. Now, you know that—

NATE: Oh, for goodness sakes, Pop, if that white man had asked for nine hundred, he'd have beaten you into less than that!

MILTON: I wouldn't have done anything of the kind! I'm getting sick and tired of you telling me what I'm supposed to do with white people!—

NATE: Maybe if you'd just listen to me just once—just once!

MILTON: I've been dealing with these people longer than you were born! And you're trying to tell me! (*Pacing, ranting.*) Took my trowel long before you were born! Brought it across that man's face— Jake Ricker—man calling me out of my name! Jumped on him and beat him to the floor—slurring me—the white devil! Beat him down! And you trying to tell me about white people!—

NATE: I'm giving you my opinion—all right?

MILTON: I didn't ask you for any opinion! I know what you're calling me!

NATE: Oh, let's just forget it—forget it! I'm trying to tell you how I feel! If you don't appreciate it, then—

MILTON: I don't want to know how you feel! . . . I'm trying to feed and clothe you—I don't want to hear another word! I don't want you to bat an eye around here from now on! (*Pacing.*) Here I am trying to work and keep my dignity— I'm spending a year in jail beating up that man . . . learning to keep my dignity—keep my reputation—and I have to get some smart lip from you! I'm surprised at you, Nathan! You ought to be ashamed of yourself! Well, I don't want to hear another word! (MILTON *turns, sees* LOU, *and crosses to him.* LOU *rises and backs onto the porch.* GREMMAR, *who has heard the noise, starts down the stairs, carrying the Scrabble game.*) And you are working for me this summer, young man—as long as I need some help—next summer too, whether you're willing or not! You don't have nothing to say about it! I'm your father, and you are going to respect me! You hear me? (GLORIA *appears at the porch, interrupting* MILTON'S *tirade.* GREMMAR *moves toward the porch, but stops just inside the living room entrance.*) Can I help you? (LOU *crosses upstage on the porch behind the bench.*)

GLORIA: Mr. Edwards?

MILTON: Yes?

GLORIA: I'm Gloria Townes . . . Tom's wife.

MILTON: Yes?

GLORIA: Can—can I talk with you a minute?

MILTON: (*Pause, frowning.*) Would . . . would you like to come in?

GLORIA: (*Glancing nervously at* LOU.) No, I . . . I . . . (*Pause.*)

MILTON: (*Looking strangely at her.*) What—what can I do for you, Mrs. Townes?

GLORIA: Well . . . (*Again looking at* LOU.) Could I . . . could I . . . see you down here a minute?

MILTON: Please come inside, Mrs. Townes. (GLORIA *enters the living room, nodding to* GREMMAR *as she passes.* MILTON *follows.* GREMMAR *goes to the porch and sits on the bench with* LOU *to play Scrabble.*)

GLORIA: (*Standing up center behind table.*) I don't have much time, Mr. Edwards, I just come over for Tom's pay.

MILTON: (*Behind stage right armchair.*) His what?

GLORIA: I said, his pay, Tom says you haven't given him his pay—the last three weeks before you laid him off, you haven't given that man nothing!

MILTON: Oh now, Mrs. Townes!—

GLORIA: And that's not right!

MILTON: (*Crosses to* GLORIA.) Mrs. Townes, I'm a deacon in the church now—

GLORIA: Mr. Edwards, you shouldn't be hiring nobody if you can't afford to pay them— (LOU *and* GREMMAR *stop playing to listen to the conversation.*)

MILTON: Mrs. Townes, your husband is lying—

GLORIA: My husband hasn't got no right to lie to me—

MILTON: I paid Tom every cent he earned—every cent!—

GLORIA: Well, he said—

MILTON: And some days he wouldn't even show up, and I'm depending on him—

GLORIA: Mr. Edwards, I think it's a shame for colored people to treat other colored people the way you're treating my husband—

MILTON: Mrs. Townes, why would I want to cheat Tom, huh?

GLORIA: I don't know! That's up to you to answer. All I know is—

MILTON: The man coming to work drunk half the time—half can't do his work—

GLORIA: (*Her voice rising.*) I beg your pardon! I beg your pardon! Tom hasn't never left my house drunk—hasn't never! Mr. Edwards, if you have the money, I'd appreciate having it. My children's get colds, I'm running out of things. We are poor Negroes, Mr. Edwards—

MILTON: Now, wait a minute—wait just a minute! I want to show you something here! (*Moving quickly to the desk to get the ledger.*) Isn't that something?

GLORIA: It's a shame!—a damn shame!— It's awful! (MILTON *crosses to the table, carrying the ledger; puts it on the table and attempts to show it to her.*)

MILTON: Every cent! My boy Nathan puts it in here promptly every week—doesn't miss a one. Now, look here, Mrs. Townes—

GLORIA: (*Turning away.*) Mr. Edwards, Tom needs his money!

MILTON: (*Turning to the payroll section of the ledger.*) I'm trying to show you, woman. Look—here it is! I have to pay taxes! You think I want the government down on my back?

GLORIA: Mr. Edwards, I ain't hardly interested in reading no book!—

MILTON: You want to know the truth, don't you? (*Pointing to the page.*) Here's the last week the man worked—right here!—all his pay! And the week before that . . . and before that. It's all in here! Now, if you don't want to believe that, then I feel sorry for you! (MILTON *crosses stage right.*) Right in here! (*She reluctantly looks as* MILTON *crosses back to the table and points to the page again.*) Right there!—and there—and right there!—I'm not trying to cheat your husband, Mrs. Townes. (*She looks closely at the page.*) And then coming up to this house—my house—and throwing a brick through my window because my boy Nate wouldn't lend him some money—drunk!

GLORIA: (*Stunned, steps to* MILTON.) Tom did?

MILTON: Yes, ma'am—that's right!

GLORIA: (*Softly.*) He didn't get laid off?

MILTON: Indeed, he did not! . . . I had to fire your husband!

(*She is silent, fighting back tears.*) Did Tom send you up here, Mrs. Townes?

GLORIA: (*After a moment, softly, her voice breaking slightly.*) No . . . I . . . I . . . just come . . .

MILTON: Well, I'm sorry you did . . . He should've told you not to . . . I'm sorry . . . (*She stands for a moment, sighing heavily and resisting the desire to cry. Turning, she hurries out, exiting stage left off the porch.*)

GLORIA: That bastard! (GREMMAR *rises and enters the living room.*)

MILTON: (*Standing, looking after her.*) Isn't that something? . . . Tom's nothing but a fool!—nothing but a plain fool!

GREMMAR: (*Crosses to* MILTON.) Milton, I don't want to meddle now—I never did do that with you children—but why don't you give the woman a few dollars—just a couple. She's in trouble, son—

MILTON: Momma, I feel sorry for the woman, but—

GREMMAR: It's not her fault, Milton. I'm not taking the blame off him, but the Lord will deal harshly with him. She does have some little children. Be charitable, Milton. You know the Bible talks about being charitable to others. Others, son. Go on over there, or send one of the boys and just give her a little present. It doesn't have to be much—just a little present. She'll appreciate it. She will. Remember your Bible, son. Remember it, and trust in it . . . Trust in it . . .

MILTON: (*After pausing thoughtfully, nods his head.*) I'll do it myself, Momma.

(*They both move to the porch, and* MILTON *exits stage left.* GREMMAR *looks after him, her thoughts again turning inward; lights fade to special on* GREMMAR. *The lights rise simultaneously in* LUCRETIA'S *room as the special fades out.* GREMMAR *and* LOU *clear stage left.* LUCRETIA *enters.* HARPER *follows from upstage right as she puts her purse on the dresser.* HARPER *puts his hat on.*)

LUCRETIA: You have to go now, Harper?

HARPER: Yes, ma'am . . . Have to go to work in the morning.

LUCRETIA: What time do you have to be up?

HARPER: Oh, four o'clock thereabouts . . .

LUCRETIA: You have to be down in the mines at four o'clock?

HARPER: 'Round about then . . . four . . . four-thirty.

LUCRETIA: Lord, at four o'clock I won't be thinking about waking up, unless Little Sam or Edna does it.

HARPER: Yeah, well, it's . . . early, all right—it's early. Can't say I like it, but that's when my shift has to go down.

LUCRETIA: (*Crosses to* HARPER.) Well, you can stay a bit longer if you want. It won't be imposing on me none. Mrs. Darden, my landlady's got the children for the evening, and she don't mind keeping 'em as long as it's not too late. You sure you won't stay a minute?

HARPER: (*Shyly.*) All right . . . if—if it won't be imposing too much.

LUCRETIA: (*Crosses stage center.*) Heavens no! I'm always up late. Mrs. Darden says I must be a night owl or something, my light's on so much. (*Pulls a chair downstage center.*) Have a sit-down, and I'll be right with you. (*Takes his hat, goes to the dresser, and takes off her hat; puts both on dresser.*) I want to thank you for taking me to the services down at the church tonight. Harper, I really enjoyed it.

HARPER: You're certainly welcome. (*She primps at the dresser, catching him staring admiringly at her. He smiles bashfully, dropping his glances.*)

LUCRETIA: You like my beads, Harper? . . . Pretty, aren't they?

HARPER: Yes, they are . . . yes . . .

LUCRETIA: Thank you. My husband gave them to me before he passed on—Sam Green? I hope you don't mind me mentioning his name.

HARPER: No, ma'am, go right ahead.

LUCRETIA: He was good to me, Sam was . . . Yes, he was. (*Moving away to the bed and sitting opposite him.*) There now, I feel better now that I freshened up a bit. (*She smiles, and he shyly returns it.*) A woman should freshen up as much as she can . . . One thing I can't stand is a woman who don't keep herself cleaned up and looking nice. Of course, they get jealous of you if you do—swearing you're trying to steal their menfolk—but it's just being jealous, that's all. (*She smiles again, pleased at herself, a silence following.*) Would you like some tea or something? . . . Won't be no trouble. I usually have some this time of night . . . Helps me to stay awake. I just hate to go to sleep at nights, it seems. I don't get company that often—gets kind of lonesome for a widow like me. (*She rises.*) You're welcome to have some.

HARPER: No, thank you . . . I—I appreciate the offer.

LUCRETIA: (*Pause as she sits on the bed.*) How . . . how's your studying for the ministry coming along now, Harper?

HARPER: Fine, just fine . . .

LUCRETIA: (*Pause.*) Reverend Lockwood going to make you a preacher soon?

HARPER: Well . . . I preach my trial sermon and . . . and he says I'll be just about ready. (*Pleased.*)

LUCRETIA: You—you have a church all lined up when you finish your practicing?

HARPER: Reverend Lockwood says he get me one over in Greensborough—folks over there, they needs somebody.

LUCRETIA: Lord Jesus, you must be excited, aren't you?

HARPER: Yeah . . . yeah, I guess I am . . . Yeah . . . it's . . . it's kinda scary, a little. One day I'm just a man way down in the mines, mining coal . . . wasn't even thinking about religion hardly—just making a living—hating it—hating it! And the next day I'm hearing the call of the Lord—hearing it as clear as I'm hearing you now—

LUCRETIA: What'd it sound like?

HARPER: Just as . . . as clear as a bell!—and pretty—just as pretty! The voice of the Lord is sweet! . . . And it's saying to me—saying to me: "I need you, Harper Edwards, to do my will—to preach the gospel—my gospel! I need you!" Well, I'm thinking at first—I'm going crazy or something, and I'm trying to shut it out!—

LUCRETIA: Ain't that something!—

HARPER: "Go 'way from here," I'm saying, "go 'way!" But it wouldn't. Kept after me—a couple of weeks, I guess. And . . . well . . . here I am . . . ready to preach and do his will . . . a shepherd looking after his own flock . . . Yeah, I—I get kinda tense when I think about it.

LUCRETIA: Oh, Harper, you're going to be a good preacher— I know you will!

HARPER: Well . . . I'm going to do my best, Miss Lucretia— with the help of God.

LUCRETIA: Sure you will . . . (*Pause as she rises and steps to the mirror and primps.*) You . . . you go on over there to Greensborough, and I bet I won't be seeing you no more, I bet, will I?

HARPER: (*With difficulty.*) I—I was going . . . I was going to . . . to ask you . . . I—

LUCRETIA: Ask me what?

HARPER: Well . . . if . . . if I could come a-courting—

LUCRETIA: Oh, Harper—isn't that lovely! That's lovely! Of course you can!—

HARPER: You're a fine woman, Miss Lucretia—

LUCRETIA: Oh, Harper, I haven't done nothing special. I'm

. . . I'm just a . . . a widow trying to look after her children with the little bit of money her husband left her—that's all.

HARPER: Well, you been doing a fine job—yes, ma'am . . . Little Sam's a fine-looking boy—a fine-looking lad! And Miss Edna's just as pretty as a picture—

LUCRETIA: (_Crosses to the foot of the bed and sits, facing audience._) I done my best, Harper—with the Lord's help. He's watched over us. Yes, he has, ever since I come here—the kids too young for me to work much, and hardly no women's jobs at all in this little mining town. He's made it possible for me and the children to make it somehow on the little bit of savings I had.

HARPER: Well, a man—especially if he's going to be a preacher—needs a fine woman—somebody who's gonna be an inspiration to his soul and light to his path and his children's path. And—and I been praying a long time, Miss Lucretia. And I see you at the church . . . and the Lord spoke to me and told me . . . the same voice I heard in the mine—told me as clear as a bell—you was the one.

LUCRETIA: That's so kind of you, Harper. (_Pleased._) I know the children are wild about you. Yes, they are! They know a good man when they see one. (_Both laugh softly, nervously and are silent, groping for words._)

HARPER: (_Pleased with himself._) Well, I best be going . . . I— I done stayed past my time.

LUCRETIA: I'm not sleepy if that's what's troubling you. But . . . if you have to go, since you have to be up so early.

HARPER: Yes, ma'am—four o'clock.

LUCRETIA: Lord, I'm telling you—four o'clock!

HARPER: (_Rising and standing awkwardly._) Well . . .

LUCRETIA: (_Also standing._) I want to thank you again for the time at the church, Harper. It was real nice.

HARPER: You're more than welcome, Miss Lucretia—more than welcome.

HARPER: Well, good night . . . (HARPER _crosses stage right._)

LUCRETIA: Aren't—aren't you going to . . . kiss me good night, Harper? (HARPER _stops and turns to_ LUCRETIA. _She reacts quickly to his being taken aback._) You can . . . we're courting now, aren't we? You're going to court a woman, you have to learn to kiss her on the cheek or hand or something. (_Holding out her cheek._) Right there—just a little peck, that's all. (_He does so, shyly._) There now, that wasn't so bad, was it?

HARPER: (_Smiling._) Good night . . . Miss Lucretia . . .

LUCRETIA: Your hat, Harper, don't forget it! (*She moves quickly to the dresser and gets the hat and places it on his head, simultaneously kissing him. He exits upstage right, stunned. She laughs gaily. Blackout. In the blackout* LUCRETIA *clears stage left.* GREMMAR *and* LOU *get into place as the lights rise again on the porch; a special on* GREMMAR. MILTON *enters from stage left, the special goes out on* GREMMAR.)

GREMMAR: You get it straightened out with her, baby?

MILTON: Yeah . . . yeah . . . couldn't help feeling sorry for the woman, though . . . (GREMMAR *begins coughing suddenly—heavy, wracking coughing.*) Do . . . do you feel all right, Momma? (*Sitting beside her as* LOU *stands, equally concerned.*)

GREMMAR: (*Slowly.*) Oh, I'm all right, son . . . just a little headache . . . a little one . . . The heat, I guess . . . I'm a little tired . . . Probably should go on upstairs and rest some . . . No sir, can't do like I used to . . . not like I used to . . .

MILTON: Oh, Momma, you're still as spry as—

GREMMAR: (*Decisively.*) Oh no . . . no . . . no, sir . . . No, I can't lie to myself . . . Not going to do me one bit of good . . . No, son, I'm not a young woman no more . . . I know the road . . . Momma used to recite a poem to me. She used to say:

> "Oh, the old sheep, they know the road,
> The old sheep, they know the road.
> The old sheep, they know the road;
> Young lambs must find the way."

Yes, the young lambs must find the way . . . I know the road . . . Well, let me get up from here with this Scrabble and go upstairs for a while . . . A little rest may help me. (MILTON *helps* GREMMAR *to her feet, and she crosses into the living room with* MILTON *and* LOU *following.*) You all don't bother about waiting for me for dinner. I'll eat something a little later on.

MILTON: Put the fan on up there, Momma. Louis, help her upstairs, will you? (LOU *rises, crosses to* GREMMAR, *takes her arm, and they move up the stairs.* MILTON *follows to the foot of the stairs and stands watching—concerned.*)

GREMMAR: The old sheep, they know the road . . . the young lambs must find the way . . . find the way . . . (GREMMAR *stops at the top of the stairs, gives the Scrabble game to* LOU, *who exits stage right. She exits upstage right.* MILTON *returns the ledger to the writing table. He stands, thinking for a moment, then sits at the table stage right chair, staring distantly, painfully.* HATTIE *enters from the kitchen and crosses stage center.*)

HATTIE: (*Softly.*) Milton, are you all right?

MILTON: (*Sighing.*) Yeah . . . I'm all right. (*She frowns curiously at him, then begins to remove the tablecloth.*)

HATTIE: Milton, I'd like to set the table.

MILTON: (*Turning to look up the stairs as* HATTIE *is folding the tablecloth.*) I don't know, Hattie, but . . . every time I think about . . . (*Pause.*) Momma used to be so . . . active . . . spry . . . cutting up and on the go—going here and there— just had to be doing something—doing something! Busy! . . . It just doesn't seem to . . . make sense! (*Sighing again— pause.*) I look at her now and . . . in some ways . . . she's . . . not even the same person . . . It's . . . somebody else— not Momma . . . somebody else . . . Somebody almost like her, but like a stranger— Somebody that—that reminds me of her . . . has the same walk . . . same kind of laugh . . . same way of talking, but— (HATTIE *crosses behind* MILTON *and puts her hands on his shoulders.*)

HATTIE: Your mother's not a young woman now, Milton, she—

MILTON: I know, I know. (MILTON *rises, sighing.*) Well, I guess I'll go on outside for a while. Weeds are taking over the string beans.

HATTIE: (*Crosses down to a level with* MILTON.) Milton, do you know how hot it is out there?—do you? You'll get yourself a stroke! (*Wiping his brow.*) Look at yourself now—sweating and all! You already worked half the day, plastering! It ought to be enough for you! Sit down and rest and be sensible! You're not one of the boys!

MILTON: I used to . . . used to be able to work out there in that heat when I was younger . . . didn't think nothing of it—

HATTIE: Well, you certainly aren't younger now!—

MILTON: Momma would—would come all the way out to me . . . a mile near . . . worrying about me, trying to get me to slow down or stop. "Sun can't hurt me, Momma—can't hurt me!" Always so worried about me.

HATTIE: Milton, you can't stop living now. If I'd stopped the day I realized my mother and father were old people, I'd be no more good today. Now, all of us, if the Lord spares us, has to grow old and leave this world, and your momma's one of them. So just make up your mind to it. Besides, there's nothing more beautiful than somebody that's grown old as gracefully as that woman has.

MILTON: (*Turns to* HATTIE.) Yeah, I suppose you're right.

HATTIE: If you're a Christian, I'm right.

MILTON: You're right, you're right, Hattie.

HATTIE: I know I'm right. -

(*They hug.* HATTIE *picks up the centerpiece,* MILTON *the tablecloth. As they exit to the kitchen,* MILTON *repeats: "The old sheep they know the road; young lambs must find a way." Blackout to denote passage of time. As lights rise on the porch and living room,* GREMMAR *enters from downstage left, wearing a straw hat and carrying the garden spade. She crosses into the living room, but suddenly suffers a dizzy spell stage center. She pauses, regaining her composure, and crosses to the piano, putting her hat and spade on top of the piano, and sitting on the stool. As she does,* LOU, NATE, *and* HOPE *enter from kitchen carrying a birthday cake, a pitcher with punch, and glasses. They are singing "Happy Birthday." As* LOU *and* NATE *hug* GREMMAR, HOPE *lights the candles, and* HATTIE *and* MILTON *enter from kitchen.*)

LOU: (*Joined by* NATE *and* HOPE.) Speech—speech!

GREMMAR. (*Crosses to upstage center and sits at the table.*) Oh now, you all didn't have to go to all this trouble!—

MILTON: Wasn't any trouble, Momma— (EDNA *enters slowly from stage right, down the stairs carrying a gift-wrapped package.*)

GREMMAR: And me looking a mess!—

NATE: (*Teasing.*) That's all right, Gremmar, you're among kinfolk.

GREMMAR: Well, I want to thank you—all of you. Thank you so much.

EDNA: (*Crosses to* GREMMAR *and gives her a gift.*) Happy birthday, Momma! (*As they exchange kisses.*)

GREMMAR: Thank you, baby. When'd you get here? Nobody told me.

EDNA: Couldn't spoil the surprise, Momma. Anyway, you was out in the garden just a piddling and poking around.

GREMMAR: Well, it's good to see you, baby—yes, it is. (*Seeing* HOPE.) Lord, what a pretty face. How are you, dear?

HOPE: Fine, Mrs. Edwards. Happy birthday. (HOPE *gives* GREMMAR *a kiss and then a small gift which she brought in on the tray.*)

GREMMAR: Thank you, sugar.

NATE: Okay, Gremmar, it's time to blow out the candles!

GREMMAR: Lord have mercy, I'm not that old, am I? How many of these things you have on there?

LOU: Just sweet sixteen, Gremmar.

GREMMAR: Oh child, I know that's not true. No, sir—a long time since I was that!

HATTIE: Come on now, Momma, time to blow now.

GREMMAR: Now, I know I'm not that big a bag of wind, am I? You all trying to tell me something?

EDNA: (*To the laughter of the others.*) You have to try anyway. Come on, Momma. There isn't that many.

GREMMAR: All right . . . lemme see here . . . Where'll I start? . . . All right. (*She blows—*)

(*Blackout, the lights rising upstairs.* LUCRETIA *sits on the bed and* HARPER *in the chair.* LUCRETIA *looks at him with excitement and admiration.*)

LUCRETIA: I keep saying to myself: That's Reverend Edwards— Reverend Edwards!

HARPER: (*Smiling, trying to restrain his joy.*) Yeah . . . yeah, I—I guess that's me, all right.

LUCRETIA: Yes, and that was a wonderful sermon you preached for your trial one—a wonderful sermon!

HARPER: Yeah, it felt good . . . yeah . . . After it was all over, Reverend Lockwood grins and says, "Well, looks like you made it, son. You're a preacher now!"

LUCRETIA: (*Exuberant, she crosses downstage left of the chair to the dresser and puts her hat down.*) Lord, you had them folks just a-shouting and carrying on—getting happy! And you were just a-preaching on—a-preaching on!

HARPER: (*Laughing, pleased.*) Couldn't help myself. The Lord was talking to me.

LUCRETIA: Well, he certainly must've been! And—and the collection basket was full up too! Some of them folks was putting in dollar bills! That shows you! Colored folks ain't going to put nothing in the collection basket unless they enjoys it— put in a lot of pennies maybe—

HARPER: (*Pleased.*) Yeah . . . yeah . . . they don't like something, they'll let you know about it one way or another. (*Looking at her with admiration as she takes his hat and puts it on the dresser, then crosses to bed and sits.*) You was a hit too, little lady—all the folks looking at you—

LUCRETIA: (*Frowning.*) They . . . they were looking at me? (*He nods. They exchange smiles and a lengthy stare.*)

HARPER: Yeah . . . "That man certainly couldn't've done no better for somebody who's going to be a preacher's wife! She's a pretty thing!" (*Laughing nervously.*) They're . . . right about that.

LUCRETIA: (*Crosses to* HARPER.) I—I didn't hear nothing. I— I was so busy watching you after the service—making sure none of those other ladies was trying to steal you. (*Laughing coyly.*)

HARPER: No need to worry about that . . . no . . . ! (*They exchange a lengthy, warm stare. He drops his eyes and rises, crossing downstage right as* LUCRETIA *crosses downstage left.*) And . . . and one of the members ups to me after the service and says, "That sure is a pretty child, Reverend . . . Used to be a child that looked like that in Roanoke a while back. Belonged to a family—

LUCRETIA: (*Quickly, fearfully—turning to* HARPER.) I—I've never been to Roanoke—never. I—

HARPER: That's what I told him . . . I couldn't imagine nobody in Roanoke as . . . pretty as you. (*He grins, pleased with his boldness.*)

LUCRETIA: Never in my life . . . (*Crossing to the dresser, avoiding contact with him.*) Who—who was this . . . gentleman that was asking?

HARPER: (*Crosses to chair.*) Oh, a short little dark fellow. He's been around White Rock off and on since I been attending. Drops in and out—

LUCRETIA: (*Attempting to collect herself.*) Who—who—what was this girl's name—the one he thought I was?

HARPER: He plum forgot, it's been so long since he's been back there.

LUCRETIA: Oh . . . (*Feigning gaiety.*) Well, it couldn't have been me, since I've never been there! Must've been my double or something.

HARPER: "Sure is pretty and familiar-looking pretty." (HARPER *sits as* LUCRETIA *crosses behind the chair to sit downstage on the bed.*)

LUCRETIA: Well . . . the next time, thank the gentleman for me. (*Nervously.*) It's—it's been so hot out . . . seems like . . . we haven't had a breeze all summer. (*Pause, silent, breathing more heavily and reacting nervously to* HARPER'S *admiring look.*) I . . . I think I hear the children . . . downstairs . . . I think . . . Did—did you hear 'em? Little Sam probably wants me now . . . Edna wakes up because he does. (*He rises reluctantly, and she does also.*)

HARPER: Well, I best be going . . . It—it don't seem possible I won't be going down in that mine tomorrow . . . I been going down in all that blackness for so long, it just seems strange, you know? . . . Lord knows I'm glad I don't have to . . . you've been a blessing to me, Lucretia. The Lord's done answered my prayers all the way 'round, he has.

LUCRETIA: (*Sighing heavily.*) Thank . . . thank you, Harper . . . You've been a blessing to me too. Well, I guess I'd better be getting to the children. (*She crosses to the dresser and gets his hat.*)

HARPER: (*Starting to go, but stopping stage right at the foot of the bed.*) Won't be long before you'll be the good reverend's wife—

LUCRETIA: (*Crosses to* HARPER.) Yes, yes, that's right . . . I'd better . . . go, Harper. (*Giving the hat to* HARPER.) You— you have a good time over there in Greensborough. And— and don't you let none of them pretty-looking sisters over there turn your head, now—

HARPER: (*Wanting to kiss her fully, but restraining.*) No need to worry about that . . . no need at all. (*Staring at her and then turning to go, his reluctance visible.*) Well . . . good night . . .

LUCRETIA: Harper? (*He stops.*) That—that man—the one that asked you about me?—the girl he thought I was?— Well, I'm . . . I'm glad it was me and not her that has you. (*He smiles and then kisses her almost fearfully on the cheek. He looks at her warmly and then leaves. She watches his departure and then turns and crosses stage center.*) Never . . . never been to Roanoke in my life—not even near it . . . wouldn't know it if I stumbled over it!

(*As the lights black out on* LUCRETIA, *exiting stage left, applause is heard, and lights rise on the living room.* GREMMAR *leans over the candles, having blown them out. The others are applauding. She begins to cough slightly.*)

MILTON: You all right, Momma?

GREMMAR: (*Feigning.*) I'm all right . . . Just a little cough . . .

HATTIE: Sit right there, dear, I'll cut the cake for you.

GREMMAR: After all that huffing and puffing, I need to.

HATTIE: (*Cutting the cake.*) You all come and help yourselves. I'm not waiting on nobody but Gremmar tonight. This is her night! (*They respond, moving to the table and helping themselves to punch, cake, and the other food. After getting various items,* NATE *and* HOPE *sit in stage left armchair.* LOU *sits at the table in stage left chair.*)

EDNA: (*Crossing between the table and stage right armchair.*) You don't have any "tea" in here, do you, Milton?

MILTON: (*Standing behind stage right armchair.*) Tea? . . . What "tea" are you talking about?

EDNA: The "tea" that makes you high.

MILTON: (*Crosses downstage and sits in the chair.*) Girl, you better go 'way from here!

EDNA: (*Laughing along with the others.*) Lord, Milton would have a fit if some "tea" was in here.

HATTIE: (*Crosses downstage of the table to upstage left of* MIL-TON.) Milton's not fooling nobody. Doctor Walker told Milton he should take some of that mess for his cold—said it would help him—and, Lord Jesus, there wasn't any trouble at all getting that man to take his medicine.

MILTON: Hattie—

HATTIE: Three o'clock in the morning and Milton's getting out of bed, creeping downstairs. "Where are you going, Milton, this time of night?" "Have to take my medicine!"

MILTON: Hattie, now, why you want to—

HATTIE: Three o'clock! Usually you have to get the law almost to get him to take some medicine! (*Sits on upstage arm of stage right chair.*)

NATE: (*Teasing.*) I heard him going downstairs.

MILTON: You all know I was just doing what the man told me—

EDNA: Tasting away, huh, Milton? Making sure to get his medicine *on time!* (*He waves away her laughter.* GREMMAR *begins coughing again.*) So how you feel, Momma? Milton says you haven't been feeling too well.

GREMMAR: Oh, I'm all right, baby—just a little cough . . . little cold or something. I'm all right.

EDNA: Well, besides that, you're looking good.

GREMMAR: I ought to go up and change this old rag I got on.

MILTON: Momma, you look fine. Stop worrying . . . Momma's always worrying.

EDNA: Well, it wouldn't be her if she didn't. (*She crosses downstage left of* LOU.) Well, Louis, Nathan's got his girlfriend—where's yours?

LOU: (*Slightly embarrassed.*) Oh, I have more important things to do, Aunt Edna.

HOPE: Well, I like that, Louis!

LOU: (*As the others laugh, again embarrassed; rising and crossing upstage to* HOPE. EDNA *sits in the chair he vacated.*) No, I mean . . . I mean, I have to do a lot of studying if I want to be a doctor . . . or a . . . scientist . . . I mean . . . after I finish up there'll be lots of time . . . Being a doctor's the most important thing right now . . . We need a lot of doctors and things. I mean . . . someday . . .

HOPE: That's right, Lou—try and squirm out of it.

GREMMAR: (*Reaching out to take* LOU'S *hand.*) He's right . . . Yes, plenty of time . . . No need to rush things . . . He's such a handsome boy, the Lord'll send him one when he's ready.

EDNA: Yes, him and Nathan's good-looking boys—good-looking!

NATE: I keep telling Mom that.

HATTIE: (*As the others laugh.*) Lord Jesus! Hope, don't pay no attention to Nathan now. He's just showing off!

HOPE: Don't worry, Mrs. Edwards—I don't. (NATE *frowns mockingly at her.*)

EDNA: Yes, good-looking!

GREMMAR: (*Patting* LOU'S *arm. They exchange smiles.*) No, no need to rush . . . no need . . . plenty of time!

(*Lights fade down to special on* GREMMAR. LUCRETIA *enters the bedroom from stage left and moves the chair upstage as lights rise.* HARPER *enters from upstage right, shouting happily.*)

HARPER: I got my church, Lucretia! I got me . . . a . . . church! (*He laughs unrestrainedly, crosses stage center and puts his hat on the chair.*) Those folks in Greensborough, they liked me! . . . They . . . they said . . . "You're the one we want, son! You're the one the—*good* Lord sent us!" That's what they said, Lucretia! I got me a church, woman! (*Laughing happily.*)

LUCRETIA: Harper . . . that's—that's beautiful—that's beautiful!

HARPER: (*Happy, wanting to let go fully.*) I'm telling you . . . I'm telling you . . . I'm just so . . . tickled . . . I . . . I just want to . . . I just want to holler again!

LUCRETIA: Why don't you just go on?

HARPER: Yeah . . . yeah . . . The Lord won't mind if I holler a little, will he?

LUCRETIA: (*Laughing.*) Of course not! Go ahead, man—holler! (*He lets out a yell.*) Do it again! Feel real good about it,

Harper—go ahead! (*He yells again, and then stops. They exchange glances, laughing softly at first. Their laughter begins to build. They rush suddenly toward each other, laughing, holding hands and swinging almost childishly in a circle, dancing. They stop suddenly, continuing to hold hands, and stare at each other. They rush suddenly at each other, embracing, kissing, feeling, and touching. He starts to break away but cannot, continuing to react to his passions. As they begin to sink slowly toward the floor, the lights fade out and as they clear, the stage left lights rise in the living room, where everyone is laughing.* EDNA *takes a piece of cake and crosses downstage of the table, up to the piano.*)

EDNA: Hattie, this is some scrumptious cake, girl! (EDNA *sits on the piano stool.*)

HATTIE: Thank you, dear.

MILTON: (*After a slight pause.*) Hired me a white fellow Saturday.

EDNA: Yesterday?— A white man? Lord Jesus! Milton Edwards, my brother, is carrying on some! Going big time! Has it turned around! Got them working for him!

MILTON: (*Restraining his pleasure, crosses to the table and puts his plate down.*) Come around looking for work, so I tried him out. (*Crosses upstage to* NATE.) Works pretty good, doesn't he, Nate?

NATE: Yeah, at least we don't have to prop him up after lunch like we did Tom.

MILTON: Lord, no! . . . Quiet . . . Don't say much . . . Just does his work . . .

EDNA: (*Rises.*) Maybe he's afraid of you niggers!

MILTON: I wish you wouldn't use that word, Edna.

EDNA: Well, that's what we are, aren't we?

MILTON: Well, maybe that's what you are!

EDNA: Well, whether we are or not, I'm going to have another piece of cake! (*Going to the table and getting a piece of cake.*) I can't help it if I like to eat. I guess it don't matter. The Lord takes 'em fat, skinny, short, and tall. He ain't prejudiced. That's one thing about him.

NATE: (*Rising and taking* HOPE'S *hand.*) We have to run over to Hope's house. We'll be right back.

EDNA: Getting tired of us old heads, huh?

NATE: No, we'll be right back—just a couple minutes. Hope's got an errand to tend to.

GREMMAR: All right, you all have a nice walk now.

HOPE: (*As they leave.*) We'll see you later. (*They leave, exiting off the porch.* EDNA *sits in stage right armchair.*)

EDNA: Yes, Lord, I'm telling you! Momma don't come over to see me no more!

MILTON: (*Crosses to stand behind* GREMMAR.) Edna, you know Momma hasn't been well all weekend. I told you that.

EDNA: I don't mean this weekend! I'm talking about before. Kids say to me: "Where's Grandma? How come she don't come over and stay here like she does at Uncle Milton's?" I say: "I don't know, you have to ask her!"

GREMMAR: Oh now, Edna, child—

LOU: She really has been a little tired this weekend like Pop said, Aunt Edna. (GREMMAR *reaches down and pats his hand, holding it.*)

MILTON: And you know you don't have room over there like we have.

EDNA: Burgess died last year. Momma could sleep with me. The kids they can double up. Yes sir, they wouldn't mind for Momma. No, Momma's just got to be with her baby! (*Laughing, a trace of bitterness contained.*)

MILTON: Edna's just messing now.

EDNA: Well, Milton, you are the baby of the family!

GREMMAR: Oh, child, you know your momma didn't play no favorites. Treated all my children equal—even Little Sam before he passed on—

EDNA: Oh no! One of us messed with Milton, and we liked to've got the devil knocked out of us!

MILTON: Edna, Momma used to spank us all!

EDNA: Me maybe—but not you and Sam much. (*Rising, getting another piece of cake.*) Yes, Jesus. Momma comes home on the weekends, and before I know it, she's gone on back to work.

MILTON: (*Crossing to stage left armchair and sitting.*) Edna's just trying to start something on Momma's birthday—

EDNA: I'm not trying to start nothing, Milton! I'm just wishing she'd come over and visit me a little more than she does! That's all I'm talking about!

GREMMAR: I will, baby, I will . . . Just as soon as I get over this cough—little headache. All right?—

(*Lights fade to specials on* GREMMAR *and* LUCRETIA. HARPER *enters in darkness from stage left and drops his coat and tie on the floor, upstage of dresser. The lights rise fully upstairs.* LUCRETIA *sits on the stage left foot of the bed, her clothing awry.* HARPER, *equally dishevelled, sits next to her— stage right—his face buried in his hands.*)

LUCRETIA: You shouldn't fault yourself, Harper, you shouldn't—

HARPER: I let him down, that's what I did! I let him down!—

LUCRETIA: Harper, you didn't . . . Harper, you're . . . you're a—a man!

HARPER: I'm a minister! You hear me? I'm a minister!

LUCRETIA: You're a man too!—

HARPER: A weak one—

LUCRETIA: Harper . . . Harper . . . we both—we both have feelings—

HARPER: We only had a couple of weeks to wait—just a couple more!—

LUCRETIA: Oh, Harper, what's the difference? A couple of weeks is supposed to make it right? . . . Harper, it just happened! It can't make us wrong the rest of our lives—

HARPER: (*Standing slowly and crossing stage center.*) I . . . I went to Greensborough today . . . Lord knows, it was a pretty day! Lord knows! The sun . . . just shining . . . birds flying and jack-rabbits running . . . And I'm sitting in that old buggy, and I'm scared. I'm scared, but I'm happy! I'm scared and happy and filled with the . . . (*Turns to LUCRETIA.*) the spirit of God! . . . It's his day . . . and yours too . . . and the children's, because I'm thinking about all of you and just hoping to God those folks'll accept me into their fold—just hoping . . . Scared some . . . And—and I gets there . . . and they're waiting for me . . . just waiting! Can't wait for me to get down to the ground—can't wait—hands reaching for me—starved to hear the word of God, I'm telling you! Just a-thinking, thanking God for sending me to them! (*Turning to face her.*) I just . . . I just got me a church, Lucretia!

LUCRETIA: Harper, I know . . . I know! And . . . and you're going to be a wonderful minister!—

HARPER: (*Turning away.*) No sooner than I leave 'em . . . here I am . . . acting . . . acting like I don't have the first bit of sense, like some—

LUCRETIA: (*Rises and crosses to him.*) Harper, stop it! . . . Stop! . . . Don't—don't make me feel wrong! I'm not going to let you make me feel wrong! . . . I . . . you . . . you were so happy! I looked at your face and you were so . . . so happy!

HARPER: (*He takes* LUCRETIA'S *arms and turns; they counter cross.*) Pray with me, Lucretia, and—and ask for his forgiveness. It's a guilty stain against our record, girl, and we have to—have to . . . wipe it clean—

LUCRETIA: Oh, Harper! . . . it—it just happened! We—we were just as happy about you getting your church. It—it just happened!

HARPER: (*Sighing.*) Get on your knees with me, Lucretia . . . Will you do that with me?

LUCRETIA: (*Trying to prevent him from assuming a prayerful position.*) Harper, don't—please!

HARPER: Do you want to be banished from the Kingdom, Lucretia? Is that what you want? Do you want his thunder and lightning to . . . to come down here in this room and—and strike us down?—do you?

LUCRETIA: (*Crosses down left center.*) Harper, I don't *want* . . . I don't want to be a part of no kingdom like that!—

HARPER: (*Following, shaking her.*) Don't you say that! Don't you say that to me! You're talking about the Kingdom he called me to lead folks to! That's what you're talking about! Don't you ever say that to me again! We're going to pray—right now—you and me! (*Assuming a prayerful position at the foot of the bed.*) Our Father, who art in heaven . . . hallowed be thy name . . . Thy kingdom come . . . Thy will be done . . . on earth as it is in heaven . . . Give us this day our daily bread . . .

LUCRETIA: Harper—please!

HARPER: And forgive us our trespasses, as we forgive those who trespass against us—

LUCRETIA: (*Again trying to break his position.*) Harper, we don't have to be doing this—we don't!

HARPER: And lead us not into temptation . . . but deliver us from evil, for thy name's sake—

LUCRETIA: It isn't wrong—it's not! You—you're just making it wrong yourself!

HARPER: For thine is the power and the glory, forever and ever . . . amen. (*He rises quickly, straightening his clothing, and moves and picks up his coat and tie from the floor, and his hat from the chair.*)

LUCRETIA: Harper, where are you going? (*He doesn't respond.*) Harper—Harper, you're not . . . leaving me, are you? (*Rushing, grabbing him. He wrenches away.*) Harper, don't be silly! Come on back here, please! (*He exits upstage right. She follows as the lights fade out. Lights up in the living room.*)

EDNA: (*Laughing.*) Sometimes . . . sometimes I think the only reason Momma don't come over is because my daddy was *white!* And Milton and Sam had black ones!

(LOU *looks up slowly at* GREMMAR, *his face registering shock. He slowly slides his hand away from hers and glances at her.*)

HATTIE: (*Also looking at* LOU.) Edna . . .

MILTON: (*Rises and angrily crosses stage center.*) Now, that isn't right, Edna! That's not a nice thing to say to Momma at all!

EDNA: (*As* LOU *turns away in deep thought.*) I'm just teasing Momma . . . He *was* white, wasn't he? Momma knows I was just teasing, don't you, Momma?

GREMMAR: Edna always did like to tease.

MILTON: Just as determined as she can be to spoil Momma's birthday with her foolishness! (MILTON *crosses stage left to the armchair.*)

EDNA: Milton—

HATTIE: (*Crosses upstage of the table to* LOU.) Let's have a good time now, you all . . . (*Looking at* LOU, *who is more absorbed in thought.*) Louis, you want some more to eat? . . . He eats like a bird now.

GREMMAR: You should eat, son. That's how you get your strength now. (*Reaching over and rubbing his arm.*)

LOU: (*Rising suddenly and moving away from the table.*) I— I'm . . . going on the . . . porch for a while . . . It—it's hot in here . . . (*He smiles tautly at* GREMMAR *and then moves out to the porch, where he stands mesmerized.*)

MILTON: (*Crosses to* EDNA.) I certainly wish to heaven you'd stop your tomfoolery sometimes, Edna.

EDNA: (*Rises and crosses downstage of the table to stage left.*) I don't know why everybody is so down on me. The man was white, wasn't he? Momma knows—

GREMMAR: All right, baby. Momma'll be over her next day off—next weekend—all right?

HATTIE: Momma, why don't you play us a little song? You feel like it?

MILTON: Edna is just jealous!

HATTIE: Milton!

EDNA: Milton knows I'm telling the truth!—

MILTON: (*Crossing to the kitchen with* HATTIE *following.*) Why don't you stay home sometime, and don't come over to my house no more!

EDNA: (*Following.*) Now, wait a minute! I'll come over and see my momma any time I want to.

GREMMAR: All right, children, don't fuss. Momma's going to play now. (*She goes slowly to the piano and collapses suddenly on the stool. The lights fade to special on* GREMMAR. *Lights also rise in the bedroom as* LUCRETIA *enters from upstage right with a basket of clothes and sits in the chair. As she sits,* HARPER *enters from upstage right, where he stands staring icily at* LUCRETIA.)

LUCRETIA: (*Rises and crosses down to* HARPER.) Harper— Harper, what's the matter? . . . Don't . . . you feel good? . . . Something happened? (*He continues to stare and then begins toward her, seething, stopping near her.*)

HARPER: You . . . you lied to me, didn't you?

LUCRETIA: I what?

HARPER: You lied to me, didn't you?

LUCRETIA: (*Avoiding his stare.*) Lied?

HARPER: (*Taking a step closer.*) Didn't you?

LUCRETIA: I—I don't know what you're talking about. (*Attempting to pass him.*) I—I better go now . . . the . . . the children—

HARPER: (*Lunging, grabbing her arm and twisting it.*) You tell me the truth!

LUCRETIA: (*Screaming in pain.*) Harper, you're—my arm, Harper! Harper, what's wrong—what's the matter with you?

HARPER: You ain't never had no husband!—you *never*, did you?

LUCRETIA: Harper, I did—

HARPER: Liar! . . . You liar! . . . You *never!* You never! Now you just tell me the truth!

LUCRETIA: Oh God!—my arm!

HARPER: (*Exerting more force.*) You been to Roanoke before, haven't you? Haven't you?

LUCRETIA: I told you—

HARPER: And they run you out, didn't they?—made fun of you and run you out—because you was a . . . a—whore, wasn't you? That's what you was, wasn't you?

LUCRETIA: I wasn't . . . I wasn't, Harper—Harper . . . I . . . I can't . . . breathe!

HARPER: That little old dark man remembered—just upped and remembered!—

LUCRETIA: He's a liar, that's what he is! . . . Sam Green was!—he was! He just—just got killed, that's all! . . . He— was coming back . . . and—

HARPER: Just another lie! Just another . . . lie! That little old dark man . . . He wrote your momma a letter.

LUCRETIA: (GREMMAR *rises and crosses downstage to stage right arm chair.*) Momma?

HARPER: Yeah, your momma! And she wrote him back . . . asking you to . . . to come back home with your sinful self!—your lying, sinful self! You ain't never been no widow! You ain't never been nothing, have you? (*Twisting her arm fully and making her scream, and then letting her go. Simultaneously, as* LUCRETIA *falls,* GREMMAR *sits in the chair.*)

LUCRETIA: (*Dropping to the floor and whimpering softly.*) No, no, no, no, no.—no, no!

HARPER: (*Crosses downstage right.*) People laughing . . . calling the preacher a fool! . . . a fool! . . . The preacher!—

LUCRETIA: (*Rising.*) Oh, nigger, why—why don't you stop thinking!—stop your . . . your . . . *thinking* and feel something—just . . . just . . . *feel* something!

HARPER: I—I don't deserve no church!—don't deserve none! . . . Making them laugh . . . Nothing but a fool! . . . a . . . a fool! Don't . . . don't even deserve . . . God! . . . Not even him! . . . (*Pausing, breathing heavily, thinking.*) He's . . . he's telling me . . . telling me . . . telling me . . . He's . . . Don't even want me! . . . Don't even want me! . . . Don't want me! Don't want me! (*He stands mesmerized—"listening." He turns, stares at her, and then starts suddenly toward her. She rises quickly, trying to retreat. He lunges, missing, and then chases her, catching her and ripping her clothing—pawing and mauling and kissing her roughly.*)

LUCRETIA: Harper, don't—don't be crazy! Please don't be crazy! (*He forces her down on the bed. She screams.*)

(*Blackout, except for special on* GREMMAR. *The No. 1 blackout drop is flown in, the No. 3 wall and No. 2 blackout drop are flown out.*)

GREMMAR: (*Softly, distantly.*) He . . . he never did become no minister—Harper . . . Never did . . . Went back to the mines again . . . way down in them mines . . . (*Pause.*) Folks . . . folks told me—told me they never did see much of that man again . . . except that when they did, he was drinking a lot . . . always . . . always . . . drunk. (*Pause.*) He . . . fell out one day . . . Fell out dead . . . Harper . . . drink on his breath . . .

(*The lights rise slowly in the living room and on the porch as* GREMMAR *rises and crosses to the piano stool and sits. After a moment* HOPE *and* NATE *walk up on the porch, where* LOU *sits staring blankly.*)

NATE: What's the matter, the party over?
LOU: (*Softly.*) No, it's . . . still going on. (NATE *takes* HOPE'S *hand and brings it close to* LOU'S *face.* LOU *looks at the ring, forcing a smile.*) Con—congratulations . . .
HOPE: Hey, don't I get a kiss?
LOU: Sure . . . (*Kissing her cheek.*)
NATE: Getting a sister-in-law, man! (*They go inside,* LOU *again caught up in thinking.*) Hey, everybody, I have an announcement to make! (MILTON *enters from upstairs,* HATTIE *from the kitchen, with* EDNA *following.*) We're engaged!— (*Everyone reacts happily*—GREMMAR *rises and applauds. She grasps her head suddenly and slumps to the floor, groaning. There is a brief moment of stunned silence, and then near panic as* MILTON, NATE *and* HATTIE *rush toward her, calling her name.* EDNA *begins to cry, while* HOPE *stands uncertainly.* LOU, *hearing the noise, rushes into the room.*)
HATTIE: (*As* NATE *and* MILTON *hover over* GREMMAR, *trying to revive her, calling her name.*) Louis—quick!—call the doctor! Hurry! Lord, let me get some water! . . . water! (*Rushing toward the kitchen.*)
MILTON: Wake up, Momma!—Momma, wake up!

(MILTON *and* NATE *pick* GREMMAR *up and carry her up to bed, with* EDNA *following—crying.* HOPE *precedes them and turns back the bed covers. As they place* GREMMAR *in bed,* HATTIE *enters and crosses upstairs with a glass of water. The lights fade to black. In the blackout,* EDNA *continues crying as* GREMMAR *puts on a bed jacket and the No. 1 blackout drop is flown out. When the change is complete, Edna stops crying, and the lights rise slowly in the bedroom.* LOU *stands outside the door to the room.*)

LOU: (*Enters and crosses stage center; he pulls the chair up to the head of the bed and sits.*) Gremmar? . . . Gremmar? (*She opens her eyes slowly, weakly, dazedly, seeking him, and looks foggily at him for a moment.*)
GREMMAR: Nathan? . . . Is . . . is that you, Nathan?
LOU: (*Softly, hesitantly, somewhat anxiously.*) No . . . it's me . . . Louis . . . Louis . . .

GREMMAR: Louis? . . . Yes . . . yes . . . (*Beginning to fade away.*) Yes . . . yes . . . come up to see me . . . come to see me . . . yes . . .

LOU: (*Quickly.*) How—how do you feel? . . .

GREMMAR: (*Still drifting.*) Come up to see me . . . knows I'm not . . . not feeling well . . . yes . . .

LOU: Gremmar . . . (*Pause.*) Gremmar . . . why . . . why didn't you . . . didn't you . . . tell me?

GREMMAR: (*Opening her eyes.*) What—what's that, child . . . ?

LOU: Why didn't you . . . tell me? Why— (*Stopping, having difficulty.*) Why did you lie to me?

GREMMAR: (*Speaking partly to herself.*) No . . . no . . . no . . . I never . . . I never lied to you, son . . . oh, no . . .

LOU: Gremmar, you did . . . You did . . . (*Smoothing the covers and then watching her sympathetically.*)

GREMMAR: Not knowingly . . . no . . . no . . . not knowingly . . . no sir . . . I wouldn't do that, child . . . no, no . . . (*Coughing.*)

LOU: Are you . . . all right? (*Pause.*) Gremmar?

GREMMAR: (*Distantly.*) I'm all right . . . (*He takes her hand and begins to stroke it.*)

LOU: You—you always did the right thing . . . always . . . your . . . whole life. So perfect . . . never did anything . . . wrong . . . never . . . lying . . .

GREMMAR: I had my needs, son—yes, I did, child . . . oh yes . . . (*Silent again, tired.*) I had my men—yes . . . I was a young woman once, child—yes, I was . . . Wasn't always your grandmother, wasn't always tired . . . No, child . . . wasn't always tired . . . (*She reaches for his hand, grasping it.*) No, baby, don't . . . don't close your eyes to my needs. Don't close your eyes. They were real . . . God knows they didn't have nothing to do with right or wrong . . . nothing to do with them . . .

LOU: Gremmar . . . don't . . .

GREMMAR: Don't make me no more than what I was, son . . . Don't fault me for my feelings . . . That's what you're doing . . . that's what you're doing . . .

LOU: Gremmar . . . Gremmar . . . you could have—have said . . . something . . .

GREMMAR: (*Speaking softly.*) Some things are mine, baby . . . mine . . . just mine . . . I had feelings . . . Yes . . . needed loving . . . touched . . . held— (LOU *rises and steps stage left.*) Held in my men's arms . . . That's what my body was for—oh yes! Wasn't easy to be all by yourself in them backwoods . . . No, no . . . I had my feelings—

LOU: (*Crosses stage center.*) Gremmar . . . just . . . just . . . stop . . . That's just what they think . . . just what they think . . . That we're so dumb . . . Nothing but . . . dumb and . . . stupid and inferior! . . . Sex maniaes . . . degenerate, and all that crap! . . . Lazy . . . black . . . coons! (*Pause.*) You . . . you . . . call them liars and . . . and . . . punch them out and . . . for what? . . . (*Pause, angrier, crossing to the bed.*) All this time . . . all this time . . . you were just the opposite, weren't you? . . . just the opposite . . . just another one of those . . . those old . . . phonies . . . Just another . . . phony—

GREMMAR: (*Sitting up.*) I was nothing of the kind! (*Pause.*) Nothing of the kind! I was a colored woman!—life in my bones! And they were tender to me! . . . tender to me! . . . They . . . they understood . . . They knew! Yes, they did! I'm still your grandmother, Louis—I still am! . . . That's something different, baby—something different, child—didn't have nothing to do with you—nothing to do with you and me—

LOU: Gremmar . . . Gremmar, it . . . did! . . . It did! . . . I—I—who . . . who do you think I was listening to . . . around here, Gremmar? (*Pause.*) Doing things . . . Testifying . . . Telling those white kids off! . . . I'm . . . I'm . . . behaving . . . going to church . . . all that—

GREMMAR: Lord, Louis—Louis, child, get off your high horse, son . . . Don't be some old . . . old . . . goody-goody—some old—

LOU: (*Angrily.*) Gremmar, I'm not! (*Hurt.*) I'm not!

GREMMAR: Yes, you are—that's what you are—some old goody-goody! Talk like some old maid, some—some little old sissy! Some little old . . . prude—that's what you are! (*Lou is shocked by her words.*) Lord, Louis, you're a man, son! You're a man! He gave you something to use—to use! Don't you know it? (*He looks at her in disbelief, and with embarrassment.*) It don't have nothing in this world to do with what you want to be—don't let folks tell you that!—no, it don't! (LOU *turns away, shaking his head, trying to find a way to shut out her words.*) Stop thinking there's something so special about it, Louis—stop thinking so much and . . . and . . . *feel,* son. That's what you're missing—that's it . . . It's there, baby . . . Don't deny it's there—don't deny what it's for.

LOU: (*Turning away.*) I . . . I . . . know what it's for . . . Don't you think I . . . haven't . . . done . . . some—some things? Just because I—I haven't said anything . . . I know . . . what—what it's for! I . . . don't have to go . . . boasting about it—

GREMMAR: You're ashamed, son—

LOU: Ashamed of—of what?

GREMMAR: Ashamed of us, Louis . . . Ashamed of your family—your father . . . your mother . . . Nathan . . . and me, too. That's—

LOU: (*Turning to face her, stricken.*) Gremmar, I'm not ashamed! . . . When—when was I ever—ever—ashamed? When—when was I . . . ashamed? . . . I—I have a right to my opinion! Does everybody have to be—to be the . . . same? What do you mean, ashamed? . . . You—you didn't mean that, did you? Huh? (*Going to her, grasping her hand.*)

GREMMAR: Yes, I did, son—oh yes . . . yes. I seen you . . . I seen you when I come to your school—I come there looking for you—I seen you . . . eating your lunch with your hand in your bag so's nobody could see what you were eating. I knew what you were doing! (*He starts to protest.*) You're ashamed—ashamed of being a black boy! I know it! I can sense it in you—you're ashamed!

LOU: (*Jerking away from her.*) I was not! I just—it—it was . . . nobody's business, that's all! I keep telling you I'm not! . . . I'm not! . . . You're . . . you're just a . . . a— (HATTIE *hearing the noises, enters from the kitchen and crosses upstairs.*) just a . . . nigger, that all! That's all you are! Just a . . . a . . . a . . . sex . . . pot, that's all! . . . Just a nigger!—

GREMMAR: (*Her breathing more difficult.*) Ashamed of your skin . . . your skin—your family . . . me—

LOU: (*Angry.*) Just a . . . lying . . . nigger! You're a nigger, that's what!— (*She begins gasping.* LOU *looks at her in horror, yet is caught up in his own rhythm.*)

GREMMAR: (*Gasping.*) Ashamed! Ashamed! (*He moves to her, sitting, grasping her hand, holding it tightly.*)

LOU: Will you stop saying that! (*Moving closer to her, his arms around her, rocking her.*) Stop saying that!

GREMMAR: Ashamed!

LOU: (*Crying, rocking her.*) A black . . . nigger, that's all!

(MILTON *scurries down the hallway, meeting* HATTIE. *Together they rush into the room. Unaware of them,* LOU *hud-*

dles close to GREMMAR, *continuing to rock her and sob.* HATTIE *and* MILTON *look at him in horror.*)

HATTIE: (*With* MILTON.) Louis!
LOU: A nigger! . . . Just a nigger! . . . A nigger! . . . A nigger!
MILTON: (*Lunging, trying to wrestle him away.*) Let—let go of her, boy! You—
HATTIE: (*Trying to assist him.*) Be careful now, Milton!— Unhand her, Louis! . . . Louis!
LOU: (*Resisting.*) She knows what she is! (MILTON *wrenches him away and begins to half drag, half push him across the room.*)
GREMMAR: Ashamed!—yes! Ashamed! . . .
LOU: (*Screaming.*) Nigger! . . . Nigger! Nigger, nigger, nigger!— (MILTON *drags* LOUIS *to the stairs and pushes him down them.*)
MILTON: Break your neck—break your neck!
LOU: (*Gasping, crying, muttering.*) Just a . . . nigger, that's all—

(HATTIE *takes* GREMMAR *in her arms and begins to fan and mop the perspiration from her face.* MILTON *pushes* LOU *through the living room onto the porch. As they appear,* NATE *approaches.* MILTON *shoves* LOU *to the upstage left corner of the porch.* NATE *moves quickly onto the porch to prevent a possible continuing altercation.* MILTON *hovers near* LOU.)

MILTON: You big . . . dummy! . . . Going in there . . . going in there and—and disturbing her and calling her names, and . . . and . . . doing the things you were doing to her! I'll break your neck! (GREMMAR *groans wrackingly. Both* MILTON *and* NATE *turn in horror.* MILTON *moves quickly toward the door.*) Don't you move—don't you move off this porch! You hear me? (*As he goes up the steps.*) Break your neck! (*He hurries upstairs into the room. He and* HATTIE *talk in whispers.* MILTON *takes* HATTIE'S *place, rubbing her arms, while* HATTIE *begins fanning and patting her face. Stunned,* NATE *glares at* LOU, *who rises, turning his back and glancing at him from the corner of his eye.*)
LOU: (*After a moment, softly, intensely.*) Three of them!— three! . . . Just another—another . . . nigger, that's all! Didn't even marry any of them—not even—not even—one!
NATE: Oh man! . . . You— Lou— You stupid idiot! (LOU *turns and lunges at him, swinging.* NATE *ducks and retaliates,*

knocking him down. LOU *rises, charging back. They grapple,* NATE *getting well the better of it.*) You dumb bastard!
LOU: (*Crying, shouting.*) You nigger! . . . black nigger!

(NATE *knocks him down again.* LOU *is ineffective as* NATE *pummels him.* GREMMAR *begins to suddenly sing, blurting out a song—a spiritual.* HATTIE *and* MILTON *react with surprise and then join her. Oblivious to it at first,* NATE *jerks up, listening.*)

NATE: What the hell . . . They're . . . singing . . . They're . . . they're singing, Lou . . . Lou, listen! (*On his back,* LOU *groans, covering his face.*) Listen—listen, goddammit! . . . It's . . . her! . . . It's . . . it's—yeah! I swear to God, it's her singing, man! (*He moves to* LOU *and pulls him to a sitting position.*) You hear her, man!—the coarse one? . . . the crackly one?—the one coming—coming in behind . . . behind Mom's and Pop's . . . You hear it? (LOU *nods vigorously.*) She—she hasn't done that—I mean, since . . . since yesterday, you know? I mean—hey—hey—maybe she's gonna make it, huh? Maybe she's . . . she's gonna be—be all right. You know, I think she's gonna do it, man!
LOU: (*Laughing, half sobbing, half crying.*) Yeah . . . yeah . . . yeah! (*The singing stops.* GREMMAR *gasps and is still.* HATTIE *and* MILTON *stare at her in shock. After a moment* MILTON *nudges her, calling her name several times. He then sits, dazed.*)
NATE: They've . . . they've stopped singing.
MILTON: (*Slowly rises from the bed, crosses to the stairs.*) Killing my mother! . . . Killing my mother!— Killing her!
HATTIE: (*Moving after him.*) Milton—Milton, now wait a minute!
MILTON: Killing her!—
HATTIE: Milton, will you listen to me! (*As they move down the steps.*)
MILTON: (*Moving onto the porch and confronting* LOU.) Killing my mother! Going upstairs, upsetting her and—and—killing that woman!
HATTIE: (*Moving in front of him.*) Now calm down, Milton— just calm down. She was— (NATE *gasps slightly and stands between* MILTON *and* LOU. LOU *stands transfixed, tears welling.*)
MILTON: (*His voice breaking.*) Calling her names . . . calling her names and killing her! (*Lunging toward him.*) I'll kill

you, nigger! (*He grabs* LOU. *As he does,* NATE *grasps and struggles with him.*)

NATE: Come on now, Pop—ease up now! He didn't know what he was saying!—

HATTIE: (*Trying to assist* NATE.) Lord God!—fighting and killing, and she isn't hardly gone! Let go of him, Milton!

MILTON: I'll break his neck!

LOU: (*Gasping, crying.*) I'm . . . sorry . . . I'm sorry . . . (*Crying, whispering to himself.*) Oh God! . . . I'm—I'm sorry! . . .

MILTON: No good! . . . No good! . . . You lie! . . . You lie—do nothing but lie! . . . Good as that woman was to you! You ought to be thankful to her as long as you live! You ought to be thankful! I'll make you remember this night . . . *nigger!*

(*He wrenches away from* NATE *and glares at* LOU. LOU *flings himself off the porch, stumbling and falling and crawling a few paces away. Hesitant,* HATTIE *moves quickly off the porch and stands near him.* MILTON *turns and rushes quickly upstairs, where he sits beside the bed, holding* GREMMAR'S *hand. Dazed,* NATE *stands emptily for a moment and then crosses upstairs and sits at the foot of the bed.* HATTIE *sighs heavily, trying to catch her breath, unnerved. She looks toward the house.* LOU *is in a kneeling position on the ground, gasping and crying softly.* HATTIE *turns again to him and sighs, softening somewhat. She moves slowly to him, hovering a moment.*)

HATTIE: Louis, why didn't you do what I told you? . . . I told you to leave it down the drain—that's exactly what I told you!—exactly! (*She turns away, sighing heavily and shaking her head. She looks out into the street, staring blankly, whispering to herself.*) Lord have mercy! . . . (*Taking a step toward him.*) Louis—

LOU: I didn't . . . I didn't . . . mean to . . . to . . . to kill her!

HATTIE: (*Sighing.*) She . . . she was on her way out, Louis . . . She was . . . We all . . . knew it . . . we knew it . . . She was going . . . It didn't help any—what you did, but . . . she was . . . going . . .

LOU: (*Almost uncontrollably.*) I didn't mean to . . . I was . . . I was just . . . just . . . trying to tell her how—how I felt . . . That's all . . . I wasn't trying to . . . to *kill her!*

HATTIE: (*Sighing heavily again.*) Well . . . (*Pause.*) I don't

know, Louis . . . I don't know . . . (*Pause.*) All I know is
there's been a lot of trouble around here tonight.

LOU: (*Stands, crosses to downstage right of apron.*) I wasn't
trying to cause any trouble!— (HATTIE *crosses stage right to*
LOU. LOU *whispers to himself, trying to control his sobbing
but failing.*) I wasn't trying to kill her!

HATTIE: (*Suddenly tired, numb, sounding almost emotionless.*)
That's your father talking, Louis—

LOU: I . . . I . . . loved her . . . I wasn't trying to hurt her.
(*Pause.*) More than . . . than . . . anybody! . . . Anybody!
. . . She—she should've known that! Anybody around here!
. . . She knew that . . . Nate . . . Pop and—and—any of you!
She knew that!

HATTIE: (*Hurt, trying to mask it.*) I'm . . . I'm sure she did,
Louis, . . . I'm sure . . . (*Turns* LOU *around and embraces;
he sobs silently.*) It always . . . always comes so hard when
it comes . . . Crashes down on you no matter what you say
you are—like a fist!—no matter how prepared you think you
are for it . . . (*Sighing again.*) She was a good person, Louis
. . . a good person . . . (LOU *nods slowly.* HATTIE *looks
toward the house and then crosses stage left.*) Such . . . such
lovely hands . . . lovely . . . Long, pretty fingers . . . You
wouldn't have thought it, all the housework and things she
did over her life . . . But she did . . . (*Looking at her own
hands.*) Much as I try, I can't get mine like that . . . Soft,
pretty hands . . . She liked her hands—took pride in them
. . . (*Both are silent, thinking.*) And such . . . a pretty laugh
. . . Just as clear as a bell . . . came from way down inside
. . . Made her shake all over . . . (*Pause.*) Face would light
up . . . eyes would shine . . . (*Both are silent, thinking.*)

LOU: (*After a moment crossing stage left to* HATTIE.) She used
to . . . to wear that . . . floppy-looking hat out in the sun
. . . in the garden . . . (HATTIE *nods.* NATE *rises from bed.
He moves to* MILTON, *patting his shoulder, and then crosses
down the steps through the living room to the porch and sits
on the bench.*) Made her look like some . . . some creature
from outer space . . . some Martian in the garden. . . . (HAT-
TIE *smiles slightly, murmuring agreement.* LOU *pauses, looking out into the street.*) We used to . . . to . . . sit out here
at night and . . . see things . . . Make up things . . . Listening
to the crickets and things and . . . and staring out into the
woods . . . into the dark. (HATTIE *turns, following his
glance.*) We'd conjure up things and . . . all sorts of things
. . . cowboys . . . Indians . . . monsters . . . tanks, ships,

castles . . . pirates . . . all kinds of . . . crazy things . . . A game . . . just a game . . . (*Pause.*) It's so dark out there now . . . just seems so . . . dark . . . Hardly see anything out there . . . Like—like there was a . . . a . . . power failure and the whole town is blacked out . . . nothing . . . So small . . . so little . . . a big power failure . . . (LOU *and* HATTIE *cross onto the porch.* NATE *rises suddenly, reacting to a breeze that has suddenly begun to blow. He opens his shirt, throwing his head back.*)

NATE: Oh man! . . . Oh man, it's about time! . . . It's about time!

(*The lights fade out slowly as* LOU *and* HATTIE *turn toward the direction of the breeze.*)

EDEN

A DRAMA IN THREE ACTS

by Steve Carter

Eden was first produced at the St. Marks Playhouse in New York City on March 3, 1976, by the Negro Ensemble Company, and transferred to the Theatre deLys on May 14th. It won for its author an Outer Critics Circle Award as the season's most promising playwright, and an Audelco Award as best play of the year.

119

STEVE CARTER

Playwright, scene designer and theater administrator, Steve Carter was born in New York City of part-West Indian heritage: his father was from Richmond, Virginia, his mother from Trinidad. After graduating from the High School of Music and Art, where he majored in art and dreamed of becoming a scene designer, he served in the U.S. Air Force as a flight radio operator with the rank of staff sergeant. Returning to New York afterward, Carter gained experience with Maxwell Glanville's American Community Theater, where he designed costumes, operated lights and sound, taught body movement and wrote plays. Later joining the Negro Ensemble Company, he served as costume designer, production coordinator and director of the playwrights' and acting workshops, set designer and playwright-in-residence. In London, Carter directed a production of *Bread* by Mustafa Matura at the Young Vic Theater. A member of New Dramatists, most recently he was playwright-in-residence with the Victory Gardens Theater in Chicago. Among his awards and honors are a creative writing award from the National Endowment for the Arts, a Guggenheim Foundation fellowship, a Rockefeller Foundation award, and a grant from the New York State Council on the Arts.

In addition to *Eden*, works for the theater by Carter include: *One Last Look*, a fantasy set in a funeral parlor; *As You Can See*, a comedy about a blind con man; *Terraces*, concerning life in a terraced apartment building in Harlem; *Nevis Mountain Dew*, a West Indian family portrait, which was a Burns Mantle Theater Yearbook "Best Play" of 1978–79; and *Dame Lorraine*, about the return from prison of a Harlem son. Others are *House of Shadows*, a confrontation between two baby-faced, would-be criminals and two aging women in a Midwestern household; *Mirage* and *Tea on Inauguration Day*, described by their author as "two very short plays"; and two musicals: *Rampart Street*, based on jazz musician Buddy Bolden's life, and *Shoot Me While I'm Happy*.

CHARACTERS

(In order of appearance)

EUSTACE BAYLOR
NIMROD BARTON
SOLOMON BARTON
LIZZIE HARRIS
AGNES BARTON
ANNETTA BARTON
FLORIE BARTON
MR. JOSEPH BARTON

THE SETTING: The action takes place on 63rd Street between Tenth and Eleventh avenues in Manhattan. This section was called San Juan Hill.

THE TIME: August to December of 1927.

ACT ONE

A four-unit set, consisting of an apartment, a hallway with a window and stairs leading up to a roof, and a working door to an apartment.

EUSTACE BAYLOR *is sitting at the hallway window sketching on a large pad.* NIMROD BARTON *is on the roof, rolling up a ball of string from his homemade kite.* SOLOMON *is in his apartment, studying from his home-bound book.* NIMROD *comes down from the roof.*

EUSTACE: (*Turns in chair to* NIMROD.) Hi!

NIMROD: Hello.

EUSTACE: How you doin'?

NIMROD: Okay! You're always sketching.

EUSTACE: You always kite flyin'.

NIMROD: I like to fly kites.

EUSTACE: I like sketchin'!

NIMROD: What are you drawing?

EUSTACE: Er . . . nothing particular . . . street . . . people. Sure is a lotta people livin' on this one street. . . .

NIMROD: (*Crosses right to window upstage of* EUSTACE. *Looks out. Sneaks a look at* EUSTACE's *sketch.*) Where? I don't see a lot of people.

EUSTACE: Guess you just used to it . . . it bein' your city and all . . . things is easier in my home . . . folks spread out a bit. . . .

NIMROD: Guess so. (*Crosses left to apartment door.*)

EUSTACE: You West Indian, ain't you?

NIMROD: What of it?

EUSTACE: Don't go puttin' yourself in no huff. I was just askin' . . . is all. Ain't never really knowed no West Indians before. . . .

NIMROD: Well . . . you know one now. As you can see, we got two asses just like everybody else. . . .

EUSTACE: You sure don't talk like one.

NIMROD: What're we supposed to talk like . . . ? Besides, I was born here.

EUSTACE: Oh, so you ain't . . .

NIMROD: . . . So it makes no difference. I'm still . . .

EUSTACE: Listen, you be what you wanna be. Don't make me no never mind. A nigger's a nigger.

NIMROD: I'm not a nigger. . . . (*Throws kite down, makes a fist, and crosses right to* EUSTACE.)

EUSTACE: Look . . . (*Stands left of chair.*) I ain' been up here long. I don't wanna get started off on the wrong foot. So lemme see if I got this straight. Now, you say you was born here in these United States . . . but you's a West Indian. Your skin's the same color as mine . . . your hair is as burly as mine . . . but you ain't a nigger . . . guess it's me that's all mixed up . . . (NIMROD *crosses to kite, picks it up; crosses right to* EUSTACE. NIMROD *glares at* EUSTACE. EUSTACE *smiles back steadily. Realizing* NIMROD *is somewhat fired up,* EUSTACE *stands and stretches lazily, letting his full height be seen.* EUSTACE *sits and resumes sketching.*) Guess I'll be gettin' back to my sketchin'. (NIMROD *enters apartment, crosses left.* SOLOMON *is sitting in stage left chair at table.*)

NIMROD: Ain't you ready? . . .

SOLOMON: No!

NIMROD: (*Crosses left through arch and enters downstage room. Leaves kite offstage*). Why're you readin' that shit . . . ?

SOLOMON: In case you've forgotten . . . he'll be home today and you know he'll be asking questions. . . .

NIMROD: So? (*Enters, crosses upstage to cabinet. Takes cookie box. Crosses downstage to up center table. Places cookie box.*) Can't you fake the answers?

SOLOMON: No! And you don't do so good either! Why do you risk getting your ass torn up when it's just simpler to learn the stuff?

NIMROD: Look . . . man. (*Opens box and takes a cookie.*) It's summertime. We're supposed to be on school vacation . . . anyway, come on, we have to go and pick up that shit . . . and I want to go and play down by the docks before we have to go to Mr. Wallace's store. (*Crosses to apartment door.*)

SOLOMON: Papa told us to stay away from the tracks.

NIMROD: (*Turns, crosses to up center table.*) Oh, shit . . . it's probably gonna be the last time. Now come on . . . You can study that shit later. (*Crosses up right center to door, exits apartment, crosses up right. Exits down steps to street.*) . . . Come on.

SOLOMON: Okay. . . . (*Stands, takes cookie, crosses to door;*

puts iron inside, closes door, crosses up right, exits down steps to street.)

(The two boys leave the apartment and go downstairs.)

AUNT LIZZIE: *(From within.)* Eustace, where you? *(He doesn't answer.)* Eustace, where you at? *(To herself.)* If that don't beat all. He got the dishes clean and *(LIZZIE opens her door, crosses to stairs, turns. Sees EUSTACE.)* already, gone, Aha! . . . there you.

EUSTACE: *(He brings head in window.)* What you want . . . Aunt Lizzie?

LIZZIE: Nothin' particular. See you already washed up all the dishes while I was nappin'. Keep tellin' you . . . You don't have to be doin' that. That's woman work. I'm supposed to be spoilin' you and here you turnin' my head 'round.

EUSTACE: You never know how hard a woman work 'till you lose one. Hard work done took my mama. I ain't 'bout to 'low the only kin I got left to do no kinda hard work if I can help it. 'Sides, ain't nothin' to washin' no dishes.

LIZZIE: You sweet, boy! *(She crosses right to EUSTACE, hugs him.)* And you my sister for the world. You big like your daddy but you my sister for the world.

EUSTACE: Stop that or you gonna set yourself to cryin' again. She dead and I miss her more than fierce but I know she better off where she at. She don't feel no pain no more . . . and I expect she happy knowin' I'm up here with you . . . and if she happy . . . I'm happy.

LIZZIE: Go'n with you . . . how 'bout another piece of cobbler?

EUSTACE: 'Bout to bust now. Ain't been up here no time yet and you done fed me 'nough to 'splode a bear.

LIZZIE: Don't want my sister lookin' down and sayin' I ain't takin' care of her baby. *(She crosses into apartment, gets chair and crosses into hall. Places chair left of EUSTACE. She has brought a chair into the hall and placing it in front of her door, she makes herself at home.)* Well, it sure ain't take you no time to pick up hallway habits. What's so interestin' out that window you can't see from inside the house . . . ?

EUSTACE: Nothin'. Just cooler out here.

LIZZIE: Cooler, huh?

EUSTACE: 'Sides, I just can't get used to seein' so many folks livin' on this one itty-bitty street.

LIZZIE: Guess we all sort of pop-eyed 'bout it when we first

come up here, but you get used to it after a time. I don't
pay it no 'tention no more.

EUSTACE: But you sure can see why people holdin' court in
the hallway.

LIZZIE: In case you ain't noticed, it's only us decent folks can
sit in the hall. Them folks that live up the other end of the
street can't do it. It's nice to sit here outta the sun. You get
the breeze . . . and all the news . . . never did hold with
sittin' on the stoop. 'Sides them folks up the other end of
the street got toilets in their halls . . . and no windows in
'em. Can you beat that? Lord . . . lord when me and Anse
first come up here . . . we live up there and, Lord . . . sometimes . . . I damn near wet myself not goin' to the toilet
when I had to . . . just used to hate thinkin' 'bout performin'
my body functions. I mean sometimes you had to wait in line
. . . then you most times had to clean up behind somebody.
Eustace, be glad we livin' in these here Phipps houses . . .
we livin' good now. Four or five sets of strangers usin' the
same convenience . . . disgustin'! (*She cuts short her memory.*) Anyway . . . what you drawin' this time?

EUSTACE: Nothin' particular. Just scratchin'.

LIZZIE: That's for sure the lord's truth . . . and I know what
you scratchin' after. . . .

EUSTACE: Now, Aunt Lizzie.

LIZZIE: Don't, "now, Aunt Lizzie" me. You know I weren't
born the seventh daughter of a seventh daughter for nothin'.

EUSTACE: You ain't no seventh daughter of no seventh
daughter.

LIZZIE: Don't make no difference, I can still tell what you up
to.

EUSTACE: Like I was glass . . . huh?

LIZZIE: See right through you. At any rate, you better stop
sniffin' after who you sniffin' after. You ain't never been
caught up with no strange niggers like them next door.

EUSTACE: They ain't so bad . . . and I thought you and Mrs.
Barton was friends. . . .

LIZZIE: That's right . . . but you know I ain't never been in
that house when that man was home. Sundays and holidays,
I mean, I even fix a plate for Mrs. Barton to taste . . . and
she likewise for me . . . but like I said . . . if he's there . . .
I ain't.

EUSTACE: Can't be that bad. . . .

LIZZIE: That West Indian ain't real . . . don't even blink . . .
he be home from the hospital today and you see . . . tell me

when that streetcar hit him, his blood come our pure ice . . .
he be home. Don't like none of us homeys . . . won't even
talk to nobody unless they born 'cross the pond like him . . .
hardly talk to more than a handful of them . . . I never seen
that man walk nothin' but a straight line and folks pure get
outa his way . . . that Indian nigger can walk straight up
Sixty-third Street 'cross Tenth Avenue right into little Ireland
and none of them Irish niggers ever bother him . . . and you
tryin' to mess with one of his daughters. The way that man
hang over them two . . . 'specially the one you after . . .
you'd think they shit rose petals . . . pardon my French. . . .
Ain't you listenin' to me, boy? Bring your head in that
window.

EUSTACE: Aunt Lizzie . . . (*Stands, crosses to* LIZZIE, *tries to
lift her from chair.*) She comin' down the street. . . . Whyn't
you go'n inside?

LIZZIE: Boy, if you ain't your father when it comes to the
ladies. . . .

EUSTACE: Never knew him . . . now be my angel and . . .

LIZZIE: Well, I knew him . . . and you just him all over again.
(EUSTACE *exits right into apartment with sketch book and
pencil.*) Lord . . . when that man made up his mind to step
some gal's way, couldn't nobody (*Stands, crosses right, stands
upstage side of apartment door.*) man . . . law or God stop
him. . . . I was too through when his eye lit on your mama.
(*Crosses left, leans on back left chair.*)

EUSTACE: Can't we talk on that some other time, Aunt Lizzie?
If you just worryin' bout her father . . . forget it. (*Crosses
into hall, buttoning shirt and tucking in pants.*) I ain't set on
myself or nothin' like that but Granny told me once that
couldn't nobody who see me fail to like me . . . and maybe
somebody like me is what the ol' man need. . . .

LIZZIE: I say . . . be careful. . . .

EUSTACE: Ain't nobody gonna get hurt . . . I'm just out to fun
a little. . . .

LIZZIE: I don't wanna see that gal hurt. Lord knows . . . there's
enough gals hurtin' 'cause o' y'all men . . . but sure as hell
don't wanna see you hurt neither. . . . You and me is the last
of the blood . . . who else you got to look out for you. . . .

EUSTACE: I can take care of myself . . . it's time, you
know. . . . (*Crosses upstage to hall steps.*)

LIZZIE: I know you big . . . and you sure seen enough for your
age . . . (*Stops* EUSTACE.) Ain't nobody supposed to see

their momma go the way you did, but Eustace, you still a
baby far as this world's concerned. . . .

EUSTACE: I'm goin' downstairs now. You go'n inside. Thanks
for worryin' 'bout me. Don't never stop . . . but I told you
. . . I'm just funnin'! (*Crosses upstage, exits down steps to
street.*) Just funnin'! (*Kisses her on the cheek and goes
downstairs.*)

LIZZIE: (*To herself.*) You just your father . . . (*Takes left chair,
crosses right, places it inside apartment. Then stands in apartment door, eavesdropping.*) all over again.

EUSTACE: (*From below.*) Hello, Mistress Agnes. . . . Mistress
'Netta. How you both today?

AGNES: (*From below and affecting a Southern accent.*) Fine!
We both fine, thank you kindly! 'Scuse us, please!

EUSTACE: (*From below.*) 'Low me to help you with them bags.
Little ladies like yourselfs shouldn't have to heft things like
that up no stairs. . . .

AGNES: (*From below.*) We don't mind "heffin." In fact, we
love to heft.

EUSTACE: I insist.

AGNES: Suit yourself. (*Gives* EUSTACE *two shopping bags.* LIZ-
ZIE *exits right into apartment, leaving door slightly ajar.*)

ANNETTA: (AGNES *enters hall, crosses left, opens* BARTONS'
apartment door. ANNETTA *gives* EUSTACE *shopping bag.*)
Thank you.

EUSTACE: My pleasure . . . you sure got a lotta packages.
(AGNES *crosses upstage to hall steps.*)

AGNES: If they're too much for you . . .

EUSTACE: (ANNETTA *appears at top of steps in hall, crosses
down right center hall.*) I can handle 'em.

ANNETTA: I know you can. You're big enough to carry a
house. . . .

AGNES: Annetta!

ANNETTA: I'll bet you could too carry a house. . . . (EUSTACE
*appears top hall step with three shopping bags, crosses down
center. They reach the landing.*)

AGNES: Thank you! (*Crosses right to* EUSTACE *and takes two
shopping bags.*) We'll take these now.

EUSTACE: We here already?

AGNES: It would seem so . . . (*Crosses left, enters apartment,
crosses left to cabinet, places bags on floor. Puts groceries
from one bag in oak cabinet, folds bag, crosses upstage, places
bag in gray sink cabinet.*)

EUSTACE: I should take these in for you.

ANNETTA: Oh, no. Thank you! I mean . . .

EUSTACE: I know you can't ask me in. Listen, it's good your daddy don't want no fast-talkin' galloots in the place when he ain't home. Some guys would take sore advantage of a little thing like you. . . . I heard he coming home from the hospital today.

ANNETTA: My mother's gone to get him. That's why we've done all this shopping.

EUSTACE: A little celebration, huh?

ANNETTA: Yes.

EUSTACE: I know you be glad to see him.

ANNETTA: Yes.

EUSTACE: I guessed you missed him a lot?

ANNETTA: Yes.

AGNES: (*Crosses to platform and props door open with iron.*) Annetta, are you coming in any time soon?

ANNETTA: (*Crosses left to* BARTONS' *doorway.*) In a minute . . . or two.

AGNES: (*Props door open with iron door stop.*) Dinner had better be ready when he comes. It's not me who's the so-called "best cook in the world."

ANNETTA: Since it's me, I wouldn't worry me head, Agnes dear. (AGNES *crosses into upstage room and takes bag to front cabinet.* ANNETTA *takes bag from* EUSTACE.) I do have to go. . . .

EUSTACE: Look like we ain't gonna have no time for no niceties. . . . Shoot, you eighteen . . . this is 1927. Shoot . . . girls back home durn near grandma's . . . your age. . . .

ANNETTA: Well . . . I'm sorry. (*Starts to enter apartment.*)

EUSTACE: Now, don't go gettin' in a pout. You West Indians sure is some quick to fire. Funnin' with one of your brothers little bit ago and he look like he want to walk all over me.

ANNETTA: You know nothing of us . . . or me.

EUSTACE: I know your father don't like niggers, but shit. . . .

ANNETTA: Don't curse. . . .

EUSTACE: I ain't say nothin' but "shit" . . . and like I was sayin', I know your father don't like us niggers but all I wanna do is take you somewhere.

ANNETTA: Where?

EUSTACE: How I know? Somewhere! Anywhere, for a walk. Shit, somewhere! I wanna be seen with you. . . .

ANNETTA: I have to go inside.

EUSTACE: Aw, c'mon, 'Netta. Like I said, we ain't got too much time and I want to nail this down.

ANNETTA: Nail what down . . . ?

EUSTACE: Okay, I want you to go with me . . . and if you say "where," I'll . . . well, you ain't all that . . . I mean you ain't dumb.

ANNETTA: You don't really know me. . . .

EUSTACE: Do, too . . . and wanna know you more . . . wanna know all about you. All I really know 'bout you now . . . is that ain't nobody from the bunch I seen around here good enough for you.

ANNETTA: And you are?

EUSTACE: No! I probably ain't good 'nough for you. . . . But I'm right for you and I 'spect you know that!

AGNES: (*Enters from upstage room, crosses right to platform with typing papers and folder and red pencil.*) Girl, Papa and Mama coming down the street.

ANNETTA: (*Crosses left into* BARTONS' *door, stands on platform.*) I have to go.

EUSTACE: (*Crosses left, stands in doorway.*) What's your answer?

AGNES: You're gonna get it!

ANNETTA: Please, we'll talk soon.

EUSTACE: What's your answer?

AGNES: They're coming.

ANNETTA: I'll think about it. I really will. Please go. He'll suspect something if he even sees you in the hall.

EUSTACE: Okay . . . but only 'cause I don't want to get you in no deep water. But think 'bout what I asked you. I want a answer. (*Crosses right into* LIZZIE'S *apartment.* AGNES *replaces iron door stop and closes door.*)

LIZZIE: (*From within.*) Ow! You ain't had to push the door so hard, boy. You should guess I was standin' 'hind it. (*He closes his door.*)

ANNETTA: (*Crosses left to cabinet, places bag on floor, crosses upstage to stove, opens soup pot, turns burner. Crosses to up center table, puts cover on cookie box, crosses right with box and home-bound book. Places book on trunk, crosses stage left to cabinet, places cookie box in upstage corner of oak cabinet.*) C'mon and help me. (AGNES *starts to study her stenography.*) At least you can set the table.

AGNES: We have time. (*Crosses downstage and sits stage right chair at table.*)

ANNETTA: (*Places groceries in cabinet. Takes milk bottle out of bag, crosses left center, places bottle in icebox.*) But you said.

AGNES: I lied!

ANNETTA: What?

AGNES: I lied! It was for your own good. . . .

ANNETTA: For my own good . . . just when I had him where I wanted him. *(Crosses upstage to cabinet. Picks up bag. Folds it, crosses upstage, and places it in gray cabinet.)*

AGNES: You may have had him right where you wanted him . . . but if Papa had come in and caught the two of you "there" together . . . you know he'd put the rope to your behind . . . and then mine . . . and I'm damned sick and tired of gettin' welts on mine just because I'm the oldest and am supposed to be able to counsel you.

ANNETTA: *(Crosses to oak cabinet, opens drawer, and takes tablecloth.)* I was coming in.

AGNES: At your own convenience. You must be in love, because you ain't using your head. Well, I ain't in love, so I don't look forward to being flogged for that gorilla. He's not bad-looking . . . for one of them . . . and, lord, is he big. *(ANNETTA crosses up center of table and spreads tablecloth.)*

ANNETTA: As big as a tree.

AGNES: I wasn't referring to just his height.

ANNETTA: I don't know what on earth you could possibly mean *(Crosses left to wall cabinet, opens it and takes six bowls, crosses right to upstage table, places bowls.)*, but as "de nigguhs" is wont to say, "Thank de Lawd for dem stove-pipe pants."

AGNES: "Amen." Well, at least he's interested in you, thanks be praised. The way you've been mooning and whining whenever you see him, I couldn't have stood it much longer if he hadn't taken the bait. But please be careful . . . whatever you do. Papa would kill you both . . . not to mention . . . me. . . .

ANNETTA: Don't be silly, girl! He's bigger than Papa. *(Crosses and sits in chair at left of table.)* Besides, it's not going to get that serious. I won't let it. I'm just having a little fun . . . that's all.

AGNES: That had better be all 'cause Papa's all but got you wedded and bedded to Mr. Wallace.

ANNETTA: If he thinks I'd even entertain thoughts of that man crossing me . . . he needs dusting . . . . Besides, Mr. Wallace is more your type *(AGNES stops correcting papers, places them inside folder.)*, you being so brainy and all. He's so crazy about Papa he ought to be nuts about you. . . .

AGNES: Hah! The man I'm going to marry hasn't been born

yet. . . . (*Stands, crosses left to oak cabinet. Places folder on upstage arch chair. Opens cabinet drawer, takes six napkins.*)

ANNETTA: Don't worry . . . (*Stands, crosses up center table.*) One day your Prince Charming will come marching down 63rd Street wearing white knickers, checkered stockings, and flapped oxfords and sweep you off your feet. . . .

AGNES: As long as I land on my feet instead of my ass. (*Crosses right to* ANNETTA, *pushes left table chair under table.*) As for you, Cinderella, you just keep on dreaming about your giant-sized Prince Charming, but right now if you don't finish setting the table (*Tosses napkins on table and* ANNETTA *picks them up.*) even your fairy godmother won't be able to prevent Papa from breaking your glass slippers . . . not to mention your black behind. . . . (*She exits left through arch, chased by* ANNETTA.*)

(*A bit later, the table is set with soup plates.*)

NIMROD: (NIMROD *and* SOLOMON *enter hall from street carrying wooden tub with beef brine, cross left to Barton apartment door.*) C'mon, man. Hold up your side. . . . (NIMROD *opens apartment door.* ANNETTA *crosses to hall table and takes flowers.*) If this shit spills and stinks me up, I'm gonna . . .

SOLOMON: You ain't gonna do shit. (NIMROD *and* SOLOMON *enter kitchen.*) Think 'cause you the oldest, you gonna kick my ass all the time and I'm supposed to just stand there and let you . . . ?

NIMROD: As long as I'm the oldest . . . (ANNETTA *crosses right to kitchen table.*)

AGNES: You two had better stop talking like street niggers and (*She stands and crosses to boys.*) . . . what in the hell is that. . . .

ANNETTA: (*She crosses up right to boys.*) Get it out of here!

SOLOMON: It's Papa's beef brine!

AGNES *and* ANNETTA: What?

SOLOMON: Beef brine. (NIMROD *and* SOLOMON *cross left, place tub in front of oak cabinet.*)

NIMROD: He has to soak his foot in it from now on . . . every night. (SOLOMON *crosses right, sits on trunk.*)

ANNETTA: (*She crosses, puts flowers in center of table, stands up center of table.*) The doctors said that . . . ?

NIMROD: *He* said it. Mama told us this morning.

SOLOMON: And we have to get it from Mr. Wallace's store everyday and bring it home. . . .

AGNES: (*She crosses right to* NIMROD.) You brought that through the streets?

NIMROD: Where else? We can't fly . . . we're the Barton brothers . . . not the Wrights.

AGNES: As if we weren't laughed at enough. . . . (AGNES *crosses right, places folder on trunk.*)

ANNETTA: As if the house didn't smell enough with that pipe of his. . . .

AGNES: Now this. . . .

SOLOMON: And don't forget, we ain't even took the cover off yet. . . .

AGNES: Haven't taken. Haven't yet taken off the cover! Can't you try to speak properly? Honestly, you two get more American every day. (ANNETTA *crosses right below oval table to stage right chair [Flo's chair], crosses up right center.*)

NIMROD: We are Americans. We were born here, remember. You and Annetta is (*He stands, does monkey imitation.*) the monkey chasers.

SOLOMON: (*He does monkey imitation.*) Monkey chasers! Coconut eaters! Sugar cane suckers!

AGNES: Doesn't matter where you're born . . . you're still West Indians. (ANNETTA *picks up up right chair, crosses to up center table, places chair.*) Try to escape if you want to but you'll never be common niggers.

ANNETTA: Oh . . . I wish all this talk about niggers and West Indians would stop. We're going to hear enough about it soon enough any way. It's bad enough he's coming home and those damned Sunday parades starting up again.

NIMROD: God damn. . . . I forgot all about them.

AGNES: I didn't . . . I was thinking about conveniently losing my tin helmet . . . but I'd only have to get another.

NIMROD: Hey, maybe with him limpin' and all now . . . maybe he can't march on Sundays no more.

AGNES: Nimrod . . . do you really believe that . . . ? I mean, do you really believe that . . . ?

NIMROD. Suppose not. . . .

SOLOMON: Well, I like the parades.

NIMROD: (AGNES *crosses to* NIMROD.) Well . . . shit . . . you crazy.

SOLOMON: (AGNES *crosses to* SOLOMON.) Aw . . . fuck you.

NIMROD: (AGNES *crosses to* NIMROD.) Fuck you back in the same old crack.

ANNETTA: (*Crosses left to cabinet, takes spoons from drawer, crosses right to table, and places spoons on napkins.*) "You're not Negroes . . . you're not colored . . . you're Edenites, for you come from Eden . . . there would be no pale-faced people had not an Edenite woman in her folly wished upon the pale moon. . . . Americans have allowed themselves to remain less than men . . . and nigger this and nigger that. . . ." I just don't want to hear it . . . you understand? I'm just sick and tired of it all.

SOLOMON: What's wrong with her . . . ?

AGNES: (ANNETTA *crosses right to* NIMROD.) Annetta doesn't like to talk about niggers anymore 'cause she's got a case on one . . . next door.

NIMROD: No shit! Thought something was goin' on. Hey . . . come to think of it . . . I saw him in the hall before and he looked like he was drawing a picture of Annetta . . . tried to cover it so I couldn't see. . . .

(LIZZIE *enters hall from her apartment, sits in chair at window.*)

ANNETTA: A picture of me?

NIMROD: I couldn't say for sure. . . . He tried to cover it up so fast. . . .

SOLOMON: (*Putting on a West Indian accent and imitating his father.*) You mean, the girl has rose eyes for a south ape.

ANNETTA: (*Crosses left to table and finishes placing napkins.*) Shut up!

NIMROD: (*Also imitation. Crosses up center to apartment door.*) "Not a bit of it! Not a bit of it! You hear. Not a bit of it! No slave's leavings will ever t'row down one of my pure British subject princesses and tup dey legs across dem." (*Crosses right center and laughingly falls to floor.*)

SOLOMON: Who would dare? Not to my little lambs. . . . They've never been touched and never will be, at least not by a slave. (*Lifts* NIMROD.) A dirty, jack-leg rogue American slave. (FLO *appears in hall top of steps and looks down.*)

AGNES: Get up from there, sah! (ANNETTA *crosses to cabinet, takes glass, crosses up to brine, crosses down right center to* NIMROD. NIMROD *crosses down center, crosses left below table,* ANNETTA *follows with brine.* AGNES *crosses up center above table to left.* NIMROD *crosses up center.* SOLOMON *crosses up center to towel rack and takes towel.* AGNES *pushes* NIMROD *to floor.* ANNETTA *kneels and threatens to pour brine on* NIMROD. SOLOMON *hits* AGNES *with towel.* AGNES *fights him downstage right, crosses left to table, takes napkin and defends self against* SOLOMON, *crosses down right.*) You but a ram goat trying to make mannish water . . . and with a British subject? Not a bit of it!

LIZZIE: (BARTON *enters hall, crosses left to apartment door.*) Hey, Florie.

FLORIE: Hello, Lizzie. (*No acknowledgment from* BARTON.)

LIZZIE: I know you glad your man's home. . . . Bet he glad to be home too.

(FLORIE *nods.* BARTON *pushes open his door and discovers the kids chasing each other around the room.* MRS. BARTON *enters behind him and closes the door.* SOLOMON *sees* BARTON *[soft voice: "Papa's home"]* AGNES *stops hitting* SOLOMON, *crosses above table and left to* ANNETTA. ANNETTA *and* NIMROD *stand.* ANNETTA *crosses up right to* AGNES. [ANNETTA *stands downstage beef brine.*] LIZZIE *puts her ears to the door to hear what she can.*)

BARTON: (*Stands on landing,* FLORIE *behind him.*) Bacchanals? Bacchanals in the home? Is it revelry you want? (*Crosses into kitchen.*) Well, I can arrange it before you go to bed this night. Behaving like jamettes!

FLORIE: (*Enters apartment, crosses right to trunk, places hat and pocketbook.*) Joseph . . . sit in your chair. . . . The walk upstairs must have exhausted you. Annetta has prepared a homecoming dinner for you. The table is set. Come! (*She leads him to his chair.*) The food is ready?

ANNETTA: Yes, ma'am.

FLORIE: Gentlemen . . . please wash your hands. . . .

NIMROD: We did already. . . .

FLORIE: Then sit in your places. . . . (SOLOMON *shakes* BARTON'S *hand, crosses left below table and up center, hangs dish towel, right sink rack, crosses to downstage arch chair, crosses right to place downstage right corner to table, crosses sits down left table chair.* AGNES *tries to pull out the chair for her father.*)

BARTON: I am not a cripple.

AGNES: Sorry, Papa. I mean . . . it's good to have you home. (NIMROD *crosses to upstage arch chair, crosses to table place down stage left corner of table.* AGNES *takes* BARTON'S *hat and newspaper, crosses left through arch. Places paper on table, hat on coatrack.*)

ANNETTA: (*Crosses right to* BARTON *and kisses on cheek;* NIM-

ROD *sits up left table chair.*) I made chicken-foot soup . . .
Papa. . . .

BARTON: But naturally. (*Stands up center table.*) I am ready.
You may begin. (NIMROD *and* SOLOMON *stack bowls on
table.* AGNES *crosses to table left of* BARTON. *Gets bowls and
crosses to stove, takes ladle, uncovers soup.*)

FLORIE: Before we begin, Joseph . . . (*Crosses right, closes
apartment door; crosses down center to right of bar.*) the children and I would like to say how thankful to God we are
that you are home with us again. . . .

BARTON: As I was preparing to leave the hospital, a nurse told
me that I should give thanks that I was going home in one
piece. I believe she meant, as you probably do, Florie, that
God was responsible for my recovery . . . and was therefore
to be thanked. I told her that I do give thanks, but since I
alone was responsible for my own recovery . . . the thanks
was due to myself only! God, it would seem, has no time for
the things I have to do. Eat! (FLORIE *crosses down to down
center table chair.*)

(ANNETTA *ladles soup into bowls.* AGNES *places them in front
of* MRS. BARTON *and the seated* BARTON *men. They sit and eat
only after the rest of the family is served. Sound of* BARTON
slurping soup. Lights fade to blackout.)

During Blackout

(SOLOMON *places down right table chair at down right arch;
crosses down left; gets lamp on bookcase; 2 books off trunk;
crosses left sits stage right table chair.* NIMROD *places napkins
and spoons on cabinet up left chair to up stage arch; crosses left
sits stage left table.* AGNES *moves brine down stage front of
cabinet; gets dish towel.* ANNETTA *takes 2 bowls, puts in sink
drain, crosses to sink, gets dish cloth.* FLORIE *crosses right to
trunk, takes hat and purse, exits thru hall.* BARTON *takes cane,
exits left thru arch.*)

(*Sometime after the meal.* MR. *and* MRS. BARTON *are in their
respective rooms. The two boys are reading "home-bound"
books. The two girls are finishing the dishes.*)

AGNES: (ANNETTA *places second bowl in drain.*) I'm glad that's
the last of them. (AGNES *takes bowl from drain, dries with
towel, places with other in cabinet.*) Can't think of anything
I hate to do more than wipe dishes. . . .

ANNETTA: (*Crosses down center table, takes down center chair* [FLO'S] *and crosses right, places between bookcase and trunk; crosses left to up center table, takes up* BARTON'S *chair, places up right center left of pipe stand table.*) Try washing them for a change . . . then maybe you'd appreciate just having to dry. (*Crosses up center table, takes lamp and flowers in vase, crosses left, places upstage arch chair.*) One of these days people're going to be looking for me to cook (*Crosses up center table, takes tablecloth, crosses upstage to sink, shakes crumbs in sink.*) something or sew something or dust something and I'm going to be gone . . . just not here.

AGNES: Well . . . (*Crosses to* ANNETTA, *they fold tablecloth.*) if you think just because I will be the only daughter around here to take your place in the kitchen, Cinderella, then you have another think coming!

NIMROD: What you two whisperin' 'bout?

ANNETTA: Both of you'd better keep on studying. (*Crosses to upstage arch chair, takes lamp, crosses right, places center table; crosses left to upstage arch chair, takes vase, crosses into hall, places on table.*) You know he's going to ask you questions.

AGNES: (*Places tablecloth in cabinet drawer.*) It wouldn't have hurt if you had read a little each night. You wouldn't have been so far behind now. . . . (ANNETTA *crosses up center to sink, gets dish cloth, crosses left center, wipes icebox.*) and risk getting your behinds whipped.

NIMROD: I don't see why we gotta study these dumb old books. I don't see why I gotta study no African history. . . . I ain't African.

AGNES: (*Puts napkins in drawer.*) You're no European either and you're learning European history in school.

NIMROD: (*Stands, crosses left downstage of brine.*) You so fuckin' smart.

AGNES: What'd you say? Boy, I'm gonna get you. (*Kicks brine, top falls off.* SOLOMON *stands, crosses up left of table. She tries to kick at him but kicks the tub of beef brine . . . spilling some . . . she screams.*)

SOLOMON *and* NIMROD: Ooooooh!

BARTON: (*From within.*) What are you about out there?

NIMROD: Agnes kicked over your beef brine. (*He crosses right, sits stage left table.*)

SOLOMON: It's all over the floor Papa. (*He crosses right, sits right table chair.*)

ANNETTA: (*She crosses into arch way.*) It was an accident,

Papa. Nimrod and Solomon didn't push it all the way to the wall and Agnes . . . didn't see it. *They* didn't push it back far enough, only a little spilled.

AGNES: (*She sits up stage arch chair.*) I wish it had all spilled!

ANNETTA: (*She crosses to sink.*) Me, too.

BARTON: I'll be out just now.

FLORIE: (*She enters from up stage room with sewing basket.*) There's not much wasted, Joseph. Just a bit. (*She crosses to up right corner of table, places basket on table.*) Annetta, clean it up . . . quickly.

ANNETTA: (*She crosses to gray cabinet, takes rags, crosses to brine, wipes it up.*) Mama, it smells so bad.

FLORIE: Hush, girl. . . .

AGNES: I hope I didn't break my toe. It sure hurts.

FLORIE: Before you go to bed, soak your foot in hot water and epsom salts.

SOLOMON: Why don't you use the beef brine . . . ?

FLORIE: (*Laughing.*) Hush boy.

ANNETTA: It does stink, mama.

FLORIE: I know, girl. I know.

BARTON: (*Entering in robe and nightclothes. He enters from down stage room, takes paper from table, crosses right into kitchen.* FLORIE *crosses right, sits chair right of trunk.* BARTON *crosses right to* BARTON *chair, places right center spike marks.*) Nimrod, place that brine before my chair.

NIMROD: Yes, sir, (*He stands, crosses to ottoman places left of trunk.*) c'mon, Solomon, help me. (NIMROD *crosses left to beef brine.* SOLOMON *stands.*)

BARTON: I take it, you're not man enough to handle it alone?

NIMROD: Yes, sir. (SOLOMON *sits.* NIMROD *takes brine cover off, crosses up center, places right of sink, crosses to brine, takes brine, crosses right, places front of* BARTON'S *chair.*) Never mind, Solomon.

BARTON: All right now! (*He sits.*) Now then . . . the four of you . . . in your places. (AGNES, ANNETTA, NIMROD, SOLOMON, *line up diagonally from door, facing* BARTON). Mistress Agnes . . . (*She steps to* BARTON.) what about the typing?

AGNES: I'm not taking it anymore.

BARTON: What's this?

AGNES: I mean . . . my instructress says there's no more she can teach me. She says I'm just too fast so I'm just helping her instruct the other students. . . . She says I'm ready for work.

BARTON: It would seem she says a great many things but I will come to the school and say to her that you will no longer assist her unless you receive remuneration for your services. The shorthand?

AGNES: Same thing. . . . My speed only increases. She says I . . . if I was allowed to work you wouldn't have to spend your money on summer school. . . .

BARTON: I will be the judge of when you're ready for employment. The piano?

AGNES: Mr. Lewis says I should be preparing for a concert. If not . . . I shouldn't take lessons anymore.

BARTON: You have a lesson tomorrow evening, correct?

AGNES: Yes, sir.

BARTON: I will go there with you and inform Mr. Lewis that he is paid to teach you how to play the piano . . . and not for advice on how I invest my money.

FLORIE: You shouldn't go out so soon, Joseph.

BARTON: Nonsense! (AGNES *crosses, sits in upstage arch chair.*) Annetta . . . (ANNETTA *crosses up left of table.*) I see you've not been wasting your time. . . . The house looks as clean as it always does. You manage well on the budget.

ANNETTA: Well, I've found a store where food doesn't cost as much.

BARTON: Ah, yes. That would explain why Mr. Wallace told me he had not seen much of you. . . .

ANNETTA: The new store . . . it saves money.

BARTON: It would seem that my family doesn't think me a good provider. . . . They worry so about my ability with money. I would like some cocoa . . . if there is some. . . .

ANNETTA: There's just enough. . . .

BARTON: Then you will go to Mr. Wallace's and purchase more? And don't bring American cocoa into my house because it costs less. Is there enough for your mother to have a cup?

ANNETTA: Yes, sir. (*Crosses to center to icebox, gets milk, crosses to stove.* AGNES *stands, takes four cups from cabinet.* ANNETTA *pours milk into saucepan,* AGNES *opens cocoa, places cubes in milk.*)

NIMROD: Can I have some too, Papa?

SOLOMON: Me, too. . . .

AGNES: I thought you always said that home cocoa was too greasy for you.

NIMROD: (*Crosses to* AGNES.) I ain't said I ain't liked it. . . . I mean . . . (NIMROD *steps to* BARTON.)

BARTON: What language is this you are speaking, young sir?

Is it supposed to be English? Well, Florie, it appears that while I have been hospitalized . . . and you have been at your jobs . . . our young men have been taking the first steps to becoming . . . Americans.

SOLOMON: Not I, Papa. (NIMROD *glares at* SOLOMON.)

FLORIE: Joseph, they play with the other boys in the street. It's natural for them to pick up some of their . . .

BARTON: But they shan't bring what they pick up into my house. If this is an example of what's to come, then I shall have to put an end to their consorting in the streets with . . .

NIMROD: I'm sorry, Papa.

BARTON: I gave you leave to interrupt me with apologies?

NIMROD: I'm sorry, Papa.

BARTON: Let us see where else you've fallen down. Before I went to the hospital, I believe we were discussing Hannibal. In my absence, I presume you've continued with your reading. Tell me now, if you will, what was the name of his father?

NIMROD: (*Steps to* BARTON *up right table chair.*) Whose father?

SOLOMON: Hannibal's. (EUSTACE *enters on top step of hall, crosses to* LIZZIE'S *door.*)

(ANNETTA *and* AGNES *are behind* BARTON, *trying to mouth the answer to* NIMROD. EUSTACE *comes up the stairs, sketch pad in hand. As he goes toward his door, he flips through the pages.*)

BARTON: I'm waiting.

(EUSTACE *suddenly turns, goes to the* BARTONS' *door and knocks.*)

NIMROD: There's someone knocking at . . . (*He crosses to landing.*)

BARTON: You think me hard of hearing?

NIMROD: No, sir. (*Crosses up right of table.*)

BARTON: What I didn't hear was your answer. (EUSTACE *knocks again.*)

FLORIE: I will see who it is. (*Puts sewing down, crosses upstage to door.*)

BARTON: Why do you not admit it if you don't know? Trying to bluff me is tantamount to telling me a lie. You could have saved yourself what's to come by not taking me for an ass. . . .

(*Another knock.* MRS. BARTON *opens the door.*)

FLORIE: Oh?

EUSTACE: Evenin', ma'am.

FLORIE: Is there something wrong with your aunt?

EUSTACE: No, ma'am. If you don't mind, I'd like to talk with you . . .

FLORIE: Me?

EUSTACE: That is, I'd like to speak with your husband.

FLORIE: My husband?

BARTON: Who is this?

(FLORIE *closes door, leaves it slightly ajar.*)

FLORIE: It's Mrs. Harris's nephew . . . from next door.

EUSTACE: (*Sticks head in door.*) My name is Eustace Baylor, sir. I'd much like to speak with . . .

BARTON: (NIMROD *crosses left, stands downstage arch.* SOLOMON *crosses, sits in upstage arch chair.*) Show the young fellow in . . . Florie.

FLORIE: Come in . . . Eustace.

EUSTACE: (*He crosses into* BARTON'S *apartment.*) Thank you, ma'am.

BARTON: (ANNETTA *crosses left to arch.*) And where are you going, Annetta?

ANNETTA: I felt a little tired. I was going to lie down.

BARTON: Sudden, isn't it? Well . . . if you don't feel too tired . . . I would appreciate it if you watched the cocoa. Suppose it boiled over . . . (ANNETTA *crosses to stove, stirs cocoa.*) You must excuse me, Mr. Baylor . . . is it? My sons are in the midst of their evening lessons. . . .

EUSTACE: Evening lessons?

BARTON: It's the summer season, I know, but that's no reason for education to be neglected. Much that young men should know is not taught in the schools. It therefore behooves us . . . the parents . . . to make up the gaps with knowledge to which the teachers are not privy, would you not agree?

EUSTACE: Well . . . I can't say that I see the hook-in' 'tween education and the toilet but . . .

BARTON: You see, I have tried to instill it into my children that knowledge is power. I want my children to know that those in power in this country respect knowledge as a great equalizer. Having that kind of power gives your enemies a certain kind of fear. . . . Would you agree to that?

EUSTACE: Where I come from . . . if those kind of folks are scared of you . . . they just hang you . . . (ANNETTA *pours cocoa in cup, crosses to right of* BARTON.)

BARTON: But wouldn't knowledge allow one to avoid your enemies . . . ?

ANNETTA: The cocoa's ready, Papa.

FLORIE: (AGNES *pours cocoa into two cups, passes one to* SOLOMON.) Would you care for some cocoa . . . Eustace?

EUSTACE: No, thank you, ma'am. I just et.

BARTON: I don't think he's come for a social visit, Florie. Sit down here where I can see you . . . young fellow. (EUSTACE *crosses right, sits in* FLORIE'S *chair.*)

EUSTACE: Thank you. (FLORIE crosses right up stage of BARTON *to trunk, takes sewing basket.*)

BARTON: Agnes, (AGNES *crosses right to* BARTON.) go with Nimrod and Solomon to my room and see that they get deeply into those books. (NIMROD *and* SOLOMON *cross right to table, take books, cross left through arch, exit downstage room.* AGNES *follows boys' exits.* ANNETTA *follows* AGNES.) No, Annetta. You will stay! (ANNETTA *stops, crosses right, stands up right of table.*) Now, what can I do for you?

EUSTACE: Heard 'bout your accident. See you soakin' your foot in beef brine.

FLORIE: (*She crosses left, sits in chair left of table with sewing basket.*) You're familiar with it?

EUSTACE: Don't smell too good, but it come in handy every once in a while. Back home we use it for all sorts of ailments. (FLORIE *sits.*)

BARTON: Who is "we"?

EUSTACE: Us homeys from down the way . . . probably just something we all know about.

BARTON: Am I to believe you've come to my home to speak of cure-alls . . . ?

EUSTACE: No, sir. Well . . . I'm a man who don't like to beat 'round the bush. Like to get right down to brass tacks as they say. . . .

BARTON: Young fellow, you've come to speak with me about my daughter here. Is this not so?

EUSTACE: How'd you know?

BARTON: I was only hospitalized, sir . . . Not unable to keep track of the welfare of my family.

EUSTACE: Well (*He stands.*) . . . long as the cat's out the bag. I'd like your permission to call on Mistress 'Netta here.

BARTON: Why?

EUSTACE: Huh?

BARTON: I asked why?

ANNETTA: Papa, may I please go to my room?

BARTON: No!

EUSTACE: I'm sorry, 'Netta. I didn't want to cause you no embarrassment . . .

BARTON: Annetta . . . if you're looking for an excuse to go to your room . . . you'll soon have it. (MRS. BARTON *goes to her daughter.*) Now . . . I believe I asked you a question, sir. Why do you want to call on my daughter?

EUSTACE: 'Cause she . . . well . . . I hadn't thought . . . (*He sits.*) but I guess she's the only person I ever seen who hold herself like she do. High! You know? Don't get me wrong. Both your girls is ladies, but there's just something 'bout Mistress 'Netta that takes me . . . just takes me. First day I got here and saw her comin' down the street . . . well . . . ain't got no fancy words to tell what I was feelin'. Even forgot to tip my cap 'till she had already passed. I remember thinkin' that she won't think I got no manners . . . I was just starin' so. Durn near . . . 'scuse me . . . pretty near jump for joy when I find out she livin' cross the hall from me. . . .

BARTON: And you were able to recognize that she was a lady of some quality.

EUSTACE: More than that. . . .

BARTON: What could be more than a lady . . . ? A queen perhaps . . . ?

EUSTACE: Don't know nothin' 'bout no queens.

BARTON: But you do know ladies. . . .

EUSTACE: My mother was one.

BARTON: No doubt.

EUSTACE: She's a star! . . . that's what she is.

BARTON: Aha! A star. . . .

EUSTACE: She shines . . . for me.

BARTON: And what is a star? Something that burns the hands of those foolhardy enough to reach for it with the naked hand. "Reach" . . . because it is not easily available to you. . . . So you want to reach upward for the stars and drag one down. Drag it to earth with you and your kind. . . .

EUSTACE: My kind? What do you mean, my kind? . . . You mean . . . 'cause I'm from South? Man, you crazy. This ain't even your country. . . . It's mine and you can't talk to me like . . .

BARTON: Really? This is your country? Go out and prove it. You live where you're told. You do as you're told. They call you "Negro." Were this really, truly your country, would it not be called "Negro land"?

EUSTACE: Well, shit. *(He stands.)* If you ain't satisfied here, why the fuck don't you go back to where the fuck you come from?

FLORIE: *(Stands, crosses right to ANNETTA.)* Joesph . . . for God's sake. . . . Allow Annetta to go to her room. She cannot hear language like this. (FLORIE *and* ANNETTA *cross left through arch, exit upstage room.)* Come, Annetta.

ANNETTA: *(Crying.)* Oh, Mama.

EUSTACE: *(Crosses left to arch.)* You gotta forgive me. It slipped out. He riled me.

FLORIE: Come, girl.

BARTON: I would like you to know that I don't go back from whence I came because I think it more important to go from whence I was taken. . . . You will pardon me if I don't get up . . . good evening, sir.

EUSTACE: *(Crosses down left of table.)* That's it? . . . You think it's gonna end here?

BARTON: It's best . . . any chance you might have had . . .

EUSTACE: Aw, shit, man. *(Crosses right down of table.)* I ain't never had no chance with you and you know it full well. Don't even know what made me knock on your door. I came back to pick up my sandwiches I forgot to take to the pool room. . . .

BARTON: I'm told you spend your nights in a "pool room."

EUSTACE: I work there. My aunt owns it and I work there. Didn't your tattle-tale tell you that, too? *(Crosses right to FLORIE'S chair, takes pad and cap, crosses left to up right of table.)* 'Stead of comin' here, I shoulda followed my mind 'stead o' whatever the fuck I was following. But, no. I had to come here . . . *(Takes out sketch of ANNETTA, places on table.)* Even brought this picture I drew of 'Netta. Thought I'd surprise you . . . she ain't even know nothin' 'bout it. Figured I could show you I was somethin' more than another nigger off the corner. But you ain't nothin' but a crazy bastard . . . tellin' people . . . tellin' colored people they ain't good enough for you. You think you white. That's what's wrong with you . . . you think you white.

BARTON: To the contrary . . . I know that I am black . . . I am black, therefore I must be even more selective in how I maintain its purity. . . . I cannot allow pollution. Now leave . . .

EUSTACE: It ain't gonna end here.

BARTON: Mark me well. Come near my daughter and I will kill you.

EUSTACE: So you think I'm worth killing, monkey chaser?

BARTON: You're worth nothing, ape. But my blood is worth keeping pure. (*The two look at each other.*)

EUSTACE: (*Muttering as he goes.*) Ol' fool, that beef brine don't cure shit. (*Exits through apartment door, crosses right, enters* LIZZIE'S *apartment.*)

FLORIE: (*Enters from upstage room, through arch, crosses right to left of* BARTON.) He's gone?

BARTON: (*Begins to dry his foot.*) For now. . . . Why did you not tell me what was going on?

FLORIE: What was going on, Joseph? Annetta tells me all they've ever done is say hello to each other . . . (*Crosses to smoke stand right of* BARTON, *takes cocoa.*)

BARTON: I had to hear it from others.

FLORIE: From whom? Mr. Wallace? (*Crosses left above* BARTON, *up center to stove, pours cocoa in saucepan.*) Since he plans on Annetta for himself, I am not surprised.

BARTON: And what's wrong with his intentions? He has property. He believes in the things I believe in . . . and (*Puts house shoes on.*) most important . . . he's one of us. (FLORIE *crosses up center to sink, puts cup and spoon in sink.*)

FLORIE: (*Crosses to left of* BARTON.) So all he could do while you were lying in the hospital was to run and fill you with suspicion. Well, he seems to have had more time for visiting than I did, Joseph. I hold down three jobs a week. Everyday I come home from the laundry and I can hardly keep my eyes open. On Thursday the Jew gives me enough ironing to keep me busy for an entire week. Then the other woman tries to kill me with her work. How can I see if anything is going on when I can hardly see to walk home? You want me to tell your suspicions too?

BARTON: Call Annetta.

FLORIE: (*Crosses right, above* BARTON, *sits in chair right of trunk.*) I won't be a party to this . . . Joseph. The girl has done nothing.

BARTON: Annetta! (ANNETTA *opens door of upstage room.* NIMROD *enters from downstage room, crosses right to upstage arch.* AGNES, NIMROD, *and* SOLOMON *come out.*) I called you?

(SOLOMON *and* NIMROD *retreat.* AGNES *enters from downstage room, crosses right to left center, left of table.*)

AGNES: Papa, please. Annetta didn't do anything. Every time
he said so much as a hello, I was with her. Nothing ever
happened.

BARTON: You were in on the conspiracy also? (AGNES *crosses
left to downstage arch.*) Annetta, don't let me call you again.
(ANNETTA *crosses through arch, crosses right to up right of
table, wiping her eyes.*) I am ashamed of you.

ANNETTA: Yes, Papa.

BARTON: I expected more . . . and better from you, who of all
my children most resemble my own mother. Time and again
I have told you . . . if you hold yourself like these people,
you will be regarded as they are regarded. Why would a
daughter of mine encourage a person such as that? He'll
bring you down. What have you to say for yourself?

ANNETTA: He didn't do anything . . . neither one of us did
anything.

BARTON: Then what would lead him to believe he had the right
to barge in here and declare himself. . . .

ANNETTA: All right . . . Papa . . . it probably was my fault. I
spoke to him a few times. He asked me . . . he . . . he just
asked me if I would go someplace with him.

BARTON: Someplace like where . . . ?

ANNETTA: He just meant the moving pictures . . . and places
like that . . . like the band concerts in the park . . . block
parties . . . places like that . . . and I told him I would think
about it.

BARTON: You would think about it?

ANNETTA: I just wanted something to think about. Something
I could decide for myself . . . and I was only entertaining
the thought because it was fun. . . .

BARTON: Fun?

ANNETTA: Look, Papa, I don't do anything except cook and
clean and wash . . . and I don't really mind 'cause I know
things aren't that easy with us and I don't mind that it's
Agnes who gets all the chances at other things because she's
the oldest and she has all the brains . . . and deserves the
chance to become a good secretary or something. I know
Mama has to work and someone's got to do things in the
house, and I don't even mind Nimrod and Solomon being
treated like kings just because they're boys. . . . But, Papa
. . . you come home from the hospital and all you tell me is
that I kept the house clean. . . . You can't blame me for
wanting to be something other than a drudge.

BARTON: (*Stands, crosses around his chair to right of*

ANNETTA.) What has all this to do with your parading yourself before something unworthy of you . . . ?

ANNETTA: Don't you see, Papa . . . someone is interested in me . . . just me. Someone cares about how I feel. Papa . . . it's summertime . . . and I'm eighteen.

BARTON: Apparently an eighteen-year-old fool. . . .

ANNETTA: I only know that someone cares enough about me to walk in here even though he knows how you feel and declare himself to your face. And I love him for it. (BARTON *slaps her.*)

FLORIE: Girl, you don't know what you're saying!

AGNES: (*Crosses to left center, left of table.*) Annetta!

ANNETTA: (*Awed at her own news.*) That's right . . . ! I do love him. He came over.

BARTON: (*Goes to his room and opens the door. He crosses left to wall cupboard, gets rope from hook. To the boys.*) Come out of there and go to your mother's room. (NIMROD *and* SOLOMON *enter from downstage room, stand under arch.*)

ANNETTA: (*Crosses right, above* BARTON'S *chair to* FLORIE.) He came over.

FLORIE: (*Crosses left, passing* ANNETTA *above* BARTON'S *chair to right of* BARTON.) Joseph . . . you can't.

BARTON: Does my wife now defy me in my own house?

FLORIE: Will you beat me, too? (BARTON *crosses right to beef brine, places rope in brine,* Annetta *backs downstage right, below oval table.*) She's a young woman. You can't beat her as if she were a child.

BARTON: (*Pointing* ANNETTA *to his room.*) She has the irresponsible mouth of a child. The irrational brain of a child. Maturity has to be beaten into her.

AGNES: Papa . . . she didn't know what she was saying. She didn't mean it.

NIMROD: Papa . . . please don't.

SOLOMON: (ANNETTA *crosses left of dinner table, left center to arch;* SOLOMON *crosses to* ANNETTA, *grabbing* ANNETTA *and crying.*) Annetta! Annetta!

ANNETTA: Don't cry, Solomon.

BARTON: You want something to cry for, young man?

(NIMROD *pulls* SOLOMON *away. Both of them go crying into their mother's room.* ANNETTA *walks toward* BARTON'S *room, undressing as she goes.* BARTON *follows her into his room, closes the door. Silence. Then the sound of rope whirring through the air . . . striking flesh, immediately followed by an ear-piercing scream.)*

AGNES: I wish he had died! I do! I wish that damned streetcar had killed him. I wish it had cut his legs off. I wish . . .

(She is interrupted by a sharp slap from MRS. BARTON, *who promptly embraces her. The two of them cry,* MRS. BARTON *inaudibly. The two boys are at the open door of their mother's room, holding each other and crying all the while, more sounds of rope splitting the air and biting into flesh . . . and more screams.* MISS LIZZIE *has come out of her apartment and is listening at the* BARTONS' *door. Suddenly, silence. The boys close the door of their mother's room.* BARTON *comes out, the now blood-reddened rope in his hand and looking neither left nor right, sits in his chair.* MRS. BARTON *and* AGNES *run to* ANNETTA *in the room.* BARTON *lights his pipe as* MRS. BARTON *runs into the toilet. She comes out with a dampened towel.)*

FLORIE: *(She crosses to up right edge of table.)* I know why you did this. Mark me well, one of these days one of our children will kill you . . . in some way, one of them will kill you . . . and so help me Christ . . . I'll stand beside them before the world. I alone know why you did this. *(She crosses left, exits* BARTON *bedroom.)*

(Lights come down on scene. BARTON *puffs on his pipe,* LIZZIE *walks slowly back to her apartment, and* BARTON *rips up the drawing of* ANNETTA *that* EUSTACE *has left.)*

(Blackout.)

ACT TWO

Some days later. SOLOMON *is sitting at stage left table eating oatmeal.* NIMROD *is sitting at stage right table eating oatmeal.* ANNETTA *is standing at* BARTON'S *chair, shakes shirt.*

ANNETTA: (AGNES *enters from upstage room with folder, crosses right to* ANNETTA.) But you don't have to.

AGNES: Yes, I do. I've let you wash that whole load of clothes . . . and I shouldn't have . . . though, Lord knows, I never could get things as clean as you . . .

SOLOMON: You for sure ain't no housekeeper, that's for sure.

AGNES: (*Crosses to up center table, props basket against table.*) But I'm going to hang them to dry . . . and that's that. You just come along and sit. (ANNETTA *sits in* BARTON'S *chair.*) Let the sun get to that back.

FLORIE: *(Enters from upstage room with shopping bag, uniform in bag, crosses up left center to stove. Looks in soup pot. Places bag and pocketbook on upstage arch chair.)* I'm ready to go now. Remember . . . you are not to eat any of the soup before your father comes in from the clinic. Agnes, today is my day at Mrs. Grossman's. Meet me at the back of her house promptly at three.

AGNES: Yes, ma'am.

FLORIE: (*Crosses right to left of* ANNETTA.) Annetta . . . are you feeling okay?

ANNETTA: I'm feeling all right . . . Mama. (*Crosses up to left of* FLORIE.)

FLORIE: Well, don't do too much. You shouldn't have washed these things . . .

ANNETTA: I wanted something to do, Mama. I couldn't stay in that room . . . looking at the walls any longer. Besides, I just feel better being up.

FLORIE: (*Crosses down to* NIMROD, *kisses him on cheek.*) Nimrod, when you and Solomon get through with your porridge, you wash your bowls and you can go over to Mrs. Cammey's and play with Raymond . . . but mind you . . . be here when your father comes in . . . about three . . . (*Crosses left to*

148

upstage arch chair, turns, crosses to SOLOMON, *kisses him on cheek, crosses to upstage arch chair, takes bag and pocketbook.*) all right? I'm off. (*Crosses right to apartment door, exits to hall.* AGNES *puts basket on floor.*) Annetta . . . be careful, please.

ANNETTA: (AGNES *crosses right to door.*) I know, Mama.

FLORIE: Good-bye. (*Exits down steps.*)

AGNES: Okay, Nimrod . . . (*Crosses apartment, closes door, crosses left to upstage arch chair, gets folder, crosses right to door.*) hand me the basket. Solomon, open the door . . . come on, Annetta.

ANNETTA: Ready. (*Stands, crosses to door;* SOLOMON *stands, crosses right to door and opens.* NIMROD *stands, takes two bowls, crosses up center, places scrub board right of sink, places bowls in sink. Crosses right to basket, picks it up.*)

AGNES: (ANNETTA *crosses into hall.*) Oh, damn.

ANNETTA: What?

AGNES: Can't very well hang up clothes without clothespins. You go ahead . . . I'll get 'em. (*Closes door.* ANNETTA *crosses to hall window, looks out, crosses to* LIZZIE'S *door, listens, peeks through keyhole.* ANNETTA *goes to the roof.* AGNES *puts wash down in the hall and goes into the house.*) Okay . . . you can go ahead now, and remember afterward . . . the two of you stay on that fire escape and keep *your* eye a-cock.

NIMROD: Never mind that . . . you just drive it into Annetta's head that all four of us can get our ass kicked. . . .

AGNES: Both of you stay on the fire escape, and if one of you has to go pee or something, make sure one of you stays out there. . . .

NIMROD: Stop givin' orders and go. . . .

AGNES: Just remember. . . .

SOLOMON: Okay, okay. (*Opens door. She goes.*)

NIMROD: (*Following her.*) Agnes . . .

AGNES: What? (*She stops.*)

NIMROD: Don't you think you oughta take the clothespins with you?

AGNES: Smartie! (*Crosses left to clothespin basket up stage of icebox, crosses right, exits into hall.* NIMROD *exits to hall with clothes basket.* SOLOMON *stands in doorway.* AGNES *puts folder and clothespin basket in clothes basket, takes basket from* NIMROD, *exits up stairs to roof.*)

LIZZIE: (NIMROD *crosses right, knocks on* LIZZIE'S *door. From within.*) Who is it . . . and so early.

NIMROD: Next door, Miss Lizzie. Nimrod Barton.

LIZZIE: Just a minute. (*Opens door.*) What's wrong?

NIMROD: Nothin', ma'am. (*Crosses left to* SOLOMON.) Go'n on the fire 'scape, nigger. (SOLOMON *crosses left, exits downstage room.*)

LIZZIE: What you want?

NIMROD: I gotta talk with Eustace.

LIZZIE: 'Bout what?

NIMROD: I gotta talk with him. It's important.

LIZZIE: Where your daddy?

NIMROD: At the clinic. Ma'am, I gotta talk with Eustace.

EUSTACE: (*From within.*) Who is it, Aunt Lizzie?

LIZZIE: Nobody! (*Pulls door close.*) Go 'way. Eustace ain't gettin into no trouble with y'all Bartons.

NIMROD: (*Pushing past her and yelling inside.*) Eustace . . . it's me. Nimrod Barton.

LIZZIE: (*Grabs* NIMROD'S *collar, pulls him back into hall.*) You fresh, boy. Goin' over me.

NIMROD: Don't mean to be, but like I said . . . it's important.

EUSTACE: (*Enters, crosses into hall.*) Okay . . . Aunt Lizzie. I'll take care of it.

LIZZIE: No! No! Can't you see trouble comin'? All the time I been livin' here I been to myself . . . 'specially since Anse pass on. I ain't had no trouble with nobody. (ANNETTA *enters onto roof.*)

EUSTACE: And you ain't gonna have none now.

LIZZIE: But you gonna . . . and if you gonna . . . I'm gonna 'cause we kin, boy. Your trouble is my trouble. And we don't have to look for none. . . .

EUSTACE: Don't fret yourself, now. I want you to go'n inside.

LIZZIE: I ain't. (*Crosses right of* EUSTACE.) Whatever's got to be said . . . gotta be said in front of me. (*To* NIMROD.) Now, what you here to say, boy? (AGNES *enters onto roof, crosses to clothesline, starts to hang shirts.* ANNNETTA *sits on stool stage right roof.*)

NIMROD: Well . . .

EUSTACE: It's okay.

NIMROD: (*Crosses downstage, bringing* EUSTACE.) My sister's on the roof.

EUSTACE: Yeah? She says she wanna see me?

NIMROD: You oughta go up.

EUSTACE: She say she wanna see me?

NIMROD: You go'n up. My other sister's with her. My brother and me's gonna be on the fire 'scape watchin'. We'll let you know when . . . you know . . . I gotta go. (*Crosses left to* BARTON'S *door.*)

EUSTACE: Hey.

NIMROD: Huh?

EUSTACE: Thanks.

NIMROD: Y'all be careful. . . . It's my ass if you ain't. 'Scuse me, ma'am. (*Enters* BARTON'S *apartment, closes door, crosses left, exits downstage room.*)

LIZZIE: (EUSTACE *crosses up left to steps to roof.*) You goin', huh?

EUSTACE: My future waitin' up there for me.

LIZZIE: So you ain't gon' pay me no rabbit-ass mind, huh? Well, I'm gonna keep watch too. And when you hear me callin', don't you be lallygaggin'. Bring it on down here, hear?

EUSTACE: I hear you. . . . (*Exits upstage.*)

ANNETTA: Spread 'em out more. There aren't that many things that you have to bunch 'em up.

AGNES: Okay, okay!

ANNETTA: Well . . . it was your idea to do this. . . . how do you expect to become a proper scullery maid if you can't hang clothes properly . . . ?

AGNES: How . . . indeed. (EUSTACE *enters, crosses center.*)

EUSTACE: Hello!

AGNES: Hello!

ANNETTA: Agnes?

AGNES: It's okay. The boys are on the fire 'scape, keeping a lookout.

EUSTACE: So's my aunt.

AGNES: Now (*Crosses upstage around* EUSTACE, *crosses between them.*) Mr. Eustace Baylor. News has a habit of traveling around San Juan Hill faster than the natives can drum beat it out. No doubt, you know my sister went through close hell because of your bit of irresponsibility.

EUSTACE: Irresponsibility?

AGNES: You shouldn't have come over.

ANNETTTA: Agnes!

AGNES: He shouldn't 've. Now, let me finish. Annetta still seems to think you're worth going through what she went through . . . well, I don't. But . . . that's you and her! I personally don't think any amount of whatever you all call it is worth all that pain. If the two of you get caught doing anything together, Annetta's in deep trouble again. But that's not all. This time I'll probably get the same thing . . . probably worse.

EUSTACE: You?

AGNES: Yes . . . you can't possibly understand my father . . . but that's his way.

EUSTACE: Well, why you gettin' in it?

AGNES: 'Cause she's in it. She's my sister. My father does preach our responsibility to each other. At any rate, Annetta's not thinking very clearly right now, so someone has to . . . and that's me. I sure hope you're worth her getting her ass whipped 'cause you sure wouldn't be worth mine.

EUSTACE: Both you and your daddy some crazy 'bout me, ain't you?

AGNES: And for God's sake . . . please . . . be careful, if Nim and Solomon call you and tell you to come down . . . you go . . . (EUSTACE *goes into a fit of laughter.*) What's so funny?

EUSTACE: My aunt just told me the same thing.

AGNES: Nobody's said she didn't have sense. Well, I have to (*Picks up folder.*) go to my class. . . . Now, you two talk, hear? Just talk. Please don't . . . just talk . . . eh? (*Exits up left roof door, enters hall from roof and down steps to street.*)

EUSTACE: How you feel?

ANNETTA: (*Shrugs her shoulders.*) She didn't finish hanging these things. (*Stands, crosses to basket.*)

EUSTACE: (*Picks up basket.*) Lemme do . . . it.

ANNETTA: No. . . . I can do it. A man isn't supposed to do . . . stuff like that.

EUSTACE: No?

ANNETTA: No!

EUSTACE: What they supposed to do?

ANNETTA: I don't know. . . . Manly things, I guess.

EUSTACE: Like whip up on a girl . . . ?

ANNETTA: I don't want to talk about that because you'll think it was your fault . . . and you'll feel you owe me something. . . . (*Puts basket down.*)

EUSTACE: We gonna have to talk 'bout it 'cause it was too my fault. I been lyin' 'wake nights . . . wonderin' what made me knock on your door. I still don't know. . . . I just had to, that's all. I'm sorry you went through that. It was too my fault.

ANNETTA: Try thinking of it in another way. . . .

EUSTACE: Don't see how I can. . . .

ANNETTA: Can't you think of it . . . as my having gone through it for you. . . .

EUSTACE: That's nice . . . real nice.

ANNETTA: Forget it happened. . . . I don't want you to think about it anymore. . . . I really don't . . . just forget it happened, can you's

EUSTACE: Can you? We startin' out on somethin' so we may's well get the ratty thing cut loose . . . start clean. (*Puts his hand on* ANNETTA's *back, she winces.*)

ANNETTA: Oh . . . (*Pulls away.*)

EUSTACE: What's the matter?

ANNETTA: (*Coyly.*) Nothing . . . my back's not quite healed. . . .

EUSTACE: Let me see.

ANNETTA: No. . . .

EUSTACE: Let me see, 'Netta. (*Turns her around and pulls up her blouse.*) God damn! What am I? Why somebody hate me so much . . . they do this to their own? . . . What's so bad 'bout me?

ANNETTA: (*Crosses down right.*) You think he did this because he hates you . . . ?

EUSTACE: You think it's 'cause he loves you?

ANNETTA: Yes . . . sort of . . . I understand him.

EUSTACE: Bless you, then, 'cause I think he's the closest thing I seen to the devil this side of hell. . . .

ANNETTA: Eustace . . . he does love me. He wants what's best for me.

EUSTACE: And for him.

ANNETTA: Yes . . . and for him! I'm not saying he's right about it, but he thinks he knows what's best for me . . . and doing what he thinks best for me gives him his kind of happiness. I would like to say the same thing about you . . . Eustace. Don't you want to do what you think is best for me . . . ?

EUSTACE: Only I ain't gonna ever hurt you . . . that's the differnce 'tween him and me . . . I hope God lay me under wherever I'm standin' if I would ever raise my hand to you. . . .

ANNETTA: Well, we don't have to talk about that because I'll never give you cause. . . .

EUSTACE: Does that mean . . . you know . . . . what we talked 'bout the other day . . . you going with me?

ANNETTA: Yes. . . .

EUSTACE: I ain't gonna press you none 'bout it. I know your father don't like us niggers but . . .

ANNETTA: Didn't you hear me . . . I said yes.

EUSTACE: What . . . ?

ANNETTA: If I didn't want to . . . do you think I'd have taken that . . . ? Well, I just wouldn't have gone through it . . . that's all. You still want to, don't you?

EUSTACE: Still want to? Still want to? Man, oh man, oh man! Hey, 63rd street, look what I got. (LIZZIE *stands, crosses left to roof steps.*)

ANNETTA: Eustace, you're crazy.

EUSTACE: You got me, girl. You got me for life.

ANNETTA: How many girls have you ever told that to?

EUSTACE: None!

ANNETTA: I'll bet you had a lot of girls crazy for you . . . in your hometown. . . .

EUSTACE: Well . . .

ANNETTA: It's really none of my business what you did before me, is it? But I'll bet you knew a lot of girls. . . . (*Sits on stool.*)

EUSTACE: It was a small town. I guess you could say I knew a few people.

ANNETTA: White girls, too?

EUSTACE: Let's get that out the way. You heard that back fence talk too. Well, 'tain't true. No white man chased me 'way from my home. I let folks think whatever they want 'cause 'tain't none of they business an' 'tain't none of mine what they thinking. I come up here after my mamma died.

ANNETTA: I didn't know.

EUSTACE: Don't go feelin' sorry for her. I was happy when that old lady died. . . .

ANNETTA: Happy?

EUSTACE: Hear that? I called her "old lady" . . . even though she was only fourteen years older'n me. But damn, she looked so old. Died 'cause she was old. Worked so hard that she just couldn't wake up when the fire started. Time we got her out, she was . . . (*Sits left of* ANNETTA.) Well, she live three days with us puttin' every kinda grease on her we could get. Butter! Lard! Grease, you know! Fannin' her. And her sufferin' so much. Too much! Her eyes . . . they was burned open . . . and she just seem to keep lookin' at me. Just lookin'. Then when all the neighbors left for the night, I put a pillow 'cross her face . . . and let her go . . . (ANNETTA *gasps.*) Now see, I didn't want to get on that. Had it at the back of my mind where it belong. All I wanted to do was tell you the truth 'bout why I come up here. Anyway, after Mama pass, my Aunt Lizzie told me she could use some help with the store since Uncle Anse had passed . . . and I come!

No! No white man chased me 'way from my home. Now, we ain't gonna talk on that no more. We gotta spend all our little bit of time together being happy with each other. (LIZ-ZIE *crosses left, exits up stairs to roof.*)

ANNETTA: Eustace . . . ?

EUSTACE: Yeah?

ANNETTA: What you did . . . for your mother, I mean. . . .

EUSTACE: Yeah?

ANNETTA: It was a brave thing . . . a loving thing. I don't care what anyone might say. . . .

EUSTACE: Me neither . . . but thanks . . .

ANNETTA: Kiss me. (*She winces. He apologizes . . . He then timidly kisses her. She overwhelms him with her aggressiveness.* LIZZIE *opens door, then closes it.*)

EUSTACE: Hot damn.

ANNETTA: I knew it. I knew this would be how it felt. I just knew it.

EUSTACE: Oh, 'Netta, 'Netta.

ANNETTA: You don't think I'm being too bold, do you?

EUSTACE: No . . . no. . . .

ANNETTA: And you'll always be nice to me . . . ?

EUSTACE: I'm gonna see to it that you never have no more unhappy days. Oh, baby, I love you.

ANNETTA: Oh . . . me too . . . but we gotta be careful. Some-body might come up . . .

EUSTACE: Let 'em.

ANNETTA: No. We have to be careful.

EUSTACE: 'Netta, don't cool me down. I'm up, I'm way up.

LIZZIE: (*Enters onto roof, crosses right.*) Well, you'd better get down. . . .

EUSTACE: Damn, Aunt Lizzie. (*Stands, crosses left.*)

LIZZIE: Eustace, go'n downstairs . . . her father's comin'.

ANNETTA: He is? (*Crosses left, takes basket.*) I wonder how come my brothers . . . ?

LIZZIE: Don't just stand there, boy. Go on downstairs.

EUSTACE: Okay! 'Netta, when we gonna get together.

ANNETTA: Soon . . . I'll think of something. . . .

LIZZIE: Yeah . . . if it's in the cards the game'll get played. You want to get her and yourself in trouble again.

EUSTACE: I'm goin'. Bye, 'Netta.

ANNETTA: Bye. (EUSTACE *exits into hall.*) Thank you, Mrs. Harris.

LIZZIE: Just a minute, Miss Fast . . . you ain't got me fooled by a long shot . . . I seen you . . . heatin' him up . . . coolin' him down. . . . Playin' him like you the great big fisherman and he the mudskipper. If you think I can't see through you, you need dustin'. He's a big country boy. (EUSTACE *enters hall from roof, crosses right, exits* LIZZIE'S *apartment.*) I love him and you ain't gonna hurt him. . . .

ANNETTA: What makes you think I want to hurt him?

LIZZIE: He ain't all that innocent, but you something new to him. . . . You different. He ain't used to your kind. He need his own kind.

ANNETTA: What kind am I, Mrs. Harris? (*Puts basket down.*) What are we fighting for? You love him and so do I . . . and don't tell me I don't know anything about love because I'll be the first to admit I don't. But I know this, the first day I saw him I said to myself, "This is the one." I want him. You're talking about his kind of girls . . . like some of them that live on this block? Well, you take a look at 'em . . . I'm not the prettiest by any means . . . but Eustace doesn't know that . . . and look at this. (*Shows her back.*)

LIZZIE: Oh, God, child.

ANNETTA: Which one of those girls would go through this to have him. . . . They just don't have it.

LIZZIE: I know your father whipped up on you, child . . . but I didn't know it was anything like that. Listen, if you still bound on him after this, y'all come to my place. You can meet there as well as up here.

ANNETTA: Thank you . . . but no. I don't care what I have to do to have him . . . and if he wants me, he's going to have to risk a little too . . . but it's no sense getting everyone in trouble . . . I'll figure things out as we go along.

LIZZIE: Eustace think you a sweet young thing. Lordie! You been here before 'cause you sure act like you older'n anybody's eighteen. (NIMROD *enters from downstage room, crosses right into hall, exits up steps to roof.*) He don't really know what he gettin' into, do he? Poor thing. (SOLOMON *enters from downstage room, crosses right into hall, exits up steps to roof.*) Hah! I hope the day don't come too soon when these men realize how we got to work 'em so they can just be somethin'. (LIZZIE *and* ANNETTA *embrace.*)

ANNETTA: I knew you'd understand.

NIMROD: (*Enters roof.*) Where's Eustace? (ANNETTA *shrugs her shoulders.*) Papa's coming.

ANNETTA: (*Crosses left to basket.*) I know that. . . .

NIMROD: (*Crosses down right on roof.*) How you know? He ain't cross Tenth Avenue yet. . . .

SOLOMON: (*Enters roof, crosses up right.*) I spotted him.

ANNETTA: (*To* LIZZIE.) You said he was already . . .

LIZZIE: I knew you'd understand. Bye now. (*Exits roof.*)

NIMROD: What were you two gabbin' 'bout?

ANNETTA: Women's talk . . . ! Too much for you two to even try to think about! Go on down. (*Gives* NIMROD *basket.*) If he asks where I am, tell him. (*Crosses right, sits on stool.* NIMROD *and* SOLOMON *exit roof.* LIZZIE *enters down roof steps, crosses right, exit through her apartment door.*)

(*Blackout.*)

Some evenings later. BARTON *is drying his feet after having soaked them in the beef brine. The clothesline is soaking in the tub.* FLORIE *at oval table lights match; lights lamp.* FLORIE *is knitting. After drying his feet and putting on his shoes,* BARTON *wrings out the ropes and hangs them on the wall to dry.*

BARTON: (FLORIE *crosses up right center, opens apartment door, crosses left to wall cupboard, opens, takes out glass.*) Florie, I have decided that Annetta will marry Wallace. (FLORIE *crosses left to icebox.*) What do you think about that?

FLORIE: When will you tell Annetta?

BARTON: When it's time.

FLORIE: (*Crosses right to up center above table.*) And when will that be, Joseph? What is the proper time to tell a young woman that her life is being arranged for her?

BARTON: It's only fit and proper that we find someone. We have daughters and have the obligation.

FLORIE: Then why aren't *we* finding a husband for Agnes? She's the eldest.

BARTON: Agnes has the head to become a person of responsibility. She could command a decent salary. She could end up as a private secretary.

FLORIE: So she won't need a husband?

BARTON: We're not discussing Agnes. We're speaking of Annetta.

FLORIE: Oh, yes. (*Crosses left to icebox.*) I forgot. Well, Joseph (*Opens icebox, takes out pitcher, pours glass of water.*) I don't think Annetta will like the idea.

BARTON: And who is Annetta to like or dislike?

FLORIE: Joseph, this is 1927. We're in modern times. Girls don't want their husbands chosen for them. (*Crosses up cen-*

ter, leaves pitcher glass on top of icebox.) . . . not even our girls.

BARTON: That's enough, woman. I won't discuss it anymore.

FLORIE: Girls want love while they're young.

BARTON: Love. What is love? Can you buy bread with it? Will it pay rent? What can it do? I'll tell you what love is. Love is two people without a thought to the future . . . without a look at the past. They don't care where they come from and don't give a farthing where they're going. They talk about silly things. The moon! The stars! The heavens! Bah! Saying asinine things like "I thank God for you." Rubbish! Who is God? Who's seen him? You? (*Puts on and ties shoe.*) Then come the babies . . . conceived in drunkenness . . . and fevered passions. Unprepared for! Unthought of as a natural outcome of lunatic alliances. Unwanted! Their futures assured beneath lamp posts . . . either shooting craps or awaiting the next customer. (*Rolls pants leg down.*) Look out that window and hear the frantic bleatings of those with the razor scars across their cheeks. They are in, as you call it, love! (*Takes pipe and matches.*) That's young and irresponsible love!

FLORIE: I've never had love. All I ever had was you.

BARTON: (*Lights pipe.*) If you were dissatisfied, you should have registered your complaints. I gave as I was given.

FLORIE: I took what I got . . . to my shame. So I guess you have to tell me what it was all for. Everytime you would put me beneath you and begin to batter me so, I would wonder why I had to hurt so much. Where was the ecstacy my girlfriends told me would be there? You would loom over me with a smile on your lips, and then come into me, filling me with yourself. I would wonder, "Why isn't the man kissing me?" You see, I was young enough to think that trivial things like kissing and loving went hand in hand. . . .

BARTON: You have waited until now to take leave of your senses. (*Puts pipe down.*) We were united together because your parents sensibly decided what was best for you . . . (*Takes glasses off, puts in case, puts case in vest pocket.*) because they knew that you, like most girls, didn't know . . . and they knew that I had brains. Ambition! Ideas!

FLORIE: Ah, yes. Ideas. The children would rebuild our glorious past. The children were going to be the new beginning of Africa. I believed in you. I felt like a saint carrying the new nation within me. How fortunate I was to have been chosen. It was only after the children started coming one after another . . . like steps, Joseph . . . that I realized they were quite ordinary children. And when the last three passed on, I knew it for sure. They died like quite ordinary children . . . no different from other children right here on 63rd Street. Quite ordinary children and I was a stupid . . . less than ordinary woman. So you tell me . . . Joseph. Tell me what it was all for. (BARTON *stands, crosses left into apartment hall to coat rack.*) If you can't, then I'll just have to believe that I bore those two girls to be bartered away. The one for her brains (BARTON *puts on jacket and hat.*) and the money you think she can bring you . . . and the other to be a prisoner in a bed with a man you designate as substitute because before God, whom you fear despite (BARTON *crosses right to apartment door.*) what you say, you can't be in that bed yourself.

BARTON: (*Turns, faces* FLORIE. LIZZIE *crosses into hall.*) How dare you . . . (AGNES *and* ANNETTA *enter from upstage room, cross down through arch.*) Get back inside! (AGNES *and* ANNETTA *cross to upstage room doorway, stand.*) How dare you! How dare you befoul my home with your vile mouth. You disgrace me. You disgrace your family . . . you disgrace your people. (*Crosses to* FLORIE, *raising hand to strike her.*) You disgrace all that is decent.

FLORIE: Go ahead. Why don't you strike me? After all these years it would be a relief.

BARTON: (*Bellowing.*) Annetta! Annetta! (*Crosses down center.*) Annetta! Come out here.

ANNETTA: Mama? (*Crosses down left center.* FLORIE *crosses left, leans on icebox.*)

BARTON: I have decided you will marry Mr. Wallace. I want no discussion . . . no back sass. Now, go!

ANNETTA: I won't! I'll kill myself before I do! (AGNES *exits upstage room.*)

BARTON: You'll have ample opportunity to demonstrate the strength of your threat. Go to your room.

ANNETTA: No!

FLORIE: Go, Annetta. Go, damn it, go! (ANNETTA *goes to her room.*)

BARTON: I'll be returning late. (LIZZIE *crosses right, stands beside chair, looks out window.* BARTON *crosses up right center, exits apartment, crosses, exits down steps.* LIZZIE *sits in chair.*) You need not wait. (FLORIE *puts pitcher in icebox, takes glass, crosses up center to sink, places glass in sink, crosses right to sewing basket, places basket on trunk, takes shirt out—examines it, puts shirt in basket, crosses up right center, opens apartment door.*)

LIZZIE: Hi, Florie.

FLORIE: Oh, Lizzie. I didn't even see you there. . . .

LIZZIE: I'm easy to miss when you got so much on your mind. . . .

FLORIE: You heard?

LIZZIE: Hard not to. (*Stands, takes chair, crosses left, places chair right of door opening.* FLORIE *sits in chair.* LIZZIE *crosses right into apartment, returns with another chair, places right center.*)

FLORIE: You remember when you were eighteen?

LIZZIE: Well, now . . . it ain't been that long.

FLORIE: Remember the feeling in your blood?

LIZZIE: Blood don't change, honey. It's still there. Lord God! I had just seen Anse for the first. That big, shiny black nigger came walkin' up the road on a hot day . . . with his shirtsleeves rolled up . . . that can do it for me, you know. Love to see me a black man with his shirtsleeves rolled up and, Lord, don't let the shirt be white . . . wooeee! Anyway, he comes up the road . . . just stridin' . . . ain't lookin' left . . . ain't lookin' right. Just knowin' every eye was on him. Well, Florie, I fell. I really fell. It was so hot . . . I was so hot. . . . The sight of him and them shirtsleeves set my blood to boilin' and my little pupee to twitchin' . . . I just fell right out . . . right out in front of him. . . .

FLORIE: You ain't mean it. (*The two of them laugh.*)

LIZZIE: For true, girl. For true. He pick me up and took me down to the creek and threw some water in my face. When I open my eyes and saw him leanin' over me . . . I give him some right there on the bank. Didn't particularly give a good goddamn who saw me, and left town with him that day.

FLORIE: You must have really been happy. . . .

LIZZIE: Happy? Happy's too simple a word. You know, before he passed . . . life wasn't all roses. Can't be when a man look like him and there's other gals sniffin. He could make me downright miserable when he wanted to, but, shit, I'd go through it all again. Ain't had no other. Ain't want no other. Ain't need no other . . . and ain't no other 'round to make me forget him. Aw, Florie, you had the feelin'. . . .

FLORIE: Once . . . back home. There was a young black god. I wanted to . . . It's spilled milk. My parents decided Joseph was for my own good. Oh well, he's probably still there. He had not the slightest bit of ambition. Anyway . . . Annetta's my concern now.

LIZZIE: I know what run through her head when she see Eustace.

FLORIE: I do too . . . and I wish it was running through her head . . . but it's in her body . . . in her blood. If she was using her head, she'd be able to see the rocks in the road . . . and if I were using mine, I'd tell her.

LIZZIE: I seen 'em together and them rocks don't mean shit, Florie. They both strainin' and chompin' to get over them rocks so they can get at each other.

FLORIE: So?

LIZZIE: So . . . let 'em go, if you got the grit . . . throw 'em together. . . .

FLORIE: Things could get out of hand.

LIZZIE: They in hand now, I suppose? How many times you done lay awake wishin' you had that young West Indian boy back home layin' next to you? How many times you had to put his face on top your man's face so you could pretend you was enjoyin' it? I know it's risky . . . but hell . . . that's life in a nutshell . . . risks. . . .

FLORIE: Where would they go? Your house?

LIZZIE: No! She told me she'd never use me that way.

FLORIE: She told you . . . ?

LIZZIE: Girl, we done talked. Let 'em go to the roof. That's where they been goin'.

FLORIE: What?

LIZZIE: Little stolen time to be with each other for a while . . . not enough time to do doodledeesquat. Lemme go get him and send him on up. . . . (FLORIE *stands, crosses upstage left to roof steps.*)

FLORIE: (*After some deliberation, crosses to upstage of left chair.*) All right . . . I'm doing the right thing, aren't I? She wants the delirium. All right . . . (LIZZIE *stands, crosses into her apartment with her chair. Crosses left to* FLORIE.) let her have it before the dullness sets in. I am doing the right thing, aren't I?

LIZZIE: Unless you got somethin' else up your sleeve. Aw, Florie. Go talk to her and tell her . . . and who knows . . . maybe we can bury all this silly ass West Indian-nigger shit where it belongs . . . (FLORIE *crosses left into her apartment.* LIZZIE *closes her apartment, exits down steps to street.*)

FLORIE: (*Crosses left to upstage arch.*) Annetta! Come here . . . I want to talk to you.

ANNETTA: (AGNES *and* ANNETTA *enter from upstage room.*) Yes, ma'am.

FLORIE: Just Annetta, Agnes. (AGNES *crosses upstage, stands in doorway of upstage room. They close the bedroom door. She goes to the door of the male bedroom.*) Either of you two have to go to the toilet?

NIMROD: Not me!

SOLOMON: No!

FLORIE: Good . . . stay in your room . . . I'll be busy out here . . . (*Closes that door.*) Annetta, wipe your eyes and sit here. (FLORIE *and* ANNETTA *cross right below table.* ANNETTA *sits stage right table chair.*) Crying is for girls and you have to grow up now. (*Crosses right below oval table.*) You are to go up to the roof.

ANNETTA: The roof?

FLORIE: Don't interrupt. Someone will be coming up to meet you . . .

ANNETTA: Eustace?

FLORIE: It may be wrong what I'm doing. I pray to God it's not. But I'm not going to let you end up like me . . . without ever having one crazy dream come true. So you go up there . . . go and meet your boy.

ANNETTA: He's a man, Mama.

FLORIE: Not yet, baby. (*Crosses left to* ANNETTA.) You're not a woman either, but you go up to the roof and don't come down until you are. Now go and don't worry about things here . . . Go! . . . Go! . . . Go before I start to think. . . . (ANNETTA *kisses her mother, stands, crosses up right center to door, exits up stairs to roof.* FLORIE *sinks to her knees. She looks out window,* AGNES *crosses into room, stands near upstage arch.*) They always told me you guided our every move good and bad . . . I hope it's true . . . and I hope you know what you're doing. . . . (AGNES *has been listening and comes over to her mother.*)

AGNES: I hope the both of you know what you're doing. . . .

FLORIE: You're a very sensible girl, Agnes. I hope for your sake you don't stay that way. I'd like to think that when a piece of life offers itself to you . . . you not only taste it . . . but eat it down until you pass it out the next day. (*Blows out hurricane lamp. She crosses into archway.*)

(*Blackout.*)

Much later that evening, BARTON *enters the dark apartment from street, crosses up left center to stove, takes box of matches, crosses up right, places cane on chair. Crosses down right center to oval table, trips on brine.*

BARTON: *Artch!*

NIMROD: (*He and* SOLOMON *enter downstage room, cross into kitchen.*) Papa, that you?

BARTON: Who else lives here? Why was not this brine put away? (NIMROD *and* SOLOMON *cross right to brine; lift, cross with brine, place up center to right of sink.* NIMROD *puts cover on brine.*)

NIMROD: We didn't know it was still out.

SOLOMON: We went to bed early.

NIMROD: You told us to, Papa . . . (*Crosses right, picks towel off floor, crosses up center, places on top of brine.* BARTON *lights lamp.*) so we could get up early for the parade in the morning. (SOLOMON *and* NIMROD *cross left to arch.*)

BARTON: Aha! Well, come here . . . both of you. (SOLOMON *crosses down to left of table.*)

NIMROD: Huh? I mean . . . yes, sir?

BARTON: Sit! . . . Sit . . . sit . . . sit. On second thought, Solomon, you go into my chest and bring me my brandy. Nimrod, fetch three glasses. No need to look at each other so balefully. You did nothing wrong. Do you so fear your father that when he makes the slightest request of you, you tremble?

NIMROD: It's just that it's so late, Papa.

BARTON: Do as I say, both of you. (SOLOMON *crosses left, exits downstage room.* NIMROD *crosses up left center to cupboard, takes out three shot glasses.* BARTON *crosses up left center to stove, places matches on stove shelf.* SOLOMON *enters from downstage room with decanter of brandy.* BARTON *takes brandy, gives* SOLOMON *his hat.* SOLOMON *crosses left, puts hat on coat rack.*) Now, sit! (BARTON *crosses up center table.* NIMROD *crosses, sits stage left table chair.* SOLOMON *crosses right, sits stage right table chair.*) I am going to pour each of you a little of this and I will toast your very good health. Tonight I have concluded a piece of business that will not only help us as a family . . . but as a nation of people.

NIMROD: What was that?

BARTON: It is two years now since Garvey was incarcerated, correct? Yet every Sunday . . . rain or shine . . . I make you put on your helmets and march with me throughout the neighborhood. You hate to put on those helmets and carry the placards and march with me and the others. Is this not so?

SOLOMON: We don't hate . . .

BARTON: Nonsense! I've repeatedly asked you not to lie to me. Why do you hate to march with . . .

NIMROD: It's not that we hate the marching . . . but people laugh at us. . . .

BARTON: And who are these people who laugh at us?

NIMROD: All our friends we go to school with. They're always calling us stuck-up, crazy monkey chasers, tinheads . . . and other things.

BARTON: Your friends, you say, call you these names?

NIMROD: Yes.

SOLOMON: Papa . . . don't you hear 'em when we're marching?

BARTON: No, son. I don't hear them. I never hear them because there are stronger voices that shout in my ears. If you would only listen most carefully, you would hear them as they drown out those pitiful bleats from your "friends" . . . as you call them. Garvey screams in my ears. Africa roars . . . (*Crosses right over to table with lamp.*) bellows, "Bring my people home!" You think I always had contempt for the Americans? No, not true. Marcus and I came here with our hearts open to receive and to give. Where was there a bigger concentration of black people who needed enlightenment and inspiration to go back to the land robbed from us? (*Places lamp on table.*) . . . Where was there a greater gathering of rhythm to underscore the cadence of our marching feet as we took back what was ours before they took us? We thought it was here . . . and for a while it seemed true. We have only a handful to march tomorrow . . . but you should have seen us then. Hundreds swelled to thousands. People had never seen such black numbers. Indeed, it came as a surprise to many of our own people that we numbered so many. Is it any wonder that our power awed and put fear into those who watched in silence? It wasn't to be long before they were setting the traps. It was to be even shorter until they sprung them. Devious and dedicated forces went to work against us . . . paving their way and corrupting from within. Lies were told . . . and lies were believed. Marcus was toppled by a power far greater . . . far greener . . . far whiter . . . far blacker than any there could be in those heavens above . . . and before our ship of hope could sail . . . it sank into chasms far deeper than the deepest abyss. A few of us tried a resurrection but to no avail . . . the harpoons had been driven in securely and did their work. We ran into walls of black indifference and contented ignorance. We are trapped in this land with a people . . . who were almost ours. People who when the water got hot . . . preferred to leap from the kettle. That's why I cannot relax . . . nor can I allow you to relax. You must, at all times, hold yourselves to not be treated as these people have allowed themselves to be. The power of your brain will mark you apart. The power of your brain will get you home to Africa . . . and there you will be masters. Your sisters will be queens and fortify the land. And should a man from another race come into your kingdom and dare to cross your sisters . . . or cross you . . . or cross your threshold without your consent . . . *(Crosses up right center to door.)* you will beat him down and take what is left of his carcass and nail it to your door as a warning to all who would dare try this again . . . *(Crosses to up center of table.)* Remember, having a black skin is not a curse. Being in this country with a black skin is a curse. You are different . . . *(Crosses left to right to oval table.)* and when people laugh at you for being so . . . your affirmations shouted at the tops of your lungs to the tops of the world shall drown them . . . are you listening?

SOLOMON: Yes . . . yes, sir. *(NIMROD has drifted off to sleep.)*

BARTON: *(Crosses left to up left table, slaps NIMROD.)* Fool! I will not let you slip back . . . I will go back to Africa if I have to walk across your back to get there. . . . Go to the room . . . both of you . . . *(NIMROD and SOLOMON cross left, exit downstage room. BARTON crosses right to oval table, takes lamp, crosses left to upstage arch.)* No, Mr. Eustace Baylor . . . your people have destroyed one dream . . . you shan't wake me from another. *(Exits downstage room with lamp.)*

(MRS. BARTON comes out and seats herself in the now darkened apartment.)

(Blackout.)

(EUSTACE and ANNETTA embrace. EUSTACE crosses down center, sits.)

EUSTACE: I'm thinkin' I shouldn't hold you to me no more. Maybe you should do like your pa want and only see that West Indian nigger. Least he could show you some places.

Goddamn, 'Netta . . . I can't even show you off. Don't nobody know I belong to you.

ANNETTA: Eustace (*Crosses to right of* EUSTACE.), this roof is all the world I need. You're here. I don't have to tell anybody or show anybody that I belong to you. I just do. That's all. I know it. You know it. And when I walk down the street and people see my face . . . they know it. (*She sits.*) You don't have to be with me to be with me. You're like God . . . just everywhere I go. And the look in my eyes shows you off. (EUSTACE *and* ANNETTA *embrace.*)

EUSTACE: Every time we manage to get together, you work me up. Then you cool me down. Up! Down! Up and down! You playin' me again, 'Netta.

ANNETTA: No. I'm never going to play again.

EUSTACE: You sure? You ain't just funnin' me?

ANNETTA: I love you, Eustace. I'm going to give all my love to you. I want you to give all your love to me. I never want you to love anyone else but me. I don't want children because I don't ever want to share you. And I'll never let you die because I won't even share you with God.

EUSTACE: Oh, 'Netta.

ANNETTA: Sssssh, baby. It's time. (*Unbuttons blouse.*)

(*Blackout.*)

ACT THREE

It's December. There's a wreath on LIZZIE'S *door.*

AGNES *sits stage right in* FLORIE'S *chair correcting papers.*
NIMROD *sits on ottoman reading home-bound book.* ANNETTA
at stove stirring soup.

NIMROD: (ANNETTA *crosses left, exits to toilet, downstage of downstage room.*) You going to the toilet again? (*Stands, crosses left to arch.*) Doggone, girl, you spend more time in there lately than the law allows . . .

AGNES: (*Stands, crosses left to stove, covers soup.*) Why don't you keep quiet?

NIMROD: What'd I say . . . ? Doggone . . . hey . . . wash your hands . . . before you come out . . . I don't want you serving my food with . . .

AGNES: You're far from funny . . . (ANNETTA *goes into the toilet.*)

NIMROD: Why don't you dry up? That's right, you can't dry up no more than you are. (SOLOMON *enters hall, up steps, crosses left, enters apartment. Closes door, throws books on floor.*) Great Valentino! What war you been in. (SOLOMON *crosses left to arch.* NIMROD *stops him.*)

SOLOMON: Listen. Don't start no shit . . . and there won't be none.

NIMROD: Who the fuck you talkin' to, nigger? (SOLOMON *crosses right, crosses down table, crosses left.*) What in the fuck is wrong with you lately? (SOLOMON *crosses right, sits in* FLORIE'S *chair.*) Can't nobody say shit to you without you nastyin' off. Whoever kicked your ass probably had damn good reason.

SOLOMON: Ain' nobody kicked my ass. . . .

NIMROD: Yeah, I know. (*Crosses right to up left of oval table.*) "You shoulda seen the other guy." Well, you better watch it. You gonna go off on the wrong person and I'm gonna hafta kick your ass. . . .

SOLOMON: You and what army?

AGNES: (*Crosses to cabinet. Takes facecloth from drawer.*) If the

167

two of you don't stop it, I'm gonna kick both your asses. You sound just like street niggers. (*Crosses up center to sink, wets facecloth.*)

SOLOMON: You mean Americans? (*Crosses left to* AGNES.) Why don't you say what you mean?

AGNES: (*Crosses down to table.*) What is wrong with you, Solomon?

SOLOMON: Just sick and tired of it. Sick and tired of havin' to fight all the time just to prove that I'm just as good as anybody else. . . .

NIMROD: (*Crosses left to right of* SOLOMON.) Why you keep lettin' that old shit upset you?

SOLOMON: I beat up Willie Clay today! My best friend!

NIMROD: For what, man?

SOLOMON: He called me a "West Indian fuck." I beat him up. . . . (AGNES *sits.* SOLOMON, *stage right table chair, cleans blood from his face.*) We went down by the pier . . . we went there right after school. (NIMROD *crosses right, sits in* FLORIE'S *chair.*) We were just sitting there. We got around to talkin' 'bout Christmas comin' and I started sayin' how I wish we could keep Christmas but Papa don't believe in it. It being a white man's holiday and all . . . and he said "Aw shit, if that's all that's botherin' you, I already got you a Christmas present . . . you West Indian fuck." I hit him. I jumped all over him, he hardly had a chance to hit back. I just beat him up. My best friend. When are we going back to Africa? I want to go now! Right now! I hate 63rd Street! I hate it! (ANNETTA *comes out of the toilet.*)

AGNES: 63rd Street isn't the whole world.

SOLOMON: It is! It's the whole, entire world. 'Till we get to Africa like Papa says.

NIMROD: Africa? Shit! Use your head for something else 'sides a hat rack. (*Stands, crosses left to right of* SOLOMON.) Garvey's ass in jail and Papa ain't goin' nowhere 'cept marching with a handful of West Indians up and down 63rd to 64th Street. We don't even cross Tenth Avenue to the Irish and Italian sections. Ain't none of us ever gonna reach no Africa. You and me gotta do our damnedest to be Americans because Papa and Mama gonna die here. Annetta will marry Mr. Wallace after she graduates next month. Agnes gonna make out 'cause she got brains and gonna be a secretary. What do you and I do? We born here, damn it . . . and have to prove that we're as good as they are. (SOLOMON *stands, crosses left below table, exits downstage room.*)

AGNES: No! You're better.

NIMROD: That's Papa talking. We're as good. We're as bad. Can't nobody understand we just wanna be the same? (*Crosses left, above table, exits downstage room.*) The same, God damn it! (*He goes into the toilet.*)

FLORIE: (*From within.* ANNETTA *enters from toilet.* AGNES *crosses up center, puts cloth in sink.*) What's going on out there? (AGNES *crosses left to upstage arch.*)

AGNES: Nothing, Mama, try and go back to sleep.

FLORIE: (*From within.*) I'll be out shortly.

ANNETTA: (*Crosses up left center to stove, stirs soup.*) What was that all about?

AGNES: (*Takes upstage chair, crosses right, places down right table.*) Couldn't you guess?

ANNETTA: No, and I couldn't care less . . .

AGNES: I guess you do have other things on your mind.

ANNETTA: Meaning?

AGNES: (*Crosses up right center to* BARTON'S *chair, crosses up center table, places chair.*) I guess I wouldn't notice my brother's face was bloody either if I had your problem. You could at least pretend you're having your period. Does Mama know, you think?

ANNETTA: I wouldn't doubt it. Mama's not dumb.

AGNES: (*Crosses up right center to ottoman, crosses down right, places ottoman to right of oval table.*) Are you going to marry him?

ANNETTA: I suppose I'll have to.

AGNES: What do you mean . . . you suppose.

ANNETTA: I meant to say yes.

AGNES: (*Crosses up right to* FLORIE'S *chair, crosses left, places chair down center table.*) Papa will kill you . . .

ANNETTA: Papa better not ever put his hands on me again. I mean it.

AGNES: You're thinking Eustace will stop him? Hah! (*Crosses up right to trunk.*) Well, you wanted him.

ANNETTA: And I got him too, didn't I?

AGNES: (*Takes folder and typing papers, sits.*) You don't sound too thrilled.

ANNETTA: (*Crosses right to trunk.*) I just didn't think it was going to go this far. I hadn't really thought I'd get to marriage so soon.

AGNES: (*Puts paper in folder.*) What had you planned to do about Mr. Wallace next month?

ANNETTA: I would have thought of something. (*Sits on trunk*). I guess something would have come up.

AGNES: Something did come up and it appears to be you. When do you plan to break the news to . . .

ANNETTA: I plan to tell Mama first. Then I'll tell Papa when we're eating. I have it all planned. Don't worry.

AGNES: Good. However, I was referring to your fiancé . . . Mr. Wallace.

ANNETTA: Papa can tell him. He's more his fiancé than mine.

AGNES: None of this is his fault, you know. He worships Papa so. That's the only reason he consented to Papa's arrangement . . . but maybe it's best I tell him . . . maybe he won't take it so hard. . . .

ANNETTA: Agnes! Well, I'll be damned. Why didn't you say something?

AGNES: If I ever marry, it won't just be for love. Love gets your ass in all sorts of trouble. (FLORIE *enters from upstage room, yawning, crossing down, stands upstage arch.*)

FLORIE: What are you ladies chattering about? The food smells good, Annetta. (*Crosses up left center to stove.*)

ANNETTA: (BARTON *enters up steps with package in hand, crosses left to door.*) Mama . . . (ANNETTA *stands, crosses left to* FLORIE.) I have to talk to you . . .

FLORIE: What about? (BARTON *opens apartment door, enters.*)

ANNETTA: Oh, nothing. It can wait until later.

BARTON: Good evening.

FLORIE, ANNETTA, *and* AGNES: Good evening. (ANNETTA *crosses left to above oval table,* FLORIE *crosses to* BARTON. *Takes hat, crosses left, places on coat rack.*)

NIMROD *and* SOLOMON: (*Enter from downstage room, cross right to table,* NIMROD *upstage chair,* SOLOMON *downstage chair.*) Good evening, Papa.

BARTON: Yes.

NIMROD: We were washing up for dinner.

BARTON: The package is for Annetta. (ANNETTA *crosses up to* BARTON, *takes package.*) You may open it. It's your wedding dress. (AGNES *crosses left to* BARTON, *takes coat, crosses left, hangs coat on coat rack.* FLORIE *crosses to right of oval table.*)

ANNETTA: I'll open it later. (*Crosses right, places package on oval table.*) Dinner's ready.

BARTON: I want you to open it now. Is it every day you get a wedding dress? It was of some expense, you know. (*Places cane up center chair at table, crosses up center to sink, washes hands.*) I had thought both of you ladies would be married in the same dress as your mother, but I couldn't find it in the trunk where it used to be. . . .

FLORIE: If you had asked, I would have told you. I made up a package and sent it home years ago.

BARTON: (*Crosses downstage to table, drying hands.*) Why would you send your wedding dress back home?

FLORIE: I want my daughters to find their own happiness . . . and not duplicate mine.

BARTON: (*Tosses cloth into sink, crosses to up center table chair, sits.*) Annetta, what about the soup?

ANNETTA: (*Crosses up left center to stove, ladles soup into bowls.*) Coming just now.

BARTON: Be quick about it. Agnes, what about today?

AGNES: (*Crosses to left of* BARTON.) I stayed home today, Papa . . . I wasn't at all well. I had . . .

BARTON: I did not ask you the nature of your complaint.

FLORIE: (*Crosses left, sits down center chair at table.*) Don't forget to take some senna tea before you go to bed.

BARTON: Nimrod, what about today?

NIMROD: Okay!

BARTON: Okay! What is okay!

NIMROD: Everything went well. Nothing extraordinary.

SOLOMON: It's the same with me.

BARTON: Had I asked you?

ANNETTA: (*Takes bowl of soup, crosses down to left of* BAR-TON, *places soup on table in front of* BARTON, *crosses to stove.* AGNES *takes two bowls of soup, crosses down, places in front of* NIMROD, *then* SOLOMON; *crosses to stove.* ANNETTA *takes two bowls of soup, crosses down left of table, places one in front of* FLORIE, *places one down right table, sits down right table.* AGNES *takes bowl, crosses right, sits up right table.*) The soup is ready.

BARTON: We will continue this after supper. (*The family begins to eat.* LIZZIE *enters from her apartment, crosses left to* BAR-TON'S *apartment door. Turns, crosses right as* EUSTACE *enters from her apartment, crosses left to* LIZZIE.)

LIZZIE: I shoulda had another swig of courage before we go in there. . . .

EUSTACE: You don't need it. (*Crosses left to* BARTON'S *apartment door.*) C'mon and let's get it over with. If you don't want to, I can handle it.

LIZZIE: No . . . I feel partly to blame. Ain't nobody to blame but me. (*Crosses to right of* EUSTACE. *He knocks on the door.*)

SOLOMON: I'll bet that's Mr. Wallace.

BARTON: Nonsense! Wallace knows what time we're at table. He wouldn't visit during this hour. Whoever else it might be can wait out there or return later. Now, silence! (ANNETTA *stands, pushes chair under table.* EUSTACE *knocks again.*) Return to your seat, young woman. (ANNETTA *crosses up right center to apartment door. Ignoring him,* ANNETTA *opens door.* LIZZIE *and* EUSTACE *enter.* LIZZIE *crosses left center to left of table.* EUSTACE *crosses up center above* BARTON.)

FLORIE: Dear God. (BARTON *ignores the visitors.*)

LIZZIE: 'Evenin', Florie. Y'all 'scuse us for bustin' in on y'all's dinner but . . .

BARTON: Solomon, stop staring. Close your mouth and pay attention to your soup.

LIZZIE: Like I said . . . we didn't mean to interrupt your dinner.

EUSTACE: Hold on, Aunt Lizzie. Let me . . .

ANNETTA: (*Cautioning.*) Eustace . . . (*Crosses right to left of* BARTON.) Papa, I'm not . . . I can't marry Mr. Wallace. Eustace and I are having a baby. (EUSTACE *crosses to left of* ANNETTA.) I'm pregnant!

EUSTACE: I want us to get married Sunday next at St. Cyprian's.

FLORIE: (*Stands, sends boys to room; crosses right to left of oval table.* NIMROD *and* SOLOMON *stand, cross left to arch.*) My poor baby. What have I done.

ANNETTA: (*Crosses right to* FLORIE.) I didn't want it to come out like that . . . so cold. I wanted to say it in a nice way. What I mean is I did want to say it like that, but I'm sorry I did . . . I don't know what . . .

EUSTACE: You don't have to 'pologize.

ANNETTA: Eustace . . . please . . . (*Silence.*)

LIZZIE: We can have the weddin' celebration at my house right after . . . (*To* BARTON.) I know it ain't likely, but you welcome to come . . . if you wanna. (LIZZIE *crosses up right center to apartment door.*)

ANNETTA: Papa, say something . . . please. (BARTON *stands, crosses left center to rope, hanging left of cupboard.*)

FLORIE: No! (*Crosses to left of* ANNETTA. AGNES *stands, crosses to right of* ANNETTA. NIMROD *and* SOLOMON *step into kitchen.*) Blame me . . . I told her to do it . . . Blame me, but you shan't touch her.

EUSTACE: (*Crosses to* FLORIE.) He ain't touchin' nobody. 'Specially 'Netta. 'Netta, you get whatever you takin' 'cause you ain't stayin' here this night. . . . (*Crosses to up center of table.*) Listen, old man, I ain't come here to pack no trouble with you. 'Netta said she just didn't want you to . . . just find out. . . . (BARTON *crosses down right table, rope in hand.*) Lord knows why she wanna be sparin' you after all you done to her. But that's okay 'cause I'm gonna take her 'way where I can love her away from this place, away from you and your meanness. I love her. She and me is havin' this baby and ain't nothin' you can do 'bout it. . . .

BARTON: You listen to me, abomination . . . (LIZZIE *crosses to up left table.*)

LIZZIE: What?

BARTON: For the second time you show how unworthy you are. You people drift through life . . . infiltrating good people with your filthy ways . . .

LIZZIE: Filthy ways? Eustace, don't let him talk to you that way . . .

BARTON: Lying! Cheating! Sneaking! Lazy! Drifting through life without cause! Going where you're not wanted! I hate you. . . . (*Crosses right to* ANNETTA. FLORIE, ANNETTA, AGNES *cross left to above table.*)

EUSTACE: Hate me? (*Crosses right to* BARTON, *stage left of table.*) Is that all? I expected more than that from you . . .

BARTON: Maybe you understand this better . . . (*Whips* EUSTACE *with rope.*)

LIZZIE: (*Crosses right, taking razor from pocket, crosses to right of* EUSTACE.) I'ma cut your ass, you . . .

(NIMROD *and* SOLOMON *disarm her. General chaos as* BARTON *continues to flail the caught-off-guard* EUSTACE, *who tries to protect himself.*)

BARTON: Ineffectual bastard! Ineffectual bastard. Trying to destroy me . . .

LIZZIE: (NIMROD *and* SOLOMON *cross right to* LIZZIE, *pull her upstage, take razor from her.*) Let me go, dammit! Let go me! What's wrong with you, Eustace? . . . Kill him! (EUSTACE *grabs* BARTON, *shakes him.* BARTON *drops rope.*)

ANNETTA: Stop . . . Eustace . . . stop!

FLORIE: Oh, God. Leave off him! Leave off him!

EUSTACE: Gimp-leg motherfucker . . . you got no right . . . (BARTON *has stroke.* EUSTACE *lowers* BARTON *to floor.*)

FLORIE: Oh, God . . . (*Crosses right below table to* BARTON. *At* BARTON'S *head.* NIMROD *and* SOLOMON *crosses down to* EUSTACE, *pull him off* BARTON. ANNETTA *crosses right below table to* BARTON'S *feet.* EUSTACE *grabs* ANNETTA. NIMROD *and* SOLOMON *cross to* BARTON'S *side.* AGNES *crosses right [above table] to* BARTON'S *side.* LIZZIE *crosses to up left corner of table.*) my God . . . Joseph . . . Joseph . . .

LIZZIE: God got him. He don't like ugly and care very little for pretty . . .

AGNES: Shut up. Shut up and get out.

ANNETTA: Eustace . . . go!

EUSTACE: Not without you.

ANNETTA: How can I go after what you've done?

EUSTACE: After what I done . . . ?

FLORIE: Nimmie, go for the doctor. (NIMROD *crosses left, exits through arch to downstage room.*) Joseph . . . Joseph . . . don't look at me so. Close your eyes. Die if you have to, but don't look at me . . . so. Annetta, do something . . . somebody . . . help me.

EUSTACE: 'Netta . . . ain't you understand . . . you can't stay here no more . . .

ANNETTA: Stop pulling at me . . .

AGNES: Didn't anyone see through to this? . . . Didn't any think that something could happen?

LIZZIE: Eustace, back off. Don't you be the one to force her . . . else she blame you if he dies. (EUSTACE *lets* ANNETTA *go.* ANNETTA *kneels at* BARTON'S *feet.*) Young miss, you gotta do some thinking now. It's your man or your daddy. Florie, I'm truly sorry all this happen. We shoulda thought this through. I'm just sorry. (NIMROD *enters from downstage room with coat, hat, and scarf, crosses right to apartment door.*) You stay here, boy. This woman need all her family with her now. Eustace . . . you go get Doctor Taylor.

EUSTACE: 'Netta? (*Crosses apartment, exits to hall, crosses right to* LIZZIE, *enters her apartment. She doesn't respond.*)

LIZZIE: Go on, Eustace. (*He goes.* LIZZIE *goes.*)

NIMROD: (*Crosses to up right corner of table.*) Maybe we can all lift him and take him to bed. . . .

FLORIE: No! We don't move him. Get a pillow for his head . . . and a blanket . . . (AGNES *and* SOLOMON *cross left, exit upstage room and return.* AGNES *has pillow,* SOLOMON *has*

blanket. AGNES *crosses right above table to* BARTON'S *side.*
SOLOMON *crosses right below table to* BARTON'S *feet, upstage
of* ANNETTA. FLORIE *lifts* BARTON'S *head.* AGNES *puts pillow
under.* SOLOMON *and* AGNES *cover* BARTON *with blanket.)*
Gentle . . . (EUSTACE *enters hall with coat and hat, exits
down steps to street.) . . . gently . . . gently. (*LIZZIE *closes*
BARTON'S *door, crosses right, exits into her apartment).*

(Blackout.)

(Next Sunday, BARTON *in wheelchair is pushed onstage from
up right bedroom hall.* SOLOMON *has home-bound book.* BAR-
TON *has afghan over legs. He crosses stage right above table
to upstage center rug.* BARTON *sits throughout scene staring.*
SOLOMON *moves table upstage of ottoman. There's a peal of
laughter from* LIZZIE'S *apartment.)*

SOLOMON: Listen to 'em. Laughing and carrying on as if the
   world was still the same . . . can I get you anything? How
   about a smoke? You want your pipe? I'll light it for you.
   (SOLOMON *crosses to pipe stand, takes pipe, matches, crosses
   right of* BARTON, *lights pipe, puffs.)* You know . . . it's not
   too bad. Still smells, though. (*Places pipe in* BARTON'S
   mouth. More laughter.) Can you hear 'em? (*Takes pipe,
   crosses to* BARTON. *Places left hand in lap, crosses right to
   ottoman, takes book.)* They're all over there and havin' a
   good time. Well, I'm still here and I'm going to always be
   here. *(Stands, crosses to left of* BARTON, *kneels.)* Look, see
   what I'm reading? I'm deep into the histories now . . . just
   like you always wanted. I see it all now like you said. And
   I got my future and the future of the people uppermost in
   my mind. Earthly pleasures only last a minute or so. Ain't
   that what you mean? Well, don't you worry. I'll get us back
   to Africa . . . I don't know how but I'll do it . . . I'll build
   the nation for you. I'll do it. (NIMROD *enters hall from* LIZ-
   ZIE'S, *crosses left to* BARTON'S *door.* SOLOMON *stands, crosses,
   sits on ottoman.* NIMROD *enters, crosses down steps.)* Look
   who's here. Tired of laughin' and havin' fun?
NIMROD: Wasn't us. There's other folks there. How's Papa?
   (*Crosses down right of table.)* He need anything?
SOLOMON: Ask him. Don't talk (AGNES *and* FLORIE *enter hall
   from* LIZZIE'S, *cross left to* BARTON'S *door.)* 'bout him like
   he ain't here . . .

NIMROD: Well . . . (*Sits at right table chair.*) he can't answer nobody. . . .

SOLOMON: It don't mean he can't hear you. And if he needs something . . . (AGNES *enters, crosses down steps, crosses right to* BARTON, *kisses cheek, crosses left, exits* FLORIE'S *room.*) you'll know it. He's your father. (FLORIE *enters, closes door, stands at landing.* SOLOMON *crosses up left to cabinet.*)

SOLOMON: Hello, Mama.

FLORIE: You should have come over and at least had a piece of cake or something.

SOLOMON: I wasn't hungry . . . and I had a lot of studying to do . . . (*Opens cabinet, takes cup, crosses to stove, pours cocoa.*)

FLORIE: You are not fooling anyone, Solomon. However, no matter what happens, she will always be your sister. Joseph . . . you all right? (*Pats his hand.* FLORIE *crosses down steps to right to* BARTON, *adjusts blanket, crosses up left, exits.*)

NIMROD: (SOLOMON *crosses down right with cup, sits on ottoman.*) It just don't seem right . . . us being over there . . . I should lay down . . . I had a drink of that stuff she makes over there . . . I don't like it (ANNETTA *enters hall from* LIZZIE'S, *crosses left to* BARTONS' *apartment.*) but I guess it was only polite . . . my head sure feels kinda funny though. I gotta lay down. (NIMROD *stands, crosses down table, crosses up left, exits* BARTON'S *room.* ANNETTA *enters, closes door.*)

SOLOMON: (ANNETTA *crosses down steps.*) Well, you all American now . . . ?

ANNETTA: Hello, Solomon. Where's Mama? (AGNES *enters kitchen with coat and scarf from* FLORIE'S *room, crosses down left center.*) How come everybody's left? Where're you going?

AGNES: Just for a walk . . .

FLORIE: (*To* AGNES.) You have your scarf? It's cold out there . . .

AGNES: Yes . . . I won't be gone long.

ANNETTA: (*Crosses to* AGNES.) Are you coming back over?

AGNES: Maybe . . . Annetta, I'm sorry but I'm just not used to hanging out with that pool room crowd . . .

ANNETTA: I know, I'm not comfortable with them either . . . but they'll be going soon. You can't all just leave me over there by myself . . .

AGNES: Now . . . you think about that. I'll be back in a little while. (*Crosses right, exits down hall steps.* ANNETTA *crosses down left table.*)

FLORIE: (*Enters kitchen from her room, crosses to cabinet, takes spoon and napkin from drawer, cup from cupboard.*) Shouldn't you be with your guests . . . Annetta?

ANNETTA: In a minute . . . I guess I do have to go back . . . Mama, can I talk to you a minute?

FLORIE: Solomon . . . why don't you go into your room for a few minutes?

SOLOMON: I don't feel like it. Don't come over here givin' orders like you still lived here. Go'n back next door where you belong.

FLORIE: Solomon! Hush your mouth! This is your sister you're talking to. Now go to your room . . . (SOLOMON *stands, crosses to wheelchair, starts to wheel* BARTON *out.* FLORIE *crosses to stove, pours cocoa.*)

ANNETTA: No! Leave him here! I want to . . . I have to talk to both of you.

SOLOMON: Can I go downstairs then?

FLORIE: Yes . . . but dress warm . . . (SOLOMON *crosses left, exits to* BARTON'S *room.*)

ANNETTA: Mama . . . can I go into your room a minute . . . ?

FLORIE: (*Crosses with spoon, napkin, cup, right to* BARTON, *places cup on trunk, napkins under* BARTON'S *chin, spoon feeds him cocoa.*) What do you mean . . . my room? You act like this is no longer your house where you grew up. . . .

ANNETTA: I feel like a stranger already, Mama. Some parts of this (SOLOMON *enters from downstage room with coat and hat, stands in archway.*) room seems like I've never seen them before. . . . (*Exits upstage room.*)

FLORIE: You be back within the hour!

SOLOMON: Yes, ma'am. (*Crosses right to left of* BARTON.) She shouldn't have done it! She did this to him! (*Crosses up right center to apartment door, crosses into hall, exits down steps to street.*)

FLORIE: Within the hour! (*Goes over to* BARTON *and adjusts the blanket and back pillow.* FLORIE *feeds* BARTON *cocoa.*) Oh, I wish you could speak. I wish you could tell me it's all my fault. I tell myself over and over again, but that's not enough. They'll all leave us soon . . . and it's going to be us. Get well, Joseph. Get well. I just didn't think (ANNETTA *enters from upstage room, crosses to up center table.*) at the time I was doing so wrong.

ANNETTA: Solomon's really mad at me . . .

FLORIE: He'll get over it. . . . He has to have time. . . .

ANNETTA: Oh, Mama . . . I don't know what to say. . . .

FLORIE: Say what you have to, child.

ANNETTA: I am so sorry. . . .

FLORIE: I don't think you can be sorry for being in love. . . .

ANNETTA: That's just it . . . I don't know . . . I don't know if I know what love is. I only know I did this to Papa. I can't even look him in the eye.

FLORIE: Never blame yourself. It was me! You hear? Me! It was me who tried to let you experience (*Places cocoa on trunk.*) what I was too afraid to do myself. . . . (*Crosses left to right of* ANNETTA.) It was me, and your father knows it. It is me who will be responsible (EUSTACE *enters hall from* LIZZIE'S *apartment, crosses left, enters* BARTON'S *apartment with bottle and glass.*) for all the unevenness of your road from here on in.

ANNETTA: No! No! I knew what I was doing.

EUSTACE: There you are. . . . (FLORIE *crosses to left of* BARTON.) Listen, you got to come on over . . . we got folks over and they toastin' us . . .

ANNETTA: I'm busy now . . . can't you see?

EUSTACE: Listen . . . you think ain't nobody notice how y'all run out? All of y'all . . . Ain't no Bartons over there. . . .

ANNETTA: I'll be back over soon. . . .

EUSTACE: You supposed to be there. You ain't a Barton no more.

FLORIE: Your husband is right . . . I'll go over (*Takes napkin from* BARTON'S *chin, crosses up center, places napkin in drain, crosses right, exits apartment, crosses right to* LIZZIE'S *door, exits.*) Annetta, remember . . . there's nothing wrong with your father's hearing. (*She goes.*)

EUSTACE: Okay, baby . . . what's it gonna be . . . ? You comin' or not?

ANNETTA: I can't . . . (*Sits stage left table chair.*) I don't feel comfortable with those people. . . .

EUSTACE: What's wrong with 'em?"

ANNETTA: I just don't . . .

EUSTACE: They're niggers . . . that it? They from the South . . . that it? Well, let me tell you something. . . . You a nigger now . . . just like your husband . . . just like you son gonna be . . . (*Crosses to left of* BARTON.) You hear that, old man? You gonna have a Southern nigger grandson . . . so you can just keep on staring with them eyes. . . .

ANNETTA: "Those eyes" . . .

EUSTACE: What?

ANNETTA: Those eyes! Those eyes! Can't you speak correctly?
He's staring with "those" eyes. . . .

EUSTACE: So it starts, huh? My talk was good enough for you
on the roof . . . and it ain't about to change now. (*To* BAR-
TON.) You done this, old man. You put the poison in deep,
but you ain't gonna win. I'm gonna have a baby and he
gonna wipe your thinkin' clean. (*To* ANNETTA.) Hot damn!
We gotta get you from here. (*To* BARTON.) From you! I
see now we can't even live next door. That's too close. (*To*
ANNETTA.) Look at you! Look at him! He can't even talk
and he still fillin' your mind with all that hockey. We gonna
move. Even if it's gotta be as far as 61st Street. (*To* BAR-
TON.) I'm gonna have a baby and he ain't gonna be split in
half. He gonna be whole . . . dammit! There ain't gonna be
no north! No south! No east! No west! He just gonna be a
nigger. You hear me? Just a nigger! (*To* ANNETTA.) I guess
it ain't full hit you yet, but I love you. Now, you pull yourself
together. Say what you gotta say to him. Do what you gotta
do and get what you gotta get, 'cause I want you back next
door. 'Netta . . . this your husband talking. (*Turns and goes.*
LIZZIE *comes out of her apartment.*)

LIZZIE: Oh . . . here you! I was just comin' to get you. . . .
This don't look right, you know. Y'all's the guest of honor
. . . where's 'Netta?

EUSTACE: She's comin'! (*He and* LIZZIE *cross right, exit to*
LIZZIE *apartment.*)

ANNETTA: Papa, what can I say? Can't you help me? I guess
not. I guess nobody can help me now. I'm married. I thought
I would be dancing through hoops on my wedding day, but
I already start out feeling that I've done something wrong.
You were right, I guess . . . 'cause things seem so different
from what I thought they'd be. I shouldn't have done it, but
I love him . . . I guess. Oh, Papa, I'm in it now and I can't
get out. But one thing . . . Eustace is wrong. I am having a
baby, but it's not going to be like he says. I'm never going
to be far from you. When this baby is born, he's gonna be
over here more than you can say. I want him to know you
and love you . . . like I love you. I want him to be like you.
Just like you.

(ANNETTA *kisses him and hurriedly runs out, slamming the
door. We see her sadly going to* LIZZIE'S *apartment.* BARTON
sits there for a few moments. Then suddenly, but with a little

difficulty . . . he rises, his left side paralyzed. It is apparent that he has partially recovered from his stroke and has not informed his family. He looks toward heaven and smiles triumphantly. NIMROD, *awakened by the slammed door, comes out of his bedroom, stares at him a moment and then, still unseen, goes back into his room, closing the door silently behind him.*)

GENERAL HAG'S SKEEZAG

A PLAY

by Amiri Baraka

General Hag's Skeezag is published here for the first time. (It may be helpful—though it is not essential—to recall that a General Alexander Haig was prominent in national affairs during the presidencies of Richard Nixon and Ronald Reagan.)

AMIRI BARAKA

Born LeRoi Jones in Newark, New Jersey, Amiri Baraka (also known as Imamu Amiri Baraka) earned a B.A. in English from Howard University in Washington, D.C.; an M.A. in Philosophy from Columbia University; and an M.A. in German Literature from the New School for Social Research. Founder and director of the short-lived Black Arts Repertory Theater and School in Harlem (1964–65), he also founded and directed Spirit House, a Newark community arts center and the home of Baraka's Spirit House Movers, a repertory group which later changed its name to the African Revolutionary Movers. He is often referred to as the cultural and spiritual leader of the revolutionary Black Arts and Black Theater movements of the 1960s. A poet, editor, publisher, teacher and political activist as well as playwright, Baraka's list of credits, publications and other achievements is long and varied. Organizer of the Malcolm X Writers' Workshop in Newark, he has taught poetry at the New School, drama at Columbia, literature at the University of Buffalo, and was visiting professor at San Francisco State University. Most recently, he has been Professor and Chairman of African American Studies at the State University of New York at Stony Brook and visiting professor at Rutgers in Newark. Recipient of an Obie Award for *Dutchman* as best Off-Broadway Play of 1964, his other honors include a Whitney Fellowship, a Guggenheim Fellowship, a Rockefeller Foundation Award, a poetry grant from the National Endowment for the Arts, and an honorary Doctor of Humane Letters from Malcolm X College in Chicago.

Among Baraka's many works as playwright, in addition to *General Hag's Skeezag*, are: *Dutchman*, a modern allegory of U.S. race relations; *The Baptism*, a comic fantasy set in the Baptist church; *The Slave*, a revolutionary fable of a racial Armageddon; *The Toilet*, a racial allegory set among schoolboys (a Burns Mantle Theatre Yearbook "Best Play" of 1964–65); *A Recent Killing*, based on his experiences in the U.S. Air Force; *J-E-L-L-O*, an absurdist comedy satirizing the old Jack Benny radio show; *A Black Mass*, a dramatization of a Muslim allegory; *The Death of Malcolm X*, Baraka's view of the Black leader's assassination; and *Experimental Death Unit #1*, a revolutionary drama of Black militants. Others are: *Slave Ship*, a ritualistic drama set in the hold of a slave ship; *Home on the Range*, a comedy of the Black revolution; *Madheart*, subtitled "a morality drama," aimed at some Black women's imitations of white women; *Great Goodness of Life (A Coon Show)*, zeroing in on the Black bourgeoisie; *Junkies Are Full of (Shhh . . .)*, an anti-drug play; and *Sidnee Poet Heroical*, on the Black "success syndrome," with a well-known actor as target. Still others are: *Bloodrites*, a ritual drama of race and class; *American, More or Less*, a musical, written with Frank Chin, Leslie Silko and Arnold Weinstein; *Jazz Opera* (libretto, to a score by Swiss composer George Gruntz), commissioned by the Paris Opera and later retitled *Money; What Was the Relationship of the Lone Ranger to the Means of Production?*, a Marxist play; and *Boy and Tarzan Appear in a Clearing*, a satire on the long-lived Edgar Rice Burroughs creation.

Baraka's other writings include *The Dead Lecturer, Preface to a Twenty Volume Suicide Note* and *In the Tradition*, all volumes of poetry; *The System of Dante's Hell*, a novel; and *Tales*, a collection of short stories. Others are *Blues People: Negro Music in White America; Selected Prose and Plays*; and *The Autobiography of LeRoi Jones/Amiri Baraka*. He is editor of *The Moderns: An Anthology of New Writing in America; Black Fire: An Anthology of Afro-American Writing* with Larry Neal; and *Confirmation: An Anthology of African American Women*, with his wife, Amina Baraka.

CHARACTERS

JOE - a young black messenger

BURGESS - a businessman (white and middle-aged)

CHARLES BLANK - a "rival" businessman (black and younger)

FRED SWINGS - Middle-aged, dignified black (a trifle abstract) husband

HARRIET SWINGS - Somewhat younger, dignified, black (more realist) mother of

MAL SWINGS - Young, ready, interested (son of Fred and Harriet)

GENERAL HAG - a general who at one time was Secretary of State

Wandering through and out of the darkness, in some semi-darkness, a young man approaches, crossing the stage, whistling and singing snatches of a song.

> Big-time as life is
> All you big-time reachers reaching
> When you reach you got them guys teaching
> That you wasn't nothing
> But what they understand
> Ain't it grand
> Yes, you girls and guys
> You may not know you got to die
> All you big-time reachers reaching
> When you reach, you got them gals teaching
> That you wasn't nothing
> No, you wasn't nothing
> But what they understand
> Ain't it, yeah, ain't it, ain't it
> just graaaaaaaaaaaaaand. . . .

He is walking slowly but purposefully. The song seems to amuse him, and he hums and whistles snatches of it as he gets to the place he finally seems to be going. His destination is a store—a combination religious supply and book store. He seems to know where he is going. It is a black community in some large city, a city where in the distance we might see shadows that imply some familiar governmental structures. Perhaps the shadow of the Washington Monument or the Capitol. Something familiar but not definite; who knows where this is taking place? It is perhaps fall, at its early edges, and there is a hint of gusts, holding the young man upright or just a little more forward than he'd like.

The store has the blinds pulled, but we can see the name: "STORY BOOKS & RELIGIOUS ENTREPOTS," and underneath, "Brother Burgess, Prop." The young man looks at the door as if something is off, but pulls the knob to turn it, leaning back an inch or so to peep at the dark coming under the blind where he thought there should be light.

JOE: What? (*Mumbling.*) What's going on . . . this dude said he'd be here. (*Raises voice a little, calling as he jerks on the knob, then knocks.*) Hey, Burgess . . . (*Saying it as if he expected someone to come immediately to the door.*) Bur . . . gess (*Drawn out, growing irritated.*) Bur . . . gess! (*Rattles the door and knocks on the glass. The street is deserted, but he cocks a look up and down, quickly. Then he begins banging on the door, in short, fierce bursts.)* Bur . . . gess, Bur . . . gess. Goddamn it. *(He is half whispering, half talking in his normal voice.)* Boy, what kinda shit is this? If I don't get back to the joint . . . Hey, man, I know you in there . . . open the goddamn door. *(Begins trying to peep around the blind, but there is no light. Suddenly the door opens abruptly and a short white man in a leopard-skin cloth African dashiki is standing behind the door, looking nervous.)*

BURGESS: Yes?

JOE: Yes? *(Agitated.)* What you mean, yes? You crazy? You know why I'm here, don't you?

BURGESS: Do I?

JOE: You better . . . *(Trying to peep around Burgess, who is looking even more disoriented.)* Look, what's going on? I'm not supposed to have to go through all this with you. In fact, what *is* going on with you, Burgess?

BURGESS: Oh, it's Joe, Joey . . . *(He is looking at him weirdly as if he just recognized him.)* Well, Joey boy, you can see I'm closed . . . can't you?

JOE: Closed? Yeah, I can see you're closed. What's that got to do with me, Burgess? *(Changes swiftly.)* Look, man, if there's something wrong. . . . *(It suddenly occurs to him that something is way off, and he begins to step back from the door. At this point, another man, a slender, tall black man in a blue business suit, impeccably tailored, moves quickly beside* BURGESS, *pointing a gun at Joe.)*

CHARLES: You wanted to come in, come right in, mister! *(JOE is backing up.)* Don't run away, friend. Enter, by all means. *(Waving the gun.)* I insist!

JOE: Burgess, *(Stepping reluctantly into the store.)* what the hell is going on? You know you can get into a world of trouble—

BURGESS: I tried to keep you out, Joe . . . you know I tried.

CHARLES: He did try, I'm a witness. *(JOE looks at him slowly, up and down, then back to* BURGESS.*)* I was all for letting you think there was no one here, but your insistence puzzled me. You seemed to think you were expected. As if it was some private meeting. It occurred to me it might be important for me to know . . . *(Laughs slyly.)* even profitable.

JOE: *(To* BURGESS.*)* Who's this creep, Burgess?

BURGESS: He wants to rob me, but he won't believe there's nothing here to rob . . . except . . .

JOE: The books? *(Squinting his eyes at* CHARLES.*)*

CHARLES: The books. Yes. I wanted to rob him. I still intend to rob him . . . and you too.

BURGESS: How much can you get for books and religious items—the same pitiful living I make. Working at it all the time. Nobody reads, at least not seriously. Even the religious-objects business could be much better.

CHARLES: I agree. That's why I wanted to investigate. The place looked too—I dunno, too well-to-do or something. Ha, and look how plump you are, sir. I'm sure there's something here to acquire. Perhaps your friend here . . .

JOE: Ahh, man, you really outa luck. You wanna rob me, you ain't into much. I ain't got no money, man. Just carfare.

CHARLES: Then what is it you want here? You and the proprietor here are obviously old friends, acquaintances.

JOE: Ahh, man, I like books. He lets me come in late evenings to browse just before he closes.

CHARLES: You don't seem bookish to me.

JOE: How do bookish people seem . . . to you?

CHARLES: Like myself. *(Self-aggrandizingly.)*

BURGESS: But you're a thief.

CHARLES: *(Somewhat nonplussed.)* But I haven't thiefed anything from you . . . yet.

BURGESS: But you have broken in here . . .

CHARLES: I did not. I came in like a regular customer. You welcomed me. You remember, you said, "Good evening, I'm not going to be open long."

BURGESS: Yes, and then you held me here against my will, asking me where I kept my money. Now you're holding both of us with a gun. Those are the actions of a thief.

JOE: Plus, you said a minute ago that you wanted to rob him . . . and me too. Which ain't even rational, since I never carry any money, since I never have any money.

CHARLES: Yes, I want money, I won't lie. I need money, it's really a very practical endeavor. *(He is smiling a cracked little smile, holding his head to one side as if studying the two other men.)* We all, I suppose, need money, but I need a great deal of money. Yes, a great deal . . . and that's not all I need, but money will start it . . .

BURGESS: Then why on earth try to rob a book and religious-object store? There's no money in this. Even if I sold everything in this store at once, I'd still be broke. To rob me is not very practical.

CHARLES: On the surface, what you say seems true. But this was a kind of off night. And I've seen you in the neighborhood. Your store looks profitable to me for some reason. Actually, I was on my way somewhere else to get a really big haul. But I thought I'd stop for a few moments and see the inside of this place and see perhaps if there was what you'd call a pretty penny. You notice, I haven't yet looked in your cash register.

BURGESS: I wondered when you'd get around to it.

JOE: Weird robber. Nothing in this joint but these books and religious shit.

CHARLES: You're probably right, but we'll see. Now, first things first. *(Goes over to the cash register and rings it open, reaches in.)* Ahhh. *(Takes out money, picks up the inside drawer, and grabs a few more bills.)* Ahhh and double ahhh. *(Counting.)* But you're right, only forty-seven dollars total. A few more pennies. A few checks. Forty-seven dollars, not very much, my friend.

BURGESS: I told you that. Times are hard.

JOE: But anything beats a blank, eh?

CHARLES: *(Head swings almost sharply.)* Why'd you say that, friend?

JOE: What? *(Mumbling.)* How I get to be his friend?

CHARLES: You know me?

JOE: What?

CHARLES: "Beats a blank" . . . it's not that funny, you know.

JOE: 'Scuse me, my man, but I'm not sure I know what you're talking about . . .

CHARLES: That's my name . . . you knew it, didn't you? Blank, that's my name. Charlie, Charles Blank. You knew me from before?

JOE: Know you? How could I know you? I never seen you before in my life. That's just a saying. An expression. In the community. Beats a blank, you know, it means anything is better than nothing.

CHARLES: Ohoo, so you're saying I'm nothing. *(Looks half serious, one is not sure.)*

JOE: Look, mister, I'm not saying anything. And definitely nothing negative, certainly nothing negative to you. I . . . just wandered in here . . .

CHARLES: To browse . . . *(Looking at BURGESS.)*

BURGESS: Yes . . . this is a place to browse . . . not just a place crooks come . . .

CHARLES: *(Half mumbling.)* Beats a blank, indeed. *(To JOE.)* So, now empty your pockets, my friend. Let's have your wallet, let me have your treasure.

JOE: How can you really be talking about you need money and robbing me? Man, I told you I don't have anything.

CHARLES: You're probably right. But I want to verify that. Let's have it.

JOE: OK, goddamn. I told you I didn't have nothing . . . (*Takes out his wallet reluctantly and holds it without giving it up.* CHARLES *whips it out of his hand and turns it inside out, various cards and other items falling on the floor.*) Damn, man, why'd you do that . . . ?

CHARLES: Beats a blank, indeed. (*Looking through wallet.*) That wasn't funny to me. (*There are a few dollars in the wallet.*) Thirteen dollars. Oh, boy, let's just say your wallet is . . . empty—empty, get it? Not full. Keep my name out of your mouth.

JOE: Yeah, I'll be glad to. If you wasn't here, I wouldn't even have to think about you! (*Exasperated.*) Hey, man, that's my last thirteen dollars you got there.

CHARLES: Too bad, you said you had nothing. And what's more, I don't believe this is all either of you have. Let's see the real money, friends. I know you (*To* BURGESS.) have got a big stash or even a middle-sized stash around here. I know you're not open all day and took in just forty-seven dollars. Come on, let's have the rest of it.

BURGESS: (*Begins to laugh.*) You're pretty amazing. All the talk about you need more money than most, yet you're knocking off a little bookstore, a little religious-notions store. What grandiose ideas. You're not based in reality too much, my friend. Not at all. How much could I make selling books?

JOE: Yeah.

CHARLES: You want me to turn this place upside down? Dump all the books and holiness paraphernalia on the floor. I am Charlie Blank. I need money, lots of money. And I'm willing to start here. But I'm thorough and I don't like to be lied to. More money now, get it up, my friends. You too, darker brother. All money must be made to show up so I can take it in my hand and depart. I, Charlie Blank, demand all your money.

JOE: What? Man, you not well. Thirteen bucks is all you gonna get from me, unless you pawn my clothes.

CHARLES: We'll see. (*Pauses.*) Well, friend book dealer? More money or books all over the place? Huge loss for you, you'll never recover. Give up the cash, my friend. Give it up to Charles Blank, who needs it. Who needs other things, but the cash will do for a start.

(The phone begins to ring. An almost imperceptible glance between JOE *and* BURGESS.*)*

CHARLES: The phone at this time of night? Your wife, bookseller, wondering why you're lingering?
BURGESS: I dunno. Perhaps.
CHARLES: Don't you want to answer it?
BURGESS: I'm not normally here at this time. There's no reason to.

(Again, the quickly exchanged looks between JOE *and* BURGESS. CHARLES *picks it up. Listening, he shoves the mouthpiece near* BURGESS'S *lips. We hear the voice on the other end of the phone.)*

VOICE: Burgess . . . Burgess . . .

*(*CHARLES *gestures with the phone for* BURGESS *to talk into it.)*

BURGESS: Yes, yes, this is Burgess.
VOICE: What the hell's wrong? Look, where's Joe . . . I'm waiting here.
BURGESS: Yes, I know, we're wrapping it up, we're wrapping it up now . . .
VOICE: Well, tell Joe to hurry, will you? I've got things to do.

(Click of phone. CHARLES *stands looking between* JOE *and* BURGESS.*)*

CHARLES: You see, I knew it. Something is going on. What's going on, gentlemen? You see how my elaborate instinct works. I, Charlie Blank, who needs money, more money than anyone. I could sense something else was happening in here. Books and religious objects. Forty-seven dollars. Beats a blank. You'll find out, as you get to know me, that Charles Blank is no fool.
JOE: Oh, boy. *(Thoroughly exasperated.)*
BURGESS: My goodness, fellow—
CHARLES: Charles Blank . . .
BURGESS: Charles Blank . . .
JOE: I never heard of that. A stickup man who gives people his name like a commercial.
CHARLES: Don't interrupt the white man. Don't you know your place?

JOE: Yes, it's away from here. (*Turns as if to leave.*)

CHARLES: Don't do that. There's no reason to complicate things. (*There is a hint of ice in his words.*) I might want to skin frisk you.

JOE: Oh, shit.

CHARLES: Now continue. Uh, what's your name, store owner?

BURGESS: Burgess . . .

CHARLES: What's your full name, I've given you mine.

BURGESS: Samuel Burgess.

CHARLES: Sam Burgess (*Laughing.*) Nice, nice. What were you saying, Sam Burgess?

BURGESS: I wanted to know why you are prolonging this petty thievery. There's nothing else here for you.

CHARLES: I told you, I must have a great deal of money to meet my requirements.

JOE: Banks are probably better able to fulfill your requirements. We can't. We was hoping you'd get that message.

CHARLES: I sense there is money in here, somewhere. I want it.

BURGESS: There is no money here. None. Only books and religious objects. You don't understand the language or what? Are the words too complicated for you? Are you some kind of dropout? Perhaps the public schools twisted you in this manner. Or perhaps it was loud music. Loud colors. Not enough oxygen to the brain perhaps, rather typical in some cases. I won't vote for you. You can't move into my neighborhood. Not and leave those gnawed skulls in front of my house for my dream girl wife to see and be made afraid. This is not *Halloween 6* or *Rocky 12*, where the hero finally *becomes* a *schwartze*. You're making me sad, sad for the future of the world. (*Stops, panting, as if out of breath. The two others eyeball him warily.* BURGESS *looks up suddenly, adding.*) And that precisely is why affirmative action is a fraud, and undemocratic, I might add. (*Pops chest with his fist and shouts.*) Heavy!

JOE: What? (*Astonished, mouth dropping open.*)

CHARLES: I understand all of it. All of it. But I'm not accepting any budget cuts. Rant and rave if you will. I'll be a member of this gang yet. I want to enter those hallowed halls being saluted by music. I'll not retreat because you impugn my character and imply name calling.

JOE: (*Looks from one to the other, not clear what is going on.*) What happened? Did I plug something in—maybe in the wrong hole or something? (*Looking from one to the other.*)

Mr. Burgess, uh, if by chance there's any money, why not give it to the gentleman so he can be on his way? (*At* BURGESS.) And so you can be on your way. (*Raises hand.*) And so, mostly, I can be on my way. I haven't even been home from work. (*Says it before he knows it, stiffens, then peeps at* CHARLES, *hoping he hasn't attached any significance to the statement.*)

CHARLES: Yes. Yes, exactly. Work. Yes. What is your work, colored guy?

JOE: I'm a . . . uh . . . communications specialist.

CHARLES: Communications specialist. Hmm, communication of what?

JOE: Information. (*Still eyeing* BURGESS *weirdly.*)

CHARLES: You're some civil service creep, I gather. (JOE *nods guiltily.*) Hmmm. (*Looking as if he's figuring something out.*) And you don't understand. (*Gesturing at* BURGESS *and himself.*) Naive guy. A naive colored guy. I used to know a song about a naive colored guy . . . we're communicating, communicator, Sam Burgess, and me. At a higher level, that's all. We're out beyond the *New York Times*. Out beyond the *New York Review of Books*.

BURGESS: Beyond *Commentary*. Though Norman Podhoretz's teeth are my style, filed into oblong gadgets for mashing pages together, it doesn't matter, the name. We remember the struggles in the desert, the sand blowing in our nose and mouths. The grim sun choking in the sand, red and crazy. We swore revenge crossing the Nile. Our spears held high. We were half crazy, really, screaming and tinted red by the dying sun. We swore revenge.

CHARLES: I'll be sworn in with all of you looking. I'll raise my hand and be remembered as the guy who dud it. Not did it or do it, or got it done. But dud it. The way past. (*Holds up the gun.*) This is civilization as we know it. It sings and writes poems. It paints and dances. (*Waving the gun.*) Filmmaker, historian, homemaker. Believe me, millions will cheer my joining the great body. Charles Blank, they'll say, they'll call on television, telegraph, satellites. Charles Blank, it's a hell of a thing you've dud. Got the money. Got the accomplishment, they'll cheer. My campaign slogan. Got the money. Got the accomplishment!

(JOE *stares at* CHARLES *as if he's truly terrified by his craziness.*)

BURGESS: (*Suddenly lurches forward, his chin close to*

CHARLES's *chest.*) I'm Hyskos! A fisher king! We crushed your empire before. And then the choking sun disappeared.

CHARLES: History streaming into a tunnel. Blocked by madness, mindlessness. When I gathered into the fold. The money scattered at my feet. Dollar bills floating up the aisles on the sea of blood that brings me to my installation ceremonies. You see, then I'll be Ishmael. I will have survived the criticism of the insane and made my peace with Shirley Temple.' Then you'll let me tap dance down the stairs with the cameras rolling. Then you'll let my teeth be seen as white, I know the game.

(JOE *is looking from one to the other, is trying now to back out the door.*)

BURGESS: (*Suddenly begins beating his chest.*) Heavy! Heavy! Heavy! I claim science, art, music, logic, history. I've civilized everything.

CHARLES: (*Whirling around toward* JOE.) Stop it, poor sap. I'm about to be integrated into the power elite. And you want to retreat. *(Shoving gun in* JOE's *direction.)* Give me money. Colored have money. Colored have a middle class and an upper class. Colored have money. I don't know many these days I'm running so much. Getting money. Give me money.

JOE: (*Points at* BURGESS, *stopping his movement.*) I'm broke, my man, broke. *(Still contemplating exit.)*

BURGESS: We swore revenge. Even now. There's tall buildings and parking lots. (*Hits chest.*) Heavy! So my friend Joe can tell you. *(Looks at* JOE, *laughing.)* Tell him, Joe!

JOE: Tell him what? Somebody needs to tell me something. Mr. Burgess, what's going on? You know this guy?

CHARLES: That was my question to you.

BURGESS: (*Laughing at question.*) Do I know him? Yes, he's a thief who wants to raid my stash of books and symbols.

CHARLES: Don't mislead your browsing friend. I want money, pure and simple.

JOE: You both talk strange, it seems to me. I don't understand you, but you understand you. But, Mr. Burgess, Sam, you know there's certain other considerations. *(Nodding at phone.)* If there's more money to give this gentleman, let's give it to him so he can go off into the sunset.

BURGESS: Mr. Blank and I have reached some sort of understanding. We don't agree, except I think we are on the same wave length. Right, Mr. Blank?

CHARLES: I am after money, that's all. Your name is Joe, I've heard. What's your full name?

JOE: It's Seth.

CHARLES: Joe Seth. Strange name. Where's the money, Mr. Seth? I want to be initiated into the power elite of money spenders. Of expensive watches and cashmere. Of fine liqueurs and wines. Of beautiful automobiles. Of travels and private islands. Diamonds. Rubies. Tasteful, expensive, absolutely necessary fantasies.

JOE: Yes, I get that message, but why here? There's no money here. I'll turn out my pockets, take off my clothes. You want to skin search me, look up my ass if you want to, nothing up there but bowels at the ready. But see (*Glancing at watch.*) I've got . . . to go. I've got someplace to be. Mr. Burgess, if there's something you can do? (BURGESS *is smiling wider and wider. Now he's doing different poses like some warrior king being interviewed on television.*)

BURGESS: I can do most things. These books and religious symbols, they're heavy. (*Punches chest, stands at attention.*)

CHARLES: Sam Burgess, I see you posturing. I know the real deal. You're sending me the message of maintain your poverty, Blank, maintain it. That's the message.

(BURGESS *nods his head.*)

JOE: Hey, there's no money around here. We got to wind this thing up, Mr. Burgess, Sam. We've got to wind this thing up. (*Trying to point at watch again.*) I think maybe you're getting carried away in this weird conversation, Mr. Burgess. There's some important stuff I know you've got to do too. Right?

CHARLES: That watch, here, let me see it. Is it expensive?

JOE: No, man. (*Not wanting to give it up.*) It's a cheap Timex, that's all. Ain't worth nothing.

CHARLES: Give it up. (JOE *hands it over.*) Timex. (*Shakes it. Then suddenly throws it to the floor.*) Cheap shit. I hate cheap shit. You notice how tastefully attired I am. Muted colors, good materials. All my suits are tailored. Plus I go to all the right places. Piano bars in muted colors and sip cognac.

JOE: Hey, man, why you do that to my watch? Goddamn. You take my goddamn lousy ass thirteen dollars, now you fuck up my goddamn lousy ass Timex. Why you so hard on me, Blank?

CHARLES: Don't take it personally, Joe, I hate cheap shit.

JOE: Mr. Burgess, please get this guy out of here, if you can. I'm gonna lose my job.

CHARLES: Your job. I thought you were off work, you civil service slave. Was that a lie you told me?

JOE: No, but, I had some other things to do . . .

CHARLES: Yes . . .

BURGESS: There's no money for you. Rest at the outskirts of the frontier. History will not bring you to the heights you aspire to. Only fantasy. And get this, both of you are black. My friend here, Joe, is black. And the description of you, Mr. Blank, is black.

CHARLES: No money is the message.

BURGESS: If you get a job you'll get money. (*Laughs.*)

JOE: I've got to get out of here. Right away, Mr. Burgess. Mr. Blank. Let's terminate our business. Please, Mr. Blank, there are other, better places to rob. Banks. Vaults. Armored cars. Diamond-cutting operations. Concerts.

CHARLES: You don't understand that this is a confrontation, not just a robbery. The fat white man there is trying to keep me out of the power elite. He rules and I rule, but he has money and I do not. Give me money and this confrontation will cease. You want to go home, Joe. Go home, but give me money.

BURGESS: We swore revenge for the chains. Moving those rocks in the desert to build the pyramids. I ordered the libraries burnt at Alexandria. I ordered the nose blown off the sphinx. Remember the hold of the ship in the dark when you were inside chained and stinking? I owned the ship. I hired guys to whip guys like you. And that's not bragging, mind you, 'cause I love you, regardless of race, creed, or color. I was a Cub Scout when I find the diamond fields. When I stand at the Cape and see the richness and the savages unable to defend it.

CHARLES: So you don't remember how I caught the niggers and sold them to you? You're lying now again. You're claiming to have literally come in like Alex Haley said and took us off. (*Shouting at* JOE). The fool! He wants to pretend ancient honor and glory and deny me mine. I have had a history of glory and honor. I was the king that sold this stupid brother here to you. Don't deny it.

BURGESS: So you stand in my shop, books and religious objects, and wave a gun. Isn't that a violation? Isn't that a violation of the treaties? You want a race war?

CHARLES: I want money.

JOE: I would like to . . . (*Shouts.*) do my job!

CHARLES: Tell me what you want here, why you came. Otherwise, maybe I'll kill you. Not just rob you, but kill you.

BURGESS: So you want race war? Savages.

CHARLES: You were in the forest, painted blue, a cannibal in the bogs of Angle-land. I have a book showing you yourself, Sam Burgess, with a foot in your mouth.

BURGESS: You still eat people. I produced a film of you, my friend, with a fat black stomach, dazed at a swimming pool. When you were murdering niggers, no less. There were mountains of them, I remember.

CHARLES: Well, give me some respect, then. If you know what I'm capable of, the mountains of them. Was it as big a mountain as yours, I ask you? (*Smiling.*) Not for sheer competition, but for your own information. Tell us, was it as big?

BURGESS: How could it be, and I am the master of the Big Bang. The AB. The HB. The NB. The Remove Everything For All Times B, which I'm still working on.

JOE: (*Absolutely dumbfounded, but trying to get out, inserting his plaint. Shouting.*) Mr. Burgess, Mr. Blank, I've got to get out of here. Can I go? I don't have any money. Mr. Burgess, you're fucking up my deal. You're gonna make me lose my job, and you're gonna lose your deal too, Mr. Burgess. (BURGESS *and* CHARLES *now seem to be doing a slow pose and posture dance, lunging at each other without really moving, swaying back and forth, toward each other and away, lunging and swaying back.*)

CHARLES: I have an ancient history of murder and madness too.

BURGESS: I have an ancient glorious history of murder and madness.

CHARLES: But my ancient glorious history is ancienter and more glorious. Leakey places us five million years ago.

BURGESS: (*Still swaying back and forth at each other.*) Yes, you are the missing link. (*Laughs, slobbering.*) The missing link.

CHARLES: The transition from apes to men would have been impossible if you had to do the job.

BURGESS: Yes, you're ancient. And dark, that's why. But the bringing of high civilization was *my* gift. (*Leaps straight up.*) Mine alone!

CHARLES: It was I who brought in the human being, who had the evolutionary style and drive to move past animal to human. Now I see I'll have to do it again!

JOE: Mr. Burgess, let me have the stuff so I can get out of here!

(*Abashed now he has let something slip out he shouldn't.*) I mean, let me go.

CHARLES: What stuff, my friend, Joe Seth? What stuff? (*Looks at* BURGESS.) You see how ancient and glorious I am. The pygmies I killed near Burundi, did you hear about that? Shit, and wait till I get the goddam AB, NB et cetera, you ain't seen nothing. Wait till you read about that explosion on the front pages of *Ebony*! First rich black guy, ancient black historical black guy with the powbowbang!!! You think Vaseline is the only grease, don't you, white boy? You think that goddamn *Life* magazine can outlast *Jet*, don't you? Afro Sheen will smash Wildroot cream oil. No one will want baloney when they've wrapped my sausages around their teeth. Goddamn it, I'm gonna be rich and very, very mean. (*Turning to* JOE.) What stuff, Joe? What're you talking about, and no lies or I'll take your pants off and shoot you. Throw you in the middle of the street, down near where the fine foxes are, with no pants. They'll see you shot and embarrassed. That's the way you'll be remembered—bare assed and blown away. All for a . . . what? Joe?

JOE: Mr. Burgess. (*Gesturing at phone.*) Mr. Burgess, you've wasted time talking to this guy. Now we're in trouble.

BURGESS: We? I am never in trouble. (*Pops chest.*) Heavy!

CHARLES: What stuff, Joe?

BURGESS: (*Goes into wallet and pulls out several large bills.*) Here, you missing link. Here's three, four hundred dollars, be gone. I've had enough sport for the evening.

JOE: You mean you never even looked in his wallet? Damn, what a poor ass crook.

CHARLES: (*Snatches the money, counts it.*) Give me all the money in the wallet.

BURGESS: No, there's too much money in there. There's thousands of dollars in it, you wouldn't know what to do with it. You'd do something stupid. Make a bomb. Another pogrom. A ghetto somewhere. You'd screw up something. Three or four hundred is enough for you. (*Now* CHARLES *turns to* JOE. JOE *doesn't understand why* CHARLES *doesn't insist on the money.*)

CHARLES: What stuff, Joe? You thought I forgot about "the stuff" you blurted out, but the stuff, Joe, what is it . . . ?

JOE: What? Three or four hundred . . . (*Looking at* BURGESS *who's patting his fat wallet and stuffing it back into his pocket.*) Hey, what kind of crook are you? You want to know about my . . . stuff? Some fantasy. Yet that guy's got a wallet full of dough. No offense, Mr. Burgess, Sam buddy, but there's a murky cloud over the light I'm seeing and what the hell . . .

CHARLES: There are things you don't understand, you're right . . . leave it at that. Like "beats a blank," dumb shit like that . . . like this gun . . . like this robbery . . . like your white friend there.

BURGESS: He means he can't understand why you just settled for the three hundred I peeled off. (*Lazily yet arrogant.*) Or was it four? (*Laughs.*) Charles Blank can't tell you because if he does, he won't get the prize I've got him up for. (*To* CHARLES *suddenly.*) You knew that, didn't you, Charlesie, that I'd put your name up for the prize. That line about how you survived the rule of savages, I liked it, boy. I liked it. I also—and this is grudging praise—liked the way you wouldn't settle for the forty-seven dollars. (*Laughs.*) Yes, indeed, I liked it. I said to myself, Sam boy, that kid's got the makings of a testicle or two, that's for sure.

CHARLES: (*To* JOE.) You see. You didn't know that, did you, the respect I engender? It's my whole style. And what I know. What I remember. What I want to be. All that's taken into consideration. You thought I was just a well-dressed ne'er-do-well, didn't you? My name goes back in history. Now, about the stuff, Joe? What is it and where is it?

JOE: And you ain't gonna pursue my man's loot over there?

CHARLES: He gave a brilliant thesis as to why I can't deal with it. You hear it. Didn't you understand what he said? Didn't you sense his determination not to be robbed? You want to see slides of Hiroshima? You know who made the yellow stars for those ill-fated aliens to be identified before they were snuffed? Our friend there. This bookshop, this store-house of the metaphysical, all dangerous stuff. You've seen the books (*Snatches a few up and tosses them at* JOE.) *Death Stalks the Good Guy* or *Diamonds and Pussy.* What about *Naked Passion Jogs with the Disco Espionage Gang*? How's this, *Jazz, Another White Creation*? You see the criminal brutality. The soulless animal illogic. What about this? *I Eat Pork and Am Proud to Be a Devil.* Doesn't that make you shudder? What about this, *What Shit Will Be Like After the Big Explosion*? Terrifying tribal stuff. And all white, white as the coldest of all things. (*Shudders.*) Whew. (*Now turns back to initial intention.*) What stuff, Joe?

JOE: You won't take the rest of this guy's money, but you want to beat me out of some imaginary stuff. This is a wig, a nut-

out. Mr. Burgess . . . (*The phone rings again.*) Mr. Burgess
. . . you know who that is and why they keep calling? Let's
get this guy out of here. You seem to be in control of him
or something.

CHARLES: Is that what you got out of this, that he's in control
of me? Why? Because I don't take the rest of the money?

JOE: You said you wanted money.

CHARLES: That was then. Now I want the stuff you
got . . .

BURGESS: He doesn't have any stuff, I've got the stuff. He's
just a messenger. So it's my stuff, not his. And you can't
take it for the same reason you can't get the thousands,
maybe even millions I've got in my wallet. You wouldn't
know how to use it.

CHARLES: Is it a naked fight you want? A return to savagery.
I smell that savagery odor. Animal odor. That's why I
became a human being in the first place, to get away from
that odor.

BURGESS: No, it's because you didn't know what to do with
your tail.

JOE: Are you going to answer the phone?

(*The rings have gotten stylized. They ring. Then stop. Then
double ring. Sometimes they seem syncopated.*)

JOE: Ow, the old man's signaling.

CHARLES: Signaling.

BURGESS: It doesn't matter. There's nothing else here now.
You heard you were going to get the award. The prize. I'll
arrange for it to be made at the U.N. It'll be big, and gold.
It'll say, "To the Lone Survivor." You can dress up. It'll be
formal. It'll be well advertised. It'll signal human importance
is coming your way. You'll find doors opened to you everywhere. You can wear a top hat. A cane. You can drink
wine even while you receive the prize. Everyone will cheer.
There'll be plenty of cheers. Everywhere you go, they'll
cheer you. They'll call you up morning and night and cheer.

JOE: (*Picks up phone.*) Yes, yes, it's Joe. Yes, I'm here, been
here, but Burgess is acting weird.

CHARLES: I could kill you, you know, take off your pants. The
fine women will see you in the square, dead with a shriveled-
up little Johnson. They'll laugh.

JOE: I came as I was supposed to, but Burgess is acting weird.

BURGESS: (*Comes over and snatches phone.*) Yes, it's Burgess.

Yes, I'll resolve the problems immediately. Just settle down. Settle down, I say! It's coming. Don't get excited. Fail you? Look, don't you think it's the other way? Just settle down and hope you remember your role in all this. (*Hangs up phone.*)

JOE: Did somebody else get on the phone?

BURGESS: Somebody else? No. It was the person you spoke to.

JOE: Really? Mr. Burgess, you amaze me.

BURGESS: I never amaze myself. You are ignorant, that's all, cigarette lighters amaze you. The *Downbeat* awards. Grammys. Oscars. All-star teams. They all amaze you. *New York Times* editorials. Even Charles Blank, who is about to leave now, amazes you.

CHARLES: The stuff, you think you can just waltz out of this without my knowing what you're up to?

BURGESS: The stuff is heroin, of course. And this is a nigger taking it to a customer.

CHARLES: You sell heroin.

BURGESS: (*Laughing.*) Sell it? No, I give it away, of course. I sell books and religious objects. I give away real dope. At least to the people I deal with. I would sell it to you. In fact, I sell it to you now, don't I? No, to somebody else, who sells it to you. The international patriotic fund sells it to you, is that right?

CHARLES: I want money. I'm not addicted to heroin. I'm addicted to money. I want money.

JOE: Burgess, why're you telling this guy . . . ?

BURGESS: Why not, he told us his name. He revealed his innermost plans. So I'm telling him ours.

JOE: Hey, but I want something to say about that . . .

CHARLES: You're not even civil service. Just a carrier through dark nights of the downtown, to perforate your fellow ghetto dwellers with the nasty stuff. You traitorous bastard, selling other niggers white man's dope. You should be killed. I should kill you.

JOE: What? I don't sell no dope. You don't know nothing about me. I just carry it and drop it off to a guy. I don't sell no dope.

BURGESS: Don't mind Charles, Joe, he thought you were getting into his stuff, that's all. Charles sells it to niggers, right, Charles?

CHARLES: Of course, but it's black dope. "Do for Self" is my motto, black dope, prayed over by some black words. We say the holy words, money and accomplishment. We summon the ancient gods. We dance. We murmur the name of the one god who resides in northern Nigeria, and the dope becomes clean and black and has a different function. It is magical, black dope. It fills you full of grand vision and asymmetries. Bones come out of nothing and are thrown and tell us things. Computers burn and the bones dance and whistle. The tunes then are written for Millie Jackson on her way to South Africa. And the black dope lights a path in the sky for her to descend. The white dope would give you Frank Sinatra, you see the difference?

JOE: What? Man, you crazy. Burgess, gimme the thing and let me make it. OK, my man, Mr. Blank, let me go out into the night and do my lowly delivery number and cut you dudes loose, OK?

CHARLES: You going to tell me who the dope's for, at least?

BURGESS: Do I ask you for the names of the people you sell to?

CHARLES: You snotty 'cause you think it's just ghetto types. You don't know. I tell you a name, you tell me a name.

BURGESS: It'll be amusing . . .

JOE: Mr. Burgess, gimme the number, lemme split . . .

CHARLES: OK?

BURGESS: OK. You first.

CHARLES: Amin.

BURGESS: Truman.

CHARLES: Ummm. Nice. But contemporary. No old stuff. Contemporary. Mobutu.

BURGESS: John Mitchell. Martha Mitchell.

CHARLES: Contemporary.

BURGESS: That's contemporary.

JOE: Mr. Burgess, please, I've got to go.

CHARLES: Shaddup. This is serious. Who's he taking the stuff to, is what I want to know. Some big guy?

BURGESS: A big guy, but not so big . . . a small big guy . . .

CHARLES: Hey, I got the Ayatollah, Louie SuperKing, all kinds of holinesses and master teachers and those in touch with various gods, and spooks and spirits and *orishas, loas*, saints, vision givers and lightning and thunder dudes. Who's he taking the stuff to?

BURGESS: You won't settle for my Gerald Ford disclosure? Spiro Agnew doesn't interest you?

CHARLES: No more than Arap Moi or Seaga interests you.

BURGESS: That does interest me, really.

CHARLES: Who, then?

BURGESS: A nobody, really. It'll disappoint you. It's Al Hag, that's all.

CHARLES: What, that small-time piano-playing junkie . . .

JOE: (*Mouth drops open.*) Mr. Burgess, what are you doing . . . the general ain't gonna dig this—

CHARLES: Aha, not the bebopper, the goddamn . . . what is he now . . . secretary of your snakes.

BURGESS: Yeah, small potatoes. You caught me on a bad night. The weekends we get to actors and their wives.

(JOE *covers his face with his hands.*)

BURGESS: (*Reaching under his counter for the dope. It is wrapped in a flag. He tosses it to* JOE.) Two pounds of pure shit, boy. Pee-You-Are-EEE. Two pounds pure stuff. Ahh, it warms me to see the boy take it off into the night, knowing the warm flow up the guy's sleeve. The red mark where the syringe goes. The shit flowing warmly, warmly. Carrying the info inside him, you see, up into the cortex, into the brain pan, into the idea box, the shit flows, so that when Al opens his trap, yours truly comes out. Funny thing, like when he calls up and talks to me on the phone it's like me listening to myself. Very amusing. But the shit flows warmly up into the mouth box, the tongue room, the image maker. It's my shit, my words flowing. Like I'm in charge here or Bomb the Iraqi reactor, destroy Lebanon, great. I watch TV and laugh at myself. Myself laughing at myself. It's great. Best show on TV.

CHARLES: That's why the only shit I can get is *Soul Trane.* But wait 'till you see my twenty-four-hour disco in pictures channel. It'll put your shit to shame.

JOE: I'm going, Mr. Burgess. The general going to be warm as hell.

BURGESS: Tell the general to shut up and shoot up, or I'll send him a hot shot!

(*Now there is a* tap-tap-tap *at the door and the phone rings again in its strange hypnotic syncopation. Even though it's ringing, we hear a voice chortling, "I want my dope, I want my dope, I want my dope" like a deranged infant, a thirty-foot-tall infant with an atomic bomb clutched in its kiddish mitt, baffled by reality. It cries and wheezes.*

BURGESS *and* CHARLES *are in their jungle motion dance,*

though it is clear that CHARLES*'s gun is a blank.* BURGESS *puts
his mouth on it, and they sway, vibrate like a very slow jungle
pas de deux. But soon it is clear that it is, indeed,* BURGESS*'s
dance. That he is directing it. The knocking on the door goes
on.*)

JOE: Mr. Burgess, Sam, should I open the door? I've got to
　　go. You hear the phone. My God, aesthetics at a time like
　　this.
BURGESS: Since I am George Balanchine and Nijinsky, I say
　　peep outside and see who it is. Since you are my messenger,
　　I could call you Muhammad were I ironic or cruel. But
　　instead I will call you Cassius, noticing your lean and hungry
　　drool.
CHARLES: You can't get away until I get in. I am the tar baby
　　and you are no doubt Farmer Brown.
BURGESS: Do you care for hors d'oeuvres? I am the creator of
　　caviar and crêpes suzettes. What about you, what have you
　　done?
CHARLES: I've done everything you have, older, crazier, mad-
　　der, bloodier. The Anheuser Busch book of kings and
　　queens. The Nabisco Black Writers Hall of Fame. There's a
　　hall of fame now attached to the real one. For Old-Time
　　Black Athletes. All of whatever there is, we got and had.
JOE: (*Peeping under the shade on the window.*) It's some black
　　people out there. A man, a woman, and a young boy.
BURGESS: Huh? Do they look harmless?
JOE: Yeah, harmless enough. I'll find out.
CHARLES: Be careful, Joe, nothin' to disturb our little confron-
　　tation here, you know. Amidst the books and symbols.
BURGESS: Droll.

(JOE *opens the door and the black family comes in. The man
is tall and dressed in casual clothes, his wife also, the child
almost as tall as they but young and rangy, still to bulk up.*)

FRED: Thank you. We need some help. We're passing through
　　this city and we're looking for some of our relatives who live
　　around here somewhere. (*All three have stepped inside.*) It
　　looks like it's clouding up. I just thought perhaps you could
　　help us. Here's this card with the number on it. This is the
　　street we're on, but there's no such number.
JOE: Relatives, well, you're in the right city. All our relatives
　　must be here.

MAL: (*Spying the bulky flag-wrapped package of dope, draws his mother's attention to it.*)

HARRIET: Perhaps it's a different section of the city we're to go to. This is the first time we've been to this city.

JOE: Hmm. This is the street, all right.

(BURGESS *and* CHARLES *are not quiet, they are mumbling more softly than before, rocking and lunging, but they have modified it so it looks as if they are discussing books, having a friendly cocktail party tête-à-tête. Occasionally the phone will ring, with its staccato syncopation.*)

JOE: Mr. Burgess, this number 999 Allover Street. That's this street, all right, but it doesn't go that high. This is in the 600's, this store.

BURGESS: 999 was probably torn down, urban renewal.

CHARLES: I could have made money off that, for instance. Why wasn't I cut in?

BURGESS: I know for a fact you were.

FRED: You mean the house is gone. Torn down.

JOE: Looks like it. (*Phone chirps up.*) Mr. Burgess, I'll be going now. It's very late.

HARRIET: Oh, my goodness, the house is gone. We should have known when we didn't get a response from the letter. Fred, what'll we do?

FRED: I'll call Margaret and get the information. She'll know where those Turners have moved. May I use the phone, sir?

BURGESS: Of course, please do. Excuse my aloofness, my name is Burgess. I am the proprietor of this establishment. My friend Joe you've met. This gentleman here is Mr. Charles Blank, a (*Pause.*) colleague.

CHARLES: (*Smiles and does a small bow in gratitude.*) How gracious. S.B. How do you do, folks?

FRED: I'm Fred Swings. My wife, Harriet, and son, Mal.

JOE: Swings? Really, that's a coincidence, ain't it. I got people in my family, somewhere named Swings. My name is Seth, Joe Seth. (*Looking frantically at watch. Also, now outside, the rain begins to plummet down.*) Wow, that storm. And I've got to go out in it. I could have been gone by now, except for certain mad interruptions. And interruptions of interruptions. Not meaning you all. Just an unusual train of events.

CHARLES: But you learned something. You browsed a bit longer. Found out some things.

JOE: Found out why you ain't got all the money you need, in your chosen profession, that's for sure. I'm wondering why you even in the business. (*Holds up hand.*) But I won't press it . . . I've got an errand. Nice to meet you Mr. and Mrs. Swings and you too, Mal, I've got to go.

HARRIET: (*Laughing lightly.*) Mr. Seth, before you go, a question. I hope it's not too personal or prying. But my son and I, he first wondered, what is in that perfectly fascinating-looking package wrapped up in the flag?

BURGESS: Hah, books and religious objects.

CHARLES: Money.

JOE: It's heroin for General Al Hag, the Secretary of Snakes of the United States of America.

(*The three* SWINGS *look at each other in disbelief. Then suddenly without warning the door is slammed open and in comes a man dressed in a general's uniform. It is Hag.*)

HAG: I came myself. (*Breathless, flushed, coming down with junky sickness, early stages.*) I was getting sick. (*Pushes up the uniform sleeve.*) I was getting sick, so I disguised myself. Slipped away from my aides and came down. I thought I could trust you, Joe. And you, Burgess, you've made my life miserable. You were the responsible man on this caper. What I'm doing is dangerous, on the face of it. Gimme that package, Joe.

(JOE *gives it up but tries to indicate others in the store.*)

BURGESS: This is very dangerous, A.H., you don't know how dangerous.

CHARLES: I knew I picked the right place to come. The correct ambience. (*To the* SWINGS.) What you'd call vibes. Don't worry about me, anybody. I'm gonna make some money before I die.

JOE: Never more than three or four hundred dollars, though.

HAG: Who are these people in here, Burgess? Our spot of rendezvous has become a train station. Perhaps it's become a church? Are these (*Pointing toward the family and* CHARLES.) some kind of singing group?

FRED: Singing . . .

HARRIETT: No, we just lost our way.

FRED: We were looking for some relatives. We wanted to use the phone.

MAL: Are you Al Hag?

JOE: Look, why don't you all go over and use the phone?

BURGESS: General, come into the back room with me.

CHARLES: There's money in this. I could dramatize it. Put it to music. I could do a series, soaps. I could rob—

BURGESS: You have your quota, Blank. All these people are under my protection, as it were. Of course, the family (*Nodding toward the* SWINGS.) after they leave here, that's somethin' else again. (*Gruffly to* HAG.) Come along, General.

HAG: (*Is absorbed in unwrapping the flag. He gets it unwrapped. It is a huge pile of heroin.*) I've got my spike with me. But, Joe, you promised me a new set of works.

JOE: (*Embarrassed and taken aback by all this going on in the presence of the family.*) But, General, shouldn't we wait till these good people make their phone call and are gone on their merry way?

HAG: Get outa the way. I can't depend on anyone but myself. In this crazy world. You gotta do everything. You can't even run a country anymore. You have to *be* the whole country. Imagine. (*He's moving toward the back but scooping off some of the scag to shoot.*) Joe, how's this stuff? I hope you didn't try to burn me, Burgess.

BURGESS: General, you're making a spectacle of yourself.

HAG: Boy, there would have been a real spectacle if I had got sick at the goddamn press conference. Throw up all over Roger Mudd!

MAL: Mama, that really is heroin he's got there? I always wondered what went on in these religious stores. I've seen that guy on television.

HARRIET: Mal, please. Let your father make the phone call and let's get outa here. In fact, Fred (FRED's *dialing and watching the proceedings.*) hurry it up, will you? There must be some other place to call Margaret from. Come on, Fred, let's get outa here, please.

FRED: (*Dialing, listening to phone ring.*) Margaret, yeah, it's Fred. Yeah, we're on Allover Street and can't find the Turners' house. . . . No . . .

MAL: Daddy, Mama sez we oughta get outta this crazy house.

FRED: Where, they moved where? (*Talking as if he can't hear, still watching Hag and others and fascinated by it.*)

HARRIET: Yo-hoo, Fred, let's go please!

JOE: (*Over his shoulder while helping* BURGESS *take* HAG *into a back room.* HAG *is still scooping up scag, and now trying to get his works out.*) Yes, Mrs. Swings, you all probably should get in the wind.

BURGESS: General, you're acting a little too wild, you know.

HAG: Wild? I'm getting sick, Sam, you *sabe* sick, throw up, sweaty sick?

HAG: People? Bah, messenger gibberish. I am everybody. Whoever is not me does not exist.

JOE: Burgess here.

HAG: In a way, he's me too.

BURGESS: Pompous dope friend, you're me!

HAG: (*Puffing up.*) You're me!

CHARLES: (*Gesturing toward* BURGESS *and* HAG.) I'm y'all!

JOE: All y'all, nowhere.

(*Family fixed, torn between laughter and sense of danger.*)

HAG: (*To* JOE.) Except you're *my* messenger. And I don't even need you. Damned affirmative action. Didn't need any colored messenger. But (*Seeming to "nod" a little.*) now they got Messenger Nobel prize. Messenger Pulitzer. Messenger fellowships. All got to go to somebody.

HAG: (*To* CHARLES.) You see how wild they get, these various messengers? How independent? Remember that.

(CHARLES *almost salutes.*)

JOE: General, it's too public.

HAG: Everything is under my control.

BURGESS: You're not high enough. That's the problem. (*Laughs.*) You're not even you!

(*Family looking at* JOE *and the others and at each other.*)

HAG: No, I'm not high enough. I've got to get higher than this. So I can be everybody. (*To* JOE.) Right, messenger?

BURGESS: (*To* CHARLES.) Messenger to messenger relationship. (*Suddenly to* HAG.) OK, OK, make it short. (*Half mumbling.*) Foolish junky, you're getting carried away. I am the Man—the *main* man. You're just on the main line.

(*Scene becomes electric boogie-ish.* HAG, BURGESS, CHARLES, *and* JOE *are like break-dancing "robots" rap-running. The family sways in "slow motion" counterpart during this.*)

BURGESS: You're just the button I mash. That's why your nose is Red, Button man. And you (*To* JOE.) the button's button . . . (*To* CHARLES.) and you just the usurping aspirant to my finger would be pusher chief . . . *soi disant me be-er*, a petty villain, barber monger.

CHARLES: But I can pat my feet
to the funky beat of your funky house falling
in the funky street

BURGESS: It fall with y'all.
(*Minstrel gestures.*) You inside
Can't go nowhere you here for life
(*In contrast.*) We're locked together by mutual villainy . . . and contracts

JOE: Damn. Put all of every them in place! My cue, I guess, to finally space. (*The idea surprises him—he likes it.*)

HAG: (*Draws himself up as if to fight. Moans suddenly.*) Ohhh, I'm gonna get sick.

CHARLES: (*Also drawing himself up to resist* BURGESS. BURGESS *quickly draws his wallet like a gun and makes* CHARLES *dance by sliding money in and out of the wallet.*)

(*Like a disco, the mood passes.* JOE *is visibly estranged from* BURGESS, CHARLES, *and* HAG.)

HAG: Don't feel superior to me, because you don't have a habit. You don't have the pressures I've got either.

CHARLES: (*Following them, trying to look at everything close up.*) There's money in this, you see. Big Money. I know. I've studied it. Just stay close to the big boys. That's how to get rich.

FRED: (*Still at phone and following the action with his eyes.*) So it was urban renewal . . . yeah . . . I dunno . . . Some funny store. Books and religious objects. Maybe a bit of an insane asylum too . . .

HARRIET: Fred, we've got to leave immediately. Now, either get the number and let's get outa here, or hang.up. This place is crazier than you suspect . . .

(HAG *is placed in a chair. There is a black curtain they throw to cover his activities, but he is squirming and trying to get the works. He is trying to cook up behind the curtain.* JOE *runs out from the curtain to get a glass of water for* HAG.)

JOE: Yeah, y'all, Mr. Swings, you should get outa here right now.

MAL: Daddy. What about you, Joe? Why're you in here?

JOE: Why? I work for ol' man Burgess.

CHARLES: (*Looking over his shoulder but helping* BURGESS *and* HAG.) He's a communications specialist. (*Laughs.*)

JOE: I don't *sell* no drugs!

FRED: (*Getting the number, writing it down.*) OK, 102–112 264th Street. Why's that familiar? Tell me how to get there . . .

HARRIET: Mr. Seth, my son, don't be offended by him, he's aggressive. Young. Not that it's a bad question. Fred, will you speed it up?

HAG: Joe, bring the damn water so I can get off, will ya? Quit bumping your goddamn lips together with those singers.

HARRIET: This is some kind of joke, isn't it—a burlesque, a happening. This is nightmare craziness, isn't it? Mr. Seth, (*He's rushing past them.*) there's no chance they won't let us out of here, is it?

CHARLES: Communications specialist. He just carry dope back and forth to Caucasian crib.

MAL: Only people we know name Swings related to us. You probably are some kinda cousin or something. Mama, when we see Uncle Nathaniel, we should ask him, any other Swings in this city related to us Southern Swings.

JOE: Probably some relation. (*Gives water and stuff to* HAG *and* BURGESS. BURGESS *begins to look back at the family now.*)

HARRIET: Fred, will you get off that phone before I pull the plug out. You are in this place with some nuts, and you calmly making a phone call.

(HAG *now has the stuff in a big spoon cooking up. He is winding a big belt around his arm, the curtain has been pushed back by his gyrations, and we see him filling up the syringe.*)

BURGESS: Joe, when the General gets off, we have to talk about our friends.

JOE: (*Stiffens a bit.*) Talk about them. Why? They going to visit they relatives.

FRED: (*Finishing getting the number.*) OK, Margaret, we'll see you when we get to Mississippi. Harriet sends her love, and Mal. We loved that last group of poems you sent out to the family. They were so powerful and beautiful.

HARRIET: (*Forgetting the danger for a moment.*) Weren't they? Tell her we'll see her soon . . . (*Remembering.*) Now, for goodness sake, Fred, hang up the phone and let's get outa here now.

FRED: OK, I got the number. We can go now. (*Gestures at* HARRIET *and* MAL, *as if they have yet to see the madness.*) Whew-ee, this is some crazy goings-on in here. Must be some hippy place or something. Gurus all over this country these days making a fortune.

(HAG *has now got himself all tied up and is shooting up in some exaggerated position, arms and legs akimbo, a look of painful pleasure on his face.*)

FRED: Harriet, Harriet (*Hunches at her, indicating* HAG *shooting up.*) What? Do you really think that's . . . that's some smack?

HARRIET: Who cares? Let's go.

MAL: Yeah, Dad, it looks like some skeezag to me . . .

HARRIET: Skee-zag? Boy, you better bring your tail outa here.

BURGESS: (*To* JOE.) Joe, don't let those people get outa here. Mr. Blank, will you help restrain everyone till order is restored?

JOE: (*Stepping back away from the goings-on.* HAG *in scag heaven,* BURGESS *trying to keep him from toppling over.* CHARLES *hopping from one foot to the other, mumbling the O'Jays' "Money."*) No, nobody gettin' in their way. Them *my* relatives. Nobody gettin' in their way.

FRED: Joe, can you tell us how to get to this address . . . (*Holding up card.*) 264th Street?

HARRIET: Better yet, Joe, why don't you come on outside with us and point out which way?

MAL: Yeah, Joe, it's time to blow!

BURGESS: Joe, we've business . . .

CHARLES: Give me a great deal of money and I will restore order.

JOE: Yeah, I'm gone. Let's go. I'll show you where that street is. I used to have some relatives live up that way.

(HAG *is sitting now, spun around where we can see him. He is slowly pumping blood back and forth into his arm, then back into the syringe.*)

HAG: They're not going to stay and sing . . . (*Getting high and in singsong dope ecstasy.*) Bomb the bastids . . . bomb 'em . . . bomb me . . . bomb every fucking thing . . . bomb bomb bomb . . . (*The family and* JOE *are leaving.*)

HARRIET: The rain's stopped, the sky's clear. The stars up there so bright.

JOE: 264th Street is up in that direction, so to speak. You know, I heard you talking to someone about poetry.

FRED: Yeah, my old aunt's a beautiful poet.

HARRIET: She sure is.

JOE: I always wanted to be a writer. I always did.

MAL: Well, right on!

(*Laughter.*)

(*Blackout.*)

LONG TIME SINCE YESTERDAY

A DRAMA IN TWO ACTS

by P.J. Gibson

Long Time Since Yesterday was first produced at the Henry Street Playhouse in New York City by the New Federal Theater on February 1, 1985, and repeated there in October of the same year.

P.J. GIBSON

Patricia Joann Gibson was born in Pittsburgh, but was raised in Trenton, New Jersey, and now resides in New York City. Her B.A. is from Keuka College, and she holds an M.F.A. in Theater Arts from Brandeis University, which she attended on a Shubert Fellowship to study dramatic writing. She lists among her mentors J. P. Miller, author of *Days of Wine and Roses*, and Israel Horowitz, author of *Indian Wants the Bronx*. Gibson has had a varied career as writer, teacher and theater administrator with, among others: Boston College; WGBH-TV in Boston; Rites and Reason Theatre, Brown University; the Frederick Douglass Creative Arts Center, New York City: Playwright-in-residence, CETA Arts Program, Cultural Council Foundation/Black Theatre Alliance, New York City: Artist-in-residence, Music and Drama Institute, Khartoum, Sudan; the College of New Rochelle; and the Office of Youth Development, U.S. Department of Health, Education and Welfare. Among her awards are a National Endowment for the Arts playwriting grant; two Audelco Awards—one for playwright of the year, and the other for production of the year (1985), both for *Long Time Since Yesterday*; and the Key to the City of Indianapolis.

Gibson's work for the theater includes: *Konvergence* and *Void Passage*, a double bill; *Spida Bug*, a children's play; *My Mark, My Name*, an historical drama of the first Black regiment of Rhode Island (commissioned by the Rhode Island Committee for the Humanities); *The Androgyny*, a surrealistic drama, first produced in Frankfurt, Germany; and *Ain't Love Grand?*, a poetic drama with music. Others are: *Miss Ann Don't Cry No More*, a Northern urban drama; *The Unveiling of Abigail*, about a dying college professor (first presented at the Torino, Italy, Black Arts Festival in 1981); *Brown Silk and Magenta Sunsets*, exploring the mind of a wealthy recluse; and *Clean Sheets Can't Soil*, the odyssey of a singer with gospel roots.

CHARACTERS

Young Janeen Earl, a cute eleven-year-old. A follower. Weak in fortitude.

Young Laveer Swan, a cute eleven-year-old. A maker of dreams come true. Full of fortitude.

Alisa Myers-Reynolds, woman of thirty-nine, married. Director of a preschool program.

Panzi Lew McVain, woman of thirty-eight. Single. Physical therapist.

Thelma Carlson, woman of thirty-nine. Single. Medical doctor.

Babbs Wilkerson, woman of thirty-seven. Divorced. Anchor news person.

Laveer Swan, woman of thirty-eight. Single. Professional artist/painter.

Janeen Earl-Taylor, Deceased woman of thirty-eight. Married.

THE TIME: Late summer. The Present

THE PLACE: Ewing Township, New Jersey

ACT ONE

SCENE I

In darkness, the sound of the young JANEEN *and* LAVEER *can be heard singing a child's song.*

JANEEN & LAVEER: (*Voice over. Singing.*) Three, six, nine. The Goose drank wine. The monkey spit tobacco on the streetcar line. The line broke. The monkey got choked and they all went to heaven in a little rowboat. Quack. Quack. Quack. Quack. Quack. Quack. (JANEEN, *singularly continues to sing the "quack quack" portion of the song.*)

(*The lights rise on* JANEEN *and* LAVEER.)

LAVEER: Wait a minute. Wait a minute. I got a better one.

JANEEN: What? (LAVEER *places her leg up on the porch step.* JANEEN *sits on the step and watches.*)

LAVEER: (*Singing.*) Put your foot on the rock. Swooooo ah, swooooo ah . . . (*Does pelvic gyrations on the "swooooo ah" section.*) And let the boys fill your . . . (*She takes a beat of silence to imply the unspoken word.*) Swooooo ah, swooooo ah. Don't be afraid. Swooooo ah, swooooo ah. 'Cause your momma did the same.

JANEEN: Oooooo. Where'd you learn that?

LAVEER: (*Proud. She sits beside* JANEEN *on the step.*) From some girls. Oh, got another one.

JANEEN: What?

LAVEER: (*Singing. Complete with all gyrations.*) I want a pickle with a bone in it. Ungh, ungh. . . . (*Emphasis and gyrations on the "ungh, ungh" section.*)

JANEEN: Oooooo, Laveer. . . .

LAVEER: What?

JANEEN: That's nasty.

LAVEER: (*Laughs.*) I know. Come on. (*Coaxing* JANEEN *to join. She sings.*) I want a pickle with a bone in it . . . (*To* JANEEN.) Come on. I want a pickle with a . . .

(JANEEN *softly joins in. She is awkward and less confident with her movements.*)

JANEEN & LAVEER: I want a pickle with a bone in it. Ungh, ungh.
LAVEER: (*To* JANEEN.) You got to put more in it, Janeen. (*Demonstrates.*) Ungh, ungh.

(*The girls start the song up again.* JANEEN *puts more into her singing and gyrations. She enjoys it.*)

JANEEN & LAVEER: I want a pickle with a bone in it. Ugh. Ungh. (*The girls laugh.*)
LAVEER: I like that one.
JANEEN: It's nasty.
LAVEER: It's fun.
JANEEN: (*Insisting.*) It's nasty!
LAVEER: (*Insisting.*) It's fun! (*Silence.*) Hair time. (*She unbraids her hair.*) I want a real different style today.
JANEEN: What kind?
LAVEER: Different. Grown-up, but different. And not like Miss Robinson's. (JANEEN *begins to comb and style* LAVEER's *hair.*)
JANEEN: You know what I want to be when I grow up?
LAVEER: A princess.
JANEEN: A lady of leisure.
LAVEER: (*Laughing.*) Where'd you hear that one?
JANEEN: (*Confused and embarrassed.*) From Miss Thomas. I heard her talking with my mother.
LAVEER: You know what a lady of leisure does?
JANEEN: No. What? (LAVEER *looks around her and then whispers in* JANEEN's *ear.* JANEEN *is shocked.*) You lie! . . . Who told you that?
LAVEER: Read it.
JANEEN: Where?
LAVEER: In a book.
JANEEN: What book?
LAVEER: The one my mother hides.
JANEEN: You lie.
LAVEER: Cross my heart. The bookcase next to the window. Besides, why should I lie? You learn a lot from reading those books.
JANEEN: Those are grown up books. You can't read all the words in those books.

LAVEER: That's what dictionaries are for.

JANEEN: What else do they say? They talk about sex?

LAVEER: (*Nonchalantly.*) Yep.

JANEEN: (*Excited.*) They do?

LAVEER: Yep.

JANEEN: I don't believe you.

LAVEER: I can prove it.

JANEEN: How?

LAVEER: (*Retrieves a book from her school bag, flips through pages, then reads.*) "He took me as I had always dreamed, tenderly, passionately. . . ." (*Stops and looks at Janeen.*)

JANEEN: "Passionately. . . ." Well, don't stop.

LAVEER: Like it huh? . . .

JANEEN: (*Embarrassed.*) Laveer . . . (JANEEN *quickly finishes* LAVEER's *hair and sits beside* LAVEER *and listens attentively.*)

LAVEER: "I knew I would let him. I would let him take me with the strength of his man. Allow him to move through the channel of my life giving waters and explode. . . . Oh . . . to have him explode like the most violent of volcanoes. To have him erupt his passion. . . . Consequences . . . I have no concern for consequences. I care only for this now, for his touch, his lips, his loving. I am his. I am his to take me, take me as he so sees fit." (LAVEER *stops reading. She savors the words for a moment and then replaces the marker in the book and then buries the book once again in the book bag. She turns to* JANEEN *whose face is still marked with astonishment.*)

JANEEN: Wow wee . . . Did you hear that?

LAVEER: Nope. I read it.

JANEEN: How many times?

LAVEER: Four or five.

JANEEN: You read that five times?

LAVEER: (*Touching her hair, approving.*) Yep.

JANEEN: The whole book or just those pages?

LAVEER: The whole book.

JANEEN: It got any real nasty parts?

LAVEER: Yep. Want to take it home?

JANEEN: (*Hesitant.*) I'd like to . . . (LAVEER *digs into her book bag.*) But. . . .

LAVEER: (*Replacing the book.*) But what?

JANEEN: Well . . .

LAVEER: Well what?

JANEEN: Suppose I get caught?

LAVEER: You won't get caught, unless you go around announcing it. *(Placing her hands about her mouth and making a megaphone.)* "I'm reading dirty books!"

JANEEN: Shuuuuu . . .

LAVEER: Or you run around with guilt written all over your face. Or you get caught breathing too hard when you're supposed to be in bed sleeping.

JANEEN: You do that?

LAVEER: What?

JANEEN: Breathe hard.

LAVEER: Only on the real nasty parts.

JANEEN: Wow.

LAVEER: Won't you take it home and read it for yourself?

JANEEN: I can't.

LAVEER: Why?

JANEEN: I don't know . . . No backbone, don't have straight legs.

LAVEER: Oooooo, I hate that expression of yours. Where'd you get it from, anyway?

JANEEN: Grandpa.

LAVEER: You ought to give it back.

JANEEN: He says people who are afraid don't have backbone or straight legs.

LAVEER: That's a yyyulky way to think about yourself, you know. You ought to wrap up all your grandfather's sayings and give 'em back.

JANEEN: You're weird. How do you think things like that?

LAVEER: I'm ahead of my time. I'm a nonconformist.

JANEEN: A nonconformist? Who told you that?

LAVEER: I read it, and after careful examination I decided that I am. It's what I want to be, besides a painter. I'm going to be a famous, famous painter. Anyway, the two seem to go hand in hand.

JANEEN: What?

LAVEER: Nonconformist and painter. *(Runs her fingers over her new and unusual hairstyle.)* This feels great. *(Referring to her hair.)*

JANEEN: Your mother's going to kill you.

LAVEER: Nope. What's she gonna do is . . . *(Demonstrates.)* Grab her heart, back herself into a corner, look up at the ceiling and ask God what she did to deserve all of this, meaning me. Then . . . after her speech *(Points her finger and shakes it at* JANEEN, *mimicking her mother.)* "Haven't I told you about . . ." And then she'll list them. She'll tell me to go upstairs and comb this mess out of my hair.

JANEEN: So why do it if you know she's going to yell and she's going to make you comb it out?

LAVEER: Why not? Besides, it feels good.

JANEEN: My mother says going through life feeling things can get you in a lot of trouble.

LAVEER: And your mother's frustrated most of the time too.

JANEEN: She's not.

LAVEER: She is.

JANEEN: (*Holding her ground.*) She's not!

LAVEER: You told me so yourself.

JANEEN: I didn't.

LAVEER: You did.

JANEEN: When?

LAVEER: Last September. We were sitting on my back porch eating pomegranates. Remember?

JANEEN: (*Remembering.*) Well . . .

LAVEER: Well, hell . . .

JANEEN: Laveer . . . your mouth.

LAVEER: What about my mouth?

JANEEN: It's filthy.

LAVEER: So.

JANEEN: It's not ladylike.

LAVEER: But it's fun. Besides, I'm not sure I want to be a lady.

JANEEN: Everybody should want to be a lady.

LAVEER: Not if we have to end up like our moms. Yelk! Too many "I can'ts" or "I shouldn'ts" for me.

JANEEN: They're respected.

LAVEER: So who cares about being respected? I want to be daring, risky. I want to . . .

JANEEN: Be like Francine Willis.

LAVEER: Bet she has more fun than we do. And what's so great about being a virgin and never kissed? I want to kiss somebody. I want to stick my tongue in . . . (*Thinks.*) Darrel Rivers' mouth and let him put his hands right here. (*Indicates her small breasts.*)

JANEEN: (*Shocked. Looks around. Whispers.*) You don't mean that.

LAVEER: Yep.

JANEEN: Your tongue in his mouth?

LAVEER: Yep.

JANEEN: That's nasty. It's swapping spit.

LAVEER: It's French kissing. Doris Day and Rock Hudson

don't kiss the way real people kiss. Anyway, I think Darrel has cute lips.

JANEEN: You're going to get in trouble.

LAVEER: If you ask me, most of life is gonna get you in trouble. Might as well have some fun. You gotta stop being a scardy cat.

JANEEN: I'm not.

LAVEER: You are.

JANEEN: Am not!

LAVEER: Are!

JANEEN: Well, everybody can't be like you! Anyway, my father said, if it weren't for the weak there wouldn't be the strong.

LAVEER: Your father, your grandfather, your mother . . . sometimes you make me so mad with all the things you believe your family says.

JANEEN: They're older and wiser.

LAVEER: They're jerks.

JANEEN: They are not!

LAVEER: I don't mean to talk about your family, but . . . they're too boxed in for me. Look, Janeen, you can't go around doing things 'cause somebody said this or that about it. You got to do what you want to do sometimes.

JANEEN: And get in trouble.

LAVEER: So you get in trouble.

JANEEN: And you get put on punishment.

LAVEER: So you get put on punishment. I stay on punishment, but I also have fun. *Sometimes* it's worth it. Besides, who gets hurt? Nobody.

JANEEN: If you kiss Darrel you might get pregnant.

LAVEER: I didn't say I was going to do it with him. I said I wanted to tongue-kiss him. You think I'm crazy? I do it with Darrel and my daddy finds out . . . He'd skin me alive and then swing me off the front porch. I ain't crazy.

JANEEN: I wish I could be like you.

LAVEER: You don't want to be like me. You want to be like you. Just do things you want to do. Okay?

JANEEN: How do you know so much about life?

LAVEER: I read dirty books.

JANEEN: But you're not afraid to do things.

LAVEER: That's 'cause I'm going to die when I'm twenty-one.

JANEEN: You are not.

LAVEER: I am. You see. I've decided I'm going to be an artist. That's because I'm ahead of my time. And I'm going to do everything, travel all over the world, have great lovers . . .

see all kinds of things and be famous, but . . . I'm going to have to experience tragedy. Artists have to do that, you know. So I'm going to die at twenty-one.

JANEEN: Nobody knows when they're going to die.

LAVEER: I do.

JANEEN: You don't.

LAVEER: I do. But . . . in the meantime, I am going to live, and be the best artist ever.

JANEEN: (*Staring at* LAVEER.) I wish we were real sisters, twins. Then I could be like you.

LAVEER: Janeen! Will you stop that? It's okay being Janeen. 'Sides, how you gonna be my twin? You can't draw. And forget that lady of leisure. You don't have what it takes to be a lady of leisure.

JANEEN: Promise me you'll always be my best friend. Promise.

LAVEER: Promise.

JANEEN: I mean . . . mean it.

LAVEER: I do.

JANEEN: Really mean it.

LAVEER: (*Frustrated.*) I do.

JANEEN: You'll always be my best friend and my sister.

LAVEER: Promise.

JANEEN: And help me to have straight legs?

LAVEER: Janeen! . . . I promise.

JANEEN: Swap hair on it.

LAVEER: Jesus . . . Again?

JANEEN: Swap hair on it.

LAVEER: You're gonna make me bald with all this swapping. (*The two girls pull hair from one another's head.*)

(*The lights dim.*)

SCENE II

Sound. A song. It is sung in darkness by the voices of young female adults. It is a spoof on a traditional college alma mater.

WOMEN: (*Singing.*)
And through the thick and thin
Racial words and snarling grins
We will persevere until the end
And make their small minds spin

We are the first
We are the best
We are the ones to hold the final conquest

And in the end
They'll look back and say
Those Rainbow Six
They were more than a credit
They were more than erotic

Those Rainbow Six
With their brainy brains
They surpassed the pains

Those Rainbow Six
A few pranks and tricks
Those Rainbow Six

Those Rainbow Six
Those Rainbow Six
They were the best.

(*A twenty-seven-year period has lapsed between the previous scene of the young girls and this. Lights rise on modern living room of a split-level dwelling. A staircase and landing protrude over playing area. [This is* JANEEN's *domain.] There are bookcases laden with medical and educational books and a special section on erotica. A modern plush designer sectional sofa dominates the furnishings. It is accented with several throw pillows. A tall chrome floor lamp hovers over one section of the sofa. Other furnishings dressing the set should be quality items reflecting the upwardly mobile status of the inhabitants.*

Enter LAVEER SWAN, *attractive woman of thirty-eight. She is a professional painter/artist.* LAVEER *dangles a loose set of keys in hand. She is followed by* ALISA MYERS-REYNOLDS, *attractive woman of thirty-nine. She is the director of a preschool program.* ALISA *wears glasses and walks with a stylish, quite feminine walking cane.* PANZI LEW McVAIN, THELMA CARLSON, *and* BABBS WILKERSON *follow* ALISA.

PANZI LEW McVAIN, *extremely attractive woman of thirty-eight. She has a beautifully proportioned and shapely figure. She is a physical therapist.*

THELMA CARLSON, *less attractive than the other women.*

She is more the Plain Jane. She wears little or no makeup and hides attractive eyes behind thick glasses. Her clothing is much darker than that worn by the other women. She is a medical doctor opening a new medical clinic.

BABBS WILKERSON, *very fair, attractiveness attributed to makeup and the art of application. She is thirty-seven and the most fashion-conscious of the women. She is an anchor person at a news station in Minneapolis.*

All women wear suitable attire and colors reflecting the past funeral service. The women carry single-stem flowers and/or programs from the internment. PANZI and THELMA are most conservative in their dress, both wearing tailored suits or attire. LAVEER is the exception among the women. She wears an artsy, almost sensual, bright mint green and black dress. She is laden in authentic and interesting jewelry, mostly gold, from her years of traveling. LAVEER also wears a huge black sun hat with veil which requires great distance between her and the others. With the veil drawn back, she wears the hat for a lengthy portion of this scene.

There is a tone of somber memory and grief as the women move into the environment.)

BABBS: (*Studying the environment.*) "Dark emptiness."

ALISA: (*To* BABBS.) What?

BABBS: A little something I once heard regarding life after death. (*She scans the room.*) "Dark emptiness."

THELMA: Yes . . . (*Studying the environment.*) This could keep Walter away. You know, they say he hasn't stepped foot back in here since he found Janeen.

ALISA: Grief sometimes does that. (LAVEER *draws open the curtains. A flood of sunlight spills into the room.*)

BABBS: Now, that's better. (*Observing the environment.*) Beautiful. One thing you could always say about Janeen, she had taste.

THELMA: That she did.

ALISA: (*Before the library.*) Fine collection.

BABBS: (*Joining* ALISA *at the library.*) And as usual, everything in its place. (*Reading book titles.*) An education section. (*To* ALISA.) Your area. (*Continues reading titles.*) Ah, Thelma . . . Good old medicine. Must be Walter's section. (*Continues reading titles.*) And erotica. (*She turns to* LAVEER *as in playful accusation.*) I wonder who influenced this. (*She takes a book and flips through the pages.*)

THELMA: (*To* ALISA.) So tell me about that leg of yours.

ALISA: Nothing much to tell. A tractor trailer jumped the median, caused a pile-up of five cars on the interstate, and left me with my souvenir. (*Indicates her leg.*) Almost lost it but for a lot of help from a good friend. (*Indicates* PANZI.)

BABBS: Oh . . . Madame Panzi Lew McVain, therapist, to the rescue. Now tell me networking doesn't pay off.

PANZI: She was a good patient, a real worker. She could have lost complete use of that leg.

ALISA: So they told me. Anyway, I've resigned myself to the distinguished look of my customized cane.

THELMA: (*Embracing* ALISA *while walking to the sofa.*) We all have our crosses to bear.

ALISA: So we do. Besides, it wasn't all as bad as it seems. During that dreadful cast-wearing stage . . . (*To* THELMA *and* PANZI.) You know, the itching part right smack in the middle where the pencil and the ruler don't reach . . . Lloyd and I discovered some nice kinky positions.

THELMA: Do tell.

BABBS: A noted reason why the Reynolds clan continues to grow.

ALISA: Well, someone among the group has to perpetuate the growth of mankind.

BABBS: (*To the group of women.*) Now, is that a dig or is that a dig?

LAVEER: (*To* ALISA.) How many is it now?

ALISA: Five.

LAVEER: Jesus.

BABBS: Jesus had nothing to do with it.

THELMA: How do you have time to run that preschool of yours?

BABBS: Half of the students are hers. (*Laughs.*)

LAVEER: (*To* ALISA.) You're not teaching anymore?

ALISA: Nope. Having the babies opened my eyes to the need for preschool environments for the working mother . . . So . . . with a lot of help from Lloyd and a little help from the bank . . . I've got my own school. (PANZI *and* LAVEER *have both taken positions on the exterior during the course of the dialogue between the women.* THELMA, ALISA, *and* BABBS *are more central in their positions. Periodically* PANZI's *and* LAVEER's *eyes meet from their opposite postions. It is obvious there is tension between them.*)

THELMA: (*To* ALISA.) I admire that in you.

ALISA: What?

THELMA: You've got the best of both worlds.

ALISA: So what's stopping you? In fact, what's stopping all of you? As you know, dear ladies, life will not stop and wait for you. You've got to get on in here and get your piece of this pie before the child-bearing years are a thing of the past.

BABBS: Count me out. The thought of two a.m. feedings and diaper charges . . . Ooooooo. (*Shrugs her shoulders and shakes.*) Reminds me of the time I was living in New York with this thigh-high poodle . . . (*Demonstrates the dog's height.*) Lady was her name. God, I was forever having to take that dog for a walk. Got rid of it as quick as I could. Can you see me doing that to a baby? (*To* ALISA.) I leave the child-bearing and rearing stage of life to you, with my compliments.

THELMA: (*To* ALISA.) I'm not going to be quite as dramatic, but you'll excuse me if I do the mothering thing vicariously.

ALISA: Give me one good reason why.

THELMA: Well, some of us—

BABBS: (*To* THELMA.) Don't you dare bring up that tired-ass excuse from yesterday. If you do, I will personally strangle you with these two hands.

THELMA: Well, you've got to admit, when God gave out beauty, I was somewhere in line getting seconds on brains.

BABBS: You see that! That kind of thinking is not healthy. Oooo, you make me so sick with that kind of thinking. I mean it. You are not ugly, Thelma. I have seen ugly people in my day, and believe me, you are not ugly. You could stand to fluff up some, but . . . (*To the group.*) Have you seen her eyes? God gave Thelma the most beautiful pair of eyes with naturally long lashes. (*To* THELMA.) If you'd just fluff up some, throw those ugly-ass grandma Lulibelle glasses of yours in the garbage, invest in some contacts, makeup, and a new wardrobe, you'd be surprised what you'd find. God, if I didn't spend half my money at the cosmetic counter, I'd look like Miss Plain Jane myself. Cosmetics do do wonders, don't they? (*Flamboyantly models and laughs. To* THELMA.) So . . . get your show on the road. (*Crosses to* THELMA.) You know I love you, but I hate, hate, hate it when you put yourself down. I really do. (*Turning to the group.*) Would anyone know the whereabouts of the bathroom?

LAVEER and PANZI: (*Simultaniously.*) It's off the hall, down the left and . . . (*They stop. Silence. The two women stare at one another. A rising wave of tension permeates the room.*)

BABBS: (*To* LAVEER.) Lavy, would you be so kind as to escort me? It's this cystitis again. Can't seem to break the cycle of reoccurence. I drink the cranberry juice, but . . . stop the cystitis? (BABBS *and* LAVEER *exit. Silence.*)

PANZI: The nerve. I mean, the gall of it all. What's she doing here?

ALISA: I think you call it mourning the death of a friend.

PANZI: Laveer was never Janeen's friend.

ALISA: That's a matter of opinion.

PANZI: You were always on Laveer's side.

ALISA: I beg your pardon. I was never on anyone's side. That feud was between you, Janeen, and Lavy.

PANZI: And did you see how she strutted up to Walter and asked for the keys to this house? Like she and Janeen had been bosom buddies.

THELMA: From the way the story goes, they used to be, remember? It hasn't been that long.

PANZI: Used to, as in past tense. I can't stand the bitch.

ALISA: All right, Panzi.

PANZI: Sashaying around with those keys like she was a friend to Janeen. I was Janeen's friend.

ALISA: So we all were. Is Thelma raising her blood pressure over those keys? Am I? What is with you, Panzi? Caaaaarist! Walter gave the keys to Lavy and that's that.

THELMA: (*To* PANZI.) Had you considered the man is still in shock? Besides, I heard Mrs. Earl tell Lavy to get the keys from Walter and bring us over here. I'm sure there was no malicious thought intended.

ALISA: The girls go back to elementary school. What do you expect at a time like this? Who's thinking logically? Obviously you're not. •

PANZI: (*Fighting tears.*) You don't understand. I was her friend. (*Breaks.*) I was . . . Me . . . They ignored me. The whole family.

ALISA: No one ignored you.

PANZI: I tell you, they did. (*Fighting her emotions.*) Not once did Walter ever come over to me. He didn't even respond to me when I offered my help with the funeral arrangements. I was Janeen's best friend, me, not that—

THELMA: But Panzi . . . the three of them grew up together. People forget about quarrels and falling-outs at times like this.

PANZI: I have stood by Janeen ever since graduation. Me. I was her maid of honor . . . I . . . Laveer wasn't even invited to the wedding. (*Fighting the tears.*) They treated me like

. . . I wasn't consulted about anything. (ALISA *crosses to* PANZI *to comfort her.*) Not even the flowers, I could have helped with the arrangements. But no, who did they contact? Who did they bring all the way up here from Mexico? That damn . . . bitch has always been in my fucking way!

ALISA: Calm down, Panzi. I know how you feel.

PANZI: No, you don't know how I feel! Neither one of you *know* how I feel.

(LAVEER *and* BABBS *enter. Their voices can be heard offstage.*)

BABBS: I loved Mexico. It was one of those romantic ventures we used to read about in those romance books. You know, the kind we used to read under the sheets by flashlight. Remember those? You know, erotica with a little taste. Anyway, Acapulco was a chapter straight out of one of those *nicer* kinds. Frank and I spent our honeymoon there. Too bad we couldn't have lived there, might have kept the romance going, but . . . We came north, my rose-tinted glasses cleared, Frank changed into the bland, non-spirited, noncommital man of the seventies and my marriage went to putt.

THELMA: Where's he now?

BABBS: Frank? Who knows? Who cares? We got a quick one-two-three divorce in the Dominican Republic. And . . . you won't believe, but . . . we weren't through signing all the legal documents when Frank had visions of sugar plums in his head. The divorce formalities were finished at eleven. He was married to young Miss twenty-two-year-old Madilane What's-her-name at three p.m. There she was, a complete carbon copy of me, right down to her hairdo. Twenty-two and I was thirty-four . . . The child even flew down on the same plane as me. I remembered thinking I liked the dress she was wearing when she walked past me to the ladies' room. It wasn't until after the divorce and Frank's new marriage that I realized that her dress was very similar to the dress he had bought me for my birthday a year before. I think I drank a case of brandy that evening all by myself. (*To* THELMA.) No, I do not know where Frank is, and I could care less.

ALISA: (*Silence. To* LAVEER.) I've been hearing some good things about you and your art. You're in Mexico now, aren't you?

LAVEER: San Miguel de Allende.

THELMA: There's an artist community down there, isn't it?

LAVEER: A few.

ALISA: Elizabeth Catlett still there?

LAVEER: Not in San Miguel, but she's still in Mexico.

THELMA: I've got to get down to Mexico.

LAVEER: You're always welcome.

ALISA: (*Proud.*) Lavy, our world traveler. How many countries is it now?

LAVEER: Jesus . . . don't make me count.

ALISA: Well, you always said you wanted to travel.

BABBS: And travel she did. You ought to have her tell you about this Egyptian who wanted her to be his . . . (*To* LAVEER.) what number wife was it? Third?

LAVEER: Third.

BABBS: And the Nigerian prince or whatever he was . . . You ought to see the gold those two men had her dripping in. (*Crosses to* LAVEER. *She inspects* LAVEER'*s hands and wrists.*) Ah yes . . . she didn't pawn them.

ALISA: That's right, you and Lavy have kept in touch over the years.

BABBS: She better have. I would have killed her if she had forgotten me. This child lives a life straight out of the romance books. A man in Paris, one in Italy, two in South America, one on this island, four or five on that . . .

THELMA: (*Laughs. To* LAVEER.) You'd better watch out for herpes.

LAVEER: Precisely why I'm down in San Miguel. One man, one quiet life and my paint brushes. It's safer.

BABBS: That'll last only until they find a cure for herpes. (*The group laughs. All except* PANZI.)

PANZI: Listen, would anyone care for something to drink?

ALISA: I could use one. Bourbon.

THELMA: Wine, white.

BABBS To hell with the cystitis and the medication. I want a brandy snifter filled with about this much . . . (*She indicates about two inches.*) of brandy. (*To* THELMA.) And Dr. Thelma Carlson, don't you say one word about what I should or should not be drinking.

THELMA: If you want to kill yourself, go right ahead and kill yourself. (*The room falls into weighted silence.* THELMA *exhales.*) I sure didn't mean for that to come out like that.

ALISA: One of us was bound to say it sooner or later.

BABBS: I can't believe she did it. Now me . . . I have the potential for the dramatic, but Janeen . . . suicide?

LAVEER: She was weak.

PANZI: And Miss Laveer Swan, pillar of strength, knows it all.

LAVEER: Janeen was weak.

PANZI: You think because you went to kindergarten, junior high, high school, and college with her that makes you an authority on who and what Janeen was, well, it doesn't. You know nothing about her. Nothing! And you know what? I resent you being here. I resent you standing there all high and mighty, dressed like you were going out for afternoon cocktails, standing there like you were God herself, voicing profundities of "She was weak." What do you know of anything?

ALISA: Please. Let's have a little peace, for Janeen's sake. Please.

PANZI: Peace? How do you have peace with her around? We're supposed to be in mourning and Miss Arteeeeeeest here takes center stage discussing the many men of her life.

BABBS: Wait a minute, I brought that up.

PANZI: (*Ignoring* BABBS, *To* LAVEER.) Who gives a good damn how many men you've screwed to get a couple of rings and a bracelet? Who gives a damn? If I had had my way, you would not be here.

LAVEER: And if you had not *had* your way, Janeen might still be alive.

PANZI: Meaning?

LAVEER: Don't push me, Panzi. Just don't push me. I will tolerate just but so much of your shit. You log that into your brain. I tolerate you only because I loved Janeen. Only because I loved . . .

PANZI: Love?! Women like you don't know the first thing about love.

LAVEER: Like I said, don't push me or . . . (*Pause.*) You back up off me, Panzi.

ALISA: Panzi, come. Let me help you with the drinks. (PANZI *resists.*) Come on, Panzi. I could use a good, stiff bourbon right about now and so could you.

PANZI: (*To* LAVEER *while exiting.*) Bitch.

ALISA: (*To* LAVEER.) Forget it, Lavy, it's the day, the funeral. You know? What are you drinking?

LAVEER: Nothing.

ALISA: Lavy . . . I'm not mad at you, you're not mad at me. So what are you drinking?

LAVEER: Brandy.

ALISA: Thank you.

LAVEER: You're welcome. (*The two women embrace.* ALISA *exits.*)

THELMA: (*Silence.*) Can I ask you a question, Lavy?

LAVEER: If I were to say no, would it stop you?

THELMA: No.

LAVEER: (*Pause.*) Well . . .

THELMA: It's sort of tied into what's got Panzi in such a huff.

BABBS: If you ask me, she's always in a huff when you put her and Lavy in the same room. It's like watching a cockfight.

LAVEER: Please, Babbs, a cock I am not.

BABBS: Well, you two fight like two cocks.

THELMA: It's about the keys.

LAVEER: What about the keys?

THELMA: She feels, because she was Janeen's closest friend, Walter should have given the keys to her instead of you.

BABBS: A bit juvenile, but . . .

THELMA: What with you and Janeen having been on the outs for so long, and her being so close to her, she feels the family should have consulted her instead of you concerning the service.

LAVEER: And the question.

THELMA: It's been a good seventeen years since that flare-up at graduation . . .

LAVEER: And . . .

THELMA: It does appear strange the family called on you instead of her.

LAVEER: Possibly.

THELMA: What's really going on?

LAVEER: Life. (*She crosses to the window.*)

THELMA: You're not going to answer, are you?

LAVEER: You're very perceptive.

THELMA: (*Releasing the subject.*) Okay.

LAVEER (*Silence.*) What is there to say, Thelma? She committed suicide. (*Silence.*) Some things are best left alone. You know?

THELMA: Okay.

LAVEER: Some things are best left just where they are.

(*Silence. The lights begin to change.* THELMA *and* BABBS *freeze. Lights rise on the adult* JANEEN EARL–TAYLOR, *attractive woman of thirty-eight. She is located on upper protuding landing with phone in hand. This area is* JANEEN's *spiritual and flashback domain. All subsequent* JANEEN *scenes are flashbacks.*)

JANEEN: Lavy? (*She waits.*)

LAVEER: (*Confused.*) Yes, this is she.

JANEEN: Lavy, this is a voice out of your past. Janeen. (*Silence.*) Are you there?

LAVEER: Yes.

JANEEN: Please, don't hang up. You won't hang up, will you?

LAVEER: No.

JANEEN: Good. I was afraid you would. I . . . I got your number from your mother. Our mothers are still members of the Trees.

LAVEER: I know.

JANEEN: Mother talked Walter and me into joining. Oh, I married Walter.

LAVEER: I know. Are you happy?

JANEEN: Boy, you still go straight to the point. Am I happy? . . . I guess so. He's still fine as ever. Great lips. Still kisses good. I guess so.

LAVEER: Why'd you marry him?

JANEEN: Why? Why do most people get married? Besides, you know my parents and his parents sort of decided we'd be a couple back at our first Christmas party. Remember? We were about five . . . Sort of like the old days back in history, right out of one of those books . . . huh? (*No response.*) You still there?

LAVEER: Umm-hum.

JANEEN: Boy, this is good reception. I didn't think I'd get good lines calling into Mexico. How's the weather?

LAVEER: Fine.

JANEEN: And your love life? Your mother says you've got a new beau, a sculptor.

LAVEER: Yes.

JANEEN: Older, I hear.

LAVEER: Twelve years.

JANEEN: Perfect. For you, I mean. For me . . . I'd turn him into my father. You know me.

LAVEER: Janeen, I'm no longer mad with you. I no longer think you're a spineless twerp, so . . . relax and tell me why you've called.

JANEEN: You're not? I mean, still mad?

LAVEER: Jesus . . . you know how many years ago that was?

JANEEN: Long time. I was wrong, you know. And sometimes I am a spineless twerp.

LAVEER: Maybe not quite a spineless twerp.

JANEEN: Sometimes. I don't want to be, but . . . Decisions and

me . . . never quite my forte. Seems sort of silly now, looking
back on the fight.

LAVEER: We were younger.

JANEEN: I guess I felt you abandoned me, reneged on your
promise.

LAVEER: What promise?

JANEEN: You promised you'd always be my friend.

LAVEER: I've never stopped being your friend.

JANEEN: But you said . . .

LAVEER: I said I would not befriend Panzi and you ought to
grow up.

JANEEN: Yeah . . . I guess I still do. It's just that . . . I didn't
know how to have the two of you in my life at the same
time. It was so hard. Always so much friction. I was always
in the middle.

LAVEER: That's a long time ago, let's bury it, okay?

JANEEN: (*Relieved.*) Okay . . . Lavy?

LAVEER: Humm?

JANEEN: We still sisters?

LAVEER: (*Laughs.*) You're still such a little girl . . . Yes,
Janeen. Now, why'd you call?

JANEEN: Daddy died.

LAVEER: I'm sorry. When?

JANEEN: Last night. I . . . I don't know what to do. I mean,
everything seems to be falling apart, giving way . . .

LAVEER: Where's Walter?

JANEEN: He's on a lecture circuit, recruiting students into his
med school. He wants to come home, but I told him to stay.
He won't, of course, but . . . Mother's handling everything
in grand fashion. The Trees are helping out as usual and . . .
can you come? I'd like for you to be here. Would you come?

LAVEER: You sure you want this?

JANEEN: Oh yes. Please. Daddy would have wanted you to be
here.

LAVEER: And what does Janeen want?

JANEEN: Janeen needs her friend. I still have your hair.

LAVEER: (*Laughs.*) You lie.

JANEEN: Truth, I do. It's in a little antique box. You won't
believe how many strands of your hair I have.

LAVEER: Please don't tell me. My scalp aches at the mere
thought. (*Pause.*) Janeen. One more question. Panzi.
Where's Panzi?

JANEEN: She's on vacation in Switzerland.

LAVEER: (*Understanding.*) I see.

JANEEN: (*Quickly.*) No, it's not like you think. I could have called her. I mean, I just talked to her three days ago. I have her number there. She would come . . . but . . . I want you here . . . Do you hear me, Lavy?

LAVEER: Yes.

JANEEN: It is easier with her there, I mean, I don't feel like I have to take sides. Will you come?

LAVEER: I'll take the first flight out.

JANEEN: (*Surprised.*) You will? (*Excited.*) Oh good. I'll pick you up at the airport. Then we can stop off for an Italian hoagie and gorge ourselves while you tell me firsthand the news I've been reading on your work. (*Pause.*) Lavy . . . thanks. I love you.

(*The lights dim on* JANEEN. *The lighting shifts back to that of the previous scene.*)

BABBS: (*To* LAVEER.) You all right?

LAVEER: Fine. (*Insistingly.*) Fine.

BABBS: Okay. (*To* THELMA.) Our own doctor in the family. (*To* LAVEER.) And she's opening her own clinic. She's moved right along since the grand old days? Yes?

LAVEER: (*To* THELMA.) Your own clinic?

THELMA: I have a couple of partners. Nothing special, just a little something for the community.

BABBS: Note the tone of modesty. (*To* THELMA.) I'm elated for your progress, but I wish you'd gone into gynecology. If I get cystitis one more time . . .

THELMA: Could be your diet.

LAVEER: Have you ever seen what her diet consists of? Pepsis, Cokes, and brandy. She doesn't know what water is.

BABBS: Water's nasty.

THELMA: Water does not have a taste.

BABBS: It tastes like chloride.

THELMA: Okay, don't check your diet. Just lay off the sodas, the booze, and the heavy lovemaking. Try a more gentle position.

BABBS: 'Round about this moment I'd love to try any position. You know the last time I had some?

LAVEER: (*Laughs.*) Last night.

BABBS: Nine months . . . (*Thinks.*) Three weeks . . . No, let me not lie. (*She opens her bag, retrieves her appointment book and checks.*) Three and a half weeks and about . . . (*Checks her watch.*) thirteen hours. November the fifteenth, to be exact. His name was Sean Meers, a bore, wealthy, couldn't kiss and was less than desirable in the sack. A real Wall Streeter. Spent most of his time running his fingers through my hair and questioning the amount of Caucasian blood in my veins. (*Disgusted, she closes the book and drops it back into her bag.*) Enough to make a person consider hara-kiri. (*She stops herself.*) Not quite appropriate, huh? (*Pause.*) I wonder where they went to get those drinks.

THELMA: (*Silence.*) Hard to believe she did it.

BABBS: Suicide and me, yes . . . Janeen . . . (*She shakes her head.*)

LAVEER: What do you mean, you yes?

(*Enter* ALISA *and* PANZI *with the drinks and a tray of light hors d'oeuvres.*)

BABBS: I tried. (*To* ALISA *and* PANZI.) Ah, finally. (*Crosses to them.*) And munchies . . . (*Picks from the tray.*) Caviar? Like I said, Janeen always did have taste. (*Takes her drink.*)

LAVEER: (*To* BABBS.) What do you mean, you tried?

BABBS: I tried.

LAVEER: When?

BABBS: Two weeks ago.

THELMA: You're putting us on.

ALISA: Putting us on about what?

BABBS: Suicide.

ALISA: What is happening with us?

BABBS: I don't know about us, but . . . I took myself a sensual bath, in a tub of perfumed bubbles. Put on my sexiest gown. Fluffed up my face. Turned on the oven. Blew out the pilot. Reclined my body on my bed in a manner befitting Cleo herself and waited . . . Unfortunately, my neighbor's car alarm went off for the sixth time that week. The ringing gave me a headache, the gas was giving me a headache, so . . . The rest is history. I opened the windows, got dressed, went out for some fresh air, and much to my chagrin am very much alive.

THELMA: Why?

BABBS: Why am I alive or why did I do it? (*Laughs. Gulps down her brandy.*) Because . . . (*To* PANZI.) Would it be too much to request a refill?

PANZI: You sure you don't want a Coke or . . .

BABBS: I'd like another. (*Indicates the glass.*) Please. (PANZI *takes the glass and exits.* BABBS *calls to* PANZI.) It might be easier on your legs if you just brought the bottle back with you. (*To the group.*) Please. Shocked stares and gaping mouths do not appeal such an illustrious group.

LAVEER: What are you doing to yourself, Babbs?

BABBS: (*Chuckles.*) I don't know. Engrossed in self-pity.

THELMA: Pity . . . For God's sake, why?

BABBS: Little things . . . big things . . . I guess it's a matter of perspective.

ALISA: And what's your perspective?

BABBS: Mine? Babbs tried to commit suicide. Janeen committed suicide and . . . God, what I'd give to be back in Stevens Hall, blanketed by the safety of college life. (*To* THELMA.) You used to tell me I was lucky to have this hair and these eyes. Remember? Well . . . it's not so lucky. Sometimes I look in the mirror and I think all of this . . . (*Indicates her being.*) a curse. It's so middle-of-the-road, not connected to anything, close enough to everything . . . It shits. Life shits. (*Pause.*) I've been doing a little assessment thing on my life. You know what I found? All the opportunities, all the fine things I get out of life . . . These eyes, this hair, this coloring . . . (*She indicates.*) the calling card. A noted reason I hold the anchor spot in Minneapolis. It's called not being offensive to the eye.

THELMA: You don't believe that.

BABBS: The hell I don't.

LAVEER: We're supposed to believe it has nothing to do with your skills?

BABBS: In Minneapolis? It's a safe route. White men who want a black woman . . . safe. (*Pats her chest.*) Black men who want a white woman . . . safe. (*Pats her chest.*) Corporations who have to fill a quota . . . safe.

(*Enter* PANZI *with* BABBS's *brandy snifter and a full brandy decanter.*)

BABBS: (*To* PANZI.) Thought you got lost. (*Taking the brandy snifter.*) Thank you. (*Drinks.*) Where was I?

PANZI: I hope off the subject of suicide.

BABBS: (*To* PANZI.) And I love you too, darling. (*To the group of women.*) Did I tell you Frank married a woman who looked just like me?

LAVEER: Yes.

BABBS: Tells you where his head was—still is, for that matter. Wonder why men are like that?

ALISA: Now don't go lumping all men into that basket.

BABBS: Okay. You're right. I'm wrong. Ninety-nine percent. (*To* ALISA.) That all right with you? (*To the group.*) You know what I'd like? Charles Bishop. He was thirteen and I was twelve. He wore thick Coke bottle glasses, was deep dark chocolate brown, and loved the hell out of Babbs Wilkerson just because he thought I was nice. Sure wish I knew where he was today.

PANZI: You know what I wish? I wish you would all respect this day for what it is.

ALISA: Just what is this day?

PANZI: Oh, cute.

ALISA: It wasn't meant to be cute. I'd like to know. What do you expect out of us?

PANZI: A class reunion this isn't.

ALISA: So a class reunion it isn't, now what? What are we supposed to do? Sit around in a circle, rock back and forth, cry out 'wos'?

THELMA: I come from a family who believes in rejoicing at a death.

PANZI: If you call Miss Drunk here (*Indicates* BABBS.) a sample of rejoicing at a death . . . Do excuse me. I've got a phone call to make. (*Exits in a huff.*)

BABBS: (*To exiting* PANZI.) Well la-di-da to you, Miss Thing. (*Sits.*)

THELMA: I'm for some fresh air. (*Rises and opens the front door.*)

ALISA: Janeen's death really has her in a tizzy.

LAVEER: It ought to.

THELMA: She did have one point.

BABBS: What?

THELMA: The way we've been going on, you'd think we had nothing to be thankful for.

ALISA: I beg your pardon. I've got a man who's hooked on my good loving, children I adore, good health, a good life, and no regrets . . .

LAVEER: I have no complaints.

BABBS: Well . . .

ALISA: (*To* BABBS) Your problem is you don't know how to take life by the horns and use it. You make life too complicated. You have assets, use them. A man sees you for something other than you are, use him until the one with some sense comes along. And prepare yourself for reality. The one with some sense may never come along.

THELMA: God forbid.

ALISA: (*To* BABBS.) If he doesn't, what are you going to do? Stick your head in the oven? All this talk about suicide and depression . . . what did it get Janeen? A beautiful woman down the drain . . . Why? Life promises you nothing. No guarantees. Nothing. We each have to do the best with what we get.

THELMA: And some of us should have been as lucky.

BABBS: (*To* THELMA.) All right, that's it. I've had it with you and that piss-poor attitude you have about yourself. (*Crosses to* THELMA.) Sit down.

THELMA: What are you talking about?

BABBS: I'm talking about you. Sit. How you ever made it through the sixties and missed the "Black is beautiful" spirit is beyond me. Sit. (*She pushes* THELMA *into the chair.*) Today Dr. Thelma Carlson, you're gonna get a glimpse of what you have. Take off those glasses. (BABBS *retrieves a makeup kit from her rather large, stylish handbag.*)

THELMA: (*To* BABBS.) And what, may I ask, are you about to do?

BABBS: Appease me.

THELMA: Appease you? (LAVEER *and* ALISA *laugh.*)

BABBS: Appease me. I've been dying to do this for years. (*Studying* THELMA'*s face.*) You might find you even like the end result.

THELMA: Babbs, don't waste your—

BABBS: Don't worry about what I waste. Just keep still, sit back, and let the master do her thing.

LAVEER: (*To* THELMA). Why don't you just enjoy the ride?

ALISA: You must admit, Babbs has taken an abrupt upswing of spirit. (*Observing* BABBS *with the makeup.*) Puts you in mind of the time Janeen had her making up Lavy's face for that mock funeral.

THELMA: Do Jesus.

ALISA: Janeen, convinced Lavy was going to die at twenty-one.

LAVEER: (*Laughs.*) I was.

BABBS: Sure you were.

ALISA: I can still see the three of them, Janeen, Lavy, and Panzi, coming out of that small-town fashion shop with that bright red dress.

THELMA: Bright Chinese orange red.

BABBS: Janeen rattling on about everyone getting everything just right. Panzi mumbling all the way to the bus stop about how ridiculous the whole thing was.

LAVEER: I have you to know it was not ridiculous.

BABBS: Tell that to Panzi.

LAVEER: I'd rather not.

ALISA: (*Reminiscing.*) Lord, that loud red dress?

LAVEER: I liked red in those days.

BABBS: (*Steps back to get a better look at her makeup work on* THELMA. *To* THELMA.) You're going to love this when I'm through.

ALISA: (*Crosses to* THELMA, *gives an approving nod. To* LAVEER.) What was the name of that morbid poem you used to recite?

LAVEER: Emily Dickinson's "My Life Closed Twice Before Its Close" is not a morbid poem.

BABBS: You repeated it a thousand times the week before the funeral.

THELMA: That was the best thing out of the whole shebang, the funeral. Janeen's orchestration of Laveer lying in state in the dorm lounge . . .

ALISA: For three whole hours. God . . . The entire campus marching around you (*Indicates* LAVEER.) lying there, hands clasped over your breast and that fire engine red dress . . .

LAVEER: Chinese red.

ALISA: Whatever.

THELMA: And Panzi giving that eulogy.

LAVEER: Horrendously . . .

ALISA: Ah ah ah . . . Now, you, Janeen, and Panzi were like three little peas in a pod in those days.

LAVEER: Panzi and I were never anything in *those days*.

ALISA: Now, Lavy . . .

THELMA: (*To* LAVEER.) It took me months to get used to calling you Lavy instead of Laveer. Janeen correcting everyone, all the time saying . . .

GROUP: (*Simultaneously.*) "Lavy."

BABBS: I'll never forget it. February the twenty-fifth.

ALISA: (*Correcting.*) A snowy February the twenty-fifth.

THELMA: Quite snowy . . .

BABBS: Janeen waved her hands over the reclining Madame Swan . . . (*Waves her hand over* THELMA's *head.*)

ALISA: Wait . . . (*Demonstrates over the sofa.*) "Rise, Lavy. Rise, Lavy. Laveer has gone to rest, but rise to life, Lavy. . . . Venture no longer in darkness. Step from. . . ." And I just loved this line. . . . "Step from beyond the veil. . . ."

THELMA: Oh God, that's when Panzi waved this white lace

thing they had dyed this grotesque gray over Lavy's body and . . .

ALISA: "Rise, Lavy . . . We need you, Lavy. We love you, Lavy. Life is here, Lavy. . . ." And the child rose.

BABBS: Pure theatre. Janeen missed her calling. (ALISA, THELMA *and* BABBS *laugh.*)

LAVEER: I have you to know we got an "A" in drama for that event of which you are now making mockery.

ALISA: (*To* LAVEER) So much for you dying at twenty-one.

LAVEER: I died didn't I?

ALISA: And you rose, but don't expect me to gather the multitude and follow you down into Mexico. . . . Funny, Janeen was the one who thought we were all going to live forever. I'd have never thought she'd . . .

BABBS: She was a light bulb wasn't she?

LAVEER: On the days she believed in herself, yes.

THELMA: Always good for a laugh.

(*Enter* PANZI. *She crosses to her bag and retrieves a cigarette.*)

ALISA: Yeah, you could always count on Janeen's theatrics to pull you out of a slump.

BABBS: Into everything. (*To* LAVEER.) I'm glad you and Janeen got things straightened out before . . .

THELMA: To tell you the truth, I was really hurt when the three of you fell out on graduation day. I mean, graduation day . . . Lord what a time to do a thing like that.

BABBS: Well, things have improved a bit over the years. Now if you and Panzi could just patch things up I'd feel even better.

ALISA: I'll second that. I've never been one who cared too much for friction, except that kind of friction me and Lloyd make beneath the sheets.

THELMA: Do tell.

BABBS: She always did have sex on the brain. (*Refers to* ALISA.)

ALISA: I did not. I do now, but then . . . I did not.

LAVEER: Ha. As I recall there was a night we all stayed over your room . . .

BABBS: The night we had that freak snow storm.

LAVEER: The precise night. Janeen's feet got cold and you told . . .

ALISA: Oh no . . . Please don't bring that up.

LAVEER: *(To* ALISA*)* You told Janeen to get a pair of socks out of your drawer and she found a pack of . . .

THELMA: Prophylactics. And Alisa had to spend the entire night telling Janeen step by step what it was like to have sex.

LAVEER: I mean, step by step. Alisa was the only one out of the six of us who wasn't a virgin.

PANZI: Oh, you were not a virgin, Laveer.

LAVEER: I was.

PANZI: Why lie?

LAVEER: Why should I lie? I was a virgin.

PANZI: You were not a virgin.

LAVEER: *(Tension building.)* How are you going to tell me what I wasn't?

PANZI: Because I know.

LAVEER: Would it be too much to ask how? You inspect me with your little finger while I was sleeping or something?

ALISA: Okay, you two . . .

BABBS: I told you you can't have the two in one space without . . .

LAVEER: Telling me what I wasn't.

PANZI: You weren't.

ALISA: Can't you two be in the same room without . . . ?

LAVEER and PANZI: *(Simultaneously.)* No.

LAVEER: On that we do agree.

BABBS: Well, that's progress.

LAVEER: I need a refill. *(Refers to her glass.)* Anyone care to replenish their goblet?

BABBS: *(Extends her glass. To* THELMA*.)* And don't you say a word.

THELMA: Who's saying anything. I have a toll-free number to AA, remind me to give it to you.

BABBS: *(To* LAVEER*.)* I'll take a refill.

ALISA: I could use another one.

LAVEER: Why don't I just bring back the bottles, then we can all use that toll-free number to AA. *(*LAVEER *exits. Silence.)*

ALISA: *(To* PANZI*.)* I thought you were going to try to be civil.

PANZI: I am being civil.

BABBS: What is it between you two anyway?

PANZI: It's simple. I can't stand the . . .

BABBS: Bitch. We know, the question is why?

PANZI: I don't like her type.

ALISA: Oh God, we're back to graduation day again.

BABBS: Do you know how many years ago that was?

THELMA: Too many for all this ruckus.

PANZI: Look, Laveer is a . . . a mold of a type, and they're all the same: self centered, preoccupied in their beauty, their acquisitions, conquest, and a lot too little concern for others' needs and feelings. . . . Janeen needed a friend who was genuinely concerned about her.

BABBS: Panzi Lew McVain.

PANZI: Time proved who her friend was.

BABBS: With a little help.

PANZI: Like I said, time and actions proved who Janeen's friend was. (BABBS *turns her attention to the cosmetic makeover of* THELMA.)

THELMA: Panzi . . . how are you and that chess game of yours doing?

PANZI: My game? (*With light humor.*) Superb as usual.

THELMA: (*Referring to* PANZI.) A little short on modesty, isn't she?

ALISA: (*Laughs.*) What do you expect from the woman who held the northeastern championship among the women's colleges? She's moved from those minor victories to the chessboard tournaments of Europe.

THELMA: Do tell. Well, now, tell me our class didn't graduate and become the Who's Who of this world? (*Laughs. To* PANZI.) Let me be the first among the ladies here to say I am quite proud of you.

PANZI: Thanks.

THELMA: But how you manage to work those tournaments into your hospital routine is beyond me. I'm lucky if I can make time to have a full-course dinner.

PANZI: That's because the therapy world is a lot different than your doctor world. Besides, every now and then I luck up on a patient who has a good game. Keeps my game sharp.

ALISA: I say bravo to anyone who can deal with that game.

BABBS: Too long and arduous for me.

THELMA: Never could quite handle it.

PANZI: (*Lighting a cigarette.*) It's all about skill, strategy, and waiting out your opponent.

BABBS: Like I said, too long and arduous for me.

ALISA: It does go on forever, and without the benefits of Monopoly, no Get out of jail free cards, no buying up Park Place, Boardwalk . . .

BABBS: (*To* THELMA.) See what having babies does to you? (*Referring to* ALISA.)

ALISA: I beg your pardon, I've been playing Monopoly since I was a kid. You can learn a lot from Monopoly.

PANZI: You can learn a lot from chess.

ALISA: Chess lacks pizzazz, color. It's gray. Like battlefields. A little move here. A little move there. Wait. Move. Wait. Think. Wait . . . I like spontaneity. Jump on in there and do it kind of spontaneity.

BABBS: Oh yeah, that we know.

THELMA: Don't we? (*To* ALISA.) Eloping with Lloyd the way you did, without as much as a hint.

PANZI: Her chess game indicated she was capable of doing that.

BABBS: How?

PANZI: She plays chess the way she lives her life.

ALISA: Oh God, please . . . I play chess terribly.

PANZI: You're spontaneous, like you said. You're also lucky.

BABBS: (*To* ALISA.) I think that's a dig back to the day you beat her at her own game.

PANZI: It was not, but she is lucky. How did she obtain her real estate portfolio? A dollar bill, a federal government housing program, and what does she own today? Two apartment buildings.

ALISA: They're only two-story, eight-apartment dwellings.

PANZI: And five houses on the top of Tioga Street. The neighbors call the area Reynolds Landing. (THELMA *and* BABBS *laugh*.)

BABBS: Reynolds Landing? You can start your own nighttime serial.

PANZI: And all from a dollar.

THELMA: Do tell.

PANZI: From the way she told me the story, she woke up one morning, glanced through the paper, saw an article on the government's new home-buying program, and the rest is history. Now, is that spontaneity and luck or is it spontaneity and luck?

ALISA: (*Reflects on the phrase.*) Spontaneity and luck . . . Always amazes me how other people see things. Distance does that. (*Crosses to the window.*) Luck . . . (*Turns to* PANZI.) I was about . . . ten, my sister, Joyce, nine, Raymond fourteen, when our parents looked into our faces, looked around the room—the small kitchen, the living room with secondhand furniture—the house and family who'd gotten too much for them . . . They made a decision to leave. (BABBS *sits.*) Just like that, leave. And they did. They placed a box of Cheerios and Kellogg's Corn Flakes on the table, a half gallon of milk we'd gotten from the Borden's milk man

and left. Never came back. We waited, Raymond, Joyce and
I . . . We waited, but they never . . . Raymond called a
family meeting over the Monopoly game we'd started to pass
the time. The topic, our next move. Another pang of reality
after hopeless periodical peeks at the clock and front door.
Raymond said, after seven long days of waiting and seven
longer nights . . . He said we were going to keep the family
together. And we did.

THELMA: Dear God.

ALISA: Throughout the *whole* summer, until the fall, until
school, nosy neighbors and teachers had the welfare agency
at our door . . . We were placed in separate foster homes.
(*To* THELMA.) Separate new families . . . (*To* PANZI.) Until
that lucky morning I put a dollar bill on a piece of real estate
and put together what the neighbors call Reynolds Landing.
Maybe it should be called Myers-Reynolds Landing 'cause I
reunited Joyce and Raymond . . . and that's all of us up
there . . . All of us. (*Silence.*) So much for "luck."

PANZI: You know, if I had known I wouldn't have—

ALISA: Why should you? Why should any of you? All of you
coming from respectable families. What was I supposed to
do? Announce I had dogs for parents? No, not dogs, turtles.
Turtle mothers drop their eggs and then walk away. Was I
supposed to tell you that? No. I let you believe what you
wanted to believe. In the long run it was better for everyone.
I hated my parents less and got on with living and learning;
you do the best you can with what you get. (PANZI *lights
another cigarette.* ALISA *stands before* THELMA *and studies*
THELMA'*s transformation. The makeup and new hair style
have brought out her hidden attractiveness.*) Well, would you
take a look at our lady doctor?

THELMA: What?

BABBS: Well, get up and take a look. (THELMA *rises and
crosses to the mirror.*)

PANZI: (*Approvingly.*) Real nice.

THELMA: (*Excited.*) Really?

BABBS: Will you hurry up and look in that mirror?! (BABBS
follows THELMA *to the mirror.* BABBS *stares between the
mirror and* THELMA'*s face to read her reaction.* THELMA *is
pleasantly surprised.* THELMA *stares at herself. Silence. To*
THELMA.) Well . . .

THELMA: (*Staring at her reflection.*) I, um . . .

BABBS: Articulate.

THELMA: Alisa . . . would you pass me my glasses?

BABBS: Oh please, Thelma. Not those things. What you've got to do is get yourself some contacts.

THELMA: What I've got to do is see. (*Holds her glasses up to her eyes to get a clearer view. She does not put the glasses on, but holds them up to see through the lenses. To* BABBS.) What did you do?

BABBS: You like?

THELMA: (*Tickled. Pleased.*) Like?

(*Enter* LAVEER *with a tray holding the bottles of wine and spirits.*)

LAVEER: I just spoke with my mother, and the Trees are sending over something to eat . . . (*Surprised by* THELMA's *transformation.*) Thelma?

BABBS: Our very own.

ALISA: Beautiful, yes?

THELMA: Can you believe?

BABBS: Now, if she'd get herself a pair of contact lenses, she can show off those lashes.

THELMA: First chance I get. (*She embraces* BABBS.)

BABBS: That a promise?

THELMA: Um-humm . . . Thank you. Now, can I hire you to do this on a daily basis?

BABBS: (*To the group.*) Now see that? Taking advantage of me already. (*To* THELMA.) You may now look like a Nubian queen, but don't let your head swell too big. (*The women laugh and refreshen their drinks, all but* PANZI. PANZI *crosses to the window.*)

ALISA: (*Crosses to* PANZI.) How are you doing?

PANZI: I should be asking you that. I'm sorry about earlier. I had no idea.

ALISA: That was a long time ago. But I am worried about you. You're okay?

PANZI: Yeah . . . You know, it wasn't more than two months ago that we were sitting here in this room laughing, Janeen and me. Watching one of those Lou and Costello reruns. Janeen laughing that laugh only she could laugh.

(*Sound:* JANEEN's vibrant laughter.)

PANZI: She had such a great laugh.

ALISA: That she did. Puts me in the mind of our first year together. Most of us were in Blylor Hall . . . You, Janeen, and Lavy getting yourselves in this thing or the other. Janeen always laughing . . .

THELMA: Like the time Fat Lucy tried to climb out the window on those blankets to see that acne-faced towny boy . . .

BABBS: Oh God . . . (*Laughs.*) Janeen hanging out her window watching Lucy screaming: "You're going to fall on your behind."

THELMA: No. You've got to say it the way she used to say it, in that little-girl, proper voice of hers.

ALISA: (*Mimics* JANEEN.) "You're going to fall on your behind."

PANZI: (*Laughs.*) And she started that laugh of hers.

ALISA: You mean that whoop. God, can you hear it?

THELMA: Hear it? Can't you just see Lucy hanging on for dear life on those blankets? All two hundred pounds of Lucy hanging out of the second-story window of Blylor Hall.

BABBS: And when Janeen said—

LAVEER: (*A perfect imitation of* JANEEN's *voice.*) "If you fall, I'm going to scream. I mean it, Lucy. If that blanket rips and you fall, I'm going to laugh at you." (*The women laugh violently. Then the laughter stops. They stare at* LAVEER.)

ALISA: (*To* LAVEER.) If you didn't just sound like Janeen . . . Just like her.

THELMA: Just like her. (PANZI *is not impressed.*)

BABBS: (*To* LAVEER.) You might be able to imitate her speaking voice, but that laugh . . . Nobody, but nobody could do that but her. (*Summons up the laughter again.*) 'Cause when Lucy fell . . . when that blanket ripped and big Fat Lucy hit those bushes, bounced up, and sprawled herself out on that pavement—

THELMA: Janeen let out that—

ALISA: Whoop of hers.

THELMA: And all hell broke loose.

ALISA: Didn't it?

BABBS: I thought the child had killed herself. I mean, Lucy was laying out there all sprawled out like a whale beached up on the sand and—

LAVEER: Janeen laughed so hard she peed on herself.

THELMA: She wasn't the only one. (*She points to* ALISA.)

ALISA: I didn't.

THELMA: Tell the truth.

ALISA: Well . . . shit. Did you see Lucy? One leg over here . . . (*Demonstrates.*) The other one hidden somewhere under that twenty tons of lard she carried around . . .

THELMA: Her mouth all hung open like . . . (*Demonstrates.*)

BABBS: And that towny boy standing over her, staring down at her like he was crazed.

THELMA: The man was in shock. I mean, how many times do you get to see Dumbo do her flying act and her ears fail?

BABBS: And fail they did, 'cause Lucy just bounced. . . . I mean, the girl just bounced off the bushes and splashed.

ALISA: You know, whenever I get a little low, when my spirits drop, I think on Fat Lucy hanging onto those blankets, Janeen hanging out of that window . . .

PANZI: And that laugh.

ALISA: All I have to do is do an instant replay on that and . . . depression gets a backseat on the back burner.

LAVEER: Sometimes she could make me so mad, but . . . when Janeen laughed.

ALISA: When she let out that whoop . . .

THELMA: Hard to believe anyone who had that much life in her could . . .

PANZI: I miss her. I really do.

(*Lights dim.*)

ACT TWO

SCENE I

Lights rise on BABBS *as she enters singing off key and with a slight variation on the melody.*

BABBS: (*Singing.*)
Save me. Miss your lovin' arms.
You can save me. I been captured . . .

(*She refills her glass and drinks.*)
(*Enter* ALISA, *unnoticed. She observes* BABBS's *actions.*)

BABBS: (*Singing.*)
Save me. Miss your lovin' arms.
You can save me. I been captured
By your . . .
By your . . .
By your . . .
Shit! How'd those lyrics go? (*Drinks, then continues singing.*)
By your charms. Come on, save me.
Don't know what to do . . .
'Cause I'm . . .

ALISA: It might help if you had the right melody and sang it in the right key.
BABBS: All of us were not blessed with melodic voices. Besides, I've been told singing is good for the soul. My soul likes to sing. (ALISA *stares at* BABBS *and the brandy snifter. To* ALISA.) Yes?
ALISA: What?
BABBS: What's wrong?
ALISA: Why do you ask that?
BABBS: You're giving me one of those motherly concerned looks.
ALISA: *Moi?*
BABBS: Yes, you.

BABBS: Yes, you.

ALISA: Well, it wasn't my intention to give the impression—

BABBS: You're not spying on me, are you?

ALISA: Spying? Why should I be spying?

BABBS: You seemed quite comfortable in there.

ALISA: I could say the same of you. (BABBS *stares at* ALISA. ALISA *stares at* BABBS.)

BABBS: Alisa, I am simply trying to remember the lyrics to this song Janeen used to sing. (ALISA *nods.*) Panzi said it was a Supremes' song, I know better. (*Drinks down the contents of her glass.* ALISA *stares at her.*) Alisa! Will you stop that?

ALISA: What? What am I doing?

BABBS: Okay, all right. To allay any mounting fears or growing doubts . . . I came in here simply to retrieve my glass. This glass. (*Indicates the snifter.*) A very elegant and beautiful brandy snifter, I might add, a tribute to Janeen's impeccable taste. (*Refills the brandy snifter.*) You could say I've grown attached to its touch.

ALISA: I see.

BABBS: (*Turns to* ALISA.) What do you see, Alisa?

ALISA: You've grown attached to its touch. (ALISA *and* BABBS *fix their eyes on one another.*)

BABBS: Sometimes you see too much.

(LAVEER *enters.*)

BABBS: (*To* LAVEER.) Got a little too crowded in there for you?

LAVEER. You could say the air's a bit fresher out here.

BABBS: It was on the verge of getting a little too crowded in here as well. (*Smiles, crosses to* ALISA, *and then embraces her. To* ALISA.) But I love you anyway. (*To* LAVEER.) You must tell your mother's club. . . . What's the name of that group again?

LAVEER: The Trees.

BABBS: Right. Well, relay a great big thank-you for such a lovely meal.

ALISA: Ditto.

BABBS: It's scandalous anyone can fry a chicken the way that bird turned out. What's the name of your mother's club again?

LAVEER: (Correcting.) The correct term is "social and cultural enrichment organization."

BABBS: Oh, excuse me.

LAVEER: (*Cynically.*) Cynicism for a group whose social morals determine the rising and setting of the sun? Why should you sense a bit of cynicism?

BABBS: (*To* ALISA.) Looks like you popped the cork on the wrong bottle.

LAVEER: The Trees, they're . . . ticks. Old, powerful, domineering, meddlesome, and—let us not forget—benevolent and caring ticks.

BABBS: Who also know how to fry chicken.

LAVEER: Bloodsucking ticks who dictate what you can and cannot do, when you should or should not do, to whom you should or should not do or marry. They're a nasty little batch of mothers and fathers who rule lives. My parents, Janeen's parents, Walter's parents: a dangerous select group of decent—and I do stress the word *decent*—family-oriented professionals who promise success. See to success making you a doctor, lawyer, judge, wife of a doctor, lawyer, judge . . .

BABBS: Sounds reminiscent of my family clan.

LAVEER: You should not be blessed with such a family. The Trees seep like the morning fog. You look up and you're dead.

ALISA: That's what you think happened to Janeen.

LAVEER: They contributed their fair share. (*Crosses to the bookcase.*) Life, people, and complications.

BABBS: Things would be a lot less complicated for me if I could get the rest of these lyrics . . . (*To* LAVEER.) Remember that song Janeen used to sing, "Save Me"? (LAVEER *nods.*) Now listen . . . (*Singing off key.*)
Save me. Miss your lovin' arms.
You can save me. I been captured by your charms.
Come on and save me. Don't know what to do.
'Cause I'm . . . 'Cause I'm
Well, help me out.

LAVEER: (*Thinks. Speaking lyrics.*) "Lonely without you. And my world's turned all blue. Tell me, what should I do. 'Cause I'm lonely, lonely, lonely without you. Come on and save me."

BABBS: (*Excited.*) That's it! (*Singing off key.*)
'Cause I'm lonely without you.
And my world's turned all blue.
Tell me, what should I do.
'Cause I'm lonely, lonely, lonely without you.
Come on and save me.

Come on and save me.
I got it!!! Now to make Panzi eat mud. (*Crosses to exit. She quickly turns and retrieves her glass. To* ALISA.) What can I say? I've grown attached to its touch. (*Exits. Silence.* LAVEER *scans the titles of the books.* ALISA *crosses to the window.* BABBS *can be heard offstage singing "Save Me" off key.* THELMA *joins her, bringing the song on key and into the right melody. Periodic bursts of laughter interrupt the singing.*)

LAVEER: (*Listening to the singing.*) "Save Me" . . . Could stand for someone to do that . . . Alisa, what do you know about power?

ALISA: It's a great asset when the tenants' rents are due.

LAVEER: I mean ultimate power, the kind which . . . (*Snatches a tissue from the tissue box.*) Like this, representing lives. (*Indicates the tissue.*)

ALISA: Whose lives?

LAVEER: (*Thinks, and chooses not to be specific.*) Lives. Power gives you the ability to . . . (*Crumbles the tissue.*) I can do this, with lives, the lives of people I love.

ALISA: Ever thought of leaving the lives right there in the tissue box?

LAVEER: That's all I've been doing lately, thinking, but I'm being pushed. Damn it . . . Pushed, and pushed too hard.

(*Voices can be heard singing offstage. The women are singing the spoof on their alma mater. They sing off key, and in many cases they have forgotten some of the lyrics. There are intermittent intervals of laughter.* BABBS *can be heard singing off key.*)

ALISA: (*Listening.*) Babbs never could hold a tune.

LAVEER: Neither could Janeen.

ALISA: She said they sang in L sharps and M minors. (*Listens to* BABBS.) That is definitely an L sharp. (*Crosses to* LAVEER.) Interesting reading?

LAVEER: A long time ago, yes. Janeen and I used to read passages from this book on the back porch. I can't believe she even remembered the title. Funny what you learn about a person after they're gone.

ALISA: Yes, I guess it is.

LAVEER: I'm partially responsible for what happened.

ALISA: How?

LAVEER: Expected too much from her. Demanded too much.

Don't be such a spineless twerp! Try something you want to do! Who's it gonna hurt?" (*To* ALISA.) It hurts everyone, Alisa. Sometimes there are consequences . . . I remember coaxing Janeen into flipping the swings. Barbara Reeks and I . . . we'd done it a thousand times. Pumped the swings as high as we could and then flip them over the top bar.

ALISA: That was good and dangerous.

LAVEER: Who thought of danger? Correction, Janeen thought of the danger. Worried she'd fall, get hurt, her mother'd find out. I called her chicken one time too many and . . . the one time she tried, she fell. Blood was everywhere. Her mother had a fit and . . . I just wanted her to be strong, her own person, but . . . some people should be left alone. There're consequences for messing with lives. (*Replaces the book on the shelf.*)

ALISA: I think you're being a little too hard on yourself.

LAVEER: Maybe, maybe not.

ALISA: Well, I'm going to take in a little of this suburban porch sitting. Care to join me?

LAVEER: Later.

ALISA: Okay. Lavy . . . don't think too hard on things which were never in your hands. (*Pats* LAVEER *on the shoulder.* ALISA *exits.*)

(*The lights change. Enter* JANEEN.)

JANEEN. The roast ought to be done in a few more moments. (*Stares at* LAVEER.) I'm glad you came. (*Stares at* LAVEER *in her environment.*) I never could figure out what was missing here. I mean, I bought this and that and that and this and still I kept getting the feeling something was missing . . . you.

LAVEER: You flatter me.

JANEEN: I don't. But I have something which may be of interest to you.

LAVEER: What?

JANEEN (*Crosses to the wall unit and retrieves a small antique box. She crosses to* LAVEER *with the box.*) This.

LAVEER: And what, pray tell, is this?

JANEEN: Guess. (*Handing* LAVEER *the box.*)

LAVEER: I haven't the foggiest. (*Shakes the box.*) Well, what is it?

JANEEN: Patience. (*Crosses to the bookshelf. She removes a book and then retrieves a small key which has been hideen under it. She unlocks the box.*) Okay, open it.

LAVEER: (*Opens the box.*) You're kidding.

JANEEN: No.

LAVEER: These are mine?

JANEEN: Every single strand.

LAVEER: You know, I didn't believe you still had these.

JANEEN: Why wouldn't I? You're my friend . . . I'm glad you came. I really am. (*Silence. The two women quietly observe one another.*) You don't feel awkward, do you?

LAVEER: Why should I feel awkward?

JANEEN: I don't know, it's been a long time . . . a lot of years. Tell me about your life. Are you happy?

LAVEER: Yes.

JANEEN: I like that about you.

LAVEER: What?

JANEEN: The way you can say it all in so few words, yes.

LAVEER: I'm a painter. It's the writer who's abundant with words. Why'd you ask if I was happy?

JANEEN: Because I want to know. Gee, can't a friend ask a friend if she's happy or not?

LAVEER: Are you?

JANEEN: What?

LAVEER: Happy?

JANEEN: Sure. Why shouldn't I be? I've got Walter, a home, two cars, and a partridge in a pear tree.

LAVEER: Do you love him?

JANEEN: Why ask a question like that?

LAVEER: I want to know.

JANEEN: You're mocking me.

LAVEER: Well . . .

JANEEN: On the subject of love. He loves me.

LAVEER: Janeen.

JANEEN: He finally got his practice started—a relief to his family and my mother. I mean, now we can start a family and that would make our families very happy.

LAVEER: And what would make you happy?

JANEEN: I am happy.

LAVEER: Do you love him?

JANEEN: (*Quickly.*) Yes. (*Pause.*) Really, I do. I really do.

LAVEER: But . . .

JANEEN: Lavy! . . . Sometimes I think you can read my mind.

LAVEER: Don't change the subject.

JANEEN: Do I love him? Sometimes and sometimes . . . things

just didn't turn out the way I thought they would. Like in the books. Remember? I keep waiting for the earth to move, explosions . . . something.

LAVEER: Still standing out on the peripheral . . . Janeen, you make it move—that is, with a little help. Walter . . . lousy lover?

JANEEN: No! I mean . . . who do I compare him with? Rayford Jones is hardly anyone to compare anyone with. I've only had two men in my life . . . no, I lie, three but the third doesn't count. Three men, isn't that a disgrace?

LAVEER: No.

JANEEN: Lavy!

LAVEER: It's not.

JANEEN: How many men have you had?

LAVEER: Too many to count.

JANEEN: You see.

LAVEER: Three men in your life is not a disgrace. I should be so lucky.

JANEEN: Really?

LAVEER: Does Walter make you feel good? Now, don't lie.

JANEEN: Yes.

LAVEER: He's versatile?

JANEEN: (*Embarrassed.*) Lavy! . . . Yes.

LAVEER: You reach orgasms?

JANEEN: (*Embarassed.*) Yes.

LAVEER: Why are you so embarrassed? You're married to the man, aren't you?

JANEEN: Yes, but . . .

LAVEER: But what?

JANEEN: This is embarrassing.

LAVEER: Why?

JANEEN: I don't know. I get this way. On our honeymoon I kept getting this vision of everyone in the church and reception standing around the bed watching us. It was embarrassing.

LAVEER: Why?

JANEEN: I told you, I don't know.

LAVEER: You act like you were a virgin before you married Walter.

JANEEN: Half the world didn't know I was going to make love before I got married. You should see how those people look at you. Even now . . . Sometimes, when I'm shopping at the supermarket. One of the Trees will come up to me, look down at my stomach, and give me that look which says,

"When are you going to put that screwing you and Walter are doing to some use? When are you going to make a baby?" I tell you it's embarrassing.

LAVEER: It shouldn't be. Not if you're in love and you're happy. Why should you care what people think about what you do with your personal life?

JANEEN: I don't know, I do . . .

LAVEER: You're not in love with him.

JANEEN: I am.

LAVEER: Okay.

JANEEN: I am. He's a really sweet man.

LAVEER: And your mother approved of him.

JANEEN: Well, it's important for your parents to approve . . .

LAVEER: You're not in love with him.

JANEEN: I am. I don't know if he knows that I am, but I am. Lavy, sometimes, when he kisses me it's like . . . being in an elevator. You ever get that elevator sensation? I like kissing him.

LAVEER: Liking his kisses is not the same as loving him.

JANEEN: I like talking to him . . . I'm just afraid I'm going to fuck things up.

LAVEER: Fuck? Janeen said the word *fuck*?

JANEEN: I know how to swear.

LAVEER: I see. Tell me, why do you think you might fuck things up?

JANEEN: I guess I worry too much about too many things. I guess it's getting in the way.

LAVEER: Tell you what. While you're adding four-letter words to your vocabulary, add a little spunk. The next time you and Walter get together in the sack, and the eyes of all the township are standing around your bed, give them a little show. Screw Walter's ears off, their eyes out, and give yourself one hell of a good time. Those visions, they're only visions of your mind, like the boogy man. Remember?

JANEEN: You know why I missed you?

LAVEER: I know, my radiant personality.

JANEEN: No.

LAVEER: What?

JANEEN: I don't know. I just missed you. (*Bursts into her laughter.*) Oh! My roast. Walter should be home any minute and . . . I forgot to tell you, he's bringing Julian Ray with him. (*Again bursts into her vibrant laughter.*)

LAVEER: Julian Ray? Janeen!

JANEEN: (*Laughing.*) What?

LAVEER: Janeen!
JANEEN: (*Laughing.*) What? (*Exits laughing.*)

(*Lights change back to setting of previous scene.* LAVEER *replaces the antique box on the bookshelf.*)

SCENE II

Enter BABBS, *high spirited. She carries with her a dessert plate. She stops her stride noticing* LAVEER *handling the antique box. She assesses the moment and then enters.*

BABBS: (*In her anchor person voice.*) Good evening. This is Babbs Wilkerson with the Eyewitness News. This evening we are in the suburban community of Ewing Township, New Jersey. Before us is the illustrious and attractive visual artist, Laveer Swan. (*Approaches* LAVEER.) Miss Swan, we are told you fly once a year to partake in the Trees' annual German Chocolate Cake Eating Spree.
LAVEER: (*Laughs.*) Once a year for the . . .
BABBS: (*Coaxing* LAVEER.) Trees' annual German Chocolate Cake Eating Spree.
LAVEER: Ah, yes. Well . . . I certainly try.
BABBS: (*In her anchor person voice.*) Our Eyewitness cameras visited the kitchen of this lovely abode and found . . . Well . . . (*To imaginary audience.*) It is almost unbelievable what this cake does to one's behavior. (*Hands the plate to* LAVEER.) There is a Dr. Thelma Carlson in the kitchen hovering over the cake with a very sharp carving knife. (*Demonstrates.*) And she has threatened to stab and pierce anyone who attempts to take another slice of this most delicious cake. (*Fingers a piece of* LAVEER's *cake. To* LAVEER.) Please tell our viewing audience . . . (*Looks into area of imaginary audience.*) has this always been the effect of your mother's baking?
LAVEER: (*Laughs.*) Thelma's doing what?
BABBS: (*In her normal voice.*) I thought I'd bring you a slice before there wasn't a slice left, or before it was sautéed in blood. This cake brought out the worst in Thelma. (*Steals another small portion of* LAVEER's *cake.*)
LAVEER: I see she's not the only one who's gotten addicted.
BABBS: What can I say? Your mother can bake her ass off. (*Pause.*) How are you holding up?

LAVEER: You know me. I always hold up.

BABBS: You've been a little too quiet for me, both you and Panzi. (*Examines the antique box.*) Beautiful.

LAVEER: (*Eating the cake.*) Yes.

BABBS: Lavy . . .

LAVEER: Umm.

BABBS: Tell me if I'm getting out of line, but . . . this thing between you and Panzi and Panzi and Walter.

LAVEER: What makes you think there's something between Panzi and Walter?

BABBS: I was there when he gave you the keys, and I saw his reaction to Panzi a little earlier in the day.

LAVEER: And your reporter antennae are still operative. Yes?

BABBS: You don't lose the knack simply because you move from the college newspaper to the anchor spot on the evening news. Care to talk?

LAVEER: We are talking.

BABBS: I retreat. Okay? (*Moves about the room admiring the furnishings and decorations.*) I'm told Walter's going to get rid of all of this.

LAVEER: So they say.

BABBS: And he hasn't been back since he found her.

LAVEER: No.

BABBS: Must have really loved her, to react like that.

LAVEER: Different people grieve differently.

BABBS: Grieve . . .

LAVEER: Still fishing up a story?

BABBS: No, no. So . . . what have you decided about Bahia? Still going?

LAVEER: Maybe in the spring. What I'd like to do is go home, have a couple of Juan's Margarita Bombs, pull out my brightest tubes of reds, yellows, oranges, turquoises, paint, and think.

BABBS: About Janeen.

LAVEER: About a lot of things. And yes, Janeen. Jesus, you're persistent. (*Pause.*) I guess you know she called me.

BABBS: I was told.

LAVEER: The day before she washed the pills down with champagne. She as much as announced it. But then, how many times had Janeen said . . .

(*Lights rise on* JANEEN.)

JANEEN: I fucked up, Lavy. This time I really fucked up. You know what I'd like to do? Close my eyes and start it all over again. (*Lights dim on* JANEEN.)

BABBS: Feeling guilty?

LAVEER: Guilty? No. Hurt, yes. You know, I heard it in her voice, the seriousness.

(*Lights rise on* JANEEN.)

JANEEN: I'd like to close my eyes and sleep right through all of this. (*Lights dim on* JANEEN.)

LAVEER: It was as though there was more than desire behind her words, there was the sense of decision. I couldn't shake that sound. Caused me to reroute my ticket and book myself on the first flight coming here. Too late . . .

BABBS: You tried.

LAVEER: I wonder if they give Brownie points in heaven to all the people who tried but didn't succeed. (BABBS *refills her brandy snifter*.) Ahh, enough of that. When did all this heavy drinking start?

BABBS: We TV world people live highly stressed lives. It's par for the course. (*Drinks.*)

LAVEER: You're going to end up with cirrhosis of the liver.

BABBS: So I get cirrhosis of the liver.

LAVEER: (*Pause.*) What are you doing to yourself?

BABBS: What am I doing to myself? What haven't I done? I'm thirty-seven, single, divorced, lonely, and stuck in a rut. Great subject for a Sunday evening special, hosted by . . . Babbs Wilkerson. (*In her anchor person voice.*) Good evening. Babbs Wilkerson. Our topic for the evening, "Where are the men of the sixties?" or . . . (*In her normal voice.*) "God, I'd just love to run up on one of those fine-spirited, driven, dreamin', doin', basketball-playin', DuBois readin', rhythm-and-blues-lovin', nation-buildin', woman-lovin', brothers of the sixties." (*To* LAVEER.) Long on the title, huh? (*Pause.*) I'm still in love with Frank. How many years is it now? And I'm still in love with him.

LAVEER: Ever thought of seeing him? It would save your liver.

BABBS: I did. About a year ago. You know what I found out? I'm not really in love with Frank, but I'm in love with Frank. You see the little Medford, Mass. girl fell in love with that New York Harlem Frank he was in the sixties. Remember the sixties? I'm hooked on midnight navy blue-black, six-four, suave-talking, intelligent, pretty teeth, good-kissing, fine-loving, "I'm going to be somebody," nation-building, brothers of the sixties. I'm hooked. Shit! . . . Try to find one today.

(*Enter* THELMA *and* PANZI.)

THELMA: Try to find one of what today?

LAVEER: The brothers from the sixties.

THELMA: Who's looking for the brothers from the sixties?

BABBS: I am. (*To* LAVEER.) I did a special on our penal system about a year ago. My way of finding out just how many of our men are rotting away in there. You wouldn't believe. Fine ones, kind ones, shy ones . . .

PANZI: Sounds like a song to me.

BABBS: Okay . . . laugh it off but . . . they're in there, all kinds of charges: nickel bags, subversion, being a Panther, being a friend of a Panther. All these fine brothers from the sixties behind bars, my heart . . .

THELMA: (*Softly, to* LAVEER.) How'd we get on this?

LAVEER: Frank.

BABBS: You know, I felt good about myself in the sixties. The brothers were men. You didn't have to worry about the color of your skin.

PANZI: She's rhyming again.

BABBS: (*Drinks.*) Damn, I miss the sixties. (*To* THELMA.) How you ever missed the spirit of the sixties is still beyond me. And the men . . . the confidence, drive, determination. That stuff moved mountains. Damn the seventies and eighties . . . Everything's changed. Look at Frank. He's complacent. Harlem, revolutionary Frank . . . I need me a man with a mixture. You know? A street-wise, book-wise, cognac and Budweiser mixture. (*Pause.*) You think I'll find that in Minneapolis? Maybe I ought to buy a home in Dorchester and work in a community center.

THELMA: Now I know she's drunk.

BABBS: I beg your pardon. I am not drunk. (*Crossing to* THELMA.) Tell me something, Thelma. Now stop me if you think I'm getting out of line but . . . you know, I always thought you were a beautiful woman. I know what you think, and I think you have a piss-poor opinion of your God-given . . . (*Thinks.*) attributes . . .

LAVEER: Come on, Babbs, let's go out on the porch for a little air.

BABBS: I don't need any air. (*To* THELMA.) I'm really confused about some things . . . And I don't mean to offend you—

LAVEER: Come on, Babbs.

BABBS: I told you, I don't need no air! (*To* THELMA.) Where was I? Oh yeah . . . How did you make it through the sixties and not come out with a better way of feeling about yourself? That was the dawn of Essence. How'd you do it? Dark clothes, thick glasses, corner of the room. I mean, that was the time to step forward and shine, and you stepped backward and hid. Why? (*Silence.*) Would it be too much to ask for an answer?

THELMA: (*Silence.*) You want an answer? I don't have one. What do you expect? Why is the sky blue? Why is one child to healthy parents born brilliant while the other retarded? I don't know. You understand? You met my sister, Ava, my brothers James and Dawson . . . You get a good look at them? Hum? Could have come from your family, right? Now you look at me. Get yourself a good look at me. (*Pause.*) In my house, my family . . . My people ooh and ahh when a baby is born with light eyes, light hair, and God bless the lightest skin possible, your skin . . .

BABBS: That doesn't say your brothers and sister are more beautiful because—

THELMA: You did not grow up in my house! You understand? You did not live through the subtleties. I did. I had to be better than everyone. Become a doctor. Did they? You don't shake that kind of pain overnight. Neither you, the sixties, Martin Luther, Stokely, Rap, Malcolm, or a new make over (*Indicates her face.*) is going to change what I feel. You don't think I've tried? My mirrors don't reflect back the same reflection as yours.

BABBS: It's not supposed to.

THELMA: In my world it is. Now if that sounds sick, it sounds sick and you'll pardon me if it takes me a little longer to work this thing through. Who knows, I might surprise you. Wake up one morning healed, like in a hands-on service. But right now . . . I don't want to talk about it, especially to you. (*Crosses to the door.*) Now, if you don't mind, I'll excuse myself for a little of this northern porch sitting. Maybe the east wind will cleanse me, heal me. I might even return glowing with whatever it is you'd like me to have, but right now I need some air. (*Exits.*)

BABBS: (*Silence.*) Well, I guess I fucked up that time, didn't I? Guess this is giving me a bit of cirrhosis of the brain.

(*Places the brandy snifter on the table.*) Now to eat crow and beg her forgiveness. (*Crosses to the door and exits. Silence.* PANZI *and* LAVEER *maintain their perimeter positions.*)

LAVEER: Are you going to continue to grit your teeth and shoot mental daggers, or are you going to get what it is off your chest?

PANZI: You are one nervy bitch. How dare you presume yourself on this moment?

LAVEER: I didn't know I was "presuming" myself on the moment.

PANZI: What are you doing here?

LAVEER: I thought that was obvious.

PANZI: I resent you being here.

LAVEER: Panzi, it's been a long four days, an especially longer day today, so if you please . . .

PANZI: Just what went on between you and Janeen during her last week?

LAVEER: Not that it's any of your business, a few phone calls.

PANZI: I'm supposed to believe that?

LAVEER: Frankly, I don't care what you believe. (*Replenishes her glass.*)

PANZI: A few phone calls and she commits suicide.

LAVEER: Are you implying I had something to do with her suicide?

PANZI: What did you two talk about?

LAVEER: Let's get one thing straight, right now. I am a thirty-eight-year-old woman. It has been some thirty odd years since I was a child, so don't you speak to me in that tone.

PANZI: I want to know what was going on between you and Janeen before—

LAVEER: You want . . . You think I give a good shit about what you want? It was your wants that brought all this to a head in the first place. (*Sarcastic mimic.*) You want . . .

PANZI: What are you getting at?

LAVEER: I am getting at nothing. I am stating facts. Given me via the horse's mouth.

(*The lights change. The lights rise on* JANEEN.)

JANEEN: (*Meekly, on phone.*) Lavy?

LAVEER: Umm-humm.

JANEEN: It's me . . . Janeen. I was hoping I would catch you. Are you still going to Brazil?

LAVEER: First thing tomorrow morning. (*Silence.*) Janeen
. . . is there something wrong?

JANEEN: I'm pregnant.

LAVEER: Congratulations. (*No response.*) You are happy,
aren't you? (*No response.*) Didn't you say you had decided
to have—

JANEEN: He raped me.

LAVEER: Who raped you? (*No response.*) Janeen? . . . Who
raped you?

JANEEN: I don't blame him. I mean, if I had been in his shoes,
I guess I—

LAVEER: Janeen, what are you talking about? Who raped—

JANEEN: I didn't mean to hurt him.

LAVEER: Damn it, Janeen!

JANEEN: I'd like to just close my eyes, go back to June, and
change it, but it's not that easy, is it?

LAVEER: Who raped you?

JANEEN: Walter.

LAVEER: (*Astonished.*) Our Walter? Why? (JANEEN *paces and
cries.*) Janeen . . . are you still there?

JANEEN: (*Meekly.*) Yes.

LAVEER: Jesus . . . what happened?

JANEEN: I want you to promise me something. Promise me
you'll never walk away again . . . I'm not sure I can handle
all this by myself. Promise me, Lavy.

LAVEER: I'm not going anywhere.

JANEEN: Promise you'll stay my friend.

LAVEER: Janeen!

JANEEN: Promise!

LAVEER: I promise. Whatever you want me to promise I promise. Now, tell—

JANEEN: I thought everything was going to bounce back to
normal. Nobody's ever died in my family before. Death . . .
it changes things. Leaves holes. All of a sudden there were
so many holes . . . I've been going through a crying binge.
I can't seem to stop crying. Like a week or so after Daddy's
funeral, I was walking through the park and all of a sudden
I started crying, for no reason, crying, right in the middle of
the lawn—

LAVEER: That's normal, Janeen.

JANEEN: I couldn't stop. Tears everywhere, brought on by
everything . . . Talk about losing control. And Walter, God,
it seemed his lecture and conference schedule just picked up.
For the first time in our marriage I didn't want him to go. I

didn't want him to go. I didn't want to sit here in this silence.
I needed him to . . . especially that weekend. I needed him
to . . . but he was giving the opening speech or something
and how could I ask him to stay? What grounds did I have?
The crazies, a spell of the cries? I called Panzi. She canceled
weekend plans and came down . . .

(*Lights change.* LAVEER *freezes.* PANZI *participates in the
flashback. It is a flashback within a flashback.*)

PANZI: You should have called me earlier.
JANEEN: Yes, but . . .
PANZI: No buts, you should have called. What are friends for?
JANEEN: I seem to have become such a pest these days.
PANZI: You should have—
JANEEN: Called. I'm sorry.
PANZI: Just make sure you remember what friends are for, the
    next time. (*Tastes the caviar.*)
JANEEN: You like? (*Refers to the caviar.*)
PANZI: Not bad.
JANEEN: (*Astonished.*) Not bad?!
PANZI: It's not bad. What amazes me is how you can have an
    obsession for caviar and on the other hand be so repulsed
    by sushi.
JANEEN: Shushi! Raw fish? Yelk . . . Ooooouuu . . . (*Shrugs
    her shoulders.*)
PANZI: Janeen, I know a few hundred thousand people who
    would say, "Fish eggs? Yelk Oooooouuuu." (*Mimicking*
    JANEEN.)
JANEEN: I'll have you know those are not just any fish eggs
    you are eating there. My dear, what your palate is now
    enjoying is Russian sturgeon.
PANZI: (*Playfully.*) My, my, the good stuff. I'm honored.
    Champagne (*Indicates the bottle.*) and Russian sturgeon. And
    it's not a wedding reception. To what do I owe the honor?
JANEEN: Friendship.
PANZI: I'm truly honored.
JANEEN: And memory.
PANZI: I see. "And memory." Does that mean I'm sharing this
    with someone, or something else?
JANEEN: Daddy gave them, the champagne and caviar, to Wal-
    ter and me for our anniversary, a whole case of both. He
    always had great taste, and I thought it would be nice to

have some today since I woke up with Daddy, caviar, and champagne on the brain. So in honor of your coming . . . (*Raises her glass. She then crosses to the window. Her mood is that of reflection. She fights tears. Turning to* PANZI.) I'm sorry . . . Going through another one of my crying spells . . .

PANZI: What are friends for? (*Wraps her arm around* JANEEN. *The two embrace.*)

JANEEN: You are a good friend. Thanks. (*Touches* PANZI's *face and then moves away.*) This is all so new . . . These feelings . . . God, does it ever end?

PANZI: Yeah.

JANEEN: When? Death . . . God, it's something you can't prepare yourself for, is it? Did you feel this way when your mother died?

PANZI: My mother? (*Crosses away.*) I didn't feel much of anything when she died. She wasn't the kind of woman who'd let a daughter child love her. No, we didn't have the relationship you had with your father.

JANEEN: I feel so empty.

PANZI: It'll pass. It takes its own time.

JANEEN: I hope time is on my side. This is making me crazy. Sometimes, when I'm in here alone . . . all of a sudden, out of nowhere I hear Stanley Witherspoon singing "Precious Lord" and . . .

PANZI: You need to get away.

JANEEN: Where? I can't shut off the voices inside my head, the memories, the emptiness . . .

PANZI: You need a fun spot, bright sun, fun, leave-your-worries-behind kind of spot.

JANEEN: What kind of a fun spot?

PANZI: An island, Caribbean, Mediterranean . . .

JANEEN: (*Crosses to the antique box. She fingers it.*) I've got the right place. Hawaii.

PANZI: Now, that's the kind I mean.

JANEEN: God, I hadn't thought about that in years. Funny how things make you remember. (*Fingers the box.*) When I was a kid, Lavy and I would take Daddy's *Trenton Times*, cut it up into strips, tie the paper around our waists, and do the hula on the front lawn. There was a time, the only place we ever wanted to visit was Hawaii.

PANZI: You and Laveer?

JANEEN: Umm . . .

PANZI: Giving this a little thought, you know there are closer paradise islands. Right off the East Coast . . .

JANEEN: My mind's made up. Hawaii. I don't think I'll have to work too hard to get Walter to come along. He's due for a vacation. Thanks. (*Pats* PANZI *as she crosses to the champagne.*) That was a great suggestion. More? (*Offering* PANZI *the champagne.*)

PANZI: A little.

JANEEN: Hawaii . . . Funny how you forget things. Maybe seeing Lavy helped bring it to the surface.

PANZI: Laveer?

JANEEN: Umm-humm.

PANZI: She was here?

JANEEN: Yeah. For Daddy's funeral.

PANZI: That was . . . (*Calculates.*) five months ago.

JANEEN: Yeah.

PANZI: Were you going to tell me or was it a slip of the mouth, a thought out of place?

JANEEN: Yes, but . . . I forgot.

PANZI: I see.

JANEEN: Besides, talking to you about Lavy isn't the easiest of things, you know. And they were close, Lavy and Daddy. So out of deference to him I thought she should know, so I called.

PANZI: I see.

JANEEN: God, Panzi . . . it's been years since that fall-out and people change. She's changed.

PANZI: I see. (*Crosses to the window.*)

JANEEN: (*Assessing* PANZI's *mood.*) What do you see?

PANZI: What do I see? It's still raining.

JANEEN: Please don't do this. Panzi, I need you to not do this.

PANZI: I didn't know I was *doing* anything.

JANEEN: She's different.

PANZI: I see.

JANEEN: Will you stop saying that? "I see. I see."

PANZI: What am I supposed to say? This hurts, you know.

JANEEN: Why? Lavy came up for Daddy's funeral. Why should that hurt you?

PANZI: What did I say when you called me in Switzerland about your father?

JANEEN: You offered to come back to the States.

PANZI: And what did you say? Humm? It wasn't necessary. You'd be alright. Right? Was that after you'd contacted Laveer? . . . I'm supposed to be your friend, your "closest friend" as you put it, but what did you do? What corner of the world did you pull her out of?

JANEEN: Mexico.

PANZI: Mexico. You call her in from Mexico and tell me to stay in Switzerland. I feel hurt because . . . as a friend, your close friend, I should have been here.

JANEEN: Panzi, Lavy and Daddy were close. Besides, Lavy's—

PANZI: If you don't mind, I don't want to discuss Laveer.

JANEEN: I need all of us to be friends again. (*No response.*) I've given it a lot of thought. Why can't we leave the arguments and the past in the past? Daddy's death . . . it's gotten me to thinking, and asking questions. We're here on this planet for what, a brief moment? All the seconds are important. And I've been asking myself, What have I done? What have I known? What have I seen, felt? Having friends around you, who share things with you, they make you feel. Living makes you feel and . . . I wonder if Daddy ever lived, ever felt, ever really shared with anyone . . . He was so safe. Everything done just so, arranged just so. His life monitored by his parents, the Trees, Momma . . . I ask myself if *I've* lived, if *I* ever felt anything and . . . the times I felt, truly enjoyed, they were the times I shared with you and Lavy. God, it seems so long ago, those yesterdays . . . Those were the good times.

PANZI: That was a long time ago.

JANEEN: It wasn't about being safe. Remember? Everyone was discovering, finding, trying . . . I should have used those years. I wish I could have used them because . . . (*Turns to* PANZI.) I've got great big holes in me and I want them filled again. I know it sounds selfish, but I feel empty and I want to feel something. I want to enjoy something before I die.

PANZI: What are you really trying to say?

JANEEN: I don't know. (*Inhales and exhales.*) Walter's not filling them. I mean, he's a nice man. God, please don't get me wrong. He's a good man, a good husband. He's a good person . . . He's . . . safe. He's not passionate. Lacks passion. There's no passion in his living, in what he does . . . and that's boring. Ewing Township is boring. My life is boring. Teaching is boring . . . And there're these giant holes. Everyplace, giant holes . . . (*Tries to pull herself together.*) I feel whole when I'm with you and Lavy. I wish the two of you could just . . . make up. Life was so much fuller when we were back at—

PANZI: You can't go back.

JANEEN: Why?

PANZI: Time moves on. Life changes. People change.

JANEEN: I know, but . . .

PANZI: Do you understand me? *People* change.

JANEEN: Yes! Lavy's—

PANZI: I don't want to talk about Laveer! I do not want to talk about Laveer. I'm talking about me . . . about you. (*Pause.*) Janeen, what do you want from me?

JANEEN: I don't know . . . I don't want to be safe anymore.

PANZI: (*Silence. She stares at* JANEEN. *She checks her watch.*) It's almost show time. I'd better make that popcorn before the film festival starts.

JANEEN: You ever think about the old days, the dorm, late-night talks? . . . The sentences we didn't have to complete, thoughts we didn't have to translate into words. We kind of just knew . . . That strange closeness women have with women. We just knew, like . . . fine tuning. I . . . I wanted Walter to sense I needed him here this weekend. He didn't: I didn't want to have to come out and ask him. I wanted him to sense it, know it, like I know when he needs me. He doesn't have to ask. And . . . he's not a bad person because he didn't know I needed him. I don't love him less because of it. I just needed him to sense . . . I'm just realizing there is a difference between men and women.

PANZI: Yes, there is.

JANEEN: It would be so nice if you and Lavy and I could be close again.

PANZI: Janeen, there was never any true closeness between Laveer and I.

JANEEN: But you wanted it. I know, I saw . . . I did try.

PANZI: Yes, Janeen, I know, but some things you can't force. I learned that from a great one, a great teacher—my momma. (*Pulling herself back to the moment.*) Look, I'd better get to that popcorn. We don't want to miss the show, do we?

(*The lighting shifts back to previous scene.* PANZI *freezes.*)

JANEEN: You know, that Sunday was strange from the start. The sun and the rain kept doing crazy things. You remember when it rained while the sun was out, we used to say the devil was beating his wife. You remember?

LAVEER: Yes.

JANEEN: We talked, Panzi and me, talked about things I hadn't voiced to anyone before, new revelations . . . I mentioned you had come up for Daddy's funeral. That went over like a thunderbolt.

LAVEER: I'm sure it did.

JANEEN: She made popcorn, we opened another bottle of champagne and watched a film festival of Bud Abbot and Lou Costello on the set . . . I hadn't laughed in what seemed like years. I remember thinking that while watching Lou get himself into one jam after another and then . . . I was crying. I don't even know the transition from laughter to tears. Everything was garbled, confused . . . and I couldn't stop crying. The images, thoughts racing through my mind: Daddy, Walter, new needs, thoughts . . . I missed him, Daddy. I needed Walter. (*Pause.*) She took a hanky and wiped my eyes. I could hear her voice saying everything would be all right, but I couldn't stop crying. She kissed my forehead. I remembered the softness of her kiss and my mind . . . I saw Walter. For a minute I saw . . . She kissed me. (*Silence.*) I remember going upstairs. Panzi undressing me. Panzi touching me. Her fingers, the softness . . . Her kisses and . . . my mind. (*Silence.*) Say something.

LAVEER: What do you want me to say?

JANEEN: Just say something. Please, don't you be silent. Say something.

LAVEER: What can I say? I'm not going to judge.

JANEEN: I do . . . Oh, God, I do. But for a moment . . . I wasn't safe. I didn't care what anyone thought. I finally made a move without consultation and approval, and I felt something. I felt . . . Then my eyes, my mind, I couldn't get them out of my eyes . . . Reverend Johnson, Sister Miller, Aunt Louise, Momma, Daddy—all of them standing around the bed, watching Panzi and me . . . Their disappointment . . .

LAVEER: Their disappointment is not important; what is, is how you felt.

JANEEN: How I felt? God forgive me. I felt good. I needed . . . to be held. I needed arms, kisses . . . And her words . . .

PANZI: (*To* JANEEN.) I need you.

JANEEN: So softly, over and over again . . .

PANZI: (*To* JANEEN.) I love you.

JANEEN: God forgive me, but I wanted her, that moment, that passion. I felt something and it was good . . . But those eyes hovering over us, they wouldn't go away . . . They wouldn't go away . . . And I couldn't run. I couldn't. She was giving me something I needed. I couldn't run, I couldn't. (*Freezes.*)

(*Lights rise on the* PANZI *and* LAVEER *scene.*)

LAVEER: (*To* PANZI.) I know what happened.

PANZI: Just what do you know?

LAVEER: Don't play games with me. God knows, right now, I'd serve a long term in hell for what I could do to you. But that won't bring her back, will it? (*No response.*) Will it?! (*No response.*) Ironically, I don't even care about your sexual preferences.

PANZI: My sexual . . .

LAVEER: Believe me, you can screw cows, trees, and bumble-bees for all I care, but Janeen . . . She was not ready for you.

PANZI: I see, you're an authority on Janeen.

LAVEER: I knew her, yes.

PANZI: How well? How well did you know her?

LAVEER: Implying?

PANZI: You're jealous, aren't you? You're jealous of what Janeen and I had.

LAVEER: Jealous?

PANZI: I always knew you had a thing for her.

LAVEER: A "thing" . . . If that means friendship, yes.

PANZI: Is that what you call it? I'm straightforward with mine. Care to come out of your closet?

LAVEER: My closet? Panzi. I'm going to set one thing straight with you right now. *If* I had loved Janeen sexually, I would have loved her. You get what I'm saying? I would have loved her. No pretense. No hiding. No lying. No desertion. I would have loved her.

PANZI: Really.

LAVEER: That check you can cash, deposit, and draw interest on. So you count your blessings I was never your competition.

PANZI: I suppose I should be grateful.

LAVEER: Oh yeah.

PANZI: Pretty sure of yourself.

LAVEER: Undoubtedly. (*Pause.*) You had not right to do that to her.

PANZI: Do what to her? You act as though she was a child.

LAVEER: In many ways she was.

PANZI: She was a woman and she made a woman's choice.

LAVEER: Janeen never made a choice about anything. You seduced her with the same tasteless scruples as an old man turning out a young girl.

PANZI: Janeen was a woman.
LAVEER: You're a disgrace.
PANZI: Am I?
LAVEER: And you mock every woman-to-woman relationship based on love and respect.
PANZI: I loved Janeen.
LAVEER: You fucked Janeen. She was nothing more to you than another piece of ass.
PANZI: Really? You know what I think's got you all fluffed out, you wanted her all for yourself.
LAVEER: You're disgusting.
PANZI: Like I said before, jealous. That is the key to all this, isn't it?
LAVEER: The key, the key . . . Yes, let us deal with the key. These keys . . . (*Refers to the house keys.*) You know these, the ones which had you bent out of shape. I think you were distressed at Walter's attitude toward you, why he didn't give these to you. His reason: a scene he happened upon, in his home, in his bed, between his wife and you.
PANZI: I'm supposed to believe that.
LAVEER: Try the process of deduction. Who did he give the keys to?

(*Lights rise on* JANEEN.)

JANEEN: I didn't see him. Neither did Panzi, but he saw and he changed. Everything changed. I should have known . . . It was weeks before we made love. Weeks of silence, a change in his mood, our eyes never meeting. I should have known . . . Then one Sunday morning—strange, they've taken on a whole new meaning, Sunday mornings—he made an announcement, said we were going to make love. Imagine? A command about making love. He rode me. Hard . . . just took me. Didn't even give me time to put my protection in. Told me not to worry while he pounded away. I kept saying to myself, "He wants to hurt me." I didn't know why, but there was no tenderness, no love . . . When he finished, he got up, showered, gnarled his mouth, and spit the kisses into the basin. (*Pause.*) This past Friday I told him I was pregnant. His face . . . emotionless. Walter's face, the man who wanted a house full of children. There was only silence, long silence, the kind that gives headaches. Thick silence . . . He told me everything, a replay of every detail he had seen. I wanted to vomit. I couldn't . . . The knot lodged itself in my throat and just sat there torturing me. He was torturing me. The silence, his eyes, everything torturing. You know what he said? "See if Panzi can do that. See if your lady lover can make you a baby."

(*Lights dim on* JANEEN.)

LAVEER: (*Stares at* PANZI. *Silence.*) You killed her.

PANZI: Oh, did I?

LAVEER: Just as if you poured the champagne and fed her each pill one by one.

PANZI: I see. Let me get this straight. Walter is supposed to have "walked in on" (*Places the phrase in quotation marks.*) Janeen and I.

LAVEER: Unfortunately.

PANZI: And Janeen is supposed to have taken the pills because of this?

LAVEER: Undoubtedly.

PANZI: I'm supposed to buy this?

LAVEER: Totally.

PANZI: You know, I don't have to accept this. In fact, I don't have to stand here and listen to you try to put me through a guilt trip. (*Crosses to the door.* LAVEER *blocks her exit.*) Get out of my way.

LAVEER: When I'm through.

PANZI: You're through now. (*Tries to open the door.* LAVEER *impedes her.*) I'm going to ask you one more time . . .

LAVEER: And then what? And *then* what? What you gonna do? Huh? You don't frighten me, Panzi, so just what are you going to do if I don't let you out the door? (PANZI *forcefully pulls the door ajar.* LAVEER *once again impedes her.* LAVEER *pushes.*) Just give me a reason, Panzi! Pleeeeeease, just you give me a reason to knock you clean clear 'cross hell and back!

(LAVEER's *raised voice and the tussle bring* ALISA, BABBS, *and* THELMA *in.* THELMA *assists* PANZI. PANZI *resists.*)

ALISA: (*To* LAVEER.) What's going on, Lavy?

LAVEER: (*Laughs.*) "What's going on?" You ask what's going on? (*To* PANZI.) Care to answer? Hum? Fill them in on all the nice, sordid details.

PANZI: (*Searching.*) Where's my purse?

LAVEER: Ahhhhh, no. If you think you're going to waltz out

of here this evening before owning up to what you did, you are out of your fucking mind. You got that?

ALISA: (*To* LAVEER.) Calm down, Lavy.

LAVEER: Calm down? I haven't started yet. Have I, Panzi?

PANZI: I don't have anything to discuss with you.

LAVEER: Oh, but you do. In fact, I think you owe this one to all of us.

PANZI: (*Unable to find her purse.*) Where's that goddamn purse?!

THELMA: (*Handing* PANZI *the purse.*) Here.

PANZI: (*Crosses to the door.* LAVEER *once again impedes her movement.*) Somebody get this woman out of my path. (ALISA *crosses to* LAVEER.)

LAVEER: (*To* ALISA *while continuing to look* PANZI *in the eye, she neither blinks nor flinches.*) Alisa, I have no qualms with you. So please, back off. (ALISA *steps aside. To* PANZI.) Now you tell them. You tell them how you came in here, to this very, very house, in this very room, and set off an avalanche she couldn't stop. You tell them what sweet, nice Panzi did to Janeen. (*Silence.*) Don't have the heart, do you? Can't live up to your deeds, can you? (PANZI *crosses away.*) I thought not.

THELMA: Will someone please tell me what the hell is going on?

BABBS: I need a drink. (*Crosses to the brandy. She refills her glass and drinks.*)

PANZI: (*Lights a cigarette, crosses to the window, and stares out. Silence. Turns to the group of women.*) I want one thing understood. What I do with my life, how I live it, needs no sanctioning from any one of you. (ALISA *sits.*) In the name of setting things straight . . . Janeen and I were lovers. (*Silence.* ALISA *exhales slowly.* THELMA *sits.* BABBS *stares into her brandy snifter.*) I loved her. I don't expect any of you to understand, but I did love Janeen.

ALISA: We all loved Janeen . . .

THELMA: It just didn't manifest itself in the bed.

PANZI: Look, I don't owe you anything, I owe you (*Clicks her fingers.*) nothing!

LAVEER: Right! But what about Janeen? You owed her explanations. All the whys . . . why that day? Why that moment? After all those *years* of *platonic friendship*, why that moment? Why the sudden distance, the immediate silence? And you talk about love? You strung her out, turned her out, and dropped her. So much for your love.

PANZI: I did not turn her out.

LAVEER: You left her without the least bit of concern for what you'd done.

PANZI: "For what I'd done."

LAVEER: For what you did.

PANZI: Just what did I do? Tell me? Since when is loving some- one a crime?

LAVEER: Loving? You mock the concept.

PANZI: Why? Because we were both women?

LAVEER: Because she was Janeen.

PANZI: Oh yes, sweet, weak, vulnerable, confused Janeen. Well, pardon me if I don't subscribe to that depiction.

ALISA: She was.

PANZI: I would expect you to agree with her. (*Refers to* LAVEER.) You've got minds like the Bobbsie Twins.

ALISA: If you're working on alienating me, you're off to a good start.

PANZI: The shit I care, Alisa. The shit I care what any of you think.

THELMA: What do you care about, Panzi?

PANZI: Don't you cross-examine me, Thelma. None of you in this room have a right to judge me.

ALISA: No one is judging you. Personally, who you screw is of absolutely no concern of mine, truly. What you do is what you do.

PANZI: And . . .

ALISA: And? Three a.m., when my head is on my pillow, my mind and my soul, they're at peace.

PANZI: (*Sarcastically.*) So much for not being judgmental. (*She turns to* BABBS.) Babbs?

BABBS: What am I supposed to say? I'm surprised? I'm not.

PANZI: No?

BABBS: I suspected. Not between you and Janeen, but I sus- pected. I'd even developed a kind of respect for you, liked the way you handled good female platonic relationships. Kind of dispelled my vampire image of lesbians.

PANZI: And now?

BABBS: I'm disappointed.

PANZI: Disappointed . . . My, how righteous you all are.

ALISA: Don't you try to put us through a guilt trip. In many ways Janeen was a little girl, innocent and naive—

PANZI: Janeen was a woman.

ALISA: And you used her.

PANZI: No, you used her! All of you used her. In your own

little blood-sucking ways you used her "innocence," "naivete." Janeen wanted to be a woman. She wasn't weak, vulnerable, innocent, or naive. She was a woman finding her own.

THELMA: And you helped her.

PANZI: I gave her what she wanted and needed.

LAVEER: You paint a revealing portrait except you negate the true colors, the blacks and grays . . . You asked what we talked about during her last week. You. Sometimes two, three times a day. You. Your distance. Her feeling of being conquered. Where were you? Too busy living?

PANZI: I'm supposed to be the bad guy because I care about my relationship with Arlene?

LAVEER: Janeen had a relationship, a husband, Walter, or have you forgotten?

PANZI: I never asked her to change her life. I never suggested she leave Walter.

LAVEER: What a shame you never sat her down and taught her the rules. Let me fill you in on something. That Sunday, while you were up there rolling around in the sheets . . . (*Indicates upstairs.*) After Walter got a bird's eye view of the two of you, he went off. Chose a Sunday and went off, raped her. Later giving her the motive, a vivid account of what he had seen.

ALISA: No.

LAVEER: Then, two weeks ago, after telling him she was pregnant . . . (PANZI *is shocked by this news.*) I'm not surprised you didn't know. But she was. And guess how Walter viewed the baby? Guess! Something you couldn't give her.

ALISA: Oh, God . . .

LAVEER: Do you know how many lives you've screwed? Do you know what you did to that man? You don't care, do you? I know, I've been watching you. Trying to understand, put the pieces together. It's never been about Janeen, has it? Looking back over the years, you know what I see?

PANZI: I could give a damn about what you see.

LAVEER: Give a damn. You give a damn. Janeen is lying out there in a plot at Ewing Cemetery. You damn well better give a damn.

PANZI: Or what?

LAVEER: Winning! All about winning. Graduation day, Janeen gave me an ultimatum concerning our friendship. You motivated that, orchestrated it. Years of friendship down the drain and why? Pawns, rooks, kings, *queens* . . . It was too much Janeen and I had become friends again. You had to top that, had to win. Well, you won! You won! How's the victory feel, Panzi? Tell me, how's the victory feel?

THELMA: *Stop it! Jesus God! . . . Please! . . .* Please . . . (*Silence.*) What's happened to us? Will somebody please tell me what's happened to us? Look at us. Listen to us. All those years of dreaming: the places we thought we'd be, things we thought we'd be doing . . . And what have we become? Drunks, dykes, nonconformists, crusaders, hiders . . . (*Crosses to* PANZI.) What you did was wrong. There's no debate on the subject. What you did with Janeen, what you do is wrong. It defies what we stood for. It defies the laws of nature, the laws of God, and when you defy the laws of God you—

PANZI: Don't you preach to me about God. I know about God and his laws.

THELMA: Do tell . . . what God?

PANZI: Your God, a God who abandons . . . And one of his laws in particular; Exodus twenty, twelve. You know it?

THELMA: I'm not up to game playing with you, Panzi.

PANZI: No game playing. Your God set out a law: "Honor thy father and thy mother, that thy—"

THELMA: Watch it, you're on the verge of being sacrilegious.

PANZI: (*To Thelma.*) "That thy days may be long upon the land which the Lord thy God giveth thee." Some law . . . Seems to me your God forgot an important one. "Parent, honor and love thy children that they may not know pain, may not know hurt, may not be neglected." (*To* ALISA.) You understand the need for that one, don't you, Alisa? (*To* THELMA.) Did your God simply forget to add this or did it simply not matter? (*To* ALISA.) Do you think you were the only child on this green earth to suffer in youth? You don't hold a patent on it! All of us don't grow up to be quite so sanctimonious and perfect!

ALISA: I'm sure—

PANZI: No! I have the floor! My turn! . . . I was born the soul daughter to Adrelline Lucinda McVain. A very beautiful, shapely, silky-haired Adrilline Lucinda McVain. A woman known for her knowledge of beauty secrets . . . jewelry. (*Directs "jewelry" at* LAVEER.) A mother of three; two boys and one girl. A woman who loved men almost as much as her reflection in the mirror. She had to have her ego stroked continually, had to have euphoric adulation gracing her ears never endingly. My mother, she had four husbands. All legal.

Discarded them when they ran out of adjectives to describe
her beauty. I used to wonder if she'd divorce me one day,
discard me. I had nightmares of my brothers coming down
to the breakfast table and finding my chair vacant and Momma
explaining in her sweet, sultry voice, "Panzi didn't know how
to talk to Momma. Momma don't share her roof with nobody
who don't know how to talk to Momma." We'd heard that
many times after Daddy disappeared, after Daddy Rudolph,
Daddy Jimmy, Daddy Mason . . . My brothers, they learned
early, caught on quickly, how to talk and stroke Momma.
They'd hug her, kiss her, stroke her ego . . . and she'd repay
you well for flattery. Buy you . . . presents. All you had to
do was be a man and know how to compliment Momma . . .
(*To* ALISA.) And you talk of innocence. When my flat chest
began to grow, Momma's eyes got colder, her words more
bitter. There was no room for a girl child in my momma's
house. When I was nine, I asked Momma for a Susie Walk-
mate Doll. It was the only thing I wanted for Christmas. I
did everything just the way Momma liked them done to get
that doll. (*Pause.*) Christmas Eve morning Momma got a
phone call. I knew it was from a man because she took a
long lavender perfume bath after she hung up the phone.
She put on her makeup, her satin robe with the fuzzy feath-
ers, her pink high-heel slippers . . . I knew it was a man by
the way her eyes bit into me. I hid when Mr. Jones rang the
doorbell. I held my head low when he gave my brothers and
me presents. I tried to disappear when he told Momma I
was growing into a beautiful young lady. I prayed Mr. Jones
hadn't messed things up. Christmas morning, no Susie Walk-
mate. Her excuse: the store had run out . . . Momma never
held me. On her dying bed in Mercy Hospital, she clutched
my brothers' heads to her breasts, but never looked at me
with those eyes . . . (*To* LAVEER.) Your eyes. (*To* THELMA.)
Where was your God and his laws then? Your God did not
soothe me. A woman soothed me. She put her arms around
me one cool winter evening while I was still young and she
loved me, made me feel like I belonged in this world. A
woman gave me that. (*To* LAVEER.) And Janeen, that Sunday morning, she needed these hands . . . I understood her.
I knew her longing. I'd been there. (*Fights tears.*) I didn't
plan for things to . . . Why did you have to come back, stir
up all the needs, desires, longings for . . . replicas? At first
it was only friendship I needed, but the more you rejected,
the more I wanted and . . . you became my sickness. Why

couldn't you have just stayed? You had to conjure up all that wanting, needing, rejecting . . . Cut from the same cloth. That same beauty, same cutting edge. You and *Momma* . . . Tell me, Laveer, what was wrong with me? *What was wrong with me?*

LAVEER: Nothing . . . I simply don't like you.

PANZI: (*Stares at* LAVEER. *Silence.*) Just like that. (LAVEER *does not respond.* PANZI *laughs.*) Just like . . . I got rid of you once, stopped the pain . . . Janeen was mine. Things were simple. Why couldn't you have just stayed? (*Silence. To* ALISA *and* BABBS.) I loved Janeen. (*To* THELMA.) Don't you think I'd change things if I could? (THELMA *turns away.* BABBS *places a nearly full glass of brandy on the table as if in affirmation of sobriety.*)

LAVEER: (*Crosses to the wall unit and retrieves the erotica book.*) We used to sit on the back porch, read erotic passages from dirty books . . . She'd sit there all wide eyed, drawn into the rawness . . . Yesterday.

(*Lights dim to black.*)

BACCALAUREATE

A DRAMA IN THREE ACTS

by William Branch

Baccalaureate was first produced at the City Hall Theater in Hamilton,
Bermuda, by the Studio Theater on April 15, 1975.

WILLIAM BRANCH

Playwright, journalist, and media writer-producer William Branch was born in New Haven, Connecticut, but grew up in the suburbs of New York City, in Charlotte, North Carolina, and in Washington, D.C. His B.S. in speech is from Northwestern University, and his M.F.A. in dramatic arts is from Columbia, where he also did postgraduate study in film production. Later he spent a year as a resident fellow in screenwriting at the Yale School of Drama. Performing briefly as an actor on stage (*Anna Lucasta, Detective Story*) and in radio and television, Branch became convinced that African Americans could not rely upon others to truthfully write and produce properties involving people of color. Since then, he has written, directed and produced extensively for the stage, TV, radio and films for, among others, NBC, CBS, ABC, PBS, the Maryland Center for Public Broadcasting, and Universal Studios, in addition to establishing his own media consulting and production firm. A teacher as well, he has been visiting professor at the University of Maryland Baltimore County, the University of Ghana, and visiting playwright, scholar and guest lecturer at numerous other colleges and universities. A resident of New Rochelle, N.Y., he is currently Professor of Theater, Dramatic Literature and Communications at the Africana Studies and Research Center, Cornell University.

Among his awards and honors are a Guggenheim fellowship in playwriting; a Yale University–American Broadcasting Company fellowship in screenwriting; a Robert E. Sherwood Television Award; and a citation from the National Conference of Christians and Jews (NCCJ), the latter two for his NBC television drama *Light in the Southern Sky*, about African American educator Mary McLeod Bethune. Others are an American Film Festival Blue Ribbon Award and an Emmy nomination—shared with fellow producer William Greaves—both for their PBS documentary film *Still a Brother: Inside the Negro Middle Class*; an NCCJ Citation for his PBS drama *A Letter from Booker T*, which was commissioned by its stars, Ossie Davis and Ruby Dee; and a Hannah Del Velcchio Award in playwriting from Columbia.

Besides *Baccalaureate*, Branch's works for the theater include: *A Medal for Willie*, about the ironies of a presentation to the mother of an African American soldier, killed in battle overseas, of his posthumous award for bravery; *In Splendid Error*, an historical drama about Frederick Douglass's involvement with John Brown just prior to the Harper's Ferry insurrection; *To Follow the Phoenix*, a biographical play on the life of civil-rights pioneer Mary Church Terrell, commissioned by the Delta Sigma Theta Sorority; and *A Wreath for Udomo*, a drama of the rise and fall of an African prime minister, based upon the novel by Black South African writer Peter Abrahams (produced in London after its premiere in Cleveland). Others are *Light in the Southern Sky*, a stage version of his award-winning NBC television drama; *Experiment in Black*, a musical and dramatic revue; *The Man on Meeting Street*, a documentary drama on a Southern white defender of civil rights, Federal Judge J. Waites Waring of Charleston, S.C., commissioned by the Alpha Kappa Alpha Sorority; and *Fifty Steps Toward Freedom*, a stage documentary subtitled, "A Dramatic Presentation in Observance of the Fiftieth Anniversary of the National Association for the Advancement of Colored People," commissioned by the national office of the NAACP.

CHARACTERS

MARTHA HILL
DOCKERY HILL
ANGELA WILLIAMS
ROGER SAMPSON
DICKIE HILL
JOHNNY HILL
CHARLIE
MRS. WEMBLEY
KENNY POWERS

THE SCENE: The entire action of the play occurs in the apartment of the Hills, an African-American family, on the second floor of a two-family house in a Midwestern university town during a spring in the late 1950s.
The play is in three acts.

ACT ONE
Scene One

Music rises out of the darkness . . . a plaintive, nostalgic strain, reminiscent of glee clubs, ivy-covered walls and ceremonial processions. Then, fading into view, projected upon a scrim, is the image of a clock tower. The clock chimes the three-quarter hour, then dissolves again into darkness.

Behind the scrim, light filters up upon the Hills' apartment. Three small rooms are visible: the front bedroom at left; the living room center, and a kitchen at right. Sandwiched in between the living room and kitchen is a tiny bathroom.

A doorway in the back wall of the bedroom leads to "the kids' room," while another up right center in the living room is the entrance to ANGELA's *room. The main entrance to the apartment is up left center, while the back door, at far right through the kitchen, opens onto a small wooden landing with a flight of stairs leading down to the first floor and the yard below. Off in the distance, glimpsed over trees and rooftops, is the clock tower of the university.*

As the scrim rises, the apartment is dimly lighted, for the shades at the picture window in the bedroom are drawn, and the slanting rays of a late-afternoon sun reach in their fingers only through the kitchen. DOCKERY HILL *is in the bed at left, asleep. He is, as he describes himself, "a working man" in his late thirties. The sound of his heavy breathing is counterbalanced by the cries of children outside at play.*

A moment later, slow footsteps are heard climbing creaking old stairs. They halt. There is the sound of keys being jangled, then one is fitted into the door. It opens to admit MARTHA HILL. *Several years younger than her husband,* MARTHA *is a not unattractive woman, though she betrays a tendency toward plumpness. She carries a large bag of groceries in her arms.*

MARTHA *closes the door, leans against it, and gives a little sigh. She peers into the bedroom at the sleeping* DOC.

MARTHA: (*Softly.*) Doc . . . ?

279

(There is no response. She takes her package into the kitchen and sets it down on the table. She takes meat, eggs, and other perishables from the bag and puts them in the refrigerator, distributing other grocery goods to the pantry up right. This done, she crosses again to the bedroom.

Taking off her coat, she hangs it neatly on a hanger dangling from a wall light fixture. Her hat goes on the dresser.

Then, in the dim light, she squints her eyes and leans over to check her wristwatch against the alarm clock on the dresser. Just then the alarm goes off, startling her until she grasps it and shuts it off. She gazes over at Doc, *who stirs in his sleep and turns over. She comes to the bed.)*

Doc . . . Doc. *(Shakes his shoulder gently.)*   ·

Doc: *(Waking.)* Huh—what?
MARTHA: Wake up, Doc, it's time for you to get up.
Doc: *(Yawns and stretches.)* Oh. Okay . . .

*(*MARTHA *turns and pulls off her dress over her head while* Doc *subsides again into sleep. She drapes the dress over the back of a chair and reaches into the closet for a housedress.)*

MARTHA: *(Noticing* Doc *asleep again.)* Doc!
Doc: Huh? I'm—I'm awake. *(Sits up in bed rubbing his eyes.)*
MARTHA: Well, get up then. *(Turns to shrug into her dress.)*

*(*Doc, *yawning heavily, swings his legs out of bed and sits there, hands to face. When he looks up,* MARTHA *is standing before him with her back to him, wriggling the dress over her head. His eyes grow live, and he reaches out his hand to touch her thigh.)*

MARTHA: *(Drawing away.)* Stop it, Doc! You know it's time for you to go to work. *(Finishes pulling her dress down.)* Besides. You know what I told you.
Doc: *(Turning away.)* All right, all right, we don't have to go all through that again.
MARTHA: Well, I should hope not! Any other woman would leave her husband, after a thing like that.
Doc: Go ahead, leave! Go right ahead. Two kids, a new vacuum cleaner and television set to pay for—go ahead, who's stoppin' you. *(Rises and pulls on his pants.)*
MARTHA: Well, I would if I had just half the chance! *(Mimics.)* "I didn't want any more kids, but Martha got careless."

DOC: Aw, for chris'sakes—!

MARTHA: And saying it to Ed Harris, of all people!

DOC: Well, hell! He's your brother-in-law. Can I help it if he had'a go and tell that blabber-mouth sister of yours?

MARTHA: Suppose you leave my sister out of this! Gracie only did what any other woman would do under the circumstances. Tell her sister what's being said about her.

DOC: (*Tying his shoes.*) Yeah, but did she have to tell the whole town first?

MARTHA: You should talk! You couldn't even wait until I'd been to the doctor's.

DOC: Okay! So you been to the doctor's and he said you wasn't pregnant, so now what you bitchin' about? For chris'sakes!

MARTHA: No, and I'm not going to be, either. You can try sleeping by yourself for awhile and see how you like it. Think I'm going to get in the same bed with you after a crack like that, you got another thought coming!

DOC: (*Rises.*) Hell, you can't sleep in there with Dickie forever! Besides, Dickie's gettin' to be a pretty big boy nowadays, and—

MARTHA: Dockery Hill! If you're insinuating that your own son—

DOC: I ain't insinuatin' nothin'! I'm tellin' you, it just ain't decent, that's all.

MARTHA: Well, decent or not, that's where I'm going to sleep, and if you don't like it, that's just too bad.

DOC: (*Starts for the bathroom.*) Go ahead, hold out as long as you want to! As for me, I ain't sayin' I am.

MARTHA: Doc, you just let me hear tell of you running around—

DOC: (*At the bathroom door.*) You won't have to hear tell of it. I'll tell you myself! (*Slams the door.*)

(MARTHA *stands furious for a moment. The telephone rings. She goes to the phone in the living room and picks up the receiver.*)

MARTHA: Hello? . . . Angela? No, she's not in at the moment, she's still at school . . . Oh, usually about five-thirty . . . Yes . . . Well, is there any message, when she comes in I can have her call you . . . Oh! Mr. Sampson—well, it's been so long since I've heard your voice . . . She should be coming in any time now, her last class is over at four-thirty . . . Yes . . . All right, I'll tell her you'll call later . . . Well, so nice to hear from you again, Mr. Sampson, I didn't know if you were alive or dead! (*A little laugh.*) All right, then, I'll tell her you called . . . Yes, and be sure and call back now, she'll be awfully disappointed if you don't . . . All right, good-bye.

(*She hangs up, puzzled for a minute, then rises and goes to the kitchen. She takes out a frying pan and puts it on the stove. From outside a boy's voice is heard calling: "Miz' Hill! Oh, Miz' Hill!" MARTHA goes to the screen door.*)

MARTHA: Yes, Charlie, what is it?

CHARLIE: (*Off.*) Dickie's got my bicycle and he won't give it back! I let him loan it for a little while, and now he won't give it back.

MARTHA: (*Goes out onto the landing.*) Oh, my goodness . . . (*Calls.*) Dickie! Dick-ie, do you hear me?

CHARLIE: He hears you, all right, he just ducked aroun' behind the Donovans' fence.

MARTHA: (*Starts down the stairs and disappears.*) Dickie I want you to come here to me this minute, do you hear?

(*There is silence for a moment. Then quick footsteps are heard on the steps outside. The door opens to admit ANGELA WILLIAMS. She is a quite attractive young woman in her early twenties, and she carries an armful of textbooks. She closes the door and leans against it, blowing at the exertion of running up the stairs.*)

ANGELA: (*Looks around.*) Martha . . . ? (*Goes into the bedroom and looks in.*) Martha . . . anybody home? (*Satisfied, she puts her books down on the sofa, takes off her light jacket and starts for the bathroom. Just then the flush of the commode is heard, and an instant later DOC emerges, wiping his neck with a towel flung over his shoulder. He stops upon seeing ANGELA.*)

ANGELA: (*Stops also.*) Oh. Hi, Doc.

DOC: Hi.

ANGELA: Is Martha home?

DOC: Yeah, she's . . . (*Glances around.*) out in back or someplace.

ANGELA: Why, Doc, that's my towel!

DOC: (*Looks at it.*) Is it? Oh, I hadn't noticed. Guess I just grabbed up the first thing handy.

ANGELA: (*Taking it from him.*) I wish you'd stick to your own towels. I have enough laundry of my own to take care of now, without having to wash behind you, too. (*Makes a move as if to go past him,. He stands with arms folded and smiles. She feints to his other side, but he does not budge.*) Doc, I have to go to the bathroom.

DOC: (*Moves a little to one side.*) Oh, I'm sorry, I didn't know.

(ANGELA *hesitates, then tries to move past him quickly. He reaches out and grabs her.*)

ANGELA: Doc! Doc, stop it. You let me go!

DOC: (*Pulling her to him.*) I'm not gonna hurt you, Angela. I just want you to be nice to me.

ANGELA: (*Struggling.*) Will you stop it, Doc! If you don't, I'm going to tell Martha on you!

DOC: (*Trying to kiss her.*) You wouldn't wanna do that! Now, would you—

ANGELA: Doc! Do you hear me? Doc—*stop* it. (*Manages to break his hold and runs away a few steps.*)

DOC: (*Breathes heavily and grins.*) Hell, you can't blame a guy for tryin', can you?

(*He takes a step toward her. She darts quickly into the bathroom and slams the door.*)

(*Just then* MARTHA *is seen climbing the back stairs.* DOC *glances up quickly and strides into the bedroom, where he busies himself putting on his shirt.* MARTHA *enters the kitchen and continues through to the bedroom.*)

MARTHA: Doc, you're just going to have to do something about that Dickie. He's getting out of hand.

DOC: What'd he do now?

MARTHA: He's been out there fighting over Charlie's bike.

DOC: Well, I told you to get him one of his own.

MARTHA: But I don't want Dickie to have a bicycle. You just don't know, I have trouble enough now keeping the kids near home. God only knows where they'd be or what they'd be doing if they had a bike to go running around on.

DOC: (*Rolling up his sleeves.*) Aw, you're bringin' 'em up to be a bunch a' faggots, that's what.

MARTHA: Well, if you were home more often, maybe you could do better!

DOC: Hell, how can I be home when I'm workin' three jobs to take care of this crew! And then, when I do get home, what do I have to put up with? A wife who won't sleep with her husband!

MARTHA: You brought it all on yourself.

DOC: The hell I did!

(*The commode is heard to flush.*)

MARTHA: (*Looks up.*) Who's that?

DOC: Your sister, who'd you think?

MARTHA: Oh. She had a call a while ago from that Roger Sampson.

DOC: (*Combing his hair.*) Yeah? What'd he want?

MARTHA: I don't know. Said he'd call back later, wouldn't leave a message. First time he's called here in a long time.

DOC: Never should be soon enough.

MARTHA: Now, what have you got against Roger Sampson? He never did anything to you. He's a nice boy from a nice family, and he got his law degree last winter.

DOC: Huh! Who the hell cares about him gettin' a law degree? Law degree, bachelors degree, master's degree—that's all I ever hear around here! Well, just you let me tell you one thing, I'd rather be just what I am, see? A custodian. Custodian—that's French for just plain ordinary hardworkin' janitor, and that's what I am. I'd rather be just that, see? A janitor with three buildings to take care of, than one a' them punk-ass smart-aleck niggers with a "collitch" degree, walkin' around dressed so sharp all the time, ain't got one nickel to rub against the other!

MARTHA: Well, Doc, nobody said anything about you.

DOC: (*Wound up.*) And another thing! I don't see you complainin' when it comes to pay the bills around here about the kind of work I do! I'm workin' three buildings, three different jobs, to make enough money to take care of you and the kids. Yeah, and that smart-ass sister of yours, too!

MARTHA: Shh, Doc! She'll hear you. Besides, you know Angela's in school. She does the best she can, she pays her board.

DOC: Hah! The money she puts into this house wouldn't take care of the shit paper for a week. And I don't care if she does hear me!

MARTHA: Doc!

DOC: And the way she walks around with that superior air of hers. "Hi, Doc" and "Good-bye, Doc"—that's all she ever says to me!

MARTHA: (*Suspicion forming.*) Doc . . . Doc, have you been after Angela again?

DOC: What? Are you kiddin'? What for?

MARTHA: You know what for! Doc, you know I warned you the last time.

DOC: Well, for chris'sakes—this is ridiculous! Who said I been after her, did she say anything to you? Huh?

MARTHA: No. But—

DOC: Well, what're you talkin' about, then? Shee-it, here I am workin' my ass off and she accuses me of a thing like that. (*From a distance, the clock tower begins tolling the hour, after which it strikes five.* DOC *speaks at the first chime.*) There, listen to that, will ya? You're gonna make me late—here, gimme my hat! I gotta go to work. (*Picks up his hat and jams it onto his head.*)

MARTHA: (*Following him to the door.*) Don't you want something to eat?

DOC: Naw, I'm not hungry. Just have my dinner hot for me when I get back at nine. (*Goes out, slamming the door.*)

(*Just then* ANGELA *emerges from the bathroom and starts for her room.*)

ANGELA: Oh—hi, Martha.

MARTHA: (*Gazing at* ANGELA *reflectively.*) Hi . . .

ANGELA: (*Stops.*) Whoa! What's the matter?

MARTHA: Matter? Oh, nothing. Nothing at all.

ANGELA: Well, you certainly have got a peculiar look on your face.

MARTHA: Have I? I didn't mean to.

(*There is a pause.* ANGELA *starts to gather up her books.*)

MARTHA: Uh, Angela.

ANGELA: Yes?

MARTHA: Has, uh . . . has Doc said anything to you lately?

ANGELA: Said anything? Like what?

MARTHA: You know. Like before.

ANGELA: Oh, Martha, you know better than that. Whatever put such a silly question in your head?

MARTHA: Then he hasn't, huh?

ANGELA: Of course not! Honestly, Martha, sometimes I don't know what to think about you.

MARTHA: (*A little sheepish.*) Well, I didn't know. You know, Doc and I haven't been getting along so well lately.

ANGELA: I know. (*Smiles.*) Dickie told me you slept in his bed last night.

MARTHA: (*Blushes.*) Yeah . . . I—I guess it seems kind of silly. But then, you don't know what Doc said about me.

ANGELA: Oh, yes I do. Gracie told me all about it.

MARTHA: (*Sits disgustedly.*) Gracie! Honestly, Angela, I just don't understand Gracie anymore! Why did she have to go and discuss this with everybody in town before she even told me, her own sister?

ANGELA: Well, you know her better than I do. You two came along together.

MARTHA: And I'll bet she's even written down home to Momma about it by now.

ANGELA: Now Martha, Gracie wouldn't do a thing like that.

MARTHA: Oh, yes she would, too, you just don't know.

ANGELA: Well, anyway, you aren't going to have a baby now, are you? So forget about it.

MARTHA: Forget about it? How can I forget about a thing like that! And the thing that hurts most is I really wanted to have another baby.

ANGELA: You did!

MARTHA: Yes. I was so happy when I thought I was pregnant. It was such a lovely feeling, thinking that again I was going to be able to bring another life into the world. Another brand-new person that would never have ever been, if it hadn't been for me. Well, me and Doc. I—I guess I sound rather silly, Angela, but that's the way I felt. For a whole two weeks I went around the house just singing, I was so happy. And . . . and then . . . After I told Doc, and he didn't sound so happy about it . . . And after the doctor told me it was a mistake. And then to hear from Grace about the awful things that Doc said, oh, I was crushed! Just crushed, that's all. You don't know how it feels, Angela. You've never had a baby to cuddle in your arms and hold at your breast. And you've never had a husband who could hurt you so.

ANGELA: Thank God!

MARTHA: Oh!—by the way, I meant to tell you. Roger Sampson called.

ANGELA: He did? When?

MARTHA: About half an hour ago. I asked him if there was any message, but he said he'd call you back later.

ANGELA: (*Reflectively.*) I see. Thanks.

MARTHA: (*Clears her throat.*) Roger hasn't called in quite some time now, has he?

ANGELA: All right, Martha. You don't have to pry.

MARTHA: Well, I'm not prying, I'm just interested. After all, I did promise Momma I'd take care of you.

ANGELA: (*Rises and takes up her books again.*) Well, you don't have to bother. I'm a big girl now, twenty-three, remember? And I'm perfectly capable of taking care of my own affairs. (*Goes into her room.*)

MARTHA: I'm sure you can, Angela, but I just thought it might be rather nice if you wanted to . . . to discuss them with someone a little older and more experienced than yourself.

ANGELA: (*From her room.*) No, thank you! It's precisely that: discussing *your* affairs with *your* older sister that's got you into all your trouble now!

MARTHA: (*Hurt.*) Well, if that's the way you feel, you can take your own phone calls from now on! (*Goes quickly into the kitchen and busies herself by opening a can of food.*)

ANGELA: Oh, for goodness sakes! (*Appears at her door.*) Martha? . . . (*Goes into the kitchen.*) Look, Martha—I'm sorry, I shouldn't have said that. But you do always have to know all about my business, and there are some things a girl would rather keep to herself. (MARTHA *does not answer; she keeps on with her dinner preparations.*) Oh, all right, if you must know! Roger and I had a fight, two months ago. I told him I didn't want to ever see him again, and he said that would suit him just fine.

MARTHA: (*Slows down her work.*) Oh? That's a shame. Well, what happened, that you had to have a fight about?

ANGELA: (*Exasperated.*) Do you want to hear all the gory details? A blow-by-blow description? Suffice it to say that he was just out for what he could get. Men! They're just swine. All of them!

MARTHA: So it was like that, was it? I'm surprised, I always thought Roger was such a nice fellow, always so courteous and smiling and everything.

ANGELA: Oh, he can be that way, all right. That's when he calls himself being "charming"—one of his "charming days," you know. But 'way back in his little beetle brain is the same old thought!

MARTHA: Hmm . . . Well, of course, I hate to say this to my own baby sister, but—

ANGELA: Then save it. I've been familiar with the little birdies and bees for quite some time now.

MARTHA: Oh, you have? Well, long as you're careful . . . But you do have to think of your future, Angela. Yes, I know you're in school and all, going to finish up your master's and go out and get a position and such. And there's nothing wrong with that, not in the least. I don't blame you—sometimes I wish I'd stayed on and finished, and gotten a good job and worked awhile longer before Doc came along. But sooner or later you're going to want a home and children and everything that goes with it, Angela. And you know well as I do, when it comes to eligible men with an education and some kind of promise, we just don't have the widest choice in the world. Take Doc—oh, I love Doc, love him dearly—but I'll admit, I can't help wishing he had a degree and worked at something else. I don't think Momma will ever really forgive me.

ANGELA: (*Shakes her head.*) I don't know, Martha. Sometimes I think all this emphasis on middle-class values is just ludicrous.

MARTHA: Well, let's face it, honey. The one thing that distinguishes people like us from the rest of that bunch out there is a little education. That and some home training, and a little ambition and get-up-and-go. What's that you told me once—life-style?

ANGELA: Well, yes, but—

MARTHA: So even if Doc does work three buildings instead of a nine-to-five, at least he keeps me out of some white woman's kitchen. Don't you want to get married someday?

ANGELA: Oh, I suppose so, eventually. But I'd like at least to be able to go into a relationship on a halfway equal basis. With dear Roger it's just, "Roll over, baby, and drop 'em down!"

MARTHA: Well, you've got to consider that Roger has his law degree now. If I were you, I wouldn't see anything wrong with using a little behind to get ahead.

ANGELA: Oh, Martha, cut it out! (*Smiles despite herself.*)

MARTHA: It's the truth!

ANGELA: Thanks anyway, but I don't need anyone to tell me how to handle Roger Sampson. I walk by guys like him every day without even turning my head.

(*The phone rings.*)

MARTHA: Oh! That's probably him.

ANGELA: Speak of the devil . . .

(*The phone rings again.*)

MARTHA: Well, aren't you going to get it? Angela!
ANGELA: All right, don't get excited, Martha, that's not the sound of my master's voice! (*Goes into the living room. She lets it ring once more before picking up the receiver.*) Hello? . . . Yes, this is she . . . Well, now, isn't this a cozy little surprise . . . I'm fine, Roger, how are you? . . . Oh, not a thing, what's new with you? . . . Oh? Well, I'm very glad for you . . . That would be rather nice sometime . . . Tonight—well, I'm afraid I'm going to be busy. I have a lot of work to do for a class tomorrow morning, and I'll be spending the evening with my books . . . Well, I've got to keep up with my work, Roger, I just can't— . . . I know, I know, but— . . . Well, to tell you the truth, Mr. Sampson, I don't see why you called in the first place! . . . No, I don't . . . Well, it seems to me we came to a pretty definite understanding the last time we saw each other . . . It wasn't? . . . Well, it certainly was to me, and I see no reason to— . . . What? . . . Uh-huh . . . (*Smiles.*) Oh, you do, do you? (*She laughs.* MARTHA, *who has been straining to hear from the kitchen, smiles also and goes back to her work.* ANGELA *laughs again.*) Now, listen, Roger, just because I laughed is no reason to think that I— . . . What? . . . Well, I don't know . . . But I can't! . . . Well, maybe for a little while . . . But I'll expect a very different standard of behavior on your part than the last time, Mr. Sampson! . . . Yes, I will . . . Okay . . . All right, good-bye. (*Hangs up and sits there, reflecting.*)

(MARTHA *looks up, apparently expecting* ANGELA *to return to the kitchen, and when she does not,* MARTHA *goes to the living room.*)

MARTHA: Well?
ANGELA: He's coming over.
MARTHA: That's nice. When?
ANGELA: Right now. He said he's parked not far from here.
MARTHA: Oh? I didn't know he had a car.
ANGELA: I didn't either until he told me. He says it's a new Buick.
MARTHA: Oh! Fancy that. He must be doing right well.
ANGELA: Probably stole it.

MARTHA: What a thing to say. (*Coyly.*) Well, Angela, I've told you the best I can. It's all up to you.

ANGELA: All right, Martha, you've written your column for today! (*Jumps up and goes into her room, touching at her hair.*)

MARTHA: (*Follows her to the door.*) Why don't you put on your new blue skirt? And—and that white nylon blouse I gave you for Christmas. You know, the sheer one?

ANGELA: (*From her room.*) I'll do nothing of the kind! I'm just going to put on fresh lipstick, that's all. And touch up my hair a little.

(*From outside comes the sound of an automobile pulling up to the curb.*)

MARTHA: (*Looks up.*) That sounds like a Buick! Hurry, dear! (*Runs into the bedroom and, standing to the side, peeks through the curtains at the window. A car door is heard slamming.*) It's him, Angela! And it is a Buick! It's kind of a powder blue, a beautiful, shiny, brand-new Buick! (*Turns to look again.*) Oh, he's coming up! Hurry, Angela! (*Excited, she jumps around like a child on Christmas, suddenly deciding that she, too, needs some quick repairs. She looks in the mirror, puts her hands to her hair. Quickly she takes up a brush and swipes away at it. Conscious of her dress, she rushes to the closet, but then decides she hasn't time for that as heavy footsteps sound on the stairs outside.*) Angela! He's here! Hurry! (*Grabs up a lipstick and smears it quickly on, then, lips together, "sets" it in a hurry. The footsteps halt and a knock is heard at the door. With a last glance in the mirror and a pat to her hair, she rushes out of the bedroom and starts for the door. Just then ANGELA appears from her rom, coolly and confidently groomed.*)

ANGELA: Uhn-unnh! (*Strides to the door.*) I'll greet Mr. Sampson.

MARTHA: (*Stops.*) Oh. Yes, well . . . (*A knock sounds at the door. ANGELA stands waiting for MARTHA to leave.*) All right, I'm going! (*Starts for the kitchen. The knock sounds again. MARTHA stops and turns, but ANGELA still stands waiting. MARTHA finally turns and goes into the kitchen. ANGELA opens the door.*)

ROGER: (*Outside.*) Hello, Angela.

ANGELA: Well, hello! Come in, come in, don't just stand there.

ROGER: Thanks. (*He enters. ROGER is tall and large, giving the*

impression of a rather genial overgrown schoolboy who'd be
much more at home on a football field. He glances around
and stands waiting for ANGELA, *who is closing the door.*)

ANGELA: Have a seat, won't you? (*As he starts to sit gingerly*
in a small armchair.) No, not that one, I wouldn't want you
to have to sue in case it didn't hold up. Sit here. (*Indicates*
the sofa.)

ROGER: Okay. (*He sits.*)

ANGELA: (*Sits beside him, at a respectable distance.*) Well,
you've put on weight. Life must have been good to you
lately.

ROGER: Oh, I can't complain. Things haven't been too bad.

ANGELA: That's nice. I'm glad to hear it.

(*There is a pause.* ROGER *fidgets uncomfortably.*)

ROGER: And—and what about you?

ANGELA: Me? Oh, still in school, still working on that master's.
Seems like forever, but I'm hoping to finish up in June.

ROGER: That's swell. I'm glad to hear that, really I am.

ANGELA: Thank you.

ROGER; And—And what are you going to do after that?

ANGELA: Oh, try to get some sort of position and go to work,
I suppose. That's what I've been after this degree for. You
can get a better salary in social work if you have your master's, you know.

ROGER: Oh—yes, of course. I'm sure you can at that, sure.
That's all right—I'm glad things are working out for you,
Angela. I'm really glad.

ANGELA: (*Puzzled.*) Well, thank you again. (*There is another*
pause. ANGELA *eyes him uncomfortably.*) I . . . I understand
you're with a law firm now. In the City. I think Martha
mentioned running across something about it in one of the
papers.

ROGER: Oh—oh, yes. Last month, I joined them. Pretty fine
firm, too. Uh, I'm the first . . . you know . . . colored with
them. Here, let me give you one of my cards. (*Fumbles in*
his pocket for his wallet, takes out a card.)

ANGELA: (*Taking it.*) Oh? (*Reads.*) "Wellington, O'Neal,
Columbo and Friedman." My, that certainly sounds impressive, doesn't it? Sort of like the United Nations. (ROGER
fidgets, uncomfortably.) Well, I think that's very nice of them
to take you in like that, when you're just starting out and
all. They must be very fine people to do a thing like that.

ROGER: Yes. Well, they are.

ANGELA: (*Casually laying aside the card.*) I'll be sure and put this away safe someplace, and if I ever need any legal work done, I'll be sure to look you up. (*Almost under her breath.*) Sitting by the door.

ROGER: (*Does a double-take, then tries again.*) Oh, I got a new car, too, did I tell you? A Buick. Buick Roadmaster.

ANGELA: (*Flatly.*) Yes, you mentioned it on the phone, how very nice . . .

ROGER: Uh, would you like to see it? Take a ride? It's really a very smooth machine. Rides like a living room sofa.

ANGELA: Well, thanks, Roger, but I'm already *on* the living room sofa.

ROGER: Oh. Well . . .

ANGELA: (*After another pause.*) Say, look, Roger—what's the matter with you? What did you come all the way up here to see me about that you said was so important, and then just sit up here and make with the polite talky-talky? What is this?

ROGER: Well, Angela, you see, I . . . I . . .

ANGELA: Well, go ahead. If you've got something to say, then go ahead and say it, you don't have to play coy with me. You never have. (*Turns.*) Though come to think of it, that would be quite a change.

ROGER: Look, Angela, I'm awfully sorry about what happened that time, honest I am. I apologize for it, really I do.

ANGELA: You don't have to apologize to me, Roger, we both made ourselves perfectly clear to each other that night and I don't see any point in bringing up the subject again—

ROGER: Well, I didn't bring it up, you did.

ANGELA: (*Going on.*) —and if that's all you came up here to see me about, you could have saved your gas and the tires on your shiny new car because I don't want to hear it!

ROGER: Look, will you wait a minute and give me a chance to say something?

ANGELA: And furthermore, Roger Sampson, I don't see that—

ROGER: Will you listen to me for a minute, please!

ANGELA: But I don't understand why you don't—

ROGER: *Please?*

ANGELA: Oh, all right, go ahead!

ROGER: Whew! What a temper.

ANGELA: Now, just a minute—!

ROGER: Okay, okay—I withdraw the remark, let it be stricken

from the record! There . . . Now maybe we can get down to business.

ANGELA: (*Suspiciously.*) What kind of business?

ROGER: Well, I, uh . . . You see, it's this way, Angela . . .

ANGELA: Yes? Go on.

ROGER: I am, I am! Now, you see . . . Well, what I mean is . . .

ANGELA: My, my! And you're supposed to be a lawyer.

ROGER: Now, let's don't start wrangling again!

ANGELA: All right, but why don't you go ahead and say what this is all about?

ROGER: Look, I can't talk here. I feel . . . closed in. Almost as if somebody with big ears were listening in.

ANGELA: (*With a glance toward the kitchen.*) You're probably right about that one.

ROGER: So, what do you say we go out for dinner, huh?

ANGELA: But Martha's fixing my dinner right now. Why?

ROGER: Because I asked you to, that's why.

ANGELA: Well, I can't see why you can't talk right here. I'm perfectly comfortable and I can hear every word you're saying, really I can.

ROGER: Angela, will you do what I'm asking you? For once, will you?

ANGELA: Well . . . (*She rises.*) Where are you taking me?

ROGER: Anywhere you say. Anywhere at all.

ANGELA: If we go somewhere in town, I suppose we could go to Parchesi's. Unless you had somewhere else in mind.

ROGER: Parchesi's is fine with me. I just love Italian food.

ANGELA: Okay, I'll get my coat, it's rather cool out. And listen, Roger, I have to get back in a little while. I really do have some work to get done for class tomorrow.

ROGER: I promise! I'll have you back here in an hour if you like. Even half an hour, if you insist.

ANGELA: Look, I want more to eat than a meatball!

ROGER: Anything on the menu, it's yours. Now, will you get that coat and let's get going?

ANGELA: Be with you in a minute. (*Goes into her room.*)

(MARTHA, *in the kitchen, has from time to time been trying to listen in on the conversation while getting dinner on the stove. Now she looks in, sees that* ANGELA *is not there, and determines to take advantage of it. First she wipes her hands on a towel and touches up her hair. She comes into the living room.*)

MARTHA: My, if it isn't Mr. Sampson.

ROGER: (*Gets up quickly.*) Oh! Hello, Mrs. Hill, I didn't know you were back there. How are you?

MARTHA: I'm just fine, how about you?

ROGER: Couldn't be better.

MARTHA: Oh, now you didn't have to get up just on my account, I was just going in the other room to get something or other. Please sit down.

ROGER: (*Obeys.*) Thank you.

MARTHA: Well, it's certainly good to see you again after so long. You mustn't stay away like that. We've missed you.

ROGER: That's awfully nice of you, Mrs. Hill.

MARTHA: Yes . . . (*Clears her throat.*) My, that's a nice automobile I saw you drive up in, Mr. Sampson. Is it new?

ROGER: Yes—yes, as a matter of fact, it is. I just got it last week.

MARTHA: How nice! You know, as soon as we saw it, Angela said to me, "Oh, I just must have a ride in that lovely car!"

(*Something falls with a clatter of glass in* ANGELA's *room.*)

ROGER: What was that?

MARTHA: Probably the kids playing ball out in the back. You know how children are, always breaking things . . . (*Clears her throat again.*) Tell me, Mr. Sampson, I understand you're with a law firm in the City now, aren't you? Seems to me Angela said something about reading the announcement in the paper.

(*At this,* ANGELA *comes storming out of her room, flinging a coat over her shoulder.*)

ANGELA: Excuse me for butting in, but shall we go, Roger? (*Sends daggers' points at* MARTHA.)

ROGER: (*Rising.*) Sure. If you're ready.

MARTHA: Oh—are you going out?

ANGELA: Yes, we are. You needn't fix dinner for me.

MARTHA: Oh, that's all right, don't worry about it. Where are you going?

ANGELA: He's taking me to dinner, do you mind?!

MARTHA: Oh no, not at all. I think that's nice, very nice.

ROGER: We won't be gone long, Mrs. Hill. I promised to bring her back very early.

ANGELA: If we don't get out of here this second, you won't

have to bring me back at all! Come on! (*Takes him by the arm and propels him to the door.*)

MARTHA: Have a good time, now!

ROGER: Thanks, Mrs. Hill. (*Opens the door for* ANGELA.)

MARTHA: (*To* ANGELA, *mouths coyly.*) And remember what I said . . . !"

ANGELA: Good-*bye*, Martha! (*She and* ROGER *exit.*)

MARTHA: (*At the open door.*) Good-bye! . . . Have fun! . . . And be careful!

(*She watches for a moment as they descend the stairs. Then she closes the door and pauses, smiling inwardly. Now she gathers herself together, stands alert and tall, chin and stomach pulled in. Raising one hand, she adjusts an imaginary veil, fluffs out her "train," while with the other she tenderly grasps a "bouquet." Then, summoning up an expression of sweet-sad beatitude, she does a slow march down the "aisle" to the swelling strains of an imaginary wedding march.*)

(*The lights dim out.*)

Scene Two

When the lights fade up again, it is evening. In the darkened living room, DICKIE *and* JOHNNY HILL, *together with their neighbor* CHARLIE, *are watching a Western movie on television.* JOHNNY, *nine or ten, is seated on the floor, while* DICKIE *and* CHARLIE, *both about twelve, occupy the sofa.*

After a time, voices are heard from the back stairs, and first MARTHA *and then* MRS. WEMBLEY *come into view.*

MARTHA: (*Enters the kitchen and holds open the screen door.*) That's all right, but you know you have no business climbing these stairs.

MRS. WEMBLEY: (*She is a stoutish woman in her seventies, though she looks somewhat younger.*) Oh, now don't you say a word, Martha Hill, don't you say a single word. I'll be seventy-four years of age this August, and I can still dance just as good as when I was a girl of seventeen. Look. (*Hoisting her skirts, she dances about a little, laughing at herself.*)

MARTHA: Mrs. Wembley! If you don't sit yourself down . . .

MRS. WEMBLEY: (*Makes a fair-sized kick.*) Whee! How's that for an old lady, pretty good, huh? Aw, there's a lot of life left in the old nanny yet! (*Stops, out of breath, and sits heavily.*) It just . . . takes me . . . a little while . . . to get my breath sometimes . . . that's all!

MARTHA: There, I told you to behave. Honestly, you're worse than some little child. Do you feel all right?

MRS. WEMBLEY: Oh, yes, I'm . . . I'm all right now, thank you. Quite all right, don't you worry about me. Why, it's been so long since I've had a real sickness now 'til I can hardly remember.

MARTHA: Well, you just sit right there and rest awhile.

MRS: WEMBLEY: And I thank the Lord, thank him every day, that he's given me the health and strength to carry on through all these many years. Oh, I have my little aches and pains occasionally, but you know what I do?

MARTHA: (*With a "here-we-go-again" expression.*) I wonder what? (*Goes to get a pie from the pantry.*)

MRS. WEMBLEY: Whenever I feel a pain or a chill coming on, I stop right still and I say this: Jesus is my strength and my salvation, in Him I find the manifestation of perfect health and mind and I will not be subject to the infirmities of the wicked! That's what I say, Martha, and you'd be amazed at how it works. And then, sometimes in the evenings, if the pain tries to creep back, I sit down and write a little letter off to the people at Unity, over in Dayton, Ohio. They have a prayer band every evening, you know, and I ask them to pray for me. Of course, they never get the letter until a day or two later at the earliest, but just putting it on paper and holding the thought is just as good as if they'd already gotten it and said a special little prayer just for me. 'Cause when I wake up in the morning I feel so refreshed and comforted, and every little ache or pain has just vanished out the window! Oh, I'm telling you, Martha, you ought to try it sometime. There's nothing in the world so wonderful as the power of God through Unity. Oh, no, Martha, please! Don't cut such a big piece like that for me, I couldn't eat it all.

MARTHA: Go ahead and try. Eat as much as you can.

MRS: WEMBLEY: No—now, please! Make it smaller. That's better, right about there. That's lovely, Martha. My, it looks so good, and the crust is so tender and flaky, did you use my recipe?

MARTHA: No, not this time. I used a can of ready-mix. Glass of milk?

MRS. WEMBLEY: Oh, now you know you shouldn't use that awful stuff—yes, I believe I will, thank you. Why, I wouldn't have a can of it in the house. (*Takes up her fork and tastes, considering.*) 'Course, you probably added a little egg white and milk and butter to it, didn't you, but using things like that to cook with's like inviting ptomaine poison! I don't for the life of me see why they allow such things on the grocery shelves. (*Digs in heartily.*)

MARTHA: (*Smiles.*) Well, if anybody gets ptomaine poison around here, I'll write a letter off to Unity and say, "Jesus is my strength and my salvation."

MRS. WEMBLEY: (*Recites.*) "Jesus is my strength and my salvation, in Him I find the manifestation of perfect health and mind and I will not be subject to the infirmities of the wicked." Say all of it, Martha, and you just watch and see. Mmmm, this is good.

MARTHA: Excuse me a minute, I want to look in on the kids.
MRS. WEMBLEY: You go right ahead, Martha, don't you worry about me.

(MARTHA *goes to the living room and leans against the portal.*)

MARTHA: (*Squinting her eyes.*) Hey.
JOHNNY: Hi, Mom.
CHARLIE: Hello, Miz' Hill.
MARTHA: It's about time for all of you-all to be in your beds.
JOHNNY: Aw, Ma, we're lookin' at the pit-cher!
DICKIE: It's almost over now, leave it alone!
MARTHA: All right, but just as soon as it's over I want you to turn it off and start getting ready for bed, hear?
JOHNNY: Okay, Mom.
MARTHA: Did you hear, Dickie?
DICKIE: Sure, I heard you, wat d'ya think I am, deaf or somethin'?
MARTHA: Now that's about enough out of you, young man. Charlie, how's your mother?
CHARLIE: Okay, I guess.
MARTHA: That's nice. Tell her I'll see her Monday night at the PTA.
CHARLIE: Yeah, sure.
MARTHA: (*Returns to the kitchen.*) How 'bout some more? I made two—there's plenty.
MRS. WEMBLY: (*Finishing up.*) No, no thank you, dear.
MARTHA: Another glass of milk?
MRS. WEMBLEY: Unh-unnh! I've had all I care for, thank you. It's not good for me to eat so much. Besides, Melvin's been telling me lately I'm looking too fat.
MARTHA: (*Sits.*) Oh, I've been meaning to ask about Melvin. I haven't seen him around lately.
MRS. WEMBLEY: No, well he's working now, you know.
MARTHA: I didn't know.
MRrS. WEMBLEY: Yes, he's been on the job over a week now. He's working at a printing plant this time, down in the City.
MARTHA: How nice.
MRS. WEMBLEY: Yes, I think so, too. I kept telling Melvin the thing to do was stop sitting around the house moping, and to get up and get out and get another job to prove to himself and everybody else that it didn't bother him in the least that he got fired from that other place.

MARTHA: Oh, was he fired? I thought he said something to me about resigning because the position didn't offer enough challenge to a person of his capabilities, or something like that.

MRS. WEMBLEY: Oh, now, Martha, you didn't really believe that, did you? Even if Melvin is my own dear son, I don't see any reason to have to lie about it. It's wicked to lie and there's no good can come of it. No, Melvin got fired from that place he was at before. Kept getting into quarrels with the people on the job, and they finally got tired of it and let him go. I kept telling him, "Melvin, don't you talk so much on the job and you won't get into arguments!" But he kept right on, talk-talk-talking, 'til he talked himself right out in the street. (*Sigh.*) I don't for the life of me know where he gets it from, his father was such a quiet man.

MARTHA: Well, I hope he can keep this one for a while.

MRS. WEMBLEY: I hope so, too. He's such a strange boy, sometimes I don't think I know him at all. It's funny, things like that, about your own flesh and blood.

MARTHA: I know. Angela gets like that sometimes, too. There are times when she just won't let anyone get near her, thinks everybody's trying to pry into her affairs, just because you try to seem interested.

MRS. WEMBLEY: Oh, but Angela's such a lovely girl, Martha. I'm sure she doesn't mean anything by that.

MARTHA: You don't know . . .

MRS. WEMBLEY: Well, maybe she needs to get married. You know how it is with these girls who stay in school too long. After a while they start getting nervous and irritable, and they don't know which way to turn almost. What Angela needs is a man.

MARTHA: Oh, I agree. But don't you dare say that to her! Whew!

MRS. WEMBLY: Oh? Why not?

MARTHA: Because she thinks men are about the lowest order of creature God ever made. She hates 'em all!

MRS. WEMBLY: Oh, but I saw her out the window just a while ago driving off with some young man in a big shiny car.

MARTHA: Yes, Mr. Sampson. But don't let that fool you. This is the first time she's seen him in going on two months.

MRS. WEMBLY: Well, a lovely young girl like Angela, it's just because she's been in school too long, that's all. I wouldn't worry about it, Martha, you have enough on your hands taking care of your own lovely family. And by the way, Martha, what's this I hear about you starting to have another baby and then changing your mind and having an operation? Oh, I know how it is to want to keep up with these modern trends—I'm not a bit old-fashioned myself. But don't you think that's dangerous, taking a chance like that when you—

MARTHA: (*Stunned.*) Mrs. Wembley, what are you saying! Where on earth did you get a tale like that?

MRS. WEMBLEY: Oh? You mean it isn't so? Well, I was certain that if your own sister, Grace—

MARTHA: Oh, no! Did you get that from Gracie?

MRS. WEMBLEY: Well, not directly, of course. But I was sure if it was such common knowledge, then— (MARTHA *gazes about wildly, then puts her hands to her face and sobs.*) Oh, dear! Now here I've gone and got you all upset. I should have known it was just a case of malicious old gossip. (*Rises and goes to comfort* MARTHA.) There now, dear. Let it all out and you'll feel better.

MARTHA: Oh, one of these days I'm going to get so mad I could kill, kill!

MRS. WEMBLEY: I know how you feel, dear, but think of your children, what would they tell their friends? Now, your nerves are all on edge, Martha dear. Sometimes mine get that way, too. And you know what I do? I stop and stand right still and say: "Jesus, envelop me in thy tender love that my days may be brighter in the service of the Lord." And then I write a letter off to the people out at Unity. In fact, I think I'll write to them tonight, Martha. I'll ask them to pray for you, dear, and tell them all about your troubles.

MARTHA: (*Sobbing loudly.*) Don't you dare . . . !

MRS. WEMBLEY: Well, I, uh . . . Martha, I know just what you need. A nice cup of hot milk to settle your stomach and quiet down the nerves. Now, you sit right there and I'll have it for you in a wink! (*Gets a saucepan and begins to heat some milk, as outside the clock tower tolls the half hour.*)

(*Meanwhile, in the living room, the movie has ended.* CHARLIE *rises and stretches, then turns to* DICKIE, *who is still sprawled on the sofa, eyeing the screen with melancholy.*)

CHARLIE: Guess I better head for home or my ma'll whale the daylights outa me.

DICKIE: Okay.

CHARLIE: Comin' by on the way to school tomorrow?

DICKIE: Yeah. Guess so.

CHARLIE: Okay. I'll see ya. So long.

JOHNNY: 'Bye, Charlie.

CHARLIE: (*Crosses through to the kitchen.*) 'Bye, Miz' Hill. Oh, hello, Miz' Wembley.

MRS. WEMBLEY: (*At the stove.*) What? Who's that? Oh, hello there, Charlie. How's your mother?

CHARLIE: Oh, she's fine.

MRS. WEMBLEY: That's nice, dear. Tell her I asked about her.

CHARLIE: Yes, ma'am, I will. Good night. (*Pushes through the screen door and darts down the back stairs.*)

MRS. WEMBLEY: Good night, Charlie . . . My, he's such a sweet boy. The whole family of them, always so cheerful and smiling. Don't guess they mind being West Indian at all . . . Here now, your milk's all ready. (*Pours the milk into a cup and gives it to* MARTHA.) Drink it while it's hot, dear, and you'll feel ever so much better.

MARTHA: (*Raises her head from her arms and sips at the milk. Then she turns her head and calls.*) Dickie!

DICKIE: (*Jumps up and turns off the set.*) Wha-at!

MARTHA: I want you to turn off that thing and both of you-all start getting ready for your beds.

DICKIE: It's already off, what you hollerin' about? Come on, Johnny. (*Heads for the kids' bedroom,* JOHNNY *following.*)

MARTHA: Oh, that Dickie. I don't know what to do with these kids. I hate to beat them, I didn't like it at all when I was a child.

MRS. WEMBLEY: Well, before my husband passed, he used to handle mine. All I had to do was threaten to tell their father.

MARTHA: Yes, but threatening never did scare my kids.

DICKIE: (*Appearing at the door to his room.*) Hey, Ma! You gonna sleep in my bed again tonight?

MARTHA: (*With a quick glance at* MRS. WEMBLEY.) Oh, I don't know, Dickie, don't worry about it.

DICKIE: Well, I don't see why you can't sleep in your own room anymore. (*Returns to his room.*)

MARTHA: (*To* MRS. WEMBLEY; *on the spot.*) I, uh . . . Dickie's been having such terrible nightmares lately that I've had to sleep in his bed to keep him from getting scared. (*Forces a weak smile.*) Silly of him, isn't it?

MRS. WEMBLEY: I know, Martha, didn't I have six of my own? (*Pause; slyly.*) And I used to get mad at my husband too. Sometimes it's only natural.

MARTHA: (*Her secret is out.*) Oh, honestly, Mrs. Wembley, you make me tell you everything.

MRS. WEMBLEY: Well, what are downstairs neighbors for if not to listen to upstairs neighbors' problems?

MARTHA: It's not *just* the downstairs neighbors I'm worried about.

MRS. WEMBLEY: Oh, now, Martha, what an unkind thing to say. You know you can trust me. (*Clears her throat.*) Well?

MARTHA: Tell you what, I'll be right back. I have to go look after the kids. (*She rises.*)

MRS. WEMBLEY: But that's not fair, now!

MARTHA: You have another piece of pie. I won't be a minute. (*Crosses to the living room. At that moment, footsteps are heard running up the stairs. ANGELA enters.*) Well, I'm certainly glad to see you. (*Calls.*) Here's Angela, Mrs. Wembley!

ANGELA: Is she up here again? Why doesn't she stay downstairs and practice taking off on her broomstick?

MRS. WEMBLEY: (*Calls.*) Angela? Come here and let me see you, dear.

ANGELA: (*With a dirty look at* MARTHA.) Ughh! (*Goes into the kitchen.* MARTHA *continues on into the kids' room.*) Hello, Mrs. Wembley, so nice to see you again.

MRS. WEMBLEY: Well, will you just look at this lovely child! Come here, my dear, and let me get a better look at you. My, one of these days some man is going to be awfully happy, awfully happy!

ANGELA: (*Under her breath.*) Some men should live so long!

MRS. WEMBLEY: And just who is the lucky beau these days? Or should I make that plural, a beautiful girl like you?

ANGELA: Oh, nobody in particular, Mrs. Wembley, I don't have much time for romance. My books keep me pretty busy.

MRS. WEMBLEY: Oh, but you can't fool me. I saw you out the window driving away in that big shiny car.

ANGELA: That doesn't mean a thing, Mrs. Wembley. Not a thing.

MRS. WEMBLEY: Well, your time will come soon, you just wait and see. As a matter of fact, my Melvin was saying just the other day, "I wonder why that Angela doesn't get married."

ANGELA: Oh? And how is dear Melvin these days?

MRS. WEMBLEY: Just fine, just fine. He's working again, you know. Has a very good job at a printing plant down in the City.

ANGELA: How nice. And does he plan to stay there awhile? A week or two, maybe?

MRS. WEMBLEY: Oh, now you shouldn't say such unkind things

about Melvin, Angela. After all, you know, Melvin's very fond of you. Yes, he is! As a matter of fact, it's been one of my dearest hopes ever since you came here to live with your sister that perhaps you and Melvin . . . Well . . .

ANGELA: Save your hopes, Mrs. Wembley. Melvin could never see anything in me.

MRS. WEMBLEY: But you're wrong entirely! Why, I happen to know—

ANGELA: Then let's make it the other way around, shall we?

MRS. WEMBLEY: Well, I didn't know it was as definite as all that.

ANGELA: I'm sorry, but it is.

MRS. WEMBLEY: I see. Well . . . (*Gives a light laugh.*) can't say as I blame you any. Melvin's my own dear son, but to put up with him it'd take a woman of . . . uncommon forebearance. Tell me, Angela, how's the school work coming?

ANGELA: I can't complain. They're certainly keeping me busy, though.

MRS. WEMBLEY: I can imagine. And just when do you get your master's degree?

ANGELA: In June, if I can hold out that long.

MRS. WEMBLEY: You will, you will. My, but I do envy you young folks nowadays, with opportunites opening up right and left. In my day, if you got your degree, it was strictly limited. Teaching, that's all most of us got a chance to do, and were we grateful for even that little bit, I tell you. Why, when I think of that brilliant, brilliant man, Dr. W. E. B. Du Bois, stuck down there in a little school like Atlanta University, teaching a bunch of virtual illiterates like me and my classmates, when he should have been off writing the great books and leading the great movements that he did later on . . . !

ANGELA: (*Shows interest.*) Oh, you mean you studied under Dr. Du Bois?

MRS. WEMBLEY: For two and a half years.

ANGELA: Gee, I'll bet that was exciting.

MRS. WEMBLEY: It certainly was. "Dr. Dubie," we used to call him. Behind his back, of course. (*Mimics.*) "Dr. Dubie, Dr. Dubie! (ANGELA *laughs.*) Even then we all knew he'd be a great man someday. Greater even than Booker T. Washington, who hated him with an abiding passion.

ANGELA: Oh? But why?

MRS. WEMBLEY: You mean you never heard of the great

debate between Dr. Du Bois and Booker T.? Child—I don't know what they teach you in these big white schools, but somehow it seems to me you need to know something about your own people. Why, we had to have a course in Negro history before we could get our degree at Atlanta University. They made sure you knew where you'd *been* before you started out on where you wanted to *go.* Anyway, Booker T. Washington—you know who *he* was, don't you?

ANGELA: (*Smiles.*) Yes, Mrs. Wembley. I've read about him.

MRS. WEMBLEY: I imagine so. If the white folks taught you anything at all, I'm sure they brought up Booker T.! Well, Booker T. Washington started his school over in Tuskegee, Alabama, and he had to get money from wealthy white folks to keep it going. So he publicly advised Negroes not to upset the good white folks by such things as voting and insisting on equal rights and getting too much education—except at *his* school, of course, where they taught you masonry without mathematics and "science" with a "domestic" in front of it. Well, dapper young Dr. Du Bois, who had his doctor of philosophy degree from Harvard and who had studied and traveled abroad, took great issue with Booker T. Yes, we need our farmers and bricklayers and cooks and maids, he said. But we also need to have our physicians and scientists and men of letters and culture, just like the other folks. No race, Dr. Du Bois used to tell us—no race can rise without its thinkers as well as its laborers, its men of inspiration as well as perspiration. And he talked about the "talented tenth"—a group of educated colored men and women who would be in the forefront of the fight to move our race forward against all the obstacles placed in our way. Oh, he could teach, that man could! But Booker T. Washington knew where *his* bread was buttered. He spoke out against people like Dr. Du Bois "gettin' outta his place" and assured the white folks that we didn't want any such-a thing as equality. So he and Dr. Du Bois debated the issue for years, in speeches and articles right and left. But the white folks rallied to Booker T. and not Dr. Du Bois, because they knew where *their* bread was buttered, too.

ANGELA: I see. But what happened? After that?

MRS. WEMBLEY: Oh, just about the climax of all the big controversy, Booker T. Washington up and died.

ANGELA: Well, did Dr. Du Bois take over?

MRS. WEMBLEY: I wish to God he had! No, it wasn't long before there were others on the scene, pointing and pulling in first one direction, then another. And all the time, Dr. Du Bois kept on speaking and writing, the lone voice in the wilderness, the prophet without honor, so-to-speak.

ANGELA: The last I heard, they were trying to put him in jail for being a subversive.

MRS. WEMBLEY: You see what I mean? (*Pause. Tired now.*) Well, I guess I'd better get back downstairs and wait for Melvin to come home. If he is coming home tonight, I never know . . . 'S funny, the girls never seem to take to Melvin much, but that doesn't discourage him any. (*Pulls herself to her feet.*) Tell Martha thanks for the pie, it was simply delicious.

ANGELA: All right. And Mrs. Wembley. I—I'm sorry. That I was so cross with you earlier.

MRS. WEMBLEY: Now, you think nothing of it, child, nothing at all. I know I'm an old bore that doesn't even live in the same world with you young folks anymore. But we get lonely sometimes. And scared. And the only thing that helps is to have someone to talk to once in awhile. And somebody else to talk about. Tell Martha I'll see her in the morning when she comes down to pick up the mail. Good night . . . Good night, Angela. (*She is out the door and moving slowly down the stairs.*)

ANGELA: Good night, Mrs. Wembley.

(*Stands reflectively for a moment, then starts for her room. At the same time,* MARTHA *appears from the kids' room, eyeing the kitchen apprehensively.*)

MARTHA: Is she gone?

ANGELA: Yes.

MARTHA: Good. (*Joins* ANGELA *in the living room.*) She's really a sweet old soul, but every once in a while she gets on my nerves. My, I certainly didn't expect to see you back so soon tonight. What happened, had another fight? Oh— I'm sorry, I forgot. I'm not supposed to pry.

ANGELA: (*Smiles.*) I'll let you by this time.

MARTHA: Oh? Then, tell me, what happened?

ANGELA: Well, to make a long story short, he proposed.

MARTHA: He did? Marriage? Well, I mean—

ANGELA: As a matter of fact, this time it was marriage he had in mind.

MARTHA: (*Pleased.*) Well! And did you accept?

ANGELA: No.

MARTHA: (*Disappointed.*) Oh . . . Well, I suppose you know what you want to do, Angela, there's not much else I can say.

ANGELA: (*For the first time a little unsure.*) Oh, Martha, I *don't* know. I don't know at all! Why is it a person can't just be left alone to live her own life by herself without having to get all involved in relationships and obligations? I just hate to be obligated to anybody.

MARTHA: Well, whether you want to or not, you just can't live by yourself in this world. Was Roger very disappointed? I mean, did he act as though he wasn't going to see you again?

ANGELA: No, not exactly. I didn't accept, but I didn't tell him no, either.

MARTHA: (*Cheered.*) Well!

ANGELA: I told him I'd give it a lot of thought, but that I couldn't possibly begin to consider it until after I'd finished school. I'd go out with him, if he liked, and if he still wanted to, he could ask me again in June.

MARTHA: Oh, well, Angela. (*Laughs a little in delight.*) I think that was a very wise thing to do, very wise. After all, you could do a lot worse than Roger Sampson.

ANGELA: I suppose so. But why do I have to do at all? Oh, Martha . . . (*Puts her arms around* MARTHA *and buries her face against her side.*)

MARTHA: (*Stroking her.*) There, there . . . you poor dear. Having such a hard time, aren't you, baby? But I think you've handled the whole situation remarkably well, really I do. Why, I remember when Doc first asked me to marry him, I came out with a plain old fat "No!" (*Laughs.*) And poor Doc, he was so crushed. He just crawled away to lick his wounds, and I didn't see him for almost a week. He wouldn't call, he wouldn't come by, and I didn't want it to be like that at all—I just didn't want to get married right away. I was staying with Gracie and Ed and going to school just like you are now. But then, after a while I called—I mean, he called, and . . . No, I don't have to hide it, I called him. Yes, and I told him Grace and Ed had been wondering about him, why he'd stopped coming by all of a sudden, and of course you know that was a lie! (*Laughs lightly.*) Gracie never could *stand* Doc, and Ed had only met him once or twice! But it worked, and he came over, and I don't think it was more than a week after that that we were standing up before Reverend Mayberry saying, "I do." . . . (*Sighs.*) My, that's the first time I've thought about that in a long time.

(*Looks down.*) By the way, Angela, what compelled Roger
to come by all of a sudden like that, after so long? And to
propose, right out of a clear blue sky?

ANGELA: Oh, he's decided it's about time his rambling days
were over, now that he's joined up with this law firm, and
that he might as well get himself a wife and a home, to add
to his new car. All very practical and businesslike.

MARTHA: Now, Angela. He didn't say that, did he?

ANGELA: No, but I can read between the lines. Roger took
me out to dinner at one of those intimate little French places
on the North Side—candlelight, filet mignon, wine, the
works! Then after he'd filled his stomach, he gave me the
business about having been in love with me for some time
and only just recently having realized it for sure. And how
he went through agony wondering what I'd say when he
called, and how he just must have me for his own or his life
won't mean a thing. Oh, you know the sort of things men
can dream up after a big meal, with a little wine and music
to lull them into a romantic stupor!

MARTHA: Why, it all sounds perfectly lovely to me. Why, I
think I'd still be there, talking by candlelight, or else go out
dancing under the stars or something. Angela, sometimes I
think you just have no sense of romance.

ANGELA: (*Rising.*) Romantic or not, I have to meet the *man*
in the morning. And if I can't give him more than hearts
and flowers on that Anthropology panel, I just might as well
flunk his course.

(*Just then* DOC *comes in. He looks at* MARTHA *and* ANGELA
quizzically, then closes the door behind him.)

ANGELA: (*Blandly.*) Hi, Doc. (*Goes into her room and closes
the door.*)

DOC: Uh, hi. (*To* MARTHA.) My dinner ready? (*Goes into the
bedroom and takes off his hat and coat.*)

MARTHA: (*Following.*) Yes, it's all on the stove. All I have to
do is heat up the chops.

DOC: (*Rolling up his sleeves.*) Good.

MARTHA: Doc . . .

DOC: (*Steels himself.*) Yeah?

MARTHA: Doc, I think we ought to get the kids a bicycle after
all.

DOC: (*Relieved but masking it.*) Well, that's what I told you.

MARTHA: And, Doc . . . ?

DOC: (*Wary again.*) Yeah?

MARTHA: Did you really think I meant it when you asked me to marry you that first time and I told you no?

DOC: (*Pauses, turns, and looks at her disgustedly.*) Of all the damn fool questions to be askin' a man. Thirteen years too late! Hell, if I'd really had my choice about it—

MARTHA: (*Grins.*) Never you mind. (*Goes to him and puts her arms around his neck.*)

(*Doc starts to raise his hands, hesitates. He looks at her questioningly. She nods her head and kisses him lightly on the lips. With a deep sigh, Doc draws her to him and begins moving his arms up and down her back. Their breathing becomes heavy, and she rains little kisses on his neck and ears, her eyes tightly closed.*)

(*There is the sound of a tussle in the kids' room, and* MARTHA *looks up, startled. She pushes* DOC's *hands away.*)

MARTHA: Not now, Doc—the kids! (*Calls.*) Didn't I tell you-all to put out that light and go to sleep? I don't want to have to come in there. (*The light goes out and there is silence.* MARTHA *looks at* DOC *and smiles.*) Come on in the kitchen and I'll give you your dinner. (*Turns and crosses to the kitchen.*)

(*Doc loosens his collar, rolls his sleeves a bit higher, and starts to follow, whistling aimlessly. As he passes* ANGELA's *room, he slows his step and his whistle and glances in at the crack of the door. Then he resumes whistling and continues on to the kitchen.*)

(*The lights fade.*)

Scene Three

When the lights rise, it is morning a few days later. The stage is empty, but sounds of life are heard coming from ANGELA'S *room. After a moment* ANGELA *appears at her door, pulling a dressing gown on over her slip. She yawns and stretches.*

ANGELA: Martha . . . ? (*Comes forward to look into the front bedroom, then turns toward the kitchen.*) Anybody home . . . ? (*There is no answer. Finally she turns and goes into the bathroom, closing the door.*)

(*A moment later, the telephone rings. It rings again. After the third ring, the commode is heard to flush and* ANGELA *comes rushing out of the bathroom in just her slip. She picks up the phone.*)

ANGELA: Hello? . . . Oh, hi . . . (*Slumps into a chair.*) No, I'm up, I was in the bathroom . . . I feel all right, I guess, how about you? . . . (*Laughs lightly.*) Oh, now Roger, it couldn't be as bad as all that! . . . Well, you had no business getting so amorous, I told you beforehand nothing was going to happen . . . Well, you get right up and take another cold shower and then you'll feel better . . . Hmm? . . . Well, while we're at it, let me give you a little tip about these things, Roger. If a girl ever does become inclined, it's certainly not going to happen on a couch in some stranger's house during a party. And especially not in the rumpus room! . . . Well, I should think you could learn a little more tact about these things, after all . . . Why should I give you another chance, I don't think you deserve it . . . Well, I'm sorry, but you goofed . . . Yes . . . What? . . . Now, Roger, I've told you I don't want to even think about that until after school's finished. Just because of last night don't get the idea I've changed my mind or anything. . . . Well, today's Saturday and I have a lot of things to get done. And since it's nearly eleven already, I'd better get started . . . No, this afternoon I'll be over at the library . . . Yes. (*Footsteps have*

*been sounding, coming up the stairs, and now there is a knock
at the door.* ANGELA *looks up.*) Just a minute, there's someone at the door. (*Calls, holding her hand over the mouthpiece.*) Yes? Who is it?

VOICE: (*Outside.*) Uh, Kenny Powers, ma'am!

ANGELA: Who?

KENNY: Kenneth Powers. May I see you for a moment, please?

ANGELA: Well, just a minute, I'm on the phone!

KENNY: That's all right, I'll wait, ma'am.

ANGELA: (*Back on the phone.*) Hello? Look, Roger, I have to
go now, someone's at the door . . . Tonight? Well, okay,
but don't get the idea I'm promising you anything . . . Oh,
about eight-thirty or so . . . Okay, see you then, good-bye.
(*Hangs up quickly and starts for the door. Suddenly remembering she is not dressed, she runs back into the bathroom for
her dressing gown and puts it on before going to the door.
She opens it.*) Yes?

KENNY: (*Without.*) Uh, good morning, ma'am, my name is
Kenny Powers and I'm a student over at the university.
Here's my ID card in case you like to . . .

ANGELA: (*Looking.*) Uh-hunh.

KENNY: Now, ma'am, I'm taking a poll of this area in connection with a class of mine, and I wonder if you'd mind if I
asked you a few questions. It won't take more than a few
minutes of your time, I assure you, ma'am, and I'd be
awfully grateful for your cooperation. You see, this is a class
in public opinion, and we have to draw up and conduct our
own polls—like Dr. Gallup, you know. And then we take
them all back to the classroom and analyze and interpret the
percentages. It's quite simple, really it is, and we'll be
through before you know it. Now here's—

ANGELA: What class is this for, Dr. Herbowitz in Sociology?

KENNY: No, it's for Dr. Henry in Political Science. (*Grins.*) So
you're a student too, I take it? Just my luck.

ANGELA: That's all right, I don't mind helping out. Come in
and I'll answer your questions for you.

KENNY: Well, uh, thanks anyway, but we're supposed to try
and get ordinary people from the community at large. Oh, I
suppose it would be easy to just hand out a bunch of questionnaires among my friends and all, and tell them to put
down fictitious names. Some of the kids in the class are doing
it. But I'm trying to avoid that. I kinda like this course, if
you get what I mean.

ANGELA: Sure. And I admire you for it, it's the only way to

really get something out of it. Well, it's a shame you had to climb all these stairs for nothing. Did you try downstairs?

KENNY: (*Grins.*) Did I? It took me over half an hour to get away from that lady. Said she didn't mind giving me answers. But first she wanted to rewrite the questions! (ANGELA *laughs.*) Well, thanks anyway, I better be making tracks. Got a lot of questionnaires to get filled out before Tuesday.

ANGELA: Aw, what's the hurry, you look a little tired. Come on in and sit down for a minute, I think I'd like to see your questions anyway.

KENNY: Well, thanks a lot, but I—

ANGELA: Would you like a glass of water?

KENNY: No, thank you, I—

ANGELA: There's some cold beer in the refrigerator.

KENNY: No, I . . . I . . . Well, it is a pretty warm day, I guess it wouldn't hurt any.

ANGELA: Then come in. (*As he enters.*) Hmm, I must be slipping. Why, I can actually remember when I wouldn't have had to use a can of beer to lure a young man my way!

KENNY: Oh, it's not that, it's just—

ANGELA: Oh no, now! No excuses whatsoever. I'll just have to spend a little time figuring out what Pabst Blue Ribbon's got that I haven't. Sit down, won't you, and I'll have it for you in a minute. By the way, my name's Angela. Angela Williams. (*Extends her hand.*)

KENNY: And I'm Kenny. Kenny Powers. Glad to meet you, Angela.

(*They shake hands.*)

ANGELA: (*Thinking.*) Kenny Powers, Kenny Powers, where have I heard that name? Oh, I know! You're the one who ran last year for the Student Senate!

KENNY: Well, I ran, but of course, you know . . .

ANGELA: That doesn't make any difference, the important thing is you ran. I voted for you, too.

KENNY: (*Smiles.*) Well, what do you know—a constituent! Almost, anyway.

ANGELA: I hope you'll be running again this year. I mean, somebody should.

KENNY: You're right, but it won't be me. I finish up in June. And what about you? In school, I mean. Are you a senior, junior or what?

ANGELA: Ha! Don't flatter me. I finished last year and now I'm doing graduate work in sociology.

KENNY: A grad student? Allah, Allah! (*Raises his arms and bows.*) Say, come to think of it, haven't I seen you around? Weren't you in old Merriweather's Shakespeare class winter term last year?

ANGELA: Yes, I was!

KENNY: Hey, I remember you. Used to sit over to the left, about five, six rows from the front.

ANGELA: That's right.

KENNY: Used to wear a big long Santa Claus cap to class sometimes, hung way down to your . . . your back!

ANGELA: (*Laughs.*) That silly old cap, a girlfriend gave it to me for Christmas.

KENNY: Well, what d'ya know. Small world, isn't it?

ANGELA: Hang on a second and I'll get you that beer. And then I'd better run and get some clothes on. (*Starts for the kitchen.*)

KENNY: Oh no, I wouldn't do that! That would spoil the whole effect, ruin the whole thing. Bring the beer, yes. But put on clothes, unh-unnh!

ANGELA: (*Laughs as she goes to the refrigerator.*) My mother told me never to let strangers into the house. But I guess dirty old men are an exception!

KENNY: (*Rises and goes as far as the portal.*) Ha! I guess you heard the one about the two little kids, didn't you? This liittle girl was in her pajamas getting ready to go to bed, and this little boy wanted to come in her room. And the little girl said, "No, no, Tommy, 'oo tan't tum in, 'cause Mommy says it isn't nice for 'ittle boys to see 'ittle girls in their nightie." So the little boy gave up and started to go away, but a minute later the door opened and the little girl stuck her head out and said, "Oo tan tum in now, Tommy. I took it orf!"

(*They both laugh as* ANGELA *brings a cold can of beer, a glass and an opener from the kitchen.*)

ANGELA: Oh, now really!

KENNY: Ain't that a hot one, though? Here, I'll get that. (*Takes the opener and opens the can.*)

ANGELA: I brought you a glass, if you want.

KENNY: That's all right, can's okay. (*Takes a long draught.*) Mmmh . . . (*Inadvertantly looks down at* ANGELA's *legs, peeping out from under the dressing gown. He takes another swig of beer.*)

ANGELA: (*Catches this. She rises.*) Excuse me a minute, will you, while I dress? I won't be a minute.

KENNY: Oh, no—really, don't bother on my account. I have to go now anyway. Got a lot of questionnaires to get filled out. (*He rises.*)

ANGELA: Well, you can stay for just a minute, can't you?

KENNY: I'm tempted, really I am. But I've set aside today to work on this, and I don't believe in letting . . . ah, distractions interfere with my work.

ANGELA: Oh?

KENNY: No, you see, I'm not rich like some of these white fraternity boys, riding up and down in their shiny convertibles, always out on a spree—wine, women and song, don't worry about the tab, father's check is in the mail. I've had to get mine the hard way. I'm on a little scholarship and I've got a board job over at the cafeteria, and I can't afford to waste the opportunity. Oh, sure, I like to run around and have fun once in awhile just like anybody else. But I like to think I'm here for a special purpose, and I want to make the most of it.

ANGELA: Is that so?

KENNY: Yeah. (*Grins.*) Oh, I guess some people'd call it my messiah complex. But somehow I've managed to convince myself that I was put down here for more than just to eat and sleep and take up space. I believe I have a goal in life—predestined, if you will. And somehow I've got to fulfill that destiny.

ANGELA: You sound like a minister. Are you taking theology?

KENNY: (*Laughs.*) No, nothing like that.

ANGELA: Then what are you talking about?

KENNY: It's a little hard to explain.

ANGELA: Try me.

KENNY: Well . . . (*Has some more beer.*) Back in Columbus, my old man, he works in the post office. Been there for more than twenty-five years. He's a graduate of Howard University in Washington, D.C. Pre-med. But he didn't have the money to go on for doctor's training, so he went to work in the post office, hoping to earn enough for his first year at least. Well, I guess you can guess what happened. He met Mom and they got married, and a little later, first my brother and then I came along. And Dad never did get to med school.

ANGELA: What a shame.

KENNY: So, all along, Dad's been telling the two of us, my brother and me, that it's up to us to go ahead and do whatever we really want to do in life. "Go to school," he said, "and stay out of the post office. Be whatever you want to be, but stay away from the post office." Well, we listened and nodded and all, but it didn't mean too much to me until my brother got ready to finish high school. He was all set to go to Ohio State on a basketball scholarship when—

ANGELA: I know. He got married . . .

KENNY and ANGELA: . . . and went to work in the post office!

KENNY: (*Grins.*) So that leaves me. I just gotta make something out of myself, don't I?

ANGELA: You sure had better, boy!

KENNY: 'Cause, if I don't . . .

ANGELA: It's off to the post office! (*They laugh.*) But what's all this about predestination? So you're not a preacher, but what are you—some kind of mystic?

KENNY: No, don't get me wrong. It's a lot more basic than that.

ANGELA: So?

KENNY: Besides my father, there are some others I think about, too. Some of the kids I went to grade and high school with, kids in my neighborhood. They kind of looked up to me because I got good grades and stayed out of trouble, and was lucky enough, I guess, to keep up with the white kids in my classes better than they could. In fact, most of the time, I led the whole class. (*Takes a quick swig of beer.*) Oh, I guess I sound like . . . I mean, I don't want to give the impression that—

ANGELA: Oh no, go on! You go right ahead.

KENNY: Well, somehow I've got the feeling that it's up to me to use my education not just to get ahead and "be somebody big" like my father would like. I think whatever I do, I owe those kids something, too. Owe our *people* something. I think it's up to those of us who've had a few advantages to take at least some time out to plow back, you see, so we can all benefit a little. Get what I mean?

ANGELA: Umm . . . Yes, I guess so.

KENNY: My father tells me I'm crazy. "Them niggers ain't nothin' and they ain't never gonna be nothin'," he says. "You better go 'head and do somethin' for yourself, 'fore they drag you down with 'em!" But I hafta overlook Dad. He means well, but this society we live in has him so brainwashed he thinks of himself as part of some highfalutin Black bourgeoisie that's separate and distinct and looks down on most of the rest of our people. He really doesn't understand that we're all in the same boat together.

ANGELA: (*Swallows.*) Oh, are we . . . ?

KENNY: You better believe it. Our folks may have their silly little class and color distinctions among themselves. But when The Man gets ready to slam the door in your face, he couldn't care less if you've got a college degree. All he wants to know is your race.

ANGELA: But aren't we getting over that sort of thing nowadays? I mean, sometimes we bring these things on ourselves, you know. Isn't it about time we started to forget about race and thought of ourselves as just people like everybody else? No matter what race or color we are?

KENNY: (*Smiles and shakes his head.*) Yeah, I've heard that before, too. But while we're fooling ourselves sittin' around thinking we're "just people" like everybody else, you can bet your bottom dollar The Man over there's still looking at you and thinking: "Nothin' but a bunch of stinkin' niggers." (ANGELA *blinks. He notices.*) Oh, I'm sorry if I've shocked you. But I believe in calling a spade a spade. (*Sips his beer.*)

ANGELA: (*Recovered.*) Well, it's just that you sound so . . . so negative about it all. We can't help it if we were born colored, can we?

KENNY: By no means, and neither should we *want* to help it, Angela. Why, I think being born "colored," as you call it, is one of the most beautiful things in the world! We should be proud of being Black. It's no badge of inferiority—unless we let The Man brainwash us into accepting it as such. It's a distinction to be justly, vastly proud of! It means, despite all the hell we've taken from Western civilization in the past four hundred years, we've survived. Despite all the sickness of those who have used us and then cast us aside, we are stronger than they are, physically and morally. It means that if there is any hope for the survival of this hypocritical American Dream, it depends largely on what happens to us. Don't you see?

ANGELA: Hmm . . . But why should you feel as if we have to have some kind of special obligation to each other? Isn't there another way of looking at it? If you make the most of your opportunities and go out and succeed in whatever your field may be—isn't that helping, too, in the long run? I mean, isn't that what we're all after, ultimately?

KENNY: Should be, should be, and I hope it is someday. But a lot of our people need help now, before we get to the point where everybody can sink or swim on their own. And somebody's got to do it. Not by going off and doing their own thing, but by coming back and putting their skills to work for us all.

ANGELA: Well, that all sounds very noble. But I just hope you aren't fooling yourself.

KENNY: How?

ANGELA: Because you feel a little guilty right now over those poor kids you left behind. Once you get out and start making some money, are you sure you won't forget all about these fine ideals?

KENNY: (*Nods solemnly.*) I've thought of that. And I can't really answer that in advance. Nobody can. But come graduation, I'm going down into the Mississippi Delta with a group of volunteers. We'll be working with small community groups—in small towns, back in the piney woods, out on the plantations. Working and living with "the folks," the grass roots of our people. And if I have any temptation to forget, well, they'll remind me.

ANGELA: (*Smiles.*) "The talented tenth," eh?

KENNY: What's that?

ANGELA: Nothing. Just thinking out loud. Uh, tell me, Mr. Powers—

KENNY: Kenny, please.

ANGELA: All right, Kenny. You don't mean that you don't even go out with girls, now, do you? I mean, you sound like you're on such a Spartan schedule.

KENNY: (*Smiles.*) You can be real funny, you know?

ANGELA: I'm not being funny at all. I'm very serious.

KENNY: But why?

ANGELA: Because I want to know.

KENNY: Well, sure, I go out occasionally. With girls. But I usually ask them.

ANGELA: Then you mean you wouldn't go out on a date, say, with me, if I asked you?

KENNY: But why should you? An . . . an attractive girl like you, you must have lots of boyfriends.

ANGELA: Then you wouldn't, huh?

KENNY: Wouldn't what?

ANGELA: Go out with me if I asked you.

KENNY: But you can't be serious.

ANGELA: I was never more serious in my life.

KENNY: You don't know me, you don't know anything about me!

ANGELA: What better way to find out?

KENNY: (*Shakes his head.*) Boy, I just can't believe it.

ANGELA: Why not?

KENNY: I don't know what to say.

ANGELA: It's very simple. Say yes or no.

KENNY: You mean it? (ANGELA *nods her head gravely.*) Well, just when did you have in mind?

ANGELA: Oh, anytime it's convenient with you. How about tonight?

KENNY: Well, let's see. Tonight I'm supposed to go to a lecture down in the City.

ANGELA: A lecture? On Saturday night?

KENNY: Well, yes. Eric Bentley is speaking on "The Death of the Living Theater."

ANGELA: Well, if you can stand it, I can.

KENNY: You mean you'd like to go to the lecture? With me?

ANGELA: Does that seem so strange?

KENNY: Well, if you really want to go . . .

ANGELA: I want very much to go. With you.

KENNY: Okay, I guess you know what you want. Shall we say about seven, then? Sorry I can't invite you to dinner, but I have to be at my board job.

ANGELA: Oh, that's quite all right, seven o'clock will be just fine.

KENNY: Then I'd better be moving along.

ANGELA: All right.

KENNY: I'm certainly glad to have met you, Angela. I'll be looking forward to tonight.

ANGELA: So will I.

KENNY: (*At the door.*) Thanks for the beer.

ANGELA: You're very welcome.

KENNY: So long!

ANGELA: So long. Until seven.

(KENNY *exits.* ANGELA *closes the door behind him and leans against it thoughtfully for a moment. Then, going to the phone, she picks it up and dials.*)

ANGELA: Hello? Is Mr. Sampson in, please? . . . Well, I'd like to leave a message. Please tell him that Miss Williams called and that she won't be able to keep her appointment for this evening . . . Yes . . . And she'll be tied up the rest of the day . . . That's right, will you see that he gets it, please? . . . Thank you so much, good-bye. (*She hangs up.* ANGELA *smiles. Then she grins. Then she chuckles. And finally she laughs out loud. With a gay, springy step, she whirls off into her room and out of sight.*)

(*Quick curtain.*)

ACT TWO
Scene One

Again music swirls, bringing with it the image of the clock tower upon the scrim. The clock strikes the quarter hour, then dissolves.

It is two months later. At rise, MARTHA *and* MRS. WEMBLEY *are seated at the kitchen table having coffee. It is late morning.*

MRS. WEMBLEY: . . . and I said to him, "Melvin, that's no reason, no reason at all for you to go and quit your job!" But then he just stood there, looking so pitiful, as if I were accusing him of some heinous crime. And he said, "But, Momma, they just don't appreciate intelligence down there. When I finally went and *told* the foreman he didn't know what he was doing and offered to show him how, he called me out of my name and told me to take my black so-and-so back to my bench and mind my own business. And Momma, you *couldn't* expect me to stay on, after that!"

MARTHA: Unh-*unnh!*

MRS. WEMBLEY: 'Course, the sad part about it is I can't help but agree with him. For all the schools Melvin's quit or been kicked out of for one reason or another, he *is* too intelligent to be down there working in a printing plant. And that man had no business calling him those names. Just as prejudiced as they can be.

MARTHA: I know. That's why Doc says he'd rather take care of three buildings. So, what's Melvin going to do now?

MRS. WEMBLEY: I don't know, Martha. He was supposed to be trying to make some money so he could start up the paper again, but now I just don't know.

MARTHA: You know, I really miss that little paper, with all the community news—funerals and weddings and trips and such. It's a shame.

MRS. WEMBLEY: I thinks so, too, especially since it's what he really wants to do. But you can't run a paper, even a little weekly like Melvin's, unless somebody's paying the bills.

319

And what few little advertisers he got pulled out after he started his editorials.

MARTHA: (*Smiles.*) Well, after that one about the mayor, what could you expect?

MRS. WEMBLEY: I know, I know. I told Melvin, no matter how much of a quarrel he had to pick with the school board over discrimination, that was no reason to start speculating over the mayor's paternal ancestry. Why, I knew his father well!

MARTHA: Well, don't worry, he'll find another job soon. Have you written off to Unity?

MRS. WEMBLEY: Oh, indeed so. I told them all about it and asked them to pray for him.

MARTHA: (*Shakes her head.*) It must be just fascinating to be a member of that prayer band.

(*Quick footsteps have been heard on the steps, and now the door bursts open and* DICKIE *and* JOHNNY *enter. They head at once for the kitchen.*)

DICKIE: Hi, Ma. Lunch ready?

JOHNNY: (*Holding up a piece of paper.*) Look, Ma. I got one hundred in spelling. Hi, Mrs. Wembley.

MRS. WEMBLEY: Why, hello there, children.

MARTHA: (*Gets up and goes to the stove.*) One hundred? That's fine, Johnny. Now if you can only work on your arithmetic a little harder.

DICKIE: (*Looking as* MARTHA *uncovers a pot.*) What we havin'? Stew?

MARTHA: No, vegetable soup.

DICKIE: Aw . . .

JOHNNY: We havin' dessert, Ma?

MARTHA: Yes, I think there's some Jello left over from last night. Dickie, get the soup bowls and some spoons.

MRS. WEMBLEY: (*Rising.*) Here you are. Sit here, children.

MARTHA: Oh, now, you don't have to get up.

MRS. WEMBLEY: That's all right, I've been up here too long already.

JOHNNY: (*As* DICKIE *places bowls on table.*) Hey! Why can't I have the blue one?

DICKIE: 'Cause I got it, so shut up.

JOHNNY: But I always eat outta the blue one!

DICKIE: Not today you don't.

MRS. WEMBLEY: Don't argue, children, one's as good as the other.

JOHNNY: But Dickie's got mine! Hey, Ma!

MARTHA: Give him the blue one, Dickie, and stop all the fuss.

DICKIE: Aw, Ma . . . !

MARTHA: Dick-ie . . .

JOHNNY: (*As* DICKIE *reluctantly gives up the bowl.*) There, I told you!

(DICKIE *raises his spoon, ready to bop* JOHNNY *on the head, but stops as* MARTHA *brings the pot of soup to the table.*)

MRS. WEMBLEY: Well, I'm going on down, Martha.

MARTHA: All right, now. See you later on. (*To the kids.*) Watch out! This is hot.

(MRS. WEMBLEY *exits rear.*)

JOHNNY: (*Tasting the soup.*) Ow! It's hot!

MARTHA: I told you that. Wait till I finish giving it to you, Dickie!

(*The front door opens again and* DOC *enters.*)

JOHNNY: Gimme a cracker.

DICKIE: Stop grabbin'!

MARTHA: (*Pouring milk.*) Look out, now, you'll make me spill this milk! (*Looks up as* DOC *comes into the kitchen.*) Hi, Doc.

JOHNNY: Hi, Daddy! I got one hundred in spelling.

DOC: Oh, you did, did you?

MARTHA: Ready for your lunch?

DOC: Not now, a little later.

(*The phone rings.*)

MARTHA: Get that, will you, Doc? My hands are full.

DICKIE: (*Jumping up.*) I'll answer it!

MARTHA: You sit right back down and finish your lunch.

DOC: (*Goes to the phone, gets it.*) Hello? . . . Uh, just a minute and I'll see. (*Puts down the phone and returns to the kitchen.*) Angela in?

MARTHA: No, she said she was going to the library. Who is it?

Doc: Sounds like that lawyer guy. You go and talk to him.

MARTHA: Oh, all right. (*Wipes her hands and goes to the phone.*) Hello? . . . Oh, hello, Roger, this is Martha . . . Yes . . . No, she's not in right now, I think she went to the library . . . Didn't she call you last night? I gave her your message . . . Oh? . . . Well, I don't know, Roger, I was sure she was going to call you . . . Not until this evening, I don't think.

(*Footsteps are heard coming up the stairs.* Doc, *hearing them, comes into the front room. The door opens and* ANGELA *enters with* KENNY *behind her.*)

ANGELA: (*To* Doc.) Hi.

KENNY: How are you, Mr. Hill?

Doc: Oh, hello. Uh, Angela? (*Indicates the phone.*)

MARTHA: Oh! Well, now, just a minute—hold the phone, will you? (*Covers the mouthpiece with her hand.*) Angela! It's for you. Shall I say you're home?

ANGELA: Who is it?

MARTHA: (*With a glance at* KENNY.) Well, you know. Oh, hello, Kenny.

KENNY: How are you, Mrs. Hill?

ANGELA: (*Shakes her head.*) Tell him I'm not in and you'll tell me to call him later.

MARTHA: But that's what I told him last night. Now, Angela—

ANGELA: Oh, all right! (*Comes to the phone.*) Hello? . . . Oh, hi, Roger, how are you? (*Indicates for* KENNY *to have a seat.* Doc *goes into the bedroom and sits near the window, scanning a paper.* MARTHA *still stands nearby in the living room.*) Well, I just this minute walked in the door . . . What? . . . Oh, yes, but it was so late when I got back and I was dog tired . . . I know, Roger, but . . . (*Looks at* MARTHA *with hostile eyes.* MARTHA *retreats to the kitchen.*) Well, I'm sorry, but I've been very busy . . . I can't help that, you know I'm trying to graduate in a few weeks now . . . Look, Roger, we can talk about that later, I've got to go now . . . Oh, you can call me tonight if you want, around dinnertime. Or I'll call you later, now I really must go . . . What? . . . No, Roger, I expect to be very busy on my thesis all weekend . . . Well, you call me and we'll talk about that later, all right? Good-bye! (*Hangs up. To* KENNY.) My goodness! Can't he understand a simple word like no?

KENNY: (*Smiles.*) Another one of your boyfriends?

ANGELA: That was the same one. He never gives up!

KENNY: (*Takes her hand.*) I don't blame him. I wouldn't, either.

(*They gaze at each other for a moment. Then* ANGELA *turns away.*)

ANGELA: I'll go look for that notebook, Kenny. And you'd better hurry if you're going to make your board job! It's nearly twelve-thirty. (*Goes to her room.*)

(*In the kitchen, the boys have finished their lunch and now* DICKIE *comes into the living room.*)

DICKIE: Hi.

KENNY: Hello there, Dickie. How's the boy?

DICKIE: Fine. Say, when you gonna help me work on that model airplane? I can't do nothin' with it, you'll have to show me.

KENNY: Okay, I'll give you a hand. Maybe I can get by Saturday for awhile.

JOHNNY: (*Joining them.*) Hi, Kenny.

KENNY: Hey, there!

JOHNNY: When you gonna bring me another book?

KENNY: Oh? Did you like the one I gave you?

JOHNNY: Sure did. That was some story. It sounded so real.

KENNY: That story *is* real. Frederick Douglass was a real man. He actually lived.

DICKIE: (*To* JOHNNY.) See, I told you.

JOHNNY: Kenny, what you doin' here in the daytime? I thought you only came by at night to see Angela.

KENNY: Well, aren't you the observant young man.

DICKIE: Say, are you gonna marry Angela?

(*In the kitchen,* MARTHA, *who has been cleaning up, stops short and raises her head. So does* DOC *in the bedroom.*)

KENNY: Well! Whatever put a question like that in your head, Dickie?

DICKIE: Oh, I don't know. Curiosity.

KENNY: (*Rumpling his hair.*) Curiosity killed the cat!

(*MARTHA and* DOC *slowly subside and resume their previous activities.*)

DICKIE: Well, are you? Are you and Angela in "luv"? (*He mugs.* JOHNNY *laughs and* DICKIE *joins him.*)

MARTHA: (*Coming quickly from the kitchen.*) Now, you kids go on outside and stop pestering Kenny, hear? Go on. Both of you.

JOHNNY: Aw, we wasn't pesterin' you, was we, Kenny?

MARTHA: Go on, now! It'll soon be time for you to go back to school anyway, so scat!

DICKIE: Come on, Johnny. (*Mugs again.*) I think I'm fallin' in "luv"!

(*He and* JOHNNY *collapse with giggling as* MARTHA *shoos them out the door and closes it.*)

MARTHA: (*To* KENNY.) Sometimes they can really get on your nerves, the way they're always asking questions, questions.

KENNY: Oh, they don't bother me at all, Mrs. Hill. I like kids.

MARTHA: Well, that's nice . . . (*Looks cautiously all around, to be sure* DOC *and* ANGELA *are not listening. Then she clears her throat.*) Uh, Kenny, there's something I've been wanting to ask you.

KENNY: Yes?

MARTHA: Well, I don't know just how to put it. But . . . well, just what plans do you have for the future? I mean, after you graduate.

KENNY: Well, what kind of plans do you mean, Mrs. Hill?

MARTHA: Well, are you going back to Ohio? That's where you're from, isn't it?

KENNY: Yes, ma'am, it is. Columbus.

MARTHA: I see. And are you thinking about getting married and settling down there, or just what did you have in mind?

KENNY: (*Grins.*) Oh. In other words, you're asking my intentions, is that it? Toward your sister.

MARTHA: (*Turns her head to glance to* ANGELA's *door.*) I guess, something like that, yes . . .

KENNY: (*Still grinning.*) You're kinda like the kids and their curiosity, aren't you, ma'am? Well, you see, since you're asking, I—

(ANGELA *comes out of her room with an old notebook.*)

ANGELA: Here it is. I had to go through practically the whole closet. I hope you can read my scribbling.

KENNY: (*Rising.*) That's swell. Boy, is this going to save me a whole lot of trouble.

ANGELA: Now you'd better get out of here. You're going to be late.

KENNY: Okay, see you tonight. (*Turns to* MARTHA.) Oh, I'm sorry we didn't get a chance to discuss that more thoroughly, Mrs. Hill. Maybe again sometime.

MARTHA: (*With a weak smile.*) Yes . . .

KENNY: (*Chucks* ANGELA *under the chin.*) See you, Beautiful.

(*He exits.* ANGELA *closes the door and turns to face* MARTHA.)

ANGELA: And what was that all about?

MARTHA: Huh?

ANGELA: What did Kenny mean?

MARTHA: Mean? About what?

ANGELA: Oh, come on now, Martha. What have you been up to?

MARTHA: Why, nothing at all. What in the world are you talking about?

ANGELA: Look, Martha, I don't know what this is all about, but just for the record, let me tell you now. Don't put your nose in my business!

MARTHA: Well, who's putting their nose in any business of yours, tell me that?

ANGELA: Just in case!

MARTHA: Honestly, Angela, I don't see why you have to go around with a chip on your shoulder all the time. You're too—too aggressive, that's what you are. You go around alienating people all the time. One of these days you'll be needing friends and you may not have them, the way you go around acting!

ANGELA: Okay, I didn't mean to alienate you, Martha. I just want to make it clear, perfectly clear—

MARTHA: All right, all right, you said that once! (*Turns and goes into the kitchen.* ANGELA *follows.*)

ANGELA: Listen, Martha . . .

MARTHA: (*Busies herself with the dishes.*) I don't want to hear any more, do you hear? Any more at all!

ANGELA: Okay, if that's the way you want it! (*Folds her arms and looks away.* MARTHA *goes on with her work.* ANGELA *slowly turns her head to look at* MARTHA. *Finally she relaxes.*) Martha?

MARTHA: What?

ANGELA: Martha, what would you say if I were to tell you I was thinking about getting married?

MARTHA: (*Stops, turns slowly.*) Well, I'd say that depended upon who to.

ANGELA: You're a bright girl. You can add two and two.

MARTHA: Oh . . . But what about Roger?

ANGELA: What about him?

MARTHA: Well, I—I thought that you and he were . . . were practically engaged. You said yourself that he wanted to marry you and you told him to wait until you finished school. Well, you'll be getting your degree in a few weeks now. So what about Roger?

ANGELA: Hasn't it been perfectly obvious to you for some time now, Martha, that I've lost all interest in Roger Sampson? You were the one who was so impressed with him in the first place, as I recall. Well, you can have him if you like. I bestow dear Roger upon you! He's yours to do with as—

MARTHA: Has Kenny proposed to you, Angela?

ANGELA: (*A slight pause.*) Well . . . not that it's any business of yours. But no, he hasn't. Yet. But I've made up my mind, that's the important thing. I wouldn't be surprised if Kenny made up his any day now.

MARTHA: (*Quietly.*) Listen . . . Angela, honey. I don't want to sound like I'm preaching to you or interfering in your life or anything like that. But, baby, believe me, you don't know what you're doing.

ANGELA: (*Turns angrily.*) Now, Martha, I—

MARTHA: No, wait, please let me finish! Angela . . . Angela, Kenny is a very nice boy. A very charming and admirable young man. I like him, really I do. I liked him the first time you had him over to the house. He's kind and considerate, and he has nice manners, and he brings things for the kids. I'm sure you like him very much—even love him, I don't know, you can answer that better than I can. But, Angela, Kenny is not ready to settle down. He's not the marrying kind. No, now wait—I'm not through! I don't mean that he's frivolous or dallying with your affections or means any harm—I'm sure he has the highest respect for you, Angela. But Kenny is a young boy who's got his head 'way up in the clouds, with a whole lot of talk about "being proud" and helping "our people" and fighting for "self-determination" and all such as that. Oh, I'm not against that—in principle— don't get me wrong. And, to give credit where credit's due, he's the kind who'll probably go out and do some of these things, too. He has that kind of . . . of light in his eyes when he talks, as if he sees things out there that nobody else can see. But while he's out crusading, trying to change the world, where does that leave you? Who's going to pay the bills and make a home and raise a family while he's out God-knows-where—maybe getting into trouble, maybe getting hurt, maybe getting thrown in jail, for all you now? Let's face it: The Man out there's not just going to fold up and crumble because somebody announces that Kenny Powers is on the scene! And don't think you can change him—you try that and he'll resent you for the rest of his life for keeping him from doing what he really wanted to do. Angela . . . I know it won't be easy for you, but forget him. He's not right for you. Right after graduation, he'll be gone. But Roger will still be here. Angela? Please. Don't be angry with me for saying what's in my heart. I know it hurts, baby, but I just don't want to see you make a mistake!

ANGELA: (*Pause, then quietly.*) No. I mustn't make a mistake. I must keep my head clear, and be practical, and just forget all about the bright young man who's selfishly out to change the world. "Don't waste your time chasing after him. See? Here's Sure-Thing Roger Sampson instead!" No, Martha, you mustn't let me make a mistake. (*Turns away with a frown.*) I have a headache. (*Crosses quickly to her room and closes the door.*)

(MARTHA *looks after her with deep concern.*)

(*The lights fade.*)

Scene Two

It is night. MARTHA *and* DOC *are seen dimly, asleep in the bedroom. The lights are out in the living room and it is empty. But in the kitchen, bright shafts of moonlight illuminate* ANGELA *and* KENNY, *seated in passionate embrace.* ANGELA *has on her dressing gown, which is unbuttoned, and wears only bra and panties underneath.*

The radio atop the refrigerator is on, and a piano concerto plays softly in the background. After a time they stir, and their lips part.

ANGELA: (*Softly.*) I love you. Oh, how I love you.
KENNY: Shh . . . Don't talk. Let's just sit here quietly.

(ANGELA *lays her head against his cheek. He stares out into the darkness.*)

ANGELA: (*Presently.*) I don't ever want to forget these nights. If time could only suspend itself in space and keep us here, in each other's arms, like this. Oh, Kenny! (*Ecstatically, her arms entwine him and she runs her fingers through his hair. He buries his face in her hair.*) I do love you.
KENNY: Shh . . .
ANGELA: I love you, I love you, I love you!
KENNY: But you shouldn't.
ANGELA: But I do, I do.
KENNY: I know you do. And I know that I love you. And I know that we should not love each other as we do.
ANGELA: Who's to say we should or should not? Our love is a fact. It lives, it breathes, it exists! Who is to deny that it exists? And if it exists, then what do we care about anything else in the world . . . except that we love each other?
KENNY: (*Gently but firmly removing one of her arms from about his neck.*) Angela . . . We've been all through this before.
ANGELA: I know. And we'll go through it all again and again and again until you say that you love me.

KENNY: I've already said that.

ANGELA: Then nothing else matters! Nothing else.

KENNY: Except . . . except that this night will not last forever. Already it is slipping away, and this moonlight will give way to the harsh light of another day.

ANGELA: But there will be other nights, my darling. Other nights, each more glorious than before.

KENNY: (*Looks at her.*) Will there, Angela?

ANGELA: (*Huddles close to him.*) Oh, please! Please don't talk that way.

KENNY: But I must.

ANGELA: No!

KENNY: Yes.

ANGELA: Then why! Tell me why you've made up your mind against me.

KENNY: I haven't made my mind against you.

ANGELA: But you have! I've begged you and begged you to consider me in your future. I've told you I want to follow you for the rest of my life.

KENNY: But I can't allow you to do that, Angela.

ANGELA: Then make me understand it! Tell me why. Oh, God! (*Buries her face in his shoulder.*)

KENNY: Angela . . . Angela, baby, the last thing I want in the world is to hurt you.

ANGELA: If I hear that just once more from a single solitary soul I'll scream.

KENNY: But you're making it so that you can't help but be hurt.

ANGELA: Aaaahh! (*It is a muffled, restrained scream, but* KENNY *starts. He freezes tensely. In the bedroom,* DOC *stirs, wakes, and sits up, listening. In the meantime, the piano concerto on the radio has ended and the announcer's voice breaks the stillness with a station identification and sign-off credits. The strains of the national anthem come crashing loudly over the air, and* KENNY *reaches up to turn it off.* DOC *continues listening for a moment, then lies down, turns over, and is silent. After a long moment,* KENNY *reaches out and turns* ANGELA'S *face around so that he can see her. She is weeping softly.*)

KENNY: Angela? Oh, Angela! (*Covers her face with little kisses. He kisses her neck and throat, and then begins to slide her gown from her shoulder.*)

ANGELA: (*Suddenly.*) No! No, Kenny. Not tonight. Please!

KENNY: (*After a pause.*) All right.

ANGELA: You'd better go now. The radio's gone off. It must be after two.

KENNY: All right. If you want. (*Leans forward to kiss her cheek, but she turns her head away.*) What's the matter?

ANGELA: Nothing. Nothing at all. I'm all right now.

KENNY: You're sure?

ANGELA: Yes. I'm sure. (*Disengages his arms and stands, pushing back her hair.*)

KENNY: (*Rising.*) I . . . I wish I could say something more to you, Angela. But the project begins very soon, now. And once I leave, it will be utterly impossible for you to come to me.

ANGELA: But I've told you, you won't have to worry about me! I can get a job, I can take care of myself. And when you're free, you can come to me.

KENNY: That would be great, Angela, but—

ANGELA: And who says we have to get married right away? I don't mind waiting. If you'd only let me, Kenny?

KENNY: I can't.

ANGELA: But if we love each other—

KENNY: We cannot base such a decision upon love alone! You've got to understand that what I and the other volunteers are about to do is something dangerous. We could be killed, any of us! It happens all the time down there—on a dark highway in the middle of the night, or even on the courthouse steps in full view of the noonday sun.

ANGELA: Then why risk it? Why go?

KENNY: Because it's got to be done. Our people have got to be liberated from fear. They've got to learn how to band together, to learn their true strength, how with a little help they can take hold and change things. How—

ANGELA: Then let me come with you, Kenny. I want to help, too!

KENNY: You don't understand. This is like working behind enemy lines in wartime. It's no place for a girl like you.

ANGELA: What if I come anyway? What if I follow you?

KENNY: You can't do that.

ANGELA: Why not? If I want to?

KENNY: Because you won't know where I am. I'll be on the move like the others—first here, then there. Free spirits ready to soar to wherever we're needed most.

ANGELA: What? You mean I won't even hear from you?

KENNY: I wouldn't count on it. Secrecy is part of our discipline.

ANGELA: But I can keep secrets, too. Let me come. I want to be with you!

KENNY: Will you listen to what I'm trying to tell you?

ANGELA: Oh, I've heard enough. Enough! I'm sick and tired of hearing you say it. All right! So we won't have a future together. You're going away on some—some foolhardy crusading scheme, and I'll never even hear from you again. Go ahead! Go now! And don't come back. Good-bye!

KENNY: (*Pause.*) Well, don't put it that way, I—

ANGELA: You heard me. I want you to go now.

KENNY: Angela . . .

ANGELA: And not to come back. Tomorrow, or the next day, or ever!

KENNY: Are you certain? You're sure you mean that?

(ANGELA *suddenly strides across into the living room and on to the door. She jerks it open, then stands silently as* KENNY *comes to the portal.*)

KENNY: Angela . . .

(*She stands adamant. After a long pause, he starts for the door. Before he can reach it,* ANGELA *shuts it quickly and clings to him, her shoulders shaking silently. Gently but firmly, he takes her arms from around his neck and holds her away. He opens the door, takes a final look at her standing there breathlessly, then leaves, closing the door softly behind him.*

In the front bedroom, DOC *has again awakened. He sits up in bed and listens.*

ANGELA *stands where she is for a long moment. Then she takes a deep breath and goes into her room, closing her door.*

DOC *listens. Finally he reaches for a cigarette on the night table beside him. He strikes a match and lights up. Then he lies back upon his pillow, blowing the smoke in a long stream up into the air.*)

(*The lights fade.*)

Scene Three

A few days later. It is late afternoon and the yellow sun pours in through the front windows. As the scene progresses, the light gradually deepens, until toward the end it is nearly red. At rise, the stage is empty, but from ANGELA's *room comes the sound of typing. After a moment the typing ceases and* ANGELA *appears. She removes a pair of glasses and passes her hand over her eyes wearily. Then she goes into the bathroom, opens the medicine cabinet, and takes out a box of aspirins. She takes two, gulps them down with water.*

Meantime, footsteps sound on the stairs, and DOC *enters from work. He closes the door, goes to his room and takes off his hat.*

ANGELA: (*Looking out.*) Is that you, Doc?

DOC: (*Glances back.*) Yeah.

ANGELA: Oh, hi.

DOC: Hi. (ANGELA *comes down into the living room slowly.*) What you doin' in on a nice Sunday afternoon like this? Thought you'd be out gettin' some air.

ANGELA: No, I have a report to get in tomorrow at school. It's the last one, thank God, after this I'm all through.

DOC: (*Rolling up his sleeves.*) I see. Well, that's pretty good. (*Pause.*) Martha go to the movies?

ANGELA: No, I think she went over to Gracie's with the kids. She left your dinner on the stove.

DOC: Good. Thanks. (*Enters the living room and starts for the kitchen.*)

ANGELA: Doc?

DOC: (*Stops, turns.*) Yeah?

ANGELA: Doc, I wanted to see you a minute.

DOC: Oh? What about?

ANGELA: Well, it's . . . it's about a rather private matter, and I wanted to talk to you about it. When you have a little free time.

DOC: No time like the present. (*Seats himself on the arm of a chair.*) What is it?

332

ANGELA: Well . . . I really hate to have to bother you with something like this, but . . . Doc, I need some money.

DOC: Yeah? How much?

ANGELA: Quite a lot, I'm afraid.

DOC: Oh? Well, about how much?

ANGELA: You see, some things came up at school at the last minute, and I have to take care of them right away. And then, there's quite a bit more expense than I'd thought connected with commencement. And . . . and there are some private things I want to take care of, too. So, that's why.

DOC: I see. How much?

ANGELA: I really didn't want to have to come to you about it, Doc. You and Martha have helped out so much already, and I thought I was going to be able to get through without it, but . . . But, as I say, these things came up at practically the last minute, and I—I just find myself in somewhat of a hole. You understand.

DOC: Sure. Yeah, I understand. Now, uh—how much? How much did you have in mind.

ANGELA: Well . . .

DOC: Go ahead, how much? Just say it right out.

ANGELA: Doc, I need three hundred dollars.

DOC: (*Gives a low whistle.*)

ANGELA: (*Hastily.*) I told you . . . it was quite a lot.

DOC: You can say that again. Boy, I knew it cost a lot of money to graduate these days. But three hundred dollars— for that they must be gonna name a hall after you!

ANGELA: No, Doc. It really isn't so much, considering. You see—

DOC: Now, wait a minute, let's just try and figure this thing out. Now, how much is tuition this quarter?

ANGELA: It's . . . it's a hundred and eighty dollars. But, Doc—

DOC: A hundred and eighty dollars, I see. But I thought you paid that already. Didn't your mother send you some money, and I thought Gracie and Ed were helpin' you out some?

ANGELA: They did, Doc, but this is something else!

DOC: Oh, this is something else. Well, let's get it down now, shall we? Okay, your tuition is paid for. What else do you have to take care of?

ANGELA: Well, there's a graduation fee of twenty-five dollars.

DOC: Twenty-five dollars. Okay, what's next?

ANGELA: Well . . .

DOC: Go ahead. I'm keepin' track.

ANGELA: But, you see, Doc, it's . . . It's just that—

DOC: Well, go ahead and we'll see if we can figure it out. So far you said you had to pay twenty-five dollars. So what's next?

ANGELA: Well, there's fifteen dollars rental for my cap and gown.

DOC: Fifteen bucks just to rent one of them black nightshirts? That's highway robbery! If I was you I'd boycott them exercises. They'd give you your diploma without it, wouldn't they?

ANGELA: Doc, that's not the point!

DOC: Okay, I can guess what you mean. After puttin' in all this hard work, you wouldn't wanna let a thing like fifteen dollars stop you from marchin' in the parade. Okay. Twenty-five bucks graduation fee, fifteen cap and gown. That's forty bucks so far. Go on.

ANGELA: Oh, Doc, this is all so silly.

DOC: The hell it is! Three hundred bucks don't grow on trees, baby, and I want to know what it's going for.

ANGELA: But I don't want you to give me the money, Doc. I only want to make a loan. After I get out and get a job I'll pay it back, every cent of it, in installments.

DOC: Tell me. Have you ever heard of a place by the name of the First National Bank?

ANGELA: I know, Doc. If I could have gotten it from the bank I'd never have bothered you in the first place, I assure you.

DOC: Now wait a minute here. Do you mean to imply that it is personally distasteful to you, perhaps, to come to me to borrow money and that you do so only as a last resort? Is that what you mean to imply?

ANGELA: Of course not, Doc! Oh, you're making a mountain out of a molehill.

DOC: Molehill, she calls it. Huh! Three hundred bucks is a molehill.

ANGELA: No, it's not!

DOC: Well, what are you talkin' about then?

ANGELA: I just want to—

DOC: (*Interrupts.*) —borrow three hundred bucks, three hundred hard-earned smackers, just about two weeks' pay from all three of my buildings, right?

ANGELA: Oh, if I'd ever known it was going to be like this, I—

DOC: You'd what? Say, by the way, why are you askin' me about this? You're the one who never has anything to say to me, remember? It seems to me it'd be a lot easier under the circumstances to talk to Martha about it and get her to come to me, don't it?

ANGELA: (*Patiently.*) Because, as I told you before, this is a private matter and it doesn't have to concern anybody but you and me. I told you I'd pay it back just as soon as I can get a job, and I'll give that to you in writing if that's what you want.

DOC: Unh-hunh. I see. Well, what's the difference if you pay it back directly or through Martha? I don't get this.

ANGELA: (*Trying again.*) Doc . . . Doc, haven't you ever had certain things that you wanted to keep to yourself? That you didn't want anybody else to know anything at all about if you could possibly help it? Just private business you didn't particularly care to discuss with anyone at all? Haven't you?

DOC: Uh-huh. Go on.

ANGELA: Well, that's the way it is about this. No, I don't need it for school expenses, if that's what you want to know. But I've never been frivolous with money, you know that. I've managed carefully, as carefully as I possibly could, to stretch every cent in order to continue with my studies. I am aware that three hundred dollars is a lot of money, and I wouldn't come to you and ask you to loan it to me if it weren't absolutely necessary.

DOC: I see. I see. And you want to keep Martha out of this, I take it.

ANGELA: Yes, I do.

DOC: Uh-huh. And you say it's not for school expenses after all.

ANGELA: No—but, please believe me, it's very important.

DOC: Okay, okay. I believe you. You don't have to convince me of that any further. It's important—it must be or you'd never take the trouble of comin' to me.

ANGELA: I didn't mean it that way, Doc, I—

DOC: Okay, so forget that point. The fact is, you did come to me, and I'm your brother-in-law, in the family and all, and it's up to me to help you out. If I can.

ANGELA: What do you mean by that? You mean you can't do it?

DOC: Well, now, let's not get ahead of ourselves, I didn't say that either. Please. Don't put words in my mouth. I got enough of my own.

ANGELA: Well, I'm sorry . . .

DOC: Okay. So let's see where we are now. The question is: have I got three hundred dollars that I can spare until you get a chance to pay it back? That's the question. Now. Let me think . . . (*His lips move in silent computations aided by his fingers and hands. Finally.*) Well, I guess I could, at that. In a pinch. At great sacrifice, mind you.

ANGELA: You mean, it's all right?

DOC: Well, I was just figurin' that loanin' you three hundred dollars would mean I'd have to spread that amount over a period of ten weeks at thirty dollars a week, or twenty weeks at fifteen, or thirty at ten.

ANGELA: (*Alarmed.*) But, Doc! Don't you understand—I need the money all at once?

DOC: I understand that all right, take it easy. I was just figurin' out for my own benefit how I'd have to think about it so's it wouldn't bother me about handin' out a whole hunk of dough like that at one time. Okay. So, I think I can afford it. Based, of course, upon the fact that you are going to get to work on paying it back, say, by the middle of the summer?

ANGELA: Yes, yes, even if I have to go to a factory or somewhere.

DOC: You're kidding, of course. People with college degrees don't work in no factories. Especially people with the degree of master of arts!

ANGELA: All right, Doc, you don't have to rub it in.

DOC: Oh, I'm sorry. I'm sorry if I was taking unfair advantage and I apologize. Now. Okay, you want me to lend you three hundred dollars and I figured out that financially I could do it, right?

ANGELA: Oh, Doc, you don't know how much this means to me.

DOC: Don't—don't let's get into that yet, Angela. So far I only said I was *able* to let you have the loan, right?

ANGELA: Now, what do you mean?

DOC: Well, in most business transactions of this kind, there is usually a small amount of return involved in addition to repayment of the principal. Is that the right terminology? I never did study economics or anything like that when I was in school.

ANGELA: (*Wearily.*) All right, Doc, I don't mind in the least paying you a fair amount of interest. How much do you think would be fair?

DOC: Well, now, we're getting ahead of ourselves again, Angela. Let's take this thing step by step, one thing at a time.

ANGELA: But didn't you just say—

DOC: If you'd listen a minute you'd hear what I say!

ANGELA: Okay, I'm sorry. I apologize for the interruption.

DOC: That's not necessary. I can understand, with your combination of youth and brains and beauty you may not always consider that the rest of us are not necessarily quite so . . . so alert as you are. As mentally or intellectually quick on the trigger! It sometimes takes us quite awhile to get something straight, so just have patience with we uneducated ones, will you?

ANGELA: Doc . . . please! Oh, I've got that headache again! (*Passes her hands over her eyes.*)

DOC: Probably been studyin' too hard. You know, they tell me it ain't so good for a young girl to try and use her head too much of the time, on account of they ain't—pardon me, "aren't"—built for the stresses and strains of too much psychological pressures and things like that. Think I read it in a book once, in my younger days, when I did quite a bit of readin' and such.

ANGELA: All right, Doc, I'll be okay. So can we get on with it?

DOC: Anything to accommodate. Where were we before—

ANGELA: You were saying you thought I should pay you interest and I said okay, how much?

DOC: I see. Well, that's a difficult question to decide, right on the spur of the moment, right like that. I don't know just what would be a fair arrangement at all, just exactly. Unless, of course, you have any suggestions.

ANGELA: None at all. Set any reasonable figure you like and I'll pay it.

DOC: All right. Then what would you say would be within the realm of a "reasonable figure"?

ANGELA: I just said, that's up to you to decide.

DOC: Well, I know that, but I thought it might be a good thing to have the benefit of your advice upon the subject. So what do you think is a good figure?

ANGELA: Oh, I don't know. The usual kind of thing with the banks is about five percent or so, isn't it?

DOC: Five percent? Now, there's a figure for you. Let me see, five percent . . . (*Again he is off on calculations.*)

ANGELA: (*Interrupting.*) Five percent would be fifteen dollars.

DOC: Fifteen? Oh, yes. Fifteen. Well, that's not a bad figure, do you think?

ANGELA: Whatever you decide. I'll pay you thirty if you want.

DOC: Oh, no—no, now. There's no point in getting too commercial about this. After all, it's all in the family, isn't it? Just a token payment is all that's necessary, just a gesture of good faith, that's all. As a matter of fact— Hmmm . . . (*He thinks.*) As a matter of fact, Angela, I think we can wrap this whole thing up very quickly and easily. Yes, I think we could. Very.

ANGELA: Then let's do, please. My head is just splitting!

DOC: Oh, that's a shame. Maybe it's the wrong time of the month or something, eh?

ANGELA: What? Doc, whatever makes you say a thing like that!

DOC: Well, I'm interested, that's all. Is it?

ANGELA: Is it what?

DOC: The wrong time of the month?

ANGELA: That's none of your business, Dockery Hill, and I'll thank you not to ask that again!

DOC: (*Spreading his hands.*) Well, what can I say? I was just about to go into how we could wind this whole thing up, and when I ask you a . . . a pertinent question, you don't wanna talk about it. So, what can I say?

ANGELA: Pertinent question? You mean . . . Doc! You're not suggesting . . . (*Sinks onto the sofa, revolted.*) Oh, God . . . !

DOC: Now, as I say, let's not get ahead of ourselves for a single minute. Step by step, that's the way to discuss things, step by step. Why, I remember one time I was havin' a discussion with a fellow—

ANGELA: (*Sick.*) Doc . . . Doc, you couldn't be so low.

DOC: Just a minute, just a minute! Let's not start calling any names here! Because it can be a matter of opinion, a matter of some discussion as to just who is low! Now, so far I have managed to keep my temper in this whole thing. But I am not so sure that will be possible if you want to start calling names! It just so happens I know a few of my own. And it will not take much more for me to unload them and display them before you! So let's not get into descriptions of personalities, please!

(ANGELA, *head in her hands, moans.*)

DOC: Oh, so now you can only sit with your head in your hands and make sounds. Well, for your information, this is not the first time I have heard you make sounds. No, not the first or the second or the fifth or the fifteenth!

ANGELA: (*Weakly.*) Doc, please . . .

DOC: Oh, no! You started this by bringing in personalities, so now just let me throw in a few for good measure, huh? Will you allow me to do that?

ANGELA: I'm sorry if I called you any names.

DOC: Oh, so now you are sorry! Hah! For several years now you have been walking around this apartment. Walking around with your nose stuck in the air and your ass on your shoulder.

ANGELA: Doc!

DOC: No, let me finish! Ever since you came here, you have walked by me like I was dirt. Cheap dumb niggah, that's what you thought about me, wasn't it?

ANGELA: No, I didn't, I—

DOC: Wasn't it!

ANGELA: Doc, please!

DOC: All you ever had to say to me was "Hi, Doc" and "Goodbye, Doc" and "Yes, Doc" and "No, Doc." You looked down your turned-up nose at me, and you despised your sister for living with a "low-class" nigger like me. Didn't you!

(ANGELA *moans.*)

DOC: And now you sit there and make sounds, long moaning sounds. Well, I am not impressed! I have heard such sounds before, under somewhat different circumstances. You see, as it happens, I am a very light sleeper—

ANGELA: For God's sake, Doc, stop it! (*Begins to sob.*)

DOC: A very light sleeper! And though I do not have cat eyes, eyes that see in the dark, I have a very good imagination for putting two and two together. Night after night, low moaning sounds, sharp quick sounds, long sighing sounds. Sounds in the night, all coming from the general vicinity of the kitchen! (ANGELA *sobs.*) And now, after all those lovely sounds, all those spicy, wonderful sounds, you come and ask me for three hundred dollars and think I don't know what you need it for! And then you have the nerve, the cotton-pickin' gall to start and call me names. Me! Why, if it hadn't a been for the fact that I don't want to talk about such things in front of my wife and kids, I'd a' thrown you out of this apartment weeks ago! And you start callin' me low—

ANGELA: (*Rises, sobbing wildly.*) Doc . . . Doc, stop it! I won't listen to you! I won't listen!

DOC: Oh, yes you will, you'll listen to every goddamn word, and you'll like it, too! Hah! So you're gonna graduate from the university, gonna be a "master of arts." And if I don't loan you three hundred bucks, when you walk down the aisle to get that diploma, underneath all that fancy cap and gown your fuckin' stomach's liable to be stickin' out! (ANGELA *turns and runs sobbing into her room, slamming the door. Her sobs are still heard as* DOC *moves to the door and stands in front of it, shouting.*) Well, all right! I'll show you what kind of a guy I am. I'm gonna give you a break. I'm gonna let you have your three hundred bucks. But I want my interest in advance! So open that door. Open that goddamn door! (*Raises his arms as if he were going to smash in the door, but then thinks better of it. He backs away and folds his arms.*) Shee-it! I'm not gonna break the motherfucker down, I don't have to! Because you're gonna open it yourself. Yes, you are! You're gonna open that door and I'm gonna come in, and when I come out again you can mark the interest—aw, what the fuck, the whole thing!—paid in full. That's fair enough, ain't it? Now, open that door . . . Open it, I say! . . . *Open that goddamn door*!

(*There is silence for a moment.* DOC *stands tensed, waiting. Then, after a long pause, the door slowly opens.*)

(*Curtain.*)

ACT THREE
Scene One

Music. The clock tower. It chimes the half hour, fades.

A few evenings later. There are cries of children at play from out in the back. The apartment is empty at rise, but a moment later the front door opens and ANGELA *enters, a little hurriedly. She closes the door and looks cautiously about to see if anyone is there, then leans back against the door, breathing deeply. Suddenly she grimaces, draws in her breath sharply and bends over in pain. She comes to the sofa and sits, eyes closed, hands tightly clenching as waves of pain come and go, finally subsiding. She leans her head back and wipes her brow.*

MARTHA *enters from off right, climbing the porch stairs with a basket of dry clothes and humming a little to herself. She enters the back door and continues through the kitchen toward the living room.* ANGELA *looks up, startled, and tries to get up, but* MARTHA *is upon her before she can rise.*

MARTHA: (*Stops as she sees* ANGELA.) Well, what's the matter with you?

ANGELA: (*Sits back, trying to appear casual.*) Oh! I—I must have been dozing. And you startled me, that's all.

MARTHA: (*Continues into the front bedroom.*) Well, you couldn't have been there long—I just now ran down to get the rest of the clothes off the line. Did you get your dinner? It's in the oven. (*There is an ironing board set up in the front bedroom.* MARTHA *places the basket of laundry on the bed, and proceeds to sprinkle the pieces preparatory to ironing them.*)

ANGELA: Oh . . . Thanks, but I'm not hungry.

MARTHA: You'd better stop this stuff about not eating, girl, you're going to make yourself sick. Are you supposed to be on a diet or something? You certainly don't need to *lose* any weight—why just yesterday Gracie was commenting how much better you looked lately, that you must have gained a few pounds. (*No answer.* ANGELA *has closed her eyes and clenched her fists again.*) Angela?

ANGELA: Oh—! I heard you, Martha.

341

MARTHA: Why don't you turn on a light in there, it's getting dark.

ANGELA: No, it's all right. I'm . . . just going to sit here a minute. How—how was Gracie when you saw her?

MARTHA: She's okay. Been having a little trouble with her sinus. Bought a cute little hat to go with her blue taffeta, she'll probably wear it to the commencement Thursday. Oh, she wanted to know how we're going over. Ed's working and he'll have the car or she'd drive us herself. (*Pause. She clears her throat.*) I told her I didn't know, but I thought maybe Roger Sampson might be up and drive us over in his new car . . .

ANGELA: (*Looks up.*) Who?

MARTHA: Why, Roger, of course. Haven't you invitied him for the exercises?

ANGELA: No, I haven't.

MARTHA: Well, I don't see why not. I'm sure he'd be just glad to come. Why don't you see if you can get him on the phone right now and ask him?

ANGELA: Martha, are we going to have to go through all that again?

MARTHA: Now, really, Angela, I just don't understand you. I don't understand you at all!

ANGELA: You're in good company. So don't let it worry you.

MARTHA: Well, what do you think you're doing? You don't discuss anything with me anymore. And when I try to ask you a simple little question once in awhile you bristle up like a porcupine!

ANGELA: (*Closing her eyes.*) Oh, Martha, let's not start wrangling again now. I just don't feel like it.

MARTHA: Well, all I want is to know what you're planning to do. I think I have some right to that, don't you? I've never wanted to put it on that kind of a basis, but after all, Angela, you are living in my home and I think I have a right to know what's going on under my own roof.

ANGELA: There's nothing going on! Nothing at all.

MARTHA: Then suppose you explain to me why Kenny hasn't been coming over lately? Or didn't you think I'd noticed.

ANGELA: I don't care whether you've noticed or not, what difference does it make?

MARTHA: Well, what's happening? Are you and Kenny planning on getting married?

ANGELA: Whatever gave you that idea?

MARTHA: Have you two broken off with each other? Or what?

ANGELA: I told you, I don't want to talk about it, I—

MARTHA: (*Puts down her work and comes to the doorway.*) Tell me, Angela—please! I think I have a right to know.

ANGELA: A right, a right! Why is it that everybody seems to have rights but me?

MARTHA: What do you mean?

ANGELA: Everybody! Everybody has a right to do anything they please but Angela! They can live their own lives, make their own decisions, take care of their own business any way they see fit. But just let me get the bold idea of trying it and unh-unnh!

MARTHA: (*Steps into the room.*) Angela, what are you talking about?

ANGELA: Just let me try to take things into my own hands! Try to run my own life and set sights on what I want to do and where I want to go. Just let me catch a glimpse of a dream and try to follow it! And what happens? Blam! And after that, the buzzards descend.

MARTHA: What buzzards? I don't understand. What's this got to do with Kenny?

ANGELA: Kenny's gone! You don't have to worry about him anymore. He's gone.

MARTHA: Oh? Well, I mean—gone where?

ANGELA: I don't know. Just gone. Left right after exams. Nobody knows just where.

MARTHA: (*Pauses.*) I see. Well . . . So then it's all over? Between you two?

ANGELA: (*Softly.*) Yes, Martha. It's all over now. He'll never know.

MARTHA: (*Delayed reation.*) Never know what . . . ? Angela! (*Reaches out to touch her.*)

ANGELA: (*Drawing away.*) Don't touch me! Just leave me alone. I don't want anybody to bother me—ever again! (*Pushes herself to her feet.*)

MARTHA: But, Angela, baby! You're not yourself, there must be something wrong!

ANGELA: No, there's nothing wrong. Not anymore. And I am myself. For the first time in my life, I'm myself! (*Turns and goes into the bathroom, closing the door behind her.*)

MARTHA: Angela! (*Stands for a moment, looking toward the bathroom door, then, frustrated, returns to her ironing. She works furiously for a moment, then begins to mumble to herself, as if storing up arguments with which to confront* ANGELA *when she returns.*) . . . nobody's asking anything they don't have a right to know . . . Just can't understand why you have to be so hostile all the time . . . You want to make a big mess out of your life, go ahead, see if I care! (*Stops ironing, looks toward the bathroom and listens. There is no sound. She irons a bit more.*) . . . After all, I am your sister, and I only think it's right to tell you what I think . . . If that's what it is, just wait'll Momma hears about it, she'll never forgive you and she'll *kill* me! (*Stops again, looks up and listens. Puzzled, she puts down the iron and goes to the doorway. After a pause she calls.*) Angela? (*There is no answer. She comes to the bathroom door, listens, then knocks softly.*) Angela, can I come in? (*No answer. She frowns and starts to turn away. Then, impulsively, she returns to the door and tries to open it.*) Angela, baby, come on out of there. I want to talk to you. (*The handle turns, but when she tries to push in the door, she meets resistance. She tries again. It still won't budge. Alarmed now.*) What's the matter? Let me in, Angela, it's only me. (*Pushes harder, and the door gives way slightly. She looks in, stops stock still for a moment, then closes the door and gazes about wildly. Softly.*) Dickie . . . ? (*Turns and runs to the front door. She jerks it open. Her cry is a wail.*) Mrs. Wem-bley-y-y-y . . . !

(*Blackout.*)

Scene Two

Two days later. Morning. At rise, DICKIE *is seated on the sofa reading a comic book. He is all dressed up in a dark suit and white shirt with tie, and his hair is neatly combed. In the front bedroom,* JOHNNY *stands idly by the window, gazing out. He, too, is in his Sunday best. The bathroom door is closed, as is the door to* ANGELA's *room. From the ktichen, the radio blares forth a current tune.*

JOHNNY: (*From the bedroom window.*) Here comes a Buick! Oh, no, it's the wrong one.

(MARTHA *opens the bathroom door and looks out. She is in her slip, and her hair is bound up with a scarf. She has been applying makeup and holds a powder puff.*)

MARTHA: Dickie? Go turn that thing down, will you? It's getting on my nerves.

DICKIE: (*Looks up from his comic book.*) Aw . . . Okay. (*Goes into the kitchen and switches off the radio as* MARTHA *returns to her toilette.*)

(CHARLIE *appears at the back door.*)

CHARLIE: (*Looking in through the screen.*) Hey, Dickie!

DICKIE: Oh, hi, Charlie. You wanna come in? (*Opens the door.*)

CHARLIE: (*Entering.*) What you doin' all dressed up in the middle of the week? Goin' to a funeral?

DICKIE: Nah, silly. We're goin' over to the university. My Ant Angela's gonna graduate today.

(*They cross to the living room.*)

CHARLIE: Well, how many times is she gonna do that? I thought she did that last year.

DICKIE: She did, but she gotta do it again. This time they're gonna give her a master's degree.

CHARLIE: A what?

DICKIE: A master's degree.

CHARLIE: What's *that*?

DICKIE: I don't know, exactly. But it's what you get when you go through college after you been through the first time.

CHARLIE: You mean your ant flunked out and had a' repeat a grade? I thought you said she was so smart.

DICKIE: Naw, she didn't flunk! She went back because she wanted to, that's all.

CHARLIE: Well, I don't get it. If she was so smart, what'd she have to go back for?

DICKIE: I told you, they're gonna give her a master's degree.

CHARLIE: Say, is that somethin' like a third degree?

DICKIE: No. It's only a second degree.

CHARLIE: Well, if that's what she wants.

JOHNNY: (*Coming in from the bedroom.*) What time did that guy say he was comin', Dickie? Oh—hi, Charlie.

DICKIE: I don't know, don't ask me. Why don't you go ask Angela?

JOHNNY: I would, but Momma said not to bother her 'til she comes out. She still ain't feelin' so hot.

CHARLIE: What's the matter with her?

DICKIE: Oh, she's been a little sick the past coupla days. In bed. Had the doctor even. But she's a lot better now.

(*The bathroom door opens and* MARTHA *comes out.*)

MARTHA: Johnny, I thought you were looking out for the car. Hello, Charlie.

JOHNNY: I was, Ma, but I didn't see nothin'. Maybe he ain't comin'. (*Follows her into the bedroom and stations himself again at the window.*)

MARTHA: Oh, he'll be here, all right. Going to drive us all over to the university in his shiny new Buick. (*Seats herself at her bureau and begins to take out the curlers in her hair.*)

CHARLIE: Well, you guys are busy. See you this afternoon maybe, huh?

DICKIE: Oh, sure. We'll be back.

CHARLIE: Okay. Maybe we can go roller skatin' or somethin'. Geez, you know? Since we been outta school this time, I don't hardly know what to do with myself.

DICKIE: You can go back if you want to. I'm glad vacation is here.

CHARLIE: Well, anyhow. Least we don't have to mess aroun'

wit' no degrees. See you. (*Crosses to the back door and exits.*)

(*The telephone rings.*)

MARTHA: Answer that, Dickie, that may be Mr. Sampson!

DICKIE: Okay. (*Picks up the phone.*) Hello? . . . Oh, hello, Ant Gracie. (*Calls.*) It's Ant Gracie, Ma!

MARTHA: (*Rising.*) All right, I'm coming.

DICKIE: (*Into phone.*) Momma's comin', hold on. (*Puts down the phone and goes back to his comics.* MARTHA *gets to the phone.*)

MARTHA: Hi . . . Well, just about, Gracie. The kids are all dressed and I'm just finishing up my hair . . . Oh, she's in her room resting, she's all ready. All she has to do is put on her cap and gown . . . Oh, I think she'll be all right. She ate a good dinner last night, and I made her take some breakfast this morning. She's looking much better, you should see . . . Well, me too. I was nearly out of my wits. I told you, I stayed up with her all night long, I thought she was going to— (*Breaks off as she realizes* DICKIE *is listening.*) No, she still won't talk about it, Gracie, and I don't think it's right to keep after her. The important thing is she'll be all right . . . Well, the doctor said there was no infection and whoever did the job knew pretty well what they were doing. He says we should all just forget the whole thing, forget it all happened . . . Yes . . . Well, I've got to get my dress on and finish my hair, so I'll see you over there . . . Yes, he's coming by to drive us over and he ought to be here any minute. So, I'll be looking for you when we get there. We'll try and save a seat near us, all right? . . . Okay, Gracie, good-bye. (*Hangs up.*) Dickie, get your feet off the couch. (*Eyes* ANGELA's *door and starts to go toward it, but changes her mind and returns to the front bedroom.*) Nothing yet, Johnny?

JOHNNY: Nothing yet.

(*Slow footsteps are heard climbing the stairs and there is a knock at the door.*)

MARTHA: (*Calls.*) See who it is, Dickie, I'm not dressed!

DICKIE: Okay! (*Goes to the door and opens it to admit* MRS. WEMBLEY. *She is elegantly attired in a full-length summer dress, and wears a broad-rimmed hat trimmed with roses.*) Wow! Come in, Mrs. Wembley.

MRS. WEMBLEY: Good morning, Dickie, how are you? My, you look so nice in your suit and all. Where's Martha?

MARTHA: (*Calls.*) In here! I'm just getting dressed.

MRS. WEMBLEY: (*Going to the doorway.*) Oh, there you are.

MARTHA: (*Beams.*) Well, will you just look at this lady today! My, my!

MRS. WEMBLEY: (*Enjoying it.*) Oh now, Martha, stop! Just stop, now. I don't want to hear any of your foolishness.

MARTHA: It's not foolishness at all, is it, Dickie? Doesn't she look wonderful? Look at that darling hat. And that dress makes you look about thirty years younger.

MRS. WEMBLEY: Oh, now, Martha . . .

DICKIE: (*Grinning.*) Yeah, you look real good, Mrs. Wembley.

JOHNNY: (*From the window.*) I think she looks a hundred years younger!

MRS. WEMBLEY: Now, if all of you-all don't just stop, stop this instant, I'll go right back downstairs and take these things off, and I just won't go, that's all! (*Seats herself in a chair in the living room.*)

MARTHA: (*Turns back to the mirror.*) Now, you know you couldn't do that. Angela'd be so disappointed if you weren't there today. Hand me that box of bobby pins over there, Johnny.

MRS. WEMBLEY: And how is the graduate this morning? I don't see her anywhere.

MARTHA: I told her to lie down and rest for a bit. She's all ready, she'll be out soon.

MRS. WEMBLEY: Well, that's nice, poor dear. Did you give her that tea I sent up for her?

MARTHA: Uh—yes, yes, of course. She drank it down, piping hot, just like you said.

(DICKIE *looks up at his mother strangely, then flops back on the sofa with his comic book, shaking his head.*)

MRS. WEMBLEY: That's fine, I'm sure it'll do her a world of good. I said a little prayer for her this morning, first thing when I got out of bed. I'm going to keep on holding the thought for her all day long, that God will envelop her in his tender mercies and give her the strength to go through this day and from now on, poor dear. (*Shakes her head.*) I still can't get it out of my mind. Beautiful young girl like Angela, intelligent and educated and full of life, lying there on the floor like that looking for all the world—

MARTHA: Yes, Mrs. Wembley, but we decided we weren't going to talk about it anymore, didn't we? It's all over now, so we're supposed to forget the whole thing, that anything ever happened. That's the best thing in the world we can do, the doctor said.

MRS. WEMBLEY: Yes, of course, my dear, and he's right, too. You'll just have to overlook me when I do things like that. I'm getting like Melvin, I talk too much.

MARTHA: That's all right, I know you didn't mean it. (*Picks up her dress, which is laid across the bed, and shakes it out. Then she slips it over her head.*)

MRS. WEMBLEY: My, that's a lovely, lovely dress, Martha. Is it new?

MARTHA: No, I've had it for nearly a year now. Just haven't worn it much.

MRS. WEMBLEY: Well, you should, it's very becoming.

(*There is the sound of an automobile drawing up and stopping.*)

JOHNNY: (*At the window.*) Hey, Ma, look! It's the Buick. It pulled up right out in front!

DICKIE: (*Dashes in to take a look.*) Yeah! We gonna ride in that? Oh, boy!

MARTHA: Good, he's here. (*To* MRS. WEMBLEY.) It's Mr. Sampson, he just drove up.

MRS. WEMBLEY: Oh well, that's fine. I'm all ready. (*Pats her hat and makes sure she has her gloves.*)

DICKIE: Shall I tell Angela he's here?

MARTHA: No, Dickie, I'll go in in a minute. There's no big hurry.

JOHNNY: He's comin' up the stairs!

(*He and* DICKIE *rush into the living room. Footsteps sound on the stairs.*)

MARTHA: Now, you kids stop all that running around.

(*DICKIE opens the door, and in a moment,* ROGER *appears. He is carefully dressed in a well-tailored suit, and carries two orchids in transparent cases.*)

ROGER: Hello, Dickie! Hi ya, Johnny!

BOYS: Hi!

(ROGER *enters*. MARTHA *comes to greet him*.)

MARTHA: (*Smiling*.) Well, Mr. Sampson! I see you got here in good time.

ROGER: Hello, Mrs. Hill. Yes, I was afraid I'd be late. Had to stop by the florist's on the way up. (*Handing her one of the boxes*.) This is for you, and this one's for . . . (*Glances about for* ANGELA.)

MARTHA: (*Beaming*.) Oh, how lovely! You didn't have to do that, Roger, especially not for me. Oh, Mrs. Wembley, just take a look! You remember Mrs. Wembley, don't you, she's the lady from downstairs.

ROGER: I certainly do, forgive me, Mrs. Wembley. (*Takes her hand*.)

MRS. WEMBLEY: (*Flattered*.) Well, how are you, Mr. Sampson? I was wondering when you'd get around to little ol' me. (*Looking at the flowers*.) My, how perfectly lovely! Just simply gorgeous.

ROGER: If I had known, Mrs. Wembley, I'd have brought you one too. Only—

MRS. WEMBLEY: That's quite all right, don't give it a second thought. My, I just know Angela's going to love that.

JOHNNY: Lemme see, Ma!

DICKIE: Hey, that's pretty nice.

MARTHA: Have a seat, Roger, Angela'll be out in just a minute. All she has to do is put on her cap and gown.

ROGER: Is she, uh—

MARTHA: She's feeling fine, just fine. All over her little illness. Here, let me take this in to her right now. You children sit down, now, out of the way. (*Goes to* ANGELA'*s door and opens it gently*.) Angela? (*Enters and closes the door behind her*.)

ROGER: (*Sitting*.) Well, Mrs. Wembley, how have you been?

MRS. WEMBLEY: Just fine, just fine for an old lady, I guess. (*She giggles*.)

ROGER: Come, now. I'd say you didn't look a day over forty. Not a day.

MRS. WEMBLEY: (*Laughs*.) Oh, you lie so charmingly, Mr. Sampson. I'll have you know I'll be seventy-four years of age in August.

ROGER: Why, that's incredible. You can't expect me to believe that.

JOHNNY: You can believe it, she's awful old.

MRS. WEMBLEY: (*Sniffs*.) Out of the mouths of babes . . .

Well, Mr. Sampson, it's been quite a little while since I've
seen you up this way. But I just knew you wouldn't want to
miss Angela's graduation.

ROGER: Uh, no, of course not. Uh, Mrs. Wembley? (*Looks
around and moves a little closer.*) Do you mind if I ask you
something?

MRS. WEMBLEY: Why, certainly not, Mr. Sampson. You go
right ahead.

ROGER: Well, uh . . . I don't quite know how to put this to
you.

MRS. WEMBLEY: Oh, you just put it any way you choose.
You'll find I have a willing ear, a willing ear!

ROGER: Well . . . you've been neighbors with the Hills for a
long time now, I take it. Or rather, they've been neighbors
of yours.

MRS. WEMBLEY: Yes?

ROGER: And I suppose you've known Angela ever since she
came here to live with the Hills and go to school and all.

MRS. WEMBLEY: That's quite true. Of course.

ROGER: So I guess you know Angela about as well as anybody
here in town, wouldn't you say?

MRS. WEMBLEY: Oh, I suppose that's true, Mr. Sampson.
After all, when you live right downstairs under people and
see them most every day . . .

ROGER: Yes, that's what I mean. Well, Mrs. Wembley, would
you say that Angela has ever been a . . . a sickly girl? Since
you've known her, I mean?

MRS. WEMBLEY: Well now, I don't know what you're driving
at, but no. Oh, she's had her colds and regular ups and
downs like anybody else, I guess. But I wouldn't say she was
a sickly type at all. And if she was, I'd pray for her and
write a letter off to Unity. Oh, do you know about Unity,
Mr. Sampson? Let me tell you—

ROGER: Yes, you've told me before. But let's get back to
Angela. You don't think she's a sickly type, you say. Fine,
I'm glad to hear it. But just tell me one thing, will you, Mrs.
Wembley? What's wrong with Angela?

MRS. WEMBLEY: What's . . . wrong? With Angela?

ROGER: Yes. Right now, in there. What's the matter with her?

MRS. WEMBLEY: (*Cautiously.*) Well . . . haven't you talked to
Martha?

ROGER: Oh, I talked to Martha.

MRS. WEMBLEY: And what did she tell you?

ROGER: Martha told me Angela was . . . that Angela had . . .

Well, she said it was just a slight case of female trouble and that she'd be all over it in a day or two.

MRS. WEMBLEY: Well, then. If Martha told you that, then that's all there is to it.

ROGER: But that isn't all and I know it! In fact, there's quite a bit of mystery surrounding this whole thing, and I want to get to the bottom of it.

MRS. WEMBLEY: Why, what makes you say that?

ROGER: Because . . . Because, well, you know, don't you, that I've been seeing Angela off and on for some time.

MRS. WEMBLEY: Oh, yes. Why, I used to look outside my window 'most anytime and see you driving up in your nice big car.

ROGER: And you know the past couple of months I haven't been by nearly so frequently. And you also know why.

MRS. WEMBLEY: (*Turns away.*) Now, Mr. Sampson, I'd rather not get involved in all this. I try to mind my own business. I do try . . .

ROGER: But you know that Angela has been seeing quite a lot of somebody else lately, don't you?

MRS. WEMBLEY: (*Uncomfortable.*) Now, you may be a lawyer, Mr. Sampson, but I'm not on the witness stand, and I—I think you'd better ask Angela anything you want to know.

ROGER: (*Darkly.*) I intend to. I intend to ask Angela everything!

MRS. WEMBLEY: (*Worried.*) Oh, but uh . . . Well, I'd be a little careful just now if I were you. After all, this is Angela's graduation day, and then, too, she's been through quite a lot.

ROGER: Oh, she has, has she? Well, I've got news for her. So have I been through quite a lot!

MRS. WEMBLEY: (*Testily.*) Well, you do what you want to, young man, but just let me tell you this: there is no use under the sun as long as it shines in the heavens in spending your time looking for the perfect woman. There's no such creature on God's green earth, and if there were, and you were lucky enough to find her, Mr. Sampson, it just wouldn't do you a bit of good because she'd be busy looking for the perfect man! So don't let yourself be a fool and do something you might regret for the rest of your life just because Angela may have made her mistakes and is paying for them now.

ROGER: Wait a minute, Mrs. Wembley—you don't understand!

MRS. WEMBLEY: That's all I care to say, thank you. Now, goodness gracious, what time is it getting to be? We don't

want to be late for the commencement exercises. (*Calls.*)
Martha? Oh, Martha, it's getting late!

MARTHA: (*Inside.*) All right, we're coming! Just a minute.

MRS. WEMBLEY: (*Has risen.*) Come, come, children! Let's get
ready to go. We ought to be getting downstairs to the car if
we're going to be on time, and I think we'd better—

(*She breaks off as* ANGELA's *door opens and* ANGELA
*appears in the doorway. She is garbed in her ceremonial gown,
beneath which she wears a simple white dress. The orchid is
pinned to her gown, and she carries her cap, folded, in her
hand. Prompted by* MARTHA, *she steps into the room,* MARTHA
following. Her face is calm, her gaze impersonal.)

MARTHA: Well, folks, here she is. Our graduate.

MRS. WEMBLEY: Why, she's beautiful, just beautiful! I've
never seen her looking more lovely. (*With a sharp glance at*
ROGER.) Isn't she, Mr. Sampson? Just look at Angela, isn't
she lovely?

(ROGER *stands, looking at* ANGELA *as if stricken.*)

MARTHA: Say hello to Roger, dear. He's come to take us to
the exercises.

ANGELA: (*When she speaks it is softly and calmly. She is in
command of all of her faculties; she is only changed, sub-
dued.*) Why, hello, Roger. So nice of you to come for us.
And thank you for the corsage.

ROGER: (*Finding his voice.*) I . . . yes . . . hello, Angela. It's
. . . nothing. Nothing at all.

MARTHA: (*At* ANGELA's *elbow, coaching.*) And here's Mrs.
Wembley, you haven't said hello to Mrs. Wembley.

ANGELA: Yes.

MARTHA: Isn't she just stunning in that outfit? She's going with
us to the exercises.

ANGELA: You look wonderful, Mrs. Wembley. I'm so glad
you're going with us.

MRS. WEMBLEY: Oh, now that's so sweet of you, Angela, my
dear. Yes, I wouldn't miss seeing you get your degree for
anything in the world.

DICKIE: Why don't you put on your hat, Angela?

MRS. WEMBLEY: Oh, yes! Let's have a preview of you in the
graduation procession. Come on, get your cap on, now.

MARTHA: (*Helping* ANGELA.) All right. Here, dear. (*Helps*

ANGELA *adjust the cap.*) Now, wait a minute, let me pin it for you . . . There.

MRS. WEMBLEY: Oh, isn't that lovely?

JOHNNY: Hey, that's swell!

MARTHA: Does the tassle go on the right side or the left? I've forgotten.

MRS. WEMBLEY: It goes on the left until they give you your diploma, and then you switch it over to the right. All right, now, Angela! Let's see you march. Come on, now! Da-dee, dee, dum! Da-ta-ta dee dee dum pum da, dee! (*Sings the traditional processional by Mendelssohn, waving her arms and directing.* ANGELA *hesitates.*) Oh, come on now, dear. We want to see you walk! Da da, ta-ta, de dum, pum-pum!

MARTHA: Go on, Angela. Try it.

(ANGELA *takes a halting step, then another and another in time with the music.*)

MRS. WEMBLEY: That's it, Angela! You're doing fine. Da dee, dee, dum!

(ANGELA *takes another step or two, then suddenly stops, with her hands up to her ears.*)

ANGELA: No! Stop! Please stop it!

MARTHA: (*Rushing to her.*) That's all right, baby, that's enough for now. It's all right. Here—have a seat and rest yourself. (*Helps* ANGELA *to a seat.*)

MRS. WEMBLEY: Oh, I'm so sorry, Martha! I didn't mean to—

MARTHA: It's all right! She's just a little nervous. Suppose you and the kids go on down and get in the car. We'll be along in a minute. It's getting late.

MRS. WEMBLEY: Yes, of course, that's the thing to do. Come on, boys. Let's start down now, and get in the car.

DICKIE: I'm gonna sit in the front!

JOHNNY: I'm gonna sit in the front, too!

MARTHA: (*Crossing to the front bedroom.*) Just let me get my hat . . .

MRS. WEMBLEY: (*Comes up behind* ANGELA *and puts a hand on her shoulder.*) Angela? Angela, darling . . .

ANGELA: I'm . . . I'm all right now, Mrs. Wembley. I'm sorry.

MRS. WEMBLEY: That's quite all right, dear, I shouldn't have gotten you upset. I'm going on down now. And, Angela? (ANGELA *looks up.*) I'll be holding the thought. (*A little*

sternly.) I'll be holding one for you, too, Mr. Sampson!
(*Calls.*) Martha, we're going down!

MARTHA: (*Pinning on her hat.*) All right, we'll be right with
you!

MRS. WEMBLEY: (*To* DICKIE *and* JOHNNY.) Come on, boys.
(*Turns, and with one hand on* DICKIE's *shoulder, she exits
with the boys, chanting.*) "Jesus is my strength and my salvation. In Him I find the manifestation of perfect health and
mind . . .

(*After they are out of sight,* ROGER *turns toward* ANGELA.)

ROGER: Angela . . . Angela, I—

MARTHA: (*Comes out of the bedroom, pulling on her gloves.*)
I guess we're all ready now. We can go. Angela?

(ANGELA *rises.*)

ROGER: Mrs. Hill. If you don't mind, I'd like a minute to—

MARTHA: Oh, of course! I'm sorry. I'll go on down and wait
with the others. Don't be long, now! (*Turns to go, then
comes back to* ANGELA.) Angela . . . baby. Is everything all
right?

ANGELA: Yes, Martha. I'm fine.

MARTHA: Good. (*Kisses her quickly on the cheek.*) And when
you march down that aisle, past those stands, I want you to
have your head held high. (*Goes to the door, then turns
again.*) Mr. Sampson, that's a mighty beautiful master of arts
you've got there. (*Turns and goes quickly down the stairs,
closing the door.*)

ROGER: Angela . . .

ANGELA: Yes, Roger?

ROGER: I . . . I want you to know that I . . . I . . .

ANGELA: Yes, Roger? What is it?

ROGER: Can you forgive me, Angela?

ANGELA: Forgive you? For what?

ROGER: For . . . for doubting you. For being such a stupid,
pig-headed ass! For thinking even for a moment that you
might not be . . . well . . . That you might've . . . Oh, I
don't know.

ANGELA: What? Roger, I don't know just what you're talking
about. But if it has anything to do with my pregnancy, then
I can only say it's all over now, and no one has to worry
about it anymore.

ROGER: (*Stunned.*) What . . . did you say?

ANGELA: Yes, Roger, didn't you know? Didn't Martha tell you? Oh, you poor dear. I see she's been trying to be her usual diplomatic self. Don't blame her, she means well. She's really a wonderful woman. I don't suppose I'd be alive today if it weren't for Martha.

ROGER: Angela! Do you know what you're saying?

ANGELA: Of course.

ROGER; Then it *is* true. It really is. This throws a whole new light on the situation, Angela. I can't, with this . . . !

ANGELA: Can't what? Please, Roger, I'm trying to follow you.

ROGER: (*Clenching his fists.*) Oh . . . God!

ANGELA: Roger, are you all right?

ROGER: And I . . . I was going to . . . to propose to you! To ask you to be my wife beside me, the mother of my children! To introduce you to my family and business associates, to come home to you at night and sleep with you! (*Pulls out a small box, opens it, and shows a ring.*) I was going to propose—see? (*Snaps the box shut.*) Damn you. *Damn you!*

(ROGER *jams the box into his pocket and stands facing her. His eyes wander down over her form. He steps forward, grasps her brusquely by the arm. Slowly and deliberately he reaches his hand to her breast.* ANGELA *does not resist, merely looks back at him searchingly. He pulls her to him and kisses her mouth, savagely at first—then, realizing she is neither resisting nor cooperating, he slowly lifts his head.*)

(ANGELA's *eyes are closed and her shoulders shake gently in silent sobs. Instantly contrite,* ROGER *loosens his grip and begins to stroke her hair and shoulders.*)

ROGER: Angela, I'm sorry . . . Please. I didn't mean . . . (*Takes out a handkerchief and tries to daub away her tears. Gradually,* ANGELA *regains control. She looks up at him and manages a wan smile.*)

ANGELA: I deserved that, didn't I?

ROGER: No! Please . . . !

ANGELA: (*Puts her fingers over his lips.*) I've hurt you terribly, haven't I, Roger? I'm sorry. I've been chasing after a dream . . . a free spirit I couldn't hold onto without snuffing out the very flame that keeps it afloat. But it can fly now. It can soar. (*Pause.*) Roger, it's flattering to know that you care. I don't know if you can be strong enough to get over it. I perhaps you'll try me again, sometime. If you'd like. Sometime when both our hurts have lessened. (*Outside, an auto horn is heard.*) We'd better be going.

(*She turns to go toward the door, but* ROGER *holds onto her hand. Worshipfully, he bends to kiss the palms of her hands.*
Footsteps sound behind the door. It opens, revealing DOC *coming in from work. They turn.*)

DOC: (*After a pause.*) 'Scuse me. (*Moves past them and starts for the bedroom.*)

ROGER: (*His spirits lifted.*) Hello, Mr. Hill. Oh, Mr. Hill . . . !

DOC: (*Stops and turns.*) Yeah?

ROGER: Don't you think Angela looks wonderful in her cap and gown? She's graduating today, you know. Doesn't she look just fine?

DOC: (*After a pause.*) Oh, yeah. She looks . . . just fine. (*Turns and goes into the bedroom and removes his hat.* ANGELA *stands gazing after him quite passively.*)

ROGER: (*To* ANGELA.) Shall we go?

(ANGELA *turns calmly and starts down the stairs.* ROGER *follows, closing the door.*
DOC *comes to the portal and looks after them. Seeing they are gone, he comes into the living room and snaps on the television set, then heads for the kitchen, rolling up his sleeves and whistling thinly.*
Outside there is a sound of a car door being slammed. Then an auto starts up and pulls away.
Ignoring this, DOC *opens the refrigerator and surveys its contents. As he does, the television sound fades up and a news announcer is heard.* DOC *selects a beer and a cold chicken leg, closes the refrigerator door and looks for an opener.*)

ANNOUNCER: ". . . so far as they were concerned, there was no evidence to the contrary. However, the local civil rights leader pointed out that the vehicle, which belonged to him, had been given a new set of brake linings less than a month ago. He stated that when he drove the car only yesterday, the brakes were working properly. He called for an FBI investigation into the deaths, claiming threats had been made against the voter-registration project and any persons connected with it. Thus far, there has been no response from FBI Director J. Edgar Hoover.

FBI Director J. Edgar Hoover.

Once again, the body of one of three persons killed in an apparent automobile accident late last night on the state highway near Greenville, Mississippi, has now been positively identified as that of a local university student, a Negro senior named Kenneth Powers, whose baccalaureate degree was scheduled to be conferred at commencement exercises only this afternoon. The other two bodies, both young Negroes, have yet to be identified, as all three were badly burned when the automobile allegedly ran off the road, crashed into a tree, and burst into flames. Authorities say they are continuing their investigation.

Turning to sports, the Chicago Cubs are in the third inning of the first game of their double-header with the Pittsburgh Pirates at Wrigley Field, and thus far there is no score in the ballgame. In other contests—

(*During the above,* DOC *opens his beer, takes a swig or two, and begins gnawing on his chicken-leg, oblivious to the newscast. At the mention of the Chicago Cubs, however, he quickly grabs his beer and hurries back to the television set. He turns the dial frantically until we hear the roar of a baseball crowd during an exciting play and a sports announcer's voice shouting over the action.* DOC *adjusts the picture a bit, then steps back and sinks into an easy chair. He crosses his legs, makes himself comfortable and resumes his lunch, his eyes firmly glued to the screen.*)

(*The curtain falls.*)

SHERLOCK HOLMES AND THE HANDS OF OTHELLO

A DRAMA IN TWO ACTS

by Alexander Simmons

All inquiries concerning rights should be directed to Dark Angel Productions, 3967 Saxon Avenue, Bronx, N.Y. 10463.

Sherlock Holmes and the Hands of Othello was first produced at the Westbeth Theater in New York City by Dark Angels Productions on October 7, 1987. (For additional information on Ira Aldridge and his daughter, Amanda, see *Ira Aldridge: The Negro Tragedian* by Herbert Marshall and Mildred Stock, New York: Macmillan, 1958.)

ALEXANDER SIMMONS

Born and raised in New York City, Alexander Simmons graduated from the Arts and Design High School, where he studied illustration and advertising. After several years working at CBS as a "day-of-air logging coordinator," he turned to acting, appearing in several off-off-Broadway theater productions, doing radio voice-overs and commercials, and working as a film extra. He has been Artist-in-Residence at the Westco Children's Theater Company; the Creative Arts Team Conflict Resolution Theater Company; and the Westchester school system, for all of which he taught creative writing and acting. He is currently Artistic Director for the Bronx Creative Arts for Youth, Inc.

Simmons has published a number of children's books, including *The Adventures of Shelly Holmes, The Ghost of Craven Cove, The Case of the Funny Money Man* and *The Ghost of Shockly Manor.* In addition, he has written and directed scripts for video and screen, including *If at First*, an educational drama on youth employment produced for national distribution by the Creative Arts Team; and scripts for radio, one of which won the Ohio State Award for Radio Drama. He has also written over thirty songs, including "Stardust Lady," recorded by Noel Pointer for United Artists, and the song lyrics for several theater productions.

Besides *Sherlock Holmes and the Hands of Othello*—which is his first play—Simmons has written two others to date: *Starchild* and *Once upon a Miracle.*

CAST OF CHARACTERS
(in order of their appearance)

AMANDA ALDRIDGE
NINSKY
VLADIMIR
THE GHOST OF IRA ALDRIDGE
PHILLIPE MOREAU
SHERLOCK HOLMES
THOMAS KANE
ELISHA CARVER
JONATHAN BRAITHWAITE
SIR LAWRENCE PRITCHARD
COUNTESS ALEXANDRA TAMBOVA
INSPECTOR LESTRADE
CONSTABLE RUTLEDGE
WINTERS
PIKER
All characters are portrayed by a cast of eight performers.

ACT ONE

PROLOGUE

A gaslit street in London. A fog spirit night in a cold December. On stage is an entrance to an alleyway. One wall contains a poster display case which bears the title "EDWARD NELSON RECITAL HALL." It proclaims the appearance of one Amanda Aldridge, tonight December 5, 1886, at 7 p.m. The street is quiet, forbidding. AMANDA ALDRIDGE *appears from the alleyway. She is a black woman in her early twenties, attractive. She is dressed in an expensive evening dress and wears coat, gloves and hat of equal value. She seems tentative and uneasy, peering up and down the dark and lonely street. Suddenly a little man comes waddling into the soft glow of the streetlight. He is shabbily dressed, but appropriately for the weather. He stares at* AMANDA, *who appears near flight, though she stands her ground.*

AMANDA: Mr. Ninsky? (*He says nothing.*) If you are Mr. Ninsky, then we have much to discuss. If not, then please be on your way.

NINSKY: (*Leering. Quiet.*) Yes, I am Ninsky. And you, young miss, are Amanda Aldridge, no doubt.

AMANDA: (*Drawing up courage.*) I have been waiting quite some time, sir. The theater closed over an hour ago. Your note said you would meet me immediately after my recital.

NINSKY: I confess, I am not punctual, but I assure you that what I have to offer is worth your wait. Did you bring the amount I requested?

AMANDA: I shall offer no payment until I know that your information is of some real value!

NINSKY: (*Angry.*) I do not advise that you play games with such stakes at hand or with such a person as myself. The information will be of greater value to others who will pay much more.

AMANDA: Then tell what you know and be quick about it.

NINSKY: (*Getting angrier.*) Young miss, you are the target of

361

such people as would worry the very prime minister of this country. They will kill to have what they wish, and even I am not immune to their vengeance—

AMANDA: Why would I concern such people?!

NINSKY: Possession! Control, power! Now give me the money I requested, and you shall hear the details! (*Moves toward her menacingly.*)

AMANDA: I said I would pay you when I have heard your—

NINSKY: (*Lunging and grabbing her purse.*) I said, give it over!

(AMANDA *backs up against the theater wall, near the alley, as* NINSKY *rummages through her purse.*)

NINSKY: (*Murder in his eyes.*) Empty. You have brought nothing.

AMANDA: (*Frightened.*) It was impossible for me to raise the amount you asked for. I thought I might—

NINSKY: (*Reaching into his coat pocket as he moves toward her.*) You thought to use me, to make a fool of me!

AMANDA: No! I—

NINSKY: Too bad, young miss. I think I must (*Produces a wicked-looking knife.*) leave you ugly . . . and silent.

(*As* AMANDA *is about to scream,* NINSKY's *free hand clamps over her mouth and he slams her against the wall. She struggles valiantly, but in vain.* NINSKY *is about to slash her face when we hear a loud swish, and* NINSKY *suddenly stiffens. He grabs his face as if struck, releases* AMANDA, *and whirls around to see a spectral figure emerging from the fog. The figure is that of a black man dressed in the robes of a Moorish general, and carrying a tribal walking stick [five feet in length] with an ornate headpiece in his right hand. He appears in his fifties, with a striking face. He raises his left hand and points at a now staggering* NINSKY, *who falls unconscious to the ground.* AMANDA *looks on in horror as the figure turns to her.*)

GHOST: Get ye gone . . . Go, get thee from my sight. Thou art damned!

AMANDA: Father? No, please, Father, not again!

GHOST: (*Angry.*) Get ye gone!

(AMANDA *retrieves her purse and runs off, snagging her coat on the display case. She tears free and disappears into the night.*

The ghost fades back into the fog, near the alley entrance. Moments later, NINSKY moans, rises to his knees, and looks around fearfully. He tries to stand, but cannot. The sound of approaching footsteps can be heard, and NINSKY seems to panic. A man enters the lamplight from the fog. He is well dressed in evening attire, with gloves and top hat. The top hat obscures our view of his face. He approaches NINSKY, who seems to recognize him.

NINSKY: I am most sorry, friend . . . Mr. Moreau. (*Becoming more scared.*) I would not have mentioned any of your part in this business. I would have told only of the Circle and would not have mentioned their names. (MOREAU *remains silent, standing over* NINSKY) I only wanted to make a few extra pounds for my troubles . . . I would not have said . . . I swear, sir! (*A silken cord appears in* MOREAU's *hand.* NINSKY *does not see it.*) We can still work together. I will never do anything like this again!

MOREAU: (*French accent, subtle.*) You are right, my friend. You never will.

(*With a quick strong action,* MOREAU *wraps the cord around* NINSKY's *throat and strangles him to death. The body falls to the ground.*)

MOREAU: (*To* NINSKY.) I will have to inform your leaders that the Aldridge affair is now entirely . . . my contract. (*Turns slowly and walks into the fog.*)

(*Lights fade out.*)

SCENE ONE

London, the next day. Before us the famous sitting room of Sherlock Homes, 221-B Baker Street. The set contains a fireplace with wooden mantel, a chaise longue, a basket chair, and a Victorian high-back chair (the two chairs are placed before the fireplace). There is also a breakfast table with a setting for one, the food barely touched, and a stack of newspapers precariously leaning near the table. HOLMES moves about the room with marked irritation. He prepares a pipe, taking tobacco from a Persian slipper on the mantel, then begins an agitated search for something.

HOLMES: (*Disgusted.*) Blast! Where the devil are the blasted things?! (*Looking about.*) Watson must have— (*Looks at* WATSON's *chair.*) Perhaps not. (*In deep thought* HOLMES *looks at the breakfast table, the stack of newspapers, then his chair. He goes to his chair, lifts the cushion, and removes a tin box. From that he removes matches, lights his pipe, smiles, and looks at* WATSON's *chair.*) Watson, dear Watson, you would find these recent cases quite uninspiring, I'm afraid. Not at all like the Greek interpreter, or the Redheaded League, or . . . the Hound. (*Moves to the window.*) It would appear London no longer has the substance to stimulate me. Perhaps your marriage was well timed, old friend. Surely it has dominated your time these recent months. Marriage and your thriving practice. (*Looking out the window.*) But all things progress rapidly forward, and racing up the street is a young man with a definite purpose. Hello . . . it would appear I am his intention. Undoubtedly my morning appointment. Most intriguing. (*Moves to his chair and casually seats himself.*) Let us see if his troubles require my leaving the comfort of our lodgings, eh? (*Knock at the door.*) Enter, Mr. Kane.

(*The door opens and in steps a neatly dressed black man. This is* THOMAS KANE. *He appears energetic, nervous. He wears a gray suit with matching bowler, a dark winter coat draped over one arm, and he carries a pair of black gloves in his left hand. His manners are polite and friendly, but he is containing a great deal of tension as he approaches the famed detective.*)

KANE: Mr. Holmes? (HOLMES *nods.*) I am Thomas Lincoln Kane. It is indeed a unique pleasure to meet you. Thank you very much for receiving me. (*They shake hands.*)
HOLMES: Please be seated. (*Motions* KANE *to a chair near the fireplace.*)
KANE: Thank you. (*Sits.*)
HOLMES: What folly could have befallen an American actor that he would undertake the long journey from Upper Norwood at so early an hour?
KANE: Wha—how on earth did you guess that, sir?
HOLMES: Guess? No, no, Mr. Kane. As my absentee friend, Dr. Watson, would tell you, I never guess.
KANE: But in my telegram I mentioned nothing but my desire to see you this morning.
HOLMES: True. I suppose you will not be content without some

portion of an explanation. Few ever are. Your carriage is strong and sturdy, you undertake a strenuous ritual constantly, but not from labors on the docks or farmlands.

KANE: How can you be certain?

HOLMES: Your clothing is too costly to be easily afforded by a common laborer, yet not that of a man of means. More important, your hand. As I shook your hand I noted that it was devoid of calluses. And your nails were well kept, clean, save for a bit of base powder on the thumb and index finger.

KANE: I—

HOLMES: There are additional spots of makeup powder, grease paint, and rouge upon your jacket and trousers.

KANE: I had no idea. (*Tries to tidy up.*) I left in such a hurry this—

HOLMES: You fell asleep on the train.

KANE: Uh, yes, I did.

HOLMES: You left your ticket protruding from your breast pocket. The conductor came by, punched it (*Removes paper punchings from* KANE's *hair.*) and returned it to your jacket. It is slightly visible. As I am familiar with the various lines, I recognize this one (*Removing the stub.*) and allowing for the depth of your repose by the fact that you are not yet fully awake . . . It was relatively an elemental conclusion.

KANE: And that is how you knew?

HOLMES: That, and the soil sample adhering to your left boot heel. (KANE *looks at his left boot.*) It is indigenous to that particular area.

KANE: (*Amazed.*) It would appear you are all people say you are.

HOLMES: (*Whimsically.*) I should hope not *all* people. Some rather juicy adjectives have been attached to my moniker. And now, sir (*Placing his hands together at the fingertips.*), to the matter of your problem. You appear somewhat agitated.

KANE: I admit to a small—no, a large degree of upset, sir. Yet the sorrowful situation is not with me, but with the family of Ira Aldridge.

HOLMES: Oh?

KANE: You have heard of Ira Aldridge, the late Negro tragedian? He was well known throughout the Continent for his outstanding portrayal of Shakespeare's works, in particular Othello.

HOLMES: I know of him quite well. Pray continue.

KANE: (*Intense.*) Mr. Holmes, Ira Aldridge had a family of five, not including his first wife. Of those surviving members, not one has escaped being struck by some ill event or circumstance in recent months.

HOLMES: Please be more concise, Mr. Kane.

KANE: Very well. As you may be aware, Mr. Aldridge died on August 7, 1867, in a small town in Poland.

HOLMES: Lodz is a city of over thirty-five thousand people. I would hardly call it a small town.

KANE: (*Annoyed.*) I have had no opportunity to visit the city, Mr. Holmes. And I believe an unmarked grave is difficult to locate . . . nineteen years later.

HOLMES: Dr. Watson is repeatedly scolding me for my lack of tact and sensitivity. I meant no disrespect, Mr. Kane. The grave is difficult to find. It is on the plot of a family named Moes. Now, my good sir, your story.

KANE: (*Momentarily puzzled.*) No offense taken, sir. (*Rises and paces.*) The exact cause of Ira's death is still in question, but a similar ailment took his youngest son, Frederick, just two months ago, in Scarborough. At the inquest Frederick's wife came to settle his affairs. Frederick was a pianist and composer of minimal, but growing success and his tours took him to many places. For some reason, he traveled with most of his possessions and important papers. So, immediately after the inquest, his wife packed his things and left. (*Wipes his mouth with his thumb and index finger, then looks toward the window and breakfast table.*)

HOLMES: Please help yourself to some tea, sir. (KANE *is amazed but complies.*) For what destination did the lady depart?

KANE: (*Excited.*) That is unknown, principally because . . . Frederick was not married. Neither his mother nor his sisters have any idea who this woman was.

HOLMES: She has made no attempt to contact the family for, shall we say, monetary assistance?

KANE: No, Mr. Holmes. (*Wry laughter.*) I'm afraid Amanda . . . I mean, the family, is hardly in a position to make any fortune hunter a healthy gain. In recent times their fortune has slowly and inexplicably dwindled.

HOLMES: (*Intense.*) I see.

KANE: (*Anxious.*) But there is no need for you to concern yourself with that. I will pay whatever you might request . . . within reason.

HOLMES: I am not concerned, my good sir.

KANE: Oh. To continue, the oldest son, Daniel, has mysteriously vanished from his home in Australia.

HOLMES: How recently?

KANE: Three months ago. Daniel and his stepmother, the present Mrs. Aldridge, had a falling out back in February of '67. He sailed for Australia, wrote once upon hearing of his father's death, then silence. I succeeded in locating him only a year ago and wrote to him often. His disappearance was relayed to me by one of his children.

HOLMES: Thus far we have one disappearance and one death, by records, from medical causes. I take it the coroner found no evidence of foul play.

KANE: No, Mr. Holmes.

HOLMES: Then I fail to see your reasons for seeking my assistance.

KANE: (*Emotional.*) By themselves they may mean nothing. But add to the fact that the oldest daughter, Luranah, while away on tour, has twice been robbed in her hotel. No jewelry or funds were taken, but packets of papers and personal items were discovered either missing or destroyed.

HOLMES: Most intriguing.

KANE: Also, the youngest daughter, Amanda, was chased by highwaymen here in London, just last night!

HOLMES: Was the young lady injured?

KANE: No, she escaped unharmed. But at that exact moment the family home, Luranah Villa, was broken into and ransacked. If not for my early return, the thieves might have gotten away with—with, well, I am not truly certain what they came for in the first place! (*Pleading.*) I only know that too many tragedies have come at once. There are too many questions that defy answer. Mr. Holmes, it would appear that a conspiracy has been launched against the Aldridge family. A conspiracy . . . or a curse.

HOLMES: And what makes you surmise some arcane force is at work?

KANE: Because for several days Miss Amanda Aldridge has been visited by the spirit of her father. A spirit who speaks in the manner of the Bard of Avon and who wears the robes of Othello. Mr. Holmes, we need your help.

HOLMES: I can be of no assistance (*Rises.*) reclining here on the seat of ignorance. (*Energetic.*) Firsthand observations are in order. I have some affairs to settle this morning, and then I shall take the first afternoon train. I will send a telegram informing you of my exact arrival time.

KANE: (*Rising and shaking* HOLMES*'s hand.*) Thank you, thank you very much, sir. I assure you we are all at our wits end, and my . . . concern for Amanda grows more fearful with each passing day. Again, thank you and I shall meet you at the station myself. Good-bye, sir.

HOLMES: Till this afternoon.

(KANE *takes up his things and departs.* HOLMES *moves to the window to watch his new client exit onto the street below.*)

HOLMES: Well, Mr. Thomas Kane, one wonders just how good an actor you truly are. (*Turns to* WATSON'*s chair.*) It would appear, old friend, that once more . . . the game is afoot.

(HOLMES *turns away from the window to the bookshelf, takes down a large volume, and begins to scan it quickly for some particular bit of information. Lights fade out.*)

SCENE TWO

(KANE *exits 221-B and walks a few feet before being stopped by another black man. This is* ELISHA CARVER, *a man in his late forties. Their conversation is watched by a dignified English gentleman in his fifties.*)

CARVER: (*Anxious.*) There you are. Why'd you have me meet you in this neighborhood?

KANE: Because my business affairs brought me here. (*Smug.*)

CARVER: Business affairs? (*Serious.*) What are you up to now?

KANE: Setting wheels in motion. Bringing in another player for this little production. One with a star's caliber.

CARVER: Thomas, make some sense out of your talk.

KANE: I will in time, Eli, my friend. You'll just have to be patient. (*Pause.*) Trust me. (CARVER *seems puzzled.* KANE *brushes it off.*) Now then, did you bring the music charts?

CARVER: Yes, I brought them, but the cast wants to know, are you coming to rehearsal tonight so we can go over all this?

KANE: Not tonight, Eli. Too many important matters that need my attention.

CARVER: Thomas, our sponsor is expecting our show to be at its best. In two days we're going to be performing before an audience of prestige, the likes of which we have never known before.

KANE: And I assure you I will be at my best . . . as always. As to the expectations of our sponsor, it's best I keep my feelings to myself.

CARVER: Why? Sir Lawrence appears to have done you well. Putting you up at the Aldridge home and all.

KANE: (*Angry.*) I brought that about, not his lordship! And I've brought about something else also . . .

CARVER: Thomas. (*Concerned.*)

KANE: Never mind, Eli. Never mind.

CARVER: Well . . . I had better return to the theater to finish the rehearsal. Especially if I want to catch the coach back to the troupe's quarters.

KANE: (*Genuine.*) How are the living arrangements for you and the cast?

CARVER: (*Displeasure, resignation.*) 'Bout what you'd expect them to be . . . for us. No better, no worse. Don't you worry about that, Thomas. This time, it's something you don't have to experience. Good-bye, Thomas.

KANE: Eli . . . will make sense, very soon. I promise.

(*As* KANE *is about to depart, he is approached by the English gentleman,* JONATHAN BRAITHWAITE.)

BRAITHWAITE: Excuse me, sir, are you Mr. Thomas Kane?

KANE: (*Suspicious.*) Yes, I am.

BRAITHWAITE: Allow me to introduce myself. I am Jonathan Braithwaite, Esquire. I am with the firm of Wintwood, Woodmere, Westerly and Braithwaite, solicitors. My card. (*Offers his card and* KANE *takes it.*) Might I have a moment of your time?

KANE: I'm in a hurry right now. Could it wait until—

BRAITHWAITE: I am afraid not. It is a delicate matter, but one that requires almost immediate action.

KANE: Very well. What can I do for you?

BRAITHWAITE: My firm represents clients who wish us to . . . protect their interests. They feel these interests are being compromised by the existence of certain information, which is in the possession of certain acquaintances of yours. Should you prove helpful, they might prove helpful to you.

KANE: What information, and how do you mean "helpful"?

BRAITHWAITE: That I would be willing to discuss with you in a more private and comfortable atmosphere. Let us say, the pub just down the street.

KANE: Let's not, Mr. Braithwaite. I have the feeling your "clients" would not remain the only compromised party should we continue this discussion.

BRAITHWAITE: Mr. Kane, my firm is aware of your passable

standing in the theater, and of your . . . shall we say, zealous ambitions. What you desire to accomplish can best be brought about with the aid of money and friends in influential places. My clients could be such friends. All they require is information.

KANE: Certain information.

BRAITHWAITE: Exactly.

KANE: Again, I say thank you, but I think not. (*Turns to leave.*)

BRAITHWAITE: Mr. Kane, if you think you have already obtained the necessary influential contacts, in the family of Mr. Ira Aldridge, I assure you, you are mistaken. And if you feel you can . . . cement your future with them through a . . . romantic channel, I would say—

KANE: (*Contained anger.*) That you have said enough. I suggest (*Hands back card.*) that you, your firm, and your "clients" walk very carefully from this point on. I am not a man to be underestimated or threatened. (*Leaves.*)

BRAITHWAITE: (*Speaking in* MOREAU's *voice.*) Neither am I, my arrogant friend. (*Crushes card.*) Neither am I.

(*The* BRAITHWAITE *persona fades, and it is* PHILLIPE MOREAU *who walks away.*)

(*Lights fade out.*)

SCENE THREE

Luranah Villa, the Aldridge home, same day. The parlor. It is a proper representation of the upper-class British life-style. The ornate furniture includes a love seat, couch, writing table, and small wine cabinet. There is also a generous amount of bric-a-brac and such decorating the room and walls, along with two magnificent sabers on a shield mount, and awards (paper), certificates, letters from notables, and a large portrait of Ira Aldridge. The face in the portrait is identical to the ghost we saw in the Prologue. The portrait commands much of the upstage left wall, near a floor-to-ceiling bookcase. Next to that is the archway entrance to the room, and on the opposite side of the archway is another floor-to-ceiling bookcase (slightly wider.) Along the downstage right wall are French doors leading out to the grounds. AMANDA *is having a fitful sleep on the couch. She tosses back and forth, moaning and calling for her father.*

AMANDA: Father, don't kill him! Father! (*Sits up.*) Oh, my God! What—what if that man last night is dead . . . am I responsible?! (*Weepy.*) Oh, my God.

(*The doorbell sounds offstage, causing* AMANDA *to jump to her feet. She approaches the archway.*)

AMANDA: (*Calling out.*) Who is it?
PRITCHARD: (*Offstage.*) Sir Lawrence, my dear. I've come with a friend!
AMANDA: (*Relieved.*) Oh, Sir Lawrence. Just one moment.

(AMANDA *attempts to make herself presentable, then exits through the archway. Offstage we hear general conversation as she leads* PRITCHARD *and his companion back into the parlor.* AMANDA *enters first, followed by the* COUNTESS ALEXANDRA TAMBOVA *and* SIR LAWRENCE PRITCHARD. *The* COUNTESS *is a stunning woman in her early thirties. She is obviously very wealthy and carries herself with a strong seductive aura.* SIR LAWRENCE *is a handsome man in his late forties–early fifties, charismatic, commanding. He is paternally attentive to* AMANDA, *but we see a somewhat more sexual attitude when he is near the* COUNTESS. *The* COUNTESS *watches him with great interest.*)

PRITCHARD: I am pleased to introduce the Countess Alexandra Tambova, wife to the late Count Feodor Petrovich Tambov.
AMANDA: Countess, I am honored.
COUNTESS: Miss Aldridge, it is truly my pleasure to meet you. (*Moves toward the center of the room, still relating to* AMANDA *but eyeing the room with awe.*) Your home is most impressive, Miss Aldridge.
AMANDA: Thank you kindly.
PRITCHARD: The Countess and myself were present at your recital last night, and you were wonderful.
COUNTESS: It is with great sincerity that I confess my awe at your talents. Your voice was never as magnificent as at last night's concert. Breathtaking, my dear, breathtaking.
PRITCHARD: The Countess is absolutely right. We wanted to tell you so, but you left so quickly.
AMANDA: (*Tensing.*) I am so sorry to have missed you, but I suffered a migraine and simply had to come home.
PRITCHARD: Oh, so sorry to hear that, child.
COUNTESS: I hope you are feeling better and that we are not

intruding, but I felt I must make acquaintance of the gifted daughter . . . of Ira Aldridge.

PRITCHARD: I believe you will find Luranah's voice to be as melodious as Amanda's.

COUNTESS: Sir Lawrence, how rude to set gifts of siblings in comparison. (*To* AMANDA.) Forgive him, Miss Aldridge, he is sometimes forward beyond protocol.

AMANDA: Oh, that is quite all right, Countess. Luranah and I have no jealousies between us. I am forever in raptures over my sister's successes as my own.

PRITCHARD: She is abroad, on tour, is she not?

AMANDA: Yes. Her last post stated Stockholm as her next destination. I expect she is there at this very moment.

COUNTESS: Wonderful, my dear. I have not had the opportunity to see her perform.

AMANDA: I'm certain you will enjoy her talents. Sir Lawrence has attended numerous concerts given by this family. From my father to my brother Fre— (*Suddenly becomes very sad and quiet.*)

PRITCHARD: Steady there. We share your grief at the loss of young Frederick.

COUNTESS: Of course, I offer my most genuine remorse over this unfortunate event.

AMANDA: Thank you very much. Forgive me . . . at times . . .

PRITCHARD: We understand.

AMANDA: And now with all these other grotesque happenings . . . it would appear our lot has become a sour one. Because of these events, Mother has traveled to visit friends in Southampton.

COUNTESS: Sir Lawrence has told me of this terrible thing. It is fortunate you had benefit of a new acquaintance to aid you.

AMANDA: (*Studying the* COUNTESS.) Yes. Mr. Kane has indeed proven to be a true and valuable friend. If you have an opportunity, please take in his performance at the Surrey Theatre this week.

PRITCHARD: He is performing some of your father's material, is he not?

AMANDA: Some, but much of it is his own or taken from the likes of Shakespeare.

PRITCHARD: (*To the* COUNTESS.) Mr. Kane is a devotee of old Ira and came over from America with very much the same expectations. (*To* AMANDA *tenderly.*) He seems to have found a place for himself in both the theater . . . and in your family's heart.

AMANDA: I would say so. (*She smiles pleasantly.*)

PRITCHARD: One would hope that he will not supplant those of us whose affections and trust have been in long standing.

AMANDA: (*Realizing he is concerned.*) Oh, no, Sir Lawrence. You have been a friend and advisor to my mother since the passing of my father—

PRITCHARD: Since you were a child.

AMANDA: (*Warm smile.*) I know. Please don't fear for the loss of your place in our hearts.

COUNTESS: Miss Aldridge, I know of your father's tours through my country, but I have not seen his work, as I was but a child then. I have heard of the many honors bestowed upon him and wondered . . .

PRITCHARD: If she might see some of the awards and medals he received from her rulers.

COUNTESS: Perhaps even some references, letters and such, regarding his impressions of my homeland, where he was greatly loved by my people.

AMANDA: Well, I—

PRITCHARD: I realize this must seem a terrible imposition, but I assure you, the Countess is an ardent follower of your father's works and acquirements. It would give her much to share with the people of the Russias.

AMANDA: Well . . . I presume no harm can come of it, though I could only show the few things we have on hand (*Approaches the bookshelf.*), albums and the like. And these that we have mounted here, on the walls.

COUNTESS: (*Incredulous.*) These are not all of the things your father received?

AMANDA: No, much of father's things are in the hands of the bank, as Sir Lawrence will bear out.

PRITCHARD: Yes, yes, my dear. But they are in safe keeping, I assure you.

AMANDA: We do have a few things here you might enjoy. (*Approaches the* COUNTESS.) Mr. Kane was just commenting on—

(*Enter* HOLMES *and* KANE.)

KANE: Wait until you see them. These swords were a gift from Prime Minister Milczanowsky, on Ira's opening night, in Odessa! These same swords were crafted by—

AMANDA: Thomas! Where have you been? I missed you at lunch. (*Noticing* HOLMES.)

KANE: (*Taking in the room's occupants.*) I had to meet a . . . friend at the station. He—

(HOLMES *spots the* COUNTESS *and seems to recognize her. Quickly he interrupts* KANE.)

HOLMES: (*To* AMANDA.) I'm afraid I invited myself up after hearing with whom my old acquaintance was presently residing. Miss Aldridge, I am Sherlock Holmes, an admirer of your voice for all these five years.

AMANDA: *The* Sherlock Holmes?

HOLMES: Few would put false claim to such a notorious éclat as mine.

AMANDA: (*Disturbed.*) What a surprise. Thomas, you never mentioned you were friends with Mr. Holmes.

KANE: I was uncertain he would be able to visit and all . . . so I kept mum. (*Dismissing.*) At any rate, people never believe name droppers to be more than culprits seeking attention. Isn't that true, Sir Lawrence?

PRITCHARD: (*Annoyed.*) To be honest . . . I reserve my opinion for another day.

AMANDA: (*To Holmes.*) Please excuse me, I seem to have forgotten all good manners in the wake of your unexpected arrival. Mr. Holmes, the Countess Alexandra Tambova.

HOLMES: Countess. (*Appears to recognize her.*)

AMANDA: And Sir Lawrence Pritchard, a dear friend of the family.

PRITCHARD: Mr. Holmes.

HOLMES: Sir Lawrence. My brother Mycroft has mentioned you once or twice in his dissertations on the financial powers of England. (*Their eyes lock.*) I am honored.

KANE: I hope we aren't interrupting anything of . . . great importance.

AMANDA: Not at all. Countess Tambova, this is Thomas Kane.

(KANE *acknowledges the* COUNTESS, *who smiles warmly. He ignores* SIR LAWRENCE.)

HOLMES: I echo Mr. Kane's earlier remark and hope we have not intruded.

AMANDA: Certainly not. I was just about to show—

PRITCHARD: (*Checking his pocket watch.*) My goodness! (*To the* COUNTESS.) We completely forgot our appointment with Mr. Crosby. He is expecting us in one half hour and it will take just that amount of time to reach him.

AMANDA: Mr. Crosby?

PRITCHARD: Banking business, my dear. The Countess is extremely interested in ways to invest some of her late husband's securities. Countess . . .

COUNTESS: Of course, Sir Lawrence. I would hate to miss this most important . . . meeting.

PRITCHARD: We'll have to depart, Amanda.

AMANDA: Of course. Please feel free to call again. (*She guides them out of the parlor.*)

(*As they leave, the* COUNTESS's *eyes admire* HOLMES, PRITCHARD *is overly anxious to exit,* KANE *stares at the Englishman intensely, and* HOLMES *watches all without the slightest readable expression. Finally, only* HOLMES *and* KANE *are left in the room.*)

KANE: Sir Lawrence is a man of many accomplishments. A man of position, power, title . . . a man to be respected.

HOLMES: (*Looking through an album.*) No doubt.

KANE: I hate him.

HOLMES: Perceptibly so.

KANE: It's mutual.

HOLMES: Any speculation as to the reason why? (*He puts down the album.*)

KANE: No. Either he views me as a threat to Amanda's happiness and the well being of this family, or . . .

HOLMES: Or?

KANE: (*Holding back.*) I don't know. Considering the results, it matters little the cause.

HOLMES: (*Moving to the wall where the swords are mounted and looking at them.*) But it might have serious effects on your intentions towards Miss Aldridge. (*Looks to* KANE.) You two are involved in an *affaire de coeur,* are you not?

KANE: You assume much, Mr. Holmes.

HOLMES: Perhaps.

(AMANDA *enters.*)

AMANDA: This has surely been a day filled with unexpected pleasures. First, the Countess, now England's most renowned detective.

KANE: I hope Sir Lawrence did not leave so hastily because of our arrival.

AMANDA: (*Smiling warmly at* KANE.) Do you really? I suspect his companion is as much a devotée of mine as is Mr. Holmes. (*Seriously.*) Why have you come, sir? The truth, please.

HOLMES: Mr. Kane is of the impression that you and your family have fallen victim to some machination of notorious proportions. He fears you are in the utmost danger, and desires my intervention. The question arises, Miss Aldridge, do you feel this same threat?

AMANDA: (*Lowers her head, then looks at* HOLMES.) Yes, I do.

HOLMES: Do you wish my help?

AMANDA: That is another story, sir. I do sense a plot against us, but if it is from some thieves' quarters, then perhaps the police can ferret it out. (*Pause.*) If it is designed against us for reasons of extraction—race—then there is little you can do and even less the law could achieve. I am afraid our purse strings would be sorrier for the expenditure. (HOLMES *remains silent.*) We cannot afford you, sir.

(KANE *is about to speak when* HOLMES *signals him to hold.*)

HOLMES: If there is a crime in progress of the magnitude suspected, then the local constables will be at a loss for a point of origin, much less conclusion. Such has been my experience. I am their superior.

AMANDA: We can—

HOLMES: Should the true roots be buried in bigotry, then I would still fight it with all my strength. Miss Aldridge, I am what I am, not for the sake of the law but for the sake of justice. (*Pause.*) Allow me my pursuits, if only for a few days.

AMANDA: And what of your fee?

HOLMES: If I am successful, we will come to an arrangement amicable to both your family and myself. I give you my word.

(AMANDA *considers the offer.* KANE *is tense.* HOLMES *is calm but attentive.*)

AMANDA: Very well, Mr. Holmes. Your skills are certainly needed. What would you have me to do?

HOLMES: (*Energetic.*) First, make arrangements for me to stay here for a few nights. Whatever accommodations are available. Second, you will tell me all you can about your father's activities and experiences during his last year's travel. Third, and most important, you must give me your complete faith. I can do nothing without trust and cooperation. (*Looks to* KANE.) And the assistance of those closest to you. Are all these things possible?

AMANDA: (*Firm.*) Yes, Mr. Holmes.

KANE: With no reservations.

HOLMES: Excellent! Then to work. We have much to accomplish.

(*Blackout.*)

SCENE FOUR

Luranah Villa that night, the parlor. It is low lit. Into it enters AMANDA. *She seems apprehensive, fearful. She wears a nightgown and robe. She moves slowly to the center of the room, looks at her father's portrait, and waits. Suddenly it comes, an ethereal voice.*

GHOST: (*Voice over.*) Hear me, grave fathers! Noble tribunes, stay! For all my blood in Rome's great quarrel shed—

AMANDA: (*Seeking the source. Softly.*) Father? Father?

GHOST: For all the frosty nights that I have watch'd/For all these bitter tears, which now you see—

AMANDA: Father, where are you?

GHOST: (*Appearing out of the darkness.*) Filling the aged wrinkles in my cheeks: Be pitiful to my condemned sons/Whose souls are not corrupted as 'tis thought.

AMANDA: (*Seeing him.*) Father . . . why did you return? Did you kill that man last night? (*He is silent.*) Father?

GHOST: Be pitiful to my condemned sons . . .

AMANDA: (*Pause.*) Are you here because of Frederick and Daniel? (*He is silent.*) It's too late.

GHOST: O earth! I will befriend thee more with rain—

AMANDA: Daniel has been gone these nineteen years! (*Fearful.*) And Frederick is dead!

GHOST: And keep eternal springtime on thy face, so thou refuse to drink my dear sons' blood.

AMANDA: It is too late! Can you not see that?

GHOST: All my offenses that abroad you see/Are errors of the blood, none of the mind—

AMANDA: Father, it is too late. You are gone from us and us from you. You were never home . . . you can't come back now . . . You can't!

GHOST: (*Angry.*) Go get thee from my sight/Thou art exile, and thou must not stay—

AMANDA: (*Raising her voice.*) Father, I will not leave this house! It is all we have left!

GHOST: (*Advances slowly.*) Adder's fork, and blind worm's string/Lizard's leg, and howlet's wing./For a charm of pow'r-ful trouble:/Like a hell-broth, boil and bubble . . .

AMANDA: Go away, Father, you cannot stay!

GHOST: (*Retreating.*) By the pricking of my thumbs/Something wicked . . . this way comes!

AMANDA: Leave, Father! Please! (*Begins to scream.*) Go, there is no place for you here! (*The* GHOST *vanishes into the upstage darkness as* AMANDA *drops to her knees covering her eyes.*) Go! Go! Go!

(HOLMES *races in through the French doors. He is fully dressed and wearing an overcoat.*)

HOLMES: Miss Aldridge, Miss Aldridge! (*Kneels by her side.*) Steady, child, steady.

(AMANDA *begins crying against* HOLMES'S *shoulder.* KANE *runs in wearing a robe and pajamas. He turns up the lights.*)

KANE: Amanda! Mr. Holmes, what happened? (*Kneels with them.*)

HOLMES: It would be safe to assume she has seen the apparition, again. (*To* AMANDA.) Is that not true, Miss Aldridge?

AMANDA: (*Gaining control.*) Yes . . . yes, Mr. Holmes. Here is where it usually appears—

HOLMES: Usually?

AMANDA: Yes . . . I mean . . . each time I have seen him it has been in this room.

HOLMES: I see. Please continue.

AMANDA: I came down to confront him. To tell him to go find his rest. (*Pause.*) I could not make him understand.

HOLMES: In exactly what area did this visage appear? (AMANDA *points upstage.*) Mr. Kane, if you would see to the young lady . . . (KANE *takes* AMANDA *to the couch.* HOLMES *examines the room. He seems to detect an odor in the air.*) I

presume that his idioms were still those of Mr. Shakespeare?
(*Sniffs a vase of flowers on the desktop.*)

AMANDA: Passages my father had spoken many times.

KANE: Which ones in particular?

AMANDA: The last words he spoke were from Macbeth, "By the pricking of my thumbs/Something wicked this way comes."

HOLMES: (*Looking at* AMANDA.) You are familiar with the Bard? (*She nods yes.*) I see. (*Turns back to his studies, finding scuff marks on the floor.*) Curious . . . curious. (*Moves to the French doors.*) In this matter there is much which warrants my attention.

KANE: You have found something, Mr. Holmes?

HOLMES: Time will tell, sir. When did the ghost first appear, Miss Aldridge?

AMANDA: Eight days ago. Tuesday, to be precise.

HOLMES: And did anything of particular importance occur on Tuesday last?

AMANDA: Not that I recall.

HOLMES: Perhaps on the previous day?

AMANDA: (*Pause.*) There was a wire from Luranah. Oh yes, Sir Lawrence informed me of someone's interest in purchasing this house. I told him we had no intention of selling.

HOLMES: Anything else?

AMANDA: (*Pause.*) Thomas finally told me of his letters from Daniel, and of Daniel's wife and children in Australia. (*Softly.*) I'd like to see them someday.

HOLMES: (*Studying her.*) Regarding your experiences last night. You still maintain that you were chased, you escaped, and there was no other incident?

AMANDA: (*Pause.*) Yes, Mr. Holmes.

HOLMES: (*Thoughtful.*) I see. (*Smiling.*) I would suggest you seek the comforts of your bed, Miss Aldridge. You've had a nasty jostling, and a good night's sleep will do you wonders.

AMANDA: Perhaps you're right.

HOLMES: Of course.

AMANDA: Good night, gentlemen. (*Rises and exits.*)

HOLMES: Well, what do you make of it all?

KANE: I am at a loss for ideas. She obviously saw something or someone, but how to lay hands on the thing is quite out of my league.

HOLMES: Truly? When did your troupe first come to London?

KANE: (*Pause.*) Friday last. We opened that very night.

HOLMES: Twelve days . . . let us be honest, sir.

KANE: What do you mean?

HOLMES: (*Sharp.*) I would venture to say you have formed quite a few theories regarding this case, some of which might hold an element of validity.

KANE: You are mistaken. I have—

HOLMES: No respect for my intelligence, sir. You came to me expecting to enlist my services, no matter what the opposition. You even saved the report of the ghost for the last, to guarantee my interest. Tell me, Mr. Kane, what do you make of the ghost?

KANE: I assure you, Mr. Holmes, you do me too much credit! I have no clear comprehension of these events!

HOLMES: Rubbish! Either you anticipated a disturbance this night or you were party to it, for you have not been to bed. Your dressing gown is in perfect order. Your arrival upon the scene was only seconds after my own.

KANE: I am a light sleeper.

HOLMES: Then most certainly to the point of levitation! For I note your hair is also in perfect disposition.

KANE: I swear there is no malice in any of my actions or ambitions.

HOLMES: I should hope not, sir. For the price would not be worth the acquisition!

(*A loud explosion sounds offstage.* HOLMES *and* KANE *are shaken.*)

KANE: My god! That came from upstairs!

HOLMES: I'd say from the left wing of the house!

KANE: That's—that's where Amanda's room is!

(*They both dash off through the archway. Blackout.*)

SCENE FIVE

Luranah Villa the next day, the parlor. It is late morning. Present are HOLMES, KANE, *and* INSPECTOR LESTRADE *of Scotland Yard. They are in a deep discussion about the previous night's events.*

LESTRADE: And I'll say it again, Mr. Holmes, the bomb that blew that room to bits could have been chucked in through the window just as easy as set. And there ain't no way a provin' it, no matter.

HOLMES: On the contrary, Lestrade, the proof would be more than obvious had you spent time studying the premises. I must admit your lack of thoroughness was below even your usual limits.

LESTRADE: Here now! Let's not lose sight of who represents Her Majesty's official department of investigation here!

HOLMES: A point as sharp as a pin and carrying as much relative weight!

KANE: (*To* LESTRADE.) Why aren't you out pursuing the people responsible? They have to pay for this and pay dearly!

LESTRADE: (*Bitter.*) Don't you worry none. Scotland Yard knows how to handle its affairs without the benefit of your opinion . . . sir.

KANE: The way you handled the burglary and the assault attempt?

LESTRADE: (*Angry.*) We're still looking into the matter!

KANE: With a blind eye, I'll wager!

LESTRADE: Listen, you waistcoated heathen—

HOLMES: Lestrade! Kane! This line of thought will bring us no closer to our goal!

LESTRADE: Well, I'll be having none of his lip! I'll do my duty in me own time.

KANE: Your own time? Amanda may be—

AMANDA: (*Entering.*) Unable to rest for all this noise.

KANE: (*Moving to her side.*) I'm sorry. We became . . . involved in conversation. How are you? Here, please sit down. (*Leads her to the couch.*)

HOLMES: I concur, Miss Aldridge. Rest is the best cure for the shock you received.

AMANDA: Having nearly obtained the "final rest," I can only think of activity, to the most extreme degree. Moreover, were those not the very words that sent me upstairs last night? (*Smiles.*)

HOLMES: (*Returning her smile.*) Touché, madam.

LESTRADE: Well, I'm a busy man, so let's get on with just a coupla questions, if you don't mind . . . missy.

AMANDA: Not at all . . . Sergeant. (*She sits.*)

LESTRADE: Inspector, if you please. Now, you say you went upstairs, stopping outside your parents' room before proceedin' to your own, is that so?

AMANDA: Yes.

LESTRADE: Why?

AMANDA: I was thinking about my father's ghost and wondering if the room contained anything that might shed some light on the matter.

LESTRADE: (*Sardonic.*) Oh, yes, the spook, you claim you saw. (KANE *tenses.* HOLMES *looks coldly at* LESTRADE, *then moves over to the swords and removes one idly.*)

AMANDA: I did see the ghost, regrettably, as clear as I see you now. (KANE *smiles at* AMANDA.)

LESTRADE: Well, it's not likely your ghost had anything to do with the bomb, now, is it? So suppose we stick to the facts.

HOLMES: (*Sarcastically.*) Finally, a concrete course of thought. (*Takes down second sword, appearing absorbed.*)

LESTRADE: So after thinking about . . . the ghost, you continued on your way to your room.

AMANDA: Exactly.

LESTRADE: And just as you're a few feet from your door, the bomb goes off, correct?

AMANDA: Correct.

LESTRADE: Now, you told Mr. Holmes you heard no crash'n of glass or such before the explosion?

AMANDA: Also correct.

LESTRADE: But you admit your mind was on this "ghost" and your parents' room, so you might not have heard anything happening around you. Now, isn't that possible?

AMANDA: (*Pause.*) That is possible, sir.

LESTRADE: Well, that'll be all for now, I think.

(*The doorbell sounds.* HOLMES *replaces both swords.*)

KANE: I'll see to that—

AMANDA: Thomas, this is still my house and I am not an invalid.

KANE: (*Smiling.*) Very well, I stand corrected. May I accompany you?

(AMANDA *nods affirmatively and the two go to answer the door.*)

HOLMES: (*To* LESTRADE, *annoyed.*) Lestrade, you have gone out of your way to be particularly disrespectful to these people, and I cannot fathom why.

LESTRADE: Oh, come now, Mr. Holmes, their likes don't expect no better. Acting all high and mighty don't change the truth.

HOLMES: The truth? There are unexplored levels of your character that have escaped my awareness 'til now.

LESTRADE: I am a simple man with simple principles, Mr. Holmes. I ain't tryin' ta change the world. Things are what they are.

HOLMES: *Homo sum; humane nihil a me alienum puto.*

LESTRADE: (*Indignant.*) I beg your pardon?

HOLMES: "I am man; I count nothing human indifferent to me." Latin, Lestrade.·

LESTRADE: The language of the British empire is good enough for me, thank you.

(KANE *and* AMANDA *return, preceded by the* COUNTESS *and* PRITCHARD. *They are also accompanied by a constable.*)

KANE: Inspector, I believe he (*Indicating the constable.*) is for you.

CONSTABLE: (*Saluting.*) Rutledge, sir. The Yard thought I should come along to assist you.

LESTRADE: They did, did they? More than likely Gregson's doing.

CONSTABLE: I beg your pardon, sir?

LESTRADE: Never you mind. Just place yourself in that corner 'til I need you. (*Indicates·a corner near the bookcase and archway.* CONSTABLE *complies.*)

AMANDA: (*Introducing the* COUNTESS *and* PRICHARD.) Inspector, these are friends of mine who have come to offer their assistance—

LESTRADE: (*Sarcastically.*) Lovely. Now, as I was saying, I don't expect no more trouble to come your way. Seems to me you've got yourself a few hotheads who don't side with your . . . style of living. They'll probably leave you alone soon enough, but I'll give a look into the matter, see what I can see.

PRITCHARD: (*Strong.*) Well, I certainly hope you will put your best men on the job, as quickly as possible. I expect results from your investigation that will give this child some peace of mind.

LESTRADE: Oh, you do, do you?

PRITCHARD: Definitely, Inspector.

LESTRADE: Well, you just keep a cool head about you, my good sir, and I'll do the same.

PRITCHARD: Sir, are you putting me off?

LESTRADE: (*Sharp.*) If the braces fit.

PRITCHARD: (*Cold.*) Do you know who I am?

LESTRADE: No, sir, I don't, but to tell you the truth, I couldn't give a brass farthing for the knowledge. Scotland Yard will not be bullied by a—

HOLMES: Lestrade, you positively amaze me. In one single morning you managed to play the jester in three courts.

LESTRADE: (*Indignant.*) Mr. Holmes—

HOLMES: In Miss Aldridge's room, you failed to notice that the area most damaged by the explosion was by her vanity table. The wall next to that table was scorched as well as blasted, indicating its close proximity to the explosion.

LESTRADE: Well, how does that—

HOLMES: This area is some twenty feet from the nearest window. Obviously the bomb was not thrown, it was set. And it was set to injure or frighten, not to kill.

COUNTESS: Mr. Holmes, how can you be certain of this?

HOLMES: Because I found residuals of Nobel's Blasting Oil. It had been placed in the gaslight receptacle, where it heated and exploded.

KANE: Nobel's what?

HOLMES: Commonly known as nitroglycerin. Its properties are so unstable, no one would chance a precision explosion. Therefore, the villain set the trap while we were all here in the sitting room.

LESTRADE: Very fancy theorizing, Mr. Holmes.

HOLMES: Based on facts, Lestrade. Whoever our antagonist is, he is very proficient in his craft: a professional.

AMANDA: An assassin? But, Mr. Holmes, why would an assassin be sent to murder me?

HOLMES: I'm afraid it runs much deeper than you.

KANE: You believe all these hardships are not directed at the immediate family?

HOLMES: Without question. I have some knowledge of this household, and in particular Miss Aldridge and her career. (*To* AMANDA.) You have offended no one of consequence, I assure you. This problem stems from your father's travels.

KANE: But Ira had no enemies. Certainly no one who hated him so much that he would attack his family twenty years later.

PRITCHARD: I agree. Mr. Aldridge was well respected.

HOLMES: Nevertheless, it is to him we must look for a reason and a solution.

LESTRADE: Well, it's all a lot of horse flies to me.

HOLMES: No doubt. (*To* AMANDA.) In an early conversation, you told me of two incidents which occurred in Ira's last year. One, the robbery and assault on board the ship *Kusevi* on the Volga River, correct?

AMANDA: Yes, Mr. Holmes, I did say that.

HOLMES: Second, some nine months later, the curious rerouting of his luggage and freight by parties unknown, while he was returning from the city of Odessa. Before this, there were no incidents of such singular nature.

PRITCHARD: Mr. Holmes, those were two unfortunate but isolated occurrences that have no possible bearing on this present problem.

HOLMES: His travels through the Russian empire, at that particular time, have everything to do with this matter.

AMANDA: How?

HOLMES: Elements of revolt were strongly in play, and many people he knew, both common and royal, were heavily immersed in the game.

AMANDA: But my father was not politically inclined.

KANE: (*Slow realization.*) But he was a symbol. I begin to see your point, Mr. Holmes. Ira was a symbol. People from England to Russia, from Poland to Ireland, regarded him as such. And for the people in the Russias, people who had just been freed from serfdom . . . Ira—

HOLMES: Bravo, Mr. Kane! You show great possibilities. (*To the* COUNTESS.) Two political assassinations occurred while Mr. Aldridge was in your country. They occurred the night before his trip on the *Kusevi*. Both murders were kept secret for quite some time, and both revolved around a document of devastating political value.

COUNTESS: I fail to see your point . . . sir.

HOLMES: The exact nature of this document was kept under close security, but Mr. Aldridge knew both victims and had been in the company of one . . . only hours before he was killed.

LESTRADE: Ain't you stretchin' a bit far on this one, Mr. Holmes?

HOLMES: No, Lestrade, I am not. It was surmised that the assassination of Emperor Alexander II five years before, might have been connected with that very same article.

LESTRADE: I still don't—

HOLMES: Situations since have grown and intensified. Through contacts of my own, I am aware of several recent developments of great significance, for instance, a certain murder in Piccadilly the night before last. (*Looking at* AMANDA.) An unimportant little man named Vladmir Ninsky. (AMANDA *stiffens.*)

LESTRADE: What's so all-fired important 'bout him?

HOLMES: He was a courier, Lestrade. A Russian free-lancer.

KANE: But if he was a free-lance agent, then anyone could have desired his death.

HOLMES: Possibly. But the method used to kill him was quite professional, quick, and brutal. He was garroted.

LESTRADE: I suppose you know who killed him, eh?

HOLMES: I have an idea as to the killer's identity which links with this case quite logically. Yes, my friends, I would venture to say (*To the* COUNTESS *and* PRITCHARD.) there is a decidedly Russian flavor to this banquet of terror.

COUNTESS: Mr. Holmes! You offend me . . . and all the Russian people with such an accusation! I will hear no more of this! We go! (*Rises and moves to the archway.*)

PRITCHARD: Mr. Holmes, you must apologize at once.

HOLMES: For offending the Countess, I would quickly beg forgiveness, but for stating the conclusions on which I must act to save this household, I can say nothing. Even should it involve people of your acquaintance.

COUNTESS: Good day, Miss Aldridge.

PRITCHARD: Rest assured, I shall use all my prominence to guarantee your great discomfort should you carry this matter to the Countess or her family! (*To* LESTRADE.) And I'll not forget your attitude, either, Inspector Lestrade! (*He exits.*)

(AMANDA, *with a worried expression, follows* PRITCHARD *out.*)

LESTRADE: Now, just who does he think he is, carrying on like that to a member of Scot—

HOLMES: He is Sir Lawrence Pritchard.

LESTRADE: (*Shocked.*) Good Lord! Why didn't you say something beforehand?

HOLMES: You were doing so well on your own. Most certainly a jester in three courts.

LESTRADE: Well, I'll certainly be in the hole if he goes on like that to my superiors. A fine kettle of fish I've come into since I got on this case.

KANE: I hardly think your situation measures up to ours.

LESTRADE: I wouldn't expect you would. Fact is, you're probably feeling pretty important right about now.

KANE: Inspector, I am feeling pretty concerned. Amanda's life is hanging in the balance.

LESTRADE: I'm well aware of that, my good man, but I'll have you know hers is not the only case I have to investigate.

KANE: It is the only case that is important to me.

LESTRADE: The British public is not sitting in wait for your judgment of what is or isn't important. They are out there now stealin' and starvin', millin' and murderin', all without the slightest thought for how you look down on them from your high horse!

KANE: Are you speaking about me, Inspector, or about Sir Lawrence? You see, I don't judge the British public, common or otherwise, by the nature of certain individuals I meet. If I did, my respect for your country would have lowered considerably in just the past few days!

LESTRADE: Well, I never!

KANE: The benefit of having been at the bottom is that you can recognize your peers and their problems. Once you start to climb up out of it, you hold onto the memories of those times, so that you never look down on anyone less fortunate. No matter where you meet him.

(LESTRADE *is visibly affected by* KANE's *words. Not changed, but moved to thought. He hastens to change the subject.*)

LESTRADE: Well, I'm still a busy man, with no time to dawdle. I'll have another look around (*To* HOLMES.) upstairs, then be on my way. (*To the* CONSTABLE.) We'll be leaving just as soon as I return.

CONSTABLE: Very well, sir.

(LESTRADE *looks at* HOLMES, *who appears preoccupied with a large book he has removed from a shelf near the* CONSTABLE. LESTRADE *then moves through the doorway, passing* AMANDA *as she enters.*)

AMANDA: Mr. Holmes (*He moves to her, center stage.*) I am afraid Sir Lawrence and his companion have nothing but the deepest dislike for you. Your statement was most inflammatory.

KANE: I'm sure Sir Lawrence will survive. (*Moves to the French doors, his back to* AMANDA.)

HOLMES: I am greatly sorry to cause you any embarrassment, but I stated only what I believe to be the truth.

AMANDA: And do you believe that the death of Mr. Ninsky is really a part of all this?

HOLMES: I do. (*Moving her away from the* CONSTABLE.) And I know you met with him that very night.

AMANDA: How do you know that, sir?

HOLMES: I examined the body and found traces of a woman's facial makeup on one hand. At the location of his death, I found scuff marks from a woman's heel, and a bit of torn fabric on the display case from a lady's cloak similar to the one in your wardrobe.

AMANDA: I didn't kill him.

HOLMES: I am quite certain of that, young lady, but we will speak of this later. Now I must know if you wish me to continue in this matter.

AMANDA: Are you still acting in the best interests of my family?

HOLMES: Unquestionably.

AMANDA: Then do what you must.

HOLMES: That I shall. (*Moving back to the* CONSTABLE.) Constable.

CONSTABLE: Yes, sir.

HOLMES: Did you come straight from the Yard?

CONSTABLE: (*Seeming uneasy.*) Yes, sir.

HOLMES: I see. Did you muster out first?

CONSTABLE: (*Pause.*) Of course, sir.

HOLMES: I see. Very good. (*Appearing to lose interest, until.*) Although I was curious as to how you obtained that residue on your trouser cuff.

CONSTABLE: (*Looking down.*) Did I, sir?

HOLMES: Yes, right there. Just about your nonregulation boots!

(*The* CONSTABLE *makes the first move. Swiftly a knife slips from his sleeve to his right hand as he swings it upward toward* HOLMES's *heart. The detective blocks the first thrust, using the large clipping album he holds in his hands. He then flips the album away, disarming the* CONSTABLE, *who follows through with a savage kick to the detective's chest.* HOLMES *falls back across the writing table. The* CONSTABLE *makes a run for the archway, but he is grabbed by* KANE, *who spins him around, preparing to land a blow. The blow is expertly blocked and countered with two sharp rabbit punches and a right cross to* KANE's *face. As* KANE *goes down,* HOLMES *rises and moves in, and* AMANDA *runs to* KANE's *side, distracting the assailant.*

HOLMES *exhibits his boxing skills, momentarily catching the assailant off guard and driving him away from the archway and into the center of the room. Just as it appears the* CONSTABLE *will go down, he bends over at the waist and snaps a savage kick to* HOLMES'S *head, sending him sprawling to the floor.* AMANDA *leaps upon the man with a nearby vase. The man takes the blow on his arm, then delivers three blows to her face, knocking her down.* KANE *tackles the deadly* CONSTABLE, *taking them both over a nearby couch, but the man is up almost instantly and strikes two side hand blows across* KANE'S *neck as he tries to rise.* KANE *drops as* HOLMES *charges. From somewhere in his clothes the man draws forth a handful of powder and throws it into the detective's face.* HOLMES *is blinded. A silken cord suddenly appears in the man's hands. He springs onto* HOLMES, *coils the cord around his throat, and begins to strangle him viciously. Blinded and battered, the detective can put up little fight.* AMANDA *tries to crawl to his aid, but she is still stunned.* KANE *is out. As* HOLMES'S *struggle weakens,* LESTRADE *enters. At first he is caught flat-footed, but then swiftly draws his gun from a coat pocket.*)

LESTRADE: Hold on there! Stop!

(*The man releases his grip on* HOLMES *and quickly dashes out the French doors just as* LESTRADE *fires. The shot misses and* LESTRADE *gives chase, out the doors, firing several more shots.* AMANDA *reaches* HOLMES. *He is coughing and gagging but coming around.* KANE *moans as he drags himself up. Seeing that* HOLMES *is recovering,* AMANDA *stumbles over to* KANE'S *side.* HOLMES *staggers to his feet as* LESTRADE *returns.*)

LESTRADE: He got clean away! Damn his hide, he moves fast as a blinkin' gazelle! (*Helps* HOLMES *to a chair.*) What 'appened 'ere? Who was he?

HOLMES: (*Still catching his breath.*) The man . . . who killed, Ninsky . . . who set last night's explosion . . . and is responsible . . . for the assassination of hundreds. Phillipe Moreau. (LESTRADE *is visibly stunned.*) (*Anger.*) The die is cast, Lestrade. I swear, I'll run him down . . . I'll see him hanged.

(*Blackout.*)

ACT TWO

SCENE ONE

The London home of PRITCHARD. *Same day, three hours later. We are in the den, a conservative-looking room with books, desk (containing a blotter, lamp, and such), and several cushioned chairs. The daylight filters in through a small window (upstage right).* PRITCHARD *and the* COUNTESS *enter, following by* WINTERS, *the elderly butler.* WINTERS *takes their coats and scarves as they move into the room.*

COUNTESS: It could not have been better, darling. (*Moves seductively close to him.*) Thank you for a most delicious repast.

PRITCHARD: (*Puts his arms around her, then notices* WINTERS.) That will be all, Winters.

WINTERS: Very good, sir.

(*As soon as* WINTERS *exits,* PRITCHARD *turns his full passions loose on the* COUNTESS. *She responds in kind. It is a heated embrace and kiss, which the* COUNTESS *finally breaks.*)

COUNTESS: Please . . . you take such liberties, Lawrence.

PRITCHARD: Really, my dear. We need not pretend here in my own home. You have been mine since that first night in Kiev.

COUNTESS: (*Coy.*) Have I?

PRITCHARD: Of course. I am a man accustomed to having my own way. With you it was no different.

COUNTESS: No difference at all? (*Kisses him hard.*)

PRITCHARD: (*Breathless.*) Damn you.

COUNTESS: (*Teasing kiss.*) Then . . . there is some difference. (*Slipping out of the embrace.*) It was not just your desire for the list that brought us together. (*Moves away slowly.*)

PRITCHARD: (*Moving after her.*) In the beginning . . . perhaps. But now—

COUNTESS: Now you want only me. (*Tease.*)

PRITCHARD: Now I want both. And it is both I shall have. (*Another passionate kiss.*)

COUNTESS: Please do not forget the list is my goal as well. Its value to my family has been marked in blood. (*Goes to kiss him again.*)

PRITCHARD: (*Avoiding the kiss and moving away, smiling.*) Blood has not the value of money, my dear.

COUNTESS: (*Annoyed.*) When it is the blood of one's father, there is no higher value.

PRITCHARD: Your affection for your father appears as eternal as Amanda's. Are you also visited by ghosts?

COUNTESS: No. (*Moving close to him.*) But I would welcome one if he would lead me to the document. (*Begins kissing him softly.*) It is somewhere in that house . . . in Luranah Villa . . . and I want it.

PRITCHARD: (*Responding to her kisses.*) All is going according to plan, never fear . . . I will have it soon. Until then . . . allow me my moments of . . . distraction. (*The doorbell rings.*) Winters will see to it . . . and send them away.

(*Another passionate kiss. Suddenly we hear the voice of* HOLMES *moving toward the den's doorway.* WINTERS *is trying to delay him.*)

WINTERS: (*Offstage.*) But sir, the master is—

HOLMES: (*Offstage.*) I will take full responsibility for this interruption. (*Entering the den.*) Good day, Sir Lawrence, Countess. I beg your pardon for this unheralded visit, but I felt I must make amends for this morning's misunderstanding.

PRITCHARD: Mr. Holmes, this is most irregular!

HOLMES: Quite. (*To the* COUNTESS, *charming.*) Yet most urgent. I know of your anger and wish only to set things as they should be. Please.

COUNTESS: (*Coy.*) Sir Lawrence, in my country we are understanding in such matters. Allow Mr. Holmes his moment to . . . make amends.

HOLMES: Thank you ever so. (*Making himself comfortable.*) Forgive my directness this morning, but the life of Miss Aldridge is in some considerable danger. I'm certain you can appreciate my concern, Sir Lawrence.

PRITCHARD: (*Angry.*) Well, I—

COUNTESS: Do you truly feel you can prevent further harm from coming to that lovely young woman?

HOLMES: I shall give it my best efforts, Countess Tambova, though . . . I admit to some degree of apprehension.

PRITCHARD: (*Tense but curious.*) You believe these attacks will continue.

HOLMES: Without a doubt, Sir Lawrence. Without a doubt.

(*Considerable noise is heard from offstage. Children's voices shout at* WINTERS.)

PRITCHARD: What the blazes could that be?

HOLMES: (*Calm.*) It would seem your manservant has encountered an undesirable or two.

(*There is a loud crash, then the voices rise in anger.*)

PRITCHARD: Good gracious! Excuse me, Countess.

(PRITCHARD *exits and* HOLMES *quickly moves to the* COUNTESS.)

HOLMES: There is little time, Countess. This interruption will last but a moment.

COUNTESS: I'm afraid I do not . . . (*Realization.*) You are responsible for this disturbance? (*Smiles.*)

HOLMES: Yes. My street urchins will not linger long. Countess, I know who you are and I believe I know what it is you seek.

COUNTESS: I do not know what you mean.

HOLMES: You are the daughter of the late Grand Duke Nicholas Rurik Katzig.

COUNTESS: That is true, but—

HOLMES: Who was one of the leaders of a secret society of nobles, known as the Circle. They were responsible for a devastating plot to crush Russia's revolutionary movement.

COUNTESS: (*Intense.*) Lies!

HOLMES: And he was murdered, August of 1867, by the very same men he conspired with.

COUNTESS: (*Angry.*) Mr. Holmes, you are greatly mistaken.

HOLMES: Please, my good woman! There is no time for deception. Your father and his associates fabricated a lethal document. Next they falsified the signatures of some of Europe's most influential literary and political figures. And finally, affixed those signatures to that document, which sanctioned, by murder if necessary, the overthrow of the Russian empire!

Their sole purpose was to unite the existing rulers in a common bond of distrust. Distrust of anyone who had spoken out in favor of the people's rule.

COUNTESS: (*Cold.*) You seem to know much of this matter.

HOLMES: I do, Countess. And it is frightfully important that you cease your pursuit of this falsified document.

COUNTESS: (*Pause.*) Why, Mr. Holmes?

HOLMES: Because lives are at stake, madam! And not simply the Aldridge family.

COUNTESS: (*Coy.*) You fear I will be attacked by ruffians, Mr. Holmes?

HOLMES: There is an assassin in the game, and his aim is identical to yours, only at a much higher price.

COUNTESS: (*Still coy.*) How can you be certain I did not send the assassin?

HOLMES: I am certain only of the gravity of this situation. It is imperative that you realize what deadly thing you are playing in.

COUNTESS: (*Moving toward* HOLMES.) I am capable of handling my own . . . affairs, Mr. Holmes.

HOLMES: (*Unmoved.*) Your affairs, quite likely, madame. But the affairs of two nations and the lives of millions . . . of that I doubt even the merits of your charms.

COUNTESS: You doubt much, Mr. Holmes.

HOLMES: That document could create chaos and bloodshed of frightful proportions. Consider wisely your next action. I am honor bound to prevent such destruction. Good day.

(HOLMES *grabs his coat and hat, and as he exits, he brushes past* PRITCHARD.)

PRITCHARD: Leaving, Mr. Holmes?

HOLMES: I am. I will say good-bye, Sir Lawrence, but I fear we shall certainly meet again. (*He exits.*)

PRITCHARD: What did he have to say? (*No answer.*) Countess? (*No answer.*) (*He crosses to her.*) What was his reason for coming here?

COUNTESS: (*Bitter.*) Mr. Holmes has declared himself my adversary and my better. We shall see.

PRITCHARD: You don't truly believe you can counter that detective on your own?

COUNTESS: That document must come into my control and mine alone.

PRITCHARD: I think not, my darling. That list is far too valuable . . . to me. Blackmail is a lucrative business.

COUNTESS: It belongs to me. It was created by my father at a time when he was influenced by men such as you. And for his efforts—

PRITCHARD: (*Sardonic.*) He was killed. And now, twenty years later, you have taken up the torch. Well, my dear, it's a new and deadlier game. The people on that document, literary giants of several countries, saints of the theater, a prime minister of England, a czar, politicos of high status, all would be in a precarious position should the list be revealed.

COUNTESS: (*Quiet distaste.*) You would seek payment?

PRITCHARD: Much more than that. If the secret is kept, their present positions are secure. But if revealed . . . books would be burned by the hundreds, the marriage plans of two royal houses would fall. Diplomatic tensions, held in check by one man, would explode between three great countries and Europe would find itself in the midst of a continental war!

COUNTESS: (*Quiet.*) Lawrence, you would let this happen?

PRITCHARD: No, no, my dear. All this destruction could be easily averted by their simple compliance with my demands . . . whatever they may be.

COUNTESS: For what reason would you do this?

PRITCHARD: Power. Through that list I would have Europe's leaders in my hands, and through them, Europe.

COUNTESS: The list is mine and mine alone! I will have it for my needs and my purposes!

PRITCHARD: We will see about that, my la—

COUNTESS: (*Angry.*) There is nothing to see! Nothing to discuss! I will have it with or without your help, for my family—

PRITCHARD: (*Swiftly crosses to her and grabs her by the arms.*) Do not play the outraged royalist with me, Alexandra! And do not think your limited bed passions are irreplaceable, for I buy and sell women like you by the hundreds!

(*She breaks free of his grip and slaps him across the face.* PRITCHARD *returns the slap with vicious power, then grabs her arms again.*)

PRITCHARD: (*Cold and menacing.*) Listen to me. The Aldridge family will fall; Sherlock Holmes will fall; and so will you, my dear . . . if you should cross me. Nothing will stand in my way now. Nothing. (*A frightening expression crosses his face.*) For, you see, I always, always get what I want. (*With brutal force* PRITCHARD *tears her dress top and begins to force her to the floor. She struggles without much effect.*)

(*Fade out.*)

SCENE TWO

Outside the Surrey Theatre, same day, late evening. HOLMES *stands with a bent, old sailor.* HOLMES *wears his famous plaid greatcoat and deerstalker. The sailor wears a peacoat with upturned collar and woolen cap. It is obviously cold. There are some signs of the upcoming Christmas holidays, in the guise of street decorations and perhaps a passerby or two wishing each other season's greetings.* HOLMES *waits until they are alone before he speaks.*

HOLMES: And you are certain of his departure and arrival dates?

PIKER: You can bet your last fiver on it, Mr. Holmes. Got it from a boatswain off the *Trafalgar Horn*, the very ship he come offa.

HOLMES: Excellent. Very nicely done, Piker. It would appear I can always depend on you.

PIKER: Don't think nothing of it, sir. I ain't forgot what ya done for me back when.

HOLMES: (*Smiling.*) No, I don't imagine you have. How is your wife, Piker?

PIKER: (*Visibly embarrassed.*) Fit as can be, sir. Loves me like the day we was first wed . . . uh, well, just about as much, I gather.

HOLMES: I see she still bats you about.

PIKER: No, she don't, sir. Honest.

HOLMES: Come now, old fellow. She clouted you just this afternoon, I'd say. There's a rather ugly but fresh bruise peeking out from beneath your cap.

PIKER: (*Nervous smile.*) Walked into a door, that's all, sir.

HOLMES: No, no, Piker. The baking flour identifies, for all the world to see, that the cause of the wound was a distressed wife's favorite weapon, a rolling pin.

PIKER: (*Quickly wiping his face, touching the wound, and causing himself to wince from the pain.*) What flour, sir. Oh, caw!

HOLMES: (*Amused.*) You missed a bit on your left eyebrow.

PIKER: (*Surrendering.*) I suppose there's no foolin' you, Mr.

Holmes. I guess I deserves it, all right. Still and all, if it hadn't been for you clearin' me of that murder charge—

HOLMES: By proving you were with another woman at the time.

PIKER: Uh, right you are, sir. Well, I'm still grateful. If ya hadn't cleared me, I wouldn't be here for her . . . (*Losing his enthusiasm as he gingerly touches the bruise.*) to be . . . battin' about, sir.

HOLMES: (*Still amused.*) A very accommodating way of viewing things, I must say.

PIKER: Thank you, sir.

HOLMES: Now, off you go and see if you can be as successful acquiring the balance of the information I requested. (*Hands* PIKER *money.*)

PIKER: All right, sir. He'll be a bit harder ta track than the first gent, but don't you worry none. I'll have it for ya by midnight tonight.

HOLMES: Piker.

PIKER: Yes, sir?

HOLMES: (*Concerned.*) Keep a careful watch. This is a very deadly business, I promise you.

PIKER: Don't you worry none, Mr. Holmes . . . (*Crafty.*) Eyes in the back of me head, I have. Nothin' can happen, 'cause nothin' can sneak up on me, so nothin' can harm me.

HOLMES: (*Indicating the bruise on* PIKER's *head.*) Nothing, old fellow?

PIKER: (*Gingerly touching the bruise.*) I see your point, sir. I'll be careful. Midnight it is. (*Exits singing.*)

(HOLMES *turns and looks at the theater's marquee. It carries a poster announcing an evening's entertainment by talented Negro performers.* KANE's *name is high on the billing.*)

HOLMES: Now, Mr. Kane, let us see how good an actor you truly are.

(HOLMES *enters the theater. A moment later, there is movement in a nearby shadowy doorway. Someone has been watching* HOLMES. *The figure moves offstage as the lights fade out.*)

SCENE THREE

The dressing room of Thomas Kane. It is sparse, drab, but neat. In the background we can hear applause dying down and a music hall fanfare concluding. HOLMES *stands before the makeup table, his pipe in hand. His coat and hat are draped on a standing coat rack, which also contains* KANE'S *street attire.* HOLMES *is fingering the makeup items and a tintype of* AMANDA *as* KANE *enters.* KANE *is wearing a white tuxedo with a red carnation in the lapel. He is surprised to see* HOLMES.

KANE: Mr. Holmes! Were you in the audience this evening?

HOLMES: For your portion of the performance, yes. I am pleased to say you are a man of certain raw but exceptional talent.

KANE: Thank you, Mr. Holmes . . . I think. (*Closes the door.*) Make yourself comfortable. (*Crosses to the makeup table and sits down.*)

HOLMES: Thank you. (*Takes a seat next to* KANE.) I am finding my exposure to this case an illuminating experience. It is not often I find myself traveling in theatrical circles.

KANE: Not since 1879, at any rate?

HOLMES: You know of my brief period on the stage?

KANE: Brief but notable. You were in New York in a production of . . . that Scottish play (HOLMES *and* KANE *exchange smiles.* KANE *begins to remove his makeup, tie, jacket, and shirt collar.*), billed as Mr. William Escot. It was a good evening, so I was told.

HOLMES: Did that evening have any bearing on your seeking me here in London?

KANE: Some. (*Continuing to clean up.*) You were involved in several mysteries while on tour in America. Your skills were recognized, and you were considered a man of many levels.

HOLMES: Perhaps no more than you are, Mr. Kane.

KANE: (*Realizes* HOLMES *is leading up to something and therefore becomes uncomfortable.*) Perhaps. (*Pause.*) Has any more come of this Russian plot you uncovered?

HOLMES: The intrigue grows deeper. And yet, I expect I will cut through it in time.

KANE: Well, if there is anything I can do to be of help to Amanda, I—

HOLMES: You can be frank with me, Mr. Kane.

KANE: (*Stunned.*) I have been earnest with you. You are aware of all my knowledge and concerns in this matter.

HOLMES: I am aware of many things, Mr. Kane. Unhappily, few of them were encompassed in your narrative. You told me one of Daniel's children informéd you of his disappearance. You did not say you were there in Australia when he vanished.

(KANE *is caught speechless. He sits rigid and silent. Suddenly the door opens and a black man enters. He is of medium build and wearing a black tuxedo with a red carnation in his lapel. He is in his early forties, but he appears slightly older due to stress and anxiety. He is* ELISHA CARVER.)

CARVER: Tom, I have to talk to— (*Spots* HOLMES.) Oh, I'm sorry. I didn't know you had company.
KANE: (*Rallies.*) Eli! No, no, don't worry. Come right in and meet Mr. Sherlock Holmes. Mr. Holmes, Elisha Carver.
HOLMES: Mr. Carver. (*Quickly extends his hand.*)
CARVER: (*Surprised.*) Sherlock Holmes. (*Shakes* HOLMES's *hand with some awkwardness.*) It's a pleasure to meet you, sir.
HOLMES: I enjoyed your part in Mr. Kane's last scene. Your articulation was most impressive.
CARVER: Thank you. It's a product of my years with the African Theatre in New York.
KANE: That's where Eli and I both received our basic training, you might say.
HOLMES: Oh? Were you and Mr. Carver students at the same time?
CARVER: No. (*Pause.*) Tom came along years after I had joined. But he caught on quickly and it seemed he always would manage to get a healthy role in our productions.
KANE: It was Eli who gave me most of my instruction. Always there to guide me.
HOLMES: I see.
CARVER: Well, if you don't mind, I'll come back and talk to you later, Tom.
KANE: Are you sure, Eli? You're really not interrupting.
CARVER: No, that's quite all right. I'll see you later. It was nice meeting you, Mr. Holmes. (*Exits quickly.*)
HOLMES: (*Matter-of-factly.*) He wears a rather floral-scented toilet water, does he not?
KANE: (*Confused.*) Excuse me? I don't understand the question.
HOLMES: No matter, my good sir. To more important things.

(*Intense, he moves close to* KANE.) Amanda Aldridge, her father, the ghost, Daniel's disappearance, and your presence in Scarborough two days after the death of Frederick Aldridge, her brother! What game do you play?

(KANE's *anger grows. He rises to confront* HOLMES.)

KANE: I am the one who brought you into this case!

HOLMES: It would not be the first time that my client proved to be the culprit!

KANE: Do you think I would do anything to harm that family?

HOLMES: Sir, I would put little or nothing past you in your pursuit of glory, in your climb to eclipse Ira's distinction!

KANE: (*Enraged.*) I am a damn good actor, and I deserve what recognition I have gained!

HOLMES: At what price, Mr. Kane?

KANE: Certainly not at the cost of my dignity!

HOLMES: Or the affections of a trusting soul? Your placement and timing within this montage of events has been uncanny. Your motives therefore become quite suspect!

KANE: My motives are more than honorable! And my affections for Amanda . . . are very genuine.

HOLMES: Then why did you not tell me immediately of your presence in Australia?

KANE: (*Slumps into his chair.*) I don't know.

HOLMES: (*Studies* KANE *for a moment.*) It was because you had changed your course, Mr. Kane. Your intentions toward this family had taken a turn. (KANE *looks up at* HOLMES. *His expression denotes the truth in what* HOLMES *has surmised.*) What part did you play in Daniel's disappearance?

KANE: (*Quiet but intense.*) None, I swear it. I had met Daniel while on tour with the African Theatre. We were performing for a number of towns through certain parts of Australia. He came to see us whenever he could. He knew his father had once been a member, before he had left for England.

HOLMES: Was Daniel well when you met him?

KANE: Yes.

HOLMES: Was he in any danger?

KANE: No, not then, at any rate. He was a simple schoolteacher, he was married and had three children.

HOLMES: Did he seem nervous or agitated?

KANE: He seemed . . . defeated. Coming to see the troupe seemed to lift his spirits.

HOLMES: You became friends. You talked about his father and

he began to reveal to you the condition and resources of the family. (KANE *looks down at the floor, and* HOLMES *quickly steals a glance at his pocket watch.*)

KANE: What little he knew. He had not communicated with them since the year of his father's death.

HOLMES: (*Crossing downstage right to the opposite side of* KANE's *dressing table.* KANE *turns to face* HOLMES, *placing his back to the doorway.*) Did he give reason for his silence?

(*The door opens slowly but only partway.* HOLMES *does not appear to notice, and we cannot see who is on the other side.*)

KANE: His stepmother, the present Mrs. Aldridge. They simply could not come to terms with each other . . .

HOLMES: Go on, Mr. Kane.

(*The door opens another inch or two, and again* HOLMES *doesn't appear to notice.*)

KANE: He said, my father was never home . . . always on tour, always on stage, always. (*Seems to drift away for a moment. When he speaks again, it is as if he is* DANIEL.) My father loved and was loved by his public. They adorned him with their adoration, and he could feel it, live it every performance. The stage was his body, the plays his heart, and the cheering crowds his life's blood. (*Pauses briefly, still portraying* DANIEL *as the door opens enough to admit* AMANDA. *She quietly stands in the doorway.*) He received our love . . . his children's love . . . from a distance. We touched him through our letters, and when he came home, we hailed him with our embraces. (*Pause.*) But he was so seldom home.

(HOLMES *spies* AMANDA *at the door. There is no sign of surprise in his action. He turns his gaze to* KANE.)

HOLMES: (*Quietly.*) Having been an orphan, Mr. Kane, what did these words mean to you?

KANE: (*Coming out of his reverie.*) I was a good child, a good boy, Mr. Holmes . . . and it got me nothing. (*With great earnestness.*) I'm a good actor, but where was that going to take me if I was without people of influence to help me? Without— (*Turns to see* AMANDA *standing there. He is stunned and looks back and forth between* HOLMES *and*

AMANDA. *Finally,* AMANDA *moves toward him. She stops only a few feet away.*) I . . . Amanda . . .

AMANDA: (*Proud, stern.*) We were to be your backers, your benevolent benefactors? Were we also to be your porters and footmen? (*Her anger builds as she moves closer to him.*) Were we to bear your slippers and pipe, or simply watch and await some meager sign of benediction?

KANE: Amanda, you don't understand. I never meant—

AMANDA: Never meant what, Mr. Thomas Kane? Never meant any harm? How Christian of you!

KANE: You do not understand! You cannot possibly comprehend what it was like for me! (*Moves to her, but she turns and walks away a few steps.*) I was not as fortunate as your father.

AMANDA: (*Whirling to face* KANE.) Fortunate?

KANE: Yes, fortunate! He had a father and a mother, and a real home—

AMANDA: And when he came to Europe, he had nothing and no one to call upon! And there had been no man before him to pave the way. Yet he worked hard, and he took each painful step one at a time, and he stamped his mark on the stages across Europe, not on the backs of his intimates.

KANE: (*Controlled, earnest.*) And for this, his children loved him. For this, I worshiped and envied him. For this, I craved. (*Takes a step toward her.*) But we are not all conquerors, Amanda. Some of us are not that strong. (HOLMES *stands quietly watching.* AMANDA *looks at him, then back at* KANE.) I came here with a parasitic plan, yes, but I changed . . . I fell in love.

AMANDA: (*Quietly angry.*) With me, Thomas?

KANE: Yes, with you. Also . . . with the bond, the living essence, of what each of you means to the other. I never knew that bond until I came here.

(*There is a long silence as* AMANDA *and* KANE *look at each other.* AMANDA *is still angry, hurt, but she is trying to see into* KANE'S *eyes.* HOLMES *fingers his pipe for a moment, then takes a step toward the couple.*)

HOLMES: (*With genuine concern.*) I am sorry, but this encounter was most compulsory.

KANE: (*Turning to* HOLMES.) You knew she would be here.

AMANDA: Mr. Holmes sent me a cable earlier this evening. It instructed me to come here at this precise hour—

HOLMES: And to make your entrance stealthfully.

KANE: Did you at any time consider that your methods might draw a painful conclusion?

HOLMES: From my experience, I am aware of the benefits as well as the detriments of the truth, Mr. Kane. Too often I am forced to disregard the means by which I gain the results.

KANE: What now, Mr. Holmes?

HOLMES: Now . . . now I would suggest you change into your street attire as quickly as possible, and join Miss Aldridge and myself for a bit of cold supper and Guinness at the small pub just down the street. (KANE *looks at* AMANDA, *who remains quiet. He turns back to* HOLMES.) I feel there is still much to be discussed, and I believe a lighter atmosphere would be better suited. (*Begins donning his coat.*)

KANE: (*Resolved.*) Very well. I'll join you there in five or ten minutes.

HOLMES: Splendid. Shall we depart, Miss Aldridge? (*Takes his hat from the rack and motions for* AMANDA *as he opens the door.*) We will see you shortly. (AMANDA *steps through the door, but* HOLMES *turns back to* KANE.) By the way, are you proficient with a blow gun, Mr. Kane?

KANE: (*Shocked.*) No . . . no, I am not proficient. I don't even have one.

HOLMES: (*Thoughtful.*) I see . . . no matter. Five to ten minutes, then, at the pub.

(HOLMES *closes the door behind himself.* KANE *appears nervous as he quickly grabs his street clothing and begins changing rapidly.*)

(*Lights fade out.*)

SCENE FOUR

The street outside the Surrey Theatre, night. HOLMES *and* AMANDA *exit the front of the building.* HOLMES *attempts to light his pipe, nonchalantly scanning the night.*

HOLMES: A crisp night indeed, Miss Aldrigde.

AMANDA: (*Solemn.*) There appears to be some sense of the holiday to come. There were carolers here as I—

(HOLMES *suddenly springs at* AMANDA, *knocking her back inside the theater doorway.*)

HOLMES: Look out, Miss Aldridge!

(*There is a strange swish. Silence. After a moment we can hear the assailant running away.* HOLMES *boldly steps out onto the street, looks in the direction of the fleeing culprit.*)

AMANDA: (*Stepping out onto the street.*) Shouldn't we call the police or go after him?

HOLMES: That would prove fruitless, I fear.

AMANDA: But he'll escape us!

HOLMES: Only for a moment. (*Extracts something from his coat's cape and holds it between two fingers as he studies it with a magnifying glass from his coat pocket.*) A long slither of bamboo, poisoned, I would wager. (*Wraps the sliver in his handkerchief, then runs over to where the assailant stood. He kneels, studies the ground, and picks up several carnation petals.*)

AMANDA: (*Pacing.*) I have had enough of this nonsense! They have chased me, violated my home, and attacked my family! I will not stand for one more atrocity, not one! They will have to battle with me for whatever the reason, for whatever the prize!

HOLMES: (*Rising and approaching her.*) Bravely put, young lady, and rest assured the time will come for such a battle. (*Opening the handkerchief and showing her the bamboo.*) This projectile contains poison capable of paralyzing or killing the intended victim. Does that suggest anything to you?

AMANDA: No, not immediately.

HOLMES: Pity.

AMANDA: Why are you bothering with all this?

HOLMES: Evidence, my good woman. A necessary element when sending a man to the docket or the gallows. (*Pockets the handkerchief and petals.*) Now, let us depart, we've done all we can here. We must dispatch one or two invitations before returning to Luranah Villa.

AMANDA: Luranah Villa? I don't understand.

HOLMES: I believe we can bring this intrigue to its final conclusion tonight.

AMANDA: But what of our meeting with Thomas at the pub?

HOLMES: (Briskly.) I feel certain he will fail to keep that appointment. Now, come along, quickly! There isn't a moment to lose!

(*They rush off into the night. Blackout.*)

SCENE FIVE

Luranah Villa, that night. The parlor is in darkness except for the moonlight that filters in from the closed French doors. Night sounds can be heard in the distance. The room has a sense of death approaching. Slowly an oil lamp's glow illuminates the archway to the room, and grows increasingly brighter until AMANDA *appears in the doorway. She holds the lamp in front of her as she walks into the room. She is wearing a dressing gown tied closely around her. Her lamp barely illuminates her as she stands in the center of the parlor, listening to the calls of the night.*

AMANDA: (*Calls softly.*) Father? Father? (*Pause.*) I am here, Father . . . Help me . . . Tell me what I must do. (*Turns to look at the portrait.*) Please help me, Father. All goes poorly, and I fear I will lose. We will lose this house, our home. Help me, Father.

(*After a moment she hears the moan that heralds her father's approach.*)

AMANDA: (*Expectantly.*) Yes, please come to me, I truly need your guidance, Father.
(*The* GHOST *suddenly appears in the upper stage left corner, near the bookcase. We can just see him.*)

GHOST: It is the cause, it is the cause, my soul/Let me not name it to you, you chaste stars/It is the cause. Yet I'll not shed her blood . . .
AMANDA: (*Calmly facing the* GHOST.) Thank you for coming, Father. I beg you to bear witness to my troubles and be of some guidance—
GHOST: If heaven would make me such another world/Of one entire perfect chrysolite. (*Pause. He moves toward* AMANDA, *one hand outstretched, a pitiful look on his face.*) I'd not have sold her for it.
AMANDA: (*Standing her ground.*) Father, you speak in riddle once more. Please, make clear what it is you would have me do.
GHOST: (*Moves within two or three feet of her and extends his other hand, which holds a walking stick.*) Where a malignant and a turban'd Turk/Beat a Venetian and traduced the state/I took by the throat . . . the circumcised dog (AMANDA *raises*

the lamp close to the GHOST.) and smote him thus. (*We can
see his face clearly*.) It would have you do nothing but forgive
me, Amanda, please, for—

(*Suddenly the French doors burst open and a man rushes in.
We can only see him in silhouette*.)

KANE: Eli!

(*Just as quickly, several men rush in behind the figure in the
doorway. They grapple with him briefly, a gun goes off, and
the* GHOST *falls at* AMANDA'S *feet*.)

LESTRADE: (*Voice in the dark*.) Quick, get a light on, Wiggins!
Get a light on, I've got 'im.

(*A figure moves in the darkness toward the archway. A
moment later the gaslights come up full*. AMANDA *kneels over
the body of the* GHOST, *a look of stunned amazement on her
face*. LESTRADE *holds* KANE'S *left arm, while* PRITCHARD *holds
his right*. KANE *is handcuffed*. HOLMES *stands by the gas lamp
switch, his hand on the nozzle, and the* CONSTABLE *is standing
dumbfounded before him. There is a small section of the upstage
left bookcase opened, revealing a secret compartment or
passage*.)

HOLMES: (*Moving to the fallen figure*.) I have it, Constable.
(*Kneeling by* AMANDA.) I had hoped to prevent this.
KANE: Let me go, Inspector! Eli! Eli!
LESTRADE: No, ya don't! I've got ya and I'll find where ya
chucked your pistol any minute now!
KANE: What are you talking about? I didn't shoot him! Mr.
Holmes!
HOLMES: (*Forcefully*.) Please be quiet, everyone. He is trying
to speak. (*Lifts the figure's head gently and removes some of
the facial makeup to reveal* CARVER.) Try once more, Mr.
Carver.
CARVER: (*With painful effort*.) I am . . . so sorry . . . Amanda.
So much money . . . and I had so . . . so little. I was good
. . . a fine actor . . . (*Begins to cough violently, then
recovers*.)
AMANDA: (*Concerned, she looks from* CARVER *to* HOLMES.)
Mr. Holmes? (HOLMES *motions for silence*.)
CARVER: Tom has so much to offer . . . to gain . . . I . . . he

paid . . . (*Another coughing attack, leaving him unable to speak.*)

HOLMES: (*Cradles* CARVER'S *head.*) Please, it is vitally important you tell us who employed you. (CARVER *cannot talk.*) Will you point to him?

(CARVER *nods yes.* HOLMES *and* AMANDA *elevate him so that he can see the threesome of* LESTRADE, KANE, *and* PRITCHARD. *He points at them.*)

HOLMES: Which, Mr. Carver? Which one?

(CARVER *dies.* AMANDA *looks at the dead man, then at* KANE, *with disbelief.*)

LESTRADE: Well, that's all the goods I need.
HOLMES: Just one moment, Lestrade!

(HOLMES *rises and moves over to* KANE. *He takes* KANE'S *hands in his own and examines them thoroughly. He sniffs them, then politely lets them drop from his grip. As he steps away, the* CONSTABLE *walks over and takes* KANE *from* PRITCHARD.)

HOLMES: Your arrest would be folly, Lestrade. You have a lamb for slaughter.
LESTRADE: What are ya talking' about? We all seen 'im rush past us in the bushes out there, bust in 'ere and shoot this fellow! Now, what's a lot of hand holdin' and sniffin' got to do with the facts?
HOLMES: He may have rushed past you three, and he most certainly did burst into this room—at a most inopportune moment, I might add—but he did not fire the shot. There are no powder burns on his hands, nor any odor of cordite. (*Patronizing.*) Even you are aware of what that means, Inspector.
LESTRADE: But the shot was fired after he ran in here. If he didn't do it then who did?
AMANDA: Yes, Mr. Holmes, who did fire that shot?
HOLMES: The person who had the most to gain from the death of Mr. Carver. (*Turns to the archway.*) Countess Tambova, would you be good enough to join us please?

(*As the* COUNTESS *enters, all seem surprised.* LESTRADE *moves closer to* HOLMES *and away from* KANE. *The* CONSTA-

BLE, *looking intense, takes* LESTRADE's *place on* KANE's *right.*
PRITCHARD *stands his ground, while* AMANDA *moves up to join*
HOLMES.)

COUNTESS: (*Looking slightly bruised but graceful.*) Yes, Mr.
    Holmes?
LESTRADE: Her? But 'ow did she get 'ere?
HOLMES: I brought her myself and left her hidden. Oh, excuse
    me, Lestrade, I did not mean to imply that the Countess
    fired upon anyone. On the contrary, she has been the victim
    of our culprit's fancy for brutality.

(PRITCHARD *quickly grabs up a pistol from under a nearby
chair. He points it at* KANE *and, taking him by the shoulder,
uses him as a shield.*)

PRITCHARD: Enough theatrics, Mr. Holmes. I had intended to
    allow our imbecilic inspector to find this (*Indicating the gun.*)
    but now it serves a better cause.
HOLMES: (*Calmly.*) As I promised, Miss Aldridge, this intrigue
    begins to come to a conclusion. I detected grime footmarks
    by that bookcase (*Indicating the open one.*) last night after
    Mr. Carver's appearance. (*Looking* PRITCHARD *in the eye.*)
    You bought Mr. Carver's talents while he toured Australia
    with Mr. Kane, did you not?
PRITCHARD: (*Edges himself and* KANE *toward the French
    doors.*) Correct, as if the confirmation truly matters.
HOLMES: And you were there to oversee the abduction of
    young Daniel?
PRITCHARD: (*Gets closer to the doors.*) Speculation, Mr.
    Holmes. Guess work.
HOLMES: I never guess. A ship's passenger log may tell much.
    You returned on the same ship on which Mr. Kane traveled.
    You two would have met were he not working his passage
    to England. (PRITCHARD *reaches the doors.*) I would like to
    know your motives for this outlandish and vile trick.
PRITCHARD: Simplicity itself, Mr. Holmes. If she would not
    reveal the location of the list to her father's ghost, she would
    certainly give up this house as haunted. And if she did not
    . . . in a short amount of time she would surely go mad and
    I would purchase all. Brilliant, no?
HOLMES: Perhaps, yet with all your brilliance, you did walk
    into this trap. A criminal mind is a pathetic one, even with
    the advantage of good breeding.

PRITCHARD: (*Furious.*) You exhibit the same insufferable, smug attitude as your brother. A family trait, no doubt!

AMANDA: (*Angry.*) What would you know of families? For all these years you have acted as a friend of mine, and yet—yet you were conspiring against us!

PRITCHARD: Do not be a fool, my dear.

(KANE *suddenly whirls on* PRITCHARD. *He knocks the gun up and out of* PRITCHARD'*s hand, then strikes him double fisted [due to the handcuffs] twice across the face, knocking him down.* LESTRADE *and the* CONSTABLE *are on* PRITCHARD *in an instant.* AMANDA *rushes over to strike the fallen man, but* HOLMES *and* KANE *restrain her.*)

KANE: Amanda, Amanda, please calm down.

AMANDA: (*Suddenly turns on* KANE.) Why should I, Thomas? Has this not been a night for deception? (KANE *says nothing but looks visibly hurt.*)

HOLMES: Please, Miss Aldridge. (*She begins to relax.*) The game is not yet over, and you will need all your strength for the news to come. (AMANDA *looks at him with determination. She goes over to a chair and sits.* LESTRADE *and the* CONSTABLE *have picked up* PRITCHARD *and* HOLMES *turns to face him.*) I can honestly say that in all of my many cases, I have met no more contemptible creature than you, sir. Lestrade, you may charge him not only with abduction, assault, and murder, but also with fraud.

AMANDA: What do you mean?

HOLMES: (*To* AMANDA, *concerned.*) I am afraid you will find your father's most valued gold and silver trophies are no longer in existence.

AMANDA: I do not understand. Those items are in the hands of the bank as collateral against this house.

HOLMES: Sir Lawrence manipulated solicitors and bankers alike until they had run your properties and capital into an atrocious state. They were then able to take possession of those awards . . . and melt them down for their market value. (*Pause.*) I am truly sorry.

(AMANDA *fights to hold herself together.* KANE *motions to the* CONSTABLE, *who removes his handcuffs.*)

LESTRADE: (*Places the stunned* PRITCHARD *in a chair.*) If what you say is true . . . (*Indignant as the realization hits him.*)

Why—why, that ain't legal! I'll have warrants sworn out at once! You just name names, Mr. Holmes!

HOLMES: Gladly, Lestrade.

(KANE, *who has been watching* AMANDA's *reaction to all this, now goes over to* CARVER's *body. The* CONSTABLE *places handcuffs on* PRITCHARD, *who looks up at* HOLMES.)

KANE: He thought that I had mastered the game. (*Kneeling.*) I am so sorry, Eli . . . for both of us. (*Pause.*) May I cover him with something?

AMANDA: (*Sympathetic.*) Yes, Thomas. There is a duvet in the closet by the front door . . . and a couch on which you may place him, if you wish.

KANE: (*Still looking at* CARVER.) Thank you. I would like that very much. (*Pause.*) He treated me well, always. Like an older brother might. (*Begins to pick* CARVER *up.*)

LESTRADE: Give 'em a hand, Wiggins.

KANE: (*Quietly.*) No, thank you, Inspector. I would like to do this myself.

(KANE *lifts* CARVER's *body and carries it from the room.* LESTRADE *raises* PRITCHARD *to his feet and marches him to the archway. They stop a few feet from the* COUNTESS.)

LESTRADE: (*To* PRITCHARD, *sardonically.*) I'm so sorry we had to park our coach so far from the house, your worship, but the walk will do you good.

PRITCHARD: (*To the* COUNTESS.) Of course, you wouldn't think of giving evidence againt me, my dear Countess.

COUNTESS: (*Cold with hate.*) Of course I would . . . and will.

LESTRADE: Do you want us to take her along too, Mr. Holmes?

HOLMES: No, I think the Countess and Miss Aldridge have much to discuss. You may return for her later. (*To* AMANDA.) I believe you will find her story not dissimilar to your own. Family devotion, love, prompts us all to many different actions . . . perhaps even Mr. Kane. (*Turns to* LESTRADE, *leaving* AMANDA *to ponder.*) I believe I shall accompany you to the station, Lestrade. There are one or two ponts regarding Frederick's elusive . . . wife. (PRITCHARD *stiffens.*) Good, I see we do have much to talk of. (*Exits with* LESTRADE, *the* CONSTABLE, *and* PRITCHARD.)

(AMANDA *walks over and stands beneath* IRA's *portrait. She turns to the* COUNTESS *and motions her to the love seat.*)

COUNTESS: I am certain, to you, an apology would be most insignificant.

AMANDA: To which atrocity would I apply that apology? To the robberies; to the act of fraud; to the months of mental anguish; or to the attacks on my family?

COUNTESS: I assure you I had no part in the harm brought upon you or your loved ones. Lawrence kept from me all knowledge of his violent acts. I believed he only hired thieves.

AMANDA: (*Disgusted.*) Then surely you wore your ignorance like a bridal veil! You welcomed its translucent properties, which afforded you a single-minded view of Sir Lawrence and your goals!

COUNTESS: No more so than your own! Are you not devoted to the memory of your father? Do you not live forever in the shadow of his deeds, his mastery, his name? Forever looking to him for that which you need or desire, but that he can no longer give. Measured by and measuring your merits by his—

AMANDA: What a pitiful attempt to excuse your own insidious and clandestine actions which—

COUNTESS: If I am in error about you, my dear young woman, why then did Lawrence's ghost ploy work all too well?

AMANDA: Because he took advantage of his knowledge of me! Of my feel—

COUNTESS: Yes, of your feelings for your father. Your eternal love for him. (*Pause.*) Your father brought you fame and respect. My father brought me disgrace and shame. Shame so horrid, my younger brother could no longer endure, and so . . . killed himself.

AMANDA: Mr. Holmes, only tonight, informed me of this document you seek and its true value. Had we found it, how would you have put it to use?

COUNTESS: I would have burned it. (*Sits on the love seat.*) When it became known certain forces sought to find and use that hated letter, I swore I would have it first. I swore it would bring no more shame upon my father's name . . . upon my family.

(AMANDA *moves over to the* COUNTESS *and places her hand on her shoulder. For that moment they seem to share a common bond.* KANE *walks in, disturbing the moment. He senses this and stands speechless.*)

AMANDA: (*Politely.*) Mr. Holmes tells me I would find your story well worth the listening. If you would close the doors (*Indicates the French doors.*) I will pour us all a bit of sherry, and then we will talk.

KANE: I would like that. (*Notices the walking stick on the floor near his foot. He picks it up, easily removes the head, and displays that it is hollow.*) When Mr. Holmes asked about a blow pipe, I realized he was thinking of Eli. (*Walks to the French doors.*) I dressed and went looking for him. I couldn't find him. I then remembered your description of the ghost and . . . (*Steps out through the doors.*)

AMANDA: (*Pouring drinks.*) And? (*Turns to look for* KANE. *The* COUNTESS *does also.*) Thomas? (*Pause.*) Thomas?

(KANE *slowly backs into the room. At his forehead is a pistol. We do not see who is holding it immediately. Then we see it is* WINTERS. *He has a deadly expression on his face.*)

COUNTESS: Winters?!

(*With a simple, swift gesture* WINTERS *indicates silence. In his right hand he holds the pistol, which is aimed at* KANE's *face. In his left he holds a (sword) cane, which he uses to knock the walking stick from* KANE's *hand, then motions for* KANE *to step back one more foot. He turns his gaze to* AMANDA *after* KANE *complies.*)

WINTERS: I have not time to tarry, Amanda. The document, please.

AMANDA: I do not have this . . . list.

WINTERS: Bring it to me, please, Amanda.

AMANDA: I tell you I do not have it. (*She is getting more and more nervous.*)

(WINTERS, *using his left hand, removes his gray hair, his putty nose, and glasses. He suddenly stands erect and when he next speaks, his words are threatening and carry a French accent. He is* MOREAU.)

MOREAU: My first bullet will enter his mouth (*Indicating* KANE.) and shatter his jaw.

(*The* COUNTESS *shudders and lets out a soft gasp. For an instant it appears as if she will make a move.* MOREAU *tenses his gun hand and she settles quickly.*)

COUNTESS: (*Scared.*) I will not move.
MOREAU: (*To* AMANDA.) You are looking on the face of death, Amanda. (*Cocks the hammer.*) The list.
AMANDA: (*Frantic.*) I don't have it! Please believe me!

(*In that brief instant* KANE *attempts to knock the gun from* MOREAU'*s hand. He succeeds but* MOREAU *swiftly strikes* KANE *over the head with his cane. As* KANE *drops to the floor,* MOREAU *removes the sword and is preparing to strike when* HOLMES *rushes into the room.* MOREAU *points his sword at* HOLMES, *who quickly removes his cloak and parries several thrusts with the heavy cloth. He throws it into* MOREAU'*s face, which confuses him long enough for* HOLMES *to grab a sword from the wall mounting. Without challenge or hesitation they rush at each other. They battle fiercely, barely avoiding parries and thrusts of deadly accuracy.* AMANDA *has moved to the upstage right area in order to avoid the combatants, but the* COUNTESS *has been slowly driven upstage left near the portrait and close to the writing table. Finally, the only thing between her and* MOREAU'*s blade is* HOLMES. MOREAU *has worked it this way to divide the detective's concentration between her protection and his own survival.* AMANDA *realizes this and what is bound to happen. She waits for an opportune moment, then turns at and knocks the* COUNTESS *down and out of harm's way. This frees* HOLMES *for proper battle, but not before* MOREAU *feints a move which ends in wounding the detective's right arm.* HOLMES *reacts, but not in fear. The pain drives him on, and in a series of expertly executed moves he drives* MOREAU *toward the French doors. By the open doors, for a second* MOREAU *considers flight, and in that moment of distraction* HOLMES *delivers his coup de maitre [a master stroke].* MOREAU *drops his sword, stares at* HOLMES *incredulously, then stumbles back, and falls dead outside the French doors.* HOLMES *walks to the doors and looks down at the assassin. At that instant* LESTRADE *runs in through the archway as* KANE *rises from the floor, unsteadily.*)

KANE: (HOLMES *nods at* KANE, *then points to* AMANDA *and the* COUNTESS.) Amanda! (*Rushes over to help them up.*) Are you all right?

AMANDA: Yes . . . I believe I am. (*Smiles faintly.*)

(LESTRADE *crosses to* HOLMES *as the* COUNTESS *sits in a nearby chair.*)

HOLMES: (*Weary.*) It had not been my intention to deliver Moreau in this manner, but he gave me no alternative . . . and deserved no better.

LESTRADE: (*Looks out at the body.*) Well, I can't say I'm sorry to see 'im in that condition, Mr. H— (*Notices* HOLMES's *wound.*) Here now, what is this? Let me have a look at it!

HOLMES: It is only a slight cut, Lestrade. It is nothing to concern yourself with.

LESTRADE: (*Checks the wound.*) "It's only a slight cut, Lestrade. It is nothing to concern yourself with."

HOLMES: (*Smiles.*) Thank you, Lestrade.

LESTRADE: If Dr. Watson were 'ere, he could dress it up for ya.

HOLMES: (*Solemn.*) Again the absence of my old friend is felt. (*Pause.*) Miss Aldridge, the threat is ended.

AMANDA: Truly, Mr. Holmes?

HOLMES: Truly.

COUNTESS: But what of the document, the letter?

HOLMES: (*Brushes it off.*) I am afraid whatever fate intended for that document, it will never come to pass. It was hidden in the silver cross Ira received that very night he sailed on the *Kusevi*.

LESTRADE: You mean one of them dignitaries 'id it on 'im and he didn't even know?

HOLMES: Exactly.

COUNTESS: Then I need never fear from that cursed thing again.

HOLMES: (*Looks at the* COUNTESS, *then turns, and steps to the French doors.*) Lestrade, you will find the body of the real Winters (*Looking out at* MOREAU.) buried in the cellar at the home of Sir Lawrence. You might enjoy informing him of how close he came to death himself.

LESTRADE: You mean, he didn't know about Moreau's part in this?

HOLMES: No, he did not. Through Mycroft and the Countess, I ascertained that Moreau was employed by a small body of officials in the Russias.

LESTRADE: Well, that's good enough for me. I'll be certain ta mention your invaluable assistance in my report.

HOLMES: Thank you ever so much, Lestrade. (*Whimsy.*) Sir Lawrence's trial will bring you no end of importance. You have all the pertinent facts to relay to your superiors and the Home Office, do you not?

LESTRADE: (*Flustered.*) Well, I'll still be needin' a few bits of clarification for me records . . . (*Humble.*) if you don't mind, sir.

HOLMES: (*Smiles.*) Not at all, Inspector.

LESTRADE: (*Pleased.*) Good enough! Now, if you would all care to accompany me to the station, I'll get all your statements. (*Looks at* HOLMES's *wound.*) And we'll get someone ta fix that up for ya. (*Heads for the archway.*)

AMANDA: May I have a moment alone with Thomas and Mr. Holmes?

LESTRADE: Sure enough, Miss Aldridge, I'll wait for the three of ya outside.

COUNTESS: (*Rises.*) Wait, Inspector. I will walk with you. (*Smiles at* AMANDA, *squeezes her hands.*) Thank you. (*Then joins* LESTRADE. *She indicates that he should offer her his arm.*) Inspector.

LESTRADE: (*Offers his arm and smiles broadly.*) Countess, it would be my pleasure.

COUNTESS: (*Seductively.*) Are you a passionate man . . . Inspector? (*They exit.*)

KANE: Amanda, I—

AMANDA: (*Takes his hands.*) It is not our time, Thomas. There is too much . . . (KANE *nods that he understands.*) But please know, from this day forward . . . you have this family to call your own. (*Kisses him on the cheek, then moves to* HOLMES. *She communicates her gratitude through her eyes and gestures.*) I believe there is the matter of a fee to be discussed.

HOLMES: My fee is a simple one. (*Picks up the sword he fought* MOREAU *with, hefts it for balance.*) This will do quite nicely.

AMANDA: Surely you cannot—

HOLMES: I am a creature who lives for the art of the game, the chase. This is all I require as a sign of the winning. Will you settle the debt or leave the marker to default?

AMANDA: (*Smiles.*) With pleasure, sir, I shall consider the debt paid. (*To both men.*) Shall we join the others? (*Moves to the archway.*)

KANE: Shortly, Amanda. I wish a moment with Mr. Holmes.

(AMANDA *looks around the room as if replaying the past adventure.*)

HOLMES: I assure you, Miss Aldridge, all will be well from this day forward.

AMANDA: And if not, Mr. Holmes, I have no doubt that whatever may come . . . I shall endure. (*Proudly exits.*)

KANE: (*Moves to* HOLMES *and extracts a check from his jacket pocket.*) You may fill in the proper amount at your leisure, sir. (*Thrusts the check into* HOLMES's *reluctant hand.*) Take it. With this I am paying a debt to Ira as well.

HOLMES: How is that, sir?

KANE: Ira once said: Though we must part my best protectors, still my heart will cherish, till its fount is chill—

HOLMES: (*With feeling.*) That proudest record—the fresh memory—that here the sable African was free! From every bond—save those that kindness threw around his heart, and bound them fast to you.

KANE: How did . . .

HOLMES: Could he not have influenced two young men? Two . . . actors? Now, if you would be good enough to join Miss Aldridge, I will be along shortly.

(KANE *walks to the archway, looks at* HOLMES *for a moment, makes a grand bow from the waist, and exits.* HOLMES *eyes the sword in his hand. He carefully pries open the handle and extracts a folded document, which he reads with a grave expression. Looking around, he spots an ashtray on the writing table, carries the letter over to it, where he takes a match from his pocket and, lighting the letter, sets it to burn in the ashtray. He also takes* KANE's *check, looks at it, then with a whimsical smile, he places it to burn along with the document. Turning swiftly, he walks to archway in time to hear—*)

LESTRADE: (*Offstage.*) Are you all right, M_____?

HOLMES: Yes, Lestrade . . . I believe I a_____

(*He picks up his coat and briskly _____ except for a lone spotlight on the b_____ The spot fades out, leaving onl_____ stage.*)

THE TAKING OF
MISS JANIE

A PLAY

by Ed Bullins

All inquiries concerning rights should be directed to Helen Merrill, Ltd., 435 W. 23rd St., #1A, New York, NY 10011.

The Taking of Miss Janie was first produced at the Henry Street Settle-
ment Playhouse in New York City by the New Federal Theater on
_____ 75, and moved to the Mitzi Newhouse Theater at Lincoln
_____ of the same year. It won the Drama Critics Circle
_____ Play of 1974–75. It was also a Burns Mantle
_____ of 1974–75.

HOLMES: I assure you, Miss Aldridge, all will be well from this day forward.

AMANDA: And if not, Mr. Holmes, I have no doubt that whatever may come . . . I shall endure. (*Proudly exits.*)

KANE: (*Moves to* HOLMES *and extracts a check from his jacket pocket.*) You may fill in the proper amount at your leisure, sir. (*Thrusts the check into* HOLMES's *reluctant hand.*) Take it. With this I am paying a debt to Ira as well.

HOLMES: How is that, sir?

KANE: Ira once said: Though we must part my best protectors, still my heart will cherish, till its fount is chill—

HOLMES: (*With feeling.*) That proudest record—the fresh memory—that here the sable African was free! From every bond—save those that kindness threw around his heart, and bound them fast to you.

KANE: How did . . .

HOLMES: Could he not have influenced two young men? Two . . . actors? Now, if you would be good enough to join Miss Aldridge, I will be along shortly.

(KANE *walks to the archway, looks at* HOLMES *for a moment, makes a grand bow from the waist, and exits.* HOLMES *eyes the sword in his hand. He carefully pries open the handle and extracts a folded document, which he reads with a grave expression. Looking around, he spots an ashtray on the writing table, carries the letter over to it, where he takes a match from his pocket and, lighting the letter, sets it to burn in the ashtray. He also takes* KANE's *check, looks at it, then with a whimsical smile, he places it to burn along with the document. Turning swiftly, he walks to archway in time to hear—*)

LESTRADE: (*Offstage.*) Are you all right, Mr. Holmes?

HOLMES: Yes, Lestrade . . . I believe I am, indeed.

(*He picks up his coat and briskly exits. The lights fade out except for a lone spotlight on the burning papers in the ashtray. The spot fades out, leaving only the flames to illuminate the stage.*)

THE TAKING OF
MISS JANIE

A PLAY

by Ed Bullins

The Taking of Miss Janie was first produced at the Henry Street Settle-
ment Playhouse in New York City by the New Federal Theater on
March 13, 1975, and moved to the Mitzi Newhouse Theater at Lincoln
Center on May 4 of the same year. It won the Drama Critics Circle
Award for Best American Play of 1974–75. It was also a Burns Mantle
Theatre Yearbook "Best Play" of 1974–75.

in an affected manner to conceal her Southern background. Tender. Sensitive.

LONNIE: White. Late twenties. Hides an uneasiness behind a super-cool pose.

LEN: Black. Light-skinned. Bush hair. Intellectual-artistic-politically aware. Early twenties.

SHARON: White. Brunette. Pretty. A California lotus eater. Early twenties.

FLOSSY: Black. Sensual. Soul sister. A woman of the streets, but not a whore. Early twenties.

RICK: Black. Light-skinned. Intellectually aggressive. An early revolutionary, cultural nationalist. Early twenties.

MORT SILBERSTEIN: White. A post-beatnik mythic figure.

THE TIME: The sixties.
THE PLACE: California and elsewhere.

*An abstract depiction of a decade of cheap living spaces—
for students, artists, musicians, poets, and other transients—
studio apartments with pull-down wall beds, sofas, couches,
and cots in dingy rooms, single beds in motel rooms, etc. But
the stage is uncluttered. The locales could be Los Angeles,
San Francisco, Manhattan, Boston, etc. At rise.*

JANIE *sits on the edge of a roll-out bed, almost tearful but
attempting to communicate with* MONTY, *who lounges beside
her, half covered by a sheet, sexually spent for the moment.*

JANIE: (*Not looking at him at first.*) It's sad . . . so sad . . . I
don't even understand it . . . Once you said . . . no . . . no
. . . many times you've told me . . . that anything's possible
. . . But I wouldn't believe you. I *couldn't* believe you . . .
You made the world, life, people . . . *everything* . . . seem
so grim . . . And I knew it couldn't be that way . . . It
couldn't . . . Even while I felt sad most of the time. Even
while I suffered and had what you called "The Blues" . . .
Even though I didn't understand why you refused to give
into sadness . . . to feeling down and beat . . . I . . . I still
didn't believe, Monty. I didn't. I still didn't believe that I
have so little understanding of the world . . . Oh, Monty, I
have so little understanding of people and life . . . and I
don't know *you*, who I thought was my friend, at all . . .
And now . . . and now I don't know what to believe anymore
. . . or know what to do next. We've been friends for such
a long time. Such a long time. . . . Ten years? . . . God, it's
been that long . . . I don't know what I'll do now . . . I don't
know what's going to happen to me . . . For such a long
time I thought of you as one of my few friends. A special
friend, really. Do you understand that, Monty? . . . My special friend . . . And now you rape me . . . you rape me!
(*Begins to cry softly.*)

(MONTY *raises his head from the pillow, then reaches over
and pulls her to him and kisses her until she quiets. She doesn't
resist.*)

JANIE: (*Catches her breath.*) Oh, Monty . . . Monty . . . why
. . . why?
MONTY: (*Annoyed.*) Why what?
JANIE: (*Surprised.*) What did you say? . . . What did you mean
by that?

(*Silence except for a tinny-sounding radio playing the Beatles, off somewhere.*) Monty . . . please . . . what did you mean? I don't understand . . .

MONTY: (*Accusing.*) You understand, Janie . . . You've always understood, Miss Janie.

JANIE: "Miss Janie" . . . you haven't called me that in years. Why do you call me that now?

MONTY: (*Rolls over, caresses her.*) It's just something that I keep for you, Janie. You remember, one of the few things that's especially ours.

JANIE: (*Moves away from him and stands.*) Stop! Why are you forcing your will on me? Why are you taking me like this?

MONTY: Because I want you, that's why.

JANIE: (*Moves toward door.*) Well, you can't have me. You can't just take what you want and use me like this.

MONTY: (*Rises and stalks her.*) Shut up, bitch! . . . You phoney, whining white bitch!

JANIE: (*Hurt and tearful.*) Don't call me that . . . Please don't say that, Monty.

MONTY: Shut up, I said! I've wasted too much love and caring on you already. From the first moment you met me you knew it would come to this . . . And you've got the nerve to cry and act like this. (*Pulls her to him and kisses her and "dry fucks" her until he begins arousing some response against her will.*)

JANIE: No! No, I didn't. I wanted to be friends with you, Monty. Friends, that's all. Oh, please . . . not again . . . Not that, please . . .

(*As he corners her, the lights change and slides appear showing a college campus and college scenes. The music fades out. Campus sounds are heard.*

MONTY *and* JANIE *momentarily disappear in the darkness upon stage, and a slide comes on with their images. They are meeting, looking somewhat younger, and are dressed in the Southern California collegiate styles of the late 1950s.*

The slide holds for a moment, then the light comes up on MONTY *and* JANIE *as they play out the scene.*)

JANIE: Hello. You're in my Creative Writing class, aren't you?

MONTY: Yeah . . . I think so.

JANIE: I love the poetry you read today.

MONTY: Thanks.

JANIE: But it was so bitter.

MONTY: Oh.

JANIE: Do you call that Black Poetry?

MONTY: Hey . . . my name's Monty.

JANIE: Mine's Janie.

MONTY: Pleased to meet'cha, Miss Janie.

JANIE: (*Surprised.*) What did you say?

MONTY: What did ya think I said?

JANIE: (*Curious.*) Why did you say that?

MONTY: Oh, just a little joke of mine, I guess.

JANIE: (*Confused.*) You guess? . . . But I don't think I—

MONTY: Let's just keep it between ourselves, huh?

JANIE: (*Thoughtful.*) If you say so . . . But I don't think I understand you very well.

MONTY: Hey . . . you want to go to a party tonight, Miss Janie?

JANIE: Oh, don't call me that.

MONTY: Why? It fits you like a pair of panty hose.

JANIE: (*Blushes.*) Do you have to say that?

MONTY: Nawh. I don't have to say nothin' if I don't wanna . . . Hey . . . what about the party?

JANIE: (*Doubtful.*) Where?

MONTY: At my place.

JANIE: I don't know . . . but I might be able to come.

MONTY: Well . . . I'll be expecting you.

JANIE: Will you be reading any of your poetry that you were reading in class?

MONTY: I don't know . . . but if you come, I'll read something for you, Miss Janie.

JANIE: I don't know if I like you calling me that.

MONTY: Just let it be our little secret.

JANIE: (*Puzzled.*) You mean we've got secrets already?

MONTY: (*Winks.*) Sho' nuf, Miss Janie. Here, let me give you my address. It's not so far from here.

JANIE: If you read tonight, please don't sound so despairing . . . Tee-hee . . . you're almost scary, ya know?

(*Party music rises. The lights come up as voices are heard.*

It is MONTY'*s apartment. The party preparations are nearly complete.* MONTY *is off in the kitchen doing the last chores.*

Out front, LEN *and* RICK, MONTY'*s roommates, are in their daily ritual of debate.* LEN *wears Levis and sandals; he has a large, uncombed "natural."* RICK *wears a black suit, white shirt, white bow tie, and white bucks on his feet. His head is shaven and glistens. He wears eyeglasses that glisten also.)*

RICK: But, Brother Len, these devils are jivin'. They ain't nothin' but stone paper tigers.

LEN: I agree with you, my brother . . . at least on some of your points of argument.

RICK: What points? What points, Brother Len? That he, the devil, is going to give the Black man ten percent of this land? Five of these states of the so-called great United States of America? Can you believe the devil's gonna do that, brother?

LEN: Well, Brother Rick, I must confess that I find that a bit farfetched.

RICK: (*Excited.*) Farfetched? Farfetched, he says.

LEN: Yes. I said "farfetched"!

RICK: (*Calls to* MONTY.) Did you hear that, Brother Monty? Did you hear what this deaf, dumb and blind *negro* said?

LEN: Deaf, dumb and blind? Negro! Now, listen, Rick, just because I don't—

(MONTY *sticks his head in from the kitchen.*)

MONTY: Hey, what did you say, Rick?

RICK: (*Makes the most of the moment.*) I said that the black man has slaved in this devil's land for four hundred years. I said that the Black man must have freedom, justice and equality . . . plus self-determinism to—

LEN: You didn't say that just now! You've been mouthing those clichés before memory!

RICK: Clichés! Clichés!

MONTY: Len! Rick! Say . . . cool it!

(RICK *is on his feet, strutting back and forth like an immaculate bantam rooster.*)

RICK: The black man has slaved in this devil's land for four hundred years, Brother Len. And you call that a cliché! I know what I am saying, from hearing the righteous black work, and you call it farfetched? A cliché? Brother . . . listen to me . . . this white man is a paper tiger!

(*The doorbell rings.* RICK *moves toward it.*)

RICK: I'll get it. Your . . . ah, guests . . . must be arriving, Monty.

(*He opens the door;* JANIE *stands on the other side, wearing dark glasses.*)

JANIE: (*Shyly.*) Hello . . . I . . .
RICK: I'm sorry. You must have the wrong address. (*Slams the door in* JANIE'*s face.*)
MONTY: (*Comes out of the kitchen.*) Hey . . . man . . . what's goin' on?
LEN: Is that somebody you know, Monty?

(MONTY *opens the door;* JANIE *still stands there, a bewildered expression on her face, beneath her shades.*)

MONTY: Janie . . . c'mon in.
JANIE: (*Nervous.*) Hi, Monty . . . Is there something wrong?
MONTY: C'mon in, Janie. C'mon. You're here now.

(*He reaches out and pulls her inside. She looks around apprehensively.* LEN *gets to his feet;* RICK *has stopped his pacing and stands in the center of the floor.*)

RICK: (*With arms folded.*) Well, well, well, well . . .
LEN: (*Smiling, going over to* JANIE.) Hello . . . My name's Len.
JANIE: Hi. I hope I'm not too early.
MONTY: This is Janie, Len.
LEN: Pleased to meet'cha. Can I get you anything?
JANIE: Oh . . . I don't know.
RICK: Well . . . isn't anyone going to introduce me? I live here too, you know.
LEN: We thought that you had met her out in the hall, Rick.
MONTY: Hey, Janie . . . that's Rick over there. These two clowns are my roommates.
LEN: Welcome . . . welcome, Janie.
JANIE: Thank you . . . but it looks like I'm really early.
MONTY: Don't let it bother you, kid. Why don't you come in the kitchen with me while I finish up. Do you know how to make avocado dip?
JANIE: (*Following.*) You mean Mexican style?

(MONTY *and* JANIE *enter the kitchen.* RICK *looks at* LEN *incredulously.*)

RICK: Did you see how he brought that devil lady right in here on us?

LEN: Shhh . . . man . . . she'll hear you.

RICK: (*Raises his voice.*) I hope she does. I hope her ole red ears burn off from hearin' my words.

LEN: Hey, Rick, man . . . you knew this was gonna be a mixed party. Both Monty and myself told you that we were gonna invite people from school. And you know that's a mixed scene, man.

RICK: Yes, I knew, Brother Len . . . But I don't have to accept it.

LEN: Well, what you gonna do, man? Leave?

RICK: Leave? Brother Len, I have no intention of going anywhere tonight, except to bed, later on.

LEN: But you not gonna be draggin' the party, are ya, man?

RICK: Me a drag? On the contrary, my brother. There would be little or no party if it wasn't for me. Have the times of your young lives. I just simply don't have to accept the validity of this scene, that's all.

LEN: And why not, man?

RICK: Because it's phony, irrelevant, and it comes straight out of some of you so-called Negroes' fantasy bags.

LEN: Aw, Rick, man. Just listen to that . . . You are gonna be a big drag tonight.

RICK: Relax, Brother Len. I'm here . . . naturally. I'm in the room. You'all got your scene goin'. Swell. I just ain't gonna deal with it like I'm a part of it. I'm checkin' yawhl out, dig?

LEN: Aw, you jive turkey. Monty and I are just lookin' for some good times. We don't want to get into all that Black crap tonight . . .

(JANIE *enters, wearing an apron and carrying a tray.*)

LEN: (*Glad for the interruption.*) Well, what do we have here?

JANIE: (*Smiling.*) Who wants to try my guacamole?

(RICK *sits down, crosses his legs, and folds his arms.*)

LEN: Guacamole? How wonderful!

RICK: No, thanks, I don't want any.

JANIE: Oh, no? But it's so good. (*Places the tray down and licks the tips of her fingers.*)

RICK: I wouldn't eat anything that was touched by you, Miss Ann.

JANIE: (*Brightly.*) My name's Janie, Rick.

LEN: Now, we're not going to have any of that, Rick.

JANIE: (*Smiling.*) Is there anything wrong? Have I done anything that I shouldn't?

RICK: Yes . . . you were born.

LEN: Now, that's the last straw, Rick.

(JANIE *moves between* LEN *and* RICK. *She looks down at* RICK.)

JANIE: Len, don't take everything so personal. Rick is just doing his thing, aren't you, Rick?

RICK: You have no idea of what my thing is, devil lady.

LEN: (*Horrified.*) Rick!

JANIE: (*Sits next to* RICK *on couch.*) You're a Black Nationalist, aren't you, Rick?

(RICK *stands and steps to the middle of the room.* MONTY *enters from the kitchen. He carries bottles of beer.*)

RICK: (*With back to* JANIE.) Those who know don't say, and those who don't know don't ask.

MONTY: (*Hands out beer.*) Hey, that's heavy, Rick. That sounds like that other one you always sayin'. How does it go?

RICK: (*Refuses beer.*) It's unimportant . . . in this context, my brother.

LEN: The first last and the last first!

MONTY: (*Not quite serious.*) Yeah. What goes around comes around . . . or somethin' like dat. (*He and* LEN *slap five.*)

JANIE: Rick, please tell me about Black Nationalism.

(*The door bell rings.*)

RICK: (*Turns and faces* JANIE.) You personify that line of poetry which says: ". . . each year they send a thousand of their best into the ghetto."

JANIE: I do?

RICK: Yes, you do. You come in here with your dirty blond

hair and evil blue eyes and act the presumptuous beast that you are!

(*The doorbell rings again.*)

LEN: Do you want me to get that, Monty?

MONTY: Naw, man . . . I got it.

JANIE: (*Smiling.*) Rick. You haven't even seen me since I've been here. My eyes aren't blue . . . they're brown. And I don't know what you mean that I'm one of the thousand that—

RICK: It doesn't matter what color your eyes are. You're still one of those sent in by the Zionist Youth Conspiracy.

JANIE: Zionist? Oh, how funny, Rick . . . Tee-hee . . . I'm of German extraction . . . both sides. I'm not a Jewish anything.

(MONTY *opens the door.* PEGGY *stands there. She wears a sweater and Levis. Her hair is cut short in a boyish Afro; she wears glasses.*)

MONTY: Hey, stuff. How're doin'?

PEGGY: Okay, Monty. I'm not too early, am I?

MONTY: Naw. Come on in. Have a beer. (*Shuts the door after* PEGGY *enters.*)

PEGGY: Hey, Monty . . . you gonna read tonight? I brought some of my latest work over.

JANIE: Oh, good, you are going to have some Black poetry read tonight. I knew I should have come. I think that's wonderful!

PEGGY: Say wha—?

MONTY: Hey, Peg . . . this is Janie. Janie's in a class of mine at City College.

PEGGY: Oh?

JANIE: Hello, Peggy. Monty and I have Creative Writing together.

PEGGY: (*Sarcastic.*) Well, bully for yawhl.

MONTY: (*To* PEGGY.) You know these two clowns.

RICK: As-salaam alaikum, Sister Peggy.

PEGGY: Salaam, Brother Rick.

JANIE: (*Alert.*) What did you say?

MONTY: I gotta check out the stove, folks . . . Be right back. (*Exits to the kitchen.*)

LEN: Want somethin' to drink, Peg?

PEGGY: I'll take some wine, if you have any, Len.

LEN: No sooner said than done. (*Goes into the kitchen.*)

JANIE: What did you two say just now? ... Rick ... Peggy ...

(RICK *and* PEGGY *ignore* JANIE.)

PEGGY: Haven't seen you in a month of gospel bird days, brother.

RICK: Just tryin' to be Black here in the white wilderness of North America, sister. (RICK *and* PEGGY *embrace and give an approximation of a traditional African greeting.*) It's sure good to see your Black self here, sister.

PEGGY: It's good to have my Black self here, brother. But who's this pale thing on the couch belong to?

JANIE: (*On couch, apprehensive.*) Did you two say something? Are you speaking about me?

RICK: You'll have to get Monty to explain this beast to you, Sister Peg. If I had my way, I'd po' gasoline on the blond, brown-eyed devil and watch it burn.

JANIE: (*Stands.*) Oh, I wish you all wouldn't talk like that. You have such a strange sense of humor. I guess I just have to learn to become hep.

PEGGY: (*With raised eyebrows.*) Hep?

JANIE: (*Takes off the apron and goes behind* PEGGY *and tries to tie it on her.*) Here ... Peggy ... maybe you'd like to help out Monty some. I'm not very good in a kitchen.

PEGGY: (*Pushes* JANIE *away.*) Hey, woman ... why don't you be cool?

(MONTY *and* LEN *come out of the kitchen. The doorbell rings.*)

LEN: I'll get it.

MONTY: The gumbo's almost ready.

JANIE: Monty ... What should I do with this apron?

RICK: What is that gumbo made from, Brother Monty?

(LEN *opens the door.* LONNIE *and* SHARON *stand in the hall.*)

PEGGY: Hey ... what kind of party you got goin' here, Monty?

MONTY: Relax, Peggy. Everything's cool.

RICK: I asked you what did you put in the gumbo, brother?

MONTY: Ground beef! I put ground beef in it, man. You know I wouldn't try to get you to eat pork.

JANIE: Oh, I just love ham . . . Do you have any ham, Monty?

PEGGY: No, he doesn't have any ham.

JANIE: Are you sure?

RICK: The pig . . . pork . . . swine is the foulest diseased poison that man can consume.

(LEN *has invited the couple in.* LEN *takes* SHARON's *hand and leads her.*)

LEN: Hey, folks . . . this is Sharon . . . She's a friend of mine.

SHARON: Pleased to meet'cha.

PEGGY: I can believe that.

MONTY: (*To* LONNIE.) What's your name, buddy?

JANIE: Hi, Lonnie.

LONNIE: It's Lonnie, man. Janie asked me to come by and check her out. I'm her ole man, kinda.

RICK: (*Making a speech.*) The pig is part rodent. You can recognize its rat genes by its rodent-like tail.

JANIE: Lonnie, you're just in time.

LONNIE: (*Cool.*) Yeah . . . baby.

PEGGY: In time for what?

JANIE: I'm having such a marvelous time. Monty . . . your friends are so interesting and colorful.

MONTY: (*Annoyed.*) Say . . . there's drinks in the kitchen.

RICK: The swine is part snake . . . It can even eat other snakes without getting sick. 'Cause it's a cannibal as well.

JANIE: Who's the girl you came in with, Lonnie?

LONNIE: She's somebody who rode up in the elevator with me, dig? You can see where she's comin' from, can't ya?

(LEN *and* SHARON *are embracing, kissing, and are in private conversation.*)

RICK: The pig is part dog. It has a dog-like nature and you become part dog when you consume the beast.

MONTY: You are what you eat, right, man?

PEGGY: Exactly.

(*Intermittently some go into the kitchen briefly and return with drinks. The improvisational quality of the party remains. The doorbell rings again.*)

MONTY: Hey . . . I'm tired of goin' to the door. *Come in!*

(FLOSSY *sticks her head in the door.*)

FLOSSY: Hey . . . is this where it's happenin'?
MONTY: Hey, Flossy . . . come on in, baby.
JANIE: Monty . . . you have so many friends.
LONNIE: (*Talking to* LEN.) Yeah, man . . . I just got off a gig.
LEN: You did, huh?
PEGGY: Can you dig it? Gig.
JANIE: Lonnie blows a horn in a jazz combo.
LONNIE: (*Super-cool.*) It's my ax, baby. My ax.
FLOSSY: (*Kissing* MONTY.) This is for you, daddy.
MONTY: Thank you, little mamma.
PEGGY: (*To* FLOSSY.) I don't think we've met. My name's Peggy.
FLOSSY: Naw, I don't guess we have. I'm Flossy.
RICK: We are in the time of the Fall of America. We are witnesses to the end.

(*Music plays and some of the couples are in a semi-dance movement. The lights change in color and depth, and the shadows deepen as the room takes on a surreal quality.*)

LONNIE: I always did say spades really knew how to party.
MONTY: Hey, man. Check yourself with that spade crap.
JANIE: Oh, Monty . . . he didn't mean nothin'.
RICK: (*To* LONNIE.) Say, devil . . . how did you ever learn how to play Black music?
LONNIE: You mean jazz, man?
LEN: That's what the brother said, man.
SHARON: Len, you're not going to start anything, are ya?
LONNIE: I just went to school . . . and learned a little and started playin', man.
RICK: He went to school to learn how to play our music. Check that out, brothers.
FLOSSY: I'm scarfish as a bear. Where's the grease, Honey?
MONTY: In the kitchen, baby. It should be ready by now. Hey, everybody . . . food's on.
RICK: I never knew Germans could play jazz.
LONNIE: Maybe Germans can't, man. But I'm Jewish.
PEGGY: Jewish.
SHARON: That's what he said. So am I. There's nothin' wrong with being Jewish, is there?

RICK: A German . . . and a Jew . . . going together. That's heavy. That's very heavy.

LONNIE: Well, man, I don't feel responsible for what some foreigners did.

JANIE: Let's not talk about that. It's too horrible.

RICK: Your daddy murders six million people and it's too horrible for you to listen to, huh?

SHARON: It wasn't her father. She couldn't help what was goin' on.

FLOSSY: (Off.) Hey, Monty, baby! . . . This sangria is boss!

LEN: They've got you brainwashed, I see.

RICK: It's sad but true, brothers. The so-called Negroes in America is in love with his slave master . . . Jews are fraternizing and lying down with their executioners and exterminators. Woe woe woe . . . the last days of civilization are at hand.

(*The lights deepen more. And* MORT SILBERSTEIN *comes through the door singing and dancing a stylized rock horah.*
The room divides into two camps: one black, the other white.
MORT SILBERSTEIN *wears a greasy vest, a black bowler hat, baggy gray tweed pants, red suspenders, white sneakers, and a short-sleeved denim shirt beneath his dark brown vest. He has on dark glasses and affects an unkempt beard.*
He sings and dances about the room like a shadow as the characters make their speeches. And he passes out marijuana cigarettes to everyone, while the other characters pass in turn through a colored spotlight and give their raps.)

MONTY: (*Steps into spotlight, smokes a joint.*) This white chick, Janie, thinks she's got my nose open. Thinks she's stringin' me along. But I got news for her. She treats me like this 'cause I'm Black. Who does she think she is? I'm as good, nawh, better than any white dude she could have. Really, I'm doin' this girl a favor by payin' some attention to her. Look at all the broads around me. Peggy . . . Flossy . . . I bet I could even have Sharon if Len didn't go for her. But I don't cut into my buddies' chicks. All I got to do is snap my fingers and I could have almost any woman I wanted. So why should I get my guts tied up in knots about this blond fake? She's nothin' but a tease. Says she likes my poetry. Tell me now, how could a white broad love "Down with Whitey" poetry? Tells me she loves my mind. Ha . . . I wouldn't have much of a mind if I believed her. She came to my party, the one where I invited her, and told her corny little boyfriend where she'd be. Who does she think she is? She can't make a fool out of me. She's mine even if she doesn't know it yet. And I'm gonna take her when I'm ready. And the time's right. That's right, get her. Take her, get her, have her . . . whatever I gotta do. I dig her blond-lookin' self. And I don't care how long it takes to get her. I got all the time in the world. 'Cause the world is what you make it.

(MORT SILBERSTEIN *steps into the light with* MONTY.)

MORT SILBERSTEIN: What's happenin', brother?

MONTY: Mort Silberstein . . . I see you made it down, man. (*They slap five.*)

MORT SILBERSTEIN: Yeah, man, I brought you a lid. You know the price has gone up, don'cha, man? That bread you laid on me evaporated, man.

MONTY: Hey . . . man . . . we agreed on what it was to be, right?

MORT SILBERSTEIN: Yeah, man, but the price done gone up.

MONTY: How much, man?

MORT SILBERSTEIN: Say, look, man . . . I need me ten more dollars. Can you let me hold ten bucks, man?

MONTY: Nawh, man . . . my pockets are on empty.

MORT SILBERSTEIN: But, man, I need the bread to get myself together, man. I gotta make this rally, man. It's about your Civil Rights, ya know, man. And I ain't got no carfare or wine money.

MONTY: I'm sorry, Mort.

MORT SILBERSTEIN: But Martin Luther King's gonna be preachin' peace, man . . . and Malcolm X is gonna be rappin' some righteous revolutionary truth, man.

MORTY: I'm sorry, Mort.

MORT SILBERSTEIN: But I need it, Monty, man. Let me hold another ten. The shit's good, ain't it? We always been straight with each other, ain't we, man? But I gotta get myself together. It takes a lot of energy fightin' for the rights of you people. I'm a poet, man. Not no Freedom Rider . . . So you got to give me some consideration . . . Well, how 'bout five dollars then, man?

(*The lights go down on them. It comes up on* JANIE.)

JANIE: (*Smokes a joint, ladylike.*) I'm not really lonely. At least so I would know it. But there's not many people I can relate to . . . or even talk to. That's why I like Monty as a friend. He's nice. Sensitive. Serious. And with so much talent. That's why I can't allow him to get too close to me. I want him as a friend. That's all. It's not because of Lonnie. I'm tired of Lonnie. But he's like a bad habit I can't shake. I once thought he was the one for me. But I was younger and more innocent and didn't realize the vast differences and problems that lay between us. Lonnie will never be anything more than Lonnie, I guess. He'll never have a big name in jazz. Never really do more than be a second-rate sideman at the Whiskey-A-Go-Go. So it isn't Lonnie that keeps me from letting Monty have his way with me. Nor is it because Monty's Black and I'm white. Gee . . . I think colored people are neat. And I've made it with Black guys before. And I guess I'll do it some more. But not with Monty. He's a friend. A lifelong friend, I hope. And I know that men and women more often than not sacrifice their friendships when they become lovers. So I'll be true to Monty. To keep our friendship alive. And perhaps our relationship will mature into the purest of loves one day. An ideal Black/white love. Like sweet grapes change with age and care into a distinctive bouquet upon choice, rare wines.

(*The lights change subtly.* MONTY *steps into the light with* JANIE.)

MONTY: You called, Janie? . . . I came as soon as I got the message that you wanted to see me.

JANIE: Oh, Monty, I didn't know who else to turn to. I need your help.

MONTY: You know I'll do anything I can for you. Just ask.

JANIE: There's nobody else I could have turned to, Monty. It's so personal and private I couldn't tell my other friends. They all know one another and word would have gotten out. You are my last resort, Monty.

MONTY: What is it, Janie? What can I do? Who do you want killed, Miss Janie?

JANIE: Please don't treat this as a joke . . . Monty . . . I have to have an abortion.

MONTY: You do?

JANIE: Yes . . . Lonnie and I have broken up. I don't want to see him anymore. And I can't have a baby now anyhow. I'm at U.C.L.A. . . . and Daddy would never understand or forgive me. And I'd die if anybody knew. Will you help me? Will you? Please, Monty.

MONTY: Sure . . . sure . . . I'll drive you down to Tijuana . . . or even El Paso, if necessary. When we get back, you can stay at my place. I've got my own pad now. And nobody will have to know where you are or how you're doin' until you're ready. You can even pretend that you're my woman.

JANIE: You're such a good friend, Monty.

MONTY: (*Serious.*) You know I've always loved you, Janie.

JANIE: (*Places her fingers across his lips.*) Shh . . . Monty . . . please . . . don't say things that we'll both regret later.

MONTY: Why does it have to be this way between us, Janie?

JANIE: I don't know. It's just that I think of you as somebody special for me. And I refuse to spoil that secret, special feeling.

MONTY: You're wrong, you know, Miss Janie.

JANIE: That's impossible . . . You know that, Monty.

MONTY: Well, we better start making our plans for the trip. It'll all be over in a day or so.

JANIE: Monty . . . I won't have any money until my dad sends me my monthly allowance.

MONTY: That's okay. I've got enough in my checking account. I can stop at the bank on our way out of town.

JANIE: What would I do without you, Monty? You know, in my own way I love you very much. Please . . . let's neither of us ever do anything to destroy what we have together.

MONTY: I'll try and do my part, Miss Janie. C'mon . . . it's time to split.

JANIE: You know . . . I don't even resent that silly name you call me too much anymore, Monty. It's grown on me like you have.

(*He lifts her and cradles her in his arms. Then he carries her away as the lights go down. Lights up on* PEGGY.)

PEGGY: Now, that was a romantic scene . . . huh? Yeah . . . Monty can really act romantic when he tries. Even with me. You know, he married me finally. Yeah. One day he up and proposed. And we got married soon afterward at the county courthouse with Len acting as best man. And then he got me to drop out of school and go to work for a bank to support him and send him to school. It was halfway slick on his part. He shoulda been a con man. He had me goin' for a good while. I was strung out. See, I loved him. Really

loved him. And still do. As only a Black woman can love a
Black man. But he never loved me. Damn, I don't believe
Monty ever loved anybody except Monty. He's selfish, ya
know. And kinda cruel. But I dig him. Still do. And I had
some good moments with him. All those other girls he had
didn't matter. I knew he never really cared about them. Not
even Janie. But she's conceited enough to think they had
something going. White girls are some dizzy critters. I know.
'Cause I know about Black men better than they know about
themselves. My father was Black. And my husband, Monty,
was too. So I know. Even though I was innocent and
wouldn't believe the truth for a long time. But Monty never
treated me right. He always would be sayin' that he had to
have time to do his thing. That's why I was workin' and
gettin' my mind messed up 'cause he was doin' his thing.
Wow! . . . sure was a heavy trip. The scenes we went through
for the time we were together. We broke up about a dozen
times. I even had a baby one of the times while we was
broke up . . . and I put it up for adoption before we went
back together again. But I learned a lot from Monty. A
whole lot. And I wouldn't trade those happy moments with
him for nothin'. 'Cause loneliness is a fatal disease . . . and
I've got a terminal case . . . But that moment of love with
him was delicious. And you know . . . even the pain was
sweet though bitter.

(PEGGY *lingers in the light.* FLOSSY *joins her.*)

FLOSSY: Don't feel blue, girl. None of them are worth it. Men
are no good, that's all. They either be tricks or they be out
to put you in one, so forget 'em. We women gotta do our
own thing.
PEGGY: But why we got to get our lives cluttered up with these
white things? First these white heifers that be after our men,
then white studs who think they be after you.
FLOSSY: Well, you should know, girl.
PEGGY: Yeah, I should know somethin', Flossy Mae, 'cause after
I finally broke from Monty for good, I married me a white
boy. Yeah, a white boy. 'Cause he wasn't no man yet. I guess
that was the one way to finally get completely away from
Monty. Marry a devil. His pride was hurt so bad he didn't
even see me for years afterward. Almost finally became a real
Black Nationalist and revolutionary. But the years without him

have been very, very lonely, girl. And no little white boy or booze, scag or L.S.D. or nothin' could fill them.

FLOSSY: It's the fault of those funky white bitches who think they can lick and suck the world up like a bowl of buttermilk. Our men especially.

PEGGY: Don't blame them, Flossy. Don't blame anybody. Now, I don't blame you, do I? And you and Monty had your thing goin' under my nose, you bitch. I got out my front door to work. And you'd be in the back door with my man.

FLOSSY: Well, you know that my thing is making it with my friend-girl's ole man, honey.

(*A light comes up on another part of the stage. It shows* MONTY *and* JANIE.)

JANIE: (*Calls.*) Hello. Hello, Monty . . . Monty, hello . . .

MONTY: Hi, Janie . . . how you doin'?

JANIE: I came up to Frisco to visit you, Monty. Since you've moved up here, I've missed you a lot. You don't think Peggy will mind, do you?

MONTY: Nawh . . . nawh . . . you know Peggy always liked you.

JANIE: Good . . . then I'll stay the week with you. You can take me all around beautiful San Francisco and show me everything.

FLOSSY: (*Moves toward* MONTY; *calls out.*) Hey, Monty . . . Monty, my man. I'm here.

JANIE: Who's that, Monty?

MONTY: It's Flossy—a friend of mine. She comes over and keeps me company while Peggy's at work.

(FLOSSY *enters and she and* MONTY *kiss passionately and begin lovemaking.*)

JANIE: Oh, excuse me. I didn't know you would have company, Monty. I thought we would be alone until Peggy came. I thought we'd be able to watch the city lights from high atop here on Potrero Hill and talk of our old school days. I didn't know you had someone besides me . . . somebody real . . . somebody Black and sensual as the night who would blot out my pale image like a cloud covering a dim, far constellation.

(*Lights down on* JANIE *and* MONTY. FLOSSY *returns to* PEG-GY's *area.*)

FLOSSY: That Monty was a no-good nigger. He'd sit that old white girl in one room and have her read his poetry and stuff while he screwed me until my tongue hung out in the next room. Chile . . . it was a scream. With those thin walls you could hear a roach pee on a soda cracker . . . and the stains on the couch. What did you have in your head when you saw that, girl?

PEGGY: Ha, ha . . . I was ignorant. I thought that the cats kept gettin' up there and were messin' around.

FLOSSY: Ooeeee . . . and the way Monty would sock it to me, girl, that lil white broad musta thought we were tearin' down the house with all that humpin'. I knew she'd be gettin' hot as a ten-cent pistol 'cause when we'd come out she'd turn all red lookin' and her eyes would be waterin'.

PEGGY: Yeah . . . and when I got home from work at midnight, everybody would still be lookin' funny. Smiling secretly to yourselves. Damn, I was dumb. I thought it was because of the wine and pot.

FLOSSY: Nigger men ain't no good, Peggy. We sisters should start takin' these niggers' heads off behind the stuff they be pullin' on us.

PEGGY: Maybe so . . . maybe so . . . at least I could agree with you at one time. When I cared about men. But I'm a liberated lesbian now. See, I had to learn to cope with the world the best way I could. Sister Power is where it's at!

FLOSSY: Right on!

PEGGY: (*Tender.*) You're still my friend, ain't you, Flossy?

(*The two women embrace and kiss passionately, then walk off into the shadows, hand in hand.*)
(*Lights change. Up on* LONNIE.)

LONNIE: (*Hands in pockets, casual.*) Yeah, man, it wasn't the times that betrayed us . . . it was ourselves. We each fed on the other's weaknesses instead of gettin' it together like the rhetoric says and giving some support to each other to make it through. Yeah, I went with Janie. Was really heavy into it with her for a while. But there were too many things keeping us apart. Her fear of what her parents would say, for one. And her always lookin' to be liberated . . . or somethin'. She was a school chick. All the time in college and never knowing what she was there for or what she wanted out of it. Her mother and father went to college, ya know. So she's got to make a career of it . . . And her having her own friends, and trying to have her own scene. That cat Monty's okay, but anybody can see what he's after. But Janie won't admit it. I'm a jazz musician, see. Play electric guitar. Not a big-timer. But I make it in L.A. okay, with a few gigs in Vegas, up in Tahoe, and around Palm Springs to make ends meet. And being around spades all the time in the music business, I gets to know them, you see. They okay, if they keep their distance and know their place. Some of my best friends . . . you know? But you got to give them dudes credit. They got lots of the broads psyched out. They got a whole super stud/super spade thing goin' for them. I had to finally cut Janie loose because of our different points of view. She and her hang-ups got to be a drag. And that was a good little while ago that we broke it off. Yeah, she had three abortions while we were together. She would tell me after she got them, after it was all over. I hated seeing that happen without being able to say anything about it; ya know, being a part of that made me feel guilty. I once told her that she was murdering our spirit and soul when she did that. She told me that she didn't believe in spirit and that everyone knew that the spades had all the soul. Guess she was high on somethin'. I told her that she was killing our future. She said she was afraid of the future. And she was never happy with me after that. I guess she thought I threatened her liberation . . . And she and I have been through and done ever since. Now I'm into a new thing. I'm into the true spirit now, ya know, religion. I belong to the Baha'i World Faith. All mankind are my family.

(LONNIE *takes a pair of dark glasses from his shirt pocket and puts them on.* RICK *joins him.*)

RICK: (*Disdain.*) Well . . . if it isn't one of the Chosen People.
LONNIE: You talkin' to me, man?
RICK: Is there somethin' wrong with your eyes, devil? There's nobody here but us.
LONNIE: Hey . . . stop tryin' to intimidate me. You tryin' to start a fight, ain'tcha?
RICK: (*Ridicule.*) How could even I start a fight with a nonviolent devil?
LONNIE: Why you gotta cast me as the devil, man?

RICK: (*Self-righteous.*) Because you are the son of Yacub . . . the original devil!

LONNIE: Look, man, everyone makes their own devil. Dig it? I'm really a child of God like you are and all mankind. So I don't see why you got to be comin' down on me for somethin' I ain't had no part in.

RICK: You are equally as guilty as your brothers and your father.

LONNIE: Listen, man, you got a rap for everybody, ain't ya? You got one for your Black brothers, for chicks, and you got another rap . . . yeah, man . . . I remember when you were quotin' Shakespeare and Omar Khayyam at the Young Socialist parties to all the little white broads you say you hate now. That was only last semester, man, and now your rap for me is that I'm the devil. Your game is weak, Rick, man.

RICK: Your reign on earth is nearly up, devil. You have ruled your allotted six thousand years, and now it is time for the Black man to rise.

LONNIE: Shut up! Shut up, will ya? You're worse than those fanatic Zionists I grew up with.

RICK: First Israel will fall!

LONNIE: Hey . . . that's got nothin' to do with me. I ain't a Jew no more. Hey! I don't want to hear that crazy crap you're talkin'!

RICK: Allah will sweep you white European devils into the sea.

LONNIE: Can't you just treat me like a human being?

RICK: Your time is nearly at hand, devil.

LONNIE: You know what, man? I liked you better when you had a sense of humor.

RICK: Death to devils! Destroy the enemies of the Black people!

LONNIE: I'll see you later, man. You've lost your cool. And I never did think you'd start believing your own bullshit.

(LONNIE *exits.* RICK *stands for a moment, relishing his victory. He puffs out his chest and walks into the shadows.*)

(*The light changes.* LEN *appears.*)

LEN: By my appearance you wouldn't take me to be a great teacher, would you? But I am. A great teacher and influencer of men . . . and lover of the finer things of life, such as art, literature, theater, fast cars, good food and women, especially. In fact, I nourished those tastes in my friend Monty. And some of it has been taken and cultivated by him, especially the finer ones like drama. Yes . . . yes, indeed . . .

and it was I who first taught Rick about nationalism . . .
Black Nationalism. He read Garvey in the books I loaned
him and encountered the righteous brothers of the Nation of
Islam at my Sunday Black cultural discussions and teas. And
I was the first to explain to him who was the most Honorable
Elijah Muhammad . . . and cite the Messenger's importance
to contemporary Black America. Now, you might ask, what's
so great about pullin' his coat to things he would find out
sooner or later, but you're now seeing Rick in his neophyte
state. Before this decade is out, the sixties, he becomes a
large national figure on the Black revolutionary scene and
falls after his rise like so many of his brothers in the struggle.
But it was nationalism that lit the fires in his ambitious heart.
So don't put down nationalism. It is the stuff that fuels revo-
lutions. Agreed? One can even say that the Zionists are the
nationalists of Israel, couldn't one? And that Al-Fatah and
other Arab terrorist organizations are the nationalists of
Occupied Palestine. Nationalism translated means national
liberation, wherever that nation stands. But these are arguments that will take too long to deal with. Tonight you are
looking into some of the makings of the sixties . . . which,
of course, went to make the seventies. Just think, at this
moment in our story the Kennedys have still to be disposed
of, Malcolm X hasn't passed from the scene, Watts has to
happen, Martin Luther King, Jr., must go to the mountain—
never to return. Ah, many things are spoken of here. And
the writer of this integrated social epic hints at only some
surface manifestations of the times, for he did not know the
impact of these accidental associations. He did not know that
through me he would discover the kernel of political truth
of the era, the seminal social vision of the sweep of so much
history . . . But I have gotten long-winded. There's so much
to say and so little time. But remember, more political and
cultural phenomena came out of Southern California in the
mid-century than Richard Nixon and Walt Disney.

(*Lights change slightly, and* SHARON *joins* LEN.)

SHARON: Len . . . you're not a Black Nationalist, are you?
LEN: Why, of course not, Sharon, dear. I just know all about
it. In fact, I know about almost everything.
SHARON: Yes, you know so much about all the Black stuff . . .
but those fanatics and radicals that collect around you . . .
LEN: Sharon, I am an intellectual. I can intellectually examine

any human proposition, but I don't allow my feelings to become involved.

SHARON: Oh, how do you do that?

LEN: I can find rationalizations for everything, my dear.

SHARON: How clever. So you don't think I'm a devil after all?

LEN: Well, at least not a big one . . . ha-ha . . .

SHARON: You're cute too, Len. Ah, you're not going to think I'm a tramp when I give you some of my body, are you?

LEN: A tramp? How could I? You're from a nice middle-class Jewish background. How could I think that?

SHARON: I was pretty wild during my last year of high school and my one year of junior college.

LEN: That was mere teeny-bopper rebellion, Sharon. Adolescent adjustment to approaching maturity.

SHARON: I made it with over seventy fellas before I lost count.

LEN: There's nothing to feel guilty about. It was done in the innocence of youth. You were a child of the times, my dear.

SHARON: Guys would say that I looked like Liz Taylor, and they'd all want to make it with me. And what was a girl to say?

LEN: It must have been pretty harrowing to have come through that stage.

SHARON: At drive-ins, in the back-seats of convertibles, at their pads while their mothers were sunning themselves at the beach . . .

LEN: Come here, Sharon. Let me hold you and make you forget those terrible times.

SHARON: Actually, it was a lot of fun for a while. But I'm glad you're so understanding, Len. That's what I need: a man who is willing to try and understand me.

(*Lights change.* LEN *moves away.*)

SHARON: And we were married . . . Len and I. At the First Unitarian Church. It was a dull wedding. But my mother was happy and cried. And my sister didn't act too snobbish. Even lots of my old beaus came. And it all turned out lots better than I thought it would. I was glad, in fact. And Len and I settled down in an apartment close to City College, where Len was in his fifth year, even though it's a two-year school. And we started getting used to each other. Which was easier said than done. In fact, it was hell. You know, it took us over five years before we really sorta ironed out our difficulties. But the times we had, my God! We gave a million parties. And I momentarily fell back into my bad habits with men. But it wasn't serious, so Len and I discussed it and decided it was merely an aspect of my neurosis. And we moved at least a dozen times. Sometimes trying to get away from each other. And I tried to break away from Len when he wasn't trying to put me down or in my place or in the kitchen, and it was pretty terrible for a while. We even broke up a number of times. But that's history now. We're back together and are making it. We have a pretty large son now, who is spoiled bad as hell and looks just like Len. Len's got his own business now. I kid him about his Marxist days now that he's a working capitalist, but he reminds me that he's really an intellectual. We're one of the lucky couples. We made it. But it took a lot of doing. And let me tell you, it's not easy being married to a Black man . . . even if he's an intellectual or not. But we're making it.

(SHARON *hesitates, and is joined by* MORT SILBERSTEIN.)

MORT SILBERSTEIN: Well, well . . . if it isn't the poor little bourgeois nice non-kosher girl.

SHARON: You talkin' to me, fella?

MORT SILBERSTEIN: Nawh . . . I'm not talkin' to you, honey. I'm talkin' to the girl who lays all the spades in town, then adds racial suicide to cultural injury by marrying one.

SHARON: You're very insulting. You have no business talking to me that way.

MORT SILBERSTEIN: I have every right in the world. Every right in the world. It's because of women like you from good Jewish homes that go out and betray their heritage and upbringing that we Jews are being threatened with extinction in the world. Why do you have to go out and disgrace us by making a display of yourself?

SHARON: You've got your nerve to talk to me, Mort Silberstein. You live with a German girl. From Germany!

MORT SILBERSTEIN: Who told you that? Has Monty been talking about me behind my back?

SHARON: Who would bother to talk about a nothing like you?

MORT SILBERSTEIN: You can't trust anybody these days . . . especially spades. That's really rank . . . runnin' me down behind my back.

SHARON: Well, I'm glad you didn't try and deny it.

MORT SILBERSTEIN: Yeah, it's true. But I just live with her. I'm not marrying her.

SHARON: You have your nerve to talk like that to me. Why aren't you with a Jewish girl?

MORT SILBERSTEIN: A Jewish girl? Are you kiddin'? I had a mother who tried to drown me in chicken soup and bury me beneath lox and bagels.

SHARON: Well, don't you ever want to start a family and settle down?

MORT SILBERSTEIN: Are you serious? If I got married, I'd probably end up with someone exactly like you. You'd probably have me out selling insurance or real estate to keep you.

SHARON: What's so wrong about that? Len works. I wouldn't have a man unless he took care of me the best way he knew how.

MORT SILBERSTEIN: Haven't you girls heard of women's liberation? What are you talking about down at B'nai B'rith these days . . . the miracle of Israel? How a bunch of European imperialists made the desert green and fertile? You'd have to go get a job drivin' a cab or somethin' before I'd look at you. I'd never take care of a lazy bitch like you.

SHARON: It's a wonder you're not sniffin' around that little Janie character. Everyone else is. She could take care of you with the allowance she gets from her folks.

MORT SILBERSTEIN: I'm not much of a herd animal. Let the bucks have their dough. Besides, she's a middle-class goy. Don't you realize that I'm a radical poet? I wouldn't be caught dead near her . . . the proto-all-American plastic fascist cunt! That would be like makin' it with Tricia Nixon. Bad news. I'll leave her for the Black studs.

SHARON: What's so different about the girl you're stayin' with?

MORT SILBERSTEIN: Nina? Well, Nina's a Marxist. And a revolutionary Leninist-Trotskyite. To Marxists, race and cultural group take second and third place to the international world struggle for national liberation.

SHARON: Ahhh . . . you ex-Hasidic Jews are all nuts. Leave me alone, will ya? I have a baby who is half Black. That's the only reality I can deal with now. I don't care who killed Jesus.

(*Lights change.* SHARON *and* MORT SILBERSTEIN *disappear.* FLOSSY *appears.*)

FLOSSY: Some party, hey? I come to all of Monty's parties. Some are better than this one . . . and some are worse. I don't live around here. Hardly no Black people do except

the ones you see here tonight. That's why it's such an integrated scene. Mostly college dudes and broads. Sure is
phony, huh? But I like Monty. We buddies . . . fuckin' buddies. We make it every once in a while. I like it with him.
He makes me feel like a real woman and a lady at the same
time. He's . . . well, you know, intelligent and nice. And he
don't put me down when I act crazy or wild. Or when I can't
pronounce those big words some of them be usin' around
here or know what they mean. These other brothers here
are messed up, but Monty's gettin' it together. If he could
ever get his nose out of these white bitches' behinds, he'd
be better off. But he and Peggy might do a thing. But I
don't see no future in it. They both got a lot of hang-ups,
if you know what I mean. He don't even like her as much
as he like me, but I'm too much out runnin' the street to
have a guy like Monty depend on me. So Peggy can have
him. I'll still see him when I want. And things will be okay.
As long as he don't get too strung out behind these white
bitches.

(JANIE *joins her.*)

JANIE: Hello, Flossy, how are you doing?

FLOSSY: Okay, I guess, until now.

JANIE: Oh, why did you say that?

FLOSSY: 'Cause I fixed my mouth to say that and that's what
I said.

JANIE: Oh, don't you like me, Flossy?

FLOSSY: You're okay, I guess.

JANIE: But there's somethin' wrong. Have I done anything?

FLOSSY: Nawh, you ain't done nothin' wrong. Just be white,
that's all.

JANIE: Flossy, I didn't know you were a Black Nationalist.

FLOSSY: I was in the temple for a minute . . . but aside from
that, I just don't like the way you carry yourself.

JANIE: I don't understand. Are you talking about Monty and
I? We're only friends, that's all.

FLOSSY: We only friends too, but he don't look at me the way
he looks at you.

JANIE: Maybe he's got what he wants from you . . . and he
wants what he thinks he can get from me.

FLOSSY: Maybe. Say, you're pretty hip in your own way. I'm
gonna tell ya somethin'.

JANIE: You are? What's that?

FLOSSY: The Game. I'm gonna tell ya what it is and then show you how to play it.

JANIE: You are? It's not going to hurt or anything, is it?

FLOSSY: Nawh. It all happens in the mind. You won't feel a thing except understanding.

(FLOSSY *pulls her into a corner and begins talking in whispers.* FLOSSY *slaps five with her;* JANIE *clumsily and timidly slaps palms.* FLOSSY *cracks up;* JANIE *giggles.*)

(RICK *appears as the girls fade out.*)

RICK: Ain't this some jive! Ain't it? Here I am with my Blackness in some jive-time stuff as this. Here I am with my roommates . . . stone integrationists . . . and vanilla-fever freaks. Wow! It's sad. These so-called Negroes ain't never gonna get themselves out of slavery. Len, my old friend and once intellectual peer, is on the eve of marrying one of these devil ladies. And Brother Monty, the poor poet brother, is waitin' for Miss Ann—oh, excuse me, waitin' for *Miss Janie* to give him some lovin'. Been waitin' for a good time and will wait for years, I'm told. In fact, this whole thing is about the Negro gettin' ready to get himself some of blond Miss Janie. What a drag. I've been to better parties, I'll tell ya. My Black brothers . . . two white women lovers. Now, ain't that a blip? How sad. No wonder so many of we Black people were so confused all of the sixties and now into the seventies: we were in a war, and was lovin' the enemy. With all the sisters out here in the world, these deaf, dumb and blind Negroes are waitin' for the devil's women to give them some of their stale, ole cold, funky butts and make them feel like men. But the sisters in this scene are comin' out of some strange bags, I'll kid you not. This neighborhood is too close to Hollywood. This is Babylon! The beginning of the end. The folks here are just jiving their lives away. I just see that I have to get myself out of here. That's right. I gotta split. I can't do nothin' 'round here. I'm just about on my way too . . . soon as this party's over and I can catch me a ride downtown.

(PEGGY *walks up to* RICK.)

PEGGY: Hey, Rick. I can give you a ride. I drive a little no-top sports car now since I divorced Monty and temporarily married my new husband. That's before I cut men loose completely . . . dig?

RICK: It won't take you out of your way, will it, sister?

PEGGY: Nawh. Just let me know when you're ready to motor.

RICK: Thank you, sister. For someone who has so many problems, you're really a real woman . . . In some ways, at least . . . ha-ha . . .

PEGGY: Well, what do you think I'd be?

RICK: (*Self-righteous and pompous.*) Sister, you must admit . . . you live a very unnatural way of life . . . I know it developed over a time of suffering . . . your disillusionment with your unfulfilled life . . . your loss through resignation of your baby . . . your exploitation by your black man . . . your search for love and emotional and physical security . . . your penis envy . . . and, ah, other masculine-feminine conflicts and encounters . . . Now, take this scene. This is where your relationship with Brother Monty was nurtured. That's heavy. At wine and pot parties to impress white girls!

PEGGY: Hey, listen, Rick . . .

RICK: (*Speech-making.*) The devil has mastered his trick-nology to such a state as to turn you, sister, into a freak, and to convert your man into an animal without culture or history, hungering after pale flesh.

PEGGY: No, Rick. Don't distort things so much. We didn't party to impress white girls. Or anybody. They were just there, that's all. And we wanted them there. The girls . . . and the boys. Our heads were into that then. It was the thing to do. We believed in America. The whole trip. And America was boring and we were young. We were just thinking that that was the best way to have a good time. We had to socialize in some way, didn't we?

RICK: But nevertheless, you went from this room into an unfortunate marriage to a confused Negro which you keep mentioning, and the subsequent divorce, and then marriage to a white boy—

PEGGY: He wasn't a boy! He wasn't! Man, stop being so goddamn condescending . . . and—and . . .

RICK: Historical!

PEGGY: Awww, fuck you!

RICK: Yes, ha-ha-ha, sister . . . or should I say *mister* to you?

PEGGY: Say "Ms.," Rick. I'm not ashamed now for anything I've done or anything that I am or do now.

RICK: But to have this Western madhouse of North America drive you into becoming a freak, sister.

PEGGY: Freak! You call me a freak? Well, look what happened to you, Rick. You became something called a Cultural Nationalist. Hah! In fact, you thought you invented it. And when the media pumped your head full of your own bull, you wigged out on a Section Eight trip. What was it now? Torturing young Black women? Freaking out? Oh, I know—or at least what I heard—you were under stress and had been keeping your thing together with speed 'cause those other comic-opera political clowns—the big Black cats—were on your case after the big shoot-out and assassination out at U.C.L.A.—

RICK: Hey! Hey! You got it all wrong and backward. You don't know what you're talkin' about, sister. In fact, you are incorrect! So why don't you just keep quiet about all that? It ain't even happened yet. So be cool.

PEGGY: But you haven't let me tell all of your future yet, Brother Rick.

RICK: I already know my future. It is going to be glorious!

PEGGY: If you think so, Rick. If you think so. But do you know what?

RICK: What's that, sister?

PEGGY: We all failed. Failed ourselves in that serious time known as the sixties. And by failing ourselves we failed in the test of the times. We had so much going for us . . . so much potential. Do you realize it, man? We were the youth of our times . . . and we blew it. Blew it completely. Look where it all ended. Look what happened? (*They are looking out front at the audience.*) We just turned out lookin' like a bunch of punks and freaks and fuck-offs.

RICK: It has been said: "If one doesn't deal with reality, then reality will certainly deal with them."

PEGGY Amen.

RICK: But I am not allowing myself to be held to blame. I am not allowing myself to be other than glorious. History will vindicate me.

PEGGY: Hey, man, you know, you never left yesterday. You're confused like all of us. Hey, do you still want that ride out of here?

RICK: Nawh, sister. Not really, anymore. I'll make it the best way I can. Are you going now?

PEGGY: Nawh, brother. Not now. I'm going to stay over and sleep with Monty. Give him a little action, ya know? If I don't, I'll never get him and have him all to myself for the few years we were together. I have to try and save him from himself, don't I? I can't just let the Miss Janies dance off with the world, can I?

RICK: Go get 'em, tiger. Ya know, it be about what you make it anyway.

(*Lights fade on them. It comes up on* MORT SILBERSTEIN.)

MORT SILBERSTEIN: (*Smokes a joint.*) This is a crazy scene,
ain't it? An honest-to-God creepy insane looney bin. A picture of the times, I say. And you can't forgive the creator
of this mess for the confusion. That's what happens when
you mix things up like this. It throws everything out of kilter.
Jews, niggers, politics, Germans, time, philosophy, memory,
theme, sociology, past, drugs, history, sex, present, women,
faggots, men, dikes, phoneys, assholes . . . everything
bunched up together. Looks like the worst party of the
decade, right? Probably the worse goddamn party in memory. Huh? Hey, you got any money? Have ya, huh? How
about lendin' me ten bucks? Ten bucks, okay? How about
it? Okay? . . . No? Well, then, five. C'mon. Five fuckin'
bucks for chrissakes! Look, I ain't no crummy wino. I got
some kinda class. It takes at least five bucks to cop some
scag. Now, ain't that right? So be a good guy and let me
have ten. You won't even miss it. Take it off your taxes as
a donation to art. I'm a Beat poet from the fifties, see. Put
it on your expense account . . . or somethin'. I can get a
nickel bag of smoke and get fixed up for a ten. What? You
say I've lost my bearings and am quoting East Coast seventies prices? Wow! Dig him. A drug-culture freak. Hey, man,
I'm only tryin' to get a fuckin' high on, not earn a fuckin'
degree. (MONTY *enters.*) Hey, Monty. Tell these folks how
bad I need ten bucks.

MONTY: Hey, man, I ain't in it.

MORT SILBERSTEIN: You ain't in it? If you ain't in it, then who
is?

MONTY: You ain't serious about nothin', Mort. I gotta cut you
loose.

MORT SILBERSTEIN: Well, will ya dig that? He says I ain't
serious. Man if I ain't fuckin' serious about gettin' fixed up,
then you don't know what serious is.

MONTY: Listen, I gotta cut you loose, white boy. You ain't
nothin' but a hang-up. Messin' around with you will get
somebody killed. In fact, it already has and will.

MORT SILBERSTEIN: (*Turns away.*) Awww, you spades.

MONTY: (*Grabs* MORT SILBERSTEIN *by the collar.*) If you say
that again, I'll crush your filthy nose.

MORT SILBERSTEIN: See what I mean? See what I mean? It
always comes to this with you guys. Shit, man! We lost people in Mississippi too, hero. Where were you at Kent State,

huh, Freedom Rider? I been with you for a long time and on a long, long trip, from Scottsboro and back, and now you coppin' out with mashin' my nose and talkin' that Third World Black people's crap. The Arabs ain't Black, man? You ain't got no place in Palestine! You can't even go to Algiers no more! . . . And the Egyptians sold your mammy!

(MONTY *punches him.* MORT SILBERSTEIN *begins to cry.*)

MORT SILBERSTEIN: The whole goddamn world has gone and went fuckeroo . . . and I don't care. I'm sick and need a fix and I don't give a fuck no more about nothin'. Kiss my Lower East Side ass, blackie.

MONTY: (*Shouting.*) I don't want to be a white man, do you hear me, Mort Silberstein? I don't want to be a token Jew even. I'm me. You understand? It's taken a long time, but I know that now.

MORT SILBERSTEIN: (*Screaming.*) All I know is that I am a Zionist junkie . . . and I don't give a shit for fertilizer . . . but what are you still gettin' your rocks off a 'blond meat for and still talkin' that Black shit!

MONTY: Shut up! Shut up your goddamn mouth before I kill ya.

MORT SILBERSTEIN: (*Quieter, serious.*) You can't kill me any more than you can kill the last century. I'm in your head, nigger, like your nightmares.

MONTY: (*Scared.*) No! Nothin's in my head except Congo drums and freeway sounds and the A train bearing down on 125th Street.

(*They wrestle about the stage. The other party members move about as if sleep walking.*)

MORT SILBERSTEIN: You're in love with my father . . . and his father's father . . . not the wet-slime presence of Miss Janie.

MONTY: Shut up! You don't know what you're talking about!

MORT SILBERSTEIN: You're in love with *Marx*!

MONTY: (*Hits him and screams.*) *Mao*!!!

MORT SILBERSTEIN: You're thrilled by *Freud*!

MONTY: (*Hits him and screams.*) *Fanon*!!!

MORT SILBERSTEIN: You suck *Einstein*!

MONTY: (*Hits him again and screams.*) *Voodoo*!!!

MORT SILBERSTEIN: You're freaky for *Jesus*!

(MONTY *beats* MORT SILBERSTEIN *unconscious, then rests.*)

(*The others in the room wake and stir.*)

PEGGY: Wow, honey . . . that was some bad grass. Hey, you and Mort Silberstein have a disagreement or somethin'?

LONNIE: Say, I'm splittin' . . . This looks like a bust to me. Hey, Janie, you ready to make it, baby?

JANIE: Nawh. I think I'm gonna stick around awhile. Monty's going to tell me the story of his life. (*Exits into the kitchen.*)

PEGGY: (*Shrugs.*) In that case, I guess I better get my hat too. You need a ride, Lonnie?

LONNIE: Why not, doll?

(LONNIE *and* PEGGY *exit.*)

LEN: I'm going to bed, Monty. See you in the morning. We can clean up this mess then, brother.

SHARON: Wait for me, Len. You know . . . you're kinda frantic for me. And besides, we're getting married soon.

(LEN *and* SHARON *exit through the back door.*)

FLOSSY: (*Kisses* MONTY.) It was a boss party, baby. I'll see you next week, huh? Come on by my place and lay up some. Oweee . . . I'll be as hot as snot for you by then, sugar.

RICK: Wait up, sister. You're on your way back to the ghetto, ain'tcha? I need some company back to civilization. Well, Brother Monty, it ends the way it ends, doesn't it?

MONTY: Yeah, man, this is the beginning of the sixties . . . but it seems like forever. And I'm so goddamn tired already. We got a long way to go, ain't we?

RICK: You said it, not me, brother. Not me. Hey, anything I can do for you before I disappear?

MONTY: (*Points to the body.*) Yeah, man, throw this thing out in the trash on your way out.

RICK: Okay, brother. For you it'll be no problem. 'Cause I know you'd do the same for me.

(RICK *and* FLOSSY *grab* MORT SILBERSTEIN *and drag him out.* JANIE *comes out of the kitchen. She wears her dark glasses and has her hair combed out.*)

MONTY: I never knew it would come to this.

JANIE: Neither did I. If anyone told me that after knowing you all these years you'd turn on me and rape me, I'd tell them that they don't know you at all. Or what makes up our wonderful relationship.

MONTY: I'm sorry I disappointed you. But I never had a chance to cop before. Funny, for twelve—thirteen years . . . I've never really been close enough to you to use an opportunity to take you like I wanted.

JANIE: Oh, yes you have . . . you just never knew it, that's all. Some people have thought all you ever had to do was push me and I'd fall over backward and my legs would fly open for you. But they never really knew us . . . never knew what we had and now have lost.

MONTY: Probably. We have been good friends, you know. Really, actually, true friends.

JANIE: Should I take a bath first?

MONTY: (*Begins undoing her clothes.*) So many things kept us apart. So many things . . . You know, if our signs were compatible, I'd probably have tried to marry you.

JANIE: Oh, no, you've always been too color conscious.

MONTY: Yeah, you're right.

JANIE: Remember the friend we had who hanged herself?

MONTY: Sure. How can I forget? We were a couple of her closest friends, or so we thought.

JANIE: She just went up on Mount Tamaipais and tied a rope to a tree branch and swung off.

MONTY: Are you going to scream and fight me, Miss Janie?

JANIE: I know you too well, don't I, Monty? I'd feel so icky doing something like that.

(*The lights dim. He fully undresses her.*)

MONTY: I've never wanted anyone as much as I have wanted you.

JANIE: Don't tell me what you tell all the others.

MONTY: You . . . I'm going to enjoy this very, very much.

JANIE: She just put the noose over her head and felt her spirit dance away.

(MONTY *pushes her back on the couch and he tears the last of her clothes away and the lights go down to blackness.*)

MA RAINEY'S BLACK BOTTOM

A PLAY IN TWO ACTS

by *August Wilson*

Ma Rainey's Black Bottom opened on April 6, 1984, at the Yale Repertory Theater in New Haven, Connecticut. It opened on Broadway at the Cort Theater on October 11, 1984.

452

AUGUST WILSON

Poet, playwright and director August Wilson was born and grew up in Pittsburgh. Dissatisfied with his formal schooling, he dropped out after the ninth grade and continued his education on his own, haunting the libraries and practicing writing styles while doing odd jobs to support himself. During the 1960s, he became a part of the Black Arts movement in Pittsburgh, founding the Black Horizon Theater, where he produced and directed plays by other African American playwrights. Later moving to St. Paul, Minnesota, where he became associate playwright-in-residence at the Playwrights Center and was awarded a McKnight Fellowship in playwriting, he saw production of several early plays of his own. From there he submitted a play to the Eugene O'Neill National Playwrights Conference, whose director was Lloyd Richards, dean of the Yale School of Drama and artistic director of the Yale Repertory Theater. Richards accepted the script, entitled *Mill Hand's Lunch Bucket*, for workshop production at the conference, and the rest is history. The following year, Wilson's *Ma Rainey's Black Bottom* moved from the O'Neill Center to the Yale Repertory to Broadway, where it won the Drama Critics Circle Award for best play in 1986. The Wilson-Richards collaboration (Richards has directed all of Wilson's plays since *Ma Rainey*) has continued to mounting success with *Fences* in 1987; *Joe Turner's Come and Gone* in 1988; and *The Piano Lesson* in 1990. All have won Drama Critics Circle Awards. *Fences* also won the 1987 Tony Award. Both *Fences* and *The Piano Lesson* won Pulitzer Prizes for Drama. And *Fences*—which ran on Broadway for two years with first James Earl Jones and then Billy Dee Williams as stars— won more top awards and grossed more money at the box office than any other non-musical play in Broadway history.

Wilson is also the recipient of fellowships in playwriting from the Guggenheim, Bush, and Rockefeller foundations. At this writing, two more of his plays, *Two Trains Running* and *Moon Going Down*, are in the pipeline and poised for early production.

> *They tore the railroad down*
> *so the Sunshine Special can't run*
> *I'm going away baby*
> *build me a railroad on my own*
>   —Blind Lemon Jefferson

CHARACTERS

STURDYVANT
IRVIN
CUTLER
TOLEDO
SLOW DRAG
LEVEE
MA RAINEY
POLICEMAN
DUSSIE MAE
SYLVESTER

THE SETTING: *There are two playing areas: what is called the "band room" and the recording studio. The band room is at stage left and is in the basement of the building. It is entered through a door up left. There are benches and chairs scattered about, a piano, a row of lockers, and miscellaneous paraphernalia stacked in a corner and long since forgotten. A mirror hangs on a wall with various posters.*

The studio is upstairs at stage right, and resembles a recording studio in the late 1920s. The entrance is from a hall on the right wall. A small control booth is at the rear, and its access is gained by means of a spiral staircase. Against one wall there is a line of chairs, and a horn through which the control room communicates with the performers. A door in the rear wall allows access to the band room.

THE PLAY: *It is early March in Chicago, 1927. There is a bit of a chill in the air. Winter has broken, but the wind coming off the lake does not carry the promise of spring. The people of the city are bundled and brisk in their defense against such misfortunes as the weather, and the business of the city proceeds largely undisturbed.*

Chicago in 1927 is a rough city, a bruising city, a city of millionaires and derelicts, gangsters and roughhouse dandies, whores and Irish grandmothers who move through its streets fingering long black rosaries. Somewhere a man is wrestling with the taste of a woman in his cheek. Somewhere a dog is barking. Somewhere the moon has fallen through a window and broken into thirty pieces of silver.

It is one o'clock in the afternoon. Secretaries are returning from their lunch, the noon Mass at St. Anthony's is over, and the priest is mumbling over his vestments while the altar boys practice their Latin. The procession of cattle cars through the stockyards continues unabated. The busboys in Mac's Place are cleaning away the last of the corned beef and cabbage, and on the city's South Side, sleepy-eyed Negroes move lazily toward their small cold-water flats and rented rooms to await the onslaught of night, which will find them crowded in the bars and juke joints both dazed and dazzling in their rapport with life. It is with these Negroes that our concern lies most heavily: their values, their attitudes, and particularly their music.

It is hard to define this music. Suffice it to say that it is music that breathes and touches. That connects. That is in itself a way of being, separate and distinct from any other. This music is called blues. Whether this music came from Alabama or Mississippi or other parts of the South doesn't matter anymore. The men and women who make this music have learned it from the narrow crooked streets of East St. Louis, or the streets of the city's South Side, and the Alabama or Mississippi roots have been strangled by the Northern manners and customs of free men of definite and sincere worth, men for whom this music often lies at the forefront of their conscience and concerns. Thus they are laid open to be consumed by it; its warmth and redress, its braggadocio and roughly poignant comments, its vision and prayer, which would instruct and allow them to reconnect, to reassemble and gird up for the next battle in which they would be both victim and the ten thousand slain.

ACT ONE

(The lights come up in the studio. IRVIN enters, carrying a microphone. He is a tall, fleshy man who prides himself on his knowledge of Blacks and his ability to deal with them. He hooks up the microphone, blows into it, taps it, etc. He crosses over to the piano, opens it, and fingers a few keys. STURDYVANT is visible in the control booth. Preoccupied with money, he is insensitive to Black performers and prefers to deal with them at arm's length. He puts on a pair of earphones.)

STURDYVANT: *(Over speaker.)* Irv . . . let's crack that mike, huh? Let's do a check on it.

IRVIN: *(Crosses to mike, speaks into it.)* Testing . . . one . . . two . . . three . . . *(There is a loud feedback. STURDYVANT fiddles with the dials.)* Testing . . . one . . . two . . . three . . . testing. How's that, Mel? *(STURDYVANT doesn't respond.)* Testing . . . one . . . two . . .

STURDYVANT: *(Taking off earphones.)* Okay . . . that checks. We got a good reading. *(Pause.)* You got that list, Irv?

IRVIN: Yeah . . . yeah, I got it. Don't worry about nothing.

STURDYVANT: Listen, Irv . . . you keep her in line, okay? I'm holding you responsible for her . . . If she starts any of her . . .

IRVIN: Mel, what's with the goddamn horn? You wanna talk to me . . . okay! I can't talk to you over the goddamn horn . . . Christ!

STURDYVANT: I'm not putting up with any shenanigans. You hear, Irv? *(IRVIN crosses over to the piano and mindlessly runs his fingers over the keys.)* I'm just not gonna stand for it. I want you to keep her in line. Irv? *(STURDYVANT enters from the control booth.)* Listen, Irv . . . you're her manager . . . she's your responsibility . . .

IRVIN: Okay, okay, Mel . . . let me handle it.

STURDYVANT: She's your responsibility. I'm not putting up with any Royal Highness . . . Queen of the Blues bullshit!

IRVIN: Mother of the Blues, Mel. Mother of the Blues.

STURDYVANT: I don't care what she calls herself. I'm not put-

456

ting up with it. I just want to get her in here . . . record those songs on that list . . . and get her out. Just like clockwork, huh?

IRVIN: Like clockwork, Mel. You just stay out of the way and let me handle it.

STURDYVANT: Yeah . . . yeah . . . you handled it last time. Remember? She marches in here like she owns the damn place . . . doesn't like the songs we picked out . . . says her throat is sore . . . doesn't want to do more than one take . . .

IRVIN: Okay . . . okay . . . I was here! I know all about it.

STURDYVANT: Complains about the building being cold . . . and then . . . trips over the mike wire and threatens to sue me. That's taking care of it?

IRVIN: I've got it all worked out this time. I talked with her last night. Her throat is fine . . . We went over the songs together . . . I got everything straight,' Mel.

STURDYVANT: Irv, that horn player . . . the one who gave me those songs . . . is he gonna be here today? Good. I want to hear more of that sound. Times are changing. This is a tricky business now. We've got to jazz it up . . . put in something different. You know, something wild . . . with a lot of rhythm. (*Pause*.) You know what we put out last time, Irv? We put out garbage last time. It was garbage. I don't even know why I bother with this anymore.

IRVIN: You did all right last time, Mel. Not as good as you did before, but you did all right.

STURDYVANT: You know how many records we sold in New York? You wanna see the sheet? And you know what's in New York, Irv? Harlem. Harlem's in New York, Irv.

IRVIN: Okay, so they didn't sell in New York. But look at Memphis . . . Birmingham . . . Atlanta. Christ, you made a bundle.

STURDYVANT: It's not the money, Irv. You know I couldn't sleep last night? This business is bad for my nerves. My wife is after me to slow down and take a vacation. Two more years and I'm gonna get out . . . get into something respectable. Textiles. That's a respectable business. You know what you could do with a shipload of textiles from Ireland?

(*A buzzer is heard offstage.*)

IRVIN: Why don't you go upstairs and let me handle it, Mel?

STURDYVANT: Remember . . . you're responsible for her.

(STURDYVANT *exits to the control booth.* IRVIN *crosses to get the door.* CUTLER, SLOW DRAG, *and* TOLEDO *enter.* CUTLER *is in his mid-fifties, as are most of the others. He plays guitar and trombone and is the leader of the group, possibly because he is the most sensible. His playing is solid and almost totally unembellished. His understanding of his music is limited to the chord he is playing at the time he is playing it. He has all the qualities of a loner except the introspection.* SLOW DRAG, *the bass player, is perhaps the one most bored by life. He resembles* CUTLER, *but lacks* CUTLER's *energy. He is deceptively intelligent, though, as his name implies, he appears to be slow. He is a rather large man with a wicked smile. Innate African rhythms underlie everything he plays, and he plays with an ease that is at times startling.* TOLEDO *is the piano player. In control of his instrument, he understands and recognizes that its limitations are an extension of himself. He is the only one in the group who can read. He is self-taught but misunderstands and misapplies his knowledge, though he is quick to penetrate to the core of a situation and his insights are thought-provoking. All of the men are dressed in a style of clothing befitting the members of a successful band of the era.*)

IRVIN: How you boys doing, Cutler? Come on in. (*Pause.*) Where's Ma? Is she with you?

CUTLER: I don't know, Mr. Irvin. She told us to be here at one o'clock. That's all I know.

IRVIN: Where's . . . uh . . . the horn player? Is he coming with Ma?

CUTLER: Levee's supposed to be here same as we is. I reckon he'll be here in a minute. I can't rightly say.

IRVIN: Well, come on . . . I'll show you to the band room, let you get set up and rehearsed. You boys hungry? I'll call over to the deli and get some sandwiches. Get you fed and ready to make some music. Cutler . . . here's the list of songs we're gonna record.

STURDYVANT: (*Over speaker.*) Irvin, what's happening? Where's Ma?

IRVIN: Everything under control, Mel. I got it under control.

STURDYVANT: Where's Ma? How come she isn't with the band?

IRVIN: She'll be here in a minute, Mel. Let me get these fellows down to the band room, huh? (*They exit the studio. The lights go down in the studio and up in the band room.* IRVIN *opens the door and allows them to pass as they enter.*) You boys go ahead and rehearse. I'll let you know when Ma comes.

(IRVIN *exits*. CUTLER *hands* TOLEDO *the list of songs*.)

CUTLER: What we got here, Toledo?

TOLEDO: (*Reading*.) We got . . . "Prove It on Me" . . . "Hear Me Talking to You" . . . "Ma Rainey's Black Bottom" . . . and "Moonshine Blues."

CUTLER: Where Mr. Irvin go? Them ain't the songs Ma told me.

SLOW DRAG: I wouldn't worry about it if I were you, Cutler. They'll get it straightened out. Ma will get it straightened out.

CUTLER: I just don't want no trouble about these songs, that's all. Ma ain't told me them songs. She told me something else.

SLOW DRAG: What she tell you?

CUTLER: This "Moonshine Blues" wasn't in it. That's one of Bessie's songs.

TOLEDO: Slow Drag's right . . . I wouldn't worry about it. Let them straighten it up.

CUTLER: Levee know what time he supposed to be here?

SLOW DRAG: Levee gone out to spend your four dollars. He left the hotel this morning talking about he was gonna go buy some shoes. Say it's the first time he ever beat you shooting craps.

CUTLER: Do he know what time he supposed to be here? That's what I wanna know. I ain't thinking about no four dollars.

SLOW DRAG: Levee sure was thinking about it. That four dollars liked to burn a hole in his pocket.

CUTLER: Well, he's supposed to be here at one o'clock. That's what time Ma said. That nigger get out in the streets with that four dollars and ain't no telling when he's liable to show. You ought to have seen him at the club last night, Toledo. Trying to talk to some gal Ma had with her.

TOLEDO: You ain't got to tell me. I know how Levee do.

(*Buzzer is heard offstage*.)

SLOW DRAG: Levee tried to talk to that gal and got his feelings hurt. She didn't want no part of him. She told Levee he'd have to turn his money green before he could talk with her.

CUTLER: She out for what she can get. Anybody could see that.

SLOW DRAG: That's why Levee run out to buy some shoes. He's looking to make an impression on that gal.

CUTLER: What the hell she gonna do with his shoes? She can't do nothing with the nigger's shoes.

(SLOW DRAG *takes out a pint bottle and drinks.*)

TOLEDO: Let me hit that, Slow Drag.

SLOW DRAG: (*Handing him the bottle.*) This some of that good Chicago bourbon!

(*The door opens and* LEVEE *enters, carrying a shoe box. In his early thirties,* LEVEE *is younger than the other men. His flamboyance is sometimes subtle and sneaks up on you. His temper is rakish and bright. He lacks fuel for himself and is somewhat of a buffoon. But it is an intelligent buffoonery, clearly calculated to shift control of the situation to where he can grasp it. He plays trumpet. His voice is strident and totally dependent on his manipulation of breath. He plays wrong notes frequently. He often gets his skill and talent confused with each other.*)

CUTLER: Levee . . . where Mr. Irvin go?

LEVEE: Hell, I don't know. I ain't none of his keeper.

SLOW DRAG: What you got there, Levee?

LEVEE: Look here, Cutler . . . I got me some shoes!

CUTLER: Nigger, I ain't studying you.

(LEVEE *takes the shoes out of the box and starts to put them on.*)

TOLEDO: How much you pay for something like that, Levee?

LEVEE: Eleven dollars. Four dollars of it belong to Cutler.

SLOW DRAG: Levee say if it wasn't for Cutler . . . he wouldn't have no new shoes.

CUTLER: I ain't thinking about Levee or his shoes. Come on . . . let's get ready to rehearse.

SLOW DRAG: I'm with you on that score, Cutler. I wanna get out of here. I don't want to be around here all night. When it comes time to go up there and record them songs . . . I just wanna go up there and do it. Last time it took us all day and half the night.

TOLEDO: Ain't but four songs on the list. Last time we recorded six songs.

SLOW DRAG: It felt like it was sixteen!

LEVEE: (*Finishes with his shoes.*) Yeah! Now I'm ready! I can play some good music now! (*Goes to put up his old shoes and looks around the room.*) Damn! They done changed things around. Don't never leave well enough alone.

TOLEDO: Everything changing all the time. Even the air you breathing change. You got monoxide, hydrogen . . . changing all the time. Skin changing . . . different molecules and everything.

LEVEE: Nigger, what is you talking about? I'm talking about the room. I ain't talking about no skin and air. I'm talking about something I can see! Last time the band room was upstairs. This time it's downstairs. Next time it be over there. I'm talking about what I can see. I ain't talking about no molecules or nothing.

TOLEDO: Hell, I know what you talking about. I just said everything changin'. I know what you talking about, but you don't know what I'm talking about.

LEVEE: That door! Nigger, you see that door? That's what I'm talking about. That door wasn't there before.

CUTLER: Levee, you wouldn't know your right from your left. This is where they used to keep the recording horns and things . . . and damn if that door wasn't there. How in hell else you gonna get in here? Now, if you talking about they done switched rooms, you right. But don't go telling me that damn door wasn't there!

SLOW DRAG: Damn the door and let's get set up. I wanna get out of here.

LEVEE: Toledo started all that about the door. I'm just saying that things change.

TOLEDO: What the hell you think I was saying? Things change. The air and everything. Now you gonna say you was saying it. You gonna fit two propositions on the same track . . . run them into each other, and because they crash, you gonna say it's the same train.

LEVEE: Now this nigger talking about trains! We done went from the air to the skin to the door . . . and now trains. Toledo, I'd just like to be inside your head for five minutes. Just to see how you think. You done got more shit piled up and mixed up in there than the devil got sinners. You been reading too many goddamn books.

TOLEDO: What you care about how much I read? I'm gonna ignore you 'cause you ignorant.

(LEVEE *takes off his coat and hangs it in the locker*.)

SLOW DRAG: Come on, let's rehearse the music.

LEVEE: You ain't gotta rehearse that . . . ain't nothing but old jug-band music. They need one of them jug bands for this.

SLOW DRAG: Don't make me no difference. Long as we get paid.

LEVEE: That ain't what I'm talking about, nigger. I'm talking about art!

SLOW DRAG: What's drawing got to do with it?

LEVEE: Where you get this nigger from, Cutler? He sound like one of them Alabama niggers.

CUTLER: Slow Drag's all right. It's you talking all that weird shit about art. Just play the piece, nigger. You wanna be one of them . . . what you call . . . virtuoso or something, you in the wrong place. You ain't no Buddy Bolden or King Oliver . . . you just an old trumpet player come a dime a dozen. Talking about art.

LEVEE: What is you? I don't see your name in lights.

CUTLER: I just play the piece. Whatever they want. I don't go talking about art and criticizing other people's music.

LEVEE: I ain't like you, Cutler. I got talent! Me and this horn . . . we's tight. If my daddy knowed I was gonna turn out like this, he would've named me Gabriel. I'm gonna get me a band and make me some records. I done give Mr. Sturdyvant some of my songs I wrote and he say he's gonna let me record them when I get my band together. (*Takes some papers out of his pocket*.) I just gotta finish the last part of this song. And Mr. Sturdyvant want me to write another part to this song.

SLOW DRAG: How you learn to write music, Levee?

LEVEE: I just picked it up . . . like you pick up anything. Miss Eula used to play the piano . . . she learned me a lot. I knows how to play *real* music . . . not this old jug-band shit. I got style!

TOLEDO: Everybody got style. Style ain't nothing but keeping the same idea from beginning to end. Everybody got it.

LEVEE: But everybody can't play like I do. Everybody can't have their own band.

CUTLER: Well, until you get your own band where you can play what you want, you just play the piece and stop complaining. I told you when you came on here, this ain't none of them hot bands. This is an accompaniment band. You play Ma's music when you here.

LEVEE: I got sense enough to know that. Hell, I can look at you all and see what kind of band it is. I can look at Toledo and see what kind of band it is.

TOLEDO: Toledo ain't said nothing to you now. Don't let Toledo get started. You can't even spell music, much less play it.

LEVEE: What you talking about? I can spell music. I got a dollar say I can spell it! Put your dollar up. Where your dollar? (TOLEDO *waves him away.*) Now come on. Put your dollar up. Talking about I can't spell music. (LEVEE *peels a dollar off his roll and slams it down on the bench beside* TOLEDO.)

TOLEDO: All right, I'm gonna show you. Cutler. Slow Drag. You hear this? The nigger betting me a dollar he can spell music. I don't want no shit now! (TOLEDO *lays a dollar down beside* LEVEE's.) All right. Go ahead. Spell it.

LEVEE: It's a bet, then. Talking about I can't spell music

TOLEDO: Go ahead, then. Spell it. Music. Spell it.

LEVEE: I can spell it, nigger! M-U-S-I-K. There! (*Reaches for the money.*)

TOLEDO: Naw! Naw! Leave that money alone! You ain't spelled it.

LEVEE: What you mean I ain't spelled it? I said M-U-S-I-K!

TOLEDO: That ain't how you spell it! That ain't how you spell it! It's M-U-S-I-C! C, nigger. Not K! C! M-U-S-I-C!

LEVEE: What you mean, C? Who say it's C?

TOLEDO: Cutler. Slow Drag. Tell this fool. (*They look at each other and then away.*) Well, I'll be a monkey's uncle! (TOLEDO *picks up the money and hands* LEVEE *his dollar back.*) Here's your dollar back, Levee. I done won it, you understand. I done won the dollar. But if don't nobody know but me, how am I gonna prove it to you?

LEVEE: You just mad 'cause I spelled it.

TOLEDO: Spelled what! M-U-S-I-K don't spell nothing. I just wish there was some way I could show you the right and wrong of it. How you gonna know something if the other fellow don't know if you're right or not? Now I can't even be sure that I'm spelling it right.

LEVEE: That's what I'm talking about. You don't know it. Talking about C. You ought to give me that dollar I won from you.

TOLEDO: All right. All right. I'm gonna show you how ridiculous you sound. You know the Lord's Prayer?

LEVEE: Why? You wanna bet a dollar on that?

TOLEDO: Just answer the question. Do you know the Lord's Prayer or don't you?

LEVEE: Yeah, I know it. What of it?

TOLEDO: Cutler?

CUTLER: What you Cutlering me for? I ain't got nothing to do with it.

TOLEDO: I just want to show the man how ridiculous he is.

CUTLER: Both of you all sound like damn fools. Arguing about something silly. Yeah, I know the Lord's Prayer. My daddy was a deacon in the church. Come asking me if I know the Lord's Prayer. Yeah, I know it.

TOLEDO: Slow Drag?

SLOW DRAG: Yeah.

TOLEDO: All right. Now I'm gonna tell you a story to show just how ridiculous he sound. There was these two fellows, see. So, the one of them go up to this church and commence to taking up the church learning. The other fellow see him out on the road and he say, "I done heard you taking up the church learning," say, "Is you learning anything up there?" The other one say, "Yeah, I done take up the church learning and I's learning all kinds of things about the Bible and what it say and all. Why you be asking?" The other one say, "Well, do you know the Lord's Prayer?" And he say, "Why, sure I know the Lord's Prayer, I'm taking up learning at the church, ain't I? I know the Lord's Prayer backwards and forwards." And the other fellow says, "I bet you five dollars you don't know the Lord's Prayer, 'cause I don't think you knows it. I think you be going up to the church 'cause the Widow Jenkins be going up there and you just wanna be sitting in the same room with her when she cross them big, fine, pretty legs she got." And the other one say, "Well, I'm gonna prove you wrong and I'm gonna bet you that five dollars." So he say, "Well, go on and say it then." So he commenced to saying the Lord's Prayer. He say, "Now I lay me down to sleep, I pray the Lord my soul to keep." The other one say, "Here's your five dollars. I didn't think you knew it." (*They all laugh.*) Now, that's just how ridiculous Levee sound. Only 'cause I knowed how to spell music, I still got my dollar.

LEVEE: That don't prove nothing. What's that supposed to prove?

TOLEDO: (*Takes a newspaper out of his back pocket and begins to read.*) I'm through with it.

SLOW DRAG: Is you all gonna rehearse this music or ain't you?

(CUTLER *takes out some papers and starts to roll a reefer.*)

LEVEE: How many times you done played them songs? What you gotta rehearse for?

SLOW DRAG: This a recording session. I wanna get it right the first time and get on out of here.

CUTLER: Slow Drag's right. Let's go on and rehearse and get it over with.

LEVEE: You all go and rehearse, then. I got to finish this song for Mr. Sturdyvant.

CUTLER: Come on, Levee . . . I don't want no shit now. You rehearse like everybody else. You in the band like everybody else. Mr. Sturdyvant just gonna have to wait. You got to do that on your own time. This is the band's time.

LEVEE: Well, what is you doing? You sitting there rolling a reefer, talking about let's rehearse. Toledo reading a newspaper. Hell, I'm ready if you wanna rehearse. I just say there ain't no point in it. Ma ain't here. What's the point in it?

CUTLER: Nigger, why you gotta complain all the time?

TOLEDO: Levee would complain if a gal ain't laid across his bed just right.

CULTER: That's what I know. That's why I try to tell him just play the music and forget about it. It ain't no big thing.

TOLEDO: Levee ain't got an eye for that. He wants to tie on to some abstract component and sit down on the elemental.

LEVEE: This is get-on-Levee time, huh? Levee ain't said nothing except this some old jug-band music.

TOLEDO: Under the right circumstances you'd play anything. If you know music, then you play it. Straight on or off to the side. Ain't nothing abstract about it.

LEVEE: Toledo, you sound like you got a mouth full of marbles. You the only cracker-talking nigger I know.

TOLEDO: You ought to have learned yourself to read . . . then you'd understand the basic understanding of everything.

SLOW DRAG: Both of you all gonna drive me crazy with that philosophy bullshit. Cutler, give me a reefer.

CUTLER: Ain't you got some reefer? Where's your reefer? Why you all the time asking me?

SLOW DRAG: Cutler, how long I done known you? How long we been together? Twenty-two years. We been doing this

together for twenty-two years. All up and down the back
roads, the side roads, the front roads . . . We done played
the juke joints, the whorehouses, the barn dances, and city
sit-downs . . . I done lied for you and lied with you . . . We
done laughed together, fought together, slept in the same
bed together, done sucked on the same titty . . . and now
you don't wanna give me no reefer.

CUTLER: You see this nigger trying to talk me out of my reefer,
Toledo? Running all that about how long he done knowed
me and how we done sucked on the same titty. Nigger, you
still ain't getting none of my reefer!

TOLEDO: That's African.

SLOW DRAG: What? What you talking about? What's African?

LEVEE: I know he ain't talking about me. You don't see me
running around in no jungle with no bone between my nose.

TOLEDO: Levee, you worse than ignorant. You ignorant without a premise. (*Pauses.*) Now, what I was saying is what
Slow Drag was doing is African. That's what you call an
African conceptualization. That's when you name the gods
or call on the ancestors to achieve whatever your desires are.

SLOW DRAG: Nigger, I ain't no African! I ain't doing no African nothing!

TOLEDO: Naming all those things you and Cutler done together
is like trying to solicit some reefer based on a bond of kin-
ship. That's African. An ancestral retention. Only you forgot
the name of the gods.

SLOW DRAG: I ain't forgot nothing. I was telling the nigger how
cheap he is. Don't come talking that African nonsense to me.

TOLEDO: You just like Levee. No eye for taking an abstract
and fixing it to a specific. There's so much that goes on
around you and you can't even see it.

CUTLER: Wait a minute . . . wait a minute. Toledo, now when
this nigger . . . when an African do all them things you say
and name all the gods and whatnot . . . then what happens?

TOLEDO: Depends on if the gods is sympathetic with his cause
for which he is calling them with the right names. Then his
success comes with the right proportion of his naming. That's
the way that go.

CUTLER: (*Taking out a reefer.*) Here, Slow Drag. Here's a
reefer. You done talked yourself up on that one.

SLOW DRAG: Thank you. You ought to have done that in the
first place and saved me all the aggravation.

CUTLER: What I wants to know is . . . what's the same titty
we done sucked on? That's what I want to know.

SLOW DRAG: Oh, I just threw that in there to make it sound good.

(*They all laugh.*)

CUTLER: Nigger, you ain't right.

SLOW DRAG: I knows it.

CUTLER: Well, come on . . . let's get it rehearsed. Time's wasting. (*The musicians pick up their instruments.*) Let's do it. "Ma Rainey's Black Bottom." One . . . two . . . You know what to do. (*They begin to play.* LEVEE *is playing something different. He stops.*)

LEVEE: Naw! Naw! We ain't doing it that way. (TOLEDO *stops playing, then* SLOW DRAG.) We doing my version. It say so right there on that piece of paper you got. Ask Toledo. That's what Mr. Irvin told me . . . say it's on the list he gave you.

CUTLER: Let me worry about what's on the list and what ain't on the list. How you gonna tell me what's on the list?

LEVEE: 'Cause I know what Mr. Irvin told me! Ask Toledo!

CUTLER: Let me worry about what's on the list. You just play the song I say.

LEVEE: What kind of sense it make to rehearse the wrong version of the song? That's what I wanna know. Why you wanna rehearse that version.

SLOW DRAG: You supposed to rehearse what you gonna play. That's the way they taught me. Now, *whatever* version we gonna play . . . let's go on and rehearse it.

LEVEE: That's what I'm trying to tell the man.

CUTLER: You trying to tell me what we is and ain't gonna play. And that ain't none of your business. Your business is to play what I say.

LEVEE: Oh, I see now. You done got jealous 'cause Mr. Irvin using my version. You done got jealous 'cause I proved I know something about music.

CUTLER: What the hell . . . nigger, you talk like a fool! What the hell I got to be jealous of you about? The day I get jealous of you I may as well lay down and die.

TOLEDO: Levee started all that 'cause he too lazy to rehearse. (*To* LEVEE.) You ought to just go and play the song . . . what difference does it make?

LEVEE: Where's the paper? Look at the paper! Get the paper and look at it! See what it say. Gonna tell me I'm too lazy to rehearse.

CUTLER: We ain't talking about the paper. We talking about you understanding where you fit in when you around here. You just play what I say.

LEVEE: Look . . . I don't care what you play! All right? It don't matter to me. Mr. Irvin gonna straighten it up! I don't care what you play.

CUTLER: Thank you. (*Pauses.*) Let's play this "Hear Me Talking to You" till we find out what's happening with the "Black Bottom." Slow Drag, you sing Ma's part. (*Pauses.*) "Hear Me Talking to You." Let's do it. One . . . Two . . . You know what to do.

(*They play.*)

SLOW DRAG: (*Singing.*)
Rambling man makes no change in me
I'm gonna ramble back to my used-to-be
Ah, you hear me talking to you
I don't bite my tongue
You wants to be my man
You got to fetch it with you when you come.

Eve and Adam in the garden taking a chance
Adam didn't take time to get his pants
Ah, you hear me talking to you
I don't bite my tongue
You wants to be my man
You got to fetch it with you when you come.

Our old cat swallowed a ball of yarn
When the kittens were born they had sweaters on
Ah, you hear me talking to you
I don't bite my tongue
You wants to be my man
You got to fetch it with you when you come.

(IRVIN *enters. The muscians stop playing.*)

IRVIN: Any of you boys know what's keeping Ma?

CUTLER: Can't say, Mr. Irvin. She'll be along directly, I reckon. I talked to her this morning, she say she'll be here in time to rehearse.

IRVIN: Well, you boys go ahead. (*Starts to exit.*)

CUTLER: Mr. Irvin, about these songs . . . Levee say . . .

IRVIN: Whatever's on the list, Cutler. You got that list I gave you?

CUTLER: Yessir, I got it right here.

IRVIN: Whatever's on there. Whatever that says.

CUTLER: I'm asking about this "Black Bottom" piece . . . Levee say . . .

IRVIN: Oh, it's on the list. "Ma Rainey's Black Bottom" on the list.

CUTLER: I know it's on the list. I wanna know what version. We got two versions of that song.

IRVIN: Oh. Levee's arrangement. We're using Levee's arrangement.

CUTLER: OK. I got that straight. Now, this "Moonshine Blues" . . .

IRVIN: We'll work it out with Ma, Cutler. Just rehearse whatever's on the list and use Levee's arrangement on that "Black Bottom" piece. (*He exits.*)

LEVEE: See, I told you! It don't mean nothing when I say it. You got to wait for Mr. Irvin to say it. Well, I told you the way it is.

CUTLER: Levee, the sooner you understand it ain't what you say, or what Mr. Irvin say . . . it's what Ma say that counts.

SLOW DRAG: Don't nobody say when it come to Ma. She's gonna do what she wants to do. Ma says what happens with her.

LEVEE: Hell, the man's the one putting out the record! He's gonna put out what he wanna put out!

SLOW DRAG: He's gonna put out what Ma want him to put out.

LEVEE: You heard what the man told you . . . "Ma Rainey's Black Bottom," Levee's arrangement. There you go! That's what he told you.

SLOW DRAG: What you gonna do, Cutler?

CUTLER: Ma ain't told me what version. Let's go on and play it Levee's way.

TOLEDO: See, now . . . I'll tell you something. As long as the colored man look to white folks to put the crown on what he say . . . as long as he looks to white folks for approval . . . then he ain't never gonna find out who he is and what he's about. He's just gonna be about what white folks want him to be about. That's one sure thing.

LEVEE: I'm just trying to show Cutler where he's wrong.

CUTLER: Cutler don't need you to show him nothing.

SLOW DRAG: (*Irritated.*) Come on, let's get this shit rehearsed! You all can bicker afterward!

CUTLER: Levee's confused about who the boss is. He don't know Ma's the boss.

LEVEE: Ma's the boss on the road! We at a recording session. Mr. Sturdyvant and Mr. Irvin say what's gonna be here! We's in Chicago, we ain't in Memphis! I don't know why you all wanna pick me about it, shit! I'm with Slow Drag . . . Let's go and get it rehearsed.

CUTLER: All right. All right. I know how to solve this. "Ma Rainey's Black Bottom." Levee's version. Let's do it. Come on.

TOLEDO: How that first part go again, Levee?

LEVEE: It go like this. (*He plays.*) That's to get the people's attention to the song. That's when you and Slow Drag come in with the rhythm part. Me and Cutler play on the breaks. (*Becoming animated.*) Now we gonna dance it . . . but we ain't gonna countrify it. This ain't no barn dance. We gonna play it like . . .

CUTLER: The man ask you how the first part go. He don't wanna hear all that. Just tell him how the piece go.

TOLEDO: I got it. I got it. Let's go. I know how to do it.

CUTLER: "Ma Rainey's Black Bottom." One . . . two . . . You know what to do.

(*They begin to play.* LEVEE *stops.*)

LEVEE: You all got to keep up now. You playing in the wrong time. Ma come in over the top. She got to find her own way in.

CUTLER: Nigger, will you let us play this song? When you get your own band . . . then you tell them that nonsense. We know how to play the piece. I was playing music before you was born. Gonna tell me how to play . . . All right. Let's try it again.

SLOW DRAG: Cutler, wait till I fix this. This string started to unravel. (*Playfully.*) And you know I want to play Levee's music right.

LEVEE: If you was any kind of musician, you'd take care of your instrument. Keep it in tip-top order. If you was any kind of musician, I'd let you be in my band.

SLOW DRAG: Shhheeeeet! (*Crosses to get his string and steps on* LEVEE's *shoes.*)

LEVEE: Damn, Slow Drag! Watch them big-ass shoes you got.

SLOW DRAG: Boy, ain't nobody done nothing to you.

LEVEE: You done stepped on my shoes.

SLOW DRAG: Move them the hell out the way, then. You was in my way . . . I wasn't in your way. (CUTLER *lights up another reefer.* SLOW DRAG *rummages around in his belongings for a string.* LEVEE *takes out a rag and begins to shine his shoes.*) You can shine these when you get done, Levee.

CUTLER: If I had them shoes Levee got, I could buy me a whole suit of clothes.

LEVEE: What kind of difference it make what kind of shoes I got? Ain't nothing wrong with having nice shoes. I ain't said nothing about your shoes. Why you wanna talk about me and my Florsheims?

CUTLER: Any man who takes a whole week's pay and puts it on some shoes—you understand what I mean, what you walk around on the ground with—is a fool! And I don't mind telling you.

LEVEE: (*Irritated.*) What difference it make to you, Cutler?

SLOW DRAG: The man ain't said nothing about your shoes. Ain't nothing wrong with having nice shoes. Look at Toledo.

TOLEDO: What about Toledo?

SLOW DRAG: I said, ain't nothing wrong with having nice shoes.

LEVEE: Nigger got them clodhoppers! Old brogans! He ain't nothing but a sharecropper.

TOLEDO: You can make all the fun you want. It don't mean nothing. I'm satisfied with them and that's what counts.

LEVEE: Nigger, why don't you get some decent shoes? Got nerve to put on a suit and tie with them farming boots.

CUTLER: What you just tell me? It don't make no difference about the man's shoes. That's what you told me.

LEVEE: Aw, hell, I don't care what the nigger wear. I'll be honest with you. I don't care if he went barefoot. (SLOW DRAG *has put his string on the bass and is tuning it.*) Play something for me, Slow Drag. (SLOW DRAG *plays.*) A man got to have some shoes to dance like this! You can't dance like this with them clodhoppers Toledo got. (LEVEE *sings.*)
Hello, Central, give me Doctor Jazz
He's got just what I need I'll say he has
When the world goes wrong and I have got the blues
He's the man who makes me get on my dancing shoes.

TOLEDO: That's the trouble with colored folks . . . always wanna have a good time. Good times done got more niggers killed than God got ways to count. What the hell having a good time mean? That's what I wanna know.

LEVEE: Hell, nigger . . . it don't need explaining. Ain't you never had no good time before?

TOLEDO: The more niggers get killed having a good time, the more good times niggers wanna have. (SLOW DRAG *stops playing.*) There's more to life than having a good time. If there ain't, then this is a piss-poor life we're having . . . if that's all there is to be got out of it.

SLOW DRAG: Toledo, just 'cause you like to read them books and study and whatnot . . . that's your good time. People get other things they likes to do to have a good time. Ain't no need you picking them about it.

CUTLER: Niggers been having a good time before you was born, and they gonna keep having a good time after you gone.

TOLEDO: Yeah, but what else they gonna do? Ain't nobody talking about making the lot of the colored man better for him here in America.

LEVEE: Now you gonna be Booker T. Washington.

TOLEDO: Everybody worried about having a good time. Ain't nobody thinking about what kind of world they gonna leave their young'uns. "Just give me the good time, that's all I want." It just makes me sick.

SLOW DRAG: Well, the colored man's gonna be all right. He got through slavery, and he'll get through whatever else the white man put on him. I ain't worried about that. Good times is what makes life worth living. Now, you take the white man . . . The white man don't know how to have a good time. That's why he's troubled all the time. He don't know how to have a good time. He don't know how to laugh at life.

LEVEE: That's what the problem is with Toledo . . . reading all them books and things. He done got to the point where he forgot how to laugh and have a good time. Just like the white man.

TOLEDO: I know how to have a good time as well as the next man. I said, there's got to be more to life than having a good time. I said the colored man ought to be doing more than just trying to have a good time all the time.

LEVEE: Well, what is you doing, nigger? Talking all them high-falutin ideas about making a better world for the colored man. What is you doing to make it better? You playing the music and looking for your next piece of pussy same as we is. What is you doing? That's what I wanna know. Tell him, Cutler.

CUTLER: You all leave Cutler out of this. Cutler ain't got nothing to do with it.

TOLEDO: Levee, you just about the most ignorant nigger I know. Sometimes I wonder why I ever bother to try and talk with you.

LEVEE: Well, what is you doing? Talking that shit to me about I'm ignorant! What is you doing? You just a whole lot of mouth. A great big windbag. Thinking you smarter than everybody else. What is you doing, huh?

TOLEDO: It ain't just me, fool! It's everybody! What you think . . . I'm gonna solve the colored man's problems by myself? I said, we. You understand that? We. That's every living colored man in the world got to do his share. Got to do his part. I ain't talking about what I'm gonna do . . . or what you or Cutler or Slow Drag or anybody else. I'm talking about all of us together. What all of us is gonna do. That's what I'm talking about, nigger!

LEVEE: Well, why didn't you say that, then?

CUTLER: Toledo, I don't know why you waste your time on this fool.

TOLEDO: That's what I'm trying to figure out.

LEVEE: Now, there go Cutler with his shit. Calling me a fool. You wasn't even in the conversation. Now you gonna take sides and call me a fool.

CUTLER: Hell, I was listening to the man. I got sense enough to know what he was saying. I could tell it straight back to you.

LEVEE: Well, you go on with it. But I'll tell you this . . . I ain't gonna be too many more of your fools. I'll tell you that. Now, you put that in your pipe and smoke it.

CUTLER: Boy, ain't nobody studying you. Telling me what to put in my pipe. Who's you to tell me what to do?

LEVEE: All right, I ain't nobody. Don't pay me no mind. I ain't nobody.

TOLEDO: Levee, you ain't nothing but the devil.

LEVEE: There you go! That's who I am. I'm the devil. I ain't nothing but the devil.

CUTLER: I can see that. That's something you know about. You know all about the devil.

LEVEE: I ain't saying what I know. I know plenty. What you know about the devil? Telling me what I know. What you know?

SLOW DRAG: I know a man sold his soul to the devil.

LEVEE: There you go! That's the only thing I ask about the devil . . . to see him coming so I can sell him this one I got. 'Cause if there's a god up there, he done went to sleep.

SLOW DRAG: Sold his soul to the devil himself. Name of Eliza Cotter. Lived in Tuscaloosa County, Alabama. The devil came by and he done upped and sold him his soul.

CUTLER: How you know the man done sold his soul to the devil, nigger? You talking that old-woman foolishness.

SLOW DRAG: Everybody know. It wasn't no secret. He went around working for the devil and everybody knowed it. Carried him a bag . . . one of them carpetbags. Folks say he carried the devil's papers and whatnot where he put your fingerprint on the paper with blood.

LEVEE: Where he at now? That's what I want to know. He can put my whole handprint if he want to!

CUTLER: That's the damnedest thing I ever heard! Folks kill me with that talk.

TOLEDO: Oh, that's real enough, all right. Some folks go arm in arm with the devil, shoulder to shoulder, and talk to him all the time. That's real, ain't nothing wrong in believing that.

SLOW DRAG: That's what I'm saying. Eliza Cotter is one of them. All right. The man living up in an old shack on Ben Foster's place, shoeing mules and horses, making them charms and things in secret. He done hooked up with the devil, showed up one day all fancied out with just the finest clothes you ever seen on a colored man . . . dressed just like one of them crackers . . . and carrying this bag with them papers and things. All right. Had a pocketful of money, just living the life of a rich man. Ain't done no more work or nothing. Just had him a string of women he run around with and throw his money away on. Bought him a big fine house . . . Well, it wasn't all that big, but it did have one of them white picket fences around it. Used to hire a man once a week just to paint that fence. Messed around there and one of the fellows of them gals he was messing with got fixed on him wrong and Eliza killed him. And he laughed about it. Sheriff come and arrest him, and then let him go. And he went around in that town laughing about killing this fellow. Trial come up, and the judge cut him loose. He must have been in converse with the devil too . . . 'cause he cut him loose and give him a bottle of whiskey! Folks ask what done happened to make him change, and he'd tell them straight out he done sold his soul to the devil and ask them if they wanted to sell theirs 'cause he could arrange it for them. Preacher see him coming, used to cross to the other side of the road. He'd just stand there and laugh at the preacher and call him a fool to his face.

CUTLER: Well, whatever happened to this fellow? What come of him? A man who, as you say, done sold his soul to the devil is bound to come to a bad end.

TOLEDO: I don't know about that. The devil's strong. The devil ain't no pushover.

SLOW DRAG: Oh, the devil had him under his wing, all right. Took good care of him. He ain't wanted for nothing.

CUTLER: What happened to him? That's what I want to know.

SLOW DRAG: Last I heard, he headed north with that bag of his, handing out hundred-dollar bills on the spot to whoever wanted to sign on with the devil. That's what I hear tell of him.

CUTLER: That's a bunch of fool talk. I don't know know how you fix your mouth to tell that story. I don't believe that.

SLOW DRAG: I ain't asking you to believe it. I'm just telling you the facts of it.

LEVEE: I sure wish I knew where he went. He wouldn't have to convince me long. Hell, I'd even help him sign people up.

CUTLER: Nigger, God's gonna strike you down with that blasphemy you talking.

LEVEE: Oh, shit! God don't mean nothing to me. Let him strike me! Here I am, standing right here. What you talking about he's gonna strike me? Here I am! Let him strike me! I ain't scared of him. Talking that stuff to me.

CUTLER: All right. You gonna be sorry. You gonna fix yourself to have bad luck. Ain't nothing gonna work for you.

(*Buzzer sounds offstage.*)

LEVEE: Bad luck? What I care about some bad luck? You talking simple. I ain't knowed nothing but bad luck all my life. Couldn't get no worse. What the hell I care about some bad luck? Hell, I eat it everyday for breakfast! You dumber than I thought you was . . . talking about bad luck.

CUTLER: All right, nigger, you'll see! Can't tell a fool nothing. You'll see!

IRVIN: (*Enters the studio, checks his watch, and calls down the stairs.*) Cutler . . . you boys' sandwiches are up here . . . Cutler?

CUTLER: Yessir, Mr. Irvin . . . be right there.
TOLEDO: I'll walk up there and get them.

(TOLEDO _exits. The lights go down in the band room and up in the studio._ IRVIN _paces back and forth in an agitated manner._ STURDYVANT _enters._)

STURDYVANT: Irv, what's happening? Is she here yet? Was that her?
IRVING: It's the sandwiches, Mel. I told you . . . I'll let you know when she comes, huh?
STURDYVANT: What's keeping her? Do you know what time it is? Have you looked at the clock? You told me she'd be here. You told me you'd take care of it.
IRVIN: Mel, for chrissakes! What do you want from me? What do you want me to do?
STURDYVANT: Look what time it is, Irv. You told me she'd be here.
IRVIN: She'll be here, okay? I don't know what's keeping her. You know they're always late, Mel.
STURDYVANT: You should have went by the hotel and made sure she was on time. You should have taken care of this. That's what you told me, huh? "I'll take care of it."
IRVING: Okay! Okay! I didn't go by the hotel! What do you want me to do? She'll be here, okay? The band's here . . . she'll be here.
STURDYVANT: Okay, Irv. I'll take your word. But if she doesn't come . . . if she comes . . .

(STURDYVANT _exits to the control booth as_ TOLEDO _enters._)

TOLEDO: Mr. Irvin . . . I come up to get the sandwiches.
IRVIN: Say, uh, look . . . one o'clock, right? She said one o'clock.
TOLEDO: That's what time she told us. Say be here at one o'clock.
IRVIN: Do you know what's keeping her? Do you know why she ain't here?
TOLEDO: I can't say, Mr. Irvin. Told us one o'clock.

(_The buzzer sounds._ IRVIN _goes to the door. There is a flurry of commotion as_ MA RAINEY _enters, followed closely by a_ POLICEMAN, DUSSIE MAE, _and_ SYLVESTER. MA RAINEY _is a short, heavy woman. She is dressed in a full-length fur coat with_

*matching hat, an emerald green dress, and several strands of
pearls of varying lengths. Her hair is secured by a headband
that matches her dress. Her manner is simple and direct, and
she carries herself in a royal fashion.* DUSSIE MAE *is a young,
dark-skinned woman whose greatest asset is the sensual energy
which seems to flow from her. She is dressed in a fur jacket and
a tight-fitting canary yellow dress.* SYLVESTER *is an Arkansas
country boy, the size of a fullback. He wears a new suit and
coat, in which he is obviously uncomfortable. Most of the time
he stutters when he speaks.*)

MA RAINEY: Irvin . . . you better tell this man who I am! You
better get him straight!

IRVIN: Ma, do you know what time it is? Do you have any
idea? We've been waiting . . .

DUSSIE MAE: (*To* SYLVESTER.) If you was watching where you
was going . . .

SYLVESTER: I was watching . . . What you mean?

IRVIN: (*Notices* POLICEMAN.) What's going on here? Officer,
what's the matter?

MA RAINEY: Tell the man who he's messing with!

POLICEMAN: Do you know this lady?

MA RAINEY: Just tell the man who I am! That's all you gotta
do.

POLICEMAN: Lady, will you let me talk, huh?

MA RAINEY: Tell the man who I am!

IRVIN: Wait a minute . . . wait a minute! Let me handle it.
Ma, will you let me handle it?

MA RAINEY: Tell him who he's messing with!

IRVIN: Okay! Okay! Give me a chance! Officer, this is one of
our recording artists . . . Ma Rainey.

MA RAINEY: Madame Rainey! Get it straight! Madame
Rainey! Talking about taking me to jail!

IRVIN: Look, Ma . . . give me a chance, okay? Here . . . sit
down. I'll take care of it. Officer, what's the problem?

DUSSIE MAE: (*To* SYLVESTER.) It's all your fault.

SYLVESTER: I ain't done nothing . . . Ask Ma.

POLICEMAN: Well . . . when I walked up on the incident . . .

DUSSIE MAE: Sylvester wrecked Ma's car.

SYLVESTER: I d-d-did not! The m-m-man ran into me!

POLICEMAN: (*To* IRVIN.) Look, buddy . . . if you want it in a
nutshell, we got her charged with assault and battery.

MA RAINEY: Assault and what for what!

DUSSIE MAE: See . . . we was trying to get a cab . . . and so Ma . . .

MA RAINEY: Wait a minute! I'll tell you if you wanna know what happened. (*Points to* SYLVESTER.) Now, that's Sylvester. That's my nephew. He was driving my car . . .

POLICEMAN: Lady, we don't know whose car he was driving.

MA RAINEY: That's my car!

DUSSIE MAE and SYLVESTER: That's Ma's car!

MA RAINEY: What you mean, you don't know whose car it is? I bought and paid for that car.

POLICEMAN: That's what you say, lady . . . We still gotta check. (*To* IRVIN.) They hit a car on Market Street. The guy said the kid ran a stoplight.

SYLVESTER: What you mean? The man c-c-come around the corner and hit m-m-me!

POLICEMAN: While I was calling a paddy wagon to haul them to the station, they try to hop into a parked cab. The cabbie said he was waiting on a fare . . .

MA RAINEY: The man was just sitting there. Wasn't waiting for nobody. I don't know why he wanna tell that lie.

POLICEMAN: Look, lady . . . will you let me tell the story?

MA RAINEY: Go ahead and tell it, then. But tell it right!

POLICEMAN: Like I say . . . she tries to get in this cab. The cabbie's waiting on a fare. She starts creating a disturbance. The cabbie gets out to try and explain the situation to her . . . and she knocks him down.

DUSSIE MAE: She ain't hit him! He just fell!

SYLVESTER: He just s-s-s-slipped!

POLICEMAN: He claims she knocked him down. We got her charged with assault and battery.

MA RAINEY: If that don't beat all to hell. I ain't touched the man! The man was trying to reach around me to keep his car door closed. I opened the door and it hit him and he fell down. I ain't touched the man!

IRVIN: Okay, okay . . . I got it straight now, Ma. You didn't touch him, all right? Officer, can I see you for a minute?

DUSSIE MAE: Ma was just trying to open the door.

SYLVESTER: He j-j-just got in t-t-the way!

MA RAINEY: Said he wasn't gonna haul no colored folks . . . if you want to know the truth of it.

IRVIN: Okay, Ma . . . I got it straight now. Officer? (*Pulls the* POLICEMAN *off to the side.*)

MA RAINEY: (*Noticing* TOLEDO.) Toledo, Cutler and everybody here?

TOLEDO: Yeah, they down in the band room. What happened to your car?

STURDYVANT: (*Entering.*) Irv, what's the problem? What's going on? Officer . . .

IRVIN: Mel, let me take care of it. I can handle it.

STURDYVANT: What's happening? What the hell's going on?

IRVIN: Let me handle it, Mel, huh?

STURDYVANT: (*Crosses over to* MA RAINEY.) What's going on, Ma? What'd you do?

MA RAINEY: Sturdyvant, get on away from me! That's the last thing I need . . . to go through some of your shit!

IRVIN: Mel, I'll take care of it. I'll explain it all to you. Let me handle it, huh?

(STURDYVANT *reluctantly returns to the control booth.*)

POLICEMAN: Look, buddy, like I say . . . we got her charged with assault and battery . . . and the kid with threatening the cabbie.

SYLVESTER: I ain't done n-n-nothing!

MA RAINEY: You leave the boy out of it. He ain't done nothing. What is he supposed to have done?

POLICEMAN: He threatened the cabbie, lady! You just can't go around threatening people.

SYLESTER: I ain't done nothing to him! He's the one talking about he g-g-gonna get a b-b-baseball bat on me! I just told him what I'd do with it. But I ain't done nothing 'cause he didn't get the b-b-bat!

IRVIN: (*Pulling the* POLICEMAN *aside.*) Officer . . . look here . . .

POLICEMAN: We was on our way down to the precinct . . . but I figured I'd do you a favor and bring her by here. I mean, if she's as important as she says she is . . .

IRVIN: (*Slides a bill from his pocket.*) Look, Officer . . . I'm Madame Rainey's manager . . . It's good to meet you. (*Shakes the* POLICEMAN's *hand and passes him the bill.*) As soon as we're finished with the recording session, I'll personally stop by the precinct house and straighten up this misunderstanding.

POLICEMAN: Well . . . I guess that's all right. As long as someone is responsible for them. (*Pockets the bill and winks at* IRVIN.) No need to come down . . . I'll take care of it myself. Of course, we wouldn't want nothing like this to happen again.

IRVIN: Don't worry, Officer . . . I'll take care of everything. Thanks for your help. (*Escorts the* POLICEMAN *to the door and returns. He crosses over to* MA RAINEY.) Here, Ma . . . let me take your coat. (*To* SYLVESTER.) I don't believe I know you.

MA RAINEY: That's my nephew, Sylvester.

IRVIN: I'm very pleased to meet you. Here . . . you can give me your coat.

MA RAINEY: That there is Dussie Mae.

IRVIN: Hello . . . (DUSSIE MAE *hands* IRVIN *her coat*.) Listen, Ma, just sit there and relax. The boys are in the band room rehearsing. You just sit and relax a minute.

MA RAINEY: I ain't for no sitting. I ain't never heard of such. Talking about taking me to jail. Irvin, call down there and see about my car.

IRVIN: Okay, Ma . . . I'll take care of it. You just relax. (*Exits with the coats.*)

MA RAINEY: Why you all keep it so cold in here? Sturdyvant try and pinch every penny he can. You all wanna make some records, you better put some heat on in here or give me back my coat.

IRVIN: (*Enters.*) We got the heat turned up, Ma. It's warming up. It'll be warm in a minute.

DUSSIE MAE: (*Whispers to* MA RAINEY.) Where's the bathroom?

MA RAINEY: It's in the back. Down the hall next to Sturdyvant's office. Come on, I'll show you where it is. Irvin, call down there and see about my car. I want my car fixed today.

IRVIN: I'll take care of everything, Ma. (*Notices* TOLEDO.) Say . . . uh, uh . . .

TOLEDO: Toledo.

IRVIN: Yeah . . . Toledo. I got the sandwiches, you can take down to the rest of the boys. We'll be ready to go in a minute. Give you boys a chance to eat and then we'll be ready to go.

(IRVIN *and* TOLEDO *exit. The lights go down in the studio and come up in the band room.*)

LEVEE: Slow Drag, you ever been to New Orleans?

SLOW DRAG: What's in New Orleans that I want?

LEVEE: How you call yourself a musician and ain't never been to New Orleans?

SLOW DRAG: You ever been to Fat Back, Arkansas? (*Pauses.*)
All right, then. Ain't never been nothing in New Orleans
that I couldn't get in Fat Back.

LEVEE: That's why you backwards. You just an old country
boy talking about Fat Back, Arkansas, and New Orleans in
the same breath.

CUTLER: I been to New Orleans. What about it?

LEVEE: You ever been to Lula White's?

CUTLER: Lula White's? I ain't never heard of it.

LEVEE: Man, they got some gals in there just won't wait! I
seen a man get killed in there once. Got drunk and grabbed
one of the gals wrong . . . I don't know what the matter of
it was. But he grabbed her and she stuck a knife in him all
the way up to the hilt. He ain't even fell. He just stood there
and choked on his own blood. I was just asking Slow Drag
'cause I was gonna take him to Lula White's when we get
down to New Orleans and show him a good time. Introduce
him to one of them gals I know down there.

CUTLER: Slow Drag don't need you to find him no pussy. He
can take care of his own self. Fact is . . . you better watch
your gal when Slow Drag's around. They don't call him Slow
Drag for nothing. (*He laughs.*) Tell him how you got your
name, Slow Drag.

SLOW DRAG: I ain't thinking about Levee.

CUTLER: Slow Drag break a woman's back when he dance.
They had this contest one time in this little town called
Bolingbroke, about a hundred miles outside of Macon. We
was playing for this dance and they was giving twenty dollars
to the best slow draggers. Slow Drag looked over the competition, got down off the bandstand, grabbed hold of one of
them gals, and stuck to her like a fly to jelly. Like wood to
glue. Man had that gal whooping and hollering so . . . everybody stopped to watch. This fellow come in . . . this gal's
fellow . . . and pulled a knife a foot long on Slow Drag.
'Member that, Slow Drag?

SLOW DRAG: Boy, that mama was hot! The front of her dress
was wet as a dishrag!

LEVEE: So what happened? What the man do?

CUTLER: Slow Drag ain't missed a stroke. The gal, she just
look at her man with that sweet, dizzy look in her eye. She
ain't about to stop! Folks was clearing out, ducking and hiding under tables, figuring there's gonna be a fight. Slow Drag
just looked over the gal's shoulder at the man and said,
"Mister, if you'd quit hollering and wait a minute . . . you'll

see I'm doing you a favor. I'm helping this gal win ten dollars so she can buy you a gold watch." The man just stood there and looked at him, all the while stroking that knife. Told Slow Drag, say, "All right, then, nigger. You just better make damn sure you win." That's when folks started calling him Slow Drag. The women got to hanging around him so bad after that, them fellows in that town ran us out of there.

(TOLEDO *enters, carrying a small cardboard box with the sandwiches.*)

LEVEE: Yeah . . . well, them gals in Lula White's will put a harness on his ass.

TOLEDO: Ma's up there. Some kind of commotion with the police.

CUTLER: Police? What the police up there for?

TOLEDO: I couldn't get it straight. Something about her car. They gone now . . . she's all right. Mr. Irvin sent some sandwiches.

LEVEE: (*Springs across the room.*) Yeah, all right. What we got here? (*Takes two sandwiches out of the box.*)

TOLEDO: What you doing grabbing two? There ain't but five in there . . . How you figure you get two?

LEVEE: 'Cause I grabbed them first. There's enough for everybody . . . What you talking about? It ain't like I'm taking food out of nobody's mouth.

CUTLER: That's all right. He can have mine too. I don't want none.

(LEVEE *starts toward the box to get another sandwich.*)

TOLEDO: Nigger, you better get out of here. Slow Drag, you want this?

SLOW DRAG: Naw, you can have it.

TOLEDO: With Levee around, you don't have to worry about no leftovers. I can see that.

LEVEE: What's the matter with you? Ain't you eating two sandwiches? Then why you wanna talk about me? Talking about there won't be no leftovers with Levee around. Look at your own self before you look at me.

TOLEDO: That's what you is. That's what we all is. A leftover from history. You see now, I'll show you.

LEVEE: Aw, shit . . . I done got the nigger started now.

TOLEDO: Now, I'm gonna show you how this goes . . . where

you just a leftover from history. Everybody come from different places in Africa, right? Come from different tribes and things. Soonawhile they began to make one big stew. You had the carrots, the peas, and potatoes and whatnot over here. And over there you had the meat, the nuts, the okra, corn . . . and then you mix it up and let it cook right through to get the flavors flowing together . . . then you got one thing. You got a stew.

Now you take and eat the stew. You take and make your history with that stew. All right. Now it's over. Your history's over and you done ate the stew. But you look around and you see some carrots over here, some potatoes over there. That stew's still there. You done made your history and it's still there. You can't eat it all. So what you got? You got some leftovers. That's what it is. You got leftovers and you can't do nothing with it. You already making you another history . . . cooking you another meal, and you don't need them leftovers no more. What to do?

See, we's the leftovers. The colored man is the leftovers. Now, what's the colored man gonna do with himself? That's what we waiting to find out. But first we gotta know we the leftovers. Now, who knows that? You find me a nigger that knows that and I'll turn any whichaway you want me to. I'll bend over for you. You ain't gonna find that. And that's what the problem is. The problem ain't with the white man. The white man knows you just a leftover. 'Cause he the one who done the eating and he know what he done ate. But we don't know that we been took and made history out of. Done went and filled the white's belly and now he's full and tired and wants you to get out the way and let him be by himself. Now, I know what I'm talking about. And if you wanna find out, you just ask Mr. Irvin what he had for supper yesterday. And if he's an honest white man . . . which is asking for a whole heap of a lot . . . he'll tell you he done ate your black ass and if you please I'm full up with you . . . so go on and get off the plate and let me eat something else.

SLOW DRAG: What that mean? What's eating got to do with how the white man treat you? He don't treat you no different according to what he ate.

TOLEDO: I ain't said it had nothing to do with how he treat you.

CUTLER: The man's trying to tell you something, fool!

SLOW DRAG: What he trying to tell me? Ain't you here. Why

you say he was trying to tell *me* something? Wasn't he trying to tell you too?

LEVEE: He was trying, all right. He was trying a whole heap. I'll say that for him. But trying ain't worth a damn. I got lost right there trying to figure out who puts nuts in their stew.

SLOW DRAG: I knowed that before. My grandpappy used to put nuts in his stew. He and my grandmama both. That ain't nothing new.

TOLEDO: They put nuts in their stew all over Africa. But the stew they eat, and the stew your grandpappy made, and all the stew that you and me eat, and the stew Mr. Irvin eats . . . ain't in no way the same stew. That's the way that go. I'm through with it. That's the last you know me to ever try and explain something to you.

CUTLER: (*After a pause.*) Well, time's getting along . . . Come on, let's finish rehearsing.

LEVEE: (*Stretching out on a bench.*) I don't feel like rehearsing. I ain't nothing but a leftover. You go and rehearse with Toledo . . . He's gonna teach you how to make a stew.

SLOW DRAG: Cutler, what you gonna do? I don't want to be around here all day.

LEVEE: I know my part. You all go on and rehearse your part. You all need some rehearsal.

CUTLER: Come on, Levee, get up off your ass and rehearse the songs.

LEVEE: I already know them songs . . . What I wanna rehearse them for?

SLOW DRAG: You in the band, ain't you? You supposed to rehearse when the band rehearse.

TOLEDO: Levee think he the king of the barnyard. He thinks he's the only rooster know how to crow.

LEVEE: All right! All right! Come on, I'm gonna show you I know them songs. Come on, let's rehearse. I bet you the first one mess be Toledo. Come on . . . I wanna see if he know how to crow.

CUTLER: "Ma Rainey's Black Bottom," Levee's version. Let's do it.

(*They begin to rehearse. The lights go down in the band room and up in the studio. MA RAINEY sits and takes off her shoe, rubs her feet. DUSSIE MAE wanders about looking at the studio. SYLVESTER is over by the piano.*)

MA RAINEY: (*Singing to herself.*)
  Oh, Lord, these dogs of mine
  They sure do worry me all the time
  The reason why I don't know
  Lord, I beg to be excused
  I can't wear me no sharp-toed shoes.
  I went for a walk
  I stopped to talk
  Oh, how my corns did bark.
DUSSIE MAE: It feels kinda spooky in here. I ain't never been in no recording studio before. Where's the band at?
MA RAINEY: They off somewhere rehearsing. I don't know where Irvin went to. All this hurry up and he goes off back there with Sturdyvant. I know he better come on 'cause Ma ain't gonna be waiting. Come here . . . let me see that dress. (DUSSIE MAE *crosses over.* MA RAINEY *tugs at the dress around the waist, appraising the fit.*) That dress looks nice. I'm gonna take you tomorrow and get you some more things before I take you down to Memphis. They got clothes up here you can't get in Memphis. I want you to look nice for me. If you gonna travel with the show, you got to look nice.
DUSSIE MAE: I need me some more shoes. These hurt my feet.
MA RAINEY: You get you some shoes that fit your feet. Don't you be messing around with no shoes that pinch your feet. Ma know something about bad feet. Hand me my slippers out my bag over yonder.
DUSSIE MAE: (*Brings the slippers.*) I just want to get a pair of them yellow ones. About a half-size bigger.
MA RAINEY: We'll get you whatever you need. Sylvester, too . . . I'm gonna get him some more clothes. Sylvester, tuck your clothes in. Straighten them up and look nice. Look like a gentleman.
DUSSIE MAE: Look at Sylvester with that hat on.
MA RAINEY: Sylvester, take your hat off inside. Act like your mama taught you something. I know she taught you better than that. (SYLVESTER *bangs on the piano.*) Come on over here and leave that piano alone.
SYLVESTER: I ain't d-d-doing nothing to the p-p-piano. I'm just l-l-looking at it.
MA RAINEY: Well. Come on over here and sit down. As soon as Mr. Irvin comes back, I'll have him take you down and introduce you to the band. (SYLVESTER *comes over.*) He's gonna take you down there and introduce you in a minute . . . have Cutler show you how your part go. And when you

get your money, you gonna send some of it home to your mama. Let her know you doing all right. Make her feel good to know you doing all right in the world.

(DUSSIE MAE *wanders about the studio and opens the door leading to the band room. The strains of* LEVEE'S *version of "Ma Rainey's Black Bottom" can be heard.* IRVIN *enters.*)

IRVIN: Ma, I called down to the garage and checked on your car. It's just a scratch. They'll have it ready for you this afternoon. They're gonna send it over with one of their fellows.

MA RAINEY: They better have my car fixed right too. I ain't going for that. Brand-new car . . . they better fix it like new.

IRVIN: It was just a scratch on the fender, Ma . . . They'll take care of it . . . don't worry . . . they'll have it like new.

MA RAINEY: Irvin, what is that I hear? What is that the band's rehearsing? I know they ain't rehearsing Levee's "Black Bottom." I know I ain't hearing that?

IRVIN: Ma, listen . . . that's what I wanted to talk to you about. Levee's version of that song . . . it's got a nice arrangement . . . a nice horn intro . . . It really picks it up . . .

MA RAINEY: I ain't studying Levee nothing. I know what he done to that song, and I don't like to sing it that way. I'm doing it the old way. That's why I brought my nephew to do the voice intro.

IRVIN: Ma, that's what the people want now. They want something they can dance to. Times are changing. Levee's arrangement gives the people what they want. It gets them excited . . . makes them forget about their troubles.

MA RAINEY: I don't care what you say, Irvin. Levee ain't messing up my song. If he got what the people want, let him take it somewhere else. I'm singing Ma Rainey's song. I ain't singing Levee's song. Now, that's all there is to it. Carry my nephew on down there and introduce him to the band. I promised my sister I'd look out for him, and he's gonna do the voice intro on the song my way.

IRVIN: Ma, we just figured that—

MA RAINEY: Who's this "we"? What you mean "we"? I ain't studying Levee nothing. Come talking this "we" stuff. Who's "we"?

IRVIN: Me and Sturdyvant. We decided that it would—

MA RAINEY: You decided, huh? I'm just a bump on the log.

I'm gonna go whichever way the river drift. Is that it? You and Sturdyvant decided.

IRVIN: Ma, it was just that we thought it would be better.

MA RAINEY: I ain't got good sense. I don't know nothing about music. I don't know what's a good song and what ain't. You know more about my fans than I do.

IRVIN: It's not that, Ma. It would just be easier to do. It's more what the people want.

MA RAINEY: I'm gonna tell you something, Irvin . . . and you go on up there and tell Sturdyvant. What you all say don't count with me. You understand? Ma listens to her heart. Ma listens to the voice inside her. That's what counts with Ma. Now, you carry my nephew on down there . . . tell Cutler he's gonna do the voice intro on that "Black Bottom" song and that Levee ain't messing up my song with none of his music shit. Now, if that don't set right with you and Sturdyvant . . . then I can carry my black bottom on back down South to my tour, 'cause I don't like it up here no ways.

IRVIN: Okay, Ma . . . I don't care. I just thought . . .

MA RAINEY: Damn what you thought! What you look like telling me how to sing my song? This Levee and Sturdyvant nonsense . . . I ain't going for it! Sylvester, go on down there and introduce yourself. I'm through playing with Irvin.

SYLVESTER: Which way you go? Where they at?

MA RAINEY: Here . . . I'll carry you down there myself.

DUSSIE MAE: Can I go? I wanna see the band.

MA RAINEY: You stay your behind up here. Ain't no cause in you being down there. Come on, Sylvester.

IRVIN: Okay, Ma. Have it your way. We'll be ready to go in fifteen minutes.

MA RAINEY: We'll be ready to go when Madame says we're ready. That's the way it goes around here. (MA RAINEY *and* SYLESTER *exit. The lights go down in the studio and up in the band room.* MA RAINEY *enters with* SYLVESTER.) Cutler, this here is my nephew Sylvester. He's gonna do that voice intro on the "Black Bottom" song using the old version.

LEVEE: What you talking about? Mr. Irvin say he's using my version. What you talking about?

MA RAINEY: Levee, I ain't studying you or Mr. Irvin. Cutler, get him straightened out how to do his part. I ain't thinking about Levee. These folks done messed with the wrong person this day. Sylvester, Cutler gonna teach you your part. You go ahead and get it straight. Don't worry about what nobody else say. (MA RAINEY *exits.*)

CUTLER: Well, come on in, boy. I'm Cutler. You got Slow Drag . . . Levee . . . and that's Toledo over there. Sylvester, huh?

SYLVESTER: Sylvester Brown.

LEVEE: I done wrote a version of that song what picks it up and sets it down in the people's lap! Now she come talking this! You don't need that old circus bullshit! I know what I'm talking about. You gonna mess up the song, Cutler, and you know it.

CUTLER: I ain't gonna mess up nothing. Ma say . . .

LEVEE: I don't care what Ma say! I'm talking about what the intro gonna do to the song. The peoples in the North ain't gonna buy all that tent-show nonsense. They wanna hear some music!

CUTLER: Nigger, I done told you time and again . . . you just in the band. You plays the piece . . . whatever they want! Ma says what to play! Not you! You ain't here to be doing no creating. Your job is to play whatever Ma says!

LEVEE: I might not play nothing! I might quit!

CUTLER: Nigger, don't nobody care if you quit. Whose heart you gonna break?

TOLEDO: Levee ain't gonna quit. He got to make some money to keep him in shoe polish.

LEVEE: I done told you all . . . you all don't know me. You don't know what I'll do.

CUTLER: I don't think nobody too much give a damn! Sylvester, here's the way your part go. The band plays the intro . . . I'll tell you where to come in. The band plays the intro and then you say, "All right, boys, you done seen the rest . . . Now I'm gonna show you the best. Ma Rainey's gonna show you her black bottom." You got that? (SYLVESTER *nods.*) Let me hear you say it one time.

SYLVESTER: "All right, boys, you done s-s-seen the rest, n-n-now I'm gonna show you the best. M-m-m-m-m-m-ma Rainey's gonna s-s-show you her black b-b-bottom."

LEVEE: What kind of . . . All right, Cutler! Let me see you fix that! You straighten that out! You hear that shit, Slow Drag? How in the hell the boy gonna do the part and he can't even talk!

SYLVESTER: W-w-w-who's you to tell me what to do, nigger! This ain't your band! Ma tell me to d-d-do it and I'm gonna do it. You can go to hell, n-n-n-nigger!

LEVEE: B-b-b-boy, ain't nobody studying you. You go on and

fix that one, Cutler. You fix that one and I'll . . . I'll shine
your shoes for you. You go on and fix that one!

TOLEDO: You say you Ma's nephew, huh?

SYLVESTER: Yeah. So w-w-what that mean?

TOLEDO: Oh, I ain't meant nothing . . . I was just asking.

SLOW DRAG: Well, come on and let's rehearse so the boy can
get it right.

LEVEE: I ain't rehearsing nothing! You just wait till I get my
band. I'm gonna record that song and show you how it supposed to go!

CUTLER: We can do it without Levee. Let him sit on over
there. Sylvester, you remember your part?

SYLVESTER: I remember it pretty g-g-g-good.

CUTLER: Well, come on, let's do it, then.

(*The band begins to play.* LEVEE *sits and pouts.* STURDYVANT
enters the band room.)

STURDYVANT: Good . . . you boys are rehearsing, I see.

LEVEE: (*Jumping up.*) Yessir! We rehearsing. We know them
songs real good.

STURDYVANT: Good! Say, Levee, did you finish that song?

LEVEE: Yessir, Mr. Sturdyvant. I got it right here. I wrote that
other part just like you say. It go like:
You can shake it, you can break it
You can dance at any hall
You can slide across the floor
You'll never have to stall
My jelly, my roll,
Sweet Mama, don't you let it fall.
Then I put that part in there for the people to dance, like
you say, for them to forget about their troubles.

STURDYVANT: Good! Good! I'll just take this. I wanna see you
about your songs as soon as I get the chance.

LEVEE: Yessir! As soon as you get the chance, Mr. Sturdyvant.

(STURDYVANT *exits.*)

CUTLER: You hear Levee? You hear this nigger? "Yessuh, we's
rehearsing, boss."

SLOW DRAG: I heard him. Seen him too. Shuffling them feet.

TOLEDO: Aw, Levee can't help it none. He's like all of us.
Spooked up with the white men.

LEVEE: I'm spooked up with him, all right. You let one of

them crackers fix on me wrong. I'll show you how spooked up I am with him.

TOLEDO: That's the trouble of it. You wouldn't know if he was fixed on you wrong or not. You so spooked up by him you ain't had the time to study him.

LEVEE: I studies the white man. I got him studied good. The first time one fixes on me wrong, I'm gonna let him know just how much I studied. Come telling me I'm spooked up with the white man. You let one of them mess with me, I'll show you how spooked up I am.

CUTLER: You talking out your hat. The man come in here, call you a boy, tell you to get up off your ass and rehearse, and you ain't had nothing to say to him, except "yessir!"

LEVEE: I can say "yessir" to whoever I please. What you got to do with it? I know how to handle white folks. I been handling them for thirty-two years, and now you gonna tell me how to do it. Just 'cause I say "yessir" don't mean I'm spooked up with him. I know what I'm doing. Let me handle him my way.

CUTLER: Well, go on and handle it, then.

LEVEE: Toledo, you always messing with somebody! Always agitating somebody with that old philosophy bullshit you be talking. You stay out of my way about what I do and say. I'm my own person. Just let me alone.

TOLEDO: You right, Levee. I apologize. It ain't none of my business that you spooked up by the white man.

LEVEE: All right! See! That's the shit I'm talking about. You all back up and leave Levee alone.

SLOW DRAG: Aw, Levee, we was all just having fun. Toledo ain't said nothing about you he ain't said about me. You just taking it all wrong.

TOLEDO: I ain't meant nothing by it, Levee. (*Pauses.*) Cutler, you ready to rehearse?

LEVEE: Levee got to be Levee! And he don't need nobody messing with him about the white man—'cause you don't know nothing about me. You don't know Levee. You don't know nothing about what kind of blood I got! What kind of heart I got beating here! (*Pounds his chest.*) I was eight years old when I watched a gang of white mens come into my daddy's house and have to do with my mama any way they wanted. (*Pauses.*)

We was living in Jefferson County, about eighty miles out-side of Natchez. My daddy's name was Memphis . . . Memphis Lee Green . . . had him near fifty acres of good farming

land. I'm talking about good land! Grow anything you want!
He done gone off of shares and bought this land from Mr.
Hallie's widow woman after he done passed on. Folks called
him an uppity nigger 'cause he done saved and borrowed to
where he could buy this land and be independent. (*Pauses.*)

It was coming on planting time and my daddy went into
Natchez to get some seed and fertilizer. Called me, say,
"Levee, you the man of the house now. Take care of your
mama while I'm gone." I wasn't but a little boy, eight years
old. (*Pauses.*)

My mama was frying up some chicken when them mens
come in that house. Must have been eight or nine of them.
She standing there frying that chicken, and them mens come
and took hold of her just like you take hold of a mule and
make him do what you want. (*Pauses.*)

There was my mama with a gang of white mens. She tried
to fight them off, but I could see where it wasn't gonna do
her any good. I didn't know what they were doing to her
. . . but I figured whatever it was, they may as well do to
me too. My daddy had a knife that he kept around there for
hunting and working and whatnot. I knew where he kept it
and I went and got it.

I'm gonna show you how spooked up I was by the white
man. I tried my damnedest to cut one of them's throat! I hit
him on the shoulder with it. He reached back and grabbed
hold of that knife and whacked me across the chest with it.
(*Raises his shirt to show a long, ugly scar.*)

That's what made them stop. They was scared I was gonna
bleed to death. My mama wrapped a sheet around me and
carried me two miles down to the Furlow place and they
drove me up to Doc Albans. He was waiting on a calf to be
born, and say he ain't had time to see me. They carried me
up to Miss Etta, the midwife, and she fixed me up.

My daddy came back and acted like he done accepted the
facts of what happened. But he got the names of them mens
from Mama. He found out who they was and then we
announced we was moving out of that county. Said good-bye
to everybody . . . all the neighbors. My daddy went and
smiled in the face of one of them crackers who had been
with my mama. Smiled in his face and sold him our land.
We moved over with relations in Caldwell. He got us settled
in and then he took off one day. I ain't never seen him since.
He sneaked back, hiding in the woods, laying to get them
eight or nine men. (*Pauses.*)

He got four of them before they got him. They tracked him down in the woods. Caught up with him and hung him and set him afire. (*Pauses.*)

My daddy wasn't spooked up by the white man. No sir! And that taught me how to handle them. I seen my daddy go up and grin in this cracker's face . . . smile in his face and sell him his land. All the while he's planning how he's gonna get him and what he's gonna do to him. That taught me how to handle them. So you all just back up and leave Levee alone about the white man. I can smile and say yessir to whoever I please. I got time coming to me. You all just leave Levee alone about the white man.

(*There is a long pause.* SLOW DRAG *begins playing on the bass and sings.*)

SLOW DRAG: (*Singing.*)
If I had my way
If I had my way
If I had my way
I would tear this old building down.

ACT TWO

(*The lights come up in the studio. The musicians are setting up their instruments.* MA RAINEY *walks about shoeless, singing softly to herself.* LEVEE *stands near* DUSSIE MAE, *who hikes up her dress and crosses her leg.* CUTLER *speaks to* IRVIN *off to the side.*)

CUTLER: Mr. Irvin, I don't know what you gonna do. I ain't got nothing to do with it, but the boy can't do the part. He stutters. He can't get it right. He stutters right through it every time.

IRVIN: Christ! Okay. We'll . . . Shit! We'll just do it like we planned. We'll do Levee's version. I'll handle it, Cutler. Come on, let's go. I'll think of something. (*Exits to the control booth.*)

MA RAINEY: (*Calling* CUTLER *over.*) Levee's got his eyes in the wrong place. You better school him, Cutler.

CUTLER: Come on, Levee . . . let's get ready to play! Get your mind on your work!

IRVIN: (*Over speaker.*) Okay, boys, we're gonna do "Moonshine Blues" first. "Moonshine Blues," Ma.

MA RAINEY: I ain't doing no "Moonshine" nothing. I'm doing the "Black Bottom" first. Come on, Sylvester. (*To* IRVIN.) Where's Sylvester's mike? You need a mike for Sylvester. Irvin . . . get him a mike.

IRVIN: Uh . . . Ma, the boys say he can't do it. We'll have to do Levee's version.

MA RAINEY: What you mean he can't do it? Who say he can't do it? What boys say he can't do it?

IRVIN: The band, Ma . . . the boys in the band.

MA RAINEY: What band? The band work for me! I say what goes! Cutler, what's he talking about? Levee, this some of your shit?

IRVIN: He stutters, Ma. They say he stutters.

MA RAINEY: I don't care if he do. I promised the boy he could do the part . . . and he's gonna do it! That's all there is to it. He don't stutter all the time. Get a microphone down here for him.

493

IRVIN: Ma, we don't have time. We can't . . .

MA RAINEY: If you wanna make a record, you gonna find time. I ain't playing with you, Irvin. I can walk out of here and go back to my tour. I got plenty fans. I don't need to go through all of this. Just go and get the boy a microphone.

(IRVIN *and* STURDYVANT *consult in the booth.* IRVIN *exits.*)

STURDYVANT: All right, Ma . . . we'll get him a microphone. But if he messes up . . . He's only getting one chance . . . The cost . . .

MA RAINEY: Damn the cost. You always talking about the cost. I make more money for this outfit than anybody else you got put together. If he messes up, he'll just do it till he gets it right. Levee, I know you had something to do with this. You better watch yourself.

LEVEE: It was Cutler!

SYLVESTER: It was you! You the only one m-m-mad about it.

LEVEE: The boy stutter. He can't do the part. Everybody see that. I don't know why you want the boy to do the part no ways.

MA RAINEY: Well, can or can't . . . he's gonna do it! You ain't got nothing to do with it!

LEVEE: I don't care what you do! He can sing the whole god-damned song for all I care!

MA RAINEY: Well, all right. Thank you.

(IRVIN *enters with a microphone and hooks it up. He exits to the control booth.*)

MA RAINEY: Come on, Sylvester. You just stand here and hold your hands like I told you. Just remember the words and say them . . . That's all there is to it. Don't worry about messing up. If you mess up, we'll do it again. Now, let me hear you say it. Play for him, Cutler.

CUTLER: One . . . two . . . you know what to do.

(*The band begins to play, and* SYLVESTER *curls his fingers and clasps his hands together in front of his chest, pulling in opposite directions as he says his lines.*)

SYLVESTER: "All right, boys, you d-d-d-done s-s-s-seen the best . . . (LEVEE *stops playing.*) Now I'm g-g-g-gonna show you

the rest . . . Ma R-r-rainey's gonna show you her b-b-b-black
b-b-b-bottom.''

(*The rest of the band stops playing.*)

MA RAINEY: That's all right. That's real good. You take your
time, you'll get it right.

STURDYVANT: (*Over speaker.*) Listen, Ma . . . now, when you
come in, don't wait so long to come in. Don't take so long
on the intro, huh?

MA RAINEY: Sturdyvant, don't you go trying to tell me how
to sing. You just take care of that up there and let me take
care of this down here. Where's my Coke?

IRVIN: Okay, Ma. We're all set up to go up here. "Ma Rainey's
Black Bottom," boys.

MA RAINEY: Where's my Coke? I need a Coke. You ain't got
no Coke down here? Where's my Coke?

IRVIN: What's the matter, Ma? What's . . .

MA RAINEY: Where's my Coke? I need a Coca-Cola.

IRVIN: Uh . . . Ma, look, I forgot the Coke, huh? Let's go it
without it, huh? Just this one song. What say, boys?

MA RAINEY: Damn what the band say! You know I don't sing
nothing without my Coca-Cola!

STURDYVANT: We don't have any, Ma. There's no Coca-Cola
here. We're all set up and we'll just go ahead and . . .

MA RAINEY: You supposed to have Coca-Cola. Irvin knew
that. I ain't singing nothing without my Coca-Cola!

(*She walks away from the mike, singing to herself.* STUR-
DYVANT *enters from the control booth.*)

STURDYVANT: Now, just a minute here, Ma. You come in an
hour late . . . we're way behind schedule as it is . . . the
band is set up and ready to go . . . I'm burning my lights
. . . I've turned up the heat . . . We're ready to make a
record and what? You decide you want a Coca-Cola?

MA RAINEY: Sturdyvant, get out of my face. (IRVIN *enters.*)
Irvin . . . I told you keep him away from me.

IRVIN: Mel, I'll handle it.

STURDYVANT: I'm tired of her nonsense, Irv. I'm not gonna
put up with this!

IRVIN: Let me handle it, Mel. I know how to handle her. (*To*
MA RAINEY.) Look, Ma . . . I'll call down to the deli and
get you a Coke. But let's get started, huh? Sylvester's stand-

ing there ready to go . . . the band's set up . . . let's do this one song, huh?

MA RAINEY: If you too cheap to buy me a Coke, I'll buy my own. Slow Drag! Sylvester, go with Slow Drag and get me a Coca-Cola. (SLOW DRAG *comes over.*) Slow Drag, walk down to that store on the corner and get me three bottles of Coca-Cola. Get out my face, Irvin. You all just wait until I get my Coke. It ain't gonna kill you.

IRVIN: Okay, Ma. Get your Coke, for Chrissakes! Get your Coke!

(IRVIN *and* STURDYVANT *exit into the hallway followed by* SLOW DRAG *and* SYLVESTER. TOLEDO, CUTLER *and* LEVEE *head for the band room.*)

MA RAINEY: Cutler, come here a minute. I want to talk to you. (CUTLER *crosses over somewhat reluctantly.*) What's all this about "the boys in the band say"? I tells you what to do. I says what the matter is with the band. I say who can and can't do what.

CUTLER: We just say 'cause the boy stutter . . .

MA RAINEY: I know he stutters. Don't you think I know he stutters? This is what's gonna help him.

CUTLER: Well, how can he do the part if he stutters? You want him to stutter through it? We just thought it be easier to go on and let Levee do it like we planned.

MA RAINEY: I don't care if he stutters or not! He's doing the part and I don't wanna hear any more of this shit about what the band says. And I want you to find somebody to replace Levee when we get to Memphis. Levee ain't nothing but trouble.

CUTLER: Levee's all right. He plays good music when he puts his mind to it. He knows how to write music too.

MA RAINEY: I don't care what he know. He ain't nothing but bad news. Find somebody else. I know it was his idea about who to say who can do what. (DUSSIE MAE *wanders over to where they are sitting.*) Dussie Mae, go sit your behind down somewhere and quit flaunting yourself around.

DUSSIE MAE: I ain't doing nothing.

MA RAINEY: Well, just go on somewhere and stay out of the way.

CUTLER: I been meaning to ask you, Ma . . . about these songs. This "Moonshine Blues" . . . that's one of them songs Bessie Smith sang, I believes.

MA RAINEY: Bessie what? Ain't nobody thinking about Bessie. I taught Bessie. She ain't doing nothing but imitating me. What I care about Bessie? I don't care if she sell a million records. She got her people and I got mine. I don't care what nobody else do. Ma was the *first* and don't you forget it!

CUTLER: Ain't nobody said nothing about that. I just said that's the same song she sang.

MA RAINEY: I been doing this a long time. Ever since I was a little girl. I don't care what nobody else do. That's what gets me so mad with Irvin. White folks try to be put out with you all the time. Too cheap to buy me a Coca-Cola. I lets them know it, though. Ma don't stand for no shit. Wanna take my voice and trap it in them fancy boxes with all them buttons and dials . . . and then too cheap to buy me a Coca-Cola. And it don't cost but a nickel a bottle.

CUTLER: I knows what you mean about that.

MA RAINEY: They don't care nothing about me. All they want is my voice. Well, I done learned that, and they gonna treat me like I want to be treated no matter how much it hurt them. They back there now calling me all kinds of names . . . calling me everything but a child of God. But they can't do nothing else. They ain't got what they wanted yet. As soon as they get my voice down on them recording machines, then it's just like if I'd be some whore and they roll over and put their pants on. Ain't got no use for me then. I know what I'm talking about. You watch. Irvin right there with the rest of them. He don't care nothing about me either. He's been my manager for six years, always talking about sticking together, and the only time he had me in his house was to sing for some of his friends.

CUTLER: I know how they do.

MA RAINEY: If you colored and can make them some money, then you all right with them. Otherwise, you just a dog in the alley. I done made this company more money from my records than all the other recording artists they got put together. And they wanna balk about how much this session is costing them.

CUTLER: I don't see where it's costing them all what they say.

MA RAINEY: It ain't! I don't pay that kind of talk no mind.

(The lights go down on the studio and come up on the band room. TOLEDO sits reading a newspaper. LEVEE sings and hums his song.)

LEVEE: (*Singing.*)
  You can shake it, you can break it
  You can dance at any hall
  You can slide across the floor
  You'll never have to stall
  My jelly, my roll,
  Sweet Mama, don't you let it fall.

  Wait till Sturdyvant hear me play that! I'm talking about some real music, Toledo! I'm talking about *real* music! (*The door opens and* DUSSIE MAE *enters.*) Hey, mama! Come on in.

DUSSIE MAE: Oh, hi! I just wanted to see what it looks like down here.

LEVEE: Well, come on in . . . I don't bite.

DUSSIE MAE: I didn't know you could really write music. I thought you was just jiving me at the club last night.

LEVEE: Naw, baby . . . I knows how to write music. I done give Mr. Sturdyvant some of my songs and he says he's gonna let me record them. Ask Toledo, I'm gonna have my own band! Toledo, ain't I give Mr. Sturdyvant some of my songs I wrote?

TOLEDO: Don't get Toledo mixed up in nothing. (*He exits.*)

DUSSIE MAE: You gonna get your own band sure enough?

LEVEE: That's right! Levee Green and his Footstompers.

DUSSIE MAE: That's real nice.

LEVEE: That's what I was trying to tell you last night. A man what's gonna get his own band need to have a woman like you.

DUSSIE MAE: A woman like me wants somebody to bring it and put it in my hand. I don't need nobody wanna get something for nothing and leave me standing in my door.

LEVEE: That ain't Levee's style, sugar. I got more style than that. I knows how to treat a woman. Buy her presents and things . . . treat her like she wants to be treated.

DUSSIE MAE: That's what they all say . . . till it come time to be buying the presents.

LEVEE: When we get down to Memphis, I'm gonna show you what I'm talking about. I'm gonna take you out and show you a good time. Show you Levee knows how to treat a woman.

DUSSIE MAE: When you getting your own band?

LEVEE: (*Moves closer to slip his arm around her.*) Soon as Mr. Sturdyvant say. I done got my fellows already picked out. Getting me some good fellows know how to play real sweet music.

DUSSIE MAE: (*Moves away.*) Go on now, I don't go for all

that pawing and stuff. When you get your own band, maybe we can see about this stuff you talking.

LEVEE: (*Moving toward her.*) I just wanna show you I know what the women like. They don't call me Sweet Lemonade for nothing. (*Takes her in his arms and attempts to kiss her.*)

DUSSIE MAE: Stop it, now. Somebody's gonna come in here.

LEVEE: Naw, they ain't. Look here, sugar . . . what I wanna know is . . . can I introduce my red rooster to your brown hen?

DUSSSIE MAE: You get your band, then we'll see if that rooster know how to crow.

LEVEE: (*Grinds up against her and feels her buttocks.*) Now I know why my grandpappy sat on the back porch with his straight razor when Grandma hung out the wash.

DUSSIE MAE: Nigger, you crazy!

LEVEE: I bet you sound like the midnight train from Alabama when it crosses the Mason-Dixon line.

DUSSIE MAE: How's you get so crazy?

LEVEE: It's women like you . . . drives me that way.

(*He moves to kiss her as the lights go down in the band room and up in the studio.* MA RAINEY *sits with* CUTLER *and* TOLEDO.)

MA RAINEY: It sure done got quiet in here. I never could stand no silence. I always got to have some music going on in my head somewhere. It keeps things balanced. Music will do that. It fills things up. The more music you got in the world, the fuller it is.

CUTLER: I can agree with that. I got to have my music too.

MA RAINEY: White folks don't understand about the blues. They hear it come out, but they don't know how it got there. They don't understand that's life's way of talking. You don't sing to feel better. You sing 'cause that's a way of understanding life.

CUTLER: That's right. You get that understanding and you done get a grip on life to where you can hold your head up and go on to see what else life got to offer.

MA RAINEY: The blues help you get out of bed in the morning. You get up knowing you ain't alone. There's something else in the world. Something's been added by that song. This be an empty world without the blues. I take that emptiness and try to fill it up with something.

TOLEDO: You fill it up with something the people can't be

without, Ma. That's why they call you the Mother of the Blues. You fill up that emptiness in a way ain't nobody ever thought of doing before. And now they can't be without it.

MA RAINEY: I ain't started the blues way of singing. The blues always been here.

CUTLER: In the church sometimes you find that way of singing. They got blues in the church.

MA RAINEY: They say I started it . . . but I didn't. I just helped it out. Filled up that empty space a little bit. That's all. But if they wanna call me the Mother of the Blues, that's all right with me. I don't hurt none. (SLOW DRAG *and* SYLVESTER *enter with the Cokes.*) It sure took you long enough. That store ain't but on the corner.

SLOW DRAG: That one was closed. We had to find another one.

MA RAINEY: Sylvester, go and find Mr. Irvin and tell him we ready to go.

(SYLVESTER *exits. The lights in the band room come up while the lights in the studio stay on.* LEVEE *and* DUSSIE MAE *are kissing.* SLOW DRAG *enters. They break their embrace.* DUSSIE MAE *straightens up her clothes.*)

SLOW DRAG: Cold out. I just wanted to warm up with a little sip. (*Goes to his locker, takes out his bottle and drinks.*) Ma got her Coke, Levee. We about ready to start.

(SLOW DRAG *exits.* LEVEE *attempts to kiss* DUSSIE MAE *again.*)

DUSSIE MAE: No . . . Come on! I got to go. You gonna get me in trouble. (*Pulls away and exits up the stairs.* LEVEE *watches after her.*)

LEVEE: Good God! Happy birthday to the lady with the cakes!

(*The lights go down in the band room and come up in the studio.* MA RAINEY *drinks her Coke.* LEVEE *enters from the band room. The musicians take their places.* SYLVESTER *stands by his mike.* IRVIN *and* STURDYVANT *look on from the control booth.*)

IRVIN: We're all set up here, Ma. We're all set to go. You ready down there?

MA RAINEY: Sylvester, you just remember your part and say it. That's all there is to it. (*To* IRVIN.) Yeah, we ready.

IRVIN: Okay, boys. "Ma Rainey's Black Bottom." Take one.

CUTLER: One . . . two . . . You know what to do.

(*The band plays.*)

SYLVESTER: All right boys, you d-d-d-done s-s-seen the rest. . . .
IRVIN: Hold it! (*The band stops.* STURDYVANT *changes the recording disk and nods to* IRVIN.) Okay. Take two.
CUTLER: One . . . two . . . You know what to do.

(*The band plays.*)

SYLVESTER: All right, boys, you done seen the rest . . . now I'm gonna show you the best. Ma Rainey's g-g-g-gonna s-s-show you her b-b-black bottom.
IRVIN: Hold it! Hold it! (*The band stops.* STURDYVANT *changes the recording disk.*) Okay. Take three. Ma, let's do it without the intro, huh? No voice intro . . . you just come in singing.
MA RAINEY: Irvin, I done told you . . . the boy's gonna do the part. He don't stutter all the time. Just give him a chance. Sylvester, hold your hands like I told you and just relax. Just relax and concentrate.
IRVIN: All right. Take three.
CUTLER: One . . . two . . . You know what to do.

(*The band plays.*)

SYLVESTER: All right, boys, you done seen the rest . . . now, I'm gonna show you the best. Ma Rainey's gonna show you her black bottom.
MA RAINEY: (*Singing.*)
Way down south in Alabamy
I got a friend they call dancing Sammy
Who's crazy about all the latest dances
Black Bottom stomping, two babies prancing

The other night at a swell affair
As soon as the boys found out that I was there
They said, come on, Ma, let's go to the cabaret.
When I got there, you ought to hear them say.

I want to see the dance you call the black bottom
I want to learn that dance
I want to see the dance you call your big black bottom
It'll put you in a trance.

All the boys in the neighborhood
They say your black bottom is really good
Come on and show me your black bottom
I want to learn that dance.

I want to see the dance you call the black bottom
I want to learn that dance
Come on and show the dance you call your big black bottom
It puts you in a trance.

Early last morning about the break of day
Grandpa told my grandma, I heard him say,
Get up and show your old man your black bottom
I want to learn that dance.

(*Instrumental break.*)

I done showed you all my black bottom
You ought to learn that dance.

IRVIN: Okay, that's good, Ma. That sounded great! Good job, boys!
MA RAINEY: (*To* SYLVESTER.) See! I told you. I knew you could do it. You just have to put your mind to it. Didn't he do good, Cutler? Sound real good. I told him he could do it.
CUTLER: He sure did. He did better than I thought he was gonna do.
IRVIN: (*Enters to remove* SYLVESTER'*s mike.*) Okay, boys . . . Ma . . . let's do "Moonshine Blues" next, huh? "Moonshine Blues," boys.
STURDYVANT: (*Over speaker.*) Irv! Something's wrong down there. We don't have it right.
IRVIN: What? What's the matter, Mel . . .
STURDYVANT: We don't have it right. Something happened. We don't have the goddamn song recorded!
IRVIN: What's the matter? Mel, what happened? You sure you don't have nothing?
STURDYVANT: Check that mike, huh, Irv? It's the kid's mike. Something's wrong with the mike. We've got everything all screwed up here.
IRVIN: Christ almighty! Ma, we got to do it again. We don't have it. We didn't record the song.

MA RAINEY: What you mean, you didn't record it? What was you and Sturdyvant doing up there?

IRVIN: (*Following the mike wire.*) Here . . . Levee must have kicked the plug out.

LEVEE: I ain't done nothing. I ain't kicked nothing!

SLOW DRAG: If Levee had his mind on what he's doing . . .

MA RAINEY: Levee, if it ain't one thing, it's another. You better straighten yourself up!

LEVEE: Hell . . . it ain't my fault. I ain't done nothing!

STURDYVANT: What's the matter with that mike, Irv? What's the problem?

IRVIN: It's the cord, Mel. The cord's all chewed up. We need another cord.

MA RAINEY: This is the most disorganized . . . Irvin, I'm going home! Come on. Come on, Dussie. (MA RAINEY *walks past* STURDYVANT *as he enters from the control booth. She exits offstage to get her coat.*)

STURDYVANT: (*To* IRVIN.) Where's she going?

IRVIN: She said she's going home.

STURDYVANT: Irvin, you get her! If she walks out of here . . .

(MA RAINEY *enters carrying her and* DUSSIE MAE'S *coat.*)

MA RAINEY: Come on, Sylvester.

IRVIN: (*Helping her with her coat.*) Ma . . . Ma . . . listen. Fifteen minutes! All I ask is fifteen minutes!

MA RAINEY: Come on, Sylvester, get your coat.

STURDYVANT: Ma, if you walk out of this studio . . .

IRVIN: Fifteen minutes, Ma!

STURDYVANT: You'll be through . . . washed up! If you walk out on me . . .

IRVIN: Mel, for chrissakes, shut up and let me handle it! (*Goes after* MA RAINEY, *who has started for the door.*) Ma, listen. These records are gonna be hits! They're gonna sell like crazy! Hell, even Sylvester will be a star. Fifteen minutes. That's all I'm asking! Fifteen minutes.

MA RAINEY: (*Crosses to a chair and sits with her coat on.*) Fifteen minutes! You hear me, Irvin? Fifteen minutes . . . and then I'm gonna take my black bottom on back down to Georgia. Fifteen minutes. Then Madame Rainey is leaving!

IRVIN: (*Kisses her.*) All right, Ma . . . fifteen minutes. I promise. (*To the band.*) You boys go ahead and take a break. Fifteen minutes and we'll be ready to go.

CUTLER: Slow Drag, you got any of that bourbon left?

SLOW DRAG: Yeah, there's some down there.

CUTLER: I could use a little nip.

(CUTLER *and* SLOW DRAG *exit to the band room, followed by* LEVEE *and* TOLEDO. *The lights go down in the studio and up in the band room.*)

SLOW DRAG: Don't make me no difference if she leave or not. I was kinda hoping she would leave.

CUTLER: I'm like Mr. Irvin . . . After all this time we done put in here, it's best to go ahead and get something out of it.

TOLEDO: Ma gonna do what she wanna do, that's for sure. If I was Mr. Irvin, I'd best go on and get them cords and things hooked up right. And I wouldn't take no longer than fifteen minutes doing it.

CUTLER: If Levee had his mind on his work, we wouldn't be in this fix. We'd be up there finishing up. Now we got to go back and see if that boy get that part right. Ain't no telling if he ever get that right again in his life.

LEVEE: Hey, Levee ain't done nothing!

SLOW DRAG: Levee up there got one eye on the gal and the other on his trumpet.

CUTLER: Nigger, don't you know that's Ma's gal?

LEVEE: I don't care whose gal it is. I ain't done nothing to her. I just talk to her like I talk to anybody else.

CUTLER: Well, that being Ma's gal and that being that boy's gal is one and two different things. The boy is liable to kill you . . . but you' ass gonna be out there scraping the concrete looking for a job if you messing with Ma's gal.

LEVEE: How am I messing with her? I ain't done nothing to the gal. I just asked her her name. Now, if you telling me I can't do that, then Ma will just have to go to hell.

CUTLER: All I can do is warn you.

SLOW DRAG: Let him hang himself, Cutler. Let him string his neck out.

LEVEE: I ain't done nothing to the gal! You all talk like I done went and done something to her. Leave me go with my business.

CUTLER: I'm through with it. Try and talk to a fool . . .

TOLEDO: Some mens got it worse than others . . . this foolishness I'm talking about. Some mens is excited to be fools. That excitement is something else. I know about it. I done experienced it. It makes you feel good to be a fool. But it don't last long. It's over in a minute. Then you got to tend with the consequences. You got to tend with what comes after. That's when you wish you had learned something about it.

LEVEE: That's the best sense you made all day. Talking about being a fool. That's the only sensible thing you said today. Admitting you was a fool.

TOLEDO: I admits it, all right. Ain't nothing wrong with it. I done been a little bit of everything.

LEVEE: Now you're talking. You's as big a fool as they make.

TOLEDO: Gonna be a bit more things before I'm finished with it. Gonna be foolish again. But I ain't never been the same fool twice. I might be a different kind of fool, but I ain't gonna be the same fool twice. That's where we parts ways.

SLOW DRAG: Toledo, you done been a fool about a woman?

TOLEDO: Sure. Sure, I have. Same as everybody.

SLOW DRAG: Hell, I ain't never seen you mess with no woman. I thought them books was your woman.

TOLEDO: Sure, I messed with them. Done messed with a whole heap of them. And gonna mess with some more. But I ain't gonna be no fool about them. What you think? I done come in the world full grown, with my head in a book? I done been young. Married. Got kids. I done been around and I done loved women to where you shake in your shoes just at the sight of them. Feel it all up and down your spine.

SLOW DRAG: I didn't know you was married.

TOLEDO: Sure. Legally. I been married legally. Got the papers and all. I done been through life. Made my marks. Followed some signs on the road. Ignored some others. I done been all through it. I touched and been touched by it. But I ain't never been the same fool twice. That's what I can say.

LEVEE: But you been a fool. That's what counts. Talking about I'm a fool for asking the gal her name and here you is one yourself.

TOLEDO: Now, I married a woman. A good woman. To this day I can't say she wasn't a good woman. I can't say nothing bad about her. I married that woman with all the good graces and intentions of being hooked up and bound to her for the rest of my life. I was looking for her to put me in my grave. But, you see . . . it ain't all the time what you' intentions and wishes are. She went out and joined the church. All right. There ain't nothing wrong with that. A good Christian woman going to church and wanna do right by her God. There ain't nothing wrong with that. But she got up there, got to seeing them good Christian mens and wondering why I ain't like that. Soon she figure she got a heathen on her hands. She figured she couldn't live like that. The church was more important than I was. So she left. Packed up one day and moved out. To this day I ain't never said another word to her. Come home one day and my house was empty! And I sat down and figured out that I was a fool not to see that she needed something that I wasn't giving her. Else she wouldn't have been up there at the church in the first place. I ain't blaming her. I just said it wasn't gonna happen to me again. So, yeah, Toledo been a fool about a woman. That's part of making life.

CUTLER: Well, yeah, I been a fool too. Everybody done been a fool once or twice. But, you see, Toledo, what you call a fool and what I call a fool is two different things. I can't see where you was being a fool for that. You ain't done nothing foolish. You can't help what happened, and I wouldn't call you a fool for it. A fool is responsible for what happens to him. A fool cause it to happen. Like Levee . . . if he keeps messing with Ma's gal and his feet be out there scraping the ground. That's a fool.

LEVEE: Ain't nothing gonna happen to Levee. Levee ain't gonna let nothing happen to him. Now, I'm gonna say it again. I asked the gal her name. That's all I done. And if that's being a fool, then you looking at the biggest fool in the world . . . 'cause I sure as hell asked her.

SLOW DRAG: You just better not let Ma see you ask her. That's what the man's trying to tell you.

LEVEE: I don't need nobody to tell me nothing.

CUTLER: Well, Toledo, all I gots to say is that from the looks of it . . . from your story . . . I don't think life did you fair.

TOLEDO: Oh, life is fair. It's just in the taking what it gives you.

LEVEE: Life ain't shit. You can put it in a paper bag and carry it around with you. It ain't got no balls. Now, death . . . death got some style! Death will kick your ass and make you wish you never been born! That's how bad death is! But you can rule over life. Life ain't nothing.

TOLEDO: Cutler, how's your brother doing?

CUTLER: Who, Nevada? Oh, he's doing all right. Staying in St. Louis. Got a bunch of kids, last I heard.

TOLEDO: Me and him was all right with each other. Done a lot of farming together down in Plattsville.

CUTLER: Yeah, I know you all was tight. He in St. Louis now. Running an elevator, last I hear about it.

SLOW DRAG: That's better than stepping in muleshit.

TOLEDO: Oh, I don't know, now. I liked farming. Get out there in the sun . . . smell that dirt. Be out there by yourself . . . nice and peaceful. Yeah, farming was all right by me. Sometimes I think I'd like to get me a little old place . . . but I done got too old to be following behind one of them balky mules now.

LEVEE: Nigger talking about life is fair. And ain't got a pot to piss in.

TOLEDO: See, now, I'm gonna tell you something. A nigger gonna be dissatisfied no matter what. Give a nigger some bread and butter . . . and he'll cry 'cause he ain't got no jelly. Give him some jelly, and he'll cry 'cause he ain't got no knife to put it on with. If there's one thing I done learned in this life, it's that you can't satisfy a nigger no matter what you do. A nigger's gonna make his own dissatisfaction.

LEVEE: Niggers got a right to be dissatisfied. Is you gonna be satisfied with a bone somebody done throwed you when you see them eating the whole hog?

TOLEDO: You lucky they let you be an entertainer. They ain't got to accept your way of entertaining. You lucky and don't even know it. You's entertaining and the rest of the people is hauling wood. That's the only kind of job for the colored man.

SLOW DRAG: Ain't nothing wrong with hauling wood. I done hauled plenty wood. My daddy used to haul wood. Ain't nothing wrong with that. That's honest work.

LEVEE: That ain't what I'm talking about. I ain't talking about hauling no wood. I'm talking about being satisfied with a bone somebody done throwed you. That's what's the matter with you all. You satisfied sitting in one place. You got to move on down the road from where you sitting . . . and all the time you got to keep an eye out for that devil who's looking to buy up souls. And hope you get lucky and find him!

CUTLER: I done told you about that blasphemy. Taking about selling your soul to the devil.

TOLEDO: We done the same thing, Cutler. There ain't no difference. We done sold Africa for the price of tomatoes. We done sold ourselves to the white man in order to be like him. Look at the way you dressed . . . That ain't African. That's the white man. We trying to be just like him. We done sold who we are in order to become someone else. We's imitation white men.

CUTLER: What else we gonna be, living over here?

LEVEE: I'm Levee. Just me. I ain't no imitation nothing!

SLOW DRAG: You can't change who you are by how you dress. That's what I got to say.

TOLEDO: It ain't all how you dress. It's how you act, how you see the world. It's how you follow life.

LEVEE: It don't matter what you talking about. I ain't no imitation white man. And I don't want to be no white man. As soon as I get my band together and make them records like Mr. Sturdyvant done told me I can make, I'm gonna be like Ma and tell the white man just what he can do. Ma tell Mr. Irvin she gonna leave . . . and Mr. Irvin get down on his knees and beg her to stay! That's the way I'm gonna be! Make the white man respect me!

CUTLER: The white man don't care nothing about Ma. The colored folks made Ma a star. White folks don't care nothing about who she is . . . what kind of music she make.

SLOW DRAG: That's the truth about that. You let her go down to one of them white-folks hotels and see how big she is.

CUTLER: Hell, she ain't got to do that. She can't even get a cab up here in the North. I'm gonna tell you something. Reverend Gates . . . you know Reverend Gates? . . . Slow Drag know who I'm talking about. Reverend Gates . . . now, I'm gonna show you how this go where the white man don't care a thing about who you is. Reverend Gates was coming from Tallahassee to Atlanta, going to see his sister, who was sick at that time with the consumption. The train come up through Thomasville, then past Moultrie, and stopped in this little town called Sigsbee . . .

LEVEE: You can stop telling that right there! That train don't stop in Sigsbee. I know what train you talking about. That train got four stops before it reach Macon to go on to Atlanta. One in Thomasville, one in Moutrie, one in Cordele . . . and it stop in Centerville.

CUTLER: Nigger, I know what I'm talking about. You gonna tell me where the train stop?

LEVEE: Hell, yeah, if you talking about it stop in Sigsbee. I'm gonna tell you the truth.

CUTLER: I'm talking about *this* train! I don't know what train you been riding. I'm talking about *this* train!

LEVEE: Ain't but one train. Ain't but one train come out of Tallahasse heading north to Atlanta, and it don't stop at

Sigsbee. Tell him, Toledo . . . that train don't stop at Sigsbee. The only train that stops at Sigsbee is the Yazoo Delta, and you have to transfer at Moultrie to get it!

CUTLER: Well, hell, maybe that what he done! I don't know. I'm just telling you the man got off the train at Sigsbee . . .

LEVEE: All right . . . you telling it. Tell it your way. Just make up anything.

SLOW DRAG: Levee, leave the man alone and let him finish.

CUTLER: I ain't paying Levee no never mind.

LEVEE: Go on and tell it your way.

CUTLER: Anyway . . . Reverend Gates got off this train in Sigsbee. The train done stopped there and he figured he'd get off and check the schedule to be sure he arrive in time for somebody to pick him up. All right. While he's there checking the schedule, it come upon him that he had to go to the bathroom. Now, they ain't had no colored rest rooms at the station. The only colored rest room is an outhouse they got sitting way back two hundred yards or so from the station. All right. He in the outhouse and the train go off and leave him there. He don't know nothing about this town. Ain't never been there before—in fact, ain't never even heard of it before.

LEVEE: I heard of it! I know just where it's at . . . and he ain't got off no train coming out of Tallahassee in Sigsbee!

CUTLER: The man standing there, trying to figure out what he's gonna do . . . where this train done left him in this strange town. It started getting dark. He see where the sun's getting low in the sky and he's trying to figure out what he's gonna do, when he noticed a couple of white fellows standing across the street from this station. Just standing there, watching him. And then two or three more come up and joined the other one. He look around, ain't seen no colored folks nowhere. He didn't know what was getting in these here fellows' minds, so he commence to walking. He ain't knowed where he was going. He just walking down the railroad tracks when he hear them call him: "Hey, nigger!" See, just like that. "Hey, nigger!" He kept on walking. They called him some more and he just keep walking. Just going down the tracks. And then he heard a gunshot where somebody done fired a gun in the air. He stopped then, you know.

TOLEDO: You don't even have to tell me no more. I know the facts of it. I done heard the same story a hundred times. It happened to me too. Same thing.

CUTLER: Naw, I'm gonna show you how the white folks don't care nothing about who or what you is. They crowded around him. These gang of mens made a circle around him. Now, he's standing there, you understand . . . got his cross around his neck like them preachers wear. Had his little Bible with him what he carry all the time. So they crowd on around him and one of them ask who he is. He told them he was Reverend Gates and that he was going to see his sister who was sick and the train left without him. And they said, "Yeah, nigger . . . but can you dance?" He looked at them and commenced to dancing. One of them reached up and tore his cross off his neck. Said he was committing a heresy by dancing with a cross and Bible. Took his Bible and tore it up and had him dancing till they got tired of watching him.

SLOW DRAG: White folks ain't never had no respect for the colored minister.

CUTLER: That's the only way he got out of there alive . . . was to dance. Ain't even had no respect for a man of God! Wanna make him into a clown. Reverend Gates sat right in my house and told me that story from his own mouth. So . . . the white folks don't care nothing about Ma Rainey. She's just another nigger who they can use to make some money.

LEVEE: What I wants to know is . . . if he's a man of God, then where the hell was God when all of this was going on? Why wasn't God looking out for him? Why didn't God strike down them crackers with some of this lightning you talk about to me?

CUTLER: Levee, you gonna burn in hell.

LEVEE: What I care about burning in hell? You talk like a fool . . . burning in hell. Why didn't God strike some of them crackers down? Tell me that! That's the question! Don't come telling me this burning-in-hell shit! He a man of God . . . why din't God strike some of them crackers down? I'll tell you why! I'll tell you the truth! It's sitting out there as plain as day! 'Cause he a white man's God. That's why! God ain't never listened to no nigger's prayers. God take a nigger's prayers and throw them in the garbage. God don't pay niggers no mind. In fact . . . God hate niggers! Hate them with all the fury in his heart. Jesus don't love you, nigger! Jesus hate your black ass! Come talking that shit to me. Talking about burning in hell! God can kiss my ass.

(CUTLER *can stand no more. He jumps up and punches* LEVEE *in the mouth. The force of the blow knocks* LEVEE *down and* CUTLER *jumps on him.*)

CUTLER: You worthless . . . That's my God! That's my God! That's my God! You wanna blaspheme my God!

(TOLEDO *and* SLOW DRAG *grab* CUTLER *and try to pull him off* LEVEE.)

SLOW DRAG: Come on, Cutler . . . let it go! It don't mean nothing!
CUTLER: (*Has* LEVEE *down on the floor and pounds on him with a fury.*) Wanna blaspheme my God! You worthless . . . talking about my God!

(TOLEDO *and* SLOW DRAG *succeed in pulling* CUTLER *off* LEVEE, *who is bleeding at the nose and mouth.*)

LEVEE: Naw, let him go! Let him go! (*He pulls out a knife.*) That's your God, huh? That's your God, huh? Is that right? Your God, huh? All right. I'm gonna give your God a chance. I'm gonna give your God a chance. I'm gonna give him a chance to save your black ass.

(LEVEE *circles* CUTLER *with the knife.* CUTLER *picks up a chair to protect himself.*)

TOLEDO: Come on, Levee . . . put the knife up!
LEVEE: Stay out of this, Toledo!
TOLEDO: That ain't no way to solve nothing.

(LEVEE *alternately swipes at* CUTLER *during the following.*)

LEVEE: I'm calling Cutler's God! I'm talking to Cutler's God! You hear me? Cutler's God! I'm calling Cutler's God. Come on and save this nigger! Strike me down before I cut his throat!
SLOW DRAG: Watch him, Cutler! Put that knife up, Levee!
LEVEE: (*To* CUTLER.) I'm calling your God! I'm gonna give him a chance to save you! I'm calling your God! We gonna find out whose God he is!
CUTLER: You gonna burn in hell, nigger!
LEVEE: Cutler's God! Come on and save this nigger! Come on

and save him like you did my mama! Save him like you did my mama! I heard her when she called you! I heard her when she said, "Lord, have mercy! Jesus, help me! Please, God, have mercy on me, Lord Jesus, help me!" And did you turn your back? Did you turn your back, motherfucker? Did you turn your back? (LEVEE *becomes so caught up in his dialogue with God that he forgets about* CUTLER *and begins to stab upward in the air, trying to reach God.*) Come on! Come on and turn your back on me! Turn your back on me! Come on! Where is you? Come on and turn your back on me! Turn your back on me, motherfucker! I'll cut your heart out! Come on, turn your back on me! Come on! What's the matter? Where is you? Come on and turn your back on me! Come on, what you scared of? Turn your back on me! Come on! Coward, motherfucker! (LEVEE *folds his knife and stands triumphantly.*) Your God ain't shit, Cutler.

(*The lights fade to black.*)

MA RAINEY: (*Singing.*)
Ah, you hear me talking to you
I don't bite my tongue
You wants to be my man
You got to fetch it with you when you come.

(*Lights come up in the studio. The last bars of the last song of the session are dying out.*)

IRVIN: (*Over speaker.*) Good! Wonderful! We have that, boys. Good session. That's great, Ma. We've got ourselves some winners.

TOLEDO: Well, I'm glad that's over.

MA RAINEY: Slow Drag, where you learn to play the bass at? You had it singing! I heard you! Had that bass jumping all over the place.

SLOW DRAG: I was following Toledo. Nigger got them long fingers striding all over the piano. I was trying to keep up with him.

TOLEDO: That's what you supposed to do, ain't it? Play the music. Ain't nothing abstract about it.

MA RAINEY: Cutler, you hear Slow Drag on that bass? He make it do what he want it to do! Spank it just like you spank a baby.

CUTLER: Don't be telling him that. Nigger's head get so big his hat won't fit him.

SLOW DRAG: If Cutler tune that guitar up, we would really have something!

CUTLER: You wouldn't know what a tuned-up guitar sounded like if you heard one.

TOLEDO: Cutler was talking. I heard him moaning. He was all up in it.

MA RAINEY: Levee . . . what is that you doing? Why you playing all them notes? You play ten notes for every one you supposed to play. It don't call for that.

LEVEE: You supposed to improvise on the theme. That's what I was doing.

MA RAINEY: You supposed to play the song the way I sing it. The way everybody else play it. You ain't supposed to go off by yourself and play what you want.

LEVEE: I was playing the song. I was playing it the way I felt it.

MA RAINEY: I couldn't keep up with what was going on. I'm trying to sing the song and you up there messing up my ear. That's what you was doing. Call yourself playing music.

LEVEE: Hey . . . I know what I'm doing. I know what I'm doing, all right. I know how to play music. You all back up and leave me alone about my music.

CUTLER: I done told you . . . it ain't about *your* music. It's about *Ma's* music.

MA RAINEY: That's all right, Cutler. I done told you what to do.

LEVEE: I don't care what you do. You supposed to improvise on the theme. Not play note for note the same thing over and over again.

MA RAINEY: You just better watch yourself. You hear me?

LEVEE: What I care what you or Cutler do? Come telling me to watch myself. What's that supposed to mean?

MA RAINEY: All right . . . you gonna find out what it means.

LEVEE: Go ahead and fire me. I don't care. I'm gonna get my own band anyway.

MA RAINEY: You keep messing with me.

LEVEE: Ain't nobody studying you. You ain't gonna do nothing to me. Ain't nobody gonna do nothing to Levee.

MA RAINEY: All right, nigger . . . you fired!

LEVEE: You think I care about being fired? I don't care nothing about that. You doing me a favor.

MA RAINEY: Cutler, Levee's out! He don't play in my band no more.

LEVEE: I'm fired . . . Good! Best thing that ever happened to me. I don't need this shit!

(LEVEE *exits to the band room.* IRVIN *enters from the control booth.*)

MA RAINEY: Cutler, I'll see you back at the hotel.

IRVIN: Okay, boys . . . you can pack up. I'll get your money for you.

CUTLER: That's cash money, Mr. Irvin. I don't want no check.

IRVIN: I'll see what I can do. I can't promise you nothing.

CUTLER: As long as it ain't no check. I ain't got no use for a check.

IRVIN: I'll see what I can do, Cutler. (CUTLER, TOLEDO, *and* SLOW DRAG *exit to the band room.*) Oh, Ma, listen . . . I talked to Sturdyvant, and he said . . . Now, I tried to talk him out of it . . . He said the best he can do is to take twenty-five dollars of your money and give it to Sylvester.

MA RAINEY: Take what and do what? If I wanted the boy to have twenty-five dollars of my money, I'd give it to him. He supposed to get his own money. He supposed to get paid like everybody else.

IRVIN: Ma, I talked to him . . . He said . . .

MA RAINEY: Go talk to him again! Tell him if he don't pay that boy, he'll never make another record of mine again. Tell him that. You supposed to be my manager. All this talk about sticking together. Start sticking! Go on up there and get that boy his money!

IRVIN: Okay, Ma . . . I'll talk to him again. I'll see what I can do.

MA RAINEY: Ain't no see about it! You bring that boy's money back here!

(IRVIN *exits. The lights stay on in the studio and come up in the band room. The men have their instruments packed and sit waiting for* IRVIN *to come and pay them.* SLOW DRAG *has a pack of cards.*)

SLOW DRAG: Come on, Levee, let me show you a card trick.

LEVEE: I don't want to see no card trick. What you wanna show me for? Why you wanna bother me with that?

SLOW DRAG: I was just trying to be nice.

LEVEE: I don't need you to be nice to me. What I need you to be nice to me for? I ain't gonna be nice to you. I ain't even gonna let you be in my band no more.

SLOW DRAG: Toledo, let me show you a card trick.

CUTLER: I just hope Mr. Irvin don't bring no check down here. What the hell I'm gonna do with a check?

SLOW DRAG: All right now . . . pick a card, any card . . . go on . . . take any of them. I'm gonna show you something.

TOLEDO: I agrees with you, Cutler. I don't want no check either.

CUTLER: It don't make no sense to give a nigger a check.

SLOW DRAG: Okay, now. Remember your card. Remember which one you got. Now . . . put it back in the deck. Anywhere you want. I'm gonna show you something. (TOLEDO *puts the card in the deck.*) You remember your card? All right. Now I'm gonna shuffle the deck. Now . . . I'm gonna show you what card you picked. Don't say nothing now. I'm gonna tell you what card you picked.

CUTLER: Slow Drag, that trick is an old as my mama.

SLOW DRAG: Naw, naw . . . wait a minute! I'm gonna show him his card . . . There it go! The six of diamonds. Ain't that your card? Ain't that it?

TOLEDO: Yeah, that's it . . . the six of diamonds.

SLOW DRAG: Told you! Told you I'd show him what it was!

(*The lights fade in the band room and come up full on the studio.* STURDYVANT *enters with* IRVIN.)

STURDYVANT: Ma, is there something wrong? Is there a problem?

MA RAINEY: Sturdyvant, I want you to pay that boy his money.

STURDYVANT: Sure, Ma. I got it right here. Two hundred for you and twenty-five for the kid, right? (STURDYVANT *hands the money to* IRVIN, *who hands it to* MA RAINEY *and* SYLVESTER.) Irvin misunderstood me, It was all a mistake. Irv made a mistake.

MA RAINEY: A mistake, huh?

IRVIN: Sure, Ma. I made a mistake. He's paid, right? I straightened it out.

MA RAINEY: The only mistake was when you found out I hadn't signed the release forms. That was the mistake. Come on, Sylvester. (*Starts to exit.*)

STURDYVANT: Hey, Ma . . . come on, sign the forms, huh?

IRVIN: Ma . . . come on, now.

MA RAINEY: Get your coat, Sylvester. Irvin, where's my car?

IRVIN: It's right out front, Ma. Here . . . I got the keys right here. Come on, sign the forms, huh?

MA RAINEY: Irvin, give me my car keys!

IRVIN: Sure, Ma . . . just sign the forms, huh? (*Gives her the keys, expecting a trade-off.*)

MA RAINEY: Send them to my address and I'll get around to them.

IRVIN: Come on, Ma . . . I took care of everything, right? I straightened everything out.

MA RAINEY: Give me the pen, Irvin. (*Signs the forms.*) You tell Sturdyvant . . . one more mistake like that and I can make my records someplace else. (*Turns to exit.*) Sylvester, straighten up your clothes. Come on, Dussie Mae.

(*She exits, followed by* DUSSIE MAE *and* SYLVESTER. *The lights go down in the studio and come up on the band room.*)

CUTLER: I know what's keeping him so long. He up there writing out checks. You watch. I ain't gonna stand for it. He ain't gonna bring me no check down here. If he do, he's gonna take it right back upstairs and get some cash.

TOLEDO: Don't get yourself all worked up about it. Wait and see. Think positive.

CUTLER: I am thinking positive. He positively gonna give me some cash. Man give me a check last time . . . you remember . . . we went all over Chicago trying to get it cashed. See a nigger with a check, the first thing they think is he done stole it someplace.

LEVEE: I ain't had no trouble cashing mine.

CUTLER: I don't visit no whorehouses.

LEVEE: You don't know about my business. So don't start nothing. I'm tired of you as it is. I ain't but two seconds off your ass no way.

TOLEDO: Don't you all start nothing now.

CUTLER: What the hell I care what you tired of. I wasn't even talking to you. I was talking to this man right here.

(IRVIN *and* STURDYVANT *enter.*)

IRVIN: Okay, boys. Mr. Sturdyvant has your pay.

CUTLER: As long as it's cash money, Mr. Sturdyvant. 'Cause I have too much trouble trying to cash a check.

STURDYVANT: Oh, yes . . . I'm aware of that. Mr. Irvin told me you boys prefer cash, and that's what I have for you. (*He starts handing out the money.*) That was a good session you boys put in . . . That's twenty-five for you. Yessir, you boys really know your business and we are going to . . . Twenty-five for you . . . We are going to get you back in here real soon . . . twenty-five . . . and have another session so you can make some more money . . . and twenty-five for you. Okay, thank you, boys. You can get your things together and Mr. Irvin will make sure you find your way out.

IRVIN: I'll be out front when you get your things together, Cutler. (IRVIN *exits*. STURDYVANT *starts to follow*.)

LEVEE: Mr. Sturdyvant, sir. About them songs I give you? . . .

STURDYVANT: Oh, yes, . . . uh . . . Levee. About them songs you gave me. I've thought about it and I just don't think the people will buy them. They're not the type of songs we're looking for.

LEVEE: Mr. Sturdyvant, sir . . . I done got my band picked out and they's real good fellows. They knows how to play real good. I know if the peoples hear the music, they'll buy it.

STURDYVANT: Well, Levee, I'll be fair with you . . . but they're just not the right songs.

LEVEE: Mr. Sturdyvant, you got to understand about that music. That music is what the people is looking for. They's tired of jug-band music. They wants something that excites them. Something with some fire to it.

STURDYVANT: Okay, Levee. I'll tell you what I'll do. I'll give you five dollars apiece for them. Now, that's the best I can do.

LEVEE: I don't want no five dollars, Mr. Sturdyvant. I wants to record them songs, like you say.

STURDYVANT: Well, Levee, like I say . . . they just aren't the kind of songs we're looking for.

LEVEE: Mr. Sturdyvant, you asked me to write them songs. Now, why didn't you tell me that before when I first give them to you? You told me you was gonna let me record them. What's the difference between then and now?

STURDYVANT: Well, look . . . I'll pay you for your trouble . . .

LEVEE: What's the difference, Mr. Sturdyvant? That's what I wanna know.

STURDYVANT: I had my fellows play your songs, and when I
heard them, they just didn't sound like the kind of songs I'm
looking for right now.

LEVEE: You got to hear *me* play them, Mr. Sturdyvant! You
ain't heard *me* play them. That's what's gonna make them
sound right.

STURDYVANT: Well, Levee, I don't doubt that really. It's just
that . . . well, I don't think they'd sell like Ma's records. But
I'll take them off your hands for you.

LEVEE: The people's tired of jug-band music, Mr. Sturdyvant.
They wants something that's gonna excite them! They wants
something with some fire! I don't know what fellows you had
playing them songs . . . but if I could play them! I'd set them
down in the people's lap! Now, you told me I could record
them songs!

STURDYVANT: Well, there's nothing I can do about that. Like I
say, it's five dollars apiece. That's what I'll give you. I'm
doing you a favor. Now, if you write any more, I'll help
you out and take them off your hands. The price is five
dollars apiece. Just like now. (*Attempts to hand* LEVEE *the
money, finally shoves it in* LEVEE'S *coat pocket and is gone
in a flash.* LEVEE *follows him to the door and it slams in his
face. He takes the money from his pocket, balls it up, and
throws it on the floor. The other musicians silently gather up
their belongings.* TOLEDO *walks past* LEVEE *and steps on his
shoe.*)

LEVEE: Hey! Watch it . . . Shit, Toledo! You stepped on my
shoe!

TOLEDO: Excuse me there, Levee.

LEVEE: Look at that! Look at that! Nigger, you stepped on my
shoe. What you do that for?

TOLEDO: I said I'm sorry.

LEVEE: Nigger gonna step on my goddamn shoe! You done
fucked up my shoe! Look at that! Look at what you done to
my shoe, nigger! I ain't stepped on your shoe! What you
wanna step on my shoe for?

CUTLER: The man said he's sorry.

LEVEE: Sorry! How the hell he gonna be sorry after he gone
ruin my shoe? Come talking about sorry! (*Turns his attention
back to* TOLEDO.) Nigger, you stepped on my shoe! You
know that! (*Snatches his shoe off his foot and holds it up for*
TOLEDO *to see.*) See what you done done?

TOLEDO: What you want me to do about it? It's done now. I
said excuse me.

LEVEE: Wanna go and fuck up my shoe like that. I ain't done nothing to your shoe. Look at this!

(TOLEDO *turns and continues to gather up his things.* LEVEE *spins him around by his shoulder.*)

LEVEE: Naw . . . naw . . . look what you done! (*Shoves the shoe in* TOLEDO'S *face.*) Look at that! That's my shoe! Look at that! You did it! You did it! You fucked up my shoe! You stepped on my shoe with them raggedy-ass clodhoppers!
TOLEDO: Nigger, ain't nobody studying you and your shoe! I said excuse me. If you can't accept that, then the hell with it. What you want me to do?

(LEVEE *is in a near rage, breathing hard. He is trying to get a grip on himself as even he senses, or perhaps only he senses, he is about to lose control. He looks around, uncertain of what to do.* TOLEDO *has gone back to packing, as have* CUTLER *and* SLOW DRAG. *They purposefully avoid looking at* LEVEE *in hopes he'll calm down if he doesn't have an audience. All the weight in the world suddenly falls on* LEVEE *and he rushes at* TOLEDO *with his knife in his hand.*)

LEVEE: Nigger, you stepped on my shoe! (*He plunges the knife into* TOLEDO'S *back up to the hilt.* TOLEDO *lets out a sound of surprise and agony.* CUTLER *and* SLOW DRAG *freeze.* TOLEDO *falls backward with* LEVEE, *his hand still on the knife, holding him up.* LEVEE *is suddenly faced with the real- ization of what he has done. He shoves* TOLEDO *forward and takes a step back.* TOLEDO *slumps to the floor.*) He . . . he stepped on my shoe. He did. Honest, Cutler, he stepped on my shoe. What he do that for? Toledo, what you do that for? Cutler, help me. He stepped on my shoe, Cutler. (*Turns his attention to* TOLEDO.) Toledo! Toledo, get up. (*Crosses to* TOLEDO *and tries to pick him up.*) It's okay, Toledo. Come on . . . I'll help you. Come on, stand up now. Levee'll help you. (TOLEDO *is limp and heavy and awkward. He slumps back to the floor.* LEVEE *gets mad at him.*) Don't look at me like that! Toledo! Nigger, don't look at me like that! I'm warning you, nigger! Close your eyes! Don't you look at me like that! (*He turns to* CUTLER.) Tell him to close his eyes. Cutler. Tell him don't look at me like that.
CUTLER: Slow Drag, get Mr. Irvin down here.

(*The sound of a trumpet is heard,* LEVEE's *trumpet, a muted trumpet struggling for the highest of possibilities and blowing pain and warning.*)

(*Blackout.*)

AFRICAN AMERICAN STUDIES

Anthologies You'll Want to Read

☐ **THE EXPERIENCE OF THE AMERICAN WOMAN: 30 Stories edited and with an Introduction by Barbara H. Solomon.** A century of great fiction about the place and the role of women in America. Works by Kate Chopin, William Faulkner, Toni Cade Bamabra, Katherine Anne Porter, and many other fine writers are included. (624289—$5.99)

☐ **STORIES OF THE AMERICAN EXPERIENCE edited by Leonard Kriegel and Abraham H. Lass.** These stories, by some of the greatest writers America has produced, give vivid insight into both our complex national character and our rich literary heritage. Authors included range from such nineteenth-century masters as Nathaniel Hawthorne and Herman Melville to such moderns as Richard Wright and Nelson Algren. (009235—$5.95)

☐ **GROWING UP IN THE SOUTH:** *An Anthology of Modern Southern Literature*, **edited and Introduced by Suzanne Jones.** Black, white, aristocrat, or sharecropper, each of the 24 authors featured here is unmistakably Southern . . . and their writing, indisputably wonderful. Includes stories by Alice Walker, Maya Angelou, Richard Wright, and many more.
(628330—$5.99)

☐ **NORTH OF THE RIO GRANDE:** *The Mexican-American Experience in Short Fiction*, **edited and with an introduction by Edward Simmen.** A brilliant gathering of writers of two cultures and many visions, including Maria Christina Mena, Stephen Crane, Americo Paredes and 24 other outstanding voices. (628349—$5.99)

Prices slightly higher in Canada.
